Shrubbers World

A light-hearted, humorous solution
to saving the planet

Andy Long

Shrubbers World

A light-hearted, humorous solution
to saving the planet

Vanguard Press

VANGUARD PAPERBACK

A CIP catalogue record for this title is
available from the British Library.

ISBN 978 1 80016 977 7

Vanguard Press is an imprint of
Pegasus Elliot Mackenzie Publishers Ltd.
www.pegasuspublishers.com

First Published in 2023

Vanguard Press
Sheraton House Castle Park
Cambridge England

Printed & Bound in Great Britain

Dedicated to Liberty Grace

Special thanks to Doreen

Introduction

My reasons for writing this book revolve around my late introduction to plants, the fascination of the growing process and the diversity that the plant world offered.

It came about by an unfortunate stroke of fate, or was I purely a victim of circumstance? I had done reasonably well running my own maintenance company, until the government stepped in and screwed it all up. It was the mid 90s, money was cut from councils, banks went through a major change and a recession loomed. Needless to say, the business died.

A small parcel of land, which had been acquired to expand the business remained. The suggestion by an acquaintance, to open a garden centre, was greeted with scepticism, as my knowledge of the plant world revolved around ignorance. The word 'hardy', to me meant an American comedian of the 1930s. So, deciding to give it a go, and with nothing better to do, the next ten years were filled with studying books, learning about species, garden design and plant introductions.

Little money was made during this time; it was fraught with paying wages, rates, and all the other mundane items that go with another business. The curiosity and interest still remain to this day; it was a wonderful learning curve, and one I can recommend to anyone. Shrubbers World Garden Centre lasted till the next recession in 2007, but I did manage to discover some strange stories along the way.

Alongside the garden centre there was the landscaping business; it dealt with all the garden designs and makeover enquiries that came in. Many projects were undertaken, but there was one in particular, that stood out. It was February, cold, dry and calm, but very bright, with the occasional dusty snowflake gently descending. I had taken on this garden, which was a typically overgrown affair. There were several established pines growing through rhododendron and laurel. They stood on the bank of a gulley, which ran parallel to the rear boundary of the property. It stretched for about fifty yards before ascending to the lawn and it had become very overgrown. No-one had ventured down there for over fifty years, and it needed quite a lot of work. The brief was to create a winding path through these established trees and bushes, which would lead to a quiet area. Seating would be positioned strategically, with views, so that the owner, a writer, could gather inspiration.

I was working alone on this day, and as soon as I arrived, I had the feeling that someone was watching. Have you ever had that feeling? Looking around, I could not see anyone, and the owner was not at home. When it reached the point where the hairs would not go down on the back of my neck, it had to be investigated. There was almost a sixth sense of the direction from where this feeling came. It appeared to me that there may be something or someone on top of the bank, behind the bushes. So, clambering up the bank, to where I thought it was, I found behind the bushes, an old bench. It was silvery oak and sporting a very nice plant growing up through the middle. On the ground in front were two patches of wood anemone in full flower. In trying to make sense of it all, I assumed that it must have been a very sheltered spot, for both plants should not be growing as they were. I decided, that next day, a plant reference book would be part of my tool kit; unsure of the bench plant, I was curious to name it.

You can imagine my amazement the next day, when I went to investigate the plants at the bench – there was nothing there, no sign of anything being dug up and removed – gone.

Continuing the work, I left the bench in its original place, to be used as the central point in the wilderness. On several occasions I could sense something was watching, but it felt friendly, and so I worked with it.

It was at this time that the dreams started: of small plant like creatures who would put the weeds in the pavement cracks, guttering and chimneys – mischievous young tykes: and of an older order of timeless planters who have gardened the universe since the beginning of time, shape shifters, who could change into a plant to avoid detection.

The dreams started over twenty years ago, around the time the plant kingdom was introduced to me. The first chapter was written about that time and put in a drawer. But then, the dreams began again. It reached the stage where I had to put pen to paper, if not to just empty my head.

Chapter 1

It was a hot afternoon in June, hotter than your usual June, it was set to break all records. With the occasional bird song and the distant drone of a tractor cutting hay, there was a relaxed atmosphere, infusing contentment on the world. There was little wind and the smell in the air was intoxicating, cut grass and lavender filled the garden, while the smell of freshly cut hay piggybacked on a summer zephyr from the fields. Fields, which stretched into the horizon, beyond the garden where Jake was working.

Jake was a young landscape gardener; he had just finished his final exams at college and was tidying up at the end of a hot and sticky day. He was working on a large natural pond, some thirty foot long, which he was constructing in the shape of the Serpentine. The shade of a large willow, adjacent, gave some respite from the blazing sun. Whilst giving some shade to the pond, it had also contributed to the problems of digging. Its roots were everywhere, but he was pleased with how it was turning out.

This was Jake's first job as a newly self-employed businessman. His decision to go into gardening stemmed from his interest in all things botanical, which was often considered an affliction. His father, grandfather and even great grandfather had all shown extreme skills in producing plants and crops where many before had failed. Jake's genetically engineered green fingers had won him respect from other growers. At shows and local fetes, he had exhibited all types of produce, which he had grown. From a very young age, Jake had shown an unusual ability.

'Here you are Jake, ice cold home brew.'

Mrs. Brownlow handed Jake a glass of amber nectar; she was a prolific brewer of homemade beer, of all types and flavours, her reputation stretched far and wide.

She and her husband had settled into the village after he had retired from the police force, some fifteen years before. They had slotted in and made a home life in the village. It was a small and remote community, it consisted of around a hundred inhabitants, and the Brownlows were Jake's first paying customers.

'I've filled up the dish by the tap for Fidgit,' she said.

Fidgit was Jake's sidekick and companion, a Jack Russell who, true to form, was trouble waiting to happen. He did take notice of Jake, and could be quite obedient, but only when he was being watched. Fidgit was upside down in a puddle, where the hose leaked, in the shade of the willow at the other end of the pond. He was cooling off after chasing Mrs. B's ginger tom. It had launched itself into the safety of the willow tree. Fidget was resting with one eye open, waiting for the cat.

'This is Grand Mrs. B,' said Jake as he swigged the amber nectar.

'The pond's gonna take time to fill, may have to leave the hose running overnight, or you could turn it off later.' He put down his jar of ale and proceeded to pull the pond liner into neat folds as the water began to rise, the weight of which pressed it into its final resting place.

'Don't worry about that, I'll get Fred to turn it off later.'

Fred being her husband, was the chairman of the local bowls club. He also helped to keep the green in mint condition and had been watering the bowling green every day.

Mrs. B wandered back to the house while Jake went round the edge of the pond, making sure that the pond liner was spreading out nicely. As he returned to finish the ale, his mobile rang. It was Barney, the local estate agent in town, an old family friend.

'Hello, young Jake, I have a job you might be interested in. Can you pop into the shop on your way home?'

'Reckon so, what's the job?'

'Aah, tell you when you get here!'

Barney, whose real name was Brian Arney, was a rotund tweed-suited type, whose round face glowed red with enthusiasm when he became excited; one worried sometimes if he might explode.

'What's with the suspense?' Jake asked.

'You'll see, about five thirty, yes?' Barney had an air for the theatrical and liked to close on time.

'Ok,' said Jake, who was starting to feel the effects of Mrs. B's wonder potion.

The time was approaching five o'clock and Jake took the empty flagon back to Mrs. B in her kitchen. The radio could be heard, and the news had just begun:

'... and the strange weather affecting only a small part of the southwest continues and is set to break all records. There is no sign of abatement, everyone is reminded to keep a vigil on the elderly and neighbours, especially those who are disabled or infirm. Keep out of direct sun to prevent burning or sunstroke and use a sunscreen for protection.

The weather forecast followed:

'.. this high pressure shows no sign of moving, parts of the southwest have temperatures in the 30s which could get even higher. This freak weather pattern is a mystery, scientists intend to send a small weather rocket into the upper atmosphere to measure the ozone over the southwest.

'Drop of good stuff that, they could probably use it in that rocket,' said Jake jokingly, as he handed her the empty flagon.

Mrs. B commented on the weather forecast.

'Probably one of them thar sunspots, you've got to be careful in this heat, you need to drink plenty.'

'Can't drink too much of that, Mrs. B!' laughed Jake.

'I'm off now. I'll pop back in the morning, if you can turn the water off around nine, it shouldn't be far off full.'

'Right, you are Jake, see you tomorrow, perhaps I should name my new recipe Rocket Fuel!'

It was her philosophy that, if you were going to make something, make it to the best of your ability.

It was only a half pint of ale Jake had consumed, but it made everything look rosy, and with the prospect of another job, he was feeling pretty damn good.

As he walked towards the pool, he could see the cat inching its way down the trunk of the willow tree. All of a sudden Fidgit is up from his prone position, and like lightning, is in position beneath the cat. He leaps, but, just by the cat's whiskers, he misses it.

'Fidgit, come here!!!' shouted Jake sternly.

The cat had receded up the tree to a branch out of reach, its back arched, claws stapled deep into the wood and its fur standing on end, still and petrified. Fidgit wandered over to Jake as if nothing had happened.

‘Come on you, we’re going into town.’

They walked around the side of the house to the front drive, where Jake’s Land Rover was parked.

‘In, you!’ Fidgit took his position in the passenger seat.

Jake had inherited his father’s old Land Rover, it was a pick-up with a canvas roof, which had been removed because of the hot weather. The windscreen had been folded down onto the bonnet, and it allowed the wind to blow through. Town was really the end of the village, it had half a dozen shops and a pub. Jake pulled out of the drive onto the lane which heads on to town, waving at Mr. B on his pushbike as he cycled home.

At the end of the lane, Jake turned left onto what was known as the High Street. Over the bridge across the river, past the pub and the shops and finally he turned right, into the car park next to the estate agents. This was the last shop before the country started again. Finding a shady spot to park up, he left Fidgit with strict instructions to stay! Sitting to attention on the passenger seat, he watched Jake walk off in the direction of the shop; he knew it was his duty to stand guard.

The shop had bow-fronted Dickensian style windows and entrance door to match. When Jake opened the door to enter, the bell bounced around on the end of its curly spring, playing its tune, summoning its master to exit from the back of the shop.

‘Aah young Jake, come in come in.’

Barney turned the sign on the door to closed, pulled the blind down, dropped the latch and turned to Jake.

‘Come into the back room, young Jake, I have something to show you.’

Barney seemed rather excited and turned to get a large biscuit-type tin from the shelf above his desk.

‘Strangest thing, this parcel came by special delivery, wrapped in brown paper and tied with string. Never saw who brought it, just heard the bell ding, and when I came out it was on the counter; they don’t wrap parcels like that anymore!’ Barney handed the tin and wrappings to Jake, pointing at the writing.

‘Look at the address on the label, it’s mine, and hand-written in ink; it’s fading as though it were old, what do you make of that?’

Jake opened the biscuit tin, in it were a large bunch of really old museum-type keys and an envelope, in which was a similar hand-written letter.

Barney explained that he had received a telephone call from a firm of solicitors in Scotland that morning. They had enquired if he was willing to deal with a small matter for them, as he was the most local agent of estates in the area. Should he agree, then a package would be dispatched; its contents would be self-explanatory. Should he know of a suitable tradesperson to assist with this task, he was to contact the firm of solicitors, and confirm that matters could be dealt with.

'The funny thing is, after contacting them, the package arrived a couple of hours later,' Barney said quietly, glancing over Jake's shoulder into the shop, half expecting to see another package on the counter.

'All a bit strange, isn't it?' said Jake examining the wrapping paper.

'Your address has been written on this for ages, by the looks, and the date has been smudged.' He put the paper to his nose and sniffed, 'it even smells old, musty-like.'

He plucked the letter from its envelope, moved over to the open back door, and in the light, he started to read:

To B. Arney Estate Agents and Valuers
1 High Street
Lychet Minster
Somersetshire.

'Dear Sir,

We have been requested by our clients to arrange for the Manor house, known as Lychee, in the county of Somerset, which has been in the family for many generations, to be made available for their convenience. As you know, it has unfortunately been somewhat neglected of late and requires an element of effort from suitable tradesmen.

Our clients are botanists, plant hunters who have just completed an exhausting expedition in search of plants in the rain forests and are returning with their finds. It is their intention to arrive on the 20th June 2018.

'This date looks like it has recently been added,' observed Jake.

They will expect to have all facilities available for their use on arrival. There will be an element of botanical material which will require the greenhouses and growing beds to be fully functional. It is intended to re-establish the Manor as a growing facility for the future expansion of their business. This will require the help of responsible persons to assist in carrying out the work. The services of a young gardener will be required to tend to outside matters, preferably a well-qualified local with good knowledge of botanical matters. And, if suitable, may be regarded as a potential candidate for future work on a more permanent basis at the Manor.

Guests shall be arriving early on the 21st June and will be expected to accommodate some 12 rooms which will require preparation. We do understand that the property has not been inhabited for some time. It will require some considerable effort to render it accessible and habitable. However, there will be help en route to aid in your labours. Our clients' staff shall be arriving soon to deal with the inside preparations, and they shall also look after the guests when they arrive and manage the running of the house whilst they are there.

Our clients are of impeccable character; they have business interests worldwide and shall be travelling directly to the manor from abroad. We shall meet with you on the 20th June, when our clients arrive, which should be around noon. Whilst we appreciate there is only a short time until this date, we have great faith in your firm, and are confident matters will be dealt with efficiently, just as you have done in the past. The keys you have should allow access to all areas which need your attention, and it must be stressed that the gates are to be locked at all times. Our clients enjoy privacy, and their wishes must be observed. You may liaise with our clients' representative who shall be staying at the Manor to confirm that matters are in hand.

Yours faithfully,

Betula & Betula, Solicitors of Oaths.'

'Wow, wonder who these clients are?'

Visions of wealthy aristocratic types mused through Jake's mind.

'So, you've been looking after the place for years?' said Jake.

'Not me exactly, that would have been my father, and his father before him, but I do have stories to tell.' Barney was lost in thought for a moment.

'This is a job that has got to be done,' said Jake fanning himself with the letter.

'Phew it's hot, I need a drink! Glass of water or I shall dehydrate!' Jake made a move to the sink in the kitchen.

'Let's retire to the tavern,' said Barney.

It was his second office and the source of much of his business, and sustenance. And so, locking the doors behind them, they wandered along the street towards the pub, The River Bank Tavern. Jake whistled to Fidgit as they walked past the car park, whereby he appeared like magic at his side.

'Sounds like you might do well from this, Barney,' said Jake as they walked into the bar.

'Stay there, Fidgit, we'll be out in a minute.'

They approached the bar and Barney announced that he would like two pints of the landlord's finest ale.

'Just an apple juice for me with lots of ice, thanks. Mrs. B gave me some of her home brew earlier.'

'That's potent stuff, you don't need much of that,' said Barney, who was a keen supporter of Mrs. B's beverages. They went outside with their drinks and sat in the shade of the trees by the river, while damsel flies flitted across the water.

'Well, young Jake, what do you think of this little project? You seem ideally suited to the task.'

Barney indulged in his liquid refreshment as he watched Jake's mind working out an answer.

'You know, I was up by the Manor a couple of weeks ago, I parked at the end of the lane and took Fidgit for a walk along the river. I peered through the gates, all tangled up with some dead climber. I couldn't see much, it had grown through the railings, stretching out towards the road. I shall need to take another look at the place.'

Jake commented that what he had seen would need a lot of work, probably more than one person could deal with, he may need help.

'Local gossip tells of someone living there, on and off over the years, but I've never really seen or heard of anyone,' said Barney, rebooting his internal filing system, gathering the information to support what he was saying.

‘I can have a look at the place tomorrow, in fact I might just swing by there on the way home,’ said Jake rising to his feet.

‘I’ll pick up those keys in the morning, ok?’

Jake finished his drink and rolled the ice cubes around his mouth, crunching them in his teeth. Barney winced at the spectacle.

‘Fine, fine, see you then!’ He bade good night to his young friend, and Jake went on his way followed closely by Fidgit.

Jake had done work for Barney in the past and the projects were always unusual and challenging, which was why this strange enquiry to work at the Manor was so inviting. The Manor was in the opposite direction and required a short run through the lanes to reach it. Before the old Land Rover rattled on towards its destination Jake pulled on an old pair of flying goggles, having had enough of airborne insects drilling his retina. Soon the road swept round to the right, there was a turning on the left, this was Pear Tree Lane, a narrow road with grass growing in the centre; it stopped a little short of the river.

The imposing great wrought iron gates of the Manor hung on hand-made brick pillars; they were set back off the road in a semi-circular cut in.

Jake pulled onto the gravel area outside the gates and marvelled at the plant growing through the iron work. Its tendrils had completely intertwined both gates, making them impossible to open, and it was covered with the most amazing blooms he had ever seen, the fragrance was intoxicating. This couldn’t be the same plant Jake thought. He wandered over to the gates and looked for the lock, breaking off some of the plant to display the keyhole. Being a bit of a gardener, he kept some of the plant to try and strike as cuttings. The road leading from the gates up towards the Manor was fairly well overgrown, although he could not see the house for the trees, he knew it must be up there somewhere. It didn’t look like anyone had visited for a very long time, which gave Barney’s story little credence of someone living there. Jake plucked some of the flowers to take home; he could check through his books to possibly find out what they were. Placing several in the shelf of the dashboard for safe keeping, he turned to Fidgit. It had to be about dinnertime, thought Jake, and wondered why he had not informed him of that fact, he usually made it quite clear with a winge and a bark to let him know it was time for food.

Fidgit was sitting in the passenger seat, head to one side, one ear up and one ear down, staring through the gates as though he was waiting for someone to appear.

'What's up lad, seen something? You'll be able to explore tomorrow, let's go and get some dinner,' and so Jake set off, back the way he had come.

Driving through the town, past the tavern, like Biggles on a mission, he turned right after the bridge, towards home. He waved to Mr. & Mrs. B, who were chatting with a neighbour as he drove past, and on to the end of the lane. He turned left at the end, round the bend, and then left into the track which led up to the family home, and Jake's place, which was just the other side of the orchard.

Home was a cottage, parts of which were nearly four hundred years old and had been home to five generations. It lay back from the road, behind a line of apple trees and a grass lawn with a duck pond in the middle. The boundary was fronted by a ten-foot-high hawthorn and blackthorn hedge, which was kept very nicely trimmed. The same type of hedge continued along the right-hand side of the track, behind which were the farm buildings. They housed the farm machinery his father used to cultivate the five thousand acres of oil seed rape and apple trees. To the left, the cottage lay back from the track some twenty yards, apple trees slightly hiding it from view. A gravel drive branched off and led to the rear courtyard and kitchen. To the rear of the cottage the apple trees congregated in a crowd, forming well-spaced avenues covering several acres or so, offering many varieties. This was Somerset where the cider apples grow, and Mother's cottage industry, where she produced cider of all types.

Following the track past the orchard, he came to the old barn. This was his workshop, garage and tool shed, as old as the cottage. It had silver oak timbers, an old, tiled roof above a hay loft, and leaning stable doors, which looked like they were permanently open. Jake parked up outside the barn, Fidgit jumped out and disappeared through the hedge. Jake took the pieces of plant he had removed from the gate, cut them into usable pieces and pushed them in the ground by the storm butt at the corner of the barn, a shady and damp spot.

A short path made its way through the trees, along the hedge which separated the fields from the orchard and led to Jake's place. This was a timbered cabin which had been installed within the hedge line, having field's one side and orchard the other. It gave Jake his own space, and some independence; he also had a small portion of the field, which he used for his allotment garden. Filling a jug with water he put the rest of the plant and flowers in to keep moist, and then his phone beeped; it was a mother text, 'dinners on table.'

While putting his boots back on, out on the porch, Fidgit turned up with a rabbit flopping around in his mouth. Laying it at Jake's feet, he sat expectant of praise and a bowl full of food.

'Well done, boy.' He picked up the rabbit and one of the strange flowers.

'Come on I'm sure there's dinner for you as well,' and they both set off through the orchard, to the cottage and the back door of the kitchen. When they reached the back door, Mother was just returning from pegging out washing in the garden.

'What do you reckon to that?' Jake waved the flower under her nose.

'Gorgeous scent, what is it?' she said, placing a bowl of boiled rabbit on the floor for Fidgit.

'I'm sure I've smelled that scent before.'

Jake tied the back legs of the rabbit and hung it on the hook by the back door. This would be prepared by Mother and stored in the freezer for Fidgit's' dinner. He was a prolific collector of rabbit which enabled him to have it every day, Fidgit liked rabbit!

Jake washed up and joined his family at the table, a large old pine affair that could probably seat twelve.

There were always copious amounts of food available for whoever turned up, a proper farmhouse kitchen, with some of Mother's best cider, jugged and ready to wash down dinner.

Mom and Dad cast the same shadow, only Mother's hairdo would distinguish their silhouettes. Five foot six and portly, they were the typical farmer and his wife, who would do anything for anyone, and were respected throughout the county.

Jake sat down to eat and recounted his day to them both, of his possible future involvement with the Manor, and of his visit there on his way home. With the strange flower wedged in a vase in centre table, Jake's mother poured him some of her latest experiment.

‘It’s new, I call it Fallen Apple.’ It had been maturing for some time, and it was always her way to test new recipes on her family. Jake spluttered a little after the first swallow.

‘Wow, Fallen Apple is a good name.’

Jake’s dad started to tell an old story about the Manor and its owners. He was an excellent storyteller, his story went on into the evening, and went something like this:

The Manor had been built in the time of Cromwell and the Roundheads and had been used as a safe house for Royalists, priests and political activists. There were secret passages and priest holes, not to mention the tunnels, said to be extensive. It had been empty for years, there were stories of strange happenings, and ghostly apparitions in the grounds. A young explorer and botanist moved into the Manor house some two hundred years ago. He was a descendant of a wealthy family, who had originally built the property, it provided him with an income and the space to continue collecting rare plants. His passion took him off all over the world, sailing on those old wooden galleons to countries which were just being discovered. He would be gone for years sometimes, returning with his discoveries in chests and great boxes, which he would then spend months examining and experimenting with.

On one occasion he returned with a rather strange companion from some deep jungle, he was apparently an African king, a medicine man. He assisted the young botanist at the Manor, and would stay, working, while the young man went off on his expeditions. The last time he left, years passed by, but he never returned, there was no sign of the young botanist whose name eluded him, he just disappeared. However, the strange companion stayed at the Manor awaiting his return, until one day, he came down to the village dressed in the finest of robes, and was driven off, never to be seen again. There was a lot of history, and tales surrounding the Manor, and this was just one of them, recounted to the best of Bill’s memory.

‘Your Gran should be able to tell you more,’ he said.

‘I’ve got to swing by to see her in the morning, I’ll ask her,’ said Jake. His mother gestured to a rather large cake at the other end of the table.

‘You can take that with you, it’s for her fund raiser.’

Gran was an active Women’s Institute member.

The evening was turning to dusk, and the story had reached a pause, Mother's cider had enhanced the atmosphere and the excitement of what lay ahead. With the visit to the Manor reaching an intensity in Jake's head, it screamed at him, he needed to be up and alive in the morning. He said goodnight to his folks and made his way through the orchard, the smell of the flower filling the air, first inside, and now outside. The light over his porch activated and lit the way up the steps to his front door. Leaving his boots at the top of the steps, he wandered through the lounge, removing his clothes as he went. He reached the patio where he slumped onto a large four-people hammock, which took centre stage with views across the fields. The effect of Mother's experiment, and the intoxicating smell, in the still, but hot night air, sent Jake into a deep sleep.

Fidgit, being that sort of dog and not quite ready for shut down, went walk about. Leaving his master he left the patio, down the steps and followed the hedge along the edge of Jake's Garden and into the field. It was usual for Fidgit to go hunting about this time as there was a host of nice things to eat out there. But tonight, he was set on a path which led him to the old barn, his interest in hunting seemed to be distracted by other smells on the still evening air. Reaching the spot where Jake had put the strange plant cutting, Fidget sat and watched again, as he did at the Manor gates, waiting curiously for an event or a command, his one ear up and head to one side.

Jake's strange plant had grown, producing more of the flowers with the intoxicating fragrance, and was attracting large moths which had descended on the blooms and were feeding on the nectar. Fidget now had company, a gathering of wild animals had come to sit, and at his side were fox, hare, rabbit, mice, voles and a host of other critters. They were all sitting together, watching as the plant grew, attracting more moths, which seemed to be bigger than average. They created something of a dust storm, as the pollen turned into a cloud and enveloped its spectators and the surrounding area.

This spectacle went on well into the night, and the moths had by this time left a trail of pollen along the hedgerow, over Jake's place and off into the distance, in the direction of the Manor.

The strange audience dispersed without incident; the moths disappeared into what was left of the night. Fidgit shook himself and proceeded to return to his master, where he curled up at his feet and drifted off to sleep. The days were long, and the night was just a dimmed version of the day, with a near blue sky that faded gently into a black velvet ceiling, there was no moon, yet the light of the night was sufficient to see.

The day dawned, the sun peeped over the horizon and started to make shadows of anything vertical, the heat was intense, it was going to be hot. Jake woke to find Fidgit upside down at his feet, and with him, a yellow powder which had formed a crust around his nose, and a trail from the edge of the hammock.

Jake pressed the remote to operate the hi-fi in the lounge, bringing the local radio station into the room, he sat up to check out the mess Fidgit had made.

'What have you been up to scruff bag?' said Jake as he started to brush off some of the dust.

Fidgit stretched, rolled over and looked at Jake, wagging his tail, expecting his early morning fuss, totally oblivious of his condition.

The radio presenter explained that it was now five a.m. and time for the news. The local news proceeded to inform Jake that the extreme weather, which had only been affecting the southwest, was due possibly to freak sunspots and was set to increase in temperature. Other parts of the country had experienced average temperatures; conditions were expected to continue. The news threatened hose pipe bans but fell on deaf ears as Jake threw off his boxers and went into the shower. It didn't take him long to get ready, as his excitement in what the day had in store, was forefront in his mind.

'Come on, scruffy, let's go and get breakfast.' He flicked off the radio on his way out and proceeded on his way through the orchard to the kitchen. With Fidgit, at his heels, and the strong fragrance of the strange flower still in the air, they approached the house, where another fragrance flooded the air – bacon. Bacon and eggs, toast and two gallons of tea were the regulation breakfast at 0600hrs, come rain or shine.

'That flower's fragrance seems to be everywhere,' his mother remarked, 'you can almost drink it. I do know that smell from old, I just can't place it, it will plague me all day until I remember.'

She placed breakfast in front of Jake, on a huge plate.

'Take a flower to your Gran, she'll know what it is,' said his father, sipping a large mug of tea.

'And she's bound to have a story of the old Manor.'

Jake tucked into his breakfast, his mind wandered to the day and what it would bring. Excitement overcoming his need to sit and eat; he gulped down his tea and forced what was left of his bacon and eggs into a thick wedge of toast and made for the door.

'Just a minute, don't forget your Gran's cake, it's in that tin on the window ledge,' she gestured to the item, more like a hat box.

'Big cake huh?' said Jake.

Jake struggled to carry the two and eat at the same time, and bidding his parents good day, wandered off to the barn with Fidgit in close pursuit.

With his vision impaired from the huge cake tin, it was all he could do to tease open the passenger door of the Landy and park the cake on the seat. Taking a bite of the bacon butty, his gaze was directed to a large plant growing up the side of the barn, with his fragrant flowers on it.

'Wow, something strange here Fidgit, I don't know anything that grows that quick.' He walked over and examined where it had grown from. It had grown from the small piece Jake had put there the night before. Remembering what his dad had said, he proceeded to pick a bunch for his Gran. Plunging an old sack in the water butt, he threw it in the passenger foot well and placed the flowers on top.

'Come on Fidgit, in the back.'

With one leap Fidgit took his place in the back of the pick-up, and they set off towards the village.

Gran lived virtually opposite the tavern, in one of four little cottages that lay back behind long gardens. No-one was quite sure how old she was, she was the oracle, involved in everything, knew everyone and her door was always open.

Jake pulled up outside her cottage and heaved the huge tin from its resting place. Walking down the front path he was greeted by a 'Good morning, Jake' from Gran, who was sitting at a large oak table by the front door, drinking tea.

'Can you pop that on the kitchen table for me, there's a good lad, and there's tea in the pot if you want one.'

'Don't mind if I do,' said Jake. 'Rushing around with a bad hand butty is not the best way to eat your breakfast.'

‘Can I use this old white vase?’ asked Jake as he joined her at the table with his cuppa.

‘I’ve got something for you!’ He went off to the Landy and collected up the flowers, putting them in the vase.

Jake put the vase on the table.

‘Aah, night flowers,’ she said. ‘I haven’t seen these since I was a child. Where did you find them?’

Jake told her the story of Barney and his letter, his trip to the Manor gates and the plant growing up the barn.

‘Your great Gran worked at the manor when I was a child, that’s when I last saw those flowers. I used to play with the children in the gardens while she tended to the conservatories, and the kitchen gardens.’

Jake could see that her mind was going back to that time, opening old memories that had been shut away in dark drawers.

‘I was no more than five when the master failed to return from his travels, it was as though a darkness had descended. The children left, my mother continued to work there for some time, but then one day the gates were locked, and she never went there again.’

Gran went on to tell of grand parties that went on for days and nights, of the attendance by grand persons from foreign countries, all dressed in fine colourful robes, and children that would play hide and seek all day, in and out of the bushes and the woods.

‘They never ventured into the village but kept themselves to themselves. We rarely saw them coming or going, but I do remember the children, very polite, happy, always playing. I played hide and seek with them and it was a good time. Hide and seek was for children, not adults, so we used to pretend that if Mother saw them, they would disappear, so it was a secret I kept. I would have imaginary friends, my mom would say. They say that the flowers only bloom while the children laugh and play, and it will only flourish in the most suitable of places, a temperamental little darling. An old wives tale says pollen is collected by the fairies at midnight.’

She smiled at Jake with a twinkle in her eye, exhibiting her fondness of that memory.

‘Has it been empty since?’ Jake ventured to ask.

‘I believe a servant stayed after the gates were locked, awaiting the master’s return. He must have lived at the Manor, behind locked gates, as no-one saw him, and he never came into the village. Until one day, almost a year to the day after the gates were locked, a finely dressed black man in gold and red robes returned to the village. He went into the estate’s office at the end of the street, you know it as Barney’s, where he deposited the keys to the Manor and an envelope. He then got back into his carriage and was driven away and never seen again,’ said Ivy, in an almost dream state.

‘It looked fairly overgrown when I saw it, it may need an army to put it right. Anyway, it’s nearly 8.00am, Barney will be there shortly, and I’ve got to go and collect keys, and get over there. Thanks for the tea, Gran, see you later,’ and Jake walked off down the path with Fidgit in his shadow.

Chapter 2

Jake motored on down to Barney's with Fidget sitting in the navigator's seat, eyes forward, and with a sense of purpose. He arrived at the office just as Barney was opening up.

'Good morning, Master Jake, I expect you're looking forward to exploring the Manor, I'll get you the keys.' Barney shuffled through the front shop and into the rear office.

Jake asked Barney what he knew of the Manor, and the strange story of a black man dressed in fine robes, who left suddenly; and why he deposited keys and letters at this office. Jake explained that Gran had told him the story, but there appeared to be some secrecy surrounding the Manor, and of its comings and goings.

Barney cleared his throat and with a "hmmm," started to explain. He said it was his great grandfather who had dealt with the Manor at that time. Barney had not known him, but did know the story, which had been passed down through the generations.

The Manor had always been a busy place. He understood that it had always been owned by plants people, for back in those days it was big business. The owners would go off on expeditions all over the world; they were botanists of some repute. They travelled to unexplored places collecting specimens, and it was on one of these trips, which took them deep into the jungle, where they met, and befriended a native guide. He told them the story of a secret place, of a people who had worshipped a special plant.

The story goes, that the guide was eventually coerced into introducing the master to the chief and medicine man of these people. And after long discussions with the council elders, it was agreed that one of these sacred plants could be taken back to the Manor. The master had convinced them that he could provide a safe and secret facility to look after it, and it would never be for sale, but used only for research. And so it was, they brought this plant back, together with many others, packed in numerous crates and boxes. It all arrived, together with the dark character dressed in colourful attire, who, it was said, was a great medicine man and king in his own country.

It was shortly after he arrived, around the time of the Great War, that the heatwave came, much like today, just affecting the local area.

'While the rest of the country was suffering from cold and wet weather, it was positively tropical around here. Of course, I'm too young to remember any of that,' joked Barney.

'You see, the master was convinced, that somewhere out there, was a plant remedy for every illness that befell mankind. He had struck up a friendship with the black man, who they called Chonga; they worked together growing all manner of strange flora at the Manor. It was during the master's last expedition; Chonga had remained to continue their work, when word came that the master had disappeared.'

Work continued at the Manor for quite some time, but gradually work became less and less, until one day the gates were closed. Not long after, Chonga appeared in the village, deposited letters of instruction and the keys, gave no explanation, and then he was gone.

Barney looked a little uneasy telling this story, his furtive glances at Jake, coupled with the heat, and Barney's inability to cope with perspiration, made Jake think that Barney was not telling him everything.

'What was in the letters?' Jake asked nosily.

'Oh, just estate agent stuff,' said Barney, as he turned to tidy up some papers on the desk. He made it quite evident that he would divulge no more.

Deciding not to press Barney any further, Jake could not wait to pursue the day, and returned to the Land Rover and his trusty navigator, Fidgit.

With the heat of the day starting to roast his throat, he checked his provisions and drinks for the day, and with his Biggles goggles on, his trusty bone shaker transported them to the Manor.

It wasn't long before he pulled up outside the gates to the Manor. Removing his goggles and adjusting his eyes to a clear un-midge splattered view, he focused on the plant that was growing through the railings of the gate. Its twining tendril stems, which had grown through the gates like whipping twine, restricting access, had somehow receded. Jake turned the key and the gates opened easily - strange, thought Jake. Pulling into the drive and returning to lock the gates he noticed that there were no flowers, and on returning to the Landy, there was no Fidgit either. Knowing it would not be long before he showed himself, Jake continued up to the house. He drove up the drive, flanked on both sides by dense bushes and trees; they covered the edges of the drive, creating an air of mystery, beckoning you to continue.

Around the bend of the drive, he was confronted by a large courtyard, with the manor house dominating the north side, imposing its finery. It was covered in the most amazing plant, which had covered all the walls and roof, leaving the windows and doors clear. Jake stood there in awe of the spectacle, and he couldn't help thinking that someone had spent a considerable time pruning and maintaining its appearance.

To the left of the house was a large open barn type structure, again with a covering of amazing foliage. In it was an old sedan type car, with an open driving seat, and enclosed passenger compartment; it was, he thought, like something he had seen in an old film.

Jake parked in the shade of the trees and walked over to the front of the house, inspecting the large entrance, which consisted of a pair of oak doors, unpainted and silver with age. Two shallow stone steps led up to them, and they had a most ornate metal ring knocker.

Jake's curiosity tempted him to give it a knock, to see what it sounded like. He had not ascended more than the first step, when one of the doors opened. Jake, startled, not expecting anyone to be there, stumbled backwards nearly losing his footing.

'Ah, Good morning, Jake,' the soft voice of a small man greeted him, a dwarf dressed in a green bib and brace overall, white shirt, with sleeves rolled up.

'Sorry, did I startle you?' he smiled.

'I wasn't expecting anyone to be here,' Jake replied.

'My name is Moss, and I am here to prepare the house for our guests,' he said, stepping down towards Jake.

He was very well spoken, and he reached up, offering his hand in friendship, Jake returned the gesture and shook his hand. Moss held Jake with both hands and reassured him that he was quite harmless.

'Barney never mentioned there may be someone at the house,' said Jake, now recovered from the shock.

'Hmmm, Mr Arney, our intrepid estate agent, has a tendency to be a little thrifty with information,' said Moss with a grin.

'I don't live too far away, I arrived a little earlier than expected things to sort out, you know. Come, I shall show you around.'

Just at that moment Fidgit came hurtling out from the bushes, he turned as though to acknowledge that he was being chased, and immediately charged back in.

Jake looked at Moss quizzically.

'You will have to excuse the mad dog; I wonder what he's found?'

With a raised eyebrow, Moss looked hard at the bushes, and explained that there were all manner of creatures in and around the house, and the dog would no doubt enjoy its time there.

Jake, casting a glance back into the bushes, whistled for Fidgit, who returned unusually promptly.

The three of them then wandered through the stone arch in between the garage and the house, along an overgrown stone paved path, which Moss indicated, would need attention. All the stone paths were six feet wide; they allowed the foliage room to grow, still leaving sufficient space for two to walk side by side.

To the left was a path that led down to the river and a summer house, in front of which was a small beach which allowed access to the water. Continuing round to the right, the path led to the rear of the house, which was south facing. A large, raised patio was bordered by several stone steps, within which was a large ornate conservatory. It was half the length of the house and took pride of place in the centre. An area either side, both overlooking the river, made it ideal for entertaining and taking in the sun.

At the other end of the patio, and down the steps, there was a very overgrown path which followed the riverbank. It led you past two dilapidated greenhouses, with a larger greenhouse to the rear, all were accessed by the stone path. It continued to a weir, which effectively raised the level of the river.

Moss explained that it had been built by the second owner to provide irrigation for the estate, and to supply water to the house. A series of rills and culverts carried the water throughout, feeding the greenhouses, kitchen garden and then on to the pond. These had to be cleared of silt and roots. Walking back between the greenhouses, following the rill, there was a walled garden, and for obvious reasons, access was positioned opposite the kitchen door. There was a greenhouse within, attached to the south facing wall, which would have provided a good harvest for the household. Exiting the walled garden and returning to the courtyard, Moss pointed out the old stables to the left.

'This can be used for storage and your work base, there is a small workshop, should you need it; it has not been used for horses for some time,' said Moss.

'All the work here revolves around plants, especially the one growing at the gate. It was thought to have perished around the time the master disappeared, over a hundred years ago. Over the years, there have been a few curious observers, who have wandered past the gates, to see if anyone had returned,' he said.

'I am afraid I took a piece of the plant when I first came to look at the Manor. The flowers and fragrance were captivating, unlike anything I have ever seen, not in any book, and it grew very fast, overnight in fact,' said Jake, admitting his guilt.

Moss was surprised that he had found it in flower; he commented that Jake must have an affinity to the plant and had shown exceptional ability in growing it where he lived, as it had never been grown outside the Manor.

'There is only its creator who has tended to the night flower and its production, he may find he has some competition,' said Moss.

The greenhouses would be refreshed with soil from Africa, where the plant was first created. Jake's job was to assess everything that needed attention, and arrange for specialists where required, anything that Jake could not deal with himself, he was to inform Moss.

Organizing was what Moss did best.

He told Jake, that there were those who had worked with the plant, who knew of its properties, and were preparing to return to the Manor, hopefully to continue where the master left off.

In his absence, and on the back of his research, an empire had been built. An empire that had provided medicines, with cures for some of the most horrible diseases. And ongoing research, which was still being carried out by devoted followers.

'So, young Master Jake, if you think you are up for it, there is work to be done.'

'Certainly, up for it, but I will need help. There's a lot to do.'

'If you have someone in mind, just let me know, we have great faith in you, you may surprise yourself with what you can actually achieve here,' Moss replied.

With that last remark, Moss returned, along a narrow path through the meadow grass to the house.

Jake surveyed the expanse of work to be undertaken and pondered on what Moss had said. There was something distinctly strange about the whole set up. First Barney, with his furtive behaviour, Gran with her stories, then his mom and dad, who appear to know this family and its history. And now Moss, praising him up, it gave him the distinct impression, that there was more to this than meets the eye. Fidgit was something else, he had obviously found a friend, what or who remained a mystery.

'Now where's he gone?' Jake said out loud, smiling at the thought that he too, might be going a little doolally, talking to himself.

Next minute he heard Fidgit barking, he could see movement in the long grass and a trail where Fidgit was mowing down a dog sized path, as he charged through.

'Fidgit,' Jake shouted, and then whistled to him.

The snaking trail of Fidgit's path changed direction, towards Jake, and it appeared for a moment, that there was another similar trail converging on his.

Jake looked on in amazement as Fidgit emerged from the grass maze, the converging trail stopped, and Fidgit sat by Jake, looking back into the grassy wilderness, as though expecting a companion to join him.

'Have you found a friend in there?' said Jake, knowing that talking to your animal was allowed.

Jake looked back over the once lawn, as the rustle subsided, and was quiet once more.

'Come on, it's lunchtime, time for a drink.'

They walked back to where the Land Rover was parked, and Jake proceeded to distribute lunch, and a bowl of water for Fidgit.

The front doors of the house were open, Moss was busy with something, and he was in and out as he moved things to new positions. Moss noticed that the pair had stopped for lunch and walked over to them.

'Do you have everything you need? I could rustle up something if you like,' Moss offered, surveying their provisions.

‘We’re fine thanks,’ replied Jake, and mentioned the incident with Fidgit.

‘Badgers!’ exclaimed Moss, and turned back towards the house, disappearing through the front doors.

Even Jake knew that badgers were nocturnal; unless these were some special species, he couldn’t help thinking that he had just been fobbed off, again.

Jake took his pad and pen from the Land Rover.

‘Come on Fidgit, we’re going to make a plan of attack.’

They both wandered down towards the summerhouse, to start inspecting the work required, and to make a list for pricing. Jake was keen to appear professional in his undertaking of such prestigious works and decided to take a methodical approach to the place. He would investigate anticlockwise around the estate, and then spiral in towards the house, so as not to miss anything. Passing the gates and marching onwards, he found pathways, sculptures and evidence of old buildings long since derelict, possible follies from old. Following the boundary wall, and approaching the larger of the greenhouses, he could hear a vehicle approaching on the lane. He wondered who it could be, toying with fact that the sound was very similar to his Gran’s scooter.

Having examined all the greenhouses, he made his way to the weir, which looked larger than he had first thought. He decided that this would be where he would start; the water was required for everything else to work.

Walking back along the path at the side of the river, Jake could hear Fidgit in the bushes, he was making his sausages noise, the noise he makes when he rolls around on his back. Jake felt a determination to expose Fidgit’s secret friend, so stealthily, he crept through bushes to where he could see him. In a small clearing, Fidgit was still making that awful noise, rolling from side to side, it almost looked as though someone was rolling him around. Jake looked on for a while, amused at the spectacle, Fidgit did appear to be having a whale of a time. Jake almost felt sorry when he exited his hidey hole; it put an instant stop to the goings on of his barmy dog.

‘Come on nutcase, I think it’s time we got going.’

Jake completed his survey along the path by the river and continued on to the house.

It was Jake's Gran, Ivy, who had turned up on her scooter earlier. Moss went to investigate on hearing the engine, but it was not until she removed her helmet that he recognized her. Moss greeted her as an old friend.

'Lovely to see you,' he said, 'the years have been kind to you. You were my size last time we met, you were about four or five.'

He held Gran's hands, shaking them gently.

'You haven't changed a bit,' Gran said, soaking up the vision that lay before her. 'The years have been kind to you too.'

They went into the house and through to the patio where Moss had provided refreshments. Cosy chairs surrounded a large circular glass topped table, with the most ornate umbrella, which kept the sun at bay. There they sat and chatted about their lives, since last they met.

Moss then went on to explain the situation that had presented itself since Jake's arrival, and his interaction with a particular plant; it had brought things forward a little sooner than expected.

'I believe the time has come to tell Jake, and I think it might be best if you explained everything to him, you are family after all, and one of the last who saw the children.' Moss poured two glasses of the delicious green liquid.

'Water cress and apple,' he said, inspecting the colour, and handed one to Gran.

'Cheers,' she said, and they both sat back, taking in the view.

They chatted and laughed, and as time rolled on, Jake appeared, as if by magic, from a line of bushes, by the river's edge. Spotting his Gran and Moss on the patio, he walked over to them.

'Hello Gran, I thought I heard your little putt putt earlier.

'What are you doing here?' He gave her a gentle hug and a peck on the cheek.

'Been summoned,' she said with a grin.

Moss passed Jake a glass of the divine green liquid.

Jake said Fidgit had been playing chase with something all day. One minute he looked like he was being chased, next minute he was chasing after whatever it was, he had no idea what, having not seen anything.

Moss was about to speak when Jake jumped in.

'And I don't think it's badgers!'

Moss and Gran exchanged glances; Jake watched the pair shrug shoulders together.

'Is there something you're not telling me?' said Jake

'Oh, is that the time?' said Gran, hurriedly finishing her drink. 'I must be off; can you pop by mine on your way home Jake? I have something for you.'

'Right,' said Jake, with a curious frown, and wandered off to find Fidgit.

Moss escorted Ivy through the house to the front, and her trusty red steed.

'Things look like they are going to get busy,' said Gran, as she put on her helmet, fired up the machine and said goodbye to Moss.

'See you soon,' she shouted, as she drove off.

Jake returned to the river in search of Fidgit. He reached a point where he had a good view of the little beach area. Fidgit was sitting at the water's edge. He was watching what appeared to be fish, splashing around in the water. There must have been at least three because of all the commotion that was being made.

As Jake emerged from the bushes the splashing stopped. Fidgit turned to see Jake walking towards him and ran over, wagging his tail in excitement. Returning to the water's edge, Fidgit looked into the clear, slow running water, expecting the spectacle to continue, but all was quiet.

'What was all that about, Fidgit?' Jake looked hard into the water, but there was nothing to see.

'Come on you, time to go home.'

Fidgit followed Jake back to the Land Rover, he was ordered into the passenger seat.

'Stay!'

Jake walked over to the front door, which was slightly ajar, and finally used the knocker.

Moss appeared almost immediately.

'Are there some big fish in the river?' said Jake enquiringly, 'making 'ell of a splash about.'

Jake handed Moss a list of the jobs he thought were priority and told him that he could work a price out for them.

'Don't worry about prices Jake, I've been authorised to accept your daily rate, plus expenses and acquire your services for the foreseeable future.'

Jake thanked him and told him he would be making a start on the water supply the next day. He explained about the unfinished job he had with the Brownlows, which would need a little time to complete.

'It's been a strange old day, what did Gran come for?'

'She came to see you, no idea why, and I believe to have a bit of a nose at the old place. She remembered it from her childhood, I'm sure she will let you know later. Don't bother with the gates I will tend to them.'

Jake returned to the Land Rover, where Fidgit was fast asleep. He didn't rouse, even when the engine started and Jake drove off, exiting past the strange flower at the gates, and up the lane towards home.

The wall surrounding the Manor bordered the road, and the trees and bushes that grew up to, and over it, were looking extremely good. Jake had not really noticed them before, but they had the look of tropical origins. Driving slowly, he tried to identify them as he went. He suddenly reached the junction, and turning right he headed off in the direction of Gran.

The temperature, coupled with the wind as he drove, felt as though a hairdryer was in his face. He pulled up outside his Gran's, and parking in the shade for Fidgit, who was still out of it, proceeded to walk up the path to the house.

'Hello Gran,' said Jake. She was sitting at the table in the shade of a large patio umbrella, with a large jug of cordial full of ice cubes.

'Pour yourself a glass,' she beckoned to the cake stand, 'piece of cake?'

'Just a drink thanks. Moss said you came to see me, at the Manor, anything up?' Jake finished his drink and poured another.

'Sandra is home!' Gran watched Jake, as he reacted, by choking on his cordial.

'Really, I didn't think she would be back for at least two weeks'.

Sandra lived next door with her mother, her father died many moons ago, and she was Jake's childhood sweetheart. They had gone to school together, played together, shared their secrets together, consoled each other when needed, they were in fact very close friends, soul mates you might say.

'She has gone to see her aunt in the next village and is staying the night. I've invited her for breakfast here, in the morning, would you join us? I have something to tell you both, which may explain a few things,' she cupped the side of Jake's worried face in her hand, 'nothing serious,' she smiled.

'Ok Gran, nothing you can tell me now?' Jake probed.

'Off to your dinner now.'

Jake gave her a hug and agreed to be there for early breakfast.

'It will be nice to see her, it's been a while.'

Jake wandered down the path to the Land Rover, where Fidgit was now upside down and snoring.

The texts on his mobile indicated dinner was ready. His journey back was filled with thoughts, he barely noticed the plant by the barn. After a quick swill, and with a sluggish Fidgit by his side, he meandered through the orchard to the kitchen. He greeted his parents and sat down to eat.

'You would not believe the day I've had!' said Jake.

He then proceeded to relay the events of the day, during which Mom and Dad gave knowing glances to each other and smiles of reassurance to Jake.

They talked until late about stories of the past, and visions of the future. Eventually, rising from the table, Jake reminded Mother that he would be breakfasting with Gran. He wished them both a goodnight and made his way through the hot scented evening to his bed. The day had been eventful; his mind was busy going over all that had happened, he was looking forward to seeing Sandra. Fidgit took up his position at the foot of the bed, after digging himself a hole.

'Not going hunting?' Jake asked.

Fidgit looked at him, took up the upside-down position, and with his legs pointing skywards, snored melodically.

It was not long before a harmonious duet from them both was sent out across the fields.

Chapter 3

The sun was just starting to show itself above the hedge line across the field, it was 05:00 hrs and Jake was awake, Fidgit was stretching and rolling around, doing his vocal sausages impression. Jake flicked on the radio while he showered:

...it was going to be another scorcher, said the local radio announcer, commenting on the temperature, and his desperate need for better air conditioning in the studio.

The news followed:

'.. and the Met Office have examined the information recovered from the radiosonde sent up by a small rocket, which accurately targeted the area of hot weather that is currently causing concern in the southwest. They found no evidence of any unusual abnormalities, and the weather continues to baffle meteorologists.'

'Come on Fidgit,' Jake was raring to go.

He wandered over to the barn, noticed that the plant had no flowers, and thought to himself, something could have taken them. He had no time

to explore the reasons, so he sorted out a few tools that he might need for the day, threw them in the back of the Landy, and with Fidgit already in the co-pilot's seat, they set off for his Gran's.

On arrival, the smell of bacon wandered out to greet him. He approached the front door and patio area, where the table with its umbrella was laid, the aroma exiting Gran's front door was stomach rumblingly good.

Sandra appeared, carrying a large pot of tea and a jug of milk; placing it down on the table she turned to Jake.

'Oh, it's good to see you,' she said.

'Likewise,' said Jake, and they both hugged, an extended hug, which was broken by Gran's throat clearing.

'Ok, you two, let's have breakfast.'

Gran had made a veritable feast, which looked spectacular on the table.

‘Yes, I’ve got something for you too, Fidgit.’

Fidgit sat looking expectantly, she knew he was partial to sausages.

‘Sit, sit,’ said Gran. ‘Sandra kindly came earlier to give me a hand. She has been telling me about Oxford,’ she gave an approving nod to Jake.

As the three proceeded to enjoy breakfast, Sandra recounted the events of her last term at university.

Sandra had just finished her third year of an undergraduate course in Plant Science at Oxford University. Her interests lay in plant genetics and the production of crops that could be grown in the more desolate and drought-ridden areas of the world.

It was her intention to take a year out to do her thesis, get a job on a farm, and hopefully carry out, and monitor, a practical experiment on crops. She told them of the work involved with the course that she had enrolled on, and that there was little time to do the student revelry that many talked of. She was lucky to have accommodation within the college and be able to study at any time.

Jake recounted his time and experiences of the recent past, his first job for the Brownlows and the work he was about to undertake at the Manor.

‘And on that note, I shall take that as my cue to tell Jake something that may explain a few things,’ said Gran, pouring the tea into three large mugs.

Jake looked up at Gran enquiringly.

‘It’s the profession you have chosen, and your attraction to the Manor, Jake. You have always had a keen interest in plants, it was your ability, and understanding of them from an early age which aroused my suspicions. But events of late have confirmed them.’

Pausing for a sip of tea, Gran then went on to explain her suspicions. She was now convinced that Jake had inherited a power that she once had. She thought that his father would inherit the gift, but he showed no signs.

However, his ability for growing crops, and his understanding of the growing conditions required had stood him in good stead, and he had been successful, where other farmers had failed. She now believed that the gift had skipped a generation and had now passed to Jake; for it was at the Manor yesterday, that she felt the presence of the children, or little ones. It was a direct result of Jake’s contact and association with the night flower, which had awakened them. She had dismissed her feelings for some days, regarding them possibly as old memories wishing to return. It was not until she learned of Jake's visit to the river some weeks before, where he had walked Fidgit, and had examined the apparently dead creeper on the gates of the Manor, that her feelings were confirmed.

'It was your touch, Jake, that breathed life into the night flower, and it is that which has awakened the dormant little ones. You see it is your birthday soon, you will be coming of age. I know that sounds a little old fashioned in this day and age, but it is the age when the mind reaches maturity.'

Gran went on to ask Jake if he had come into contact with the pollen. It is said that when the flower blooms the fairies come to drink of the nectar; in fact, the fairies are a large moth, and it is only this moth that pollinates the flowers.

Jake told her of the morning he woke to find Fidgit covered in a yellow powder, it seemed to be everywhere.

Gran smiled and told him there was nothing to worry about. The night flower had announced its return to the many, and the little ones, her children, were active again.

'You wondered why Fidgit was having so much fun.'

'They ran him ragged, full of fun. They weren't badgers.' Gran's eyes were a dazzling blue and shone with renewed excitement.

'You might have noticed that the hot weather started around the same time as well. The night flower has inherited a power which resonates into its surroundings. It can affect the weather and temperature to regulate the environment and maintain its safety.'

Not giving Jake a chance to question her, she continued to explain with the enthusiasm of a lottery winner, overjoyed at the chance to be able to share this long-kept secret. When she was very young, around four, she would accompany her mother to work at the Manor, and she would play with these little ones. Her mother said she had imaginary friends, because only the animals, young children, and those whose minds were open, could see them.

Over the years, society had ridiculed those things that we do not understand, so we have had a tendency to dismiss them from our minds. Nearly everyone in the village had been involved with working at or supplying the Manor in some way. Everyone knew of the imaginary friends the children had, it was an accepted part of the work and a secret that everyone had, for they were happy times. If the little ones got excited, they would create plants with every step. If they were to become over excited, then they would just disappear, reappearing in the strangest of places. Sometimes, it would need the assistance of Moss or one of the villagers to retrieve them.

'You see the little ones could produce an abundance of plants by touch, not exactly in any order, or type, they required guidance and training to focus. They had been known to just run around planting weeds in the cracks of the pavements, chimneys and gutters. They are gardeners, shape shifters and travellers, they have been around for a very long time. They have bestowed a few chosen ones with a gift to assist them in their quest, your gift Jake, will mature and be a lot more powerful than mine ever was. Time spent at the Manor will be good for you, it will develop your skills and allow you to discover your abilities,' Gran smiled at him as she sipped her tea.

'Wow, I don't know what to say, it almost sounds like a fairy-tale.' Jake poured himself another mug of tea.

'I've been studying intelligence in the plant world at Uni,' Sandra said, 'there is evidence that they can reason, but it's all new and we are just scratching the surface.'

'Sandra, your Gran and I worked together at the Manor, I wouldn't be surprised if there was a little bit of magic in your DNA.'

Gran reached into her handbag and brought out a seed pod similar to the sea bean found washed up on many shores. Gran passed the seed pod to Jake, and almost immediately a green shoot came from it and gently wrapped itself around Jake's wrist.

'It's saying hello,' Gran said.

'I can feel it,' Jake replied, 'not loud, it just seems to override my thoughts'.

The pod returned back to its original state and Jake handed it back to his Gran. She explained that the little ones had given it to her just before the gates were closed, and that one day it would tell her that they had returned.

She continued to tell of the Master, who had left suddenly, on finding out that his friend Ade had been lost, returning home to Africa from the

Manor. He had been visiting the Master, but decided to leave, as the hostilities of war drew perilously close to his village.

When the news arrived of his disappearance, the Master was convinced he knew of his whereabouts, and there was no stopping him. Against advice from everyone, Henry set off to a badly war-torn part of the world. While en route through the jungle, he disappeared. The locals say he was out with his guide, whom he was following closely, and then suddenly, the Master wasn't there. When the guide was questioned, he said it was the spirit of the jungle. The last thing he saw was the Master's arm reaching out, then it was gone, there was a pop as the air rushed in to fill the space he had occupied.

It was after this event that things started to go wrong, it used to be such a happy place, but a sadness descended. Work did continue at the Manor for a time, but when the war ended, *Chonga*, the African, left to go in search of the Master. The plants refused to grow and there was less and less work for the villagers; they became redundant and gradually left to find work elsewhere.

'My mother was the last to leave,' Gran looked a mite sad at her recollections.

She said that over the years, she had walked past the gates at the entrance to the Manor, longing that it might return to its former happy time. The creeper on the gates had withered, with outstretched arms, pining for its master. There was nothing she could do, and it had stayed that way until now. She told of many dreams she had had since that time. She dreamt of being lost in a maze, unable to find her way out, and of the Master who beckoned to her, only to fade away as she approached.

She was convinced that the Master was alive and refused to believe that he had gone.

'Well, Jake,' Gran shook herself out of the sad memory and returned to the present.

'The gift I was endowed with gave me health, long life and the occasional vision of what might be. I have recently seen a return of the Manor's hustle and bustle and happiness, and I believe you are a major part of that.'

Jake and Sandra looked at each other in disbelief.

'It would certainly explain a few things, Gran, but this is a lot to take in.' He turned to Sandra. 'What do you think?'

‘I have read many strange things during the course of my studies, and there are new things being discovered all the time; I wouldn’t rule out the possibility of anything Gran has told us.’

Sandra had an open mind, she was keen to explore the unknown, her curious nature had had its appetite whetted.

‘Would you like to come over to the Manor with me, meet Moss and witness these crazy things? You will be expected to work too,’ Jake winked. It was his way of saying, if you accompanied him, you would end up getting your hands dirty.

‘Can’t have you standing around bored, can we?’

Sandra jumped at the opportunity and said she would just pop round next door and get a change of clothes.

Gran said she would fix them up a packed lunch and threw Fidgit three cold sausages from the table.

‘Moss will be able to tell you more, for it was he who locked the gates that day, many moons ago’.

Jake helped Gran take the breakfast things through to the kitchen, it was 08:30 hrs and they had been chatting and listening to Gran’s story for over two hours.

Sandra appeared in walking boots, shorts and tee shirt, and rucksack over her back.

‘There you are you two, picnic for the day, and sausages for Fidgit.’

Gran handed them both a parcel of food and a bottle of squash, and giving her a hug apiece, they both set off down the path, to the transport that would take them to the Manor.

Jake raised the windscreen and fixed it into position, and with Fidgit relegated to the back, they set off to the Manor.

‘I’m going to check on my pond at the Brownlow’s first, they’re on the way.’

It did not take long to get there, parking up outside their house, he told Fidgit to stay, not wanting to upset her cat again.

‘Would you like to see my creation?’ he asked Sandra.

‘Love to,’ she said, and they both wandered around to the back garden, where Jake had been working.

‘Gosh, it’s big,’ said Sandra walking around the edge of the pond.

‘Hi, Mrs Brownlow, how are you?’ Mrs Brownlow was hanging out the washing.

‘Morning Jake, hello Sandra, how was Uni?’

’Everyone’s talking about the Manor opening up again, are you going to be working there as well?’ Mrs B asked.

Jake scratched his head and asked where had she heard that?

‘Oh, it’s all round the village,’ she said.

It never failed to amaze Jake how information was passed around the village, it appeared to be common knowledge before it was even thought of the local grapevine was faster than the internet.

Jake told Mrs B that he had been asked to do a lot of work at the Manor, to help get it ready for visitors who were coming the following week. His work on her pond would be held up a little to accommodate it, but he would pop round on his way home from the Manor, during the week, to complete it.

‘That’s ok Jake, I understand,’ she filled a bowl from the outside tap and placed it on the floor for the cat.

‘No Fidgit today?’ she said.

‘He’s under orders to stay in the Landy.’

Jake smiled at Mrs B and said his goodbyes.

Sandra waved to Mrs B from the other side of the pond and they both made their way back to the Landy.

‘I reckon Barney has been talking in the pub,’ said Jake, Barney was very fluent after a couple of pints.

They reached the open Manor gates, and Jake stopped to show Sandra the plant. She got out of the pickup and wandered over to it. She touched some of its uppermost buds. Turning to Jake, she said it was quite unreal, she could feel a strange pulsation from them, like the purring of a cat. At that moment Moss came round the bend of the drive.

‘Good morning. Sandra, I believe?

Moss,’ he said, clasping his hands around Sandra’s, introducing himself.

‘Pleased to meet you, Moss, this plant is truly amazing,’ Sandra returned his handhold, and asked if it was ok to accompany Jake for the day.

'You are more than welcome Sandra; you may find the day to be full of surprises. I understand you have spoken with Gran; we should have lunch on the patio later, and we will talk, I shall leave you to find your feet and get started this morning.'

Moss proceeded to close the gates, left open after an earlier delivery for the greenhouses. Jake drove up to the barn which was to be his base for the work in hand.

Fidgit immediately jumped out and ran towards the overgrown bushes surrounding the drive.

Sandra gave a shriek and turned to Jake, and said, 'There were three small faces with large eyes, peering from the bushes where Fidgit went, then they were gone.'

'Gran mentioned children in her stories this morning,' said Jake, 'perhaps you can see them too'.

They both wandered over to the place where Fidgit had entered the undergrowth, parting the branches hoping to see what it was, but there was nothing.

'Looking for something?' said Moss who had joined them, quietly and without introduction, in their observations into the thicket.

'Oh, you made me jump,' said Sandra. Moss laughed and explained that they had nothing to fear, and that Master Jake was right, they weren't badgers.

'Your Gran must have explained a little of what the Manor is all about.' He turned to Sandra.

'I'm sure you will find some subject matter for your studies during your time here'.

Moss questioned Jake about his plans for the day.

'Are we still dealing with the water supply today?'

'Yes,' said Jake.

'Good man, perfect day for it.' Moss returned to the house and disappeared through the large front door.

They both wandered up the river to the weir which was the main source of water for the Manor. A series of rills, channels and underground culverts, constructed of stone, allowed a gentle flow of water around the estate. It provided irrigation to the greenhouses, kitchen garden and conservatory. After filling a small reservoir in the basement, it continued to the pond, exiting into the watercress beds, eventually returning to the river downstream.

On inspection of the sluice gate at the weir, it was found to be quite silted up; after years of neglect the bed of the river had risen; this required a degree of digging to free up the flow of water. The gate itself looked in good condition, and Jake decided that a dose of grease on the threaded bit would be sufficient. They decided to tackle the weir first, so with a spade apiece, they waded out into the near still water, and set about clearing a channel to the sluice.

Digging the riverbed and depositing the silty mud into the flowing water over the weir, created a cloud of murky streaks in the water as it headed downstream. They were up to their waists in the water, but it did not take very long before the area had been cleared.

Jake was busy dislodging a large branch which had buried itself into the riverbed, when all of a sudden, a large mud pie hit him squarely in the back. He turned to receive another on the top of his head, which dribbled down his face, and another squarely on his chest. The sight of Jake, now resembling the mud monster from the black bog, had Sandra in hysterics. Unable to throw because of her laughing, she stood there helpless. A return volley of a large splattering of mud covered her, and spitting out the gritty substance, she armed herself with more ammunition.

There ensued a mud battle that would have made Laurel & Hardy's custard pie fight look tame.

They both turned to the sound of clapping; Moss was standing on the bank, laughing, with Fidgit at his side.

'I thought I might come and see how you were getting on – very well by all accounts. Just to let you know, it's lunchtime.' Fidgit barked at the spectacle, two bog monsters he did not recognize.

Both Jake and Sandra surveyed the area, found a clear part of the water, swam to it, washed themselves down and returned to the riverbank.

'Yes, should be able to open the sluice gate after lunch', said Jake, clearing his throat in an effort to return to normal, unable to hide the grin across his face.

'We shall await your presence on the patio,' Moss turned to walk back with Fidgit in tow.

'Well, that was fun,' Jake said, with a grin that could span the river, 'we should be dry by the time we reach them.'

Sandra glanced at the retreating figure of Moss and Fidgit, as they approached a bend in the path. There were three small figures with them.

'Look Jake,' she pointed, but the figures had gone.

Jake just caught Moss as he disappeared behind the bushes.

'What did you see?' Jake asked.

'Strangest thing,' she said, and explained what she had seen.

Jake gathered up the discarded tools and placed them up against a tree.

'Come on, let's go eat, and see what Moss has to say.'

On their way back to the barn they passed the greenhouses, two figures were working, barrowing soil into them. As they got closer, Jake exclaimed that it was Jim and Joe Miller from the village, they shouted a greeting and both Jake and Sandra waved back to them. They continued to retrieve their lunch that Gran had provided, from the barn, then wandered round the end of the house to the patio.

It was tiring working in the heat, but their cool water episode had given them a refreshing clarity to the day. Arriving on the patio, they sat at the table where Moss had provided drinks.

Sandra began, 'When we arrived this morning, I saw something odd in the bushes as Fidgit went off to play. Again, just as you walked back to the house, I saw three small figures with you, who are they?'

'Are you sure it wasn't a trick of the light?' said Moss, pouring them all a large glass of cordial.

'Positive!' said Sandra defiantly.

'Mmmm, it would appear that you have inherited some of your grandmother's ability, gained from working at the Manor all those years ago, no doubt. Some had the gift of sight; they could see the young ones, the children of the night flower. Let me explain.'

Moss continued to tell them some of the history surrounding himself and the Manor:

'Lychee Manor is one of several locations throughout the world, which have been dedicated to the preservation, and cultivation, of what is called the night flower. The house was built at a time of great conflict. Civil war raged, religion was under attack, and people were persecuted. During the course of construction tunnels were discovered, the owners used these to hide those fleeing authority, it became a refuge for those in trouble. Many secret passages and hidey holes were built into the house, and they saved many lives. The location was chosen not only for its proximity to water, but that it also stands on an energy line, connecting the rest of the world.

'We, the *Burrbesh*, are caretakers, we have been given many names, worshipped by some, hunted by others, and we have tended this world since the very beginning. It has been our job to create the vegetation, foliage, trees and plants that would produce a world that could evolve and sustain life. It was difficult in the early days, due to the ever-shifting plates and lines of energy, many areas would be wiped out and have to be started over. It took a long time, but there was a moment when the world seemed perfectly balanced. It was a time to enjoy, practise and hone our skills, as there were new worlds being created all the time, which also required our attention.

'We were few, and it was at this time that the night flower was created, it was our way of repopulating our species, a nursery you might say. The fruits of this plant would produce our young, which was the culmination of experiments over millennia. It allowed us to increase our numbers and provide what was so badly needed throughout the universe. The little ones were not as powerful as the elders. They were erratic and subject to mood change, which reflected in the plants they created. Their growth was slow, and they required the combined effort of the elders to reach maturity. It was during this time of trials and experimentation, when, unfortunately, an experiment went wrong. The elder responsible discarded it into the oceans, not too dissimilar to the practices of today, and with similar consequences. An eon passed and animals began to appear from the waters, massive creatures that could eat faster than we could produce, flying reptiles, bugs and insects. Subsequently, it was then our duty to provide sustenance for this ever increasing, diverse population. From all the strange shapes that appeared, there would be a special type of plant to produce, which would accommodate individual feeding preferences. This kept us busy for a long, long time.' Moss took a drink from his glass, indicating that he had finished that particular bit.

'So, how old are you, Moss?' asked Sandra, curiously.

'I suppose you would say, very old.' Moss smiled as he observed their facial expressions, changing at each new revelation.

Moss explained that the elders had the ability to shape shift and travel; it was convenient for them to retain a human form, for obvious reasons.

'The *Burrbesh* had been created at the beginning of time, when chaos reigned, where anything was possible. They drifted through the fabric of space and time, protected from the elements, as seed, which would survive the most extreme conditions; it could survive forever, until required.

'That is what we do, we are gardeners, and with only a limited workforce, the amount of work required took many years. Just as we thought things were going well, a catastrophe occurred, much of our creation was destroyed and a darkness fell over this world.'

Moss shuddered at his memory of that time.

'The dark seemed to last forever and was followed by a winter, the like of which had never been seen. It was not until the spring returned, eons later, that work could start all over again. It was as though the board had been wiped clean, everything could be redone, they were confident in the knowledge that previous mistakes could be eliminated. So, the scene was set for the cultivation of the world once again, it would be done very differently to that which had gone before.

'There were continuous experiments, introduction of many and varied plants. One of the elders, who caused the chaos first time, was convinced he could change everything himself. He continued with his experiments, much against the advice of the council. He was eventually banished but continued with his work. He dreamt of creating a living Utopia, a new breed of plant that could function as the *Burrbesh* do. Unfortunately, that went wrong also, and the results escaped into the surrounding area and bred. His failure hung heavy on his conscience, and he proceeded to develop all manner of poisonous plants to try and eradicate this new breed, man.

'However, man learned, he travelled and formed new colonies all over this world. Eventually, he became helpful to our cause, and more sympathetic to his environment than the previous species that roamed the earth.

'Until recently'.

'So, what you saw, Sandra, were young *Burrbesh*, they were woken by Master Jake's unwitting contact, some weeks back,' said Moss, referring to Jake's meander.

'The little ones had joined the melancholy sulk of the parent plant, after the master went missing, and were woken prematurely. It was hoped their appearance would coincide with the solstice, as there was to be a gathering at the Manor. The Council of Libra were to meet and discuss the problems facing this world. Mankind was killing his home and seemed ignorant of the fact; it is therefore left to us to decide its fate. The indigenous tribes of the world understand this, they have assisted us in our quest, and may help again.

'These peoples, have, over time helped to keep a balance, and the *Burrbesh* secret. There are also references to us throughout history, in many guises and in many languages.'

'Are there any questions I can answer?' Moss asked.

'How many of you are there?' Sandra asked.

'Not exactly sure. Originally, I believe it was in the hundreds, that's the elders, the new ones probably thousands. But they are distributed all over the universe.'

Moss found numbers difficult.

'How do they get across the universe?' Sandra enquired.

Moss explained as best he could that everything was connected; empty space connected all things. Recent theories called it dark matter, but they had always referred to it as the fabric, a word that had stuck, in describing space.

'It certainly is a lot to take in,' said Jake, 'are these little ones here at the moment?'

'I believe they may have gone to the weir for a mud fight, having seen you pair, you may catch a glimpse if you're stealthy in your approach.'

Moss excused himself from the table and said he would catch up with them later.

'I'm keen to open the sluice gate, let's sneak up there and see if we can spot these little ones, I really would like to see them.' Jake picked up the remains of his lunch, including the sausages for Fidgit, he was sure to find him by the weir.

They wandered up the path to the weir, Fidgit could be heard barking, cutting through the bushes to where they could see the water. They reached a position which afforded them a good view; the sight that greeted them was a mud monster's party, one could only recognize the dog because he was jumping up and down, barking. His appearance was that of a termite mound, covered with mud which appeared to have been heaped on top of him, and in the water, were three blobs of mud, and mud projectiles being launched from these blobs, going in every direction. Neither Sandra nor Jake could make out any distinguishing features; all that could be heard was an infectious giggling, which set Sandra off, which set Jake off.

As a result of their hysterics, the party subsided, Fidgit shook himself, and all went quiet.

'Where did they go?' Sandra asked, massaging a stitch she had acquired from the excess laughing.

'Crazy,' said Jake walking over to Fidgit.

'Come here you; let's wash some of this crud off you.

'What have you been doing?' Jake took Fidgit deeper into the river and washed him down.

Fidgit didn't like baths.

The rest of the afternoon was taken up following the water along the rills and culverts; there was an element of digging and weed removal to be done in places where there had been the occasional blockage. The whole system worked well, Moss kept his eye on the reservoir in the basement of the house, and as the flow reached the pond, it started to fill. The pond had dried and would take a considerable time to fill, so the watercress beds would be the last to receive attention, taking out surplus soil and weed to allow the unrestricted flow back to the river.

The bushes and trees which surrounded the pond were giving just that right amount of shade. Jake's training at college allowed him to appreciate how well balanced the light was.

The day's work at the Manor was nearly complete, things had gone well, Sandra and Jake collected Fidgit, thanked Moss for an unforgettable day, made their farewells and left the Manor to do a little work at the Brownlow's.

Chapter 4

It is the year 1605, Lord Henry and Lady Mercedes Lyte had just become proud parents of a healthy nine-pound boy. He would be named Henry James Lyte, after his father, but would be called James to avoid confusion.

Henry's wife was Spanish. They met when he was returning from a plant hunting trip around the Mediterranean. Spain, which was not very friendly with England at that time, had made travel, and plant expeditions, very awkward. So, Henry had arranged to make one final stop. He was determined that he should return home with samples of Spain's finest.

Henry, having explained his plan, had convinced the captain of the ship to drop anchor just outside the small port of San Sebastian, on the north coast, where, through his contacts with English smugglers, he had arranged to pick up a consignment of plants. Henry thought his plan was quite simple. He would take a longboat, and under the cover of darkness, meet with the *contrabandista*, collect his goods and be on his way, and no one would know.

The captain, seeing a major flaw in Henry's plan, insisted that Henry be accompanied by a proficient sailor, who would take charge of the boat, row him to shore, and be ready to make a sharp exit. Setting off, they could see the light from oil lamps, shining through windows of the cottages surrounding the harbour. The light allowed his oarsman companion to navigate through the dark and set him safely ashore. The boat allowed Henry to disembark close to the beach and would wait for him a few yards out. Henry made his way up the beach, where he met his contact. He led Henry to his premises, which were not far from the beach, and took Henry inside to inspect his goods.

Unfortunately, things did not go quite according to plan; having inspected the goods and paid his contact, pandemonium happened. Just as he was about to leave, the front door flew open, and an out-of-breath young woman entered. She closed the door behind her, and turning, noticed the two startled onlookers.

Henry's contact knew the girl as Mercedes, a fellow *contrabandista.* She explained that she had been caught red handed, with contraband, and the Militia were after her. She said that she needed to escape her pursuers, who were nearly upon her.

Henry, always a soft touch for the ladies, agreed to help. His contact would attempt to stall the Militia, hopefully giving them enough time to reach the boat; he then showed them both to the back door.

Fortunately, Henry and Mercedes escaped to the long boat. Unfortunately, he had to leave some of his prize behind, but found himself with another, one that he little knew, would end up as treasure. Her command of English was enough to allow some conversation, and during the voyage home they chatted, and spent time together. The result was a relationship that blossomed into marriage.

Henry received a knighthood from Queen Elizabeth I, for his work with medicine and a cure he had affected for her. She had suffered for some considerable time with a particular malady; Henry had studied this problem and had some success devising a cure. He became a good friend of the Court, and adviser to the Queen's doctor.

He transcribed work by a French herbalist and adding his own discoveries. He dedicated this publication to the Queen, who decreed that all her subjects should have access to the healing properties found within. As a result, Henry became famous overnight, and he was given considerable lands in the County of Somersetshire. He was also given a life pension from the crown, which was enough to allow him to set about building. He would build a Grand Manor house on the estate; this would be his base for research into cures of human ailments.

Following this support by the monarchy, Henry felt a certain loyalty to the crown. He supported the Royalists during the time of the Cromwell uprising. He would help fugitives escape to safer lands; his Manor house had, built into it, many secret passages and hidey holes. He managed to avoid suspicion, and thus capture and death, as he was good friends with a large selection of the English nobility, and that held him in good stead.

His passion for the progress of medicine took him to many strange places. He was convinced that somewhere out there, was a plant waiting to be found, that either had, or contributed to, a compound that would cure a particular illness. His son James was encouraged to follow in his father's footsteps. But, as a young boy, with only the discipline of his mother, who allowed him too much freedom, he took his adventures in other directions. Although his interest in his father's work was there, it tended more towards the practical application; the theory was always put aside for more interesting pursuits.

It was on James' eleventh birthday that he was sent to boarding school. His mother and father were set to embark on an expedition to India; it was simpler, to ensure James was looked after, and this school had produced some outstanding biologists in its time. They would introduce him to the school, give him time to settle in, check on him before they went, then off to India for possibly twelve months.

James protested and made it abundantly clear that he wanted to go with them. His argument was that he would learn more with them. But it was not to be, even though his mother was sympathetic, Jamie would be taken to the school immediately; basic supplies were packed, and more extensive personal items would follow.

Gunter, their German butler, was extremely efficient; he would carry out the Master's wishes, to the letter.

Their ship the '*Erinus*' would set sail from Plymouth, in seven days. Trading had increased with India, thanks to the Dutch East India Trading Co, and it was Henry's intention to obtain many of the sacred spices, which would assist in his research.

Docking at Chittagong, in the Bay of Bengal, they would then trek across land to their destination, Kathmandu; from there, they would visit the shrines of Tibet. There had been much correspondence with a guide, who would make the arrangements, and the introductions for Henry and Mercedes. It would be an extensive trip deep into the interior, places where very few westerners had been.

With all the necessary arrangements in place, Jamie at boarding school, seemingly settled, and having made their farewells, Gunter, who had his instructions, was confidently left to run the Manor, maintaining its efficient routine.

The day came to set off for Plymouth. Their luggage, which was extensive, had gone the day before. When Henry and Mercedes reached the docks, they were in awe of the hustle and bustle, of goods being unloaded, people departing and arriving. They were led to their ship, the '*Erinus*', a solid-looking galleon, which, they were told, had made the passage many times. The captain greeted them. He informed them that they would be leaving at first light, on the spring tide, and the passage should take around four months. There would be several stops to take on fresh provisions. They would be sailing around the southern Cape of Africa, and any requests to disembark at these set points would be considered. Completing his introduction, the captain ordered the Purser to show them to their quarters.

Mercedes' concern for Jamie, left all alone at a strange boarding school, presented itself. Henry consoled her with the promise that on the next trip they would take Jamie. They settled into their cabin, and that evening, took supper with the captain, as is tradition. The morning came and they found themselves well under way; the ship had been at sea for some four hours, and there was no sign of land. The following days were taken up with planning the forthcoming trips across India, checking their luggage and packing crates for the transport of spice.

It was during this checking of their luggage that they found an empty trunk. After speaking to the captain, he ordered an investigation into the possible cause. The contents were not valuable, but it required answers. They were now a week into the voyage.

Henry and Mercedes were just getting used to life at sea, the air, the motion, and the strict rules of operation directed by the captain when they were summoned to the captain's cabin, which, full of maps, charts and seafaring equipment, also had their son, James. Startled to find their son in front them, it transpired that he had stowed away, inside the trunk that had lost its contents.

He had given the night porter at the boarding school a draught of senna, rendering him incapable of guard duty at the main entrance. He had also made a friend at the school, who had agreed to cover for him, claiming that James was suffering with an affliction, similar to the night porter, and as a consequence, bed bound. Having obtained transport back to the Manor, it had not been difficult for James to conceal himself. He had been careful not to use a trunk with important equipment, but one which would shortly be transported to the docks. James had remained concealed until the ship was well underway. He then found somewhere in the hold to remain in hiding, until he was discovered.

Mercedes could not disguise a smile, which emerged, together with a lurch forward to hug her son. Henry was dumbstruck, and after agreeing that his son had shown an element of ingenuity in carrying out this venture, tried to put on a stern face. The captain found it difficult to hide his amusement. He was curious to know the condition of the night porter, and agreed it was certainly worthy of an entry into the ship's log.

The captain then put on his stern face and explained that walking the plank could be an option, or he could be clapped in irons, and handed over to the authorities at the next port of call. Having made his position clear, he then suggested that, if Henry and Mercedes agreed, he would enlist Jamie as cabin boy, and he would work his passage off as a member of the crew. This last suggestion was acceptable, and so it was that young James became the cabin boy, his rota of duties would keep him busy throughout the voyage, and he would eat, drink and sleep with the other crew members. It was also agreed that every other Sunday, he would join the captain and his parents for an evening meal. At these occasions, both parties would have the opportunity to discuss the events, trials and tribulations of the previous two weeks.

James quickly settled into the role which had been thrust upon him. His duties would include some of the more undesirable jobs, but he took them in his stride.

It was soon common knowledge that Jamie was the son of the Lord and Lady travelling in the private cabin. There were a few who directed an element of animosity towards him, and there were those who had a concealed admiration, and shook his hand. There was the big black sailor, whose command of the English language was poor, to say the least, but understood more than he let on. He became a good friend of young Jamie, and took him under his wing, protector and teacher, even to the point of teaching him some of his own language.

As the weeks passed and turned into months, Jamie fulfilled the tasks set him and gained the respect of the entire crew. His dogged determination and stubbornness not to admit defeat, stood him in good stead. He was taught the intricacies of using the sextant to plot their position using the stars, sun and planets. The captain also taught him how to read the charts, and plot a course, using wind and tide, and of the importance of keeping a log. His favourite place on board was the crow's nest; having been taught how to climb safely, it was his escape from time to time. As a member of the crew, he was also eligible for the weekly rum ration. The crew, knowing him to be new to the liquor, had him dance a jig on a barrel, to the hornpipe, played by members of the crew, whose applause and encouragement could be heard in the captain's quarters.

It was during one of the rum-tasting sessions, when the tongue is liberated, that the African, who had taken young Jamie under his wing, told him about his life, and of his own people. His name was Gazali, he had been captured and sold as a slave, and after two years in captivity as a galley slave, he had escaped by jumping overboard and swimming to shore. Upon reaching the shore, he made his way to the local harbour, where he was offered work aboard the ship. The captain, having heard his story, assured him that one day, he would return to his people.

They were an ancient tribe, who had lived deep in the jungle for many generations, and every year they would make a pilgrimage to a sacred site. It was there that many were captured and taken as slaves. They were transported to a foreign land, where they were sold at market, like dogs. He told Jamie that for thousands of years, his people had been the keepers of a sacred plant; he had no idea what had become of it after his people had gone. He wondered what had become of them all, scattered about the world, taken from their homes and loved ones. He vowed to return one day, to find what was left of his village, and the secret that it had kept for so long. Gazali then proceeded to snore, in a rum-induced stupor, and that's the last Jamie heard of his story.

Henry and Mercedes were very impressed with the progress of their son, his ability to learn, the interesting stories he had to tell, and the fact he had stowed away, and was now with them. Henry was also very interested in the story of Jamie's friend, Gazali. He had tried to speak with the man but had never got any further than a broken English greeting.

The ship was approaching its destination, a port on the East coast of India in the Bay of Bengal, Chittagong. There was an air of excitement as the crew readied the ship to navigate the narrow channel into the harbour, where they would also load up with spice for their next trip to Australia and the Philippines.

Henry and Mercedes were also preparing for the long trek, partly upriver, and then across land. They had arranged to travel with guides who had made plans for the two of them; they would now have to accommodate a third. The day came when the ship docked in the very busy port; there were people of all nationalities, aromas of spices filled the air, the atmosphere was electric.

The captain wished Henry, Mercedes and Jamie the best of luck, and gave them the date of his expected return to port, for their return journey. The crew gave young Jamie a resounding send-off; he thanked each in turn, especially Gazali, who gave him a carved wooden bracelet, a token of good luck, to be returned when next they met. Jamie returned the favour; he gave Gazali a lucky two-headed coin, also to be returned when next they met.

They left the ship and met with their guide, Ramjit; he had been very busy setting up the trip for Henry and spent some time explaining the plans he had put into place. He and his associates would take them high into the mountains, on all manner of transport, a trip that would take at least a month. From Kathmandu, it was intended to obtain further transport to the sacred temples in Tibet. Having arranged for their extra passenger, and loaded all their equipment onto the transport provided, they set off across the Indian interior.

It was crucial that they stuck to the timetable, if they were going to avoid the bad monsoon season, which would stop them in their tracks and could delay their return to port by months. They made good progress, Ramjit had proved to be an excellent guide and organizer, and they made it to Kathmandu in less than three weeks.

The main task of purchasing herbs and spices took over; they had to await the arrival of their new guide, whose wife had just given birth and would be delayed a couple of days. Truly spectacular markets, small farms growing the strangest plants, were all visited in the quest to fill the empty crates. Jamie had been given the job of cataloguing, and keeping an inventory, a job he approached with the vigour and the stealth of an adult.

The new guide arrived, eventually, with Ramjit, who introduced his third cousin, Parmajit. He assured Henry and Mercedes that he was now available to carry out his task, and there would be no interruptions. It was expected to take a week or two to reach the sacred sites, as the terrain was not exactly as smooth as that which they had previously travelled. He agreed to set off at first light and had arranged for their purchases of spice to be stored in his brother's stables, where it would be safe.

The final step of their journey was slow; their guide knew the area well and managed to find safe passage through the mountains. The final valley eventually brought them to the entrance of a monastery, which spanned the gorge. The stone carvings were abundant, across the top of the wall, fixed onto the front walls, and guarding the gates from the top of stone pillars either side.

Their guide explained that he would set camp outside the walls, he and Mercedes were forbidden to enter such a sacred place. Henry would have to meet and negotiate with the priests, and he would have to wear respectful robes. This was a requirement to express demeanour, to accept the sanctity of the temple, and request permission to enter. Parmajit aided with the translation, and an agreement was reached; the priests of this sacred place would give audience to Henry and Jamie alone.

And so it was, that the following day, Henry and his son would meet the holy ones. It had been established that there was one priest who had an understanding of the Spanish language, which would allow conversation. Both Henry and Jamie, dressed appropriately, approached the gates, which were opened for them. Once inside, they both stopped in their tracks, for the vision that confronted them was one of extreme beauty, the peace and tranquillity had an instant calming effect.

Two priests greeted them, and led them to a garden of small trees, perfectly manicured, fragrances filled the air, and the aromas from incense burners conjured dream like visions. They were greeted by a very old man, small, hunched, holding a gnarly old stick to steady himself. He turned and walked on through the garden, to a house, with sculpted trees and shrubs in front, and beckoned to them to follow. He led them through to the rear of the house which overlooked another garden; they sat, and a young priest brought drinks for them. The gnarly one introduced himself in perfect Spanish, he was a high priest, and his earth name was Ten-zin.

Henry proceeded to explain what his own life was about, and of his search for the knowledge that was locked away in the plant world. They discussed many things; talks went on for hours, a loyal procession of devoted priests brought refreshments and snacks at regular intervals.

Jamie had been allowed to wander whilst the grownups talked, having been given strict instructions not to touch anything. This was an eleven-year-old being told not to. He found a corner of the garden, where a particular plant looked very out of place. It was not manicured like the rest but sprawling over walls and archways. Bald priests wandered all around, bowing to Jamie, who felt compelled to return the politeness, so bowed back. His interest in the unusual plant caused concern among the priests; pointing and shaking their heads, they indicated it was a no-go area. So, sitting in a very comfortable seat close to this no-go area, Jamie studied the anomaly, and promptly fell asleep.

It was whilst young James slept, that the strangeness happened; what can only be described as an inquisitive plant, came to investigate. A shoot or tendril grew towards him, it inspected the bracelet he wore, and subsequently proceeded to cocoon young James where he sat.

The vigilant priests brought this to the attention of Henry and Ten-Zin; it interrupted their conversation, and they went to investigate. On arrival at this spectacle, they found young James totally immersed within the growth of the plant. Ten-zin approached the bench and sat next to James. There was nothing to be seen of him, he put his hands on the plant, and closing his eyes, appeared to enter a trance-like state. After some minutes, Ten-zin informed Henry that there was nothing to worry about; a bonding was taking place, instigated by a particular bracelet Jamie was wearing.

Henry and Ten-Zin returned to the house, continued their conversation, which now had added subject matter, and talked until dawn. Ten-Zin explained to Henry the properties of the sacred flower and its connections with an ancient race, not seen for an age. Ten-Zin told him that it had been looked after within the temple for thousands of years, no-one outside knew of its existence. Henry was then bound by a vow of secrecy, not to say anything of what he had seen. In return Ten-zin would furnish Henry with a substantial collection of herbs and spices, to which Henry agreed.

They both went to collect Jamie, for breakfast. They found him asleep on the bench, where he had been all night, the plant was in its usual state of disarray, sprawling around. Jamie would wake, none the wiser, but for a vivid dream, which he would have recur for the rest of his life. The three retired to the patio of the house, where a breakfast banquet was served by a devoted family of priests, dedicated to a cause.

Young Jamie was quizzed by Ten-Zin, who inquired if he had been comfortable while he and his father had talked, he expressed his regret if Jamie had been too bored. He had a curiosity to know how much, if anything, Jamie remembered of his strange encapsulation, and how he had come by the strange bracelet he wore. Jamie recounted the pact he had made with Gazali, to return the gifts they had exchanged when next they met. And his night had been so comfortable, it was as though he was back home in his own bed. He had dreamed he had been everywhere; he had flown over the seas, he had floated on clouds, and he had feasted with strange beings amongst the stars.

Jamie joked that it all seemed very normal.

Ten-zin advised Jamie to relish his youth, enjoy life, and not be afraid of knowledge, for he would come to realise that everything was connected, and a harmony exists with all living things. The three sat down to breakfast, and plans were made to assemble a collection of some of the most exotic herbs and spices that the monastery had to offer.

Ten-Zin gave instructions to Henry on how to prepare and use the herbs, while Jamie did his best to write this information down in the journals they had been keeping.

The time came to leave the holy place, and laden with goods, they made their farewells to the priests and Ten-Zin, who invited Jamie to return when he was a man. Returning to camp, they packed up then set off on their return journey. Their guide led them safely back to his village, there, the rest of the cargo was loaded onto carts, and with a fond farewell to Parmajit and co, they set off for the port of Chittagong.

The trip had gone very well, they returned to port on time, to find that the *Erinus* had been in port for a week, awaiting their arrival. Everything was loaded on board, the captain explained that the monsoon season might start at any time, so they should make haste and sail on the first tide.

Jamie would not be expected to work off his passage as cabin boy but would be allowed to mix with the crew should he so desire. It was a privilege he embraced, as he had made good friends with the crew the first time, especially Gazali, who he was keen to meet up with again.

The ship sailed, Henry busied himself with the inventory, Mercedes assisted with cataloguing the different species and Jamie continued to carry out duties as cabin boy, even though his passage was paid for.

Jamie told Gazali of his exploits, the journey through the interior, the amazing monastery, and his night of dreams. Gazali refused to accept back his token of the bracelet, claiming that it had chosen young James as its new keeper, and anyway, he preferred the coin. It had won him a considerable amount, in his pursuance of gambling, money which he would use to find his way back to his village.

The ship sailed on, just managing to outrun the monsoon, which could be seen darkening the skies from whence they came. Having fair winds and light seas, they made good time, and soon approached the final leg of their journey. The captain announced that they would make landfall in two or three days. They would see Plymouth, and home, after nearly a year, in which young James had reached the ripe old age of twelve.

They docked in Plymouth and thanking the captain and crew for a safe voyage, Henry, Mercedes and James disembarked; Gazali shouted to James that he would see him in Africa one day. Having unloaded all their cargo, and then loading it onto numerous horse-drawn wagons, the family set off for the Manor.

Young James returned to the boarding school, apologized to the night porter, and settled down to his studies with renewed vigour. The friendship with his accomplice in crime, John Tremayne, grew; they both had similar ideas on current medical practices.

Henry spent the years studying and experimenting with the rich variety of herbs and spices, which they had procured in India and Tibet. Mercedes ran things, she was an excellent organiser; she arranged all of Henry's seminars, and correspondence with hospitals and colleges, and she became quite a notary herself.

As the years passed, James completed his schooling, and he became more interested in his father's work; a passion drove him to apply to Oxford. Both he and his friend John Tremayne entered Oxford at the same time; they soon made a name for themselves, arguing at seminars, and conferences, that the old medicine was dangerous. It was often the case that they would both be physically ejected by some speakers, believing their ideas to be too inexperienced. Henry was trying to introduce a new approach to medicine, his experiments with plant extracts, creating tinctures and lotions were showing promise. His discoveries, he believed, needed to be taught and explained to the medical profession.

Some years later, Henry decided that another expedition would be required, to collect more of the plants that he could not grow in his greenhouses. His goal was to find a cure for the plague. The destination, a return to Tibet. He had been working on a potion which lacked one vital ingredient, he was sure that it could be found at the monastery; he had tried to get word through to Ten-Zin, without success.

James was in his final year at Oxford, and both he and his friend John had expressed their desire to go in his father's place, as he was getting on in years, and his time would be better spent working at home. John's parents, wealthy landowners in Cornwall, would fund the trip, eager for their son to experience the world, and its potentials. And so, it was arranged, the trip to India on board the '*Erinus.*'

The captain greeted Jamie as an old friend, some of the original crew were still on board, but Gazali, had left some years earlier to pursue his roots. The guides in Chittagong were more relatives of Ramjit, and the same with the trek to the monastery from Nepal; they were big families. When they reached the monastery, Ten-Zin had just returned from a pilgrimage, which had taken him the best part of a year. He greeted young James and his friend, inviting them to stay. John was allowed to attend various classes, they included what the priests regarded as mindful medicine, while James, was taken into a sacred place where strange things grew.

Ten-Zin informed James that very few had been allowed access, he referred to the bracelet James still wore; it had refused to be removed and had virtually bonded with his skin. It was the conduit through which the plant made contact but did not guarantee the bonding that happened. This came about after it had searched his soul and found a pure spirit. It then gave him the dreams that he had.

They entered a sun-drenched piazza, hidden within the temple, and in it, was the plant, growing up walls and across balconies. It had the most amazing flowers, with a fragrance that induced a vision. Ten-Zin told James the story of the flower, of its ancestry and use, it was a timeless entity which James would have considerable dealings within the future. There were others like it throughout the world, each being looked after by a people who understood, and were at one with nature. Ten-zin would give James an offshoot of the plant to take back, together with other sacred herbs and spices that he had come for, but the plant was to be looked after, and kept secret.

Just before the intrepid explorers left, Ten-Zin told Jamie that his friend Gazali might need his assistance, and that he would soon know where to find him.

Jamie and his friend returned to England, John set up a medical practice in London, and Jamie continued his work with his father. The secret plant was given a home which had been specially built; it would allow it to grow and benefit from secrecy.

Jamie continued with the expeditions in his search for new species, and together with his father, they wrote medical journals, about their discoveries and cures. His trip to Africa did result in his reconnection with his old friend Gazali; he had re-established his village, but the plant that they had been looking after for centuries, had suffered. Gazali knew that the bracelet would help to restore the plant and told Jamie that he had spoken with Ten-Zin in a dream. He knew of young Jamie's association with the plant and was glad it was he who had been chosen.

There were many things to learn, Jamie had just started, but it was quite evident that he would be the one to bring together all the people of the night flower and become the Earthbound keeper of the plant.

Chapter 5

It was 05:00hrs; Jake's open-air sleeping arrangements now had a fly net, because the hot weather had provided a breeding ground for the horse fly. He was in between that deep sleep and the awakening; his mind had travelled to a strange place, where a tall creature was continually blocking corridors and creating doors that led nowhere, in a labyrinth that stretched farther than the eye could see. A man could be seen walking these corridors, he appeared to be searching for a way out, always thwarted by the creature, which seemed to take pleasure in its game. Jake could see the way out and was trying to tell him. He shouted but no sound came from his mouth; he tried to point the way, but in vain. The creature acknowledged that Jake was trying to help this man. It put a door in his path, not allowing any communication from Jake to get through. Jake opened the door, and another appeared, the doors appeared again and again. The sweat was now pouring down Jake's brow; he was struggling through cobwebs behind each door.

He woke with a start, tangled in the fly net, with Fidgit slobbering all over his face. Fidgit thought it was a good game and did a little mad run around the bed as Jake untangled himself.

'Phew,' said Jake, 'that was a weird dream. I suppose you think that's funny.'

Fidgit, tail wagging, head between paws, bum in the air, was awaiting the next move.

Jake had already done a day's work in that dream. He climbed into the shower to wash it all away. The radio announcer was commenting on the weather:

'...and it looks like this record heat wave of 2018 could be much longer than the summer of '76. There doesn't seem to be a let-up in the heat anytime soon.

Jake wandered out to his garden to give it a watering. Fidgit was in a playful mood and was quite happy for Jake to try and zap him with the water hose, running in and out of the bushes.

Dressed in shorts, T-shirt and working boots, Jake made his way to the front of his cabin, whistling Fidgit, who had gone a wandering.

'Breakfast!' shouted Jake and continued through the orchard to the kitchen; Fidgit was already there, having his favourite.

'You're on the ball this morning.'

His comment fell on deaf ears as Fidgit licked the bowl into a corner.

Jake entered the kitchen parlour where his father was tucking into a hearty breakfast, and his mother was putting Jake's serving on a plate.

'Cuppa?' said Mother. 'You look tired; been clubbing all night?'

'I feel knackered.' He then told them of his dream, and his futile attempt to help.

'That be your Gran's dream,' said his father, 'she's had that dream since I were a lad, strange you should have it too.'

He looked over at Mother who had that concerned look and winked.

'You'll feel better after a cuppa,' and she passed him a large mug of tea.

Jake seemed to be somewhere else over breakfast, his mind wandering again, unable to concentrate on the day.

'Talk to your Gran, she'll explain it, I wouldn't worry too much about it.' His father then went on to change the subject.

'Saw Bertie Brownlow at the bowls club yesterday, says your job on the pond is looking for pucker, he's well pleased.'

'Good,' said Jake, beginning to find renewed vigour.

'We're going to get the final planting sorted today. I've told Moss we shan't be at the Manor, we have done most of the work over the past five days, so we are going to finish Mr & Mrs B's, and have a bit of time off, catch up, you know.'

Mother gave Father that approving look and continued to wash up the crocks.

'Right, I'm off to get Sandra.' Handing his mother more washing up to do, he praised his mother's breakfast, and exclaimed it was just what he needed.

Fidgit was sitting eagerly awaiting Jake.

'Are you going to be a good lad, you know Mrs B's cat doesn't like you?'

Fidgit, one ear cocked, head to one side, knew exactly what Jake had said, then ran to the Landy; he was sitting on his favourite cushion in the back when Jake got there.

As Jake drove down the lane towards his Gran's, Mr B was out at the front of his garden cutting the hedge.

'See you later,' Jake shouted. He pulled up outside his Gran's, and walked up the garden path to where she was entertaining Sandra.

'Morning Jake, cuppa? You look tired, everything all right?' Gran looked at Sandra.

'Do you think he looks tired?'

Sandra said, 'Yep, definitely looks tired.'

'Pack it in you pair,' said Jake, knowing he was being wound up. They all laughed and blamed the weather.

Jake mentioned his dream to Gran.

'Mmmm, I had that dream too, last night,' she said.

'I'm going up to the Manor later, guests arrive day after tomorrow, lots to do. I shall speak with Moss about our man in the maze, I have an idea, I may know who it is.'

Jake told Gran of their plans to collect plants from an aquatic centre over by Bridgwater. They should complete the Brownlow's job later and be clear for the work at the Manor. They made their farewells to Gran, who wished them well, and set off to do their stuff.

After Gran had cleared the morning breakfast things away, she donned her helmet and drove off towards the farm on her scooter. She pulled up outside the kitchen door where Edna was sitting with a mug of tea.

'Would you like one, Ivy?' she said, gesturing to the teapot on the table.

'No thank you, just finished breakfast with Jake and Sandra.'

Ivy sat down tentatively, and told Edna that she too, had dreamt of the lost man. She was positive that it was Master Henry, who was being held captive inside the maze.

'Should we tell Jake what this dream means? I can see him getting frustrated. He's had a lot to take in these past weeks, so I carn't say as I blame 'im.'

Edna told Ivy that Bill had started dreaming. He had put aside many strange thoughts for most of his life, but this dream was strong. In this dream, he had seen Jake and a strange creature, it was very hazy, it looked like a fight was going on. Jake was calling to a man who kept going through the same door, over and over, getting nowhere. Jake was confronting the creature, who stood defiantly in his path, raising its arms.

'That's as far as the dream goes. Bill couldn't see what happens next, he's afeared Jake is struck by the creature.'

He woke up at that point, soaked in perspiration.' Edna continued to tell Ivy, that for years, Bill had refused to believe in the goings-on at the Manor; he had always dismissed it as folklore and superstition, until now.

'I'm off to the Manor now, I need to speak with Moss, he will know what to do,' Ivy consoled Edna, and assured her that no harm would come to Jake.

'I shall pop in on my way back,' she said, donning her helmet yet again. The sound of her scooter could be heard on the still air of the day, as she rode off into the distance.

On reaching the Manor, Ivy found Moss, Jim and Joe Miller all busy putting the night flower into crates of soil, in order to transport it to the conservatory, and its new home.

'Good day, Ivy, they are ready for you in the conservatory, we shall be with you, presently.' Moss smiled, and told Ivy he was aware of the dreams, and there was absolutely no need to worry. Ivy, a little unsure as to who *they* were, continued up the drive to the house, stood her trusty steed on its stand, disrobed from her helmet and entered the front doors. As she walked through to the conservatory, she was aware of childish gigglings, and on entering the conservatory she was greeted by three young *Burrbesh*, jumping around in the newly prepared flower beds. They turned to Ivy and rushed over to her; she hugged each one in turn, a tear in her eye, and fond memories of a childhood, where every day had been fun, came back to her, and they were exactly as she remembered. Then Moss entered.

'They did love you, my dear, in their own way, and they never forgot you.

Come, let us talk, there is much to do and very little time to do it. Jake comes of age the day after tomorrow, and we need to be prepared.'

After a wash and brush-up, Moss led Ivy out onto the patio, a rather nice place to chat. Jim and Joe, together with the less helpful *Burrbesh,* continued with their task of making the night flower comfortable, in its new bed.

With refreshments on hand to compensate for the ever-increasing temperature, Moss began to explain to Ivy the tricky situation that had arisen over recent weeks.

The great elder had summoned the Council of Libra to a meeting at the Manor; it was to take place on the Summer Solstice. This would be a particularly strong solstice, with the alignment of certain celestial bodies, which only happens everyone hundred years. There would be an increase of energy, in all the Ley lines that criss-cross the Earth; it used to be a time when great things came about. The elders would use that energy to arrive, and then communicate the results of the meeting to others of their kind.

'It will be a gathering, not seen since the last winter.'

Each, a specialist in their own field, tree planters, grass growers, hedgerow providers, everything that grows. One in particular, whose name is *Leber*, deals in dangerous, poisonous and downright nasty stuff.' Moss gave a shudder at the thought.

He continued to explain that it was he who had imprisoned the master, not with shackles but with confusion.

'You see, Master Henry had gone in search of the secrets of travel, which is our way of getting around, and a heavily guarded secret. He had spent many years studying with us, he had learned many of the *Burrbesh* ways, he thinks as we do, and has the same ideals. He is also approaching immortality, which has annoyed one of us, in particular, *Leber*. He is the rogue, who has been responsible for some of the more chaotic creations throughout time. He has been exiled on more than one occasion, but he does provide solutions to some of the more problematic Earthbound perils.' Moss took a long slow drink to refresh his palate.

'Master Henry has given up much of his earthly life to support us, and I think it is only fair that we should assist him in his escape. We are going to need all the help we can muster, to deal with what is coming, including the inimitable *Leber*.' Moss had a serious tone to his voice and Ivy was listening intently.

'My grandson comes of age on the Solstice, I have had visions of what might be, but they are vague. I know he has an important role to play, but it isn't clear. Do you know what that is, Moss?'

Ivy was looking for clarification, it had been a while since she had seen things, but the visions were becoming clearer by the day.

‘Yes, there is a plan,’ said Moss.

He grabbed the empty pitcher from the table.

‘More refreshments, I think, and a look in on how things are going inside.’

After checking the progress inside, he returned with a new pitcher of drinks and proceeded to explain.

Taking a large drink of the refreshing cold lemonade, Moss began:

‘Firstly, *Leber* has Master Henry trapped in a quandary, a confused dilemma, from which he himself cannot escape. He will need our help. *Leber* has to attend the meeting, so there will be a moment when he is distracted; this is when we shall have our opportunity. It will require all who are connected to your bloodline – you, your son, your grandson and possibly Sandra, for diversion. There will be strength in numbers, but I cannot be seen to be involved. There are times when the code of the *Burrbesh* gets in the way of common sense. Decisions made by *Leber* are usually respected by the majority.

Secondly, I have to tell you, that you are Master Henry’s daughter.’

Moss observed Ivy’s reaction to this news; it did not appear to come as a shock.

Ivy explained that her mother had attempted to tell her on several occasions. She surmised that there had been someone else, and over the years, her mother had let slip little secrets; her mother had loved this man very much. Both Ivy and her mother had lost husbands in wars, and they had both only had one child; Jake too, was an only child.

‘It may be, that Jake could be as powerful as Master Henry. As he is his great grandson, and born on the same day, the two could prove invaluable in the coming battles,’ said Moss, standing to admire the view.

‘And the Manor will be the centre of operations, which could affect the whole planet,’ Moss said, so quietly, Ivy did not hear.

Turning to Ivy, Moss said with authority.

‘So, Ivy, you need to live long, Jake also has his destiny already written, his family and friends will play a crucial role in events; the Manor is going to get very busy.’ Moss sat back in his chair, examining expressions on the face of Ivy. A silence came over the Manor, and even the little ones were quiet.

'I take it, you need me to be the conduit, just where exactly is Master Henry?' Ivy asked, trying to associate a place within her vision.

'*Leber* has him running up and down the steps to the front door, he's made the steps into a labyrinth, and told Master Henry that the front door is just at the top of the stairs. He has been looking for that door for over a hundred years.'

Moss told Ivy that Master Henry had not quite mastered the art of travel through the fabric, and it needed outside help to show him the way.

'I'm not sure if you can connect with Master Henry, but he needs to understand his position, and be ready for our rescue attempt,' said Moss.

'Master Henry needs to return; he is to play a vital role in future plans. Do you think your son could assist in this rescue?'

'He has always had an underlying curiosity for the stories I have told him. Unlike myself, when I was young, I was surrounded by the strangeness, and accepted it; it's all different today,' Ivy went on to explain.

'I think he will rise to the occasion with a passion, and do us proud, he has always been strong-willed. His devotion to duty has been paramount, which has always kept him on the right path, and his dreams under control.'

'We should both investigate Master Henry's dilemma, right now, while we have the time,' said Moss.

Ivy was finding the heat a little intense, and with the prospect of diving into the unknown, she came over a little faint. Moss refilled her glass and apologized for being a little pushy.

'I don't want to put you under pressure, Ivy, but as you are here, it may be a good time to test my theory for a rescue of Master Henry.' Moss passed her a glass of cordial and encouraged her to drink.

'I have waited so long for something to happen,' she said. 'I shall not let you down.'

'We need to let Master Henry know we are here, and have come to help, and that he needs to change the repetitive directions that *Leber* has set him. We should go down to the basement, I want to show you something.'

Moss led the way, a door in the hallway led into a small anteroom, used as a cloakroom. Oak panelling adorned the walls; he pushed on one panel which revealed a door handle. Turning and pulling, a large door opened, complete with panels. It revealed a stairway which was carved out of the stone the Manor house was built on.

'This was created by Master Henry's father. When the house was being built, it has provided refuge for many a persecuted soul. You may enjoy the cooler temperature it commands.'

Moss continued down the winding steps, on and on, dim lighting from the occasional tungsten bulb illuminating the way. Eventually reaching the bottom, he flicked on an ancient light switch; the lights revealed a cave of considerable proportions with columns creating arches all around the perimeter. These arches formed the entrance to tunnels, each one wandering off in its own direction; it gave the impression of a small cathedral.

'It's huge,' said Ivy, taking in the spectacle.

'It is a natural cave, discovered during the original construction, only those loyal to the crown were allowed to work on it. The tunnels go for miles, we use it, as you would use your underground, it is directly over energy lines, assisting us all to come and go. It is possible that Master Henry may be along one of these tunnels.'

Moss took Ivy's hands and held them tightly; together their minds wandered the maze of catacombs, which had so often been in their thoughts, but now Ivy could see them with such clarity and purpose. It did not take her long to locate Master Henry, and after observing his actions for some time, they concluded that it was going to be a little more difficult. *Leber* had effectively connected two doors together, to look as one, so when Master Henry passed through one door, the other door returned him to a corridor that led back to that same door. In effect he was back where he started, he would go round and round in circles, with no hope of escape. Releasing hands, Moss said they needed to talk.

'Do you think your family might like to come for dinner this evening? We could discuss it then.'

Returning to the heat of the day, and after inspecting the night flower, where three young *Burrbesh* had nestled in amongst the stems of mother, they both reflected on the calm silence that prevailed. Ivy thought of the calm before the storm.

'Would you like to join me? I'm going to check on the greenhouses. Jake and Sandra have done a great job, and they have both worked very hard,' Moss said, as he turned towards the patio.

'No, I shall go home, then I'll go over to the farm and convey your invitation to Bill and Edna. I may even see Jake and Sandra at the Brownlow's on the way round.

'You can count on us all coming over, it is important after all.' Ivy bade Moss a farewell and proceeded through the hall to the front door.

'We shall have staff tonight, a complement of Scottish reliables are turning up later,' Moss shouted.

These were staff, accustomed to the strange goings on at venues where Moss was involved; nothing would faze them.

Ivy rode on down the lane, and eventually arrived at the farm. Edna was in the cider house, mixing what she believed to be another masterpiece. Hammering a wooden bung securely into the top of the barrel, she said, 'It's lunchtime, fancy a scone and a cup of tea?'

'That would be nice,' Ivy replied.

They retired to the table outside the kitchen, after preparing a light feast, and sat down in the shade of a very useful umbrella.

'This heat is never ending, lovely, isn't it? It's how summers should be,' said Ivy as she sat down next to Edna. Without holding anything back, Ivy told her the full story, including Moss's confirmation that she was Master Henry's daughter.

'Well, I never,' said Edna. 'Your mother kept that secret well, and what's this talk of battles to come?'

'I'm not too sure about that; Moss said all would be revealed at the meeting, day after tomorrow.'

They both drank tea and ate their scones in silence.

Edna broke the silence, saying they would come over to the Manor, it would be around sevenish.

'Fine, I shall go and check on Jake and Sandra, they will probably be busy at the Brownlows.' Ivy thanked Edna for tea, donned her helmet and made her way to where she assumed Jake and Sandra were. Jake's Land Rover was parked at the front. Pulling up next to it, Fidgit who had been napping, sat up expecting to go with her, but Ivy said:

'So, you've been ordered to stay here, mmm, I wonder why?'

Giving Fidgit the order to stay, he reluctantly returned to his cushion.

Ivy knew Mrs B and wandered round the back. Jake, Sandra and the Brownlows were all around the pool, which was nearly all planted up, and looking very good.

'Hello Gran, what brings you here, come to admire our creation?' Jake smiled at her, as she walked around admiring the detail.

'Had to see my grandson's first job, didn't I?'

Turning to Mrs B, she said, 'Bettie, can you bring a few samples of your best amber nectar to the next meeting? Some of the bowls committee will be there, and you know they enjoy your formulas.' Then, turning to Jake and Sandra, she asked if they were free that evening around seven. Looking at each other quizzically, they turned to Gran and said yes, they had nothing planned.

'Good, that's settled, pop in on your way back, I have something for your mother, you can take with you.' Ivy said her goodbyes and returned to her transport, telling Fidgit, 'they won't be long.'

Ivy returned to her house and decided a summer frock might be in order; it was rare that she went out for dinner, and this could be a special night. Foraging around in her wardrobes, a box of photos fell from a shelf and spilled out on the floor. As she picked them up, she realized that they were of her mother's wedding, very old sepia prints. She sat browsing through them, having a moment's reminiscence, sadness at the loss of her mother's husband, so young, annoyed at the futility of war.

He had come home on a week's summer leave, only to find her mother too ill to enjoy it; a bout of Scarlet Fever had taken hold. It was the last she saw of him. He was to be stationed on the French/Belgium border; he was killed at the battle of Mons in August 1914, just twenty years old. Ivy picked up the photographs and carefully packed them away.

She managed to choose a lightweight summer frock; one she could not remember ever wearing. Memories were flashing through her mind, of her husband, who had been killed in the second war when she was only twenty-five. After that, she had immersed herself in her work as a nurse, eventually marrying a doctor, with whom she had William, Bill, her only son.

She suddenly felt the presence of Moss, who, acknowledging the dinner reservations for the six of them, for seven o'clock, conveyed his condolences for her sadness. She must remind herself to have words with him at dinner and stay out of her head.

Her thoughts then returned to the plight of Henry; he had been the one who had nursed her mother to recovery, all those years ago. He was now in need of help, and she was determined that he should be freed from his prison. She mused on the fact that her father would be four hundred and thirteen years old, the day after tomorrow.

Picking up the chosen frock, Ivy thought it needed refreshing, so off it went to the wash. Hanging it on the line, she turned to go back through the house. Fidgit announced the arrival of Jake and Sandra, by doing his mad dash, down the garden and back, tail between his legs. Ivy came through the house and out the front door.

'Hello you two, all finished. I bet you're proud of that job, it's going to look gorgeous when all those plants get established.'

She picked up the tray from the table and said, 'I need a cuppa, anybody else?'

They both agreed readily to that suggestion

'I'll come and help,' said Sandra.

'And I'll sort Fidgit a drink,' said Jake.

Having deposited all that was required for afternoon tea on the table in the front garden, they continued their chat.

'What's happening at seven o'clock then, Gran?' Jake asked.

'Dinner at the Manor with your parents, Moss and myself, I have been asked to invite you both.'

Ivy then went on to explain about Jake's dream, which his father, Moss and herself had all been witness to. She went on to explain the situation, and that with their help, they could possibly free Master Henry from his hundred-year quandary. The dinner would be an opportunity to plan the rescue attempt if everyone was willing.

'I can't get him out of my head. Since the dream he has been knocking a door; all the time I hear this door knocker, if I close my eyes, I see him. I can see him shouting but there's no sound, is this real or am I just going barmy?' Jake, evidently frustrated, was not ready for the next bombshell.

Ivy blurted out.

'He is your great grandfather.'

She could not find an easy way to say it. Jake collapsed back in his seat, unable to take in what he had just been told.

'That makes him your father,' said Sandra, 'how old must he be?'

Ivy sheepishly told them that he would be four hundred and thirteen the day after tomorrow, same birthday as Jake.

'Moss will explain this evening, are you both going to come?'

Jake and Sandra looked at each other and agreed that they could not miss this for the world. It had been agreed that Jake's father would collect them all and take them to the Manor.

'Be like going to the ball,' said Ivy, winking at Sandra, 'no glass slippers.' Ivy chuckled to herself as she took the tea things through to the kitchen.

'See, you later,' Jake gave Sandra a peck on the cheek, and went off down the front path, whistling to Fidgit as he went.

Back at home, Jake parked up in the usual place by the barn, and he noticed that the strange plant he had acquired from the Manor had gone. Fidgit had gone through the hedge, to do what he did best, and Jake went straight to the kitchen. He was a little earlier than usual, Mother was not about, he went round to her cider house, still no sign. He went back into the house and called to his mother, a muffled, 'be down in a minute', could be heard from Mother. Jake poured himself a glass of water and waited for her. She appeared, wearing a rather colourful dress, and carrying an armful of even more colourful dresses that she had been trying on for the ball.

'What do you think, Jake? Haven't been to a ball for so long,' his mother joked.

'I just don't know what to wear, and I can't find me tiara.' Jake was rather tickled by that remark and burst out laughing; this infected his mother, and they were both hysterical by the time Jake's father walked in.

'Oy, oy, what's going on?'

'Mother can't find her tiara,' said Jake, which brought on another bout of hysteria, affecting his father too.

The kitchen was filled with laughter, sides started to ache, Fidgit turned up, dropped his rabbit and howled, which only exacerbated the laughter. When eventually, normality returned, Edna explained to Bill that they had been invited to the Manor for dinner, staff had arrived, Moss was in charge, and dress was expected to be non-formal.

'Blimey, never been to the Manor,' said Bill, 'shall have to find me best braces and dickie bow.'

This brought about another spate of laughter.

Jake left before he hurt himself and wandered down to his place to get ready for the event.

Meanwhile Edna explained to Bill what the dinner was for. She said that Ivy had called earlier, and told her of the facts regarding his family, and that it involved the dream he had recently been having.

'Sounds like history is coming acalling,' said Bill, and he gave Edna a big hug.

'Let's go and do this!', and they both retired to prepare.

Jake arrived at the kitchen door to find Mother spruced up in her summer finest. Father soon followed, looking very dapper; they made Jake feel a little underdressed.

They climbed into Father's Range Rover and set off to pick up Sandra and Ivy. Arriving at Gran's, Jake went up the front path to collect them; both Sandra and Ivy were well capable of gracing any catwalk.

'You both look stunning,' said Jake and offered each an arm to escort them to their carriage. They arrived at the Manor and were greeted by a tall man in butler's attire. In a broad Scottish accent, he greeted the guests and escorted them to the patio, where Moss was giving instructions to other staff members.

'Good evening, I am Moss, your host this evening,' he said, introducing himself to Jake's parents.

'Shall we go through? I thought drinks on the patio, before lunch?' He enquired if anyone had any preferences on food, before instructing the staff to produce some tasty morsels.

Having comfortably settled on the patio with drinks, Moss began his inquisition. He needed to be sure that what was required could be supplied without question, if there was to be any hope of success.

He continued: 'If anyone has a question, please do not hesitate to interrupt; there is little or no space for error. Ivy may have informed you of the situation we have.'

Moss had his serious head on, again. He continued to explain about Master Henry's predicament, which was: whilst searching for the ancient secrets of travel, in the African jungle, he had been extracted from this world by a jealous and dangerous elder. He had been firmly ensconced in a quandary, a repetitive circuit from which there is no escape for the individual. He had been in this void for nearly a hundred years, his only hope was for his family to join forces, and focus the strengths that they had, to help break this cycle.

'Ivy, you as daughter are the strongest. Bill, you have renounced this for years, your strength is weak but growing stronger the more you believe. And Jake, your strength is very strong, and will be even stronger on your birthday. *Leber,* will not be expecting someone with your strength. Sandra, you do have some connections through your family, you may very well provide just the distraction we need.' Moss went on to describe the sequence of events for the gathering.

There would be twelve elders arriving for the meeting and they would arrive from noon onwards; they were the elected representatives for the *Burrbesh* and made up the Council of Libra. Rooms had been prepared for them, and they would return from whence they came the following day. Should the quest to free Master Henry be successful, he would be invited to attend the meeting, as the thirteenth council member.

'I expect he will be asked to take charge of the battles to come, which will be decided on the night.'

Having examined the quandary of Master Henry, there is a moment when he hesitates, approaching the door. There is another door to the left, he knows it is there, but it has been obscured by *Leber*, it is this door he must go through to break the cycle. It is this door that he needs to acknowledge, he needs to be guided to this door, and he must open it. Ivy and Bill, together, you may be able to inform Master Henry of the plan to affect his escape, and Jake, you will have to guide him to the door.

'Sandra, *Leber* will arrive at twelve noon, you shall be invited as a guest, and you may be able to distract him for a moment, for that is all we need.'

'How do I get there; how do I find the door? I have never done anything like this before,' said Jake.

'Can you see Master Henry now?' asked Moss.

'Constantly,' said Jake.

Moss continued to explain that Jake's gift would get stronger; in time he would learn to control it, but for now and with the energy available, he would have no difficulty in carrying out his task. Moss instilled a confidence within the small group, and over dinner, clarified the plan that would take place at noon, on the twenty-first.

The remainder of the evening was taken up with stories of the Manor, how it was in the early days; Moss was a good storyteller. Everyone listened, and felt more as one, as Moss eloquently captivated his audience. And as the evening drew to a close, they left the Manor, thanking Moss for an enlightening evening.

He recommended that Jake and Sandra enjoy a day off, and he would catch up with them later.

Chapter 6

The evening had been a resounding success. Bill pulled up outside Ivy's, she invited Jake and Sandra for breakfast the following morning to set them up for their day out. Making her goodnights to everyone she carried on up the path to her house. Jake walked Sandra to her front door, their hands met as they walked, her touch was gentle and comforting, it triggered a feeling in Jake. His heart missed a beat, it was at that moment that he acknowledged his feelings for Sandra; this was a man who had just realised he was in love. With a long slow kiss, and a cuddle, they bade each other good night; they had the whole day together tomorrow.

Back at home and with the night over, and so complete, everyone settled down; their thoughts were full of what had been discussed, and what the next day could possibly bring.

The night passed without incident, and a new day dawned, with magnificence. Even without rain for so long, everything looked spectacular in the rising sun. With an early morning wander around his allotment, dressed as nature intended, Jake watered everything, including Fidgit. He then proceeded to jump in the shower, turning up his favourite music, to the point where objects fell off the shelves, and he indulged.

His mind wandered to the rescue attempt, he was feeling angry with *Leber*, and very confident in what he thought might work as a plan. His world was firing on all cylinders, you could have thrown him off the top of The Shard, and he would have landed on a delivery of mattresses, not polyester but goose feather and down. He wandered over to the kitchen to see Mother, before going to Gran's.

'Mornin', sleep well?' Mother said, as she slid four fried eggs onto his father's plate.

'How's Sandra this morning?' she said, looking over at his father, giving him that mother's knowing look.

'I have no idea, Mother, you know more than I do,' said Jake nonchalantly, pouring himself a glass of milk, and downing it in one. He made his farewells and said he would see them later. Turning to his father, he asked.

'Are you ok to have Fidgit, Dad? I'm going into town with Sandra, you know he hates the traffic.' His father agreed to look after him and wished them both an enjoyable day.

'Give Sandra my love,' he said.

Jake gave his mother a peck, issued Fidgit with instructions, and then went on his way.

Master Henry was now in his mind all the time, even more so when he was alone, and even just allowing his mind to wander, Henry's predicament took over his thoughts.

He pulled up outside Gran's. Realising his shadow was not with him, he made his way up the path. Sandra greeted him.

'Good morning, sleep well? No bad dreams?' Jake gave her a hug and an early morning kiss.

'Slept like a log,' he said. 'You?'

Sandra explained that she felt a little detached from all that was happening at the moment. Although she would like to connect, she wasn't sure that she could be of benefit. At that moment Gran arrived with a tray of goodies.

'Here, let me help,' said Jake.

He and Sandra then followed her to the kitchen to collect the rest of the breakfast banquet, for Gran never did anything by halves.

They all sat down, and after the first cup of tea, began to discuss the events of the past twenty-four hours.

Gran started by asking Sandra what she thought about everything that had happened to her since she came back from university.

'I have got to admit, there is a lot that feels like it came from the Brothers Grimm, and I am concerned for the safety of Jake.'

She explained, that, although she understood the concept, she found it a little difficult to get her head around it: that in this modern age, old world gremlins were about to come forth, and possibly wreak havoc on the world.

'I suppose it could be a concern, but I don't think for a minute that there will be gremlins running around,' Gran smiled and reassured Sandra, and added, should things return to how they were when she was young, the world would be a better place.

'Anyway, what are your plans for today?' Gran asked.

Sandra told her that they planned to go into town; she was going to look for something suitable to wear for tomorrow, and then they planned to visit her aunt, for lunch, and after, perhaps a stroll along the river.

'Very nice,' said Gran, and turning to Jake, 'any ideas for Master Henry's rescue?'

'Yes, I have actually, I may need a little help from you on that, need to speak to you later.' Jake said he had a good idea where Henry was, he had seen a room with passages all around, and he had also seen his Gran there with Moss.

'Mmm, yes I know that room,' said Gran. She told Jake of her meeting with Moss and the door to the stairway.

'I shall see Moss later. But you two should go and enjoy the day, and don't worry, Sandra, nothing bad is going to happen, I can sense it.'

Jake said his visions were getting more frequent.

'They pop up anytime, but I'm getting quite used to them, comforting almost.'

They continued with breakfast, and chatted about their plans for the day, mentioning to Gran that they were now perhaps a little more than friends.

'How nice, can't say as I'm surprised though, you pair have been inseparable since you were kids.'

Finishing their banquet, and having helped Gran tidy up, the pair set off on their day out.

Gran soon set off to the farm to catch Bill before he got involved in his work; she was keen to find out how he felt about all this, and would he rise to the occasion.

When she arrived, Bill had just gone to check on the irrigation of the orchard.

'He shouldn't be long,' said Edna, and they sat outside and chatted. Ivy told her that she had fed the lovebirds, and they had gone to enjoy their day off.

'The village is full of talk about the Manor, Barney was giving his, "when I were a lad story" in the Tavern, and then there were the Millers, and you know what they are like.' Edna got to hear a lot of gossip first-hand, she did of course supply several of the shops in the high street, including the Tavern.

'Everyone is going to be at the Tavern for Jake's birthday party tomorrow. I wondered whether or not to cancel it, what with all that's been happening.'

Ivy reassured her that Jake would be there, hiding a frown.

'Morning, Mother,' boomed Bill as he suddenly appeared from round the corner.

'Blimey, don't do that! I near 'ad a conorary,' said Edna recovering from the sudden entrance. She got up, patted her heart, and said, 'I'll go and put the kettle on,' and disappeared into the kitchen.

'Jake and Sandra make a nice couple, don't they, Mother?'

'When did…?' cutting her short, Bill replied.

'Watched it develop all night, no flies on me you know, besides they didn't think I could see them kissing in the doorway.'

Ivy jabbed him in the shoulder, and said, 'you old fraud.' Bill laughed, got up and went to help Edna with the tea things.

Meanwhile, Ivy dipped into that part of her mind where she could see Master Henry who was blindly carrying out his recurring steps, and subsequently getting nowhere.

Trying to attract his attention was fruitless, there was no connection, no sound, he was in a dimension which Ivy found impenetrable on her own.

'Here we are,' said Bill, laying the tray of tea things, and a plate of homemade shortbread on the table.

Edna came to the table, poured herself a cup and made her excuses.

'I have pressing work in the cider house,' she said, finding amusement in her pun. 'I'll see you pair later,' and she wandered off to her second home.

There was a slight apprehension in the air, as they spoke about the dilemma, and what they hoped to achieve together. They had to make sure that contact with Henry was possible, and that the whole prospect of a rescue was not futile.

Finishing their tea and biscuits, Ivy said, 'What can you see, Bill?'

He described a hazy vision, of a man walking up a flight of stone stairs, he reaches a door, then hesitates. Almost unwillingly he opens the door in front of him and goes through. He cannot see the other door; when he goes through that door, he comes back to the stone stairs, and it starts all over again.

'Yes, that's what I see,' said Ivy. 'Do you not see another door, to the left of the one at the top of the stairs?' Bill admitted he could not see another door, but he did get the impression that the man looked to his left, when he hesitated.

'This is the escape door, the one which we must convince him is there, and to open.'

Ivy continued to explain that they needed to establish contact, this was his grandfather, and they needed to get him out of there. If they could both focus their thoughts on the same thing, at the same time, it may be just enough for Henry to hear their call. Ivy clasped her son's hands in hers.

'Concentrate,' she said, and they both returned to the vision of the man on the stairs. Just as he hesitated, Ivy called out.

'The other door, Henry.' There was a distinct pause in Henry's repetitive cycle. He looked over his shoulder to see if anyone was there, but he continued to go through the door. Ivy released her son's hands.

'Flippin' 'eck Mother, that's quite a grip.'

Rubbing his large work-hardened fingers, he sat back on the bench. Ivy told him that their little experiment had been very successful, there was a possibility that contact could be made. And, feeling rather proud of herself, she popped a couple of biccies into her pocket.

'For Moss,' she said, as Bill raised an eyebrow.

'I'm off to the Manor, thank Edna for the tea, see you later,' and off she went.

On arriving at the Manor, she was greeted by Moss, who was organising the unloading of a large furniture removals lorry.

'Good morning, Moss, moving house?' Ivy joked.

'Just a few items to make our guests comfortable,' he said. They looked like very old chests, wooden with iron bands, which were being taken up to the bedrooms, together with some very antique furniture.

'You look in good spirits this morning, what have you been up to?' Ivy told Moss that she needed to speak with him, and briefly described her experience with Bill.

'I'm nearly finished here; would you like to walk on down to the summerhouse with me? There has been some restoration work carried out, which I need to check up on.'

'That would be lovely,' replied Ivy.

Moss went over to the removal's men, to ensure that all had been delivered and taken inside. Ivy could hear their broad accents, and noticed the Scottish address, as they lifted and secured the rear door of the lorry. Moss waved the lorry off, as it made its way down the drive, and walked over to Ivy.

'Shall we?' He beckoned to the arch over the path, which led down to the summerhouse.

'Scotland? They have come a distance,' said Ivy, passing Moss a home-made shortbread, which he took without hesitation.

'Hmm, very nice. Yes, there will be more items coming later,' and they both disappeared into the shady tunnel of trees, towards the river.

This was nature at its finest. What a perfect time to wander down to a summer house, trees in full leaf, plants in full bloom, the smell of cut grass on a warm day. Emerging from the protection of the trees, they wandered down the path, the grass cut short either side, making it look wider. On reaching the summerhouse, Ivy commented on how well the restoration had been carried out.

'It's beautiful, it has a newness to it, almost as if it had just been built,' but she knew it was hundreds of years old, and that's how it felt to her. They entered through the double French doors, comfortable seats with large floral cushions surrounded an ornate round table, and the windows gave a panoramic view of the river. Ivy remembered the summerhouse from her youth, nostalgia started to set in, and Moss unwillingly, shook her out of that.

'So, what happened this morning?' Moss said curiously. He normally picked up on Ivy's train of thoughts, but he had not been privy to any recently.

Ivy shook herself, having allowed the sights and smells to fuel her memories long enough.

She recounted her experience with Bill earlier. As they had both been able to attract the attention of Henry, it might be possible to direct him to the correct door. She was reluctant to let her thoughts out in case *Leber* picked up on them. She quizzed Moss for information, which she could give to Sandra, in order to distract *Leber*.

'You know I cannot directly be of assistance, but, if you ask me a question, I may be able to make a suggestion,' said Moss, arranging himself in a cosy chair, awaiting twenty questions.

'If Sandra was invited as a guest, with Jake, she may find it possible to engage *Leber* in conversation, and keep him occupied, possibly asking for his expert advice on information appertaining to her thesis. It would have to be based on Sandra's studies into the intelligence of plants. Do you think that's possible?'

Moss thought for a moment and said, '*Leber* is a dark horse, he houses a chip on his shoulder, a very conceited person, he is also not the most avid fan of mankind. He does, however possess one of man's weaknesses, and that is, a pretty girl will turn his eye, and a clever pretty girl, well....' Moss left the rest up to Ivy's imagination.

Ivy said that whilst *Leber* was at the meeting, it did seem to be the ideal opportunity to help poor Henry escape. She was concerned that Sandra might be put in danger by her actions.

'You do not have to worry yourself about that,' said Moss, 'I shall be there.'

Reassured, Ivy went on to describe the birthday celebrations that had been put in place for Jake's birthday. The Tavern had been arranged, with BBQ, dance floor and live music, and if he could drag himself away from the meeting, he would be very welcome.

'I believe the meeting may go on until very late, I may be somewhat indisposed,' said Moss. But he told Ivy that Jake and Sandra were invited, and it was his intention to introduce them to the Great Elder, *Tabule*, when he arrived.

'The meeting will begin mid-afternoon; it will be strictly members of the council.' Moss explained that as it was a rare occurrence, it would be a closed affair, items of extreme importance would be dealt with. He would indicate the arrival of *Leber* to Sandra, and he asked Ivy to convey his best wishes, for luck and success in their quest.

'I believe it is lunchtime, would you like to join me on the patio?' Ivy replied she would be delighted. They wandered back to the house, chatting about all the work that was going on, and how it had impacted on the village.

After a light lunch, Ivy left. Moss would be busy overseeing various small works within the grounds, trying to complete them, on time, for the big day.

Ivy pulled up in the carpark of the Tavern, intent on ensuring that all the arrangements were in place for the festivities the next day. On walking through the garden, she could hear Mr B. Arney reciting one of his many stories, and, in a sheltered nook under a large umbrella, were Jake, Sandra and Barney.

'I thought I could hear Mr Arney, but I didn't expect to see you pair,' Ivy said, pulling up a chair into the shade.

'Hello Gran,' said Jake, 'what brings you here?'

'WI business,' she replied, always a good standby excuse.

'Would you like a drink? There's fresh lemonade in the bar, it's too ruddy hot to work,' Barney said, mopping his brow.

'That would be nice, thanks.'

'I'll go, with ice, yes?' Jake wandered off to the bar.

Ivy enquired how their day off was progressing. Had they been to town and done as they had planned?

Sandra told Ivy that she had bought a real slinky dress for Jake's party. He still had no idea what was happening, everyone had kept the secret really well, she had told him the dress was for the meeting at the Manor.

'That's why I'm here,' Ivy replied, 'to check on the arrangements.'

Barney rose and went off to refill his tankard. This gave Sandra a chance to tell Ivy that Jake's visions were getting more and more intense.

'Jake was talking to Henry as though he was next to us, in town, he even saw your attempt with his father. He has been trying to instruct this man that he has to change his direction.' Sandra said it was really frustrating him.

'Frustrating who?' Jake said nosily, as he suddenly came from behind the bush screening them from the Tavern. He handed his Gran the ice-cold lemonade.

'I was telling your Gran of the visions you've been having,' said Sandra.

‘Ah, it’s more a thinking aloud,’ Jake said. ‘Will you be in later when I drop Sandra back?’

Ivy said she had no plans to stay out late that evening, and her door would be open.

‘Right,’ said Jake, ‘no more visions, I have a good idea how to deal with our man in the maze. We’re off to see Sandra’s aunt; she should be home now.’ Jake said he would see his Gran later.

Barney arrived back just as they were leaving. He wished them a safe journey, and sat with Ivy, to chat freely about the party.

The day was hot, too hot, this summer heatwave had intensified over the last few days, and the temperature was in the high thirties. A siesta-style calm had come over the village, there was very little happening, hardly a vehicle passed down the lane, and tranquillity reigned.

Jake and Sandra went to see her aunt. They had a typical English afternoon tea and sat and chatted till late. The evening barely got dark before it was time to return home. They both thanked Sandra’s aunt for a fine afternoon, they arranged to see her again soon, and making their farewells, they set off down the lanes in the direction of home.

It was approaching 23:00. Jake told Sandra that he had been mulling over an idea for the following day. He was now more determined than ever that he should succeed, his confidence was growing by the hour.

‘Do you know, I cannot wait for tomorrow, I feel so alive and positive, perhaps I should buy a lottery ticket,’ said Jake jokingly.

He told Sandra that she should continue with her plan to side-line *Leber*. He had been working on an idea that he might try, a little earlier.

‘What?’ Sandra asked, ‘don’t get doing anything silly,’ she said, beginning to get a little concerned.

‘Don’t worry, it’s all under control.’ Jake had taken on a new persona, Sandra was unsure about it, and knowing he had not had a drink, could not blame it on that. She reached out for his hand, not sure whether it was to reassure him or her.

They arrived outside Gran’s quite late, her porch light was on, Jake walked Sandra down her path, to the front door. It was evident that Sandra’s mother had retired, as there were no lights on, she was a midwife, and a very busy one. They embraced in a very friendly way and made their goodnights to each other.

'See you in the morning,' Jake whispered. He then went through the gap in the hedge to Gran's. Her front door was open, he knocked and called to her.

'Come in, Jake, I'm in the front room, there's some coffee in the kitchen if you'd like?' Jake poked his head round the door.

'Good day?' she enquired.

'Yeah, it was good,' Jake replied.

'Would you like a coffee?' Gran declined, claiming more than one would keep her awake, Jake poured a coffee and went to sit with his Gran.

'So, what's all this about?' Gran asked.

Jake then told her of the feelings he was experiencing, and the visions of Master Henry that he had seen during the day.

'My whole body seems to be tingling, my fingers seem to vibrate when I touch things, it's like touching a tuning fork while it buzzes.' Jake continued to explain that there was a clarity in his thoughts, he could focus and examine minute details, and felt more confident with life. He realised that his feelings for Sandra had stepped up a notch and that he had always been fond of her.

'Could this be how you feel when you have stepped up a notch? Could it be love I'm feeling?' He looked at Gran, who smiled knowingly.

'Jake, at five in the morning you will be twenty-one. They say a man usually reaches maturity at this age and many things will become evident. I believe you will understand more as the days go by. It may not appear instantly, more a gradual progression; this gift will show itself in different circumstances and give you the strength to do the right thing.'

Gran continued to tell Jake of the dreams she had had over time. In these dreams she has seen Jake grow strong and develop skills which would set him apart from others. There will be much contact with the *Burrbesh*, as battles of a life and death nature are fought. She knows that Jake will be able to overcome any obstacle, and any plan he has for Henry's rescue from the maze, will surely succeed.

'Besides, I expect you here at 17:00 sharp as I have a little surprise for you, Sandra too,' said Gran raising an eyebrow, just to add an element of intrigue to the sentence.

'Will you be with dad tomorrow morning?' Jake enquired.

'That is our plan, I do intend to keep a watchful eye,' said Gran reassuringly.

'It may be that I will need a poke in the right direction, if things get sticky,' said Jake, watching his Gran's face change, as she caught a glimpse of his plan.

Then, changing the subject, Jake passed on the best wishes sent by Sandra's aunt, and said that she might be passing tomorrow afternoon. Rising from the cosy chair, Jake leaned over, gave his Gran a peck on the cheek and made his farewell.

'I think we're in for a busy day tomorrow,' she said as she saw Jake out, and waved him off.

Jake made his way home. When he arrived, all was in darkness. Quietly he made his way to the cabin, his porch light came on as he approached, lighting his way through the front door. Climbing into bed through the mosquito net, he was greeted by Fidgit, who jumped on his chest, and gave him a greeting as though he had been away for a month.

'Ok, ok, behave.' Fidgit took up his position at the foot of the bed and they both drifted off to sleep. Jake slept long and hard, until his dreams were interrupted by the radio which had suddenly come on, very loud, the local radio station was playing Happy Birthday. When the music finished, the presenter announced that:

…today is Jake Gardner's twenty-first birthday and this is a birthday message from all who love him – Mom, Dad, Gran, Sandra, Fidgit the Jack Russell, and anyone else who knows him. Jake, your mother has a special birthday breakfast waiting for you in the kitchen, so if you're listening Jake, you had better get over there pronto.

Jake could hardly believe his ears; the tune that followed was significant also, one of his favourites. He rushed a wash and brush up, and ran over to the kitchen, with Fidgit at his heels. On entering the kitchen, he was greeted with a rendition of *Happy Birthday to You,* sung by his mother and father, and not exactly in tune, which brought on Fidgit's howling, just to add a little harmony to the spectacle. His parents burst into laughter. Jake hardly knew where to put himself, but joined in the laughter, giving first his mother, then his father a hug.

'How did you work that out?' Jake asked, amazed at them both.

‘Ah, your mother phoned the radio station yesterday while you were out. She arranged for it to happen right after the news at 06:00, so I went and set your hi-fi to come at 06:10, and turned it up, simple. Bet you didn’t know I was a master with a remote control.’ Both parents burst into fits of the giggles again.

Straightening her pinny, Mother invited Jake to the table. ‘All yer favourites,’ she said, unveiling a banquet fit for a king.

‘Thanks Mom, this is brilliant. I bet the whole village heard that radio broadcast.’ Jake took his seat at the feasting table.

‘Ere, a few cards came this morning,’ and she handed Jake a handful of post.

Opening his cards, and enjoying a Michelin star breakfast, they all laughed and joked, even Fidgit had a change from rabbit. Jake had to admit defeat over the culinary delights, he had reached the stage where he would explode, and make a mess, if he had another morsel.

‘There you go, Jake, your present from me and your ma.’ His dad handed him a set of car keys.

‘It’s only that old Land Rover Discovery your mother used to have, we had it polished up a bit.’ His dad told him it was parked up at the front of the house.

Walking round to the front, Jake stepped back in awe, the sight that greeted him was a tad more than a polish, although, that was the finishing touch.

‘We gave it to Alan the coach trimmer, he titivated it up a bit,’ he said winking at Mother. Mother walked over to it and jokingly said she didn’t want to part with it anymore.

Dad gave a commentary on what had been done.

‘He’s trimmed up the inside, new upholstery, a bit of cream leather. Painted it Post Office red, I think he said, new wheels and tyres, cos’ yer ma had buckled two of ’em. Oh, and the engine’s had a tweak. Can’t ’ave you taking Sandra to the ball in that old Landy of yours, can we?’

Jake, having examined every door, and sat in every seat, exclaimed that it could not be the same car Mother used to have, it was brilliant, and thanking them both, Jake made his excuses to get ready for the Manor.

‘Sandra’s gonna love this,’ he said, then wandered back to his place to get ready.

By now it was getting on for 09:00. Having showered, shaved and changed into suitable attire, Jake made his way back to the kitchen. Gran, who had just arrived, was sitting outside, and burst into song.

'Happy birthday to you, happy birthday to you, happy birthday dear Jakey boy, happy birthday to youououou.' Gran gave him a big sloppy kiss and gave him a small parcel.

'Happy birthday, Jake, this is something you may find useful.' Jake removed the wrapping to find an Atora suet box. He looked at Gran who gestured to him to carry on.

On opening the box, he found the sea bean. It was the seed Gran had looked after all those years. As he held it, it opened and stretched out a shoot, it wrapped itself around Jake's wrist. It hardened into a bracelet, which Jake found impossible to remove. He directed a concerned look at Gran.

'It's ok, it won't hurt you, you will find it very useful, as I did.' Gran took Jake's hands and held him tightly.

Looking into her deep blue eyes, Jake felt a strength surge through his very being.

'Thanks, Gran,' Jake gave her a big hug.

'You are going to be here, with Dad, yeah?'

'I would not be anywhere else today,' she said.

He walked over to his new toy, got into the driving seat, and started her up.

'Shall have to think of a name for her,' he shouted, as he drove off down the drive.

On his way to Sandra's, there were several shouts of 'Happy Birthday.' Pulling up outside her house he was greeted by her mother on her way to work.

'Happy Birthday, Jake, heard it on the radio, did you enjoy your breakfast?' Jake was starting to feel as though the whole world would be asking him, 'What did you have for breakfast Jake?'

Thanking Sandra's mother, he made his way up the path to the front door, where Sandra was waiting. Reaching out, he held her hands and exclaimed that she should be on the front cover of Vogue.

'You look stunning,' he said. 'Come, see my new chariot,' and Jake started to lead her down the path.

On holding his hand, she noticed his wrist, and inspected the strange growth attached.

'Gran's seed,' he said; it had now grown under his skin, leaving just a proud outline of a woven bangle.

'It doesn't hurt, in fact it feels rather comfortable.'

On reaching his new car, he opened the passenger door for her.

'My lady,' he said, bowed gently, and then walked round to take his position at the helm.

'This is lovely, it smells so nice, and it suits you,' she said. They sat for a while, roof open, enjoying a cool breeze from the air conditioning, pressing the buttons to see what each did. Then, finding the play button, they set off for the Manor with favourite tunes filling their ears. Deciding to take the long way round to the Manor, they both drank in the experience given by their new chariot. Eventually, pulling up outside the Manor, Moss greeted them.

'What a fine-looking conveyance, Master Jake, birthday gift by any chance?' Turning to Sandra, Moss said, 'you look positively radiant, my dear, I am going to steal you while Jake parks his vehicle in the barn,' and Moss offered Sandra his arm to escort her into the house.

Jake proceeded to deal with the parking arrangements, which would allow space for the arrival of further visitors. Crossing the courtyard, he went in through the front doors to join Moss and Sandra, who were chatting on a large sofa. It was positioned to catch a gentle breeze blowing through the hallway, from the front door, through to the conservatory.

'Many happy returns, Jake.' Moss took Jake's arm and inspected his wrist.

'Was this a birthday gift too, don't tell me, from your Gran?' Moss recognized it and made comment that it was from the night flower.

'I meant to ask you about that,' said Jake, 'The flower that grew by the barn back home, has gone. Do you know anything about it?'

Moss explained that it had been pining; knowing that its mother was being looked after at the Manor, the moths had brought it home one evening.

'Would you both like to see it? We have time,' Moss said rising from the sofa.

'It has a new home in a greenhouse.'

‘You go, Sandra, I forgot to bring something from the car, I’ll catch you up,’ said Jake.

As Moss and Sandra left by the conservatory, Jake looked back to make sure that they had gone, and slipped into the cloakroom where the secret door was. He pushed and poked at the panels until he found the one with the door handle; turning the handle and pulling the door open, he entered the stairwell.

He descended the stairs to the large chamber, just as his Gran had described it. He could hear many voices coming from all the passageways, not just voices, but noises of activity, as though busy markets were going about their business. He tried to focus on which of the passageways led to Henry, with little success. He had explored the tunnels in his dreams, and now they all looked different.

Suddenly he felt a throbbing in his wrist where the seed had attached itself. He could see his Gran and father, they seemed to beckon him to go right, and following their directions, he continued along a passage for some distance. It eventually opened up into a large cave, possibly larger than the one he had just left. There were steep walls with seams of fluorescence that shone like the aurora, different colours, illuminating parts of the chamber in a stroboscopic effect. Some of the walls would be cast into darkness, until a burst of light brought them alive, stairs carved into the face appeared and disappeared, changing shape and direction with each changing colour. Jake ventured into the centre of the cathedral-like cave, trying to make sense of the chaos that shone before him. Not knowing which way to go he sat on a large flat stone and closed his eyes. The vision he had of Henry was now very strong. Henry was somewhere within the changing stairways that were all around him. Jake tried to call out, but no sound came from his mouth.

He felt a presence, and thinking it might be Henry, he opened his eyes, only to be greeted by the creature *Leber*, who stood before him holding a staff, his long fingers culminating in a claw-like nail, pointing at him.

‘Who are you to think you can challenge me?’ his voice boomed through the cavern, ‘you are trespassing.’

Leber was not a small person; he stood possibly over seven feet tall, and Jake was dwarfed in his shadow.

'You hold my great grandfather, and I have come to rescue him,' said Jake, trying to make his voice as loud as he could. *Leber* laughed, a sound which resembled the eruption of a volcano.

'Very well, young Jake, do your worst.'

Leber pointed his staff at a section of the wall, glowing green, and in the dim shadow of the green light, could be seen a man, ascending a flight of stairs. He disappeared through a doorway.

'Feel free to attempt your rescue, young Jake, for I have a more pressing appointment.'

Jake, with all his new-found power could not stop what happened next. He suddenly found himself on the stairway, climbing to a door, and knowing he should not go through it, goes through and returns to the stairway, only to climb again, and go through the same door, time and time again.

Leber, rather pleased with himself, emerged from his underworld kingdom, into the Manor house, immediately acknowledging the presence of the night flower, which was strong. He wandered into the conservatory, where the essence was strongest, he walked over to the plant which seemed to reach out to greet him. Its tendrils wrapped around his claw-like fingers, and they both caressed one another for a moment, until the reunion was disturbed by Moss.

'*Leber*, how is the underworld?'

'What goes around, comes around, you know how it is,' *Leber* said, with a cynical grin.

'Am I the first to arrive?'

Moss confirmed, that yes, he was, and that he would like to introduce him to Sandra, a university graduate studying plant intelligence.

'Perhaps you may be able to help her with her studies.'

Moss caught Sandra's eye and beckoned her over.

'Sandra, I would like to introduce you to *Leber*, the first member of the council to arrive.'

Moss made his excuses to deal with more guests arriving, leaving Sandra and *Leber* chatting on the patio.

Moss found a quiet spot and tried to connect with the vision of what was happening, Gran and Bill had lost Jake, they were supposed to be his back-up. Moss could see nothing, he wondered if it was worth appealing to *Leber's* conscience, and then on reflection, realised that would be futile.

Leber found Sandra intoxicating, his attitude towards mankind might even have improved, he was impressed.

Jake, however, was not having a good time, his progress was slow, he could now see Henry in a haze in front, he had to quicken his pace to catch him up. There was an element of lethargy associated with Jake's actions, which made his feet feel like lead. He concluded that this was to prevent him from reaching Henry. It took all of Jake's strength to overcome this weight and catch up with Henry. It took time, but eventually he came shoulder to shoulder with Henry, who, in turn took time to acknowledge his presence. Jake suddenly felt the presence of his Gran and his dad, it came through the throbbing in his wrist. He shouted to Henry, who turned to see who had called. Jake told him that they had to escape. Henry had no idea he was captive; he was just going to answer the door. Jake tried to explain; he told Henry that he had been imprisoned by a creature called *Leber*, and that he had come to rescue him.

It was difficult to make Henry hear him, the haze seemed to absorb the sound of his voice. He tried to tell him that he was his great grandson, and that his daughter had been waiting to see him for so long. Jake told him that the door through which he had gone so often, was his jailor, there was another door which had been obscured. He should look to the left where the other would show itself; it was through this door where he would find his means of escape.

Jake followed Henry up the stairs, and as they approached the door they had been through so often, Henry reached for the handle.

'No, the other door,' a monastic-type echo penetrated the haze. It came from the combined effort of Jake, Gran and his dad.

Henry heard this, and turning back to Jake, followed his lead. Jake felt for the obscured door and handle; on finding it, he turned the handle, a new doorway opened, and they both went through. It led to the room with the passages beneath the Manor, the cycle had at last been broken.

Closing the door, they found themselves staring at each other, Jake was first to speak. He explained that *Leber*, a *Burrbesh* elder had imprisoned Henry; he had been gone for over a hundred years. Henry, a little dazed, his faculties returning slowly, started to take in his surroundings. He appeared to be none the worse for his long incarceration. He shook Jake's hand and noticed the bracelet-style growth around his wrist.

'It would appear we have much in common, and I have much to catch up with. Thank you, young Jake, you put yourself at risk for me, for that I will be eternally grateful.

'Shall we return to the real world? I am so hungry; I could eat a horse.'

Henry told Jake that he had played in these tunnels when he was young and proceeded to lead the way out.

'I think it's about time I had words with *Leber*,' said Henry, and they started the long ascent up the stairs to the Manor.

Chapter 7

Henry and Jake made their way up the stairs to the door leading into the cloakroom. As he was opening the door into the hallway, Jake could hear many voices.

'It sounds very busy out there, should I go and investigate first, introduce you perhaps?' said Jake.

This was the most anxious Jake had felt all day, and he had not given this moment a thought, or its consequences.

'Damn them all,' retorted Henry, pushing past Jake and striding towards the dining room.

'I think I'm allowed this moment.'

He stood in the doorway surveying the scene, it looked as though most of the council members had arrived. Henry recognized *Tabule – he* was standing in the centre of the room chatting with three other council members.

He looked at Henry, and, leaning his head slightly to the left, and without losing eye contact, gave him a small nodding bow, which Henry reciprocated. There were those whom he did not recognize. They had gathered in small groups, at the table, on sofas and some were wandering in and out of the conservatory. They paid little heed to Henry and Jake, as they wandered through.

Henry was curious to know why there were so many council members there. They continued further into the room, the night flower dominated the far wall, and they were both drawn to its magnificence. Several of the visitors were already admiring the spectacle.

Henry looked around and said, 'I cannot see *Leber*, but wait a moment, who is this? Well, you are a sight for sore eyes!' said Henry, holding his arms out to greet him.

'Henry how are you?' said Moss. He turned to Jake, and told him he had done well, even though he had caused major concern as to his whereabouts; he had been gone for hours.

‘We had a search party out at one stage; you might have told someone what you were planning.’

Moss ushered them both through to the lounge.

‘Here, there’s food and drink,’ said Moss. ‘You must be hungry.’ Henry admitted he was, but thought he might see *Leber* first, to thank him for his incarceration.

‘Plenty of time for that,’ said Moss, taking two glasses of wine from a passing waiter, and offering one to Henry.

‘Jake, have you seen Sandra? She was on the patio earlier with our intrepid estate agent.’

Moss encouraged Jake to find her. Taking two glasses of wine from a waiter he went in search of Sandra.

Jake had no idea that he had been missing for over six hours, events had overtaken him, and it was now time to relax and enjoy the evening.

As he approached the doors to the patio, *Leber* entered the conservatory, chatting to two of the ugliest people Jake had ever seen. *Leber* acknowledged Jake with a raised eyebrow, and looking down his nose at him, passed him by without a word.

Jake could hear Barney but not see him, which was quite usual. He followed the sound of his voice and found him on a large sofa, in the shade, reciting a story to an avid audience, Sandra being one of them.

She had her back to Jake, Barney had seen him, but Jake, putting a finger to his lips, indicated he wanted to surprise her.

He leaned down to whisper the words in her ear.

‘Glass of wine m’lady?’

She jumped up, knocking the wine out of the glasses, which mainly landed on Barney. She threw her arms around him; it was all Jake could do to hang onto the two empty glasses.

‘Where have you been? I’ve been so worried, why didn’t you tell me? I have been looking everywhere for you, I thought I’d lost you.’

After untangling himself from her embrace, they both sat down. He apologized to Barney and his lady friend, who were mopping themselves with one of Barney’s monogrammed handkerchiefs. Jake told Sandra where he had been, and what had happened. He explained that it was the only way he could think of to rescue Henry, the idea had come to him in a dream.

Because Gran was only able to attract Henry's attention for a few moments, it was necessary to get closer to him.

'I had to get inside the quandary, the only way to help him was from within.'

If it had not been for the help of Gran and his father, at the right moment, he would most probably still be there now. From the description Moss gave him of *Leber*, he thought it would have appealed to his sense of humour, to entomb Jake in the same way. Jake was banking on being put in the same place as Henry; fortunately, his plan worked, and Henry was now free, and inside, chatting to Moss.

'Would you like to come and meet my four-hundred-year-old great grandfather?' whispered Jake.

Rising to his feet he held out his hand for Sandra, made his apologies to Barney and his lady, and they both went off in search of Henry.

Sandra had her own adventure to tell; she started by telling Jake how concerned she was when he did not return. She did have an inkling, after what Jake had told her, that he might attempt something crazy. She had struggled to remain calm and had stuck to the plan.

'*Leber* was the first to arrive. Moss introduced us, he was interested in my studies at university, and has a great knowledge of the subject.'

She said she found it difficult to believe that he was responsible for Henry's predicament, he seemed so polite, caring, and well spoken. As Jake and Sandra walked through the hallway, Moss called to them from the dining room, and beckoned them to come in; Henry was talking with *Tabule*. Moss escorted Jake and Sandra over to them. When they approached, Henry made the introduction.

'Sire, may I present my great grandson Jake and his fiancée Sandra.

Jake, Sandra, I would like to introduce you to *Tabule*, Grand Elder of the Order of Libra.'

Tabule was tall, very distinguished, with long white hair, a small growth of almost green whisker to his lower chin, and a full-length robe of greens, silvers and black.

He took Sandra's hand and pressed it to his lips.

'Charmed,' his wide green eyes spoke to her.

Turning to Jake he held out his hand. Jake, returning the courtesy, shook his hand. *Tabule,* noticing his mark, held his wrist gently with both hands, and looking deep into his soul, passed on visions of the past.

Jake shuddered at the sudden input of so much information.

'Sorry,' he smiled and released him. 'We shall speak again soon.'

Turning to Moss, he said, 'I believe we shall be staying a while longer, there appears to be much more to do than I first thought.' At that moment, *Leber* entered the room; he noticed that Henry and Jake were with *Tabule* and walked over to the group.

'I am impressed,' he said, 'you have managed to thwart my efforts this time; perhaps next time you may not be so lucky,' and leaned over to glower at Jake.

'Enough of these petty foibles *Leber*, there are more pressing issues to deal with, and we shall all need to be united in that quest. I suggest you make truce with Henry; he could be very useful.'

There was an insistence in his voice, and *Leber*, giving a slight nod of his head, said nothing, but wandered off to mingle with the others. Moss went over to a dinner gong; striking it and attracting everyone's attention, he announced that the meeting would commence shortly. He thanked all who had come and wished them a safe journey home.

Those who had come to the Manor, were all descendants of relatives who had worked there in the past; they had been invited for an afternoon tea in recognition of their loyalty. Moss told everyone that he was certain the Manor would be hosting many more functions in the future.

Now the serious stuff was about to begin.

Tabule asked Henry to stay; he would put it to the council that he should be included and make up the thirteenth member.

Jake meanwhile had wandered over to *Leber*.

'I know we have got off on the wrong foot; perhaps we could start again as strangers and not enemies?' Jake held out his hand to shake. *Leber* declined but did notice the mark he carried on his wrist.

'We shall see,' he said.

Sandra came over and reminded Jake of his appointment with his Gran at 17:00. She bid *Leber* a good night, and with her arm in Jake's, ushered him towards the door. Moss was at the front door, seeing everybody off. Henry walked over, just as Jake and Sandra were about to leave. He thanked

Jake for all he had done that day, and said he intended to be around for quite some time and expected to see them both very soon. Moss commented that he would no doubt see them tomorrow, and that Jake should go and enjoy the rest of his birthday.

They went over to the barn, where Jake's birthday present was parked, looking all shiny and new. Then in a manner befitting a Lord and Lady, they waved goodbye to Moss and Henry as they drove down the drive and made their way to Gran's.

When they arrived at Gran's, Sandra's mother, Jo, short for Josephine, greeted them and explained that his Gran was getting ready and would be down shortly. No sooner had she finished telling them when Gran appeared at the door. She was wearing her Sunday best and gave a twirl.

'Do you like it? I thought we might go down to the Tavern for a celebratory birthday drink. You can take us all in your new jalopy.' Gran was absolutely buzzing.

'A good result for the day, you can fill me in later,' and arm in arm, he escorted them down the path to his new car and they made their way to the Tavern. Parking up, they made their way to the main entrance and Jake commented that there did not seem to be many people around.

Gran ushered him through the doors, where fifty plus people burst into song, and gave their rendition of 'Happy Birthday to You.'

Then his mom and dad, Sandra's aunt, friends, relatives and all who knew him, poured out into the gardens, where banners were erected, and balloons were distributed. The pig roast was fired up and a small band started to play. Mr and Mrs Brownlow had brought Jake a present, a special brew called Rocket Fuel. Jake was totally stunned. He told Sandra that this had been a well-kept secret, he had no idea that anything like this was being planned. A small dance floor had been set up so that everyone could show off their footwork skills. Jake and Sandra sat with Father and Gran, while Mother supervised the pig roast.

Jake told them both of the day's events, and how their intervention had been perfectly timed. The party continued to attract laughter and song, and as more people arrived, it turned into a resounding success. Jake did manage to make a speech, but the effects of Mrs B's rocket fuel managed to tangle his tongue, which brought about roars of laughter, and the party continued well into the night.

Meanwhile, back at the Manor, before the meeting started, *Tabule* had attached himself to Henry. He was determined that Henry should be voted onto the council, he was doing the rounds, introducing him to everyone, encouraging a favourable vote.

Moss joined them, offering them both a glass of wine.

'Of course, you know Moss, he likes small, he tends to the small plants, the mosses and the lichens, heathers and suchlike, a very useful character to know.'

He continued to point out other members of the council and explained that they were all chosen representatives of their particular persuasion.

Before wandering over to each of them, *Tabule* pointed them out to Henry. '*Travesh*, has assisted man with food crops, *Agi*, likes to be feminine, and looks after the water plants. *Leber* of course likes to kill people, he produces anything toxic, while *Angio*, with her feminine touch, likes pretty flowers. *Maegrin* likes his grasses and savannahs, *Kretol*, we don't see much of him, he dabbles in the carnivorous, *Gantel* likes creepers and vines, *Myck*, he loves his fungi, and then there is *Marley*, who recently renamed himself after a keen follower. He grows anything that gets you stoned or affects the mind. Mankind likes him.'

One by one the three met each member, with only *Leber* remaining; as they approached him, he turned to them, and said, 'I know what you are up to *Tabule*, and you know my opinion, and that is, only a true *Burrbesh* should be allowed to sit on the council.'

Henry argued, 'My loyalties are with the *Burrbesh*, and have been since an early age, and although I don't have your contempt for the human race, I can sympathise with your intolerance of them.'

Henry went on to put his case to *Leber*. He had become more like them over the years; his concerns for the world and the effects mankind was having on it, equalled those who sat on the council. *Leber* interrupted him.

'You also aspire to travel through the fabric; that is totally unacceptable, it is only for the *Burrbesh*, we have kept that our secret for millennia, man would only abuse it.'

Leber, turning to *Tabule*, explained that it was for this reason that Henry had been placed in the quandary, and should he continue with this quest, he may find himself back there.

Leber, with a slight bow of his head to *Tabule*, turned and walked off. He entered the dining room where the meeting was about to start.

Tabule asked Henry if his quest to gain the power of travel could be set aside; he believed there was much to do on this world, without the need to go elsewhere. Henry agreed and said he would forego his research into travel if the council accepted him as the thirteenth.

'I shall send for you if the council agree.'

Tabule proceeded into the dining room. Two large butlers closed the doors behind him, and took up their positions either side, like two guardsmen.

An alignment of planets would occur around 23:35, it would create a portal through which energy would be transmitted. The focal point of this energy would be the junction of ley lines, which were just north of the Manor. It would bring about a change to all those *Burrbesh* who had taken on the form of man. They would be subjected to a period where their natural shape would predominate and would revert to their original form.

Henry was starting to feel the effects of the last hundred years; he wandered past the buffet table, and picking a selection of tasty morsels, and a glass of wine, he made his way onto the patio.

'Ah, Henry, will you join us?'

A well-dressed man with red hair, and sporting a full beard, offered him a seat. His colleague pulled out a chair for him at the table; his Scottish accent prompted Henry to assume he was one of the staff.

'You're not with the caterers, are you?' Henry enquired.

'No, no, allow me to introduce ourselves.'

We represent the firm of solicitors, *Betula* & *Betula*, I am Donald and the hairy one is my brother, Duncan MacDonald.'

They explained that their firm had been responsible for managing the will, and estate of his parents. Their firm was not unused to dealing with strange circumstances, and those clients who lived for unusual lengths of time.

They did, after all, have several members of the council on their books.

After Henry disappeared the last time, he was presumed dead, but his death had not been confirmed and his file had inadvertently been put in the pending tray.

It was at this stage, that one of the young partners of the firm took it upon himself to use the assets of the Lytes' estate, and with his power of attorney, operate it as his own. It became an obsession, and a very successful obsession; he grew the business into a global company.

'Since his death some ten years ago, the firm has been dealing with the business, and, as it was carried on in the Lytes' name, it now falls to you to inherit.'

The MacDonalds took it in turn to explain the facts. Henry was of such an age that he would need to verify his authenticity. Moss had informed them of the day's developments and of Henry's sudden appearance; they would need a little time to gather the relevant papers. They had not come prepared to do business with Henry but congratulated him on his return. By invitation from Moss, they would be staying at the Manor, and they would have further meetings with Henry, as they also had business with several members of the council, so they would be around for a while.

'Well, gentlemen, today has been full of surprises. I'm not sure I can take any more,' said Henry.

At that moment, Moss appeared on the patio.

'I think you might like to accompany me; the council have requested your attendance.'

Henry shook hands with both the MacDonalds and bade them a good night.

As they walked towards the door with its butler sentries, the clock in the hall started to strike the tenth hour. They entered the room, and there, seated around the long table, were the council members, with *Tabule* at its head. Moss took his seat next to the head of table.

'Sit opposite me, Henry,' *Tabule* gestured to the empty seat at the other end of the table.

Henry poured himself a glass of water from a pitcher on the table as *Tabule* began the meeting.

Before the main agenda could commence, it was necessary to establish the role of Henry. There had been much discussion among the council members, and the case for Henry was strong. However, there was dissent amongst some, regarding his aspirations to find the secret of travel. Henry was asked to put his case to the council and explain his intentions with regards abandoning his quest. Henry stood, and after making eye contact with all the members, he began his explanation.

'I have devoted many years to the research of plants and their uses, travelled to far distant places, and met and worked with tribes and cultures who have an affinity with the land.'

Henry went on to describe the sadness he had experienced, where cultures had been wiped out. Some, who had been entrusted with the preservation of sacred items, he had been unable to save. During his travels he had witnessed the struggle of indigenous tribes who had watched their lands disappear, taken by the greedy in the name of progress. Slavery, genocide, changes in society, had vanquished the old ways, and these were ways which he would like to protect. Wars that had ravaged the Earth, taken lives needlessly, all brought about by man, meant that he had little respect for some of the human race, so could sympathize with *Leber*. But what respect remained, he had for those whose hearts were in the right place; there were those who preferred the old ways and wanted to return to them. Henry was full of optimism for these remaining hopefuls and felt a sense of duty to assist them wherever possible.

During his explorations, Henry had found cultures which had embraced the *Burrbesh* ways, and they were proud of the secret they kept. He admitted that in the past, he had inadvertently stepped through the fabric; he could not control this power, and it had resulted in him reappearing some considerable time in the future. Losing time, missing his mother's later years, and her end, had prompted him to search for a way to retrieve that time.

He did not realise he would offend anybody by investigating the fabric, and to understand and control it. But after his unsuccessful adventures with the travel, he would be quite prepared to withdraw from any further investigations.

Leber gave a slow clap, *Tabule* interjected and spoke.

'A fine speech Master Henry, I believe a short break is called for, the time is almost upon us, this alignment may not be the big one, but we should enjoy it, nonetheless.'

The waiters brought in refreshments, and the time came when the planets were at their best. A haze enveloped those council members who had taken the human form. They changed, some resembling their chosen discipline, while others took on some quite bizarre shapes.

Illuminated only by candlelight, their green eyes fluoresced in the dimly lit room.

Henry thought that *Leber's* new look was an improvement.

There was a buzz of excitement as the spectacle revealed new forms. The windows, which opened onto the conservatory, allowed the night flower to grow through; its fragrant blooms filled the room with scent, while the little ones hopped in and out of the foliage, playing hide and seek.

Tabule stood, he towered some eight or nine feet tall. He tapped a staff he was carrying on the floor, attracting the attention of the council members.

'It is time to cast your votes. As you can see, Henry is quite sincere, and I personally think he would be ideal as our thirteenth member.'

Henry caught his own reflection in a window. His eyes were green also, but, without the strange shape shift. He retained his human form.

The council voted unanimously in favour of Henry, even *Leber*.

It was the first time that a man had sat at the table of the Council of Libra.

'And now to discuss the real matter at hand.'

Tabule sat and brought order to the proceedings.

'It is the objective of this council to maintain a balance in the worlds that we visit, to bring about a natural order that will sustain life. There are always setbacks to any project that we are involved in, and this world has certainly had its share. Setbacks of a natural origin are things we can deal with, but on this world, now, the balance has been tipped over the edge.'

He went on to describe the devastation that was evident throughout the world in the forests and oceans, areas blighted by industrial activity, pollutants in the atmosphere. He compared the future of this world with others he had seen.

There was a world not far away, a red world that once had very similar problems, where now, nothing grows. The council did nothing to save that world. But now, the need to step in, and right the wrongs of man, had arrived.

‘I therefore suggest that we make plans to address these problems; this world cannot sustain man’s attack upon it. It is time for us to take drastic action, and if needs must, we shall have to declare war.’

Tabule was passionate, his voice rang through the ears of the council. *Leber* was first to applaud.

‘About bloody time,’ he said.

The rest of the council joined in, the feeling was consentient, and everyone was of the same opinion.

Tabule went on to outline his plan, which he had looked at, long and hard.

‘There has to be a representative who can visit the places most in need, and who is capable of assessing the problems and providing a solution. There will be many, all with their own unique conditions, and where there is no negotiable solution, a more direct approach shall be taken. Recruitment of like-minded experts will be required, and plans made, if this battle gathers momentum.

The number of keepers of the night flower have declined; there are too few remaining to make an impression. There will be a great need for the use of the little ones’ abilities; this will require the re-establishment of ancient tribes, all over the world, to provide them with safe haven. It will necessitate the bringing together of these disbanded cultures, to resurrect their old ways, bringing their credibility and status back, and making them proud again. There are those who are already returning to the way of the land, and they need to be enlisted on this quest.

The growing facilities here at the Manor, will contribute greatly to the propagation of the night flower, and as the armies of safe keepers increase, then they too, can take possession of it. There needs to be instant access to the night flower, and its attributes, in every country, and every corner of this world, to provide the ammunition for a swift response.

A representative from each of the council members shall be available for advice and support, ranks are to be established, a line of command set up, and also communications where necessary.’

Tabule commented on how fortuitous it was that Henry had come back onto the scene, albeit partly destiny, he may be able to contribute greatly.

Also, there were the growing abilities of his great grandson, and the support of his young lady. They would be able to contribute to the cause, should they be so willing.

The discussion went on till dawn, the sun casting its long shadows across the patio, as the participants of the meeting spilled outside. Some of them formed small groups, and wandered around the grounds, some were seated on the patio; the discussions were deep and intense. Henry had found a solitary seat by the pond, his thoughts went back to the time of his mother and father, memories of his past flooding his mind.

He was startled back to reality by *Leber*.

'Do you mind if I join you?' he said.

Henry shuffled to the end of the bench, to make room for the still very large creature.

'It is likely that our paths will cross again very soon, and if so, I would prefer it to be as colleagues, and not enemies. I may have misjudged you, Henry. I was under the impression that you were just a glory hunter.'

Leber continued with his poor excuse for an apology, but Henry got the message.

He told *Leber* that he might have done the same, had the roles been reversed. It was his curiosity that had fuelled his need to discover the travel; having lost time by inadvertently slipping through the fabric, he was anxious to recover it. *Leber* explained that the fabric was not time travel, merely access to highways, which each took time to travel upon.

He continued: 'These circumstances in which we find ourselves have never happened before. We have never interfered with another species; it has always been left in the hands of those who inhabit the worlds which sustain life.'

He said that all of the council members had a particular affinity for this world, it had survived many traumas, and was one of those worlds which had earned respect. He confessed that he was responsible for the evolution of man, and it had hung heavily on his conscience.

'To be quite honest, I was all for leaving mankind to its own devices, but I think I may be getting a little soft in my old age, I may even feel responsible.'

Rising from the seat, *Leber* gave Henry a slight nod of the head and said he had to find *Tabule*, something urgent he had remembered.

Moss, seeing that Henry was now free of *Leber*, approached the bench and sat with him.

'Quite a day you have had, Master Henry, you must be tired!'

Henry turned to Moss and said, 'You know, I feel totally refreshed, not tired in the slightest, but I am so hungry I could eat a horse.'

'Oh dear,' said Moss, 'I don't think we have any horse; would bacon do?' Henry burst out laughing, and explained it was a figure of speech, a joke.

'I have got some catching up to do, Moss. What was that vehicle young Jake drove off in? What other things have developed since I have been gone? I shall rely on you for instruction.'

They made their way through to the kitchen, where cook dealt with Henry's hunger.

Tabule called the meeting to order, and with all the members present, put it to them, that the next meeting should include the villagers, and those loyal to Henry, and the secrets of the Manor. Word should be sent out for this meeting to convene two days hence, during which time the council should familiarise itself with possible strategies, in the war room. The Manor would be the base of operations, its unique location would allow for the communications, and the production of night flowers.

Over the coming weeks, equipment, which would enable the Manor to enter the modern world, would be bought and installed.

Arrangements would be made to accommodate the meeting of the villagers, and a plan formulated. Henry met the MacDonalds at lunchtime, and it was agreed for public appearances, that he would become the grandson of himself. Verification of his identity would take place, and his right to inherit the business and fortunes, could go ahead.

When Henry asked the value of this inheritance, there was no definitive answer, a ball-park figure of around one hundred billion pounds was mentioned.

Both Duncan and Donald, once they had completed their business at the Manor, would return with the required paperwork and figures. There would be no problems, as far as they could see. Meanwhile an account had been set up for Henry to use.

Henry meantime had a lot of explaining to do. He had arranged to meet his daughter and great grandson that afternoon.

Chapter 8

Many of the council members had returned to their place of origin, to spread the word, and prepare for the forthcoming events. The Manor was quiet; there were only a handful of council leaders, preparing for the next meeting.

Henry, having dealt with the Scottish solicitors, went to investigate proceedings within the Manor; the main front room had been taken over for operations.

Moss was organising the placement of various pieces of furniture. *Tabule*, *Leber*, *Angio* and *Myck* were sitting around a table discussing the forthcoming events, and how they might use modern technology to assist them.

Not used to dealing with such necessities, they all agreed that it was quite beyond them, and they would require help. Henry, having approached the table and heard their comments, agreed that he too, had no idea of what new inventions were likely to help, but was sure there was something. Moss suggested that when Henry took on permanent staff at the Manor, someone who could advise on these matters might be included: someone who understood the requirements, could suggest what equipment would be needed and could provide training.

Nobody noticed the arrival of Jake, Ivy and Sandra, as they meandered into the war room.

Moss greeted them.

'Good afternoon, birthday boy, I hope you took good care of him,' Moss directed his last remark to the ladies.

Henry came over to them, he held Ivy's hands and looked into her eyes, gave her a hug, and told her that he had lost too much time, and had missed so much.

'Let's go outside, we need to talk!'

They all retired to the large shady sofas on the patio.

Henry was full of regret for his lost years, and he thought it was about time he explained.

He started to give an account of his childhood; he told them of his escape from boarding school, of stowing away on the '*Erinus*' and of his trip to India. He told of the strange flower, and the bracelet, his friend Gazali and his lost tribe, the business that he had set up with his father, which had been very successful; and of his mother, who had so competently dealt with the financial side, while he and his father searched for new medicines.

It emerged that on his last trip to India with his father, the ship '*Erinus*' floundered in a massive storm, and sank with all hands. Henry had managed to pull himself onto the spar of a mast, which had snapped clean off the ship. He had drifted for days; when he came to, he was on the beach of an island, not on any map.

His rescuers were a local tribe, who took him in, and cared for him. They too were keepers of a sacred plant, and it was his wrist bangle that had identified him as a friend and saved him from being eaten.

There were no ships that passed this way; in fact, they had never seen a ship, so rescue was highly unlikely.

Many years passed, he became a trusted friend of the Chief, and was accepted into his family's bosom. He learned their language, and many of their secret ways.

He also discovered that they could travel, not just an out-of-body experience, but actually slip into the fabric, and be gone. They had perfected the art of meditation, and trance, although some who had tried, had never returned. The Chief had visited distant islands this way; he described his experiences in minute detail and warned that it was dangerous to venture too far.

Eager to understand more, Henry became obsessed with the idea; he also looked upon it as a means of escape. He ticked off the days into weeks, the weeks into months and the months into years. He meditated hard, and attempted the trance-like state, but to no avail.

It was on the night of a great storm, which could be seen heading towards their island, that Henry had decided that this storm would seal his fate one way or another and entered one of the caves along the beach.

The villagers warned him that a great wave would come, and wash him away, and that he would be safer on higher ground. Reticently, Henry sat down in the cave and adopted his lonely, cross-legged position. He found it somehow comforting as the thunder and lightning raged.

His mind wandered back to the shipwreck.

Might he see his father again?

Suddenly there was a huge crash; a wall of water stood before him. He got to his feet and made ready to accept it, but the water wall stopped halfway into the cave. He was not sure how, but believed he had crossed over into the void, where travel would allow him to affect his escape.

He turned to survey the myriad of passageways, tunnels and doorways which had opened up.

Marking his way as he went was no use, in an ever-changing scenery, his marks would move. He spent an age trying to find his way, only to end up back at the same place. It felt like an eternity wandering the dark tunnels, which never led him anywhere. Eventually a *Burrbesh* traveller passing by guided him to a way out.

When he eventually reached the Manor, he found that one hundred and thirty-six years had passed by. The Manor had been mothballed, the business had been closed for years, and the strange plant had gone. His mother had passed away but had left an instruction for the Manor to be kept ready. But over time, the caretakers of the Manor, whether through illness or lack of kin, failed to continue their duties.

And so, on Henry's return, some of the surrounding lands had to be sold to fund the repairs, restart the business and return the Manor back to its former glory. It was 1766, and in the years that followed, he buried himself in the task of rebuilding the Manor and the business. The night flower had gone; he had searched England for it, but it was not to be found. He knew that it thrived in the monasteries of Tibet but was reluctant to admit to anyone that he had lost it. During this time, he planned to continue with his explorations and expeditions. He wanted to find the night flower and to search for his old friend Gazali, deep in the African jungle.

As the years passed, Henry became restless, and having rebuilt the business, felt it was time to travel. He left a trusted work colleague and friend in charge, with strict instructions to carry out, should he not hear from Henry for more than a year.

He spent many months looking for Gazali's village.

He had returned to his people, as he had promised, and re-established his village. He had been a great leader and was given the highest honour; his death had been mourned for many years. There were many villagers with stories of the great Gazali, and of his return to his homeland, with the secret flower. They had looked after it, not knowing its purpose, but had followed the wishes of its saviour. Gazali had many children, it appeared, and the story of a friend who received his bangle as a boy, had been passed down through the generations. Henry had been accepted by the family, as that friend, and taken into their confidence.

A visit to the night flower took place; it recognised Henry, and released a bracelet for Gazali's youngest great grandson, Ade. Henry understood this to be the replacement for the bangle Gazali had given him as a boy. Ade would become a great person within the tribe.

The old wise medicine man took Henry high into the mountain, to a sacred place. He showed him areas where he obtained plants for medicine, known only to himself. He allowed Henry to collect some of these for his research, explaining that one in particular should never be used, except in sacred rituals.

It was through this plant that Henry discovered another way to enter the secret world of travel. It was the knowledge that he acquired from the medicine man, which allowed him to briefly dip in and out of the fabric. Using a combination of the plants he had collected; Henry experimented and became more confident. Convinced that he had found the answer, and eager to recover the lost time with his mother, curiosity eventually got the better of him, and Henry succumbed to the unknown.

He entered the fabric and explored the vastness within, keeping notes of directions travelled, until it was time to return. He had not noticed the movement of everything within, and subsequently, his return did not materialize. Walls, corridors and tunnels had merged; he was lost.

The passages within the fabric are a mirror of one's mind, they will change with the moods of man, making return almost impossible. This is something that Henry had not detected, and why the *Burrbesh* can move around so freely. Henry's grey matter was no competition for the *Burrbesh* green matter. Henry had got himself into a predicament, as before; he was going round and round in circles. Each time he returned to his starting point, the time inside the fabric reset, so he was not actually moving forward.

Outside the fabric, the world was ticking away as normal. Looking back, he could never have judged how long he was there, it just seemed like an hour ago.

'It was on this occasion that I met Moss,' said Henry, and continued to weave his story to the eager listeners.

He told them of the small man who had come to his aid and had noticed his wrist. It was only because of the mark he carried, that he offered his assistance. Henry began to introduce himself, but Moss interrupted; he knew Henry, and he knew a fellow *Burrbesh* had helped him in the past.

Henry, apologetic and grateful, followed Moss through the underground network, changing direction at each junction. At these junctions there were other creatures, many with strange appearances, some like man, all looking as though they were waiting for the next train. Moss explained that it was the energy lines they used that enabled the *Burrbesh* to retain their anonymity and travel undetected. There was the usual chinwag at junctions where the traffic increased. One of the chinwaggers came over to Moss and questioned him about his charge. He asked if all mankind would be allowed access to the fabric, and then, noticing the bangle on Henry's wrist, walked off. Moss explained that this individual was *Leber*, and that Henry should not get on the wrong side of him.

'It was absolutely amazing, the passages led right to the Manor, and we entered through the old secret passage I knew as a child.' Moss became a good friend – he would come and go – and on one occasion, returned the night flower.

The year was 1875. Henry had been lost for sixty years. He vowed to concentrate on the work at the Manor and regain his life.

Unfortunately, on his return, he found that his trusted friend and colleague had long since departed and it was his third generation who had taken charge of matters.

After the initial shock of Henry's return, the custodians of his estate met with Henry, and a plan was put into being. They would continue to run the business; they would run it as their own, and enjoy the benefits, but Henry would retain ownership. Henry would take charge of the Manor, the farms and productivity, and attempt to resurrect it to its former glory. He would continue his research into medicine, and the contributions that the plant world could offer. Discoveries of new medicines would become the property of the business, but unfortunately there had been very few of those recently.

'How can you be so old, yet still look like a young man?' Sandra asked.

Henry explained that it must be the influence of the night flower, and his time spent in the fabric, where time must stand still.

Jake asked Henry about the bangle on his wrist.

'It seems to have grown into my skin. Could it be dangerous?' he said.

'No, I don't think so,' replied Henry. He explained that the bangle mark on their wrists had been a saviour on more than one occasion, and he was determined to understand more about its purpose.

In the coming years Henry made progress. He recovered the land that had been sold, plus additional farms. The business was flourishing, and his eagerness for knowledge was insatiable; new medicines were introduced. He continued to explore new areas and discover new plants. More of the world was opening its doors, and Henry was making the most of it.

On one of these expeditions, Henry returned with a very colourful assistant, who was introduced to the staff as Chonga. He was a tall African, who had assisted Henry on his last expedition; he also claimed that his father was a God. His knowledge of plants and their uses was invaluable, and he would take charge of the Manor while Henry explored.

In nineteen fourteen, war had broken out, making travel very precarious. Expeditions to those countries affected, were impossible, and sea voyages were dangerous. The need for food and medicine had never been so great and he needed to retain all the help he could get to meet the demand.

He argued against the conscription of men in his employ, with some success. Unfortunately, many of the men were called up for duty. It was just after war broke out, that a visitor arrived at the Manor. He called himself Ade, another black African; he was the great grandson of Gazali, his old friend. He showed very little sign of age, probably the result of the wrist bangle, which had been granted him by the night flower. Henry remembered that night well and was a little reluctant to be reminded of it.

Ade had told him that it was the wish of his father that he should travel. It was written that he who wore the mark of the night flower, when coming of age, should search and make contact with others the same. For there would be a reckoning, a great plague would follow a war, crops would fail, seasons would change, and the gods would no longer be able to protect them. He knew of the fabric, and of the creatures that dwelt within. His people had guarded these secrets for generations, but they were convinced that life would one day change.

Henry was just glad to see him; whilst he understood that the world was having a crisis, he could not see too much long-term strife. He invited Ade to stay, and work with him for a while; he would feel at home with his friend Chonga. And, when all the commotion in Europe died down, he would gladly accompany him and assist in his search.

'You can never be so wrong,' said Henry.

When war broke out, the grey hand of death stretched far across the world; many of the men who went to fight, never returned. Henry became very hands-on with work at the Manor, and he would joke and flirt with the women. One in particular stood out, Ivy's mother, Mary. Henry could only admire from a distance as she had been writing to her beau for nearly three years. Marriage was planned next time he had leave.

Henry buried himself in the business, providing for the war effort, and extending the premises. Ade was now concerned for his people and told Henry that he must return home; he had heard that the war was approaching his village. Henry argued that this was not the safest time to travel, he could be killed. Ade told him not to worry, if all else failed he would travel the old way. Henry said that it was not that simple, besides, he would stick out like a sore thumb. He gave a brief description of Ade, a seven-foot black giant with a red dress, and a bright green hat. Henry tried in vain to prevent him from going, but he decided to leave, and one morning he was gone.

The war seemed to go on forever, it was now in its fourth year, and it was harvesting time. Mary's sweetheart had been granted three days leave, and the wedding would take place at the local church. Everything was set, the villagers dressed up the church in harvest festival style. The day was perfect, the sun shone, the couple arrived, and the service took place.

It was when the confetti petals were thrown at the church entrance that Mary collapsed. She had a fever. It turned out to be scarlet fever. Henry had her sent to the Manor, where he attended her, his knowledge of medicine was to be a great help.

Unfortunately, the man she married had to return to his unit – she never saw him leave. Henry nursed her, never leaving her side. Several weeks passed, and slowly, the fever abated, and she began to grow stronger. Luckily, she made a full recovery and returned home, where her mother took over, feeding her up, and getting her strength back. She returned to the Manor, and work.

Henry now felt guilty because of his feelings for her. He tried to keep things on a purely professional basis but found it difficult. Then one cold November morning, Mary came into the kitchen, a place where most of the workers came for a warm. She had tears in her eyes, and cook was consoling her, when Henry entered. The cook passed Henry a telegram, which read, 'missing in action, presumed dead'.

The close friendship, which had developed during her illness became stronger. Henry had to admit his feelings for her, and the length of time he had had them. And the story goes on; the pair became very intimate. Everything seemed to happen at once after their union.

Moss appeared; he brought news of Ade. He had entered the fabric to return home and was lost. Moss had attempted to follow his tracks, but to no avail; it would be the medicine man who would be able to locate him.

Then, several of the workmen stormed in, shouting that the war was over. Everyone was dancing and shouting.

After the pandemonium had died down, Henry announced that he would have to try to save his friend, Ade. Arrangements were made for Henry to travel to the old village of Gazali; it was not easy as transport was at a premium and there was talk of an epidemic spreading across the globe. Henry had managed to find a military ship which was bringing back the troops, and it was leaving in a couple of days. There was a mad rush to get aboard; he packed, spent one last night with Mary, and left. He promised her he would return as quickly as he could, and getting down on one knee, asked her to be his wife.

Chonga meanwhile, was sending telegraphs to his friends in Africa, to arrange for guides and transport to meet Henry.

Eventually reaching Africa, he managed to cadge a lift off a pilot, who was patrolling an area not far from Henry's destination.

Making contact with the guide Chonga had organised, it was not long before they entered the village. The medicine man was briefed on the situation; Ade was still lost, and it would require all their skills to find him.

Both Henry and the medicine man entered the sacred cave. They linked arms and Henry entered the fabric, while still connected to the real world. Exiting, Henry told him of a presence he could feel, he was sure Ade was not far away. Trying again, and calling to Ade within, he managed to guide him to the sound of his voice. Grabbing his arm, he pulled him out, but caught, out of the corner of his eye, another figure, advancing towards Ade.

Outside in the real world there was a sigh of relief from Ade. Henry advised a sharp exit, for the medicine man believed that they had upset the spirits. They all returned to the village and recounted their experience. Ade vowed never to enter again, and the village rejoiced on their return.

The next day Henry set off with his guide; he had made his farewells and promised to return. It was shortly into the trek through the dense undergrowth, when Henry felt a strong presence behind him, and turning, he was confronted by *Leber*, who dragged him back into the fabric.

'That is my story. I was deeply in love with your mother, Ivy, but my future with her was stolen from me.' Henry sat quietly, casting his mind back to his last night with Mary.

Moss came out to them on the patio, and taking a seat opposite, he told them that there was something else.

He told them that on the evening Ivy was born, she was taken from her crib by the little ones, and she was found next day in the vines of the night flower.

That was a summer of extreme heat, it is something that happens every hundred years, and it is known as the *Burrbesh Summer*. Realising that Henry was lost, search parties were sent out into the jungle. But they searched in vain; it was as if the jungle itself had swallowed him.

'I searched as far into the fabric as I dared. You see, *Leber* had spent most of his time there, he had learnt how to manipulate and mould its structure.'

Moss admitted that he had to be careful and continued the story.

'Chonga did a great job of running things after Henry disappeared, but there was something missing. After several years, the heart seemed to disappear from the Manor, a melancholy reigned, and the night flower became sad and sulked.

Chonga left to search for Henry, and he was never seen again. The war and the sickness saw off the trustees of the business, and it was left in the hands of the solicitors. 'If we have finished, would you like to join the council members in the war room?' It was really for this reason Moss had come outside.

Rising to their feet the group approached the war room.

'What is that vehicle you drive, Jake?' asked Henry.

Jake and Sandra exchanged glances.

'Of course, you have no idea what the world is like now, it will be mine and Jake's pleasure to show it to you.'

Sandra grabbed Jake's hand as they entered the room.

'Aah, good afternoon people. For the benefit of our good friend Ivy, my name is *Tabule*, this is *Leber*, who some of you know, and *Angio* and *Myck*,' he gestured to the others.

Tabule went on to explain a little more of what was happening, and their purpose in this world.

'We thought we had created a utopia on this world. Had mankind made use of all the species around him, and learned to live in harmony with his world, his life here would have been very harmonious. What we had not counted on was man's greed and avarice, intolerance of those less able and his impunity for rendering species extinct.' *Tabule* made it quite clear, there were issues with the decimation of species, and the effect it was having upon the world. To watch perfection disappear was not an option, there were other worlds out there with fewer species. Their respect was greater, and their future brighter. But here the future was grim. It had to be rectified, the balance had to be restored. They were the only ones who could do that.

'We need to monitor this world, we need news, and current updates of areas in need of help. Our communications have served us well for millennia, it is ours and cannot be adapted. If we are to enlist the help of mankind to assist in this quest, then he needs to be able to communicate and adapt.'

Tabule continued to explain. He had a modest understanding of today's media, he understood television, and he had a basic understanding of modern technology. But what they were proposing would need a specialist, someone up to date with the modern world. He believed that it might take an army to deal with this world's crises, and modern crises needed up-to-date solutions.

Jake intervened and suggested that he might know the very person; he was a lecturer at his college. He was always referred to as a computer geek, a solitary man whose only companion was a set of circuit boards and monitors. If he could introduce Henry to him, he might be able to teach him a few things.

It might also be a good idea to show Henry around the estate. They could take in the homes of each of them, the local pub and the area surrounding the village.

'I know you're eager to inspect my birthday present, and it would be my honour to introduce you to the rest of your family,' said Jake.

Henry stated he hadn't even looked at the grounds of the Manor since he emerged. Agreeing to the offer and making their excuses to the council members, they proceeded to the shiny new motor. Henry was very impressed with Jake's description of the vehicle's attributes.

Not really understanding any of it, he nodded his head and looked knowledgeable. Jake drove around the fields, along the tractor access routes, deep into the countryside. Driving around the boundary of the estate, Jake showed Henry which fields had been rented to other farms. His knowledge of the area was helped by the work he had done with his father over the years. Jake parked up on a small hill in the shade of a single oak tree.

Henry, eventually mastering the exit handle, got out and stood, taking in the vision before him. The river could be seen winding its way past the Manor house towards the village. The hedgerows were like back to backs, providing accommodation for the wilder side, and creating definitive borders. Ivy walked over to him and put her arm through his.

'What a splendid world this is,' said Henry, reflecting on his circumstances.

'I think I could quite happily stay here forever.'

Jake and Sandra agreed that this was the best view on the estate.

'There is lots more to see, I think we should show you the local Tavern,' said Jake.

Completing the tour around the north end of the estate they returned to the road. Driving through the village, Ivy did the commentary on shops and people, until they reached the Tavern. It was customary to partake of the amber nectar, especially on such a hot day. During their beverage, the air ambulance flew over, and trying to explain to Henry what it was, well, where could one start?

Jake continued his tour, introducing Henry to his mom and dad, and Fidgit of course. Jake explained to his mom and dad that there would be more time for a proper get together, this was just a mad day. After visiting Ivy's house, it was agreed that this whistle- stop tour would be enough for the first time. Returning to the Manor, and the proceedings in the war room they found that plans were well under way for the meeting the next day.

Moss came over and asked if they would mind joining the council members in the dining room; they required advice on a few things.

'Ah, Henry, come in, we are putting the agenda together for the meeting, and, as you are the Lord of the Manor, so to speak, we hope you will become our spokesperson,' said *Tabule.*

He was concerned about just how much the villagers needed to know, and their reactions.

Ivy said that she knew most of them intimately, and as it was a new generation, attitudes might have changed. It might be pertinent to introduce them slowly. She didn't think that an announcement of a declaration of war on the world would go down very well with some folk.

Moss appeared and asked who would be staying for dinner.

'We should really be getting back,' said Ivy.

It was getting late, and she had commitments. Jake had had little time to appreciate his new toy and would like to take Sandra for a drive.

'Henry, join me for a stroll around your estate, we need to talk,' said *Tabule*. There was a slight sense of urgency in his voice.

'Well, that settles it then, nobody.' Moss turned and disappeared through the hall.

Jake, Sandra and Ivy said good night, and said they would return tomorrow around lunchtime.

Tabule and Henry wandered out onto the patio and set off in the direction of the weir. They were not alone, the sound of giggling and rustling of undergrowth followed them.

Tabule voiced his concerns. It was not in his nature to interfere, nor did he have the knowledge for this massive undertaking. They walked and talked through the night, both putting their own views and ideas on the subject. It was light when they returned to the Manor house, the remaining council members were still debating, *Tabule* sat at the table, and said: 'Fellow elders, I have talked with Henry, and we have discussed many possibilities for dealing with this crisis. It has been an ongoing concern to us for some time; we are all unanimous in our belief that we should intervene. And I believe that we now have a plan.'

Chapter 9

The meeting with the villagers was set for 18:00. The majority would be relatives of those who had worked at the Manor. Of course, there would be new members of the community, curious to see the Manor. Memories of its history would be from stories passed down through the generations. The camaraderie that once existed would need to be developed all over again.

Henry suggested to *Tabule* that perhaps the council members should maintain a low key for the time being.

And so, it was decided that Henry would interview and assemble a loyal workforce. This would be the first item on the agenda.

Those members of the council present, convened around the table, to commence their meeting, whilst other members arrived spasmodically. *Tabule* was repeatedly interrupted as the remaining members of the council took their seats. Eventually he had their attention.

'My friends, we believe that within the next thirty years the polar ice caps on this planet will melt. The water will rise, and life will change. Plants will die, and this world will suffer. We have spent millions of years grooming and repairing previous damages. We cannot allow the work of an eternity to go to waste.'

Tabule went on to explain that their role was that of creator, not fighter and destroyer.

'Drastic measures are required, this world is quite unique in its ability to sustain life, and we would hate to lose it.' There was a passion in *Tabule's* voice as he continued:

'It was not so long ago that much of the human race thrived in their surroundings. Nature and its elements were used wisely, and mankind flourished. The night flower brought peace and harmony to many parts of this world. Alas, its presence has declined as society has turned away from the old ways.'

Tabule explained that a decision had been made.

The *Burrbesh* believed that by assisting in the repatriation of the tribal cultures around the world, safe havens for the little ones would follow. So many had looked after the night flower in the past, and hopefully would do so again. The *Burrbesh* would like to re-distribute the night flower across this world and restore it to its former glory. Time was of the essence. A speedy colonisation of the plant produced at the Manor, could see vast areas replanted.

'It is sheer destiny that has brought Henry back into the fold. For it is the nature of man to fight; it is for this reason that Henry would be the ideal candidate for the job. We should vote on giving him the responsibility of coordinating events. Man is prone to create conflict on this world; it seems to take precedence. He is unable to see the broader picture; it is as though his very nature is to destroy. Mankind seems too wound up in talking and reporting about his misdemeanours to notice the reality.'

Tabule continued to comment: He was sure that man alone could not agree on a plan to repair the world. He would be quite happy to leave the mess for future generations.

Henry interjected and said, 'The business my father and I started many years ago has flourished. Details are to be finalised with solicitors, and the facilities available within the company would be at the disposal of the council. Its global connections may prove to be a useful tool in the recruitment of allies.'

He admitted that he had a lot of catching up to do but vowed that he would stop at nothing to save this world.

It was now mid-morning, the weather was about to turn, a storm was approaching. The *Burrbesh* had a certain influence over the weather, they liked it warm, but storms were just a bit too strong to control.

The night flower, still enjoying the effects of the planets, was slowly taking over the conservatory and making its way into the meeting. It appeared to caress each of the council members in turn, as it snaked its way slowly around the room. Each member accepting of its attentions, bonding with it, giving a token of themselves.

This bond, which had never happened before, would give the night flower the qualities of each individual. The little ones, who would be produced by the night flower, would be more powerful than ever before; they would definitely need guidance. The meeting entered a moment of silence, where deep thought took over; the influence of the night flower was felt by all. Henry felt a sense of comfort and belonging and drifted into a deep sleep.

He was awoken by the arrival of Jake and Sandra, who were amazed at the sight that greeted them. The night flower had grown around the table of council members – some were wrapped in a tight embrace, and others were supported as if in a hammock.

'They all appear to be asleep. What a sight of extreme harmony they make,' said Sandra.

Jake and Sandra had been to visit the computer geek, and, as he was a local, they had invited him to meet Henry.

Sandra tugged on Jake's arm and whispered that it might be best to leave them for a while. At that moment Henry stirred, and stretching his arms, greeted them both.

'I must apologize for not being responsive; it must be the first sleep I have enjoyed for over a hundred years,' said Henry jokingly. He looked round at the rest of the council members; they were all entwined in the same way.

'It must be something in the air,' said Henry, stretching and untangling himself from the caressing plant.

'I have had the most amazing dream, or was it real? It's difficult to tell with all that's recently happened.'

Henry commented on how refreshed he felt and ushered them out of the room and into the conservatory.

There, examining the plant, was a tall skinny man. He had long hair neatly held in a ponytail and a goatee beard. He was dressed in a green velvet suit, and a green cravat with large yellow spots tied in a flimsy way around his neck. He turned to greet the trio.

'Fascinating,' he said, gesturing to the now jungle-like addition to the room.

'Allow me to introduce myself, Professor Edmund Mathews at your service.'

There was a slight Germanic inflection to his voice. He confessed that he had a passion for horticulture; his love of strange plants that seemed to defy nature, was insatiable.

'It is a hobby that often resembles an illness, rather than a pastime. Never seen anything like this.'

He turned to touch one of the unopen buds, which gave a very discernible shiver. He drew his hand back sharply, which caused a humorous outburst from the onlookers.

Henry explained that it was a unique plant, and he would give a full explanation in due course.

'What is it you specialise in at the College?' asked Henry.

The Professor went on to explain that it was computer technology, laser communication, electronics and surveillance. He admitted to being obsessive about understanding new inventions, even to the point of improving their design.

They wandered over to a quiet corner of the conservatory and sat around a table, upon which tea had been served.

'You will have to excuse the staff; they are preparing for the meeting later. We may be just out of their way here.'

Trays of nibbles and drinks were being ferried to and fro by the staff, in preparation for the throngs of villagers who were expected.

'You will have to pardon my ignorance,' said Henry. 'I have been out of society for some time and much of this new technology goes straight over my head.'

Jake tried to explain to Henry that the Professor would be able to help in providing the infrastructure required. Communication would be vital, and surveillance would play a key role in successful planning. Being able to monitor the results of what was happening and keep everything up to date, could be very useful.

The Professor said that as it was the summer break, he would be most happy to assist where he could.

'There is one other thing,' said Sandra, 'Henry is going to need educating on most things, perhaps a little more than you can imagine, Professor.'

'We may have to get you to swear an oath of secrecy,' joked Henry.

He agreed that the Professor could be a useful ally and told him that there would be no expense spared to provide the equipment required. Henry invited him to the meeting that evening and said it would be most helpful if he could offer advice.

In the meantime, it was agreed that there was much that Henry needed to know.

It was just after midday, the room went quite dark, and a great thunderclap, followed by a flash of lightning, broke the silence.

The council members emerged from their doze, *Tabule* joined Henry's party, whilst others wandered off to their respective rooms. Some ventured into the grounds to enjoy the rain, which came down in sheets.

A strange intense storm broke, very much like a squall out at sea. It passed very quickly, soon returning to bright sunshine, with increased sauna-like humidity.

Henry introduced the Professor to *Tabule*, who took Edmund's outstretched hand to shake. He questioned Edmund's interest in botany, having felt his passion through the contact.

'We are going to need the help of people like yourself,' explained *Tabule*. The Professor told *Tabule* that Jake and Sandra had given him a brief outline of the circumstances involved. He was an ardent supporter of a green earth, and he would be honoured to be considered.

Suddenly Henry stood up. He asked the Professor to join him in a walk around the grounds and, making his apologies to the rest, they both disappeared through the doors, onto the patio.

Tabule, quite content to sit and chat with Jake and Sandra, quizzed them both on matters of importance. He was keen to understand what Sandra was studying at university. There was a curiosity about Jake's thoughts on recent events, and his views on the matter. They sat chatting, and Jake gave an account of his life up till now.

They exchanged ideas on how to repair the world and the possible outcome of failure. One thing was agreed upon by all, and that was a massive reintroduction of green areas. Sandra explained that the work she found fascinating, was genetically altering plants to grow in hostile conditions. She told *Tabule* of a species that had been discovered surrounding volcanic vents, at the bottom of the Pacific. The DNA had been extracted and inserted in various lichens and mosses; they were now under trial in a toxic growing medium and were thriving.

Tabule called to Moss who was chatting with several members.

'Come, listen to this,' *Tabule* gestured to Moss to take a seat with them.

Sandra continued to explain the research which was currently ongoing. It was a bid to find a solution to the areas of the world devastated by pollution, famine and drought. Although genetically modified foods had had bad press of late, these experiments had taken a different direction and were aimed directly at climate change.

The small group continued to chat. Moss told Sandra he had created many species which had been required to withstand severe conditions. Most had outlived their usefulness, and to be quite honest, forgotten. Moss expressed his enthusiasm to work with Sandra on this subject.

Meanwhile, Henry had taken the Professor around the grounds. Henry had explained to the Professor the circumstances surrounding his life and its incarcerations. He was taking the Professor into his confidence. Henry had felt a strong sense of loyalty from this man and had concluded that they would become very good friends.

In response to Henry's forthright honesty, the Professor vowed to teach Henry all he needed to know of the last century.

They made their way back to the Manor, where villagers were starting to arrive. They met up with *Tabule*, Moss, Jake and Sandra.

Ivy, who had just arrived, was introduced to the Professor; he bowed, looked deep into her eyes, took her hand and without altering his gaze, kissed it.

It was a proper Bavarian introduction, complete with heel tap.

'Charmed,' he said. 'I am very pleased to meet you, please call me Edmund.'

'Very pleased to meet you too, Edmund,' said Ivy.

Jake and Sandra looked at each other, witnessing the chemistry and expecting another electrical display.

Although Ivy was reaching a great age, her youthfulness shone out, a product of her genetic inheritance.

There was a hustle and bustle as the Manor started to fill with people. Small groups congregated and could be heard discussing each other's historical family ties. Each person had a story to tell, secrets that had been kept for a generation were being divulged.

Jake and Sandra wandered around, stopping to eavesdrop on someone's tale. They were both quite amazed at the volume of history the Manor had created. It had been a major contributor to social life in the village; those who were employed were treated as family. Many of the villagers were speculating on what the plans were to be for the Manor.

Jake and Sandra had to rescue Henry from a group of women who had surrounded him. He explained to them that it was probably best if he introduced himself as the long-lost grandson, who had eventually been tracked down by a firm of solicitors and informed of his inheritance. As a family member, he would have been told stories, and with limited knowledge of the Manor, would be able to respond to their questions.

The three went off in search of *Tabule,* in order to get the meeting under way. There must have been forty or fifty people from the village who had turned up for the evening's event. Moss really enjoyed striking the dinner gong, and wasted no time in performing this role and informing everyone that the meeting was about to start.

Everyone except the council members, meandered into the dining room. *Tabule* had decided to conduct his own meeting, outside on the patio. He would brief the other members to support any plan Henry might come up with, and they would inform others to do the same.

'It is a bit of history in the making,' *Tabule* announced.

'It seems like an eternity since all the *Burrbesh* were united in a single cause, but for now, I must leave; there is important work I must attend to elsewhere.'

As *Tabule* proceeded to leave, *Leber* intercepted him and took him to one side.

'Sire, much has happened in the last few days, and I must admit to having a feeling of guilt. I may have been wrong about our Henry, having connected with him and felt his bond with the *Burrbesh.'*

'That's unlike you, *Leber,'* he replied.

Leber explained that he would not interfere with Henry's pursuit of the *Burrbesh* ability to travel. Should he find it necessary to use it in future campaigns, he would be more than willing to advise him on its finer points. *Tabule* was quite taken aback by this change in one who had always been a rebel in the ranks.

'I believe Henry is now more *Burrbesh* than human; his time in the quandary has changed him, all thanks to you *Leber.'*

Tabule made his farewells to the group and was gone.

The meeting was called to order.

Henry took the rostrum, albeit a basic conductor's stand, found in the attic, and began:

He introduced himself as Henry James Lyte, grandson and heir to the Lytes estate and businesses. Until recently, he had been studying cave workings deep in the Amazon jungle, which was not too far from the truth.

Having been contacted by solicitors, and dragged from his observations, he had returned to the family home. He knew much of the history of the Manor and knew how important it had been to the village. The production of a particular plant had made it a very special establishment. Many who were present would have stories of such happenings, all related to the magic of the night flower. He continued, with references to the devastation that this world was going through, and the benefits that could be achieved by the production and distribution of this magic plant. He claimed it was his intention to return the Manor to its former glory: to revitalize the area, provide jobs for the village, and to resurrect the production of the night flower. It would be distributed all over the world, to assist in restoring the balance of things.

'Nature was struggling, and it needed help.' Henry stopped for a moment to take a sip of water; there was a resounding applause.

Henry continued. He knew of the connections many had with relatives who had worked at the Manor, and explained that he too, felt connected. Not wanting to give too much away, he told of stories that had been passed down from his father, his father and his father before. He commented on how comfortable he felt on his arrival; the Manor was now his home, and he was there to stay.

He told them of his plans to build up-to-date growing facilities to increase production. There would be warehousing and training facilities; many jobs would be created. It would become a world recruitment centre for the further supply and care of the night flower.

'Those who would like to work at the Manor can take an application form from the lobby. Please fill it out and leave it before you go.' Henry gestured to Moss and told the villagers that he would be the collector of forms.

Henry concluded his oratory by inviting everyone to help themselves to food and drink. He would meet anyone who had a question for him, and he would be glad to answer.

The evening continued with enthusiasm. Jake and Sandra found themselves answering questions too.

Eventually the meeting shrunk, as, one by one, individuals made their farewells and returned home.

Moss approached with a fistful of applications.

'There are many who would like to work here,' he said.

Henry felt very pleased with the result and said that now the work could begin. Plans would need to be drawn up, to accommodate all that was intended.

'Edmund has offered to take me under his wing for a few days,' said Henry. 'I have much to catch up on and he suggested that I accompany him on his daily work schedule.'

The remaining elders, together with Henry, Jake and Sandra, retired to the dining room. They discussed the proposed works to be carried out at the Manor. Also, the planned return of tribal cultures which would be vital in the overall scheme of things.

They talked long into the night, and all agreed that it would be *Burrbesh* that would instigate the search for lost tribes; to bring them together and unite them in the quest of which their ancestors had been so proud. Any other influence that could expedite the return of these people should also be explored.

It was also agreed that the work required at the Manor would be overseen by Henry, Jake and Sandra. Suitable builders, suppliers and professionals would be drafted in to begin immediately. Jake and Sandra would make a start in Henry's absence, by using a reasonably adequate drawing of requirements, made on the back of a napkin.

As the morning was nearly upon them, Henry offered Jake and Sandra rooms at the Manor, to rest and refresh.

One by one the elders made their exit, acknowledging Jake and Sandra, and vowing to return soon.

Henry bade them a good morning and wandered outside to walk around the grounds, followed closely by three gigglers.

'We are definitely going to have to find a name for each of you three.' Henry inhaled the heady aroma of the air, fresh after the rain, then disappeared along the path.

Chapter 10

You could almost hear the Manor house emit a sigh of contentment as the sun rose on a perfect morning. Having been quiet for so long, the return of life and meaning cast a comfortable sense of purpose over the property.

Henry wandered around the estate, three sprouts in tow, reflecting on the enormity of the challenges to come. Everything seemed to be clear, his visions of the times to come had organized themselves into neat parcels of strategy.

The proposed expansion of the Manor should encourage those who had the desire to further their knowledge. It would be a base for those who had disconnected from their roots, a place to learn and be learnt, to re-establish their cultures. It would bring together those who were lost, having left the old ways, and who had tried, without success, to make it in the new world.

With an incentive and funding, the training could see a resurgence of lost traditions and secrets. Henry was excited, and slightly sceptical as to whether this could all happen. He reflected on what the coming weeks would bring.

Could he actually learn from his new acquaintance, the Professor? Would his learning of new knowledge affect his dedication to the cause and his acceptance by the *Burrbesh*?

Suspicious since a young boy that he was somewhat different to others, he had never been able to pinpoint why. His life had now taken a turning, from repetitive uselessness, to being a potential crusader, in search of the Holy Grail.

He was comfortable sitting in that place which overlooked the estate, with the river in the distance. It was the place where Jake and Sandra had taken him days before.

His three strange companions had stayed close to him, and as a result, he had connected with them more closely. He had picked up on their sadness of previous years, of their loss, as Henry had suddenly gone in search of his friend. Leaving the Manor with little thought for others, he had not had the opportunity to examine the ramifications of his actions.

The little ones poured out their feelings to him; he learned much from this and vowed it would not happen again.

The time was around 06:00, a tractor pulling a plough was approaching the small, wooded knoll where Henry sat, absorbing the world. It was Jake's father; he had taken on the rental of the fields from the estate years back.

Bill saw Henry and pulled over at the edge of the knoll. Exiting his tractor, Bill walked over to Henry.

'What you doing up 'ere this time o' day?' Bill enquired.

'Sorry, we had to leave early last night, but you know how it is. Needs must, early start, 'cos nature won't wait.'

Henry said there was no need for apologies, that he knew what farm life was like, and he understood.

Bill extracted a flask from his tractor and brought it over to where Henry was sitting.

'Cuppa tea?' said Bill.

'That would be lovely,' said Henry.

The pair sat, drinking tea, with that perfect moment of silence as the caffeine took effect.

'I hears that you have been away for a while,' said Bill.

'Yes, a while is a good word. I don't know how much you have been told,' said Henry.

Bill told Henry that he had been privy to certain information but wouldn't mind being filled in on the finer points.

Henry said, 'You must know, of course, that I am your grandfather, father to your mother, Ivy, and great grandfather to Jake.'

Bill said he found that bit a little difficult to get his head around. He only knew what his mother had told him when he was a small boy. He remembered stories of magical plants, and of lands far away, where great treasures were sought.

Ivy had told him many a tale; he had assumed they were just stories, made up for bedtime.

He told Henry that as he grew older, he started to have dreams of strange plant-like creatures. Those same dreams came every night; he thought he was going mad. He told his mother, who dismissed them as part of his growing pains. So, putting them to the back of his mind, Bill concentrated on getting on with his life. He never mentioned them again, even though they returned many times.

'Funny thing is,' said Bill, 'recently, I've bin seein' those critters again, thought I saw them last night at the meeting. And I don'ts feels too comfortable now.'

Henry laughed. He commented on how difficult it was for men to be susceptible to the unnatural. Would he believe him, if he said there were three of those little critters sitting on the branch of the tree above them?

Bill glanced furtively upwards, where three sprouts materialised; they were sitting together waving and giggling.

'Well, I'll be buggered, those critters have been in and out of my head for as long as I can remember,' said Bill, relieved he wasn't bonkers.

The trio of critters left their perch, and came to sit with Bill and Henry, just like a family picnic.

'Let me fill you in on a few details, Bill,' said Henry, and proceeded to give an account of his past history.

He spoke of his parents, his childhood travels and his bond with the night flower; of expeditions, discoveries and his run-in with the Council of Libra; his incarcerations, which had taken an age to escape from, and the one love in his life, whom he never really got to know.

They sat chatting for some time; morning turned to noon. Bill eventually said he must crack on; the fields wouldn't plough themselves. He thanked Henry for being so honest, and said he would stick to calling him Henry, as 'Grandad' would probably raise a few eyebrows.

Henry laughed, and rising to his feet, he held out his hand to Bill.

'It has been nice to talk. It's good to catch up, especially when it's family. In fact, the Professor is coming over at lunchtime to begin my education.'

Declining a lift back in the tractor, Henry decided to walk back along the bridleway situated behind the hedge. It led back to the stables at the Manor, and although very overgrown he remembered it from his last visit. So, he, and his three companions, made their way back to the Manor.

On arrival, Henry found the Professor and Ivy on the patio, awaiting his return. The Professor had taken Ivy home the previous evening, and he had brought her to collect her two-wheeled steed, which had been left at the Manor.

'Good day to you both, I have just spent a glorious morning with Bill, sitting up on the knoll in the top field,' Henry said.

'Introduced him to three friends, he was quite pleased to see them in the flesh, so to speak.'

Henry winked at Ivy, 'You never told him.'

Henry poured himself a large glass of lemonade and took a doughnut off the cake stand.

'Well, Edmund, what do you have in store for me today?' said Henry, brushing off an avalanche of loose sugar.

'I thought we should go for a drive, take in some of the neighbouring villages and towns. When was the last time you went to Bristol?' Edmund enquired.

'That would be about three weeks ago, when I left to find Ade,' said Henry.

Having no memory of the last hundred years, it was still very vivid in his mind.

He knew Bristol and the docks reasonably well. His research still revolved around plant and herbal medicines. He would regularly collect plants and soil samples from all over the world. He recalled earlier times, where the masts of ships at harbour in Avonmouth could be seen as you passed through Clifton.

'Mmmmm,' said Edmund.

'I think a visit to a gent's outfitter would be a good start.' Holding his chin with thumb and forefinger, he scrutinized the style of clothing Henry was wearing.

'Perhaps a trip to Bristol tomorrow, if that's all right with you?' said Edmund enquiringly.

Henry said he had an appointment with the solicitors three days hence, until which time, he would place himself at Edmund's disposal.

Rising to his feet, Edmund leaned over to Ivy and took her hand; kissing it, he apologised for leaving her and vowed to return. Ivy encouraged them both to go and enjoy the sights. She was expecting Jake and Sandra at any moment. They had work to do.

As Henry and Edmund entered the conservatory, there was the distinct sound of children playing. Edmund turned to Henry and enquired after the presence of children in the Manor.

Henry stopped and pointed to the top of the night flower.

'They are playing hide and seek. Show yourselves, sprouts!' shouted Henry.

Edmund, looking at what appeared to be nothing, turned to Henry, who, using Edmund's shoulder as a tripod, rested his arm and pointed.

When Edmund turned to look again, he saw the three little ones, they scurried down from their perch and disappeared out the door.

'Fascinating,' exclaimed Edmund.

'Those are our children, I keep saying we shall have to find them names,' Henry replied.

He explained the role and some of the history of the sprouts, as they walked through the hallway, and out to where Edmund's car was parked.

'They shall be put to the test very soon.'

They walked over to Edmund's car; bearing in mind he was a little eccentric, the car wasn't.

'Do you like it? She is the same age as me,' said Edmund. 'She is a 1956 Morgan 4/4 Mk II; I call her Matilda.'

She was finished in British racing green, a two-seater open-topped sports car, which oozed the character of Edmund, in more ways than one.

'Shall we?' said Edmund gesturing to the small, almost insignificant door. Henry opened the car's door and poured himself onto the very low, brown leather seat.

Edmund positioned himself at the helm, turned the key, and with a roar of the engine they set off, narrowly avoiding an incoming delivery van. As they exited the drive, Jake and Sandra were about to turn in. Edmund stopped and greeted them both. As Jake was driving his old Landy, Henry asked where the posh red one was. Jake said he was keeping it for special occasions, and enquired where they were off to.

'We are off to Wells; I shall try and ease Henry into the twenty-first century and maybe some new clothes.'

Edmund waved goodbye as he sped off down the lane.

There was still sufficient time in the day to explore the professional skills of Edmund's tailor, and the country air.

Jake continued up the drive and parked outside the barn. Fidgit, who had been dozing in the back, realised they had arrived. He immediately jumped out and ran off into the undergrowth, in search of you know who.

Jake and Sandra wandered into the Manor, greeted by Moss who was obscured by boxes. The place seemed busier than it did before the meeting.

'Moss, I know you're in there somewhere. What's happening, what's with all the boxes?' shouted Sandra.

Moss poked his head above one of the top boxes, some eight feet from the ground.

'It's started,' he yelled. 'I have lists from Henry, Edmund, Ivy, house staff, butler and the Millers, who are working in the garden.'

'I suppose that means you don't want any more lists, like this one?' said Jake, waving a sheet of A4 at Moss.

'Moss, let me help,' said Sandra, 'it just needs organising.'

There was a scream from Moss as the stack of six boxes over balanced and Moss and boxes ended up in a confused pile on the floor.

'Are you all right?' said a concerned Sandra, rushing over to him.

Jake, however, had developed a fit of the giggles, which erupted into hysteria when he saw Moss appear from beneath the cardboard. Static had charged bits of white packaging, which were now attached to Moss's person.

'I'm sorry, I have to go and measure up outside.'

His laughter intensified as he saw Sandra remove a piece of polystyrene packaging from behind Moss's left ear. Sandra inspected the boxes and assured Moss that nothing seemed to be damaged.

'No, I'm fine,' said Moss, sarcastically.

Sandra decided that Moss needed some help and stayed with him to deal with delivery after delivery. They both continued to tidy up and unpack the contents.

Meanwhile, Jake had gone out onto the patio. His Gran was sitting there, studying the drawing that had been made on the napkin.

'Ah, Jake, what do you make of this? Doesn't look like any knitting pattern I've ever seen.' Ivy passed him the sketch of squares and circles.

Jake laid it out on the table and explained that it was a sketch of the proposed alterations which were to be made at the Manor.

'You see this square, it's the Manor, these are new greenhouses, and this will be the training centre and workshops. The circle will be a rain and water storage tank.' Jake pointed out all the proposed items. He explained to her that what they needed to do now was measure up, see if these ideas were possible, what space would be required and then arrange to get the whole idea built.

'Edmund seemed to think it would be a good idea to enlist the professional help of an architect. 'Is there anyone you know, Gran?' said Jake.

Jake poured himself a large glass of the now famous lemonade, and sat back, watching his Gran think.

She was sure there was someone who could do this.

'It will come to me,' she said.

Jake said he was going to check on the greenhouses, the river level had dropped a bit and he wanted to check the irrigation. Then he would try and roughly plot out the napkin drawing. Ivy was ready to lend a hand; she said she would catch up with him shortly.

Jake got up and walked across the patio. He whistled for Fidgit, who actually came. This made Jake suspicious.

'What have you been up to, and where are your little friends?' Jake observed Fidgit's reaction, not one he had seen before. Summoning him to stay close, Jake set off up the river with the obedient Fidgit at his side.

It was about this time that Henry and Edmund arrived in Wells, having taken the scenic route to get there. Edmund had been giving a detailed account of sights that they saw, as well as answering a curious man's questions.

Pulling up outside a double-fronted tailor's shop, Edmund told Henry to have a look in the window, to see if he liked anything on display. Extracting himself from Matilda, he made his way with Edmund, past the window, browsing the displays, and into the shop. They were greeted by a shop attendant with a smart waistcoat and a tape measure around his neck.

'Good afternoon, Professor, what can I do for you today?'

'Levi, I have brought a friend. He has been away for many years but has returned and requires a new set of clothes. The airport appears to have sent them to Afghanistan, if not, they are lost!' The Professor apologised for Henry's existing clothes and was confident Levi could help.

While Henry and Edmund were in the shop, the boot of the car fell open, and there was a giggling from inside. Whilst playing hide and seek with Fidgit, the little ones had chosen the boot of Edmund's car to hide in.

Tentatively, each of them wriggled out of the boot and dropped onto the road. There was a park opposite with two large trees just inside the gates; they beckoned to the sprouts to enter. They could see a play area over the other side, with its swings and slides, a climbing frame with ropes and a tree house.

They made their way towards it, where a mother was pushing a young child gently on the swing. Not noticing the other child parked in a buggy with a sun parasol, they walked past. The infant, around two years old, noticed them and reached out, babbling something in infant; the three little ones, all together, put their fingers to their lips.

Mother turned to see the commotion, and, unable to see anything, resumed her attention to the swing.

The little ones, having touched the play tray on the infant's buggy had left a large clump of daisies. In fact, everywhere they touched resulted in daisies growing.

They were giggling and pulling faces at the baby in the buggy. In fact, the baby was laughing so much, mother turned to look. By this time, the buggy was covered in daisies, growing from everywhere. Baby had a bunch in its hand, and was waving goodbye to the three adventurers, who could not turn off the planting touch. Their footsteps turned to daisies, leaving a trail behind them.

The mother loaded the second child in the buggy and began her exit from the park.

Turning their attention to the climbing frame the sprouts became more excited, which made matters worse.

Stranger, bigger and more colourful plants appeared, covering the climbing frame as they played with slides, swings and ropes. Soon the sprouts could only be heard laughing from inside the greenery.

Back at the shop, Henry and Edmund were just leaving. The shop owner, Levi, had measured Henry, who had chosen a selection of useful garments, to be collected.

As they descended the steps to the pavement, Edmund noticed the open boot.

'I shall have to get that fixed; it's been loose for a while.'

At that moment, the mother with her two children came walking towards him, her floral buggy caught Henry's eye. He could tell they were real and was impressed that someone should go to the trouble of using real plants.

'That's quite pretty,' remarked Henry.

'Strangest thing,' she said. 'We were in the park, and all of a sudden, daisies just appeared everywhere.'

'No,' Henry became suspicious.

'I think we should just have a look at this phenomenon in the park, I think we may have had uninvited passengers.'

They both wandered over to the park entrance; they could see the play area on the far side. Walking towards it they could see a small jungle appearing. The swings were a tangle of clematis and honeysuckles, all with fantastic flowers and fragrance. The climbing frame could not be seen, the slide looked like a wild meadow, and there was a distinct sound of laughter coming from within.

Clearing his throat in a very loud fashion, which did not have the desired effect, Henry then called to the little ones.

'Ok, playtime is over.'

One by one the little ones appeared, each with its own unique shape and protuberances.

Edmund confessed he could not see a thing. He could, however, see the foliage that had wrapped around the play area.

'Mother has more control over them at the Manor, they are young, playful and unsure how to manage their gift.'

Henry grabbed Edmund's arm.

Suddenly the three sprouts were visible, each of them had become over-excited and changed shape.

'This is quite astonishing,' said Edmund.

'Can you imagine what could be achieved with hundreds of these?' said Henry, painting a picture of a mass planting of desolated areas.

'A repair circuit for the planet.'

'I think we had better get these rebels back home, don't you?' Henry took the hand of two, while Edmund took the third on his shoulder.

Returning back to the car, the little ones were ushered into the boot. Edmund decided it was best locked, just to be on the safe side.

As they sat back in the car Edmund's phone gave a beep. It was a concerned text from Sandra, they had not seen the little ones all day.

'Here,' Edmund passed Henry the phone. 'See what you can make of that.'

Edmund laughed and told Henry that this little item was not quite fully understood by most of the planet.

They set off back the way they had come. Edmund continually fed Henry information on the complexities of sending a text. It resulted in them arriving back at the Manor before the text.

Sandra came down the steps to greet them. Henry apologised for not mastering the workings of the Professor's box of tricks, in time, and then continued to explain the misdemeanours of the rebel sprouts.

Edmund opened the boot, and one by one the stowaways emerged.

Moss had just appeared and saw the state they were in.

'Oh my, Mother will be pleased,' he said, as he continued to herd them into the conservatory.

'They are all funny shapes,' said Sandra, hardly able to contain a smile.

She told Henry that Jake and Ivy were in the grounds, measuring out the napkin. It looked like there would be trees that would need taking down to accommodate the planned buildings.

'Let's go and have a look, shall we?' said Henry.

They all wandered around the house and into the grounds, where Jake and Ivy were pegging out the area for the workshops.

Sandra told them both of the little ones' recent adventure. Jake commented that Fidgit had been moping around like a lost soul all day, he knew something was amiss.

Henry came and examined the areas which had been set out for the buildings, trusting in Jake's judgement and expertise.

'It's looking good. I think we should retire to the patio for refreshments, and make plans for tomorrow,' said Henry. He felt that enough had been done for one day.

The time was approaching five o'clock, the staff were making preparations for dinner. Moss wondered how many they would need to prepare for.

'You should all stay for dinner,' said Henry.

Ivy and Jake wandered into the conservatory to see the little ones, they were back to their normal shape and being cossetted by Mother.

Fidgit gave a bark of indignation, having been left with no one to play with.

The Professor and Ivy were quite amenable about staying for dinner and returned to the patio. Jake and Sandra had to pop back, freshen up and get changed. And of course, Fidgit would want his dinner.

'6.30 for dinner then, see you later,' shouted Henry.

Joining Ivy and Edmund, Henry was updated on proceedings for the building works. Ivy said she would visit the local council the next day and inquire what would be required regarding planning permissions. She had also met an old friend whose husband was an architect. Ivy had invited them for coffee, at lunchtime the next day. He could have a look at the site, and she and her friend could catch up with news.

Edmund enquired of Henry if Bristol was still on the agenda, making sure to check for stowaways first.

This comment created a bout of laughter from them all.

'I seem to have missed the joke,' said *Tabule*, who had appeared, as if from nowhere.

Henry remarked that this was an unexpected pleasure and retold the adventures of that afternoon.

Tabule told Henry that he had been in contact with *Chonganda*, an old acquaintance who had agreed to give his support for the task ahead. He had also spoken to many of the tribal elders. They would begin the gathering of support through the grapevine. There would be much to do, many of the lands once occupied by these people, were no more.

Jake and Sandra arrived; Moss accompanied them to the patio.

'Good afternoon you two,' said *Tabule*. 'I have a project which may interest you, Sandra.' He said no more and kept Sandra guessing. He told Moss that he had a situation which would require his assistance. It would only be for a few days, but they needed to leave immediately.

Tabule and Moss excused themselves, made their apologies and left.

MacTavish came through and announced that dinner was ready and would be served promptly.

Chapter 11

Dinner went on well into the night. The topic of discussion revolved around the Manor and its history. Then into the future, and the role set out for it to play and how it would cope with the changes required. Other than gas lighting, and a rudimentary electricity supply, run off a clapped-out generator, the house had remained untouched for hundreds of years. It still had the hand pump for water outside the kitchen door. It was very obvious that there was more than Henry that needed upgrading.

Eventually the dinner guests made their excuses to leave. Edmund had agreed to take Ivy home and would collect her in the morning on his way to the Manor. Jake and Sandra bade goodnight and made their way to the shiny red present. They both laughed at the sight of Edmund feeling around in the small boot of the Morgan.

The following day was a repeat of the previous two weeks. Jake rose at 05:00 and proceeded to water his allotment, chasing Fidgit with the water spray. After a quick shower, Jake and Fidgit went for breakfast.

You could virtually eat the aroma coming from the kitchen. Sitting at the table with a breakfast that would feed four. Jake dug in. His father enquired how the plans were going for the building work at the Manor.

Answering between mouthfuls, he did manage to explain that it needed electrics, water, phones, cable, but not sure about drains.

'It needs everything,' said Jake.

Some of the trees would need moving. Henry was reluctant to cut trees down. Jake asked his father if he knew anyone with machinery that could dig up large trees and replant them.

'Yes,' he said.

He knew a forester who had a tree nursery; he provided big trees for big projects; he would give him a call and give him Jake's number.

Jake's mother said there was another one of those cakes to take over to Ivy, if he didn't mind.

Finishing his tea and walking out with a sausage in his mouth, Jake picked up the cake tin. Throwing half the sausage to Fidgit, Jake said, 'come on you, let's go and find your friends.'

With his Biggles goggles on and Fidgit firmly ensconced as navigator in the passenger seat, they set off to Sandra's. Pulling up outside, Jake could see Ivy and Sandra sitting at the table, chatting. He walked up the path, sat beside Sandra and gave her a peck on the cheek.

'Morning,' he beamed, placing the tin on the table.

'Mother's contribution!'

'It's for a fund raiser later,' said Ivy.

Her charitable work knew no bounds.

'Looks like you pair will be on your own today. You might get a visit from the architect later.'

Jake commented that the amount of work they had should keep them out of trouble for a year or so. They wandered down the path with Fidgit in tow.

'Your carriage awaits, milady,' Jake gestured to the rather grubby Land Rover.

Jumping into the back of the Landy, Fidgit, unhappy with the shape of his blanket, proceeded to dig into it.

Amused by Fidgit's enthusiasm, they never saw Edmund arrive.

'Good morning, good morning, lovely day,' exclaimed Edmund.

Caught a little off guard, the pair jumped, but before they could return his greeting, Edmund was bounding down the path to Ivy.

'I reckon there's something going on with those two,' said Sandra.

Jake just grimaced and muttered something unintelligible and continued to drive to the Manor.

On arrival, they saw Henry talking to someone, they walked over and were introduced.

'Hello, you two, this is Chris Reynolds, the architect Ivy made contact with.'

Henry apologised for having to rush off, but he expressed his confidence in Jake and Sandra's abilities.

'They probably know better than I do, what will be required.'

Before Henry had finished speaking, the roar of the Morgan came up the drive. Parking up, Edmund rushed around to open the door for Ivy.

Taking his arm, they walked over to the rest, where Ivy greeted Henry and Chris. She thanked Chris for his prompt visit and told him she would stay for a while.

'Important matters to attend to in the village later,' she said.

Edmund enquired if Henry was ready for the day, to which there was an enthusiastic, yes.

'Well, if you're ready, we can depart.'

Edmund bid farewell to the group and promised Ivy, he would see her later for dinner.

Sandra turned to Jake and gave him that 'woman knows' look.

'Told you,' she said.

Walking over to the car Henry asked Edmund if he wouldn't mind making a small detour on the way.

He began to tell Edmund the story of the Gypsies. They were a band of Romanies who came to work the farm when he last returned. They had befriended Henry and he had come to look upon them as family. One old lady in particular had become like a second mother to him. The Gypsies would travel but come back every year to help with harvest. Eventually some stayed and made the farm their home, while others would return when the harvest fell due.

Henry gave directions: the road to Bristol had two turnings off to the left, both of which gave access to fields. It would be the second turning, which was on a sweeping right-hand bend. The opening was bordered by two great oaks and the track then continued along the hedgerow. It was flanked occasionally on either side by younger oaks, which had been planted by the Gypsies. The track would lead down to the river, where a clearing would have housed the caravans, giving shelter from the winds.

Henry told Edmund that he had spent many a night with them and wondered if there was any sign of them now. He would like to see this place again just to satisfy his curiosity. They were a secretive bunch who respected the natural world and knew much about the land and its hidden treasures.

The Morgan bounced along the lane, and on reaching the relevant turning, Edmund drove in.

'It may get a little uncomfortable, these vehicles are not renowned for their soft suspension,' said Edmund.

The track could only be negotiated slowly, the car turned into a rather uncomfortable fairground ride.

Gently, they proceeded down the track, which made a slight descent towards the river. A gentle wisp of smoke could be seen rising from the small coppice ahead.

As they entered the clearing, they saw that a brown and white horse with the most amazing mane, tail and hairy boots, was tethered. The tethering pole had allowed it to wander in a circle and the grass had been eaten to resemble a bowling green. To the right, nestled in the corner, was a brightly painted Gypsy caravan, where a small log fire was burning, with a pot hanging over it.

Henry and Edmund got out and walked over to the caravan. Henry could not help but say hello to the horse; he cupped his hand under its chin and pulled it to his chest.

'Just seems like yesterday, hard to believe it's been so long,' said Henry.

'You find it hard to believe?' returned Edmund's wry comment.

At that moment, a woman dressed in a brightly coloured long dress and shawl, came out from the caravan.

'Aah, Henry, I was wondering when you might call,' she said in a deep Irish accent and wandered over to him.

She stood a little shorter than Henry, an attractive elderly woman with bronzed skin from outdoor living, and a face full of character, weathered and smiling. She opened her arms to embrace him. He returned the gesture, then looked into her devilishly playful eyes, a vivid green. She had long red hair with a white streak. The memory of a small girl with red hair came back to him.

'Shelta, is that you?' Henry asked, taking her hands.

'I don't believe it, you look so, well... young!'

She had been a little whippet of a girl, no more than four or five, when last he saw her. Always the happy laughing child, running and playing through the woods barefoot.

'Nothing changes,' said Henry, looking down at her feet.

'Except this,' pointing to the bangle mark on her wrist.

She looked at Henry and gave him a wink.

‘Where has everyone gone, are they still around, do they want to come back?’

Henry became overwhelmed with their meeting, he had so many questions. His tongue had trouble keeping up with his brain.

Shelta asked Henry if he would like her to contact others and invite them. Overjoyed, Henry agreed, and enquired how, was it telepathy?

She pulled out a mobile phone from her pocket, and just waved it at Henry. He smiled and turned to Edmund, shaking his head.

‘Listen, we are off to Bristol, I would love to come later, if that’s ok?’

‘Do you like rabbit?’ she said.

‘Love it,’ said Henry.

‘Six o’clock then.’

Edmund and Henry returned to the Morgan. They both waved as they left the clearing and continued to Bristol.

Henry explained to Edmund that Gypsy folk had been a great asset to the farm in the past. He thought that with their knowledge of the land and their travels to obscure places, they might be able to make contact with others, who understood the word of the Gypsy.

It was not long before the outskirts of Bristol were reached. Henry was in awe – cars, bridges, cranes, huge windmills, people, houses, shops. He was amazed at how much had been achieved in a hundred years.

Edmund told Henry to prepare himself for the docks, as they drove over the river Avon, on the M5 motorway.

Parking in one of the large multi-storey car parks, Edmund thought a visit to a shopping mall might capture his attention. And so continued Henry’s education, with a crash course of shops, media and entertainment.

The docks were unrecognisable, the places he had visited some weeks ago had disappeared. Henry was finding it difficult to put into perspective the time lapse in his life. Edmund could see Henry was starting to struggle with the whole experience.

‘Shall we go and pick up your clothes from the tailors?’

Edmund suggested, expecting a change of venue would help.

Henry admitted that it was a bit overwhelming, he felt that he did not fit in anywhere. Even though he was impressed with the scale of things, he could not connect to them.

‘Could be I’m just a country boy at heart,’ joked Henry.

Edmund suggested that perhaps a history lesson at the College might be more suitable, fewer people and no concrete jungles. Henry would have no problems with its architecture, it was over three hundred years old.

Henry thanked Edmund for his perseverance.

'You're a good man, Edmund. Come, let's find your carriage and exit this busy place.'

They sauntered back through the hustle and bustle, to the carpark of many floors, where even Edmund had some difficulty finding his car.

Henry took rather a fancy to a big blue shiny vehicle parked next to Edmund's, which emitted a rather shrill sound as he ran his fingers along it.

Making a hasty exit from the carpark, they drove out of Bristol, across a bridge that Henry recognised, and on to Edmund's tailors.

When they arrived, Henry suggested they take a stroll in the park; curiosity getting the better of him, he was keen to see the plants. When they passed through the gates into the park, the sight that greeted them was not what they expected.

'Blimey,' said Edmund.

'Oops,' said Henry.

The spectacle that greeted them was a veritable jungle. The plants had grown and had gradually crept halfway across the park.

There was a TV van with satellite on its roof. The crew were interviewing a lady with what looked like huge daisies on wheels.

'Do you think that could be the lady we saw yesterday with the pretty pushchair?' joked Henry.

They both wandered over to hear what the reporter was saying. They could just hear his explanation for the unusual flora, blaming the extreme weather experienced lately. However, it was to be investigated by experts from the local horticultural college.

Henry and Edmund walked around the oasis of foliage.

'Very nice, good choice of plants,' said Edmund, inspecting the perimeter.

An elderly member of the public came over to them. He told them he had been gardening all his life and had never seen anything like it.

'Sunspots!' said Edmund, in a very matter of fact voice. He suggested to Henry that perhaps they should make a hasty retreat, and giving the TV van a wide berth, continued on to the tailors.

'You will probably see it on the news later,' said Edmund.

'See it?' quizzed Henry.

'On television.'

Edmund suddenly realized that Henry had little knowledge of everyday objects.

'I may have thrown you in at the deep end, perhaps we should start tomorrow with the electric kettle.'

'Mmmmm, I do know what an electric kettle is, never used one though,' muttered Henry.

They entered the tailor's shop to collect what was ready, just in time, as the closed sign was being turned round.

Having concluded their business, they left the shop. They noticed an increased activity across the road, in the park, and assumed that it was all the nosy people who had heard the news and were keen to see what was happening.

'They are all probably keen horticulturalists,' said Edmund.

His dry sense of humour made Henry laugh.

'And where would sir like to go now? Never mind, I think I can guess.'

Edmund headed back the way they had come.

'Just drop me at the end of the track, I'll be fine, I can walk back along the river.' Henry sat back in his seat, enjoying all the smells of the country, as the air passed over the open top of the Morgan.

It wasn't long before they reached the turning that would take Henry down to the clearing by the river.

They both had dinner dates with a special woman.

Bidding each other goodnight, Henry walked on down to the clearing. As he got closer, the smell of food cooking and the fragrance of a wood fire, filled the air. He had ridden this way many times, on horseback, the smell was the just the same.

As he rounded the corner of the clearing, the caravan became visible. In the afternoon sun it took on a whole new perspective.

There was now an added item of furniture, a small table with a large candle in its centre. No chairs, but cushions to soften the ground.

Shelta emerged from behind the caravan with two logs for the fire. The cooking pot suspended above was releasing its culinary bouquet, indicating it was ready for consumption. Henry positioned himself over the pot, scooping up and breathing in the aroma, with eyes closed.

'Good timing,' she said. 'Drink?' Shelta passed Henry a glass and opened an unlabelled bottle of clear liquor.

'Poitín,' she said, 'only the best for my guest, proper Irish potato whiskey.'

A large flatbread in the table's centre acted as knife and fork, while the rabbit was just served in bowls.

They sat chatting, and Henry was keen to know where everyone had gone. Shelta attempted to fill in the gaps. She told him of the sad times when the Manor closed, of fun times in Ireland, and the adventures they had when they travelled across Europe to Romania. She had learnt much from the peoples they met on their travels and had made many friends.

When food was finished, Shelta suggested they retire to the bank of the river. Taking the glasses and the bottle, they found a spot in the evening sun. This had been dug out by her kin many moons ago; two nice chairs had been sculpted into the riverbank. Over time, the grass had grown to serve as cushions. The smell of cut hay in the air and the gentle sound of running water from the river, created an atmosphere of tranquil perfection.

Henry asked her how she had come by the mark on her wrist. She told him her story of magical times when she had sneaked into the Manor grounds. She would play hide and seek with the *fir plandaí,* as she called them, and would take the flowers from their mother back to the camp.

After Henry left, the Manor was never the same; hide and seek and the laughter went away. The last she saw of her little magical friends was the day the gates were closed. They held her hand to bid her farewell and the mark was left. She had tried to wash it away, but it just got bigger over the years. It gave her comfort and had allowed her to keep in touch through her dreams.

Many years passed, with fleeting images of strange places. Not entirely understanding what they meant, one thing she did know, was that Henry was alive and confused. She felt a connection to an old order, which involved the beautiful flower. She had visions of dense forests with mountains covered in vegetation, smoking like volcanos. She explained that these were some of the things she had dreamt of over the years. Then recently, as she had returned for the solstice, she had been graced with the knowledge that Henry had returned.

The *fir plandaí* had visited her, they had brought the flowers from their mother, and they marked the return of good times.

'Tell me about you, what happened, where have you been?' Shelta poured another drink for them both. She pointed to a shooting star.

'Make a wish,' she said, closing her eyes and crossing her fingers.

Henry told her of the council, and the task with which they were now confronted. He told her how he had rescued his old friend Ade, and his own forced entrapment in the quandary. Their chat went on well into the night and so did the Poitín. The air was full of a fragrance they both knew well.

On the opposite side of the river, a family of badgers entertained them in the dim light. An air of calm followed, and together with the mellow feeling instilled by the liquor, they both drifted into a restless sleep. Their dreams seemed to be entwined, for each dreamt of one another and of times gone by.

Eventually, Henry was woken by a gentle tugging of his shirt sleeve. On inspection he found that the sprouts were there, beckoning him to go with them. Shelta had made coffee. She watched Henry rise to his feet, clasping his head in his hands.

'Ah, I had forgotten, one needs to acclimatize to Poitín,' Henry said, checking that his head was on the right way.

'Your little friends have come to take you home. Drink your coffee, I've added a little something to help the head,' she said.

Henry drank his coffee while the sprouts were making it very evident that he should make a move. Henry made apologies for their lack of etiquette.

He was now being coerced further along the riverbank in the direction of the Manor. Vowing to return as soon as he could, he succumbed to the well-meaning actions of the sprouts and gave in. Henry had no idea what time it was, but continued the trek along the river, to the boundary of the estate.

He could hear the sprouts gabbling and giggling; he was sure they were saying, 'can't be late, can't be late'. He repeated the banter, which provoked them into even more gabble, it was the first semi-coherent conversation he had ever had with them.

They arrived at the Manor boundary; Henry noticed that his head had cleared. He thought of the Queen of the Gypsies and her potion; he did have a notion of what it was she had added to his coffee. Making his way through the grounds, the playful sprouts disappeared.

On reaching the patio, the butler, who shall be called MacTavish, was waiting. Henry enquired of the time, to be told it was only six o'clock.

'Would sir like breakfast?' enquired MacTavish.

'Excellent idea, has Moss returned yet?' Henry asked.

He was informed that Moss had not been seen since he left with *Tabule*.

'I'm going to freshen up, shall be down shortly.'

Henry went to his room and inspected the clothes that had been collected the day before; they had been neatly laid out on the bed.

Freshened and changed ready for the day, Henry, on descending the stairs, saw the door to the cloakroom open. Moss, looking very dishevelled and covered in scorch marks and soot, entered the hallway.

'What happened to you?' Henry enquired.

Moss dusted himself down and attempted to put his hair straight.

'Nothing,' said Moss curtly, and proceeded past Henry and up the stairs.

Henry carried on to the dining room. It was laid out like a hotel, food in warming trays and drinks on the side.

Henry congratulated MacTavish on the display, knowing the lack of facilities, and promised to get round to the matter of running the house.

Henry decided that the outdoors was preferable and took his food out to the table on the patio. It wasn't long before Moss joined him, having cleaned up, he poured himself a drink and sat opposite.

Henry, continuing to eat breakfast, glanced at Moss, who was unusually quiet. Pouring a large mug of coffee from a jug, Henry glanced over again. Moss was staring at Henry awaiting a response.

Henry burst out laughing.

'Well, are you going to tell me?' Henry's laughter had broken the ice.

'Bloody *Tabule,'* muttered Moss.

Moss tried to explain that a particular pet project of his, was defying all efforts to save it. Moss had been roped in to help, only because everyone else had already been there and refused to do any more.

He described the project as a new moon, very hot, and with a personality disorder. No matter what efforts were made to help it become habitable, it would just spit it out. *Tabule* had been planting an area which seemed accepting of his efforts. Moss was seconded to add a gentle planting to extend the boundaries. All of a sudden, the ground erupted in a fountain of fire and brimstone, taking Moss up in the air with it. Each patch of new planting Moss had carried out was being systematically regurgitated.

Moss, having escaped the first fountain, was chased back to '*Tabule's* area, continually being launched on fire burps.

Not happy with destroying the gentle planting, the fire rash proceeded to destroy everything.

'I suffered severe singeing, and as for *Tabule*, he can whistle if he thinks I am going back there.'

Moss joined in Henry's laughter, as the vision of Moss running and trying to escape, filled their minds.

'The last I saw of *Tabule* he was frantically trying to hold down what he had planted. But every time he moved his foot, it was spat out in a ball of fire.' This vision tickled Henry and they both rolled around, crying with laughter.

At that moment Edmund appeared, enquiring what was so funny, and that only brought about another fit of laughter. Eventually composure set in and normality, if you can call it that, returned.

Henry promised to let Edmund in on the joke later. Pleased that Edmund was so early, Henry suggested they make a start as he had many questions which required answers.

So, bidding Moss a good day, they set off to fill Henry's head.

Chapter 12

Henry left with Edmund, keen to observe the world of today and full of curiosity.

Moss was busy directing tradesmen and builders to their required areas when Jake and Sandra arrived. Moss told Sandra that she was needed in the greenhouses. There was a bit of an emergency that required her personal touch.

'Nice to see you back Moss,' said Jake.

'Ah yes, Jake, the architect is waiting for you on the site behind the walled garden. There is a monstrous machine due any minute, and the electric company want to close the road for two days,' Moss was flicking through pages on a clip board.

'Oh, and there is a part of the house which is not on the plans,' Moss was starting to get a little flustered.

Jake reassured him that everything was under control.

First, he would go and see Chris the architect, then he would see why the road had to be closed, finally he would check the house.

Jake had been charged with organising the work at the Manor, while Henry was being brought up to speed with the planet.

Jake felt reasonably confident with the outside work, college had been a good source of learning, and with support from Chris, who was overseeing the building, Jake's knowledge was increasing by the day.

He wandered over to the proposed site, where Chris was surveying the area.

'Morning, Jake,' said Chris, who was looking through his level, on a tripod.

'Henry wants to make another access through the boundary wall, for the building works. It will be used as the facility's main entrance, leaving the Manor entrance unaffected.'

They both walked through the wooded area to the wall; it was an area less populated, with more bushes than trees. There were, however, a number of mature trees on the site that Henry had chosen for the new building.

Chris enquired if this was something Jake could undertake: to clear the path and make the access.

'I have spoken with the local planning office, and we can erect a building of a certain size without permission, if it is used for agricultural use, training and the like. It will just require building regulations.'

Chris said he had a friendly contractor who could start the project almost immediately. Jake was confident that the new entrance would be ready for traffic in three days.

'No problem, there is machinery on its way,' said Jake.

He also knew of a particular bricklayer who would help with the building of the entrance and do a good job of matching the existing one.

Jake enquired why the road had to be closed.

Chris explained that all the services for the new project would have to come from the main road, and along the lane. But they could come across the field instead, if Jake's father would agree to his field being dug up.

Jake agreed to ask his father that evening.

'Moss said something about part of the house as well?'

Chris explained that when he did his survey, he noticed the size of the house did not correspond with the space within. An easily overlooked discrepancy, it had three windows indicating three floors, but only two inside.

'I expect Henry would know the layout of the house; we should ask him later.'

Jake left Chris marking out for the new building. He wandered over to the greenhouses to see why Sandra was so urgently needed.

On reaching the door to the first greenhouse, it was evident that there was something amiss. Several of the women who had been working inside, were struggling with the door; it had closed, and they were unable to open it. The women told Jake that Sandra was inside.

Offshoots of the night flower had suddenly grown, occupying all available space. The flowers had matured, buds were forming, and it was about to produce seed. Sandra wanted to collect some of the seed as it was produced. She had told the women to make their escape before they too, were trapped.

Jake tried the door handle, it opened with no resistance.

The women looked at each other in amazement; they had been struggling to open the door to no avail. Jake told them to wait there, he would investigate. The sight that greeted him was a jungle; the plant had grown into every corner of the greenhouse. He called out to Sandra. The plant seemed to open a path as Jake moved forward, closing up behind him.

'I'm over here, she shouted.' Sandra was further down the greenhouse, and as Jake made his way towards her, she suddenly appeared.

The plants had produced buds, which strangely resembled the little ones. There was a strange mist pulsating in and out of quite a number of them.

'Wow,' said Jake. 'There's hundreds'

Sandra told Jake that the buds had appeared suddenly, she presumed that the mist was seed or spores, and continually changed colour. She had a sealed collection box with some of the mist inside, floating and changing shape.

'It's fascinating,' she said. She wanted to investigate it under a microscope, and she thought that the facilities at college would be a good place. They made their way to the door and the concerned ladies outside.

Sandra reassured them that they were in no danger, and that what was growing in the greenhouse, was a success.

It was the culmination of the work they were undertaking, which desperately needed more space.

Leaving Sandra and the women to continue their work, Jake made his way to the house.

Moss was in the driveway talking to two men. On joining them, Jake discovered they were delivering the tree relocation machine. Their insurance would not cover them to bring it on site, but they needed to instruct whoever was going to use it, on how it worked.

Jake wandered off with the men, to be instructed.

Moss meanwhile returned to the house, where he found *Tabule*. He looked a little dejected having returned from his unsuccessful campaign. They walked through to the gardens, and it was obvious that *Tabule* was frustrated.

‘Never known anything like it,’ he said. ‘It has defied every attempt to create life, I do believe that it is itself alive, and has a death wish.’ *Tabule* continued to voice his dismay, trying to recount how many planets and moons he had successfully planted. He believed this moon was a new species, and wondered how it would fit into the whole scheme of things.

As they turned a corner in the path, *Leber* approached.

‘Good day to you both. We have germination.’ *Leber* had been to visit the greenhouse and the new plants within. He, more than most, was closely linked to the night flower; its successful return was something he was closely monitoring.

‘You look as if you could do with cheering up,’ remarked *Leber*, unable to miss the sorry face of *Tabule*.

‘I think we should indulge in some radical land change, see how well this new seed behaves.’

Leber had the look of devilment in his eyes, his radical was normally off the scale.

‘I believe I know just the place,’ he said.

He went on to describe an area not too far away, where man went to practise killing. It lay on the line to the Henge and was easily accessible. It had been uncultivated for many generations, which made it perfect.

Tabule admitted that his confidence could certainly do with a boost.

‘*Leber*, this could be one of your better ideas,’ said *Tabule* with a smile.

Moss confirmed that he too would benefit from a change.

Leber said that they could harvest some seed from the new plants in the greenhouse. It might slow their growth down a bit and give them a chance to build a bigger greenhouse.

‘If the seed is left unharvested, the buds will only mature; we shall have an epidemic of young *Burrbesh.*’

The three agreed that they would descend on this place as soon as possible. *Tabule* suggested that they should keep this little soirèe to themselves for now, everyone would be able to assess the outcome after the fact.

Leber wandered off to the greenhouses. He was impressed with Sandra’s knowledge of plants, and he was curious to know how strong the seed would be. Previous radical plantings had resulted in anything up to twenty-five years growth overnight; there would be an initial burst of energy, after which, the normal growing speed would be resumed.

Moss and *Tabule* wandered back to the house via the stables. On turning the corner, they were greeted by a monster machine, with Jake at the helm. Jake waved to them both, then continued on to the site to play.

Just as they reached the steps to the front door, a battered old pick-up pulled up. A rather unkempt character got out and came over to them. He had shoulder length hair in a Rastafarian style, his steel toecaps shone through the badly worn leather of his boots. He enquired of *Tabule* the whereabouts of Jake, as he had come to do some work on a wall.

Without a sound, *Tabule* pointed a very bony finger in the direction in which Jake had gone. This very obvious workman gestured as though tipping an invisible hat and marched off in that direction.

'It's getting very busy here,' remarked *Tabule*.

'It is only going to get worse,' said Moss.

They both retired to the conservatory, where the night flower was creating her offspring.

A line of ceremonial planting bowls were laid out in front of it. Overnight tendrils from the plant would rest on the special soil within each bowl. Roots would then appear and by morning a new plant, a perfect copy of its parent, was born.

These would then be taken off to the greenhouses where they would grow into mature plants. The plan was then to redistribute these plants to the tribes and cultures around the world. They would nurse and keep safe the night flower, which would be used to help restore the balance of the planet.

Tabule stretched out his arm to the flower, it gently wrapped a tendril around his wrist.

'The seed is strong, it will cover well, said *Tabule*.

Turning to Moss he said,

'I do believe we are ready to go.'

Meanwhile Jake was showing Bob, his brickie, just where the entrance was to be, instructing him to use the old bricks and to make it look exactly like the other entrance.

The rest of his day was taken up with scooping up the mature trees from the site of the new build and planting them in a new home.

There was a distinct opening beginning to appear in the perimeter wall, as Bob removed, cleaned and stacked the old bricks.

Sandra had been learning from *Leber*, and in turn, he had learnt from her whilst working in the greenhouses.

He had discovered that the seed of the new plants was good, but not as strong as the mother; however, it would certainly make an impression.

Henry returned with Edmund. After a very informative day, his curiosity for everything had kept his teacher very busy.

Edmund bade Henry goodnight, as he had a dinner invitation from Ivy, some home-cooked food. He licked his lips at the thought. Everyone descended on the patio, which had now become the main meeting place.

MacTavish, with perfect timing, provided cold drinks.

He told everyone that as soon as electricity was installed permanently, he would be stocking many of the local brews.

Henry was busily trying to explain some of his new-found knowledge to *Leber*, whose lack of interest in modern man was evident.

He told MacTavish his meeting next day could be held in the summerhouse, and that he would be leaving early that evening because he was to be collected and taken for dinner with the Gypsies.

Jake added that he and Sandra were going out that evening as well, the military were putting on a big concert. All manoeuvres were cancelled, there would be no firing on the ranges that night. It was in honour of some retiring general who had commanded the Salisbury Plain military base for thirty years.

It was a free concert and not one to be missed – by all accounts, a very rare occasion.

Overhearing this statement, *Leber* looked at *Tabule*, who in turn looked at Moss and winked.

'Tonight, it is then,' said *Tabule*.

Moss said he would have to search out his planting hat.

Leber wondered where he might have left his dibbing staff and planting pod and went off to find them.

Tabule groaned, he knew exactly where his planting coat of many pockets was; he had abandoned it, due to the irrational behaviour of a temperamental moon.

'Damn,' said *Tabule*. 'I shall have to retrieve it. It's bad luck to go planting without one's favourite jacket.'

He stormed off with a determined stride, muttering obscenities.

MacTavish appeared and announced to Henry that his transport had arrived.

Jake and Sandra accompanied Henry out to the drive.

Turning to Henry, Jake said, 'The architect, Chris, mentioned something about the house. His survey had shown some discrepancy with the number of floors it had.'

Henry told Jake that the house did have a secret. He had put it to the back of his mind.

Of course, to Henry it was not so long ago, but it now seemed that this was the right time to put past history to bed.

'We shall look at it tomorrow,' said Henry.

Henry's transport was a fine horse ridden by a Gypsy with flowing red hair, bareback and barefoot.

'Jake, Sandra, I would like to introduce you to Shelta,' said Henry. He grabbed her outstretched arm and jumped up to sit behind her.

'Pleased to meet you both,' she said.

'You may be seeing a lot more of her,' said Henry, as his chauffeur gently kicked the horse forward.

'Enjoy your evening,' he shouted, and they disappeared past the stables and into the grounds, directly towards the Gypsy camp.

Jake and Sandra wandered over to the old Land Rover.

Jake looked around for Fidgit, then realised he was not with him.

'Shall have to bring him, it's like losing your right arm when he's not around.'

They left the Manor to prepare for the evening's festivities.

Henry meanwhile had arrived with Shelta at the clearing by the river. There were five other caravans, each one elegantly adorned with decorative paintwork.

There were other horses too, tethered around the clearing.

Shelta explained that some of the Grand Council of the Gypsy folk had arrived. They were ranked as highly important and had come especially at Henry's request.

They had all seen the damage and knew that changes were needed for Mother Earth, and they were keen to help. Henry was introduced to each of the men, two of whom had their wives with them. Two of the elders were women, who both had daughters with them; the last was an elderly chap, who it was difficult to put an age to. He was introduced as one of Shelta's many uncles. She said he had always been a secretive type, but as an oracle, he was priceless.

A large table and chairs had been placed in the clearing, adorned with a wonderful array of food.

Henry was invited to sit next to the head of the table. He could foresee that this evening was going to be a long one.

Back at the Manor, Moss had found his hat, *Leber* arrived shortly after, with his dibber and pod. All of a sudden, *Tabule* appeared from the fabric. He was smoking and patting himself to douse an occasional flame that appeared. In his arms was his smouldering coat of many pockets.

Moss grabbed the jug of lemonade and threw it at the smoulders, with not a very accurate result.

Tabule, who caught most of it in his mouth, spluttered; it had caught him a little by surprise. Spitting it out brought a fit of the giggles from *Leber*, who was not renowned for his humour, but on this occasion, he provoked a bout of laughter from all three. When the laughter had subsided, *Tabule* indicated that it might be a good time to load up.

Leber laughed at Moss.

'You look like a leprechaun in that hat,' he said.

Moss had on a rather large green hat, the texture was of course, moss. Top hat in style, but it looked as if someone had tried to inflate it and failed.

'Ok, so where's your pointy hat then Merlin?' retorted Moss.

'Now, now, we have work to do,' said *Tabule*.

The three musketeers each went to their desired night flower. *Tabule* in the conservatory, Moss and *Leber* to the greenhouses.

Standing in front of the night flower, *Tabule* opened his coat. The many pockets within, now beckoned for the seed to fill them. Streams of hazy cloud made their way from the night flower and entered each pocket in turn.

In the greenhouses, Moss, having removed his hat, allowed the same, and *Leber's* pod filled itself to the brim.

It took them longer to gather their seed, as these plants were young and inexperienced. This production line was new to them, but they would learn in time. There was little left to give from the young night flowers, it had exhausted their reserves.

The time was now nearly midnight, Moss and *Leber* returned to the conservatory, all set for the night's exercise.

'Shall we?' said *Tabule*. He beckoned in the direction of the intended foray.

They all agreed that they were as ready as they would ever be, and the three of them melted into the fabric.

Salisbury plain covers a large area of some three hundred square miles. It was used by man to practise his killing, a trait not supported by the *Burrbesh*.

It was just after midnight, and the three intrepid gardeners arrived at a large area of barren waste ground, central to the plains. There were many badly damaged vehicles all around the area, all of which were used as targets for the guns. *Tabule* started the proceedings, and opening his coat, the seed spewed out from the many pockets, in streams of luminous fog.

When Moss removed his hat and *Leber* held up his pod, the air thickened. The seed and spores spread across the whole area, like Northern Lights dancing across the ground. It covered a huge area, and where the mist landed, plants began to grow.

When eventually their cargo was exhausted, they stood quietly and watched, as the extensive selection of trees and bushes, plants and grasses, began to cover the land.

Both Jake and Henry felt something had happened.

There was a tell-tale tingle affecting their wrists, with a hazy vision of what had occurred.

Jake told Sandra that he believed something big had happened, and he did not think it was too far away.

Henry decided to keep this knowledge to himself, until his meeting with the Gypsy elders had finished.

The area affected by the trio of planters could possibly stretch to ten square miles. The effect of the boost to its growing capacity meant that trees reached heights of twenty feet or more and bushes became hedgerows overnight.

Where vehicles were parked, roots had gone through them to reach the ground. Some had totally disappeared under the growth of vines and climbers. Others had been squeezed beyond recognition, as branches had wound around and around. There would be much damage to operational vehicles. Tracks and roadways were slowly turning green, and by morning it would be unrecognisable.

As they looked on, the foliage was beginning to surround them, soon they would become part of the landscape. So, pleased with their results, they returned back the way they had come, leaving little or no evidence of themselves ever being there at all.

Henry's meeting with the Gypsies went on till the early hours. They talked of the old days when man had an affinity with his surroundings. They examined the state of the planet today, its failure to cope with man's excesses. They all agreed that something must be done, and their support would be available, as and when required. Henry felt that the meeting had gone very well. His reconnection with descendants of people he had known years ago, reassured him that their loyalties had not changed.

With their meeting over, Henry told them that something had happened that evening that would begin the fight. In his vision he had seen a vast barren landscape turn green, a result of a *Burrbesh* intervention.

The Gypsies had stories of the planting people, passed down through many generations. They were aware that forces greater than man have wandered the earth since the beginning of time.

A relaxed atmosphere descended on the clearing as the sun rose, casting its rays through the trees. It picked out the brightly coloured paintings of flowers on some of the caravans.

Henry thanked each of them for coming, finishing with the ceremonial shaking of hands. The Gypsies invited Henry and his friends to a feast, before they moved on to other places. Henry willingly accepted their invitation and promised to return. He would bring with him the night flower and seed that they could disperse where needed.

'Would you like a ride back to the Manor?' Shelta enquired.

Henry declined, explaining he would accompany the three little sprouts back. They had been too shy to approach the group and were nestling in the hedgerow along the river.

He bade good morning to his new friends and told them he looked forward to their next meeting. He thanked Shelta for her offer of a ride back, and for collecting him earlier. Giving her a friendly peck on the cheek, he whispered that she held a fond place in his heart.

Henry made his way back to the Manor, collecting a trio of excited sprouts on the way. There was confused gabbling from the little ones as they tried to tell him of the last night's events.

As Henry entered the grounds of the Manor, by the weir, he met *Tabule* and *Leber* sitting on the bench.

The little ones ran over to them, and, acting like excited grandchildren, they jumped onto their laps.

'I felt the actions of something dramatic earlier,' said Henry, probing them both.

'It felt very good,' said *Tabule*.

'It felt extremely good,' echoed *Leber*.

Tabule continued to explain what had taken place earlier. He told Henry that the opportunity had dictated the event, there was little time to plan or inform anyone.

'Would you have told anyone if there had been time?' Henry enquired.

'Probably not,' said *Leber* with a grin.

Henry said an element of secrecy was going to be essential. It would obviously attract a lot of attention; he wondered how the army would react. Luckily it was far enough away to avoid immediate scrutiny, but the army might have to find another use for the land.

'I hope they don't go in and cut it all down,' said Henry.

'Jungle warfare,' said *Leber*. 'They could use it to get lost in.' *Leber's* humour was very dry.

Henry left the two midnight planters and returned to the Manor house, sprouts in tow. On arrival, he found Moss positively buzzing around the night flower, in the conservatory. The little ones had already climbed into the comforting branches of mother.

'What are you up to?' Henry enquired.

'Nothing,' said Moss, hiding his hat behind his back.

He said to Henry that there might be another deserving area where it would be good to test the seed.

Henry explained that he had spoken to *Tabule* and *Leber* on his way back. He told Moss that future sorties would need to be planned and organised. He understood that everyone had enjoyed letting off steam that evening. They just had to be careful not to draw attention to themselves, at least until the night flower could be distributed.

'Just like the old days,' said Moss.

He recalled the time when Henry's father was suspected of sorcery. It was just after the building of the Manor when witch-hunting was rife. He had to be careful then of course; everything that happened at the Manor was secret.

'That reminds me, Moss. Do you remember the upper floor?' said Henry.

'It is probably time it was re-opened. Chris the architect has commented on its existence. Jake has also asked, and we may need the space.'

Henry held a special affection for this area.

'Do you still remember how to access the stairway?' enquired Henry.

Moss, scratching his chin, thought hard. He said he was not there when the top floor was sealed, but he had been told of its secret.

Henry recalled that one of the rooms had been extended onto the landing. Great wardrobes were placed in front of a false wall; they rolled open when a lever was pulled. The stairway had not been accessed for nearly four hundred years. Henry and Moss stood at the bottom of the main staircase. They surveyed the landing and ceiling of the first floor. Unable to see where the concealed stairs went, they decided to investigate. They were only halfway up the staircase when an excited Jake and Sandra arrived.

'Have you seen the morning news, massive disruption on the Salisbury Plains?'

Sandra had the news report on her tablet.

'Come on down and we'll show you.'

'The stairs will have to wait, you three have certainly started something,' Henry whispered to Moss as they came back down.

Sandra passed the device to Henry, where he watched a video from a drone-cam flying above the whole of the military area. It showed previous footage of the firing ranges and tracks through large open areas. It now revealed lush vegetation, trees and bushes covering a vast area.

… and covering an area of some fifteen square miles came the report from the newscaster.

'Hmmmm, that's better than we first thought,' said Moss.

Henry had to admit that the greenery was a huge improvement and was impressed at the scale of it.

Today was going to be another busy one. *Tabule* and *Leber* wandered unnoticed into the dining room, as they avoided the workmen taking over the grounds.

Edmund and Ivy arrived, also curious to learn of the night's activities.

MacTavish announced the arrival of Ronald and Donald MacDonald, solicitors from Betula & Betula. He had shown them to the summerhouse as Henry had requested.

Henry made his apologies and went off to his meeting. Moss ushered everyone into the dining room, where the night's activities were explained in great detail by *Leber*, with the occasional correction by *Tabule*.

Having heard the details of the night's escapade, Jake and Sandra left to continue with their own individual tasks.

They left the three musketeers, and Edmund and Ivy, chatting, vowing to catch up with them later.

Chapter 13

Work was beginning to progress at an alarming rate. Jake met up with Chris on the site of the new building.

'I spoke with my dad; he says it's fine to take all the services across his field. In fact, we can use the lower part to store equipment and materials if we need to.'

Jake and Chris worked out the schedule of what Jake would be responsible for. The Manor house was to have new electrics, plumbing, heating, and cable. Trenches were being dug to take the new services to the house. There were workmen everywhere; Jake was tasked with organising the supply of labour and materials. The first order was to get some sort of site office to work from: somewhere to scribble notes and centralise work details.

MacTavish arrived and requested the presence of Chris in the summerhouse, there were things to be sorted.

Jake went on to the hole in the wall to see how it was progressing. Bob the brickie had been there since first light, the opening would be big enough to drive through by the end of the day.

Everyone had their part to play.

Sandra seemed to have been left in charge of the greenhouses. Ivy came to help her and had slotted into a job of her own making.

There were bases being prepared for new greenhouses, with trenches, holes in the ground and red and white tape everywhere.

The house was having proper electrics; Edmund had taken on the task of organising the installation of the more sensitive equipment.

Moss was trying to organise the refurbishment of the rooms, while MacTavish was overseeing the kitchen installation.

Jake meanwhile had scooped up and replanted some twenty large trees, using his machine. Finishing the task, he drove it down to the end of the lane ready for pick up.

He wandered over to the greenhouses to see how things were going, then realised his shadow was missing.

'I'm going to fetch Fidgit,' he shouted to Sandra who was halfway down the green house.

'Fancy some lunch down the pub?' Sandra willingly agreed, she said she was cooking, it was baking hot in the green house.

'Some of the opening roof lights need repairing, you can hardly breathe in there,' she said.

Jake reached into his back pocket, pulled out a notebook, and wrote...greenhouse windows.

Sandra, impressed with his efficiency, grabbed his arm and marched him to the Land Rover.

When they reached the vehicle, they found the little ones had rather taken to it. There was one tugging at the wheel, jumping up and down on the driving seat, one quite placid in the passenger seat and the other was dozing on Fidgit's favourite blanket, in the back.

'Out, all of you,' said Jake, sternly.

Sandra was more sympathetic, she reflected on the fact that they had not really been out much and did so love Jake's Land Rover.

'We could take them for a ride, what harm could they do?'

She gave Jake that look, which meant he could not say no. He reminded her of the last time they went out when they planted everything, even things that moved. With a sigh, Jake reluctantly gave in.

'Ok, we take them for a ride, collect Fidgit, bring them straight back to the Manor, then go and get lunch.'

Jake was going to play it safe. He had no intention of allowing the three little ones out of his sight.

Sandra gave them all a good talking to; she explained that if they were good, Master Jake would take them for a ride. There was an evident response of excitement as they took up position in the back and readied themselves for the event.

Turning left out of the drive, Jake continued on to the end of the road, waving at Bob who had created a rather large hole in the old wall.

On to the village they went, over the river, and past the pub. It did not take long to get to the farm; Jake ran over to the kitchen. His mother was just off to the cider house to do some work. He told her that Fidgit was missed, and he had popped back to get him.

'He's just had his dinner, I expect he's gone for a nap down at yours,' she said. 'He mopes about when he's on his own.'

'Thanks,' said Jake, 'I've got kind of used to having him about.'

Jake was halfway through the orchard when he whistled for Fidgit. He had scarcely finished whistling, when his intrepid shadow appeared, obviously very glad to see him and be part of the team once more. On his return to the Land Rover, Jake enquired if everything was ok.

Sandra assured Jake that he was worrying unnecessarily, the three passengers had been as good as gold.

Fidgit's appearance however had brought about an excitement.

'Ok, calm down,' said Jake.

Reversing out of the drive, Jake continued the return to the Manor.

As they passed the pub, Sandra could see a large shiny vehicle, like a coach, parked in the car park. It had a large satellite dish and an array of aerials sticking up from the roof. It was just before the bridge, Sandra shouted.

'Look, I think there's a television crew parked at the Tavern.'

She pointed through the bushes at what she had seen.

Trying to see what Sandra was pointing at, his concentration was redirected.

Suddenly he had to swerve, narrowly missing a hedgehog and the bridge. Regaining control, Jake continued on to the Manor, where lunchtime had arrived. Nearly everyone had stopped work, and were in the shade, with lunchboxes and drinks.

Parking up by the stables, Sandra commented:

'That wasn't so bad, was it?'

Turning to check the passengers, Fidgit and two of his friends were looking at her. Fidgit gave a bark and stared at them both.

'Where's the other one?' she said.

Jake jumped out and went to the rear of the motor. He checked under the blankets – not there. There was little place to hide in the open-backed pick-up.

'Where's he gone Fidgit?' said Jake.

There was a babbling from the little ones which Jake found difficult to understand.

Fidgit jumped out of the Landy and barked at the direction from which they had come.

Sandra escorted the two remainers back to the conservatory, while Jake turned the vehicle around and waited for her by the front door. When Sandra returned, they set off to back track their journey, with Fidgit firmly to attention, pointing the way.

What they didn't know, was that the hedgehog, avoiding manoeuvre, had catapulted the one sprout clean off the back of the Landy.

It had been sitting right on the corner, which was very precarious to start with. It had been launched and then sailed clean over the bridge wall, somersaulting into the river, giving an excited squeak on its way down.

A bemused heron watched as the tumbling sprout splashed into the water.

After floating down the river some distance it came ashore; it was now in a state of extreme excitement. And of course, when the sprouts get excited, they create.

Realising where it was, the sprout set off along the riverbank in the direction of the bridge, and the pub.

A trail of exotic plants, including bananas, figs and mangoes, appeared to be following the now misshapen sprout, growing to a height almost immediately.

It was approaching the bridge, on the opposite bank from the pub, when Jake's rescue party arrived at the car park.

Fidgit immediately jumped out and ran across the bridge. Jake and Sandra followed, and on looking down the river, saw the emerging foliage, with sprout at the helm.

It was treating it like a procession, almost marching, waving its arms and possibly singing.

Unfortunately, there was an audience in the garden of the pub, also watching the spectacle unfold. Luckily, there was a hedge line obscuring the path and the sprout and its procession disappeared from view.

Fidgit was the first to reach the adventurer, with Jake and Sandra close behind. Jake scooped up the little pest and parked him on his shoulders.

As they made their way back to the pub, they had to stand aside to let four excited people run past, as they made their way to the river.

'I think we should make a sharp exit,' said Jake.

Sandra, however, had other ideas; curious to learn why the TV van was there, she had a plan.

Jake was more than a little reluctant to go with another of her great ideas.

'If we park the Land Rover under the willow at the end of the carpark, it's right by the end of the garden. You can sit with these two while I go and get food and drinks.' She could then find out what was going on.

'Okay, okay, I'll babysit,' said Jake reluctantly.

He drove down to the end of the car park, which was screened a little by a large willow. He could see the opposite bank of the river from where he was and noticed the four men returning. Intent on watching what they were doing, he never noticed Barney, who had come over to say hello.

'Hello young Jake!' he bellowed.

Jake nearly had an accident.

'Flippin' eck Barney, you frightened the life out of me,' he said, composing himself.

Barney commented on how jumpy and shifty Jake appeared, unable to see his cargo in the back.

'What's with the TV people?' asked Jake.

Barney began to tell Jake that the TV crew had been up to the park where all the plants had suddenly appeared. They were on their way to Salisbury to report on the latest occurrence and had just stopped for lunch.

'They thought it was a real quaint little pub,' said Barney, speaking from experience.

Jake told Barney briefly what had just happened, and where Sandra had gone.

Barney acknowledged that these strange happenings bore all the hallmarks of the Manor. He said he had been chatting to the TV guys, until they ran off to investigate the sudden appearance of plants on the opposite bank.

Barney chuckled to himself, they were certainly scratching their heads, it would no doubt keep them thinking for a while.

Keen to re-join the group as they returned, Barney promised to keep Jake informed on his findings. Barney scurried back to the bar, tipping his brow to Sandra as she returned with refreshments.

'I think we have a spy in their camp,' said Jake, and eagerly took the drinks. She told him that burgers would be on their way.

Sandra told him the same story as Barney's, that they were just passing and decided to eat. Their food was brought out by a youngster on school holiday, earning a bit of extra cash.

They sat watching the comings and goings of customers and TV men.

Jake and Sandra's presence on the bridge had obviously not raised any suspicions, their presence passed without interruption. Eventually the four men returned to their vehicle and left. They stopped on the bridge to look down the river for a moment, then continued on their way.

'Well, I suppose we had better get this little one back home,' said Jake.

Just as they were about to drive off, Barney came over to them, red faced and in a state of excitement. He said that the TV chaps had to rush off as they had a deadline, but they would be back. They couldn't understand what they had witnessed, and it certainly needed more investigations.

'I told them it happens a lot, something to do with the peat,' Barney continued with his story.

He had told these TV people that the heat of the sun had warmed up prehistoric seeds bedded deep in the peat. Every now and then strange plants grew from deep in the ground; they popped up here there and everywhere.

Barney seemed convinced that they believed his explanation; even Sandra said it sounded plausible.

Bidding them both a good day, Barney returned to finish his liquid lunch, in the shade, by the river. Jake drove very carefully back to the Manor, while Sandra kept an eye on their ejectable passenger. No sooner had they parked the Land Rover, than both Fidgit and the sprout disappeared into the bushes.

'I don't think we'll be doing that again in a hurry,' said Jake.

Sandra sheepishly agreed and accepted that her suggestion of taking them for a ride wouldn't happen again either.

MacTavish called to Jake from the front of the house.

‘Master Jake, can you go down to the summerhouse? Your presence is required.’ He gave Sandra a blank look and told her he would see her later, then wandered on down to the summerhouse.

He could hear Fidgit, a bark he does when he’s playing, at least he knew where he was.

On reaching the summerhouse, Jake found Henry with the two solicitors. They were sitting behind a long table, desk-like in appearance, with an abundance of papers, in piles, from one end to the other. Henry beckoned to him to sit down and told him there was something interesting to discuss.

‘Did you enjoy lunch?’ said Henry knowingly.

There was always going to be that tell-tale tingle when an event took place.

Jake apologized for taking the little ones out and told Henry of the TV crew at the pub. Henry said that it was time to start educating the little ones into focusing their talents, and to create specific planting.

‘They get far too excited to be able to control anything.’

We shall have to take them out more, away from the Manor, keep things low key. We don’t want to draw attention to ourselves, do we?’ said Henry

‘Draw attention to who?’ said Ivy, entering the summerhouse.

Ronald and Donald went to rise at her entry, caught unawares, as they listened to Jake’s account of events.

Ivy was briefly brought up to speed with the events of Jake’s lunchtime romp, and then sat down, having also been summoned by Henry.

Henry began to explain that his father had been granted the title of Lord. This, even after such a long passage of time, would pass to Henry, and his immediate family. The pension from the State had been put into trust since his mother’s death and had been administered by the solicitors.

Henry sat down and left the rest of the details to Ronald and Donald. They took it in turn to explain, in detail, the ramifications of their investigations.

Henry could, if he so desired, take up his seat in the House of Lords.

The pension pot had been invested and was now a considerable amount, enough to buy back the lands to restore the Manor.

The business side had undergone substantial expansion at the hands of their colleague; it was now a global player in the pharmaceutical market, with many businesses attached.

They were still investigating the quantity and operation of these satellite companies, some of which were on the dubious side.

However, they had been instructed by the company's board of directors that Henry's claim of ownership had been accepted. This came with a rather large salary, which had been backdated to his twenty-first birthday. His current age had been declared as forty, old enough for a seat on the board with access to all business locations.

Funds had been set up for Ivy, Bill and Jake, as heirs and immediate family. Payments to these accounts would begin immediately.

Handing out various forms to Jake and Ivy, the two solicitors congratulated everyone on a positive outcome.

'I would like to offer Sandra a position within the business,' said Henry. 'She certainly has a passion for the subject.' Jake agreed and said he would tell her.

Donald handed Henry a letter with a plastic card attached. Henry took it with a knowing look.

'This is one of those payment card thingies, I know, Edmund has told me all about them.' Henry was quite proud of his new-found knowledge.

In true butler tradition MacTavish appeared with another member of the kitchen staff, carrying champagne and some very posh-looking nibbles.

He turned to Jake.

'Shall I send Miss Sandra down, sir?'

'I'll come with you,' said Jake, and walked back with him to the house.

He escorted Sandra back down to the summerhouse.

On the way, he told her of Henry's offer of employ and the basic details of the meeting. When they reached the summerhouse, they joined in the celebrations. They all toasted the solicitors, the outcome of events, the building work, each other and the weather.

It was now late afternoon when they returned to the house, a little merry, and found Edmund poring over the wiring diagrams of various bits of tech.

‘Ah, Henry,’ said Edmund. ‘The electricians and plumbers are baffled as to where the wiring should go. They can’t seem to access the loft or take their wiring through the ceiling.’

Henry now accepted that it was time to examine the top floor and open it up, something he had put off for a long time.

He went off in search of Moss, who he hoped could remember the location of the secret lever. He found him chatting with *Tabule* and *Leber* by the pond.

Henry called to Moss to join him. He explained that they needed to deal with the top floor. They returned to the hallway where everybody was chatting about the day’s events.

Henry confessed that the Manor did have a secret.

After his return many years ago, his mother’s apartment was boarded up. He had been devastated that he had missed her final years, and contrite that he been absent for so long. Not being able to bring himself to even visit her grave, he realised that now was the time to accept the facts and face them.

Henry began the ascent of the stairs, the small group followed in single file, tentatively, as if waiting for some demonic happening.

On reaching the landing, Henry opened the door facing the stairs. It led into a bedroom, perhaps a little smaller than the others, with floor-to-ceiling wardrobes all down the right-hand wall.

‘There is a lever somewhere, hidden inside a wardrobe, that when pulled, opened the entrance to the stairs,’ said Henry, admitting that he had no idea where it was.

Moss examined each wardrobe, poking and pushing, and finally admitting defeat, he stood back, scratching his head.

‘Sorry,’ said Moss.

‘Perhaps I may be of assistance sir?’ said MacTavish, making his way to the front of the queue.

He explained that his predecessors had written instructions for all the operations of the Manor. These had been passed down through generations of loyal servants who had served the family. He did know of a concealed entrance to the upper floor; it was his duty to know such things, and he was sure he could locate the lever.

Having opened all the wardrobe doors, he inspected the interior of each in turn. Then, leaning into the middle wardrobe, he reached in and pushed a square of panelling. A section of two wardrobes with four doors sprang open.

MacTavish looked at Henry for approval, Henry nodded and came to help. Together they pulled the two large wardrobes, which opened with surprising ease.

There behind, was revealed another staircase, slightly smaller but in the same style as the main stairs. The dim light exposed a bare wooden staircase with ornately carved banister and spindles. It led to another landing, heavily encrusted in cobwebs and dust.

MacTavish explained that the story of a lever was a ruse; it had been devised by those who constructed it, to maintain its secrecy.

The sight of what lay before him took Henry a little by surprise. He stepped back, tears welling up in his eyes.

Ivy grabbed his arm, and giving him a reassuring squeeze, she gestured to the stairs, and together they made the slow ascent.

On reaching the landing, Henry recognized the smell, even through the years of mustiness. He closed his eyes as memories flooded back, childhood memories, then visions of his mother and father going about their daily business. They all faded as Ivy tugged on his arm to shake him back to reality.

'You're right Ivy, no time to dwell, let's open the shutters and let the light back in,' said Henry, scraping umpteen years of cobwebs from the nearest window.

He said it only felt like yesterday to him, his memories were relatively fresh in his mind.

He asked her to give him a moment. He then made his way along the corridor, to the furthest door. This had been the main living room of his parents. Turning the large dust-encrusted doorknob, the door creaked open. As Henry entered the room bright sunlight dazzled him for a moment. The room was clean and bright, just as he remembered; his mother was sitting with a book by the fireplace.

'Ah James how are your studies coming along?' she said.

His father, who had been observing something of interest through the window, turned and said, 'Thought I might go into Bristol tomorrow, fancy coming along?'

Henry walked over to his mother, she looked up at him and smiled, he then turned to his father who was awaiting a reply.

'I would love to go with you, father,' said Henry.

Hearing voices, Ivy had wandered down to the room where Henry was. She stood in the doorway watching him.

The room had been left as it was the day Lady Mercedes died. The furniture, paintings, bookshelves and the desk at which his father worked, were all there, covered in sheets. Everywhere was covered in cobwebs and fine dust. Sunlight shone through small chinks in the shutters, which were all closed, except for the one by Henry, which had dropped a little on one side. It allowed a little more light to filter through, casting a sunbeam, which caught the dust particles. Henry had moved forward, his father was starting to fade, Henry reached out to stop him leaving.

'No!,' he shouted. As the vision of his mother and father faded, the stark realisation of reality took over.

He looked around at his surroundings, closing his eyes in one last bid to bring them back.

In his despair he felt his mother hold his hands. He opened his eyes to find Ivy with him, she was holding his hands in an effort to comfort him.

He thanked Ivy for being there and said that his vision had been so very real.

'Strange how grief affects you,' he said.

His cry had prompted the others to come hurrying, and they were all at the entrance to the room, enquiring if all was well.

Putting his arm around Ivy, he proclaimed that this was his family now. He was going to do his utmost to be the best father, grandfather and great grandfather.

'Let's open all the windows and let the world in, it has been shut out long enough,' said Henry.

He told MacTavish that a good clean was in order. He himself would assist the staff with this task; it might help him to fill in the final years of his mother.

‘Oh, and there is to be a party at the Gypsy camp tomorrow night, and everybody is invited, including you MacTavish.’

Henry proceeded to open the shutters around the room, instructing everyone to do the same in all the rooms and landing.

Henry told Edmund that his electricians and plumbers now had a route to take their services, but they should just be careful.

The whole of the top floor was now bright and showing its years of neglect. It did however have a very homely feel to it, in spite of the eerie tapestry of cobweb and draping sheets.

‘Jake, you must tell your father to visit me as soon as he has a moment.’

Henry confessed that he had only briefly chatted with him, and there was a lot more he should know.

As the group made their way back down the stairs, Henry said he was going to spend a little time on his own, collecting his thoughts and indulging in the atmosphere. He felt that the moment needed time for reflection and urged everyone to continue with their evening.

Collecting his belongings, Edmund switched on his tablet to catch the local news, as it was approaching six thirty.

Ivy and Sandra gathered around to watch, while Jake wandered outside with Moss.

The news article covering Salisbury Plains had made the headlines, a team of scientists were being despatched to investigate the phenomenon. One possibility came from reporters who had interviewed a local historian; he claimed that prehistoric seed deep in the earth had been affected by the unusual weather.

‘That was Barney,’ exclaimed Sandra.

She found this extremely amusing and went off to tell Jake that Barney was now a local historian.

Finding him with Moss, *Leber* and *Tabule* by the pond, she repeated what the news item had said.

This brought a bout of laughter from them all, and they chatted about the night the trees returned to the Salisbury plains.

Chapter 14

Henry wandered around the room where his mother had spent her final years, removing the dust sheets from various pieces of furniture. One piece in particular, was the desk, which both his mother and father had used. He removed the covers from the desk and an old wooden office chair.

He remembered, as a child, he would spin round and round on it until he was dizzy. He checked its stability, then sat at the desk and began to investigate the contents of the drawers.

In the first drawer were writing implements – pens, pencil, rulers – all of which had some sort of woodworm. They crumbled to dust as Henry examined them.

Working his way down the three-tiered drawer system and having discarded the powdered remains of the first two, he reached the bottom drawer, which contained what appeared to be a leather-bound folder.

It felt quite greasy, the cover seemed to have been preserved with something. It was embossed with the words 'Our Life.' Henry placed it on the desk in front of him.

He continued with his investigation and went through the drawers on the other side. The majority of contents turned to dust as he picked them up, a few objects survived, like the magnifying glass. Having exhausted the desk's offerings, Henry picked up the journal and wandered over to a sunny spot by a window.

He removed the sheet covering a large three-seater sofa, opened the sash window, and then sat to examine his find. It was tied with a very ornate piece of plaited leather, a substantial volume and reasonably intact.

As Henry got himself comfy, MacTavish arrived with food, a cheese board and a nice bottle of Beaujolais.

'I knew sir would not think of sustenance, so I have taken it upon myself to bring him a supper.' MacTavish placed the tray beside Henry and turned to exit.

'Most thoughtful, MacTavish,' Henry said, and thanked him for the offering.

Opening the journal to the first page, he recognised his father's handwriting. He remembered his father, with pen and ink pot, scribbling away at his desk. As a boy he would enquire what his father was writing in his journal; his father would joke that maybe one day he would find out.

The journal chronicled the life of his mother and father, of their first meeting and the adventures which ensued.

There were graphic details of many medicines which his father had discovered, with formulas on how they were made.

His mother's handwriting appeared in places, giving her account of life without Henry, whilst he was away on his expeditions.

A reference was made to a particular birth, namely one Henry James. A birth which had its difficulties, the result being that he would remain an only child.

His father's African expeditions were numerous. There were references to characters whom he had met, and who had become good friends.

As a boy, Henry recalled being introduced to many strange visitors who called at the Manor.

There were entries about his trip to India, and his introduction to the night flower, which Henry remembered as though it was yesterday.

Many references were made of this plant and the research carried out on it; it became a dominant feature in his father's life.

During his African expeditions, his father wrote of a very special character he had been introduced to at a ceremony, a ceremony which had lasted nearly a week.

Villagers came from far and wide to pay homage, they brought gifts and offerings to the gods. A large outcrop of rock towered above the trees; it was here where worship took place. They were giving thanks to the god of all plants, Chonganda, who appeared in grand robes of red and gold, wearing a garland of the most fragrant flowers.

It transpired that Henry's father, and this deity became good friends. There were many entries in the journal of the strange flower which had become an obsession; taking him to all corners of the globe in search of its secrets, he was convinced that this was the plant to cure all.

The next entry was of the expedition to India, and of a young boy who stowed away and worked his passage.

Henry smiled as he read; he believed there was almost an element of admiration from his father for those escapades.

Flicking through the pages of formulas and remedies, Henry reached an entry referring to the caverns below the house; his father had always offered refuge to the persecuted priests of the parish. They had been allowed shelter from their pursuers; they were given food and drink and told to remain below until the coast was clear.

Some were never seen again.

There were notes on this incident. Rations of food and drink were found untouched, and after extensive searching, nothing was found. The caves stretched for miles. They would branch off in directions left and right, some up and down, impossible to search.

Shortly after the disappearance of the priests, his father set off on another expedition, alone.

He wrote of his son being in his final year at university and who could not accompany him. On his way to the port the wind increased, and a storm built in strength, the severity of which brought down trees and damaged property.

His ship had not arrived, so he ventured into a local inn for shelter. There he met a small man, a dwarf, well dressed, who spoke very well. They chatted about the storm, which was getting worse, and of general things.

Then, out of the blue, he made reference to the priests that Henry had given shelter to. He assured him that they were safe and well and he was to be commended for his act of compassion.

Henry paid for the drinks from the bar, but when he turned round the man had gone. He wrote that he had turned for only a moment, it was impossible for this person to have exited the inn; it was as if the very fabric of space had swallowed him.

The storm raged for three days, Henry's ship never made it to port, his expedition was abandoned, and so he took refuge at the inn until the storm abated.

Returning to the Manor, his father continued with his research; he re-scheduled the expedition for when his son graduated from university.

Henry continued to browse through the journal as the light faded. There were many more entries, of experiments, thoughts on the state of the country, concerns for everyone's wellbeing and his life with Mercedes.

His attachment to the monarchy took up a lot of his time, while the political wranglings' of the House of Lords befuddled his head. He was no politician, he wrote.

The last of his father's entries was to document the India expedition with his son, who had received a doctorate with honours. He was very proud that his son would join him in his work and continue with the search for medicinal cures.

The next and remaining entries were made by his mother, who poured out her grief at having lost her family at sea. There was an unwillingness to accept the situation; she believed deeply that they were both alive, stranded on some remote island.

Henry could read no more, a great sadness came over him; putting the journal down, he leant back and closed his eyes. Henry drifted off into a restless sleep. His dreams were full of tantalizing situations: reaching out to people he could not touch on board a ship entering the harbour, where an evasive quay is never reached.

His dreams continued, and he found himself walking in the country, along a leafy lane with green fields and hedgerows. A greyness appears under his feet, he turns to look behind, there is a barren landscape, and everything is grey and withered. Turning back, the greyness is now travelling in front of him, the green turns to grey. There is a distinct line in front of him, and no matter how he tries he cannot overtake it.

He is forced to watch as the line of greyness marches forward, it travels across the fields, and consumes everything in its path. The dream keeps recurring; in parts there is a line of connected creatures resembling origami soldiers on parade; they are in formation all along the line, pushing the greyness in perfect unison.

Henry's dreams continue through the night; he is murmuring, tossing and turning, until he is awoken by the singing of a blackbird sitting on the windowsill.

It was four a.m. and Henry, a little unused to red wine, took himself off to freshen up. He followed the smell of cooking, down to the kitchen where he found MacTavish and Shelta making preparations for the evening.

‘Good morning,’ said Henry, pouring himself a black coffee.

‘You look a bit rough this morning,’ observed Shelta, joining him. She told Henry that the word had got out, and more important guests were arriving, the gathering was going to be quite an event.

Henry recounted his evening of memories, and of his dream, as they wandered through to the dining room.

There they met Moss who was reading a newspaper; he was keen to follow up on comments relating to his adventures.

‘And how is the world?’ enquired Henry.

Moss was positively buzzing; he admitted that there was an element of juvenile exhilaration connected to their activities.

Reading from the news report, Moss summarised the article; he told everyone that the scientific community was totally at a loss. Moss found the comments extremely amusing and would provide inspiration for future sorties.

He continued reading; a leading botanist had been to examine the park and had commented that there were shrubs from all over the world.

The news crew witnessed strange plants appearing by the river. These would require further investigations by the science team.

He concluded with the news media’s description of the phenomenon: ‘a veritable world of shrubs: a Shrubbers’ World.’

‘I think that is a perfect description, they are unaware of how accurate that description could be,’ laughed Moss, throwing the paper on the table.

‘As long as they don’t come to the Manor,’ said Henry.

‘By the way Moss, did you ever meet my father?’

Henry recounted the entry in his father’s journal and the storm.

Moss admitted that there had been brief encounters with Henry’s father. On that occasion, Moss had been tasked with ensuring Henry never sailed, it was fortuitous that the storm raged heavily. They had spoken of many things, of saving those in need of help, and his work at the Manor.

Moss put Henry’s mind at rest and told him of the fate of the priests. They had been relocated on an island in the Mediterranean, where they lived out their lives happily, and not persecuted. They were respected by the community that they served.

He went on to inform Henry that his father had been a close friend of the *Burrbesh* in the past and had assisted on several projects.

Moss had been devastated at his loss and had spent an age tracking down young Henry's location and assisting in his return.

'I had no idea,' said Henry, 'there is no mention of his association with the *Burrbesh* in the journal.'

Henry had deduced that the description of the small man was Moss but could not understand the connection.

'Your father became a very good ally of the *Burrbesh*, and one of the stipulations was that it was to be kept secret. A secret he kept well.'

Moss went on to describe the attributes of Henry's father, a man who, it seems, was held in high regard by many.

'Master Henry, you will come across many supporters of the *Burrbesh*, some have the skills and abilities much like yourself.

They have supported the task in which we are involved on your world; unfortunately, their numbers have dwindled over the years.'

Moss continued to justify the much-needed input into maintaining the health and stability of the flora, and rubbing his hands, expressed his sheer joy that things were beginning to happen.

'A fine speech Moss,' said *Tabule*, who had been standing in the doorway listening to events.

'I must admit, it does evoke an element of excitement,' he grinned.

He had come to see Edmund; he explained that he had been exploring the possibilities of distributing the seed.

The tribes in the far north and south found that at certain times, the aurora attracted massive shoals of fish to certain areas.

It was this magnetic field that he thought might control the flow of seed, having watched their last release across the plains.

He thought Edmund might know a trick or two to promote this effect and make the whole project a little more effective.

Time was approaching 07:30 hrs and tradesmen were starting to arrive.

Jake and Sandra arrived, and each having work to do, went off in separate ways.

Edmund and Ivy arrived; Ivy joined Sandra on her way to the greenhouses and Edmund needed Henry to go over the plans for the top floor.

Tabule agreed to chat later to Edmund, so he and Moss retired to the conservatory to explore the seed idea.

Henry saw Shelta out, she commented that the evening would be one to remember, and they both agreed to meet later.

Henry, returning to the stairs, went up to meet Edmund, who was in conference with three of the contractors.

They discussed the installation of new services and where they were to be sited, and the need for respect when carrying out the work.

Henry was still struggling with the fact that the top floor had been opened, and of all the memories it had revealed.

He wandered downstairs to meet *Tabule*, who was in the conservatory, deep in thought.

'What do you know about London?' Henry asked.

He continued to explain that he would soon journey to London and take up his seat in the House of Lords. And while he was there, he could assess areas suitable for the special talents of the sprouts. He was contemplating carrying out a campaign with them, to take some of the attention away from the Manor.

'What do you think?' asked Henry.

'Lots of roads and concrete, with pollution a prime candidate,' said *Tabule*.

Tabule reiterated the idea he was to put to Edmund; he said that the areas in London might be very suitable, and he would like to be involved.

Henry returned to the top floor to continue his reading of the journal; he passed Edmund who was on his way down to see *Tabule*.

'Ah Henry, I have something to show you,' said Edmund, and asked if he was going to be around.

Henry admitted that he was going to absorb the top floor for the remainder of the day.

Edmund continued on his way down to see what *Tabule* wanted. He was surprised to find him entwined in the night flower; it was difficult to tell which part was the plant and which was *Tabule*.

Moss arrived and informed Edmund that it was best to leave him for the moment, there was much preparation ongoing, and he should really not be surprised at anything he saw. Moss closed the doors to the conservatory and put a 'Private No Entry' sign across the door handles.

Edmund, now a little confused, decided to retry Henry with his news, and returning to the top floor, caught up with Henry in the end lounge.

Henry had removed the covers from all the furniture in the room. He had taken rather a shine to the sofa on which he had awoken that morning; it allowed a good view of the room.

Putting his journal down, he welcomed Edmund and told him to be seated.

Edmund explained that the new technology that had arrived would allow connections to various satellites. He spent the next two hours explaining to Henry what a satellite was, how it got where it was and what it could do. Edmund was convinced that this technology would further advance the plans that were being discussed.

Henry was more than impressed by the abilities of Edmund and of the advances man had made over the last hundred years. With Edmund's help he was sure that it would give them the technical edge to succeed.

'I want us to have the most up-to-date equipment, we cannot allow ourselves to be one step behind. I know there is much of this technology that can help us, it just seems that there is more of it than one man can absorb.

You have become a good friend, Edmund, a friend also to my daughter, I do not want you to feel under pressure to produce results. When you get to know everyone who is involved, you will find it only takes a mention to activate a solution.' Henry continued reading the instruction manual for Edmund's new gizmo, trying to look as if he understood it.

'I understand what you are saying, Henry. I know that only certain amounts of technology filter down to the general public. There is much that we do not see, that is more efficient and sophisticated.

You are in a privileged position to access these unique inventions. Your company has many dark corners that you, as yet are unaware of.

I have done a little research into some of the more obscure companies you own. You are really going to want to know what they are doing.'

At that moment Edmund felt closer than ever to Henry, it was almost a family tie. Henry stood up, he complimented Edmund on his efficiency, and admitting that there was more to do, he said:

'I think that you need to have access to these companies. We shall have to get you some inside information on these factories. But tonight, we party! Have you ever been to a Gypsy evening?' asked Henry.

He told Edmund to collect Ivy and put aside all thoughts until the morrow.

'Tonight, is a night to let your hair down,' he said.

They both wandered downstairs to find a hive of activity. Cooks were carrying loads of food out to the front, where MacTavish was loading it into the boot of the old Rolls and Moss was carrying boxes of something out from the conservatory.

'What's in the boxes Moss?' enquired Henry.

Moss told him that the night flower was going to be distributed among the Gypsy folk, as they often travelled to the most remote places.

Shelta appeared in the hallway to collect one of the boxes.

'Would Master Henry like a lift from a lowly Gypsy girl?' She bobbed her head to the side in a nonchalant manner.

'Don't mind if I do,' said Henry, picking up the box for her, and carrying it out, he said, 'We can't have an old lady picking up heavy boxes, can we?'

She stamped on his foot, provoking a quiet grimace. He carried the box out to the courtyard where a very large colourful Gypsy wagon was tethered to two horses.

Climbing up the two steps into the rear of the wagon, he was amazed to see the brightness inside. What looked like canvas cover from outside was in fact a flexible one-way-mirror-type material, he could see everyone, everything.

The inside was a giant planting area, which seemed larger inside than it did out. It housed many of the smaller night flowers and one very large, very established plant.

'You never cease to amaze me Shelta. How long have you been involved with the *Burrbesh*?'

He inspected the larger of the night flowers and complimented her on the quality of her mobile greenhouse.

He leaned out and pushed his face to the outside of the canvas, but could not see in.

Climbing onto the wagon seat, Henry asked Shelta how many other night flowers were out there. She had to admit that this was one of the few that were left when the Manor closed, she had no idea if any more existed.

She said that if there were others out there, they were being a well-kept secret.

She shook the reins and the two horses walked on.

Leaving the Manor down the driveway, they made their way along the road to the camp.

Edmund ventured into the conservatory; there was an air of contentment, the fragrance was intoxicating and *Tabule* had gone.

He continued through to the patio where he found a small army of workmen that had been invited by Moss for drinks. Chatting with Jake, Sandra and Ivy was *Tabule*, who, when he spotted Edmund, made his apologies that he needed to speak with him.

Kidnapping Edmund to a quiet corner, *Tabule* began to explain his idea.

'There are many forces on this world which greatly affect conditions on a day-to-day basis. One of them is the magnetic field; the borealis changes but the energy lines remain constant. When we released the seed, it was very reminiscent of the borealis. Could we not devise a way to control the magnetism, to make the seed go where we want?'

Edmund told *Tabule* that there were numerous inventions that man had discovered regarding the control of magnetism. It was a subject on which he had carried out some research, using satellites to monitor the earth's magnetic field. He would investigate the possibilities.

'In fact, there has been a delivery of some satellite equipment today that I was showing Henry earlier,' said Edmund.

'Good, good, we shall discuss it tomorrow. May see you later, a few friends I have to see.' *Tabule* turned to walk into the gardens. He was positively electric.

Edmund was surprised at the change in him from a few hours ago and turned to re-join the others.

Discussions were under way to arrange transport to the Gypsy camp.

Edmund offered to take Ivy, Jake and Sandra who were going to freshen up, Jake was bringing Mom and Dad and couldn't leave Fidgit. So, it was all sorted.

The evening was about to begin.

As Jake and Sandra walked through to the front drive, MacTavish was just reloading the boot with goodies, and Moss was struggling with a crate of beer.

'I recognize those bottles,' said Jake, 'that's Mrs B's rocket fuel.'

Moss had only praise for the beverage, he complimented Mrs B for creating such perfection from plant material.

He said he would be getting a lift to the venue with MacTavish; he believed that the staff would also accompany them, as Shelta had asked everyone.

'Right, we had better be making a move,' said Jake.

'See you all later.' Jake and Sandra walked over to the Land Rover to find Fidgit curled up on his blanket with the three little ones. There were distinct snoring sounds coming from them all; they looked at each other.

'We shall have to take them back inside,' said Jake.

Gently lifting the three dozing entities, both Sandra and Jake transported them back to the conservatory and placed them on a cushion of Mother's foliage. They never stirred. Sandra said they must be absolutely whacked, running around with Fidgit all day.

'Aah, I wondered where those three had got to,' said Moss, as he continued on through with his arms full.

They returned to the Land Rover, Fidgit still spark out, not waking, even when he dropped Sandra home. Pulling up outside the barn back at home, he jumped out and rushed in, to shower and change.

Finally ready, he wandered over to the kitchen where his dad was sitting at the table, waiting.

'Yer ma's just putting her face on,' he said.

'Never been to a Gypsy do before, 'course, there used to be plenty back in the day, yer Gran can tell a few stories.'

Mother arrived, looking very summery, prompting a hug from his dad.

'There is a drop of cider I thought we might take, I left it by your car Jake,' she said.

They all piled into the shiny red thing, including Fidgit who had suddenly appeared, and set off to pick up Sandra. She was waiting by the front gate when Jake arrived. Getting into the front seat, she greeted Jake's parents. She confessed that she was really looking forward to the whole event, and asked Jake's mom and dad if they had ever been to such a do.

Before they had time to answer they were there. There were quite a few vehicles parked alongside the track leading to the camp.

Jake parked up and they walked on down to where the music and food smells were coming from.

The sight that greeted them was reminiscent of a village carnival. On one side there was a small band, playing fiddle, accordion and flute. Several other instruments were parked next to seats, awaiting their performers. Further round was a hog roast, turning gently on a spit over an open fire. Next to that was a make-shift bar with beer pulls and an array of beverages lined up on shelves, with optics.

Continuing around were bistro tables and chairs, just like French pavement restaurants. The centre of the clearing had been left uncluttered for dancing and entertainments.

Strung all around the trees were lanterns which would produce light when the sun went down. Henry came over to greet them; he showed them to a table which he had reserved for them, and then proceeded to introduce them to some of the elders.

After the introductions, Jake spotted Edmund; he had joined the musicians and was tuning up a fiddle.

Jake and Sandra wandered around taking in the atmosphere. They collected a drink from the bar where Shelta was helping out. Jake mentioned the cider, which was in the back of the car, next to an upside down Fidgit.

'I'll go and fetch it after we've seen Edmund perform.'

Jake and Sandra joined Ivy at a table near the band, just as they began to play. It was a foot tappingly good sound they produced, folk music that made you want to dance.

It wasn't long before everybody was on the dance floor, the music went on for ages, until a gong was struck.

Moss announced the food was ready and people should make their way to the servery.

A large table was then placed in the middle of the dance floor, connected to a number of smaller ones. It turned into a banqueting table with tablecloths overlapping each other, providing the surface for the wealth of food and drink.

Henry was invited to head the table at one end, while Shelta took the other.

Platters of meat and pastries, bowls with all kinds of good things were systematically passed around in a clockwise direction. Jugs of beer and cider, bottles of Poitín endlessly arrived, delivered by a very efficient system – whoever empties it, replaces it.

Everyone had something to say, with the main topic being the sorry state of the world. Tales of the past were recited by the older generation, which always attracted a keen audience.

Barney also had an avid audience and was in his element telling his tales of old.

The music resumed when the food was done, it was played in a more traditional manner of slow ballads.

The occasional singer would accompany the music, some with words in their native tongue, when everyone would watch and listen in silence.

The atmosphere within that little clearing in the wood reflected what the world could be like once more.

Henry spent most of the time chatting to the Gypsy elders as the night began to turn into morning, and people started to leave.

Some of the guests were camped a little further up the river, within walking distance, while MacTavish was operating a taxi service for those who lived a little further.

Jake's parents took advantage of his offer of a lift and bade everyone a good morning, thanking them for a wonderful evening.

Jake and Sandra walked with his parents down the track, following MacTavish to the old Rolls.

Bill and Edna received hugs from them both; Bill claimed it must be the month of parties, two in a fortnight.

MacTavish held open the door for them to enter their carriage, and the smell of old leather greeted them as they got in. Waving them off Jake and Sandra turned to return to the party.

Jake checked on Fidgit as they walked past the shiny thing. He beckoned to Sandra to come and look. Three little ones had somehow got in, probably through the open sunroof.

They were all sprawled out head to toe in a triangle, with Fidgit, upside down in the middle.

They were definitely noisy sleepers, as distinctive snoring came from inside. They both crept quietly away so as not to disturb them, returning to the party, albeit now only a few groups chatting around the edge.

The musicians, including Edmund, continued to play soft haunting music that seemed so apt for the moment.

At the table in front of them were Henry, Shelta, Ivy and a very red-faced Barney. Barney was quite well lubricated and in story-telling mode.

Jake and Sandra wandered over to them, just in time to hear Barney say it was an old letter which had been sent to his grandfather. He gave a chuckle and then, startled by the sudden appearance of Jake, would say no more, but continued with intermittent chuckling.

'Pay no heed to the old fool; you know he is always keen to play tricks and create a little theatre.' Ivy leaned over and poked him.

'Isn't it past your bedtime Barney?'

Barney stood up, perhaps a little too quickly. He sat back down and admitted he could probably do with a nap.

Shelta said there were some cosy sofas around the caravans, placed there purely for that purpose.

Jake and Henry assisted Barney to a nearby cosy seat, for a nap.

MacTavish came over and enquired if Mr Arney would require his assistance. Ivy said it was best to leave him, he would have an hour's nap, then be fully recharged, that was his way.

Jake and Sandra wandered over to the river. The music took on a different sound as it floated through the trees.

They lay on the grass, watching the sun come up. The sound of the river mixed with the music was so peaceful, they both drifted off to sleep.

Chapter 15

It was mid-morning when Jake roused; the effects of the evening's physical exertions on the dance floor had left its mark.

Fidgit, recognising his master's groan, ran over to give him a refreshing wet tongue wash.

Sandra had already been over to Shelta's caravan to freshen up and was sitting with Barney and Henry, sipping coffee.

'You looked so peaceful there, it seemed a shame to wake you,' said Sandra.

Both Henry and Barney bade him good morning.

Jake poured himself a coffee and joined them. He enquired how Fidgit had escaped the car.

'I let him, and the little ones out last night,' said Shelta, emerging from the caravan, from where the smell of bacon was also coming.

'Breakfast or brunch anyone?' she enquired.

The answer was unanimous, there was nothing quite like the smell of bacon, outdoors, to set the taste buds on edge.

The clearing was now empty, except for Shelta's caravan and the mobile greenhouse, which had just arrived, having spent the night in a quieter place.

The horses, now unbridled, were being attended to by Patrick, one of Shelta's many nephews. She called him over to join them as she brought out two large plates, full of bacon, sausage and eggs.

'Help yourselves,' said Shelta.

She explained that they would be taking the vans to meet up with the others. Then they would travel across Europe, where they would meet other bands of Gypsy, and distribute the night flower.

Henry asked Jake and Sandra if they had seen the plants that would be going, and the unique conveyance in which they would be transported.

The three wandered over to the brightly painted caravan and went inside. Jake and Sandra were amazed at the size of it.

Single plants lined the one side, while the whole of the opposite side was taken up with a large well-established plant. It was in various stages of growth, flower buds about to open, flowers in full bloom and large seed heads that looked very similar to the little ones.

Henry explained that as the night flower was one of *Leber's* more successful creations, he had been giving this one a little more of his time.

'There was a need for more of the sprouts,' Henry said, and explained there would be no harvesting of this one until the seed heads matured.

Then out of the corner of his eye, Jake saw a movement within the foliage. He pointed to where it had been, and there, peeking out from behind a leaf was a smaller version of the little ones. When his eyes had grown accustomed to its shape and camouflage, he started to spot more. Pointing was wasted as there were more of them than he had fingers.

Shelta appeared behind them.

'What do you think of our little colony?' she said.

Sandra was amazed, and asked how it could be possible, they were exact smaller copies of the three sprouts she had come to know. She had witnessed the buds and the seed, but this was a part of the growing process that she had not seen.

'I shall tell you, my dear,' boomed the deep mellow voice of *Leber* who had quietly joined them.

Having given them all a start he apologized and continued to explain.

He told them how, in the early years, the *Burrbesh* had needed assistance to deal with such a massive workload. He had worked on the creation of a plant that would provide such help; the result was the night flower.

'It needs care and attention and has to feel wanted. If these three conditions are met, then it will thrive and flower; once in flower it requires a particular insect to ensure pollination. When germinated it produces seed, this it stores until near bursting point, and can be altered to grow many different species. When the elders bond with the plant, they each give a little of themselves, and the night flower takes on each of their special talents.

It cannot be grown from seed, it lays its stems down on its native soil and allows a new plant to grow. The little ones, as you call them, result from not harvesting the seed, the pods containing the seed are allowed to grow to another stage.'

Leber picked up one of the small creatures and held it with a fondness, a little out of character for him.

He went on to explain that the little ones could create a vast number of plants and trees in their footsteps. Each would need its mother plant to bond with and grow strong. The night flower would store the information from the bonding, and at any time in the future would produce the seed required by the elders. However, the little ones were still learning. They could plant up specific areas, whereas the seed would saturate a massive area, something he and *Tabule* were working on.

'With the help of yourselves and many like you, the night flower should flourish all over the world. And when the time is right, there should be enough to turn the tide of destruction that your world faces.'

Leber returned the little one gently into the twining tendrils of the night flower.

They all stepped out of the fragrant growing room. *Leber* said he had things to do and would see them later.

Henry said his farewells to Shelta, wishing her a safe journey and would see her on her return.

Jake and Sandra also said goodbye to Shelta. Jake whistled for Fidgit who came bounding out of the growing room, having made many, many new friends.

Henry and Barney were both offered a lift back to the Manor. The day had now turned into afternoon, and a gentle calm descended on the Manor as they rolled up the drive.

It was the weekend, and there were no workmen rushing around. Henry had tasked himself with the complete exploration of the upper floor.

Everyone else went off to have a relaxing time, readying themselves for the return to organised chaos on Monday.

Henry completed his task on the upper floor, and Sunday passed without incident. It had given Henry a chance to wander the grounds, to inspect the work being carried out, and study it in a little more detail.

The staff, including MacTavish, were all away; Moss and *Tabule* were obviously away too.

Henry had only the little ones for company, and even they were comatose most of the time. He enjoyed this moment of reflection; it allowed him to make peace with his new home.

The week started with the usual clatter of tradesmen busying themselves with the jobs in hand.

Henry, having taken the top floor as his own apartment, was continually off out with Edmund, who had arranged all manner of crash courses for him. He was now learning computing and phones, and he had taken a driving course to get his licence.

Edmund had been given access to the portfolio of the business empire that Henry had inherited. Having investigated each of the companies and its function, Edmund found one secretive business, it was very old and situated in a remote, secure location. He had little success in obtaining much information, other than its title, 'Magnatek', and so, would seek the help of the solicitors.

In between, Edmund was showing Henry the equipment that was arriving daily, in boxes which filled the hall and walkways.

Jake was busy with the new greenhouses and the new barn building.

Sandra and Ivy worked well together; they were preparing the new greenhouses as they were coming online, and new night flowers were in full production.

They were testing new packaging for its suitability to transport the plant to various destinations.

The whole place was a building site, there wasn't a corner of the Manor that didn't have some work going on.

In all the hustle and bustle MacTavish asked various workers if they had seen Henry.

He eventually managed to track him down on the upper floor; he was in conference with the decorators.

'The MacDonalds are here to see you sir, I've taken the liberty of showing them to the summerhouse.'

'Good man, how's your kitchen coming along?' said Henry.

He told Henry that the floors had been removed and there was little that could be done in there at the moment. So, he had sent the kitchen staff outside to plant up the watercress beds.

Henry smiled, descended the stairs, and sidestepping tools and cables that were lying about, he called to Edmund to join him.

As they made their way to the summerhouse, Henry asked Edmund what was the name of the company that was of interest. He could ask the MacDonalds for information on the nature of the business, and perhaps arrange a visit.

The meeting with the MacDonalds was very successful. Edmund got an appointment with the company he wanted, and it turned out that Henry would have to visit London, the House of Lords in fact, to take up his place.

It would need to be dealt with in the next two weeks, before parliament closed for the summer.

'I shall have to tell *Tabule*, he was keen to do planting in London, and I have still to witness this seed spectacle,' said Henry.

'It might be a good idea to get away while the bulk of this work is going on.'

Henry suggested that they both visit this company; he was curious himself about what secret research was being carried out.

He asked Edmund for his advice on the upstairs apartment. As he was going to be living there, it should be sympathetically upgraded.

Edmund assured him it was on his list.

As the workmen started to leave for the night, a calmness settled and the smell and sounds of the country reappeared, together with the aromas from the conservatory.

There would be no electricity, as the old generator had just given up the ghost; water was only available from a bowser outside, and it would be several days before the big turn-on.

MacTavish had positioned altar candles throughout, ready to light, and food was consigned to bread and cheese, or the pub.

Henry and Edmund retired to the patio, with a large glass of red, awaiting the presence of Ivy, Sandra and Jake.

'How would you like to go to London for a few days Edmund? I could use a friend to navigate me through the new city. We could take in this secret research facility that I apparently own, and see what they are up to,' said Henry, leaning back into a very comfortable cushion.

His last recollection of old haunts in the capital was very hazy, he was only young, and they had to be in and out quickly, as there was a terrible sickness.

It would slip Edmund's mind on occasion that this man had been around for so long; it was a difficult concept to keep abreast of.

Edmund said he would be more than willing to accompany Henry on a short trip. There was little he could do until the new supplies were connected to the Manor.

Voices of Jake, Sandra and Ivy could be heard coming towards the house, with another, not so familiar. As they rounded the corner and ascended the patio, *Leber* turned out to be the unfamiliar voice, his tone was becoming less harsh.

'Henry, these ladies are doing an excellent job, you should be proud,' said *Leber,* pouring himself a glass of water.

'There is some excellent Rioja,' said Henry, raising his glass.

'No, dries me up,' said *Leber,* continuing his refreshment.

Henry asked Jake how his projects were coming along, to which he replied:

'I reckon another three days will see the greenhouses ready to roll, there is only the heating to install. But with this heat, it won't be needed for a while.'

Wiping his brow, Jake took a glass of water from Sandra.

'It's all coming along really well,' he said confidently.

Henry told them that he and Edmund would be going to London on business for a few days; it might work out just right.

Edmund explained about the company and its research that needed to be investigated.

'I believe *Tabule* would be interested in your findings too,' said *Leber*.

'What would I be interested in, *Leber?*' said *Tabule,* as he appeared behind him.

With all eyes on *Tabule,* they actually watched Moss appear, as though stepping out of the fog, right next to him.

'Good trick,' said Henry, nodding his head in approval.

Henry was impressed at their perfect timing. He briefly explained the circumstances that would take Edmund and himself away for a while and knowing that *Tabule* was keen to be there in London, Henry invited him to join them.

'You may have to go without me, as things are progressing at a pace. But before we go any further,' said *Tabule*, 'we have found an old friend of your family, he is quite concerned about a particular area.'

There then entered, from the conservatory, a tall charismatic black man, dressed in fine robes of red and gold.

'*Chonga*?' shouted Henry. He walked over to embrace him.

'God, I've missed you, what have you been doing, where have you been?'

Chonga, being the shortened version of Chonganda, was the name Henry had given him when they first met.

He was not *Burrbesh*, but one of a race of deities who had been worshipped for thousands of years. There are records of others like him, all over the world, in different cultures, all with different names. Recent years had brought about a decline in those cultures who understood the balance of things.

Many members of these cultures had been forced to relocate to the cities when their homelands were destroyed.

He explained that he had wandered from one desolate place to another; the devastation was immense. The damage had become more intense with the increase of peoples and technology. Machinery was now forcing its way through the homelands of many peace-loving tribes who were unable to fight back.

'I find myself struggling to help these people, I get weaker as the plants become fewer.'

Chonga painted a bleak picture of doom and gloom.

His association with Henry all those years ago had given him hope, but he thought that Henry had been lost forever.

It was only recently that word had reached him, of a man who had taken to the *Burrbesh* way. He knew then that Henry had returned.

He explained that he had been wandering the place known as the Amazon for many years, he had witnessed much destruction and it was in desperate need of help.

Henry told *Chonga* of their plans to send the night flower all over the world; there would be many dedicated followers required to help in this task. Teaching the keepers of this precious plant would be the key to its success, for it could be temperamental, and refuse to perform. He apologised to *Chonga* for not being able to stay and spend time with him, his plans for the immediate future were vital.

'We shall be gone, but for a few days, please stay, see the country and we shall talk of old times on my return,' said Henry.

He told *Chonga* of his summons to the House of Lords and asked him what knowledge he had of new technology. *Chonga* replied that the way of man was not really his way, but he did have a young associate who was very keen on keeping up to date with the world. He would try to explain man's new inventions to him, but most of it seemed to go over *Chonga's* head.

He agreed to stay, he had much to talk about with the *Burrbesh*, and this would be a very good opportunity for catching up with news.

'That's settled then,' said Henry, 'you shall stay here, the facilities will get better, I promise.'

Jake said that they were going to get a bite to eat at the Tavern on their way home and invited everybody to join them. And so it was, a motley crew of Moss, *Leber*, *Tabule*, Henry and the brightly coloured *Chonga* piled into the Rolls, with MacTavish at the helm.

Edmund and Ivy followed in the Morgan, while Jake and Sandra with Fidgit, brought up the rear. They formed a convoy along the lane to the Tavern.

On arrival, they found that most of the staff from the house had exactly the same idea, even some of the local workforces were present.

It got very jovial, especially when Barney arrived, and immediately took centre stage. How could he resist such an audience? Even *Leber* seemed to enjoy the new-found entertainment.

As the evening drew to a close, everyone made their way back home, having been wined, dined and entertained.

Edmund had arranged with Henry to make an early start on the trip to London. Little known to Henry, was that he himself was going to drive.

Edmund felt confident enough to give him the opportunity to do a long journey, after all the crash course driving tuition he had had.

Edmund had arranged a test drive in a car that Henry had seen, and made comment on, during their visit to Bristol.

Everybody wished everybody else good night and MacTavish stood aside the Rolls, holding the door open for its passengers. With Henry and the three odd fellows aboard, the Rolls purred along the lanes with barely a sound.

Arriving back at the Manor, which had descended into a dim candle-lit stillness, they retired to the patio. The calm evening was interrupted by the occasional distant cries of fox cubs fighting and a nightingale serenading its mate. MacTavish brought out drinks for them all and bade them goodnight.

'I do like this world when it's peaceful like this,' said *Tabule*. 'It is quite unique.'

He spoke to Henry of his proposed trip to investigate the facility and the research being carried out. Of course, he was interested in being involved, but he believed that he and Edmund were more qualified to deal with it.

'You must keep me informed of your findings, but in the immediate future, I shall be arranging a meeting of the *Burrbesh*. We shall leave you and go in search of these lost tribes and cultures, in an attempt to bring them together; then they will need your help. I feel a strong sense of loyalty in you Henry, I am glad you have returned.' *Tabule* was quite passionate in his short speech.

Leber told Henry that he had already spoken to *Tabule,* and it had been agreed that should Henry find the need to use the fabric as a means of travel, he, *Leber*, would not stand in his way.

'When I'm wrong, I do it properly,' said *Leber,* shrugging his shoulders.

Moss had to have a say as well and reaffirmed his belief in the loyalty Henry had shown.

Moss almost felt like a family member, as he had watched Henry mature from a youngster. Moss's bond with the Lyte's family was very strong, and should Henry ever need his help, for whatever reason, he would be there for him.

'Well, I think I may as well tag along with you three,' said *Chonga*. 'I can show you the area of which I speak.'

They all raised a glass to Henry, wished him well and bade him goodnight, and as the night opened to allow them entry, they were gone.

A midsummer morning was just a brighter continuation of the evening, workers arrived, and the kitchen staff put on a continental breakfast.

Edmund was one of the first on the scene, he joined Henry in the dining room, admitting he had had very little sleep. The excitement of the day had taken over his mind, it raced from one possible dream to another, never allowing one to take precedent.

'Henry, I have arranged a little surprise, I hope you don't object?' said Edmund.

Henry, who was just washing down a croissant with a large orange juice and unable to speak, looked at Edmund quizzically.

Eventually he asked Edmund, 'What surprise?'

At that moment MacTavish came in and announced that there was a delivery for Edmund Mathews.

Before Edmund had a chance to take a bite of his croissant, he launched himself over to Henry's chair, grabbed him by the arm and told him he had to see this.

Escorting Henry out to the front of the house, Edmund told him to close his eyes. Guiding him down the steps and eventually telling Henry to open them, he was blessed with a vision of a Bentley Continental GT convertible, in a baby blue metallic with white leather trim. This was a car Henry had seen on their trip to Bristol the first time; Henry had claimed it was a piece of art.

'How do you fancy driving that down to London Milord? One has to look the part, doesn't one?'

Edmund smiled, as he watched Henry examine the spectacle parked on the drive.

Then, as if on cue, Ivy turned up on her scooter, followed closely by Jake and Sandra, with Fidgit of course, who immediately ran off into the bushes.

They all congregated around the new shiny vehicle, admiring its presence.

'It's very you,' said Ivy. She had known of its planned appearance, as Edmund had confided in her, having spent some time arranging its delivery.

'Let's take it for a spin,' said Edmund.

Henry ordered everyone to climb in. If it was to be his maiden voyage, he thought that everyone should enjoy it. Edmund had already spent several hours digesting the instruction manual and guided Henry through the controls and starting procedure.

The car glided down the drive and off up the lane, past Bob the bricklayer, adding his final touches, who waved, then past the army of workers who cheered. Turning left Henry manoeuvred the car with the dexterity of a seasoned chauffer.

'You drive very well, father,' said Ivy who had commandeered the front passenger seat. Edmund was fiddling with the sound system and found the track he thought would suit the excursion.

All of a sudden, the Beach Boys sang out, and everyone joined in, except Henry, who hummed.

Having completed a circuit of the lanes, Henry pulled back onto the drive and expressed his utter admiration for Edmund's thoughtfulness.

'When I first saw this car in Bristol, you understood my feelings. As I am not a great one for worldly goods, you recognised my appreciation of its beauty.

'You know, I would never have sought this item for myself. I do not know what to say, thank you Edmund.'

Henry shook his hand and said that they really should be going.

MacTavish came out with luggage to be loaded in the boot. Edmund, who was in charge of gizmos, pressed the relevant button and up popped the boot. With the luggage loaded, Henry and Edmund boarded their chariot and bid everyone farewell. Edmund pressed the required buttons, plotted a course into the sat nav, and off they went.

What went unnoticed was Fidgit; he sat at the top of the drive, watching the Bentley disappear into the lane as it went on its way. He was on his own, one ear up, one down, giving a barely audible whimper.

Chapter 16

The route to London had been decided, it would be the scenic route, as Henry could not technically drive on motorways yet. The factory to be visited was on the way, in Aylesbury, a facility set in its own grounds of five hundred acres, with fields set out for the research.

The official description of the business was Research and Development of Satellite Technology: its objective, to further the application of GPS in agriculture. On the surface, the company was using this technology to control machinery and its automation.

Edmund had been reading out the company profile from a brochure that had been provided by the solicitors.

There was an ulterior motive to the research being carried out, which was only privy to the legal team, and Henry.

Having finished with the prècis of their intended destination, Edmund proceeded to explore the controls within the car. Fiddling with all the controls, and being a techno geek, he was telling Henry the results of his findings.

Henry, not being a techno geek, was just nodding his acceptance of the facts, as the car and he became one with each hour that passed.

Edmund explained that the instructions for directions were displayed on the dashboard; he showed Henry the display for the sat nav. After choosing a suitable voice, Edmund instructed him to follow the directions given by the softly spoken female in the dashboard. Eventually Henry became more relaxed and began to enjoy the experience; he had been reluctant to tell Edmund that he was, to say the least, a little apprehensive at the start.

After driving for a couple of hours, Edmund enquired if Henry would like to stop for a break. It was agreed that a stop would be a good idea and that Henry would need to stretch his legs, it was not like riding horses. His legs felt as if they should be doing something.

So, it was agreed that at the next hostelry they would stop for refreshments, and a stretch of the legs.

It wasn't long before the perfect place appeared. The Fisherman's Inn, a hostelry positioned right next to a river supporting trout and other edibles. Pulling into the car park, the Bentley purred into a parking space in the shade of a large beech tree, and with the flick of a switch everything was silent.

Just as Henry opened the door to get out, there was a sudden movement in the car. Henry asked if that was supposed to happen. Edmund replied that he wouldn't expect that of such a fine car. Henry gestured to Edmund to stay still, he was waiting for the movement to reappear, and sure enough it did.

'There's something in the boot,' they both said, simultaneously.

They both got out and walked round to the rear of the car. Edmund pressed the button to open the boot.

Grabbing Edmund's arm, Henry gave him the opportunity to see what he could see. There, inside, were the three sprouts, arm in arm doing what appeared to be the can-can, swaying and kicking their legs from one side of the car to the other.

Henry let out a bellow of laughter, which made Edmund laugh, which only encouraged the little ones to dance even more.

When the laughing subsided, the pair tried to work out how these little troublemakers had gained entry into the boot. Not as though it would make much difference, they were a good way from home and the journey back would throw their timetable out.

They were stuck with them.

They decided that for the journey, they would put the three little ones on the back seat so they could be watched, but for now, Henry shut the boot, ordering them to behave.

Henry and Edmund continued to the Inn in order to complete their planned stop for refreshments and a stretch of the legs. Henry knew that the sprouts would not disobey him and felt comfortable while partaking of the facilities.

With refreshed vigour, Henry and Edmund returned to the car, released the little ones and positioned them on the back seat, with strict instructions to stay.

Edmund had found the TV monitors in the back of the seats and tuned in to the CBB channel; the little ones found this fascinating.

Continuing with the route the on-screen display had decided on, they set off. Henry was getting very proficient in his ability to drive, and Edmund confirmed that, by passing comment.

Their destination soon showed up on the sat nav screen and the authoritarian voice of direction lady commanded them to turn.

The entrance to the facility was at the end of a lane bordered by fields and a line of hedges. The hedgerow suddenly turned into a more cultured variety, an eight-foot beech hedge, which stretched on into the distance, perfectly upright and level. It masked a much higher, inhospitable security fence, signs of electric fence and razor wire adorned it, and a nicely mown area provided a patrolling pathway for security guards.

The entrance had a pristine frontage, with well-cut lawns and two topiarised yews, cut to four-foot square and six foot high. They guarded the entrance, standing one either side like a pair of soldiers on sentry duty.

A short way in, the drive led to a pair of military-style gates with cameras on each side. The security fence stretched far into the distance on either side. The fence was not visible from the road, as the high manicured beech hedge shielded it.

Pulling up to the gates, Henry drew next to the intercom. A voice asked his business, to which Henry replied.

Immediately the gates started to draw sideways, opening up the route which led down a winding road bordered by lime trees, to an old country house.

The drive and frontage were in the same immaculate state as the front gate; a circular, stone-built bed in the centre housed an array of colourful plants. Henry pulled up to the side of the front door, which was set back in a timbered vestibule structure with one step down to the drive.

The door, with its highly polished brass plaque in the centre, opened and out came a well-dressed man to greet them.

'Lord Lyte and Professor Mathews, welcome, my name is Professor Stiller, I am in charge of this establishment.'

He announced that accommodation had been prepared for them both, and that the itinerary would include a tour and inspection of the facility, with a seminar later. The following day would be spent with a demonstration of the research and its progress.

He thought that refreshments might be a good idea to start and had arranged for tea to be served in the dining room. If they had any luggage, he would arrange for it to be taken to their rooms.

He explained that the facility regularly had visiting scientists and experts from all over the world to stay, some were there for weeks. The staff who would be looking after them would be at home in a five-star hotel. They were very efficient, and Henry and Edmund had only to ask for anything they needed to make their stay comfortable.

A member of staff was already waiting at the doorway to assist with their luggage.

'Thank you, that will not be necessary as we have only a basic overnight bag, and please call me Henry, and my associate is Edmund.'

He did not want to draw attention to the fact that there were another three passengers on board.

'If you can show us our rooms, we shall just freshen up and meet you in the dining room,' said Henry, casting a sideways glance at Edmund.

'Excellent, I shall instruct Michael, your valet, to show you through when you are ready.'

Professor Stiller turned and went back into the house, leaving Henry and Edmund to deal with their bags, and the sprouts.

It was fortuitous that the sprouts were not visible to the uninitiated, for Henry walked past the valet, with the three little ones sitting on his bag.

The valet showed them both to their rooms, off a corridor at the top of the stairs. The rooms would not have been out of place in any of the finest of hotels.

Having instructed both Henry and Edmund on the facilities available in the rooms, the valet told them he would wait downstairs for them.

'I shall put the TV on for the little ones,' said Edmund.

'They seemed to like that, and it may help to keep them occupied!'

Edmund thought he saw them sitting on the edge of the bed, and asked Henry where they were.

Henry confirmed they were there.

'You may get to see more of them, the more you are around them,' said Henry. 'Familiarity brings you closer, you will soon see them all the time.'

Edmund went next door to freshen up; Henry meanwhile poured a little water in the large spa bath for the little ones to have a dip in.

Wandering onto the balcony, he could see the extent of the grounds and was looking forward to the coming afternoon.

He instructed the little ones, who were sitting in front of the big screen watching children's TV, to be good and not wander away from the room. Closing the door behind him, Henry collected Edmund and they both made their way downstairs.

They were greeted by Michael, who proceeded to show them into the dining room, where they were introduced to a small group of company scientists.

With refreshments and introductions out of the way, Professor Stiller invited everyone to follow him down to the labs. This was where the nuts and bolts of this establishment were being thrashed out.

The laboratories surrounded a large hangar-type construction with a high roof, in which there were many white-coated technicians, seemingly involved in the task of testing some type of drone.

Professor Stiller explained that they were experimenting with the manipulation of magnetic fields. Their aim was to construct a portable device that was as powerful as the laboratory version. With this device, and with the advances in global positioning systems combined, the goal was to control the distribution of water. In effect, send a raincloud to where it was needed most.

The theory stacked up; rainclouds have an element of static charge, the magnetic field, which if controlled, could guide these clouds like a large plane. The ejection of the contents is something that they were working on at the moment and were very close to a breakthrough.

Edmund asked if it was only water that they were interested in controlling. Professor Stiller went on to explain that water has many properties: as a gas, hundreds of tons can be carried in clouds: sand particles, frogs, and insects, have all been carried, they get caught up in the busy atmosphere and themselves become charged. It is really only the lightweight particles that, when they become electrostatically charged, can be controlled.

Edmund reached into his pocket and brought out a jar.

In it, was a sample of the seed *Tabule* had given him, the swirling effect within was almost pearlescent.

'Is this something that could be controlled?' asked Edmund.

Henry took the jar from Edmund and turning to Professor Stiller, he said, holding the jar high, that this was their main reason for coming. Handing it back to Edmund he told the group that it was Edmund who would explain their requirements, as he was the expert on this subject.

'In this jar is a seed, which, when released has the characteristics of the aurora, a magnetic field is displayed in its dispersal, but it is random.

If it were to be controlled and targeted to specific areas, then we would have a better chance of success.'

Edmund handed the jar to Professor Stiller and explained that this seed was no ordinary seed.

'It is possible to pre-determine which plants it could produce, and that, if possible, could it be used in the demonstration tomorrow?' enquired Edmund.

The jar was being passed around among the others, all of them keen to get a look at what it contained.

'We should get it down to the lab to be analysed,' said the Professor.

With their tour and seminar concluded, Henry suggested that they might retire to a quiet place.

It was now pertinent to explain the circumstances surrounding his background. Henry, Edmund and Professor Stiller retired to the lounge, a room set out like a gentlemen's club with leather chairs and small wooden drinks tables. The walls were adorned with oil paintings of landscapes from different countries around the world.

It looked out over a narrow patio, to the fields, all neatly prepared for planting.

As it was approaching the evening mealtime, Michael greeted them with menus and the opportunity to order drinks.

Henry chose a Rioja; it was his mother's favourite.

Having all agreed, a bottle and three glasses were brought in, and Henry proceeded to explain, in summary, his past, and his association with the Council of Libra.

Professor Stiller listened intently, while Edmund nodded in agreement at various points of the tale.

Henry's story had absolutely confounded the Professor; he was sure such things existed; his whole life had been devoted to the preservation of life and was grateful for the opportunity to be able to help with such a quest.

'Of course, we would expect to keep this matter to ourselves, and few should know of these plans until it is absolutely necessary,' said Henry.

They had chatted for some time. Michael came through to inform them that dinner would be served in forty-five minutes.

Henry excused himself to return to his room.

Edmund however was keen to visit the lab to see what progress was being made with the seed; Professor Stiller agreed that he too was curious to see how things were progressing.

Henry was a little unsure of what to expect when he returned to the room, the sprouts had an uncanny knack of surprising him.

Opening the door, Henry was greeted by the TV showing the channel he had left it on – ok so far.

The door to the bathroom was shut, there was a sound of running water and a distinct sound of giggling.

Not so good.

Henry was a little hesitant to open the door; he went to turn the doorknob, just as a squirt of soap bubbles came oozing out of the keyhole.

Opening the door, he was overwhelmed by an avalanche of bubbles which had completely filled the bathroom. Scooping his way through the foam, he realised that the spa was operating, it was full to overflowing, sprouts were appearing and disappearing, and giggles could be heard all around.

Henry attempted to find the controls and turn off the bubble machine; eventually finding something that resembled a tap, he turned it. This only seemed to make things worse.

At that moment there was a knock at the door of his room. Edmund came in, bursting to tell Henry the news.

By now Henry had exited the bathroom, shut the door and was standing with his back to the door, guarding its entry. What he didn't realise was that he had foam suds standing on his head and shoulders. He looked like the naughty child who had done the deed. Edmund looked at him, mouth open with a smile beginning to appear.

‘Come in, shut the door, the sprouts have made a proper mess,’ said Henry.

He opened the door to the bathroom, a dense pillow of foam began to creep into the room, like some slow-moving lava flow.

‘I can’t stop it,’ said Henry, battling his way back in and disappearing from view.

Edmund followed him in and found the right controls to slow down the foam production.

The occasional glimpse of a sprout could be seen as it submerged through the bank of suds, they could certainly be heard, even Edmund could hear the giggling.

‘I think I’ve found the drain plug,’ said Edmund, who by now was soaking wet and covered in foam.

He turned to see Henry lurch forward to catch one of the sprouts as it jumped toward the spa. He missed it and slid headfirst into the water. By now Edmund, knowing the situation had been contained and waiting for it to abate, burst out laughing. He could just see Henry’s head above the foam, complete with policeman’s helmet-shaped dome on his head, and a sprout on each shoulder.

Edmund now was beside himself; he had lost all control of his limbs; the sight of Henry was too much.

Henry, who had resigned himself to his predicament also started to laugh, they both fuelled each other’s laughter, which seemed to last for an eternity.

When a state of compos mentis returned, they surveyed the scene, and the cause of the devastation was evident.

Somehow the spa had been switched on, the water was operated by touch controls, with the plug already in, it just got deeper. Then with the swirling water, the complete supply of bath gel, shower gel, shampoo and every other bathroom condiment added, the result was pandemonium. Something the little ones knew a lot about.

Exiting the spa, Henry grabbed the sprouts and took them over to the shower where he promptly washed them down.

‘I came to tell you that the equipment that they have developed here is very advanced.’ Edmund could contain himself no longer. He explained to Henry what was being tested at the moment, it was perfect for the seed and far outreached any of his expectations. He tried to explain in layman's terms the accuracy of the magnetic field that had been achieved by the scientists at the facility. The seed contained an element not seen before, it acted as a fifth element, stabilizing the process on which they had been working without much previous success. Edmund said he was looking forward to the demonstration the next day, it should prove to be very interesting.

Henry surveyed the carnage left by the three sprouts, after their wild party.

'We shall have to get someone in to clean up this mess,' smiled Henry, as he scraped some of the foam from the wall and flicked it at Edmund.

There was a knock at the door, Edmund opened it to find Professor Stiller who, after surveying the room, smiled and said.

'My, my, it looks like someone has had an accident.'

'Not someone, but some three,' said Henry. He put his hand on the shoulder of the Professor, who suddenly saw the three little ones, huddled in a large towel at the end of the bed.

'Perhaps there is something else you need to know,' said Henry, 'I shall explain over dinner.' Henry threw a small towel to each of the sprouts and instructed them to clean up the mess.

'I want it to be spotless for when I return,' he said sternly, trying to keep a straight face.

Henry beckoned to the door.

'Shall we, gentlemen, before something else happens?'

The three then set off downstairs to the dining room.

Professor Stiller explained that he had come up to inform them both that they should see some of the past experiments. They had video footage of some successes and failures he thought they might like to see after dinner.

'A sort of, it will be all right on the night compilation,' he said.

They all sat for dinner, the three were joined by a trusted colleague of Professor Stiller, Dr Henri Chanel from INRA.

Henry told them the story of the little ones and how they came to be, and of their attributes and recent antics.

He told of the distribution that had been set up with the Gypsies; of their destinations over the coming weeks, and how they would play a major role in distribution of the plants.

Professor Stiller and his colleague both had very strong views over the decline of the planet's eco system and were ready to give Henry their full support. They reassured Henry that what was spoken of at the table would go no further, and that he could rely on them.

Dr Chanel commented that he was sure there had been a news report on a strange occurrence of mass planting in his home country recently; it appeared to be connected to a group of Gypsy travellers. Reaching into his briefcase for his tablet he tapped away and suddenly exclaimed.

'Here it is.'

He read the report from the screen:

... After an annual Country fete in the Bordeaux region, an unexplainable phenomenon occurred.

Local food and drinks producers had been displaying their wares. Livestock and rare breeds were being shown together with a range of country crafts which were being demonstrated by locals, and a visiting band of Gypsy folk.

When workers arrived the following morning to clear away the stands and marquees, they could not gain entry to the event because of a sudden appearance of a jungle. It was so dense; it had covered the whole area where the event had taken place. Special equipment was called in, but the plants proved too much for the machinery to deal with, and it was decided that the area would be left for the pleasure of the local community.

Henry smiled as he imagined Shelta dancing with the little ones all around the venue, at midnight; she did enjoy the night, he recalled.

The Gypsies would have camped quite close to the fete and would have been on their way in the very early hours.

Although there was no inference of a connection with the Gypsies, Henry and Edmund knew that there could only be one reason for the abundance of plants.

The four of them talked well into the night, a bond was forming with them, a friendship, based on a common interest shared by them all, which increased as the evening went on.

When they eventually decided to turn in, Henry thanked his hosts for their hospitality and said he and Edmund were looking forward to the demonstration the next day.

Making their way upstairs to their rooms, Henry was a little hesitant to open the door, wondering what he might find.

Bidding Edmund goodnight, he opened the door and entered; the room was polished to sparkling, not a soap sud in sight. The three sprouts were curled up in the towels they had used and were asleep in front of the TV.

Henry breathed a sigh of relief and turning off the TV, he settled down for the night.

The morning arrived with the usual intense heat that had survived for the past weeks.

Henry and Edmund made their way down to the breakfast room. Comments on the need for rain rang out from everyone in the breakfast queue, as the procession made its way along to the servery.

There were a good number of experts present to see the demonstration requested by Henry. The dining room was full to overflowing.

'Good morning,' came a voice from within the throng.

Professor Stiller pointed to a table by the window, which had been reserved for them both, and he would like them to join him.

Eventually, with breakfast well under way, both Henry and Edmund found themselves in the company of Professor Stiller, Dr Chanel and two female associates, who worked at the institute.

The excitement of the impending demonstration was electric, the topic of conversation had progressed from rain to a higher level.

The research facility had put up a viewing platform, capable of catching the whole spectacle; it was tiered, with seating for around fifty guests.

The area for the experiment would cover the size of a football pitch, and the information sheet that had been handed out explained the programme of events.

In summary, a drone with an array of technical equipment would rise to around five hundred feet, a magnetic field would then be generated which would control the shape and dispersal of a cloud of water vapour.

It was hoped that the letter H would be created in the centre of the target area. A further experiment using a specially treated cereal crop seed would then be launched into the atmosphere, where the same process would take place. Then there would be a final test of Lord Henry's offering to determine if this process could offer the same result.

Then, with everyone ready and the experiment due to start, Henry took his seat, and shook Professor Stiller's hand, who gave a sharp intake of breath at what he saw.

Henry had with him, on each shoulder, two of the little ones, the other was happily placed with Edmund.

Henry put his finger to his lips and whispered to him.

'I had to bring them with me. After last night, I thought best keep them close, and they cannot get into trouble.'

The Professor shook his head. Almost everything he had seen in the last twenty-four hours had been way off the scale, no science he knew explained what he had seen.

Continuing with the proceedings, Professor Stiller gave the order to commence.

On the back of a flatbed lorry at the edge of a field, there was mounted a rather large four-propeller drone with a considerable amount of equipment attached. It was positioned behind the target area which had been marked out using fluorescent tape.

A voice crackled over a tannoy and began to explain the proceedings while the drone rose to its destined altitude.

'When the drone reaches five hundred feet the magnetic field has an operating radius of two hundred feet. The higher it goes the wider the target radius, but the more dilute the cover. For this experiment we have decided five hundred feet would suffice,' said the voice over the tannoy.

The ground in the centre of the field had been dusted with a fine dry material to show any effects.

A high-pressure jet of water vapour was blasted into the air from a ring of pipes, it rose into the air, blotting out the sight of the drone.

Suddenly the air seemed to take on a solid form and descended onto the dusty area, where a huge letter H appeared. The water vapour had been concentrated into a dense mist; the splashdown of the letter H caught out a few of those who were a little close, probably a welcome drenching.

There was a cheer and applause from the spectators as the tannoy announced a successful result.

Henry turned to Edmund who had a worried look on his face. He told Henry that the little one he was watching seemed to be affected by the experiment. Henry agreed that something didn't quite feel right with his two, either, they seemed to shudder, something he had not experienced before. Henry suggested that he should take charge of the three, while the next demonstration was under way.

So, folding his arms he embraced the three little ones, and keeping a tight grip on them, he awaited the next experiment.

The next experiment involved the launching of a mortar containing specially prepared barley seed; it was designed to release its cargo at three hundred feet.

The mortar, already positioned at the edge of the field was given a countdown, and at zero it fired. The desired outcome was achieved, it successfully released its payload, and the drone took over.

Henry found it difficult to hold onto the little ones, as the distinct shape of the letter H descended onto the target area. When it was over, there was another round of applause and the little ones calmed down.

There was a definite area of seed within the dampened letter H on the field.

Edmund offered a reason why the little ones had been affected; the magnetic field may affect them more. Henry examined them, they all seemed to be in a state of subdued excitement, his very words of enquiry seemed to spark an increase in activity amongst them.

By now, arrangements were in place for the final experiment containing Henry's contribution of the night flower seed. Henry was asked if he would like to be involved and release the seed on the field.

With everything that was at stake Henry could hardly refuse the honour. He passed the little ones to Edmund and told him to hold them tight; this was the last experiment, and he was sure that all would be fine.

Henry made his way to the field, took possession of the container with the seed, and held it up high. Having announced the final experiment of the day the tannoy began the countdown.

On zero, Henry opened the container, the seed did not fail to perform, a cloud resembling the aurora borealis crept skywards. The magnetic field did its job, grabbing the seed in mid-air it redistributed the spectacle into a large H.

Edmund, at this moment, was having difficulty trying to keep his feet on the ground. The little ones were in a state of extreme excitement and were being pulled skywards.

Holding the little ones as tight as he could, he found himself some four feet off the ground. He was starting to bump into everything and everyone around him and, unable to hold onto the sprouts, he let them go.

He tumbled down, knocking over several spectators, while the sprouts shot skywards towards the seed. Henry witnessing all that had happened, tried to reach Professor Stiller and call a halt to the experiment. But it was too late. The seed had successfully been transferred to the target area in the shape of the letter H.

The experiment had been more successful than anyone had imagined. The little ones were right in the middle, dancing around in a state of advanced merriment. They too had been transported with the seed; they were of the same genetic make-up after all.

Then it started. The seed grew into an H-shaped field almost immediately, vines and creepers grew, exotic plants and trees shot up, growing faster than ever before.

The little ones began to dance around the field, creating a trail of vegetation, not just confined to the letter H, foliage erupted wherever they went. Henry ran onto the field, scooped up the little ones and attempted to calm them down.

The visiting scientists looked on in disbelief, while Professor Stiller took the microphone and attempted to reassure everyone that everything was under control. He believed that the magnetic field might have been a little too strong and may need recalibrating for the final experiment.

He suggested that everyone should return to the conference room to evaluate the afternoon's successful trials. Edmund ran over to meet Henry.

'I think we may have some explaining to do,' said Edmund with a smile. 'Are the little ones all right?'

Henry re-assured him that they were fine.

'But what about you?' Henry asked. 'When I saw you starting to levitate, I wondered where you were going. You certainly held onto the sprouts. Perhaps for a little longer than you intended.'

Henry looked down at the three small faces with their big bright green eyes looking back at him. Unable to contain himself, and with the vision of Edmund still firmly in his mind, he had to laugh.

More a laugh of relief.

'Well Edmund, you have had your first flying lesson.'

Edmund was analysing the experiment in his head; he said he found the strength of the magnetic field stronger than he had ever thought possible.

'I shall bring a parachute next time,' said Edmund.

As they re-joined the group, on their way back to the conference hall, they were approached by many of them with questions. The speed of growth from Henry's seed being the centre of attention.

The little ones had now calmed down enough to be left in the room. Henry gave them instructions to be good and returned downstairs.

The day's events had gone well, even with its surprises.

It was agreed after discussion, that there would need to be further tests. Everyone who had witnessed the trials of the new technology that day was sworn to secrecy.

Henry agreed to explain everything to them on his return. He had been impressed with the research at the facility and knew that it could play a vital role in the future.

The following morning, with everything packed, Henry and Edmund bade goodbye to certain dignitaries. Having explained his appointment in London to them, he vowed to return as soon as possible to continue trials with the magnetic generator.

Then, climbing into the Bentley, they drove up the drive and out onto the lane.

Chapter 17

With the little ones safely ensconced in the back seat, and settled into their entertainment, a course was plotted for London on the sat nav.

'I'm wondering what delights the sprouts have in store for us in the big city. Do you think you will be able to cope with them, while I go through the motions in the House?' said Henry.

Edmund said they were becoming more visible by the day; his close contact with them helped. Having them ride his shoulder was the best, he could almost see through their eyes, a very strange experience.

Henry agreed that the bond created with the little ones was something quite unique. Edmund confirmed his confidence in being able to look after them. He said that having experienced recent happenings, he felt he could now cope with anything.

'That's settled then, we are not going to send them by Royal Mail back to the Manor.'

Henry laughed at the thought of packaging them up in brown paper and excused himself for even thinking such a thing.

They soon came out of the countryside, and the big city loomed before them; they crossed over the M25 and entered the inner sanctum of concrete towers and tightly packed buildings.

Henry looked on with amazement at the increased size of the city, the almost unbalanced shape of towering buildings racing to the clouds.

Then the traffic slowed to London's average speed of five miles an hour.

'Where do all these vehicles come from?' asked Henry.

It was stop start, the noxious regurgitation from internal combustion engines made their eyes smart, and throats sore.

Turning to check on the little ones, he noticed a distinct change in their colouring. Instead of the cheerful bright green, they were now a dark olive, with drooping eyes, a really sad spectacle.

Edmund decided to put the roof up and with the press of a button, silence and clean air was resumed.

It was slow going through the streets of London. Edmund had booked a hotel a few days earlier, close to the House of Lords and within walking distance. The onboard sat nav worked its miracle and guided them through the inner-city chaos.

Pulling up outside the hotel, a uniformed valet came to greet them. Following him was a young lad, equally smart, with a trolley for their luggage.

Edmund popped the boot, and their luggage, albeit a small amount, was loaded onto the trolley.

Leaning into the back of the car, Henry scooped up the dozing sprouts, who were looking a lot better and placed them on top of the luggage.

'Stay there and enjoy the ride,' he whispered.

Edmund passed the car keys to the valet, and they followed the young lad into the lobby of the hotel to check in.

The young lady behind the desk greeted them, and on signing the register they were escorted to their rooms.

Henry kept fairly close to the wheeled conveyance on which the little ones sat, just in case; by now they were fully recovered and beginning to act in their usual manner.

Having managed to reach the room without incident, Henry put the TV on and gave the sprouts the remote. Instructing them to be good while he went with Edmund to inspect the restaurant, he said he would only be a few minutes.

Henry expressed a wish to visit The Globe Theatre, it was somewhere he had been with his mother and father as a boy. Henry and Edmund agreed to have lunch and then take a trip by taxi to visit his boyhood memory.

'We shall have to take the sprouts with us,' said Henry.

'We don't want a recurrence of last time, do we?'

Edmund said he had an idea on how to deal with the transport of the little ones; he was going to purchase something that might help and would return shortly.

Henry returned to his room, the little ones were happily sitting watching TV, having now mastered the intricacies of the remote control.

He explored the room and en suite; he filled the bath with two inches of water for the little ones and continued to explore the glass panelled balcony with its view. He could see the Palace of Westminster, and a large green area running alongside the river.

His thoughts were to perhaps visit this small park and let the sprouts have some free time, supervised of course.

He sat at the small bistro table laid out very professionally for four people. He poured himself a glass of water from the decanter and his mind wandered back to his first visit to London all those years ago.

He was eight years old and was accompanying his mother and father on a trip to London to see a play. It was his first trip out with his parents, he remembered that his father was excited at the prospect of attending this showing of a new play. It was about the same time of year too.

They had travelled down to stay with friends, who had a town house nearby. They went to see the play that evening; he remembered it was a packed audience with people standing outside to hear some of the performance.

The costumes of the actors were all bright colours, and Henry found it positively magical. They all returned to their friend's house for supper; they were staying for two days to see the sights, plus his father had some business to attend to.

It was the following day, when they heard the news that the theatre they had attended had burnt to the ground. His parents were thankful no one was hurt and grateful that they had seen the play when they did.

The visit to the site would be a nostalgia trip for Henry; it was a memory of his parents which was very clear in his mind.

Henry was brought back to earth by a knocking on his door. Edmund had returned, earlier than expected, with his purchase, a man bag.

'Look, it's perfect, large enough for them to hide in and with a compartment for them all to stand in and see the sights.'

Edmund seemed very pleased with his purchase.

Henry proceeded to try it out; calling to the sprouts to enter their new transport, he bundled them in. Adjusting the strap for his head and shoulder, the bag worked a treat, the little ones could look out, or slide down and disappear. Henry congratulated Edmund on his ingenuity and looked in the mirror for confirmation.

‘Man-bag?’ said Henry.

The terminology seemed to baffle Henry, not really understanding which way the media had gone with the English language, of late.

Putting the sprout carrier on the bed, Henry explained to them what the plan was, and he would be back shortly for them.

Henry and Edmund left them watching TV and went off to the restaurant. Over lunch Henry told Edmund of his reason for wanting to visit the theatre, and they also made plans for the next day, when Henry would take up his seat in the house.

When lunch was concluded, Henry ordered a taxi and went up to collect the little ones in the travelling man-bag.

He met Edmund in the lobby and they both went out to the hotel’s taxi, a comfortable black Mercedes.

Having given instructions to the driver they set off for the theatre. Henry could not get over the shape of some of the buildings that punctuated the London skyline.

Edmund gave a brief commentary on some, giving details of not only what was above ground, but projects below, also.

On arrival at the venue, they told the driver that they would walk back and take in some of the sights.

Edmund had planned a route along the river, crossing over to take in as much green space as possible.

Thanking the driver for his service they proceeded to the theatre. They were just in time to take the last tour, and Henry, having read the leaflets and listened to the commentary, realized it was not the original.

Wanting to see where he had been as a boy, they wandered along the bank. It was an impressive reconstruction, just as he remembered it, but he was not impressed by the original site.

Putting himself in the hands of his fellow navigator, Henry, with his bag of sprouts, he took in the remaining sights. Crossing over the river on a large footbridge, they continued along the riverside path with its green spaces and bistro bars.

It was approaching early evening; the restaurants and bistros were filling up with the night’s clientele.

They decided to stop at a rather nice little tapas bar, Henry liked his Spanish – an influence from his mother.

They did not have far to go to the hotel, it was just a half-mile along the river and through a park, where Henry promised to let the sprouts have a wander.

They sat chatting about the day's events, watching the illuminated riverboats go about their business.

Henry talked about the possible influence he might be able to exert on the policy makers within the House when his Lordship materialised.

Having had their fill of nice bites and a decent bottle of wine, they got up to leave. Nearly forgetting his man-bag, Henry turned back to collect it from by his chair.

'Can't let this precious cargo get lost, can I?' said Henry.

He was perhaps a little tipsy and was overheard by a couple of other diners, who turned to watch him leave.

They both made their way along the path towards a small park alongside the river. Within ten minutes they were in the tree-lined recreation area, with benches, a bandstand and nicely trimmed hedges.

Henry lifted the bag from his shoulder and, looking down at the sprouts in their travel bag, asked them if they would like to come out for a while, but no hide and seek.

Suddenly, from out of the bushes, a man appeared, there was something glinting in his hand, it was a knife.

'I'll take that precious cargo in the bag,' he said, wielding his knife around in a circular motion.

He grabbed the bag, and before either of them could comprehend what was happening, the man ran off.

The three little ones were in the bag. They had been kidnapped. Henry and Edmund began to chase after the man in the direction he had fled.

Not really expert runners, they soon slowed down to a brisk walk. The path through the park turned into a series of footpaths which led onto adjoining roads. The riverside path continued to wind its way around properties on the river's edge, never allowing a straight line of sight. They had lost sight of the man, there was no way of knowing which way he had gone.

He had disappeared into the night.

Henry wondered what he would do with the bag when he found there was nothing but invisible creatures inside.

Edmund told him that he had filled in the name tag inside the bag, the shop assistant had recommended he do so. If Henry's address was found inside, there was a good chance it might be returned. They continued back towards the hotel, looking in rubbish bins and bushes in the hope they might find it.

What they did not know, was that the man who had snatched the bag had run along the embankment towards the Houses of Parliament. He had stopped under a bridge to inspect his prize, and on opening the bag, could see nothing. He shone his mobile phone torch into the pockets, but the little ones were hiding. He could not see them.

Dejected and angry, the man threw the bag into the river, made his way onto the bridge, and was gone.

The little ones, by now, were floating down the river, hanging onto the man-bag, and every time they touched the riverbed in the shallows, something began to grow.

They bobbed up and down for some distance, and the three of them together created a powerful planting force. Many trees began to emerge from the water, from Westminster Bridge and downstream, just twenty yards from the Palace of Westminster, all the way past Victoria Tower Gardens. It was not until the little ones bumped into a jetty that they emerged from the river.

The trees were Mangroves, they started to grow at a fast pace, very visible from the bridge and were soon attracting the media. Henry and Edmund were only twenty minutes behind, they entered onto Westminster Bridge to see a crowd looking over into the river.

Curious to know what was happening, they made their way to the parapet and looked over. They looked at each other and laughed.

'They seem to be all right, wherever they are,' said Henry.

There in front of them was a line of Mangrove trees, some fifty feet tall, stretching nearly half a mile alongside the Houses of Parliament, and beyond.

These were monsters, almost prehistoric, huge-star shaped columns sat on spider-like roots. Their canopies stretched over the river and the buildings adjacent, while flashes from onlookers' cameras made them look almost animated.

'Those are some serious trees,' commented Edmund.

He was amazed that the little ones could produce such enormous specimens, and so quickly.

'It is the three together that triplicate the power, their minds act as one, and because they are all in the same situation, they do the same things,' said Henry, having witnessed the power of the three in the past.

'I think we had better follow the line of trees and see if we can find them before they get swept out to sea.'

There was an air of concern in Henry's voice, it was only natural that he did not want to lose part of his new-found family.

Edmund recalled seeing some small rowing boats, tied up at the end of a pontoon that they had passed earlier. He suggested it might be best if they could search from the river, as they would stand a better chance of finding them.

Having both agreed, they backtracked to where a small pontoon was anchored on dolphins. It had a gate with a padlock to prevent access.

Edmund pulled out a wallet, in it were a selection of lock picks, and he proceeded to fiddle with the padlock.

'Misspent youth?' enquired Henry.

Edmund assured him that it was a recent hobby, one which he had found useful on occasion.

The padlock clicked open, and they both went through to the main gangway. Edmund closed the padlock, and looking at Henry, said, 'You can never tell who's about, can you?'

And with raised eyebrows and a shrug of his shoulders, Edmund began to inspect the boats.

They both chose a rather nicely varnished wooden rowing boat, which had two seating positions. Under the seats were two waterproof jackets with hoods.

Edmund suggested they wore them, as they were going to sail under the bridge with all the spectators. It was probably best not to be photographed by a hundred cameras, especially as one of them would be in the House of Lords the next day.

So, dressed to look like fishermen, they cast off and began their search down river.

As they came out on the other side of the bridge, there was a mad flurry of camera flashes. The oars then became part of the dancing stage of a discotheque. Edmund grinned at the image Henry made as he plunged the oars into the river.

'You look quite surreal in strobe light,' said Edmund, holding back a laugh.

They were now parallel with the trees, and heading downstream, they scanned the riverbank for any sign. They were now halfway along the line of Mangrove trees, and Edmund reckoned they were now out of range of the cameras on the bridge.

The boat suddenly stopped, snagged on something under the water, then began to rise, it was caught up on a tree root. It was lifted some six feet out of the water, and suddenly, like a lifeboat, slid back down into the water to continue on its way.

Edmund recommended a further distance be kept from the trees, as they still appeared to be growing. They were approaching the end of the line of trees. Henry decided to turn in closer to the bank. It was not quite dark, but twilight, which reduced the ability to see. The roots were beginning to be a big problem, they could not get very close to the bank, and the little ones, if they were there, could easily be missed. Henry could see that further downstream, there was a large pontoon where a passenger ferry was moored.

'I think we should make for that jetty; we can moor up and walk back upstream on the bank and look for them.'

Henry was afraid they might get permanently caught up in the ever-growing roots, and that would not help their situation.

Edmund agreed, and suggested they remove the very warm jackets, as he was beginning to melt.

Henry manoeuvred the boat further out into the channel to give a wider berth to the roots, then on clearing the line of trees, turned back on a heading to the jetty.

As they approached the pontoon, Henry asked Edmund if he could hear giggling.

Edmund had to admit that his hearing was not quite as good as it had been, but the closer they got he did acknowledge the sound of a scream and a splosh.

He was quite adamant it was a splosh and not a splash.

They pulled up on the opposite side of the pontoon to where the ferry was moored. There was the distinct sound of playful sprouts. Henry put his finger over his lips and beckoned to Edmund to silently follow him.

Climbing from their boat they tiptoed along the pontoon and boarded the ferry. They sneaked along the side and went up the steps to the bridge; they could hardly believe what they saw.

Believing they may have run out of steam, planting trees, the roof of the bridge was adorned in a crown of hanging flowers. The little ones had found the perfect launch site to jump off, and then, from the bridge roof onto the tightly covered life rafts that were tethered around the sides. Finding these to be the perfect trampoline, they would then be launched into the air to splosh down in the river. And with the boarding platform and steps up the side of the boat, they could return to do it all again.

It did seem a shame to bring their adventure to an end, but Henry, with a large clearing of the throat, attracted the attention of the three little party goers.

'Come on, you lot, we had better get out of here before the crowd with the cameras arrive.'

Crouching down, Henry held out his arms, which the little ones eagerly jumped into.

Edmund was already on his way to the exit, again, a gate that was locked. He knew this lock would defeat him, so he returned to the boat.

'We shall have to row the boat around the locked gate,' said Edmund, and helping Henry aboard, cast off and rowed to the bank.

There was a short section of jetty, before the locked gate, which allowed them to disembark, and reach the bank.

Leaving the boat securely moored, they all made their way along the riverside to a small public garden.

They had escaped just in time.

A large throng of people came along the riverbank, down to the ferry. They sat with the little ones, watching the increasing crowd congregate along the river, taking in the spectacle which was continuing to unfold.

It was time they made a hasty retreat; Edmund had established a path back to the hotel on his phone sat nav. It was saying the distance, if walking, would take eight minutes.

They exited the garden without being noticed. The route back was followed meticulously, and sure enough, on rounding the final corner, there was the hotel. Entering the lobby, the desk clerk waved and bid a good evening to his Lordship and the Professor.

Unseen were the three sprouts riding the shoulders of them both. Entering the lift, they breathed a sigh of relief, they had made it back, intact, and had managed to remain incognito.

It was 22:00, Edmund switched on the TV, where the news had just started. It referred to a newsflash, just in, of a massive growth of mangrove trees in the river Thames.

There was camera footage of not one, but three lines of trees stretching alongside the Houses of Parliament.

The reporter claimed that:

.. the growth has started to subside, and there has been no activity for nearly half an hour. Luckily, this phenomenon was unlikely to affect the daily routine of river traffic but would certainly cast a shadow over the House of Commons.

Henry's new mobile phone rang, it had been left on the bedside table.

Edmund picked it up.

'It's Jake, and there are five missed calls,' he said.

Edmund answered the call and greeted Jake, telling him that their day had been full of surprises.

He passed the phone to Henry, who explained the day's events.

Henry said that they were all ok, and not to believe everything he heard on TV; finishing the call, Edmund had to remind him how to hang up.

Edmund gestured to Henry to look over at the three sprouts, they were all fast asleep on the pillows of the sofa in the corner of the room.

'I need a drink,' said Henry, and suggested a short visit to the bar downstairs.

Edmund agreed that a quick one was well deserved.

They felt confident that the little ones were well and truly shattered. To produce those size trees and continue to play, was nothing short of amazing.

'They are getting stronger,' said Henry.

Reminiscing on some of the sprouts' previous escapades, they would be out for the count almost immediately, and for a day or two.

They walked through the lobby to the lounge bar. There was no music, just the gentle sound of running water, from a beautifully planted feature along the one wall.

They chose comfortable leather armchairs adjacent to the creation and immediately a waiter came to take their order.

There were several other people in the lounge, and if one tuned one's ears, one could hear their conversations.

They revolved around the sudden appearance of the huge trees in the river Thames.

Henry and Edmund sat people watching, and earwigging, with a delightful bottle of Rioja, for a good hour.

They would not need to listen to news on the media, they had it all, across the room of the lounge. It was a very comfortable atmosphere and having listened to various arguments on how and why these trees had arrived, and having made short work of a second bottle, Henry and Edmund bade the waiter and everyone within the lounge, a goodnight.

On their way back to their rooms they made rudimentary plans for the following day. Henry's agenda was set in stone – however, Edmund's agenda was open to the imagination. He could do whatever he liked, as long as he did not draw attention to himself, and the sprouts.

Edmund confessed that the evening had made him a little more adventurous regarding the three little ones.

First on the agenda would be to obtain a replacement man-bag and bidding each other goodnight they made their way to their rooms.

The morning came round in the blink of a dream. Henry was summoned to the lobby; a car had been sent to take him to the House.

There was little time to talk with Edmund about his plans for the day, but Henry said he was getting better with his mobile phone thingy and would keep Edmund informed throughout the day.

While Henry was whisked off to be enrolled in an age-old tradition, Edmund, having looked in on the little ones, decided he had time to partake of breakfast.

His breakfast was interrupted by a waiter, who brought Edmund a package; he opened it to find the man-bag.

Some enthusiastic finder had contacted the Manor and had been given the address of the hotel, and at great expense, had travelled across London, to return it.

No name was given. The waiter, who apologised for it still being damp, admitted they had tried to dry it in the kitchen.

Thanking the young lad for his efforts, Edmund graciously accepted the item, and returned to Henry's room.

The three little ones were involved in the morning CBB channel.

On showing them the retrieved sprout carrier, they all jumped in, expecting another adventure. That was easy, thought Edmund, expecting a lack of enthusiasm.

Open spaces were the order of the day. St James Park was somewhere Edmund had never been.

He decided he would walk to the park and check on the mangrove trees on the way.

Putting the bag over his shoulder, Edmund descended to the lobby, and double checking that the little ones were still with him, he set off to begin the day's adventure.

Edmund had always been a workaholic, keen to please his employers, and had never found time to enjoy his own life. It was a refreshing change to work for Henry – there was a freedom – and he felt obliged to return the trust and loyalty he had shown him.

Having got his early-morning anxieties out of the way, he concentrated on the task in hand, which was to look after, and protect the little ones.

He thanked the doorman as he opened the door for him, and bidding him a good day, set off.

The riverbank was not far; the trees could now be seen in all their splendour. Crowds lined the riverbank, and the bridge; they had all come to see this marvel of nature.

Edmund looked down at the three of them, all gazing skywards at the canopy.

'Very impressive,' said Edmund. 'I do believe they have stopped spreading across the river.'

Edmund counted around forty trees in the first line, each had produced two others, like Russian Cossack dancers with arms locked.

One hundred and twenty trees marched down the river at fairly staggered intervals, finishing just before the ferry, where he and Henry had found them.

Leaving the riverbank, Edmund made his way towards the park. His thoughts turned to the little ones, and he realised that they were becoming more visible to him. Even their chatter and laughter seemed to be more audible.

On reaching the park, Edmund decided he would explore in a figure of eight, with a final return across the bridge.

He stopped to admire a lone *Echium*, eight-foot-tall, if it were an inch, a dinosaur triffid.

As there were few people in the park, all at the river, possibly, he mused. He thought it might be safe to let the little ones out for a while.

'Stay close, you don't want to get lost again.'

With a little hesitation he leaned down and placed the bag on the ground.

The three inseparables wandered onto the grass and walked alongside Edmund for some distance, until they found a flower bed. It was here that they played hide and seek.

Edmund sat on a bench and watched the plant movement as the little ones ran through.

Suddenly there was a movement vertically, lots of triffids began to emerge from within, and they grew higher and higher.

Edmund could only assume that they had picked up on his liking of the plant. He let out an astonished laugh, and then looked around to see if anyone had heard him.

This, he did find amusing, and when the little ones emerged from the undergrowth, they bowed to which Edmund reciprocated with applause.

It was just at that moment, that a woman who was taking her funny looking poodle hybrid, for a walk, gave Edmund a strange look, and quickened her pace.

'Ok you lot, shall we move on?'

Edmund's route took them around the outside of the park, occasionally taking a path alongside the lake.

Edmund's concern was that they would jump in and start a new mangrove forest, but they seemed quite happy playing follow the leader.

Not only was it follow the leader, but a version of do as I do. With a jump or a stamp of the foot a new plant appeared; as a result, there were circles and trails of flowering blooms wherever they had walked.

They approached a bench, which had been set in a position at the top of a bank, with fine views over the lake.

It was now the residence of a person with their home in a shopping trolley. Sitting on the bench was a rather dishevelled person, drinking from a brown paper bag.

The little ones' game took them around and around this homely spot; subsequently the flowers and blooms that appeared, totally encircled the person on the bench.

Looking on in disbelief, they then examined the contents of the brown bag, and put it aside.

Edmund found the whole thing extremely amusing.

The plants around the park bench grew to a height that totally obscured it, a fence of colour.

Leaving the poor person to deal with their surroundings, they then set off for the bridge.

Bending down, Edmund offered the man-bag to the little ones, who climbed in and took in the scenery as Edmund continued on his route.

He came within sight of Buckingham Palace and then along the mall, until a small refreshment kiosk beckoned him. Purchasing a fancy pastry and some bottled water, he retired to a shady spot on the grass, away from the eatery.

Giving the little ones a drenching, they sat with him; they had been a delight to take to the park.

Huddled together they seemed to be busying themselves with something, Edmund lay back on the grass and relaxed for a moment.

Feeling a gentle pressure on his wrist, he looked down to find the little ones; they had placed on his wrist a bangle made of clover and daisy-root.

All three held his hand as the bangle fixed itself to his wrist. He could hear quite plainly their words, they thanked him for being Henry's friend, and that he was now their friend.

Edmund was quite overcome with this small interlude and thanked them back.

Rising to his feet, he ordered them into the man bag, and continued across the now busy park bridge.

Then, where it became less crowded, he let them wander in and out of flower beds, across neatly cut lawns and in and out of the bushes.

He believed that a corner had been turned in his life; he was touched to be accepted by the little ones, and watching them produce, felt that the park could only benefit.

It was now late afternoon, Edmund had completed his tour, the day had been excellent, and it was now time to return to the hotel.

Henry had managed a text, to say that he too, was on his way back to the hotel.

Chapter 18

Edmund and Henry arrived in the lobby around the same time as each other, both had a story they were bursting to tell.

They agreed to take coffee in the lounge, but first Edmund wanted to thank the staff for the effort they had made over the man-bag, and its return. He was standing at the reception awaiting his turn, when a small child noticed the three little ones in the bag.

The mother, who was in front of him talking to the receptionist, was holding the toddler, of around two years, on her hip.

The little ones, always keen for attention, started swaying in sync, waving their arms, and the toddler reciprocated. The mother turned to see what all the commotion was, but of course there was just Edmund, who smiled.

The toddler was now fixated on the sprouts, and was swaying and waving, while the mother could see nothing, Edmund just raised his eyebrows and shrugged his shoulders.

He did eventually get to thank the staff but realized that these three attention seekers were going to require a special sort of management.

Edmund joined Henry in the coffee lounge; he told him of the episode at the reception and continued to give him a blow-by-blow description of the day's events.

Henry listened patiently, a trait he had mastered through the course of his history.

Eventually, an excited Edmund apologized for babbling on and asked Henry how his day had been.

'I see you have been bangled,' said Henry and then he began to recount his day's events.

In the House, the main topic of conversation was, of course, the sudden appearance of the trees along the river.

Most of the morning had been taken up in the restaurant at the side of the river, where he was introduced to everyone as they arrived for the afternoon's sitting.

One person in particular attached himself to Henry, Lord Archibald Dartington-Smythe. He made a comment which Henry was not expecting. He referred to the sudden appearance of trees, and at having witnessed something like it in his youth.

He told Henry his story.

When he was a young boy, his father had taken him to see his grandfather in India, and on their arrival his grandfather was suddenly taken ill. Archie had accompanied his father on a mission to find medicine in a remote village. The search took them deep into the interior looking for a religious order, one that worshipped a particular flower.

Now this, to Henry, had set alarm bells ringing.

Archie continued to explain that during this ceremony plants had erupted from bare earth. An elder used what looked like dolls, in a ritual dance. Henry said Archie's memory of the incident, which had also been witnessed by his father, was spoken about on many occasions, but people seemed to dismiss it as just a party story.

Henry felt sure there was a connection to the night flower.

'I have arranged for the three of us to meet up and have dinner at the House, in the restaurant alongside the river, and I would like to take the sprouts.

What do you think?' said Henry excitedly.

Edmund confessed that the little ones did seem to benefit and learn quickly when taken out.

He admitted that this person's account of his childhood should be investigated, and Edmund agreed.

Henry was sure that if Archie saw the sprouts, he might recognize them as the dolls in the ceremony. He might also be a very useful ally, not just in the House, but in their quest, as he had similar ideals.

Henry had booked a table for seven-thirty, a taxi was ordered for seven, and they both retired to their rooms to change.

They met back down in the lobby, just in time to be told that their taxi had arrived.

With the little ones safely back in their travel bag, they went out to meet the taxi.

On their way, Henry filled in a few gaps he had missed in the coffee lounge:

Archie was very much into wine, and in whichever country he produced wine, there was an element of agriculture. He specialized in the more obscure crops which sell to high-end restaurants all over the world. This subsidised his passion for wildlife, for on all his farms, there was a large portion planted with indigenous trees and wildflower.

He was also involved in the conservation work of each of these countries, donating to, and helping to run, the charitable foundations responsible for replanting some of the worst areas of deforestation.

The restaurant was not far, and the taxi journey was over in the blink of an eye.

Arranging for the driver to pick them up later, they thanked him and went off towards the ornate entrance of the restaurant.

They were greeted immediately by the maître d', who showed them to a table in the gallery adjacent to the river.

Shortly after, they were joined by Archie. He had been chatting with others at the bar and had seen them arrive.

The conversation immediately turned to the trees outside; Archie was in awe of them. He said he would love to have been a fly on the wall that evening, to witness whatever created them. He summarised what he had told Henry earlier, of his boyhood experience, for the benefit of Edmund.

Henry was keen to get some sort of description of what the dolls looked like; he probed Archie for answers. It appeared that Archie remembered them as being green, almost luminescent.

There were two of them, the medicine man held one in each hand, whilst carrying out a ritual dance.

He would whisper to each, words which Archie could not hear. He then placed them on the ground, and for a moment Archie swore he saw them dance.

Suddenly the ground moved, bushes began to grow.

The medicine man scooped up the dolls and disappeared into a hut. Archie said he never saw them again.

Henry looked at Edmund, who had the bag still across his shoulder.

'Archie, as you know, I too have a passion for the planet and its future. What I am about to show you must be kept secret, not a word to anyone; give me your hand,' said Henry.

Edmund, raising the bag into view, and allowing it to rest on the table, enabled the little ones to climb out and show themselves.

They stood there, and as Archie's eyes became accustomed to the vision, he gasped in disbelief.

'Meet the tree planters,' said Henry.

Edmund laughed. 'Was that a pun?' he enquired.

Henry, unsure of the joke, said he called the three, his little sprouts, others called them the little ones, but no-one had actually given them names.

Archie said, with relief, that now he knew they were real and not just a party story.

Edmund whispered to them to produce something small in the centre of table.

The three little ones huddled together, heads down, shoulder to shoulder as if in conference. Then all of a sudden, they stamped a foot and out of the table sprang a crimson rose with the most gorgeous scent.

Archie leaned over to touch it, it was firmly planted, and peering under the table he could see its roots coming through.

'This is amazing, what you could achieve with these three is nothing short of magical,' said Archie.

Henry told him that that was just part of it, he would like him to visit the Manor, to be properly introduced to the whole scheme.

They were shown to their table in the restaurant, and they dined on a fine meal.

They spent the evening really introducing themselves, giving each other an insight into their lives, getting to know one another.

They departed as friends, and Archie promised to visit the Manor as soon as he could. He had to conclude some business at his farms in Venezuela and hoped to be there within a fortnight.

A good night was had by all.

The taxi came to take them both back to the hotel; Henry had to take one final look at the mangroves he was so impressed with.

Thanking the driver, they then bid each other a goodnight and retired to their rooms for a well-earned rest; it had been a busy day.

Henry left the sprouts in their travel bag as they looked so comfy, then crashed and burned on the king-size bed.

He was awakened in the morning by a circus act. The three sprouts were doing the trampoline thing on the bed.

It was five a.m., and Henry was a little bleary. He pulled the quilt over his head but was accosted by three sprouts pulling it back off him.

It turned into a battle – the sprouts would not give in, and Henry was not ready to get up.

Needless to say, the sprouts won.

Dragging Henry's quilt across the room they then proceeded to jump up and down on him.

He gave up.

Putting them in the man-bag, he took them round to Edmund's room, and pretending he had been locked out, asked a cleaner to open the door for him.

He threw the bag of sprouts in and returned to his bed, managing to sleep for another two hours before being woken by the hammering on his door.

Henry rose and opened the door to find Edmund with the three sprouts hanging off his person.

'I suppose you found that amusing?' said Edmund.

'They love you,' said Henry.

Showered, breakfasted and then checking out, Henry and Edmund, with the bag of trouble, stepped out of the lobby.

Their car had been brought round for them by the valet, luggage was loaded in the boot and thanking the doorman with a tip, they set off on the journey home.

The three little ones had mastered the remote controls of quite a few modern appliances and were being happily entertained by the built in TVs.

Henry kept the roof up until the city was behind them, and the rural countryside began to appear.

'I'm keen to get back and see how the Manor is progressing. We can contact Professor Stiller at Magnatek later,' said Henry.

He had intended to pay him a visit on his return from London but had decided to invite him up to the Manor instead.

The trip back to the Manor would take them another two hours. Still having to take the scenic route, Henry decided they should stop for coffee on the way.

Henry had become so proficient in his driving ability that Edmund told him he would pass his driving test easily. He would have to make his application on their return.

They stopped at the same inn, with its fish menu, and choosing a place down by the river, they allowed the sprouts a little freedom.

The water was a magnet for the three little ones, starting by the bank and then becoming more adventurous.

Soon, they were ducking and diving mid-stream. Henry went over to the bank, showing his consternation.

'Stay close to the bank, and no mangroves!' he shouted.

To his utter amazement the sprouts did as they were told.

Walking back to their table, Henry smugly said, 'Authority, that's all that's needed.'

Their food arrived and they took little more notice of the sprouts until they had finished.

When they turned around to check on them, they found they had kept close to the bank, in fact they had planted the bank.

A large weeping willow had appeared, its dangling branches a positive circus act's dream, and they were using the branches to swing on.

They had purposely kept quiet to avoid detection; Henry and Edmund could only look on in disbelief.

'We are going to have to find something for them to do, and soon,' said Henry.

Edmund wandered over to where the sprouts were swinging, and holding up the opened travel bag, told them it was time to go.

With perfect precision, each of them swung out of the tree, and into the bag, a trapeze act in the making.

'Nicely caught, I think we should be on our way before anyone notices. I'll meet you by the car,' said Henry.

He went and paid the bill, looking back to see if anyone had noticed. He promptly exited to the car, and they were off.

‘Next stop home,’ and turning to the sprouts, he ordered, ‘no planting in the car, please, I’m becoming rather fond of it.’

The three little ones giggled and nodded in approval.

The roads got progressively narrower as they approached familiar territory. Recognizing various landmarks, Henry declared that they were nearly there. Sure enough, on rounding a bend in the lane, was the turning into the fields where the Gypsy camp was.

As he turned into Pear Tree Lane, there was a distinct confusion, the gate which provided the entrance to the Manor, had moved. Henry could have sworn it was further down, but here it was, not a hundred yards from the junction. Henry pulled up outside the closed gates, which were set off the road, just as he remembered.

All of a sudden, the gates opened, and Jake came walking towards the car, greeting them both.

‘What do you think? The gates are a pretty good copy of the originals, and I have set out the drive the same. Bob the bricky has done a tremendous job, even the mortar looks old. It just needs planting the same way and you won’t be able to tell the difference.’ Jake was starting to babble, he had so much to tell Henry.

‘Let’s chat at the house, we have lots to tell also,’ said Henry, reversing out and proceeding to the correct entrance of the Manor.

Parking outside the front door, Henry and Edmund were greeted by Ivy and Sandra. Jake had run from the other entrance, while MacTavish expressed his congratulations on them returning in one piece.

Henry wondered how they all knew they were coming. Edmund was waving his phone in his hand.

‘Technology, dear boy,’ he said with a grin.

Ivy noticed the mark on his phone-waving hand.

‘So, you’ve been bangled,’ she said with a smile.

The little ones were also glad to be home, their friend Fidgit was making rather a fuss of them.

‘We have water, electricity, a kitchen and provisions, the modern world has come to the Manor. Would Sir like tea on the patio?’ enquired MacTavish.

‘What a perfectly English idea,’ said Henry. ‘Then we shall take a tour of what has been achieved since we left.’

Henry could sense that Jake was itching to tell him of all that had happened.

The group settled on the patio, relating their experiences over the past days.

Jake told Henry that the new building was now complete and was being fitted out with all the equipment for the laboratories and tech workshops.

The house was nearly complete, some of the equipment was under test, and Edmund would be required to do the final calibrations.

All the greenhouses had been completed and were now in full production.

Ivy said that there had been no news from Moss, *Leber* or *Tabule*. Their sudden decision to go in search of displaced tribal members, and reconnect with them, had been impulsive.

'I have a feeling we shall hear something quite soon,' said Henry.

With refreshments over, Edmund made his excuses and left; he was very keen to get involved with the testing of all his equipment.

Accompanied by Ivy, Edmund went to visit the new laboratories, and could be heard laughing as he recounted his adventures in London to her.

Henry was quite happy to be guided around the completed work and have Jake and Sandra explain it all.

Henry, on examining the new entrance, was amazed at the detail and its exactness to the main gates.

'What you need to do now Jake, is get the sprouts to plant the drive, exactly the same as the other. I'm sure if you asked them nicely, they would oblige.'

Henry continued to inspect all aspects of the work; he praised the workmanship, which had been carried out meticulously.

They continued their tour of the estate and came across several workmen who were adding the final touches to projects. Henry chatted with them enthusiastically, feeding his curiosity, and increasing his knowledge of the modern day.

When they reached the greenhouses, Sandra took over, for this was her subject. They had installed a hydroponic system; Sandra explained the concept to Henry.

The new plants could only reproduce by layering in their native soil. She explained that *Leber* had been instructing her on the intricacies of growing and looking after the night flower.

This was one of the safety mechanisms he had designed into the plant when he first created it. The plant had to feel at home, and only he and a few trusted colleagues were privy to where the soil came from. This would prevent the night flower from being reproduced and sold commercially, although it did restrict the number that they themselves could produce, until now.

'*Leber* has helped to produce a clone of the mother plant, thirteen in total, one for each greenhouse, and the soil needed has now been incorporated, into the hydroponic system.' said Sandra.

Leading them to the end of the greenhouse, she introduced them to a larger specimen. She said they were expecting to produce new plants very soon.

'There will be four to six weeks before the new plants can be shipped out, and seed will be collected in between.

The little ones, produced at harvest, will play an important role in determining what grows when the seed is dispersed.

At the moment it is only the Council members who can manipulate the type of plants that will grow, the intention is to give the little ones more influence.

We are hoping to produce a new strain which will have more independence,' she said.

As they walked around the last greenhouse, close to the weir, Henry noticed a new structure close to the hedge.

'What's this then?' he asked.

Jake explained that as they relied on the river water for irrigation, if it were to dry up, then this would ensure a continuous water supply.

'A well has been drilled, and a water treatment system installed to provide water to the house and buildings,' said Jake.

Henry wandered inside. He said it was not like any well he remembered, with its tanks and cylinders and a panel of flashing lights.

On leaving the new well building, they were greeted outside by Chris Reynolds, the architect.

'Good afternoon, Henry, inspecting the works?' he said.

'You should be proud of young Jake, he has worked like a Trojan, and he has some great ideas. If I were starting up in business again, I'd take him on in an instant,' said Chris.

He explained to Henry that the well was Jake's idea. He knew that the water table would not be far underground, and close to the river. He also helped in the design of the new workshops and was adamant that the new entrance should be a replica of the old one.

'There's another well over by the new building, which Jake used his grandfather's divining rods to locate. The watering system in the greenhouses works on capillarity, no pumps.'

Chris continued to sing the praises of Jake's ingenuity, especially where water was involved.

'So that's why you built the Brownlow's Pond,' said Sandra with a knowing smile.

'Behave,' said Jake. 'It's not rocket science; this watering system has been about for years.'

He said it was not much different from the rills and culverts around the manor, which had fed water to areas for hundreds of years.

'You're very modest,' said Henry, suggesting an inspection of the inside of the new building before tea.

They made their way to the main entrance, which was central to the building; there were several large, raised planting areas, constructed at Sandra's request. These would be used to accommodate some experimental planting by the little ones.

Inside the lobby, there was a large stone trough, which would house a night flower.

Through the doors and past the reception was the corridor, running east to west, taking you from one end of the building to the other.

On either side were rooms small and large, all with external light, one of which had been allocated as the canteen.

Many were filled with unpacked furniture, desks, benches and boxes of electrical equipment with names no-one could pronounce, which Edmund and Ivy were busy unpacking.

Ascending the stairs to the first floor, the rooms were much larger, halls effectively, places where seminars and lectures could take place.

'I can't believe this has gone up so fast,' said Henry.

‘Steelwork, mezzanine and fancy insulated cladding,’ said Chris.

‘It really is a glorified barn, which is why we had little resistance from the planning department.’

They continued up the stairs to the top floor. This had been divided into many rooms: accommodation for visiting scholars, small and compact, each with en-suite.

‘You have twenty-five rooms each side, if they bunk up you can take a hundred students, a tight squeeze but possible,’ said Chris. ‘All the rooms came as a module, ten by fifteen foot, just a matter of lifting them into position before the roof went on, very quick.’

Henry turned to Chris and shook his hand.

‘You have done us proud,’ he said.

‘Couldn’t have been done without Jake, he is a logistics expert, you will be wise to keep him,’ said Chris.

Returning to the lobby they were greeted by MacTavish.

‘You have visitors, sir, they are awaiting you in the dining room.’

Henry again shook Chris’s hand and apologized for cutting their meeting short. He would see him over the course of the next few days, where finishing, and small problems would be ironed out.

Henry walked back to the house with MacTavish, leaving Jake and Sandra to finish their dealings with Chris.

When Henry arrived in the dining room, he knew by the sound of the voices who his visitors were.

Pushing open the double doors he greeted the travellers, Moss, *Leber*, *Tabule* and *Chonga*.

They had been on a fact-finding mission in the badly devastated part of the Amazon.

They had met displaced natives and witnessed at first hand the tyranny that had befallen them.

Logging companies were carrying out a mass exodus of vast areas, with the support of the Government.

Machinery, which had advanced over the years, was cutting faster, and transporting more efficiently.

Small areas were being cleared close together; this made access easy, eventually connecting like a large dot-to-dot puzzle. Then the area within would be cleared, four-hundred-year-old trees lost forever, and no replanting taking place.

What little soil was left would be farmed until it could sustain no more crops, then, they would move on to another location.

'These humans are raping the planet,' said *Leber*.

Moss commented that he had witnessed devastation and natural disasters but found it difficult to comprehend that man could effect such carnage.

They had been with *Chonga* to one area of some two thousand square miles, in Brazil, where there were stumps and red soil as far as the eye could see, in all directions.

'Henry, I am keen to hear of the progress your researchers have made,' said *Tabule*.

Taking Henry aside, he suggested they walk around the estate while they talked.

Leber was keen to find out the results of Sandra's work in the greenhouses; he had an idea that might increase the propagation process.

Chonga said he would meet him in the greenhouses shortly, he was going to stroll around the grounds for a while.

Moss had agreed to assist Edmund, more of a tutorial assistance, as Moss would be expected to operate the equipment now being installed in the house.

He was shortly to have a crash course on loading software onto Henry's systems.

Chapter 19

Leber, on finding Sandra with Jake and Chris, made his excuses to them both and whisked her off.

When Jake had finished his meeting with Chris, he returned to the house. He entered through the front door and wandered through the hall, he peered into the war room, checked the dining room, and came to rest in the conservatory.

There was no one about, except for Fidgit. He was upside down, on a rug, by the night flower.

Close by were the little ones, they were being cossetted by mother in the now dense foliage.

Jake sat down in a large comfortable armchair, which was almost absorbed by the twining tendrils. He stared in amazement at the size of the plant and took in its intoxicating scent.

After all the hectic work of the day, Jake reflected on how peaceful it was, total quietness reined.

Jake closed his eyes for a moment and was gone. He drifted into a deep sleep.

The night flower, sensing he was receptive, gently wound a new shoot around his fingers and wrist.

Jake began to dream, of streams and waterfalls and rivers that disappeared underground. He began to follow the water; it led to a vast subterranean lake, a reservoir within the earth. All around the lake small streams disappeared deeper into fissures within the rock, while small waterfalls fell from the sides to replace them.

Jake was now following the water along cracks no wider than his fingers; he had become the liquid he was observing, in order to see where it would go.

The distinct smell of damp earth surrounded him and when the ground became porous, he felt himself being sucked upwards. Root systems from above, vegetation, trees and the like, began to absorb his very being. He travelled along the hair-like root systems, set down to sustain the plants to which they belonged.

His journey took him along a busy motorway, two lanes coming and going, both of equal size, running parallel to one another.

A symbiotic interaction was taking place with other plants, as they each exchanged food offerings.

His journey continued; the channels were becoming wider, he passed insects which he recognised, all the size of elephants.

Up and up, he went until he came into bright sunlight, witnessing photosynthesis from the inside.

He had changed; he now carried sugars, and the water which had taken him on his journey, had become heavier and its odour had changed.

He travelled down the fine capillaries feeding a myriad of organisms on his way.

Shedding his heavy load, he escaped back into the deep fissures in the rock. Travelling at speed, he was unable to control his direction, but felt a type of comfort that he was in safe hands.

Jake could feel a distinct increase in temperature, evaporation was taking place as his journey took him to the desert.

He emerged from beneath the sand and changed from liquid to gas, rising high above the sands, until nightfall, when he descended and condensed as dew, back into the liquid he knew.

At every point in his travels the water took on a different fragrance.

He had now permeated deep under the desert, he was heavy with minerals washed from the rocks, as he sank.

Slowly rolling down the side of a stalactite, he dripped onto the floor of the cave to join a stream.

This took him along channels to a place where an upward force bubbled into an oasis: a busy place, with lots of daily activities, and as a result Jake found himself heading upwards again.

The change from liquid to gas happened so suddenly.

Drifting on winds high up, he eventually became part of a larger formation, a rain cloud. This had all manner of foreign objects whirling around inside, plastic bags, frogs, sand and insects of all shapes and sizes.

His experience of flying was one that he would not forget, as he effortlessly drifted across continents.

It was not until he could see the Manor and its surrounding countryside, that he felt himself falling. He braced himself as the ground got closer and closer and then – impact.

Jake woke with a start as he found himself on the floor in front of the chair.

He was still connected to the night flower but had slid off the chair in anticipation of his impending touchdown.

He got the distinct impression the night flower found the scene amusing, as it gently released its grip on Jake.

It was at that moment that Sandra and Ivy walked in to witness Jake sitting on the floor.

'Ok, anything we should know about?' smiled Sandra.

Climbing to his feet, Jake shook his head and said, 'I must have nodded off.' He continued to describe his dream to them both, and turning to the night flower, he acknowledged that there was a humorous side to his experience, and he gave a slight bow of the head. There was a ripple of laughter, even the night flower appeared to give a little shudder.

Edmund and Moss came down the stairs and joined the group. Jake was trying to explain the feeling of flying to Ivy and Sandra.

'Flying, who's been flying?' enquired Edmund, unable to avoid overhearing.

'Jake has been telling us of a dream he had,' said Ivy, and promised to tell Edmund all about it later.

Henry entered with *Tabule*, *Leber* and *Chonga*.

'I understand you have been on a journey Master Jake,' said *Tabule* knowingly. 'It may prove useful in the weeks ahead.'

They had agreed that the first major offensive to be undertaken would be an area known as the Amazon rain forest. Inviting them all into the war room, *Tabule* believed it was time to formulate a plan of campaign.

He accepted that the council would need to approve the action, and it would need to convene soon to discuss the matter.

Now that modern technology was available, it would be useful to understand how it could benefit the cause, and for the council to be briefed on its application.

'We have seen the devastation that *Chonga* has witnessed, for ourselves.

It is therefore our intention to coordinate a planting of this area of the Amazon. It will require a specific diversity of species to re-instate it to its former glory,' said *Tabule*.

He turned to Edmund and asked what this equipment could be used for, in their task.

This was the cue Edmund had been waiting for.

Rising to his feet, he began to explain how the equipment could benefit the revival of the area. The TV screens all around the walls could show images of the Earth's surface anywhere on the planet. Each of the fifty screens could be programmed to receive an image from any satellite, hundreds of miles up. The equipment could log onto transmissions which were being beamed back to Earth.

Edmund explained it was a simple method of intercepting the signal, deciphering the algorithm it used and using it to display the picture.

Keen to demonstrate, Edmund started to switch on banks of technical looking equipment. Different coloured lights danced across the front panels and white noise from the TV screens filled the room as the process began.

'Do we have any co-ordinates?' enquired Edmund.

'This is your area, my friend. You can direct Edmund and his magic boxes to the correct location,' said *Tabule*, giving the floor to *Chonga*.

Edmund was beginning to connect the many images from the Brazilian satellites.

The TV monitors on the walls were connecting together to form one huge picture of the country below.

Everyone's eyes were fixed on the image now appearing, getting sharper as each wave of information came in from a satellite.

Large tracts of scorched earth were becoming visible; you could even see the cut stumps of the once magnificent trees.

The river, silver like a mollusc trail, could be seen winding its way through this ex-forest.

Chonga spoke of the many fires that had burned for an eternity, taking away the once lush vegetation, and the villages of the tribes he had come to know.

He had no knowledge of coordinates but would recognize the area when he saw it.

He gave a brief description as he remembered it; it was a place where the river slowed down and became fat, it had turned into a great pool with an island in the middle.

It had been a safe place, worshipped by many tribes who had, for generations, fished and made their homes there.

Edmund zoomed into a spot on the river that resembled *Chonga's* description.

It appeared as a lagoon of some two miles in length, and where it spilled back into a river, there were several waterfalls.

The land had been washed away over millennia, forming a basin which had allowed the lake to form.

Now, it had no vegetation; the barren earth stretched for many miles.

As Edmund became more adept with the controls, he could zoom in and follow the shoreline, picking out the occasional small groups of disbanded villagers, by their campfires.

'These are the people who will not leave, they were the last forest dwellers we saw before we left.'

Chonga turned to *Tabule* and *Leber*, who agreed that they too, had witnessed the sorry plight of these people.

Edmund started to enter squares across the whole picture. As more and more filled the area, Edmund told them that each square represented the Salisbury plains effect.

Pressing a button to give a total, the figure that flashed across all the screens was sixty times the area, some two thousand four hundred square miles.

There was a silence, as each person's gaze was fixed on the image across the wall of the war room.

The silence was broken by MacTavish.

'There is a phone call for you, sir. I believe he said his name was Archie, calling from Venezuela, it was a very poor line. And a Professor Stiller from Magnatek called, can you call him back?' MacTavish enquired if cook would be required to provide dinner, and if so, for how many.

Henry told MacTavish he would raid the kitchen later and he could send cook home.

Henry then left the bemused group to contemplate the outcome of the disasters they had witnessed. He was impatient to find out the reason for his calls.

Tabule and *Leber* decided it was time to inform the other council members that a meeting was to be called and left to make arrangements.

Moss and *Chonga* sat chatting about the scale of the operation. Moss commented that in normal times it was usual to allow the planting time to deal with its own expansion, at its own pace.

There had never been anything attempted on this scale before; it would need many *Burrbesh* for it to succeed.

Jake and Sandra made their excuses and left to complete the day's chores at her stables; there was a rota, and it was her turn.

'There is a new horse coming to the stables, and it's for sale. Henry mentioned that he would like to have his own horse again, we could check it out,' said Sandra.

As they left the Manor, Fidgit came charging from the bushes with his tail between his legs, turning to bark at whatever was chasing him.

'Come on you, in the Landy,' shouted Jake.

Meanwhile back in the war room, Edmund was getting familiar with his equipment.

The time was six p.m. the news had just started, and the item that was being discussed was the strange planting in London:

...Scientists examining the strange tree occurrence at Westminster have uncovered a strange phenomenon. Samples were taken and examined in the laboratory. The results were conclusive, the DNA was a mixture of many species that had been genetically modified. There was a theory that the Americans could be behind it. It has been linked to a similar occurrence on the Salisbury plain and a small park in Somerset. All the samples taken from each site indicate that this is a new breed of plant species.

'Can you get news in Brazil?' enquired Ivy.

Claiming that anything was possible, Edmund put in a search for Amazon rain forest news.

Many stations flashed on to the screens, Edmund switched the view to multiple channels. There was no shortage of news on the devastation taking place.

Pictures of fires, displaced people living in canvas shanty towns, areas of scorched earth, loggers taking large trees out of the forest. Sawmills that could be set up anywhere; a portable pillaging business fuelled by greed and world demand.

Edmund said that the more he researched the problem of global warming, the more he found out how it impacted on human suffering. He had been immune to the problem in his working career, but now felt that he was in a position to do something about it, a very gratifying feeling.

Chonga said he had witnessed the gentle way mankind could work with nature, but over the past five hundred years, the greedy had become too strong.

As *Chonga* was reminiscing over the past, Henry stormed in and cut him short.

'There have been developments at Magnatek. We need to put our heads together and work out a plan of attack,' said Henry excitedly.

Henry believed that if the *Burrbesh* could produce the result with a combined effort, using the technology that Edmund and Magnatek could control, there would be a very high chance of success.

Henry began to explain the details of his telephone call from Magnatek.

'They have managed to fine-tune the control of the magnetic field, it can now operate a blanket cover, in any shape, using satellite coordinates.

Also, there is the facility to create holes within it, effectively creating unplanted areas anywhere within the field.' Henry was really beginning to embrace technology; his enthusiasm was contagious.

Chonga was a little in the dark, he could not see the reason for Henry's excitement.

Henry went on to explain that there was to be a demonstration; Magnatek were going to visit the Manor. A suitable field of around two hundred acres would be required. Magnatek would conduct an experiment, using any choice of seed to plant the field.

'I believe Bill has a field around that size. He was ploughing it not too long ago; I shall talk to him tomorrow. Magnatek are ready to move at a moment's notice,' said Henry.

He continued to explain that the process had been adapted to operate at higher altitudes without losing the quality. Before, the higher one went, the signal would weaken, thus reducing the target area's detail and planting would not be so tightly compacted. Henry did not fully understand the process and told them it was something to do with GSP.

'GPS,' interrupted Edmund.

'Yes, that was it,' smiled Henry.

'Max said if you were here, we could do something on the phone, in conference or something.' Henry was getting rather excited, there was a positivity beginning to transpire.

'That would be video conferencing,' said Edmund. 'I shall call him and put it on screen.'

Edmund logged on to the call Henry had made, the sound of a phone dialling came through the wall monitors, and then the picture appeared.

Max was more than life size across the wall. He greeted Edmund who then introduced the others.

With the pleasantries out of the way, Max enthusiastically explained to Edmund the breakthrough they had achieved since his visit.

Edmund clarified the technical language, and explained to everyone in simpler terms, the outcome of their breakthrough.

Every substance has a unique magnetic code, a bit like DNA: this magnetic field could be manipulated to create a picture. By altering the frequency, different elements could be placed in particular areas, and there was no limit to area size or quantity. The result would be a high-definition picture, or map, of specific elements transmitted to the ground.

For example, if you wanted to plant a field of barley with a smiley face of maize in the middle, on a hundred-acre field, it would be possible.

The seed would be treated, the maize with one signature, the barley with another. They would then be sent into the atmosphere by rocket or mortar, even a standard firework. This would then be collected in the magnetic field, operated from a drone, mapped and correlated to produce the picture required.

Of course, this would take time with normal seed, but if they used night flower seed, the results would be almost instantaneous.

'I think that just about covers it, what do you say Max?

Can this technology deal with two thousand four hundred square miles?'

Edmund faced the screens to catch Max's reaction; he did a quick calculation, and said, 'There is no reason why not, but at this moment we would need to be a lot higher for the beam to cover that size area. You would need a much bigger plane, capable of reaching at least twenty thousand feet.'

Max wanted to set a date for an experiment.

'I can phone Bill now,' said Ivy. 'Just give me five minutes.'

Edmund continued to quiz Max on the technical abilities of the new equipment, and whether an area with no planting could be programmed. He also needed to know how many different items could be dealt with at any one time.

'Bill said it's ok to use the top field, it is around one hundred and fifty acres, is that big enough?' said Ivy, interrupting the conversation.

Max agreed that that would be fine, he would action the transport of the equipment and be with Henry by noon of the next day.

Bidding them a good night, Max left the room.

'We are going to need a bigger plane,' said Edmund.

'I'm sure we have one lurking in a cupboard somewhere. I shall speak to the MacDonalds and find out,' said Henry, fascinated by the video calling.

He asked Edmund if they could be contacted in the same manner.

Edmund had uploaded all of their phone contacts into the main computer, and with the tap of a key, the dialling started.

'Let's see if Ronald will answer,' said Edmund.

A voice came across the screens, but with no picture.

'Henry is that you? What can I do for you?'

'Sorry to bother you at this hour,' said Henry, 'but we need a plane, a big one. It needs to reach at least twenty thousand feet and fly over Brazil.'

'The hour is of no matter; I am usually working till around nine p.m. most nights. Your request caught me a little off guard that's all.

Why Brazil?' replied Ronald.

Henry gave a brief explanation that the Amazon rain forest was to be the focus of their intentions.

Ronald told him that both he and his brother had been working on Henry's portfolio for some weeks.

'I do seem to remember there was a plane somewhere. Give me a few minutes to look and I shall call you back.'

Moss stood by Edmund, looking and learning as he navigated his way around the equipment.

'When we descended on Salisbury plains, we took only a modest amount of the seed, as I recollect,' said Moss.

Tabule leaned forward in his chair; he spoke of the seed being a fairly recent newcomer to the tools that the *Burrbesh* had at their disposal.

'A success attributed to *Leber*, but one which has never been measured or quantified. The old ways of the *Burrbesh* have been very personal to each individual, subsequently, each has developed their own speciality. It has been so since the beginning of time, where an individual would visit suitable areas through the fabric and leave their mark. It was then left to time to improve, and we would tend to the results, like the gardeners that we are.'

It was a profound statement by *Tabule,* who turned to *Leber* for his opinion on how this new-found work ethic would perform.

Leber, who was now accepted as the undeniable father of the night flower, began to explain the complexities of his creation. He accepted that the Salisbury plains episode was a spur of the moment decision, and that some seed was from young plants. But to measure and quantify the effectiveness of a set amount would be nigh on impossible. The type of seed harvested to deal with the Amazon project could be diverse and would have different weights and densities.

'I believe that the number of seed that could be harvested now, given all the clones of mother that have been produced, will be more than sufficient. Sandra will need to catalogue each individual species within that particular area of rain forest. Then the council can convene,' said *Leber*.

The council would ensure that the correct seed would be available to reinstate the rain forest to its former glory.

'If I have understood correctly,' said Edmund, 'every plant will have its own magnetic signature. This means that each species can be deposited in an area, accurately, to within one inch.'

Everyone was quiet for a moment, trying to visualize the outcome, when a message and ringtone indicated an incoming video call. Edmund accepted the call and Ronald appeared on screen.

'Henry, I have located the aircraft, it's an old Short C-23B Sherpa, ex-military cargo plane in Jamaica. It has been used by the company for carrying freight, but now they are using a local air service, and this is not used any more, but stored as a back-up. Would you like me to arrange its delivery?'

Henry thought for a moment, and then told Ronald he would discuss it with Max the next day and be in touch.

He thanked him for his prompt reply and bade him a good night.

He turned to *Tabule* and enquired when would the council be likely to meet? To which *Tabule* replied he was awaiting the replies of a few members and would be certain to set the date by tomorrow.

Chonga said he felt he should really be back with his people; he felt he had to reassure them that the future looked promising.

Edmund said, 'Before you go, there is a little device that would be invaluable in the organising of this venture.'

He produced a small hand-held GPS and said he would instruct him on its operation before he went.

The night was drawing in, Henry excused himself from the group and said he would try Archie again.

Edmund and Ivy also left, leaving Moss to experiment with the controls, and entertain the others, which he did until the early hours, and past sunrise, to a riveted audience. He had mastered the art of scanning the forest for activity. The thermal imagery that he had brought up on the screens was received with disbelief.

There appeared to be much more going on under the canopy than one could see on the surface.

The time was around six a.m., and the household staff were now busying themselves with daily chores.

MacTavish appeared and enquired if they had been up all night, and whether they required breakfast?

Henry was just coming down the stairs as MacTavish made his way back to the kitchen.

'Yes please,' shouted Henry.

Henry entered the war room to find *Tabule*, *Leber* and *Chonga*, seated where he had last seen them.

They were being flown over the Amazon rain forest, directed by Moss. Lights down, curtains drawn, it was a proper cinema experience, without the popcorn.

'We are really going to have to do something about those loggers,' said *Tabule*. 'They are like locusts, and they move around a lot!'

He explained to Henry that they had all had a chance to see the problems.

Chonga had suggested that there needed to be a massive return migration of tribes to the areas they once occupied.

Tabule emphasized that it needed to happen before the event, because the forest would be very dense, and probably impassable in places.

He could foresee that the loggers and the portable sawmills would need to be dealt with individually.

It was therefore necessary to distribute the night flower and its harvests to these people and educate them on its ways.

It would fall to the little ones to deal with individual targets, of which there were many.

Tribal weapons were no match for the modern methods, a stealth approach would be much more successful.

'Your new training facility has been built for just that purpose Henry, has it not?' said *Leber.*

Chonga told Henry that there were an estimated sixty villages that used to occupy this area. He was going to find the head of each village and bring them to the Manor, to prepare them for the coming event.

He had been given licence by the *Burrbesh* to use the fabric to transport them and would be going as soon as Edmund arrived.

He did not have to wait long.

'There is the most delightful aroma coming from your kitchen, Henry,' said Edmund marching into the room.

'And I see you are getting to grips with the system, Moss,' he said, looking at the screen.

Chonga told Edmund of his intentions and said he had waited for his arrival. It was for the device that Edmund had recommended he take, which would track his movements and transmit coordinates.

This would allow Edmund to log all the village areas which were to be left barren and allow enough room for the village to resurrect itself.

Edmund opened a box and took out a small device, he switched on and explained its function to *Chonga.*

'Moss, can you zoom into England for a moment, and put it on screen?' asked Edmund.

Moss, now very proficient in the controls of his new toy, zoomed in on the southwest of England.

A small pulse of light showed up where the Manor was. Moss zoomed in even closer, the Manor was now on full screen.

'Watch the pulsing light,' said Edmund, as he walked out through the conservatory, and onto the patio and back.

The pulsing light moved around, following the path that Edmund took.

He explained to *Chonga* that the device should be switched on when he was at a village location. He was then to walk around the perimeter of what was once the village boundary.

The coordinates from the path he took would be logged into the computer to create the future map of the planting.

Confident that he understood how the device operated, *Chonga* prepared to leave.

Tabule had offered his assistance to direct *Chonga* to the correct paths in the fabric, some of which could be very elusive.

Chonga admitted that his task would definitely benefit from the help of another, especially one with experience.

Henry wished them luck as they set off.

'The training facility is to have all the equipment connected today,' said Edmund. He would be busy checking its installation, and Moss would require instruction on logging the data from *Chonga.*

MacTavish suddenly appeared and announced that breakfast was served. As they entered the dining room, Ivy and Sandra walked in.

'No Jake?' said Henry.

'No. Ivy gave me lift. Jake has gone with his father to prepare the field for this afternoon,' said Sandra.

She mentioned to Henry that she had seen a horse at the stables that he might like, and perhaps, when he had a moment, he might like to see it.

Arrangements for the day's events were discussed over breakfast. *Leber* had ideas for the planting demonstration, and asked Sandra and Ivy if they could go over them this morning.

Henry was going to be dotting between everything that morning. He still had not contacted Archie.

He was now distracted by the mention of a horse, a passion of his, in the past.

'I shall try Archie one more time, then I need to get over to the new building,' said Henry.

He left the dining room and walked out onto the patio, with the phone to his ear. Almost immediately, Archie answered. He said he had just that second received his replacement phone, as his last one got run over by a lorry. He was just about to call Henry when it rang.

He said he had just landed, and asked if it was ok to come to the Manor. He had news to tell.

Henry explained the agenda and suggested it would be well worth a visit.

Archie gave his eta of around noon, which Henry agreed would be perfect, and looked forward to seeing him.

As Sandra was on her way out with Ivy and *Leber*, Henry said that he would like to see the horse this evening, if that was possible.

Sandra told him that it should be no problem.

'Good, good,' said Henry, and wandered off in the direction of the new building.

On the way over to the greenhouses, *Leber* spoke of carrying out a test, with different seed, replicating that which would be found in the rain forest.

Curious, he questioned Sandra on the magnetic field of plants, and whether man had catalogued a list of such things.

Sandra replied that an extensive study had been made of the seed from most of the plant species on the planet. The results and specimens were kept in a special facility in secure vaults to preserve them in case the plants were threatened with extinction.

During the course of her studies, she had been privileged to visit Kew, a world leader in plant science.

They had studied and measured the magnetic field of thousands of plants, and the results were available on a database, to those involved in plant research.

Each magnetic signature was unique to that particular plant.

'Do you have a list of these signatures?' asked *Leber*.

'They are available online,' said Sandra. 'Edmund would be able to access them with my password.'

He asked her if she could give him the Latin names of twenty or so plants that would be found in this area of forest.

He could produce them but had never given them names; that strange quirk rested with man who liked labels.

She would have to refer to, and gain access to the website which held that information.

They wandered back to the house in search of Edmund and his computer.

They found him with Moss, who was sitting in an umpire's chair at the back of the room. He was operating a joystick and keyboard. Edmund was instructing him on the controls, and fiddling with knobs, calibrating the on-screen display.

'Watch this,' said Moss.

The screen began to zoom into a field, which was being graded by two tractors, driven by Jake and his father.

Zooming in even closer, they could just hear the music playing in Jake's tractor.

'Good stuff, eh?' said Moss, rather pleased with himself.

Sandra told him that they needed to access her account on the website at Kew. She gave Moss her password and waited for him to enter the details.

'Edmund, I would like you to take twenty Amazon plants found in this forest and to add them to the demonstration this afternoon. It needs to be large enough to make an assessment, say five acres?' said *Leber*.

Sandra was scrolling through the list of plants and downloading a good cross-section, together with their magnetic signature.

Leber was watching intently, as he recognized and remembered the plants that Sandra had chosen.

Edmund, who was examining the data attached to the plants, agreed that it was a universal measurement, and would be easy to upload into the Magnatek equipment.

Having familiarized himself with the plants that were to be used, *Leber* wandered into the conservatory to connect with the night flower.

Sandra went back to the greenhouses just as a beeping pulse of light started to show on screen.

'Wow, that didn't take long,' said Edmund.

He instructed Moss to bring up the Amazon map again and sure enough, there was *Chonga*'s signal. They watched as the signal formed a rough circle, which took nearly half an hour, then it ceased.

'That's the first village logged, I'll set it to automatically save from now on.' Edmund was pleased his equipment had worked; rather better than he had imagined.

MacTavish appeared in the doorway, announcing the arrival of Professor Max Stiller and Dr Henri Chanel.

Edmund went to greet them, eager to inspect the progress that had been made, and to compare notes.

Henry joined them around the front of the house, where a large truck was parked.

There was a satellite dish and aerials on the roof, also steps which led to a door at the rear. Inside was equipment, floor to ceiling.

Henry and Edmund were given a guided tour of the inner workings, and then they all went off to the war room to plan the afternoon's events.

They watched on screen as Jake and his father completed the preparation of the field and began their return to the farm.

Leber came in and was introduced to Max; he enquired if Max felt confident about the afternoon's demonstration.

It was his experience that plants do not always do as you expect.

Max assured him that the system was operating very well, and he was confident of the outcome.

'I shall be in the greenhouses if anyone needs me,' said *Leber*.

Chapter 20

MacTavish came in. He announced the arrival of Lord Archibald Dartington-Smythe.

'Show him in, show him in,' said Henry.

'Please, call me Archie,' he said to MacTavish.

'Very well M'lord.'

Henry winked at Archie and shrugged. 'Old school!' he said.

'So, what's this news you have?' enquired Henry.

Archie proceeded to tell Henry about his government's plans to flood three massive areas of rain forest to build dams.

'It is very similar to the plans of the Brazilian government, the need for cheap hydroelectric energy overrides all.

Loggers have been sent into clear areas and remove whatever they like, there is no control, and it's just a free for all with no thought for the native occupants.'

Archie told him that the activity was very close to one of his vineyards. Massive fires were raging as they cut and burnt their way into the forest. It was the fear of damage to his property that had prompted Archie to go out there.

'I have taken pictures of the carnage. Last year I had the plane specially adapted for surveying and had some special high-resolution cameras fitted. The pictures I took show the loggers and their network of roads, and as I flew low over their operation to take close-ups, I was shot at. Luckily, the bullet passed through the wing without damage,' said Archie.

There had been a news blackout, the media had been forced to keep it quiet, but once his pictures got out it would make the national news.

Archie was not without friends in the news world, his pictures would be used in the next editions, anonymous of course.

'There will be a lot of noise and government denials, and there will probably be very little done about it. It will be put down to progress. I have thought a great deal of our meeting in the restaurant, and the creatures you introduced me to,' said Archie, as he continued to express his concerns.

He had thought that with the powers they possessed, some sort of retaliation could be implemented. He said it would be nice to plant great trees along their roads.

Having listened to Archie's passionate plea, Henry concluded that he was of the same mind. And so, he decided to let Archie into the secrets of the *Burrbesh*, the Council of Libra and its connection to the night flower. They could only benefit from like-minded people such as Archie.

'I shall tell you what we are planning, here, at the Manor today,' said Henry.

He told him that they were all committed to doing whatever was necessary to prevent this world from destruction.

Henry suggested they walk the grounds, and he would show Archie the work that had been done, with explanations on the way.

'There is to be a demonstration of our new technology this afternoon. I'm sure you will find it interesting.'

Shall you bc staying the night, Archie?' Henry enquired. 'I can have MacTavish prepare a room for you.'

'Very kind,' said Archie.

'But, how rude of me. You have not been introduced to the group.' Henry escorted him over and introduced him to everyone.

'The event will take place at 14:00 hrs,' said Edmund.

He had a lot to sort out with Max, and they would be going up to the field after lunch and setting up the equipment.

Henry and Archie wandered into the conservatory, and Archie began his tour. He was introduced to the night flower; he asked after the little ones he had met in London.

'They do tend to wander around the grounds playing hide and seek,' said Henry. 'No doubt we shall come across them later.'

Henry took Archie off to the summerhouse, where they could remain undisturbed while he summarized the story of the *Burrbesh*.

Edmund, Max and Henri went to check on the equipment to be used in the demonstration, while Moss continued to fiddle with his new toy.

The Manor had never been so busy.

Ivy had enlisted the willing help of many members of the WI, many with green fingers, and sworn to secrecy. They had been seconded to the greenhouses, as the need for more night flowers had increased.

Shelta and the Gypsies had requested more; they had met many more groups who were dedicated to the cause as they travelled across Europe.

The Amazon project would need a huge amount, given the size of the area, and so there was a well organised production line being set up.

Jake, having finished his work on the field, arrived at the Manor.

He pulled onto the drive in his Land Rover and instructed Fidgit to go and find the little ones and bring them to him.

Not needing to be told twice, Fidgit leaped off the Land Rover and disappeared into the bushes.

Jake intended to use their skills to complete the planting of the second entrance to the new building.

He walked over to the large truck parked by the front door; he wandered round to the rear and peered through the door.

'Hi Edmund,' shouted Jake.

Edmund was sitting at a short table upon which were monitors, and equipment with lights flashing.

'Ah, good day, Master Jake,' said Edmund. 'Allow me to introduce Professor Stiller and Dr Henri Chanel.'

Jake recognized the names from the story Henry had related, of his trip to London.

Edmund explained to Jake briefly the procedure of the afternoon's demonstration.

'Dad said he would sooner have rape seed than barley,' said Jake.

Edmund told Jake that *Leber* was going to provide the seed for their demonstration, and he would need to let him know.

'I think you will find him in the greenhouse with Sandra,' said Edmund.

Jake left the three chatting and inspecting their equipment and continued around the side of the house towards the greenhouses. On reaching the greenhouse he greeted Sandra and relayed his father's concerns to *Leber.*

'I think we can deal with that,' said *Leber*, and he wandered into the next greenhouse to see how Ivy and her army were coping.

Jake told Sandra that he was going to use the skills of the little ones to do a bit of planting.

Leaving the greenhouse, they both set off in the direction of the barking.

Jake caught up with Fidgit and his playmates, and giving orders to follow him, they all set off for the new building.

Never having had an intelligent conversation with the little ones, Jake was surprised to find a total understanding of what he was saying. Although there was no dialogue, his thoughts were clear, and the feeling of satisfaction at the understanding from the three was quite overwhelming.

The three little ones approached the new gate pillars, the ground either side of the driveway was still showing signs of building work.

They began what looked like a conga dance; they held each other at waist level and danced all over the fresh earth. When the rhythm called for them to lift a leg, one-two-three lift, one-two-three lift, green shoots emerged.

The conga became more intense, the little ones could be heard giggling as the excitement increased, and with the excitement came the bigger plants.

It did not take long before the area on both sides of the drive had grown to a height which Jake could not see over. There were trees and bushes, very similar to the original.

Jake was impressed, and he thanked the little ones for their efforts, upon which they ran off, with Fidgit in hot pursuit.

Jake made his way back to the house; he found Moss in the war room, busy with the controls of the equipment.

'Ah, Jake come and look.' Moss had the satellite imagery of the area where *Tabule* and *Chonga* were.

There were the outlines of two villages now showing on screen. Moss swore he could see *Chonga* and *Tabule* at the site of the third village.

'It looks very green around one of those villages,' said Jake. 'And the other looks like it's starting to go green too.'

Moss said it was *Tabule*, he could not resist the urge to improve an area, he had put trees all around the village, and he would probably do the same for the others.

'This really is fascinating technology,' said Moss, who was now becoming a real techie.

Pointing at the screens, Jake could see the outline of the third village starting to appear.

'I'm sure I can see *Chonga*'s bright red robe following the outline, as it appears,' said Jake, amazed at the image he was observing.

'What's happening to the heads of the villages. Are they going to come back to the Manor?' asked Jake.

Moss explained that he had been delegated to deal with the incoming students, *Tabule* had agreed to assist *Chonga* transporting them back, while Ivy would train them on the niceties of the night flower and its quirks.

MacTavish entered and announced that the time was now 13:00, dinner would be served shortly, and it would be a buffet set out in the dining room.

Edmund came in with Max and Henri, just as MacTavish announced food.

'Splendid idea,' said Henri, whose stature displayed his love of food.

Edmund was busy watching the third village outline appear on screens. He suggested that Henri and Max should explore the conservatory, and introduce themselves to the night flower, before lunch.

'It's a pity we cannot communicate with them. It would be nice to have an update on the expected numbers of tribal members,' said Edmund, riveted to the monitors.

'We do have ways,' said *Leber,* who had been observing from the doorway.

'I see *Tabule* could not resist the urge to create,' he said, observing the darkening greenery around the village rings.

'All the co-ordinates are being logged,' said Edmund. 'We shall know exactly where each village is.'

'This is amazing,' said Ivy, who had returned with *Leber*.

Henry meanwhile had been showing Archie around the grounds. After his history lesson on the ways of the *Burrbesh,* Archie had come to see a whole new chapter opening up in his life.

They returned to the house, and in the dining room, met up with Max and Henri.

Henry was curious about how they intended to deal with the Amazon area, and began quizzing Max.

'In layman's terms, Henry, we need to go bigger, more powerful equipment, higher altitude, bigger plane.

We are just beginning to calculate the logistics,' said Max.

Henry told him that there was a plane within the company that might be suitable. It would need a pilot though, to bring it back to England,

'What sort of plane are you talking about?' inquired Archie.

Henry proceeded to tell Archie all about it, and of the plans that were in place for it.

'You need look no further,' said Archie. 'I would be honoured to assist.'

Archie rarely did things by halves; when he took his pilot's licence, he took it in all manner of aircraft, including passenger jets.

An excitement began to buzz around the room, as detailed plans began to formulate. Archie enquired if a decision had been made on which airport would be used to keep it, as it would need to be worked on.

Max said the equipment would take about two weeks to install and would need to be kept low key; they did not want to attract the attention of the CAA.

He suggested Bristol airport would probably be best, as the trip to London was fraught with problems, and too much security.

'Could we not register some sort of research mission to map the old tribes of the Amazon? We could be using sonar and radar technology to map the area,' suggested Edmund.

The idea had merit; Max was sure the equipment to be installed would more than resemble traditional mapping technology.

'Sounds good, we are probably looking at about four weeks from today, if everything goes to plan,' said Henry.

Edmund came in and confirmed that the sheer logistics would take time, even without fitting the aircraft with equipment.

Edmund said there was a lot riding on the outcome of this afternoon's results. The equipment had only been tested on five specially treated seeds, under laboratory conditions.

What was intended that afternoon, was going to test the accuracy of the magnetic signatures of some twenty species.

These had been chosen by Sandra, nurtured by the night flower, collected by *Leber* and were now being programmed into the equipment by Edmund.

It had been a last-minute decision to increase the quantity of species in the equation, one which had not been passed on to Max or Henri.

'Should we inform Max and Henri of our plans, Edmund?' said *Leber* quietly, inspecting the various rows of flashing lights on the equipment.

'I don't think so,' said Edmund, tapping away at the keyboard.

'There, it's done,' he said, removing the memory stick from the machine and placing it in his top pocket.

'We should go through and let Max and Henri know,' said Edmund.

'I have just finished putting another programme together for our intended demonstration, it just needs to be plugged in,' he said.

Everyone had assembled in the dining room. They were busy chatting, too preoccupied to be seated, and they picked at their food, except for Henri, who appeared to have an appetite.

Edmund told Max that there was an alternative programme using the night flowers seed, and it was ready to be loaded. Showing him the memory stick, Edmund explained that *Leber* and Moss would be providing the seed and it would be useful to try a broader spectrum of plant species. It would be interesting to see how the new device would cope.

Indigenous flora, researched by Sandra, allocated to specific regions and dispersed with the Magnatek equipment, could have limitless uses.

'If we have any chance of recreating the natural flora for an area that man has destroyed, this would be a perfect opportunity to test it,' said Edmund.

Max agreed whole heartedly, he had been impressed with the experiment they had carried out recently, using the night flower seed, even though they had given up trying to contain it.

Leber joined them both and inquired if everything was all right.

Edmund and Max in unison said 'fine.'

Leber took Edmund to one side, as Max went over to explain the change of plan with Henri.

'*Tabule* has expressed concerns about the difficulties in finding many elders within the vicinity. He was afraid they had left for the cities or had been killed.' *Leber* said that *Chonga* may require their assistance to search.

He said that runners had been sent out from the camps to try and find their people, but they had been scattered everywhere.

‘Is there not something we could do with this technology?’ *Leber* asked.

‘I shall give it some thought,’ replied Edmund.

Max asked if anyone would like a lift to the demonstration field, as there was plenty of room for everyone in the truck.

Henry told Sandra that he would be interested in looking at the horse she mentioned, after the demonstration.

He would much prefer to ride up to the field but accepted the lift and went out with Ivy, Edmund and Archie to the truck.

‘I shall drag Moss from his new toy and meet you there,’ said *Leber*.

Jake said he would just give his father a ring, he was keen to witness the experiment, especially as it was his field.

He and Sandra would be driving up in the Land Rover and would meet them all there.

It was a perfectly calm day with not a cloud in the sky. The weather over the Manor and its estate was set to continue for weeks to come.

Max drove the truck along the lanes, with Henry instructing him on directions, telling him to turn left at a field entrance.

It was the turning before the Gypsy camp, which they had visited some weeks previously.

Driving for nearly a mile alongside the field, on a neatly mown grassy border, they eventually reached the area where the event would take place.

Max parked the truck in a position which had a panoramic view of the whole field. There was the oak tree standing proud on a small hillock in the middle.

Max and Henri busied themselves. Henri climbed the ladder onto the top of the truck and set the aerials and satellite dish, while Max shouted from inside which way to twiddle each of them, for perfect calibration.

Back at the Manor, *Leber* had managed to drag Moss away from his plaything and took him off to the conservatory and the night flower. There, they both prepared themselves with a portion of the night flower’s finest and set off for the field.

They blended into the fabric and appeared on the side of the field not far from the truck.

They walked over to Edmund who explained the proceedings, and when they would be instructed to release the seed.

Jake and Sandra could be seen driving up the field towards the truck, closely followed by his father.

Parking up and joining the rest, they selected a good vantage point in which to view the spectacle.

The audience was now assembled.

In the truck, Edmund was now sitting in front of equipment, glued to a monitor. Henri was preparing for launch, two panels opened in the roof, revealing a large drone. It was carrying some heavy equipment with what looked like a small satellite dish underneath.

Max was sitting at a table outside with the remote controller for the drone.

Suddenly there was a loud humming as the propellers on the drone burst into action, and with its six rotors the drone gently rose from its resting place in the roof of the truck.

Henri was now sitting in front of another monitor opposite Edmund; he was reading out altitude measurements.

'We need to reach a thousand feet to be effective across the area of the field,' said Henri. 'When the drone reaches the correct altitude, the field will be turned on. We shall then monitor the field to ensure the correct frequency and strength are transmitting.'

When everything had been checked and was operating correctly, he would then give the signal for the seed to be released.

Edmund confirmed that his programme had been loaded and Henri was counting up in fifty-foot increments, eight fifty, nine hundred, nine fifty, one thousand feet.

This was now being broadcast through a speaker on the roof, the whole show resembled a space launch.

'Altitude is now stable at one thousand feet, position is good, magnetic field on,' Henri paused briefly, awaiting Edmund's confirmation of stability.

'Magnetic field is stable, and pattern is correct,' said Edmund.

'Ok, ladies and gentlemen, let the event begin, release the seed,' said Henri.

Leber brought his hands together at waist height, his fingers began to extend to the ground and also upwards. They twisted and twined together to form his planting staff. His facial appearance changed to his original form, and a dark cloud came from the top of the staff and ascended.

Moss, who was at his side, had removed his large hat which now looked like a ball of sphagnum moss.

Holding it above his head, a cloud with a distinct green hue came forth, giving off a visible electrical charge, like that of a plasma globe.

The two clouds danced around each other and rose into the sky. Then they were caught in the magnetic field; almost instantaneously the cloud became a flat beam, like a laser cutting through the air. It covered the whole field, then a pattern began to emerge, and it began to descend.

'Eight hundred, seven hundred, five hundred, three hundred, gently, gently, fifty, twenty, ten and release, magnetic field off.'

Henri's voice was very matter of fact.

The cloud, which was now only inches thick descended; it came to rest very accurately, so much so, that those close to the field edge, felt they had to jump back out of its way.

Almost immediately there were green shoots appearing, the crop had begun to grow.

Leber and Moss, who had now regained their composure, walked over to everyone by the truck.

Edmund and Henri were outside now, observing the spectacle which was growing before their very eyes.

'The crop of what you call rape, has been advanced a little, two or three months perhaps. This will occur within hours, after which time it will revert to normal growth pattern. The other has been left at its twenty plus years' advantage; that may take a day or so,' said *Leber*.

'The other?' questioned Bill, who had been listening intently.

Leber pointed to the middle of the field where a large dark mass of greenery was beginning to tower over the crop.

'What in god's name…?'

The stunned Bill looked on in disbelief.

In the middle of the field was a veritable jungle rising out of the ground.

'Sorry, I did try to keep it small,' said Sandra.

Max invited everyone to observe the pictures being sent back by the drone. He had brought the vehicle down to five hundred feet, and the picture it was transmitting was on the monitor in front of the remote console.

It clearly showed that the planting had been accurately done, the field borders were intact and there was no overlap across them. The oak tree standing on the hillock within the field had a clear circular edge surrounding it, no planting had taken place there.

This had been the clear test area for potential villages that would need to be left plant-free.

The darker jungle planting had been set out in the shape of Brazil, one of Edmund's quirky ideas.

While on the far side of the field, was a distinct smiley face. That was Jake's contribution, using barley for the main picture.

'Well, I'll be blowed. I've never seen the like,' said Bill.

Jake gently punched his father on the shoulder and laughed.

'There you go Dad, crop circle.'

They all stood in silence, for ages, watching the planting, as it rose to near full maturity.

'Well, I think we can conclude that this experiment has been a total success,' said Max, as he guided the drone back safely to its resting place.

Bill inspected the now flowering rape and commented that it may not take long to harvest, but he was a little unsure about the jungle.

Sandra said she could not wait to inspect it.

'Best left till tomorrow,' said Moss.

'It will take some hours for it to slow down.'

Henry left Archie mesmerised by the event, and went to speak with Max.

'Your equipment is amazing, I'm very impressed.

What do we need to do in preparation for installing it into the plane we spoke about?'

Henri and Edmund joined them, having packed away the console and outdoor gear. Max explained that the team had looked into this and there would be some limitations using the conventional equipment.

The maximum operating area at forty thousand feet, currently stood at around forty-five miles in diameter, on the ground. The wider the angle of transmission the less accurate the mapping. However, there was a prototype under construction which would enable the transmission of the magnetic field on multiple horizontal planes, using lasers. It would allow hundreds of layers each with its own pattern and have a range of around five hundred miles in diameter.

'We shall be trialling this equipment on our return,' said Henri. 'Please, come and join us.'

Edmund said he would be more than happy to. Henry, however, had his House of Lords commitment, and had intended to travel down with Archie.

Everyone made their way back to the Manor house. There was much to talk about. It had been a successful day, but there was still a long way to go.

Moss was back at the controls in the war room. There were now five outlines of villages on the wall monitors.

Edmund mentioned to *Leber* that perhaps they might use the social media outlets on the internet to try and locate tribal members. Even if they themselves had no knowledge of how to use the internet, someone may know of them, it could be worth a try.

Henry was now keen to see the horse Sandra had mentioned. He found both her and Jake on the patio.

'What would it take to put the stable block back together?' he asked Jake.

Jake told him that there was not much to do, the stalls were still intact, he had used it for a workshop and storage, but the new building had proper facilities.

'I think it would be nice to return the stables back to their original use. Can you sort that out, Jake?' said Henry.

Jake said he would get onto it first thing.

'Second thing,' said Sandra. 'We are checking out the jungle first.'

'Yes, boss,' said Jake.

He offered them both a lift to see the horse. He had to go and give his father a hand, so could not stay.

The three walked out to the Landy, Jake whistled for Fidgit, who appeared on cue, and took his place on the blanket.

Then they set off for Sandra's stable.

Chapter 21

Max and Henri were busy chatting with Edmund and Ivy on the patio. She had no idea what all the scientific tech talk meant but did have a good understanding of the overall plan. She had arranged to go and pick up Henry on her red scooter, after giving him an hour or so to check out his horse.

Ivy rose from the comfy patio chair and excused herself.

'I'm just going to see the ladies off, find out who will be coming tomorrow, then I shall go and collect Henry,' said Ivy.

The three men gave a courteous half rise as she got up to leave.

'We shall have to make our way back soon, so we may be gone when you return. But why don't you come down with Edmund for a day or two? You would be most welcome,' said Max.

'Thank you, I shall give it some thought; see you shortly, Edmund,' and she left the men to their debate.

It was not long after Ivy had gone that Max and Henri made their farewells and left to drive back to Magnatek.

Edmund went into the war room where Moss was in charge of the visual display.

There now appeared on screen eight ringed village areas, each surrounded by an element of greenery.

In three of the larger areas, there was distinct movement.

'Are those villagers?' Edmund asked.

Leber explained that *Chonga* had sent runners out with news that the gods were returning. A great spectacle was about to happen, which needed the support and powers of the heads of each tribe. They should return to their birthplace and prepare.

'*Tabule* has also sent word that there are many, still in towns and cities – places where the runner's tongue does not reach,' said Moss.

Edmund suggested that that message could be put onto a social media site; even in the ghettos of the deepest hellhole, someone would have the internet.

Edmund sat himself at his keyboard, his monitor blinked into life, and he began tapping.

Moss watched in awe as Edmund used his eight fingers with lightning speed across the keys; he looked at his own two fingers, then at *Leber*, and then shook his head.

'There, it's done. I have put that very same message onto the net, it may encourage their return,' said Edmund eagerly.

'*Tabule* also said that there may not be enough people left to occupy the villages. Those who have returned have told stories of loggers who enjoyed hunting down those who fled. Many were killed, shot for sport, like beasts,' Moss said, painting a rather sinister picture.

However, the word was out, people were returning slowly, and it was still early days.

'We have four weeks, do we not?' said *Leber*.

The runners would continue to explore new territory.

Chonga would oversee the repatriation of the newcomers to their homelands, then, he would be able to ascertain who their leaders were, and the task of educating them could begin.

Tabule, leaving *Chonga* to his task continued his search for missing villagers.

He would need to attend a meeting of the council in two days. He knew it was short notice, but many members of the council were already about, dealing with another matter.

Henry and Ivy walked in, just in time to hear the last sentence.

'Will the meeting be here, at the Manor?' asked Henry.

Leber explained that now they had the facility to see the area on the monitors, it would be the most suitable place. And it would enable all the council members to see the magnitude of the proposed event.

Archie entered the room with a collection of papers and forms in his hand. He told Henry that he had been working on a flight plan to bring the plane back. It was parked in a hangar, at a small airfield on the west coast of Jamaica. He had mapped out a route to bring it back to Bristol airport, but because of its range, it would mean refuelling at least two or three times.

He suggested that they take the equipment over to Jamaica and carry out the modifications there.

It could then be flown directly to an airfield he partly owned, in Venezuela, and from there, Brazil and the Amazon were a mere hop, skip, and a jump away, and easily within range of the plane.

The main thing in its favour was that it did not need a long runway to take off and could quite easily be serviced by a small airfield.

The alternative would be a bigger plane, which could do the distance in one go, but would need a longer runway.

Henry turned to Edmund and asked his opinion; he personally felt it would enable them to keep a low-key approach.

Edmund agreed and suggested that they should both visit Magnatek as soon as possible. They would need to examine the new equipment and find out whether it could be fitted to the plane in Jamaica.

Archie's main question was how heavy it all might be, and if he could take it in his own plane.

Edmund asked Ivy if she would like to take up Max's offer and accompany him. He described the converted country house and its views across the countryside, as the equivalent of an up-market hotel.

Archie explained that he had to be at Westminster to vote on an important bill, which he had spent years pushing for. He would greatly appreciate the support of Henry when it came to the vote.

The bill would create a repatriation fund for indigenous tribes, displaced by conflict, and in danger of extinction.

It was a charity which Archie had long supported, and he had been a leading voice on getting the bill through the house.

Henry agreed that it was a worthy cause and that they should travel down together; they would take the Bentley.

They could then meet up with Edmund and Ivy at Magnatek on their way back, where Archie could answer their technical questions on the plane.

'I shall join *Tabule* in his recruitment drive, he appears to need a spot of help,' said *Leber*. 'I can foresee the arrival of the first heads of tribes as imminent. I shall be back tomorrow,' and with that he left them.

Henry shouted to MacTavish as he went past the doorway. He was carrying a huge box he could not see over.

'Are the rooms in the new building ready to take guests?' Henry enquired. 'It looks like there may be visitors soon.'

MacTavish said that most of the furniture had been installed and that towelling and bedding just needed unpacking.

He would instruct the chamber maids to continue making the rooms ready, first thing in the morning.

Henry suggested that they all round off the evening at the local Tavern; he had become rather fond of this hostelry.

Moss had found his vocation and was quite happy to remain and monitor proceedings, and so, they bade Moss goodnight and went off to the Tavern.

MacTavish, in the course of his duties, wandered into the war room.

'Good evening, Mr Moss, can I get you anything?' said MacTavish, gazing at the screens. He commented on how technology had changed life.

'It does not seem that long ago, when transport and communication was dealt with by the humble horse,' he said.

Moss expressed his fascination for the new technology and admitted that he was becoming a bit of a geek.

'Do you want to see something radical?' said Moss.

Moving to another keyboard and monitor, he began to tap the keys.

MacTavish, curious, pulled up a chair and made himself comfortable.

'This is a simulation of what this area will look like if everything goes according to plan,' said Moss.

The screens on the wall began to display a gentle greenery, creeping across the desolation that had been there previously. Then the image changed; it was as if a drone some twenty feet above the ground, was looking back at the oncoming greenery. The speed increased and looked as though the vegetation was catching up with the camera. It was so dense, and an almost immediate canopy filtered the sunlight into a dappled shade.

The view switched to a satellite image, and the area that was once brown, was now becoming a vivid green.

They both sat and watched in silence, as the spectacle unfolded before them.

Down at the Tavern, the four had settled at a table overlooking the river. They had met Barney, who invited them to join him for a short while.

He had a rendezvous with his lady friend shortly, and so would be leaving them.

He told them that two of the film crew who had been there a few weeks ago, had booked a room.

Barney being the inquisitive type, had probed them for their reason for returning.

They told him that they had been following leads of strange happenings, where plants had suddenly appeared.

He said they had been to Westminster to cover the sudden appearance of mangrove trees in the Thames.

After questioning waiters in the restaurant, by the water's edge, they were shown a rose, which was still in full bloom, having grown through a table.

'They also mentioned a giant willow tree which suddenly appeared in a pub about fifty miles away from here.

They had drawn a line through these incidents on a map and come to the conclusion that somewhere around here was the cause,' said Barney.

Just at that moment the two men returned to the beer garden having refreshed their glasses and walked over to Barney.

'Ah, Barney, I see you have company, won't you introduce us?' said the taller of the two in a broad American accent.

Barney briefly introduced the group, as he was becoming slightly irritated by the American's manner.

'Can we get you guys and the lady a drink?' said the irrit, pulling up a chair, intending to join them. He shouted to a young girl clearing tables.

'Yo, can we get a round of drinks here?'

She gave a sideways glance, and, being used to the occasional drunk, continued clearing without answering.

His colleague apologized for the rudeness, in a very English, well-spoken tone.

Insisting that they would sooner be left in private, he excused his rather forward and brash fellow worker, then guided him, by the upper arm to a table further away.

Barney bade them all good evening, and shrugging his shoulders, he finished his drink and went on his way.

'Well, they seem to have considerable knowledge of our comings and goings,' said Edmund. 'I don't think I like the large one.'

They sat chatting, analysing the possible problems the two reporters could create, until food came. Then the discussion changed to a more interesting topic.

Who would like to go to Jamaica?

The four pondered the possibilities well into the night.

They all had to hold back their laughter as the big American tried to walk to the bar, having had one too many.

His colleague tried in vain to steer him away from the furniture, apologizing profusely to those unfortunates who were in his path.

Eventually, out of sight and on their way to their rooms, the four could laugh about the situation.

'I shall let Moss know; he can keep an eye out for them,' said Henry.

Edmund reminded Henry that the cameras which had been installed around the grounds, should now be online.

'Very little will get past those – another toy for Moss to add to his collection,' he said.

The four continued to enjoy a quiet evening, until the lights in the garden went out, signalling the end of a fine night.

Activity at the Manor started early next morning. Sandra and Jake arrived first; she was very keen to see the results of the jungle planting.

Jake wandered into the war room to see the progress of the villages in the rain forest.

Moss was sitting chatting with two council members who had arrived a little early for the meeting.

'Good morning, Master Jake,' shouted Moss. 'It looks like we are going to have company later, there has been a flood of villagers arriving at the sites you see on screen. All thanks to the message Edmund put out on social media.'

Moss resumed his position at the com and began to tap the keyboard. He showed Jake the now twenty-seven village sites that had been established and logged on the map.

'*Tabule, Leber and Chonga* will be coming back later for the meeting, and they hope to convince three of the surviving heirs to return with them,' said Moss.

It appeared that what was left of the fractured society had been evacuated to distant relatives in order to be safe. They had been educated in the old ways but had also received schooling in the ways of modern society.

'Jake, we have to go, your father will be at the field, and I can't wait to see the results of the jungle planting,' Sandra said excitedly.

They had agreed to meet Jake's dad at the field; he too was keen to see the results, and what impact it would have on his harvesting abilities.

Jake and Sandra left to meet up with Bill.

Outside they found the three little ones and Fidgit, quietly sitting in the Land Rover. They seemed to know that the trip to the field would be happening and were awaiting patiently.

Jake and Sandra looked at each other in disbelief; they had expected the foursome to be charging through the undergrowth somewhere. But, as a result of their well-behaved manner, and the fact that there was little possibility of them getting into trouble, Jake conceded to take them. He turned to them and gave them strict instructions on the rules of behaviour and proceeded to the field.

Edmund and Ivy were already on their way to Magnatek. Edmund was fast becoming the science officer for the event; he would play a vital role in ensuring the equipment and data were fit for purpose.

Meanwhile Archie and Henry, having breakfasted, were preparing for their trip to Westminster.

'We should be back around five,' said Henry, explaining to Moss that he should be well in time for the meeting.

So off they went, Henry hopefully making his last journey as a learner driver, for on the following day, he was to take his driving test.

Bill had arrived at the field some time before Jake and Sandra, and the view that greeted him was something he had not expected. He stood there for what appeared to be an age, staring at the spectacle that had been created.

His observation was interrupted by the sound of Jake's Land Rover driving up the field. Parking fairly close, Jake and Sandra joined him. Fidgit and the little ones disappeared into the fields towards the jungle.

'Wow,' said Jake.

'Oh dear,' said Sandra.

The three stood there, looking on; the jungle experiment had surpassed all expectations. What was supposed to be a token effect had in fact covered not one, but approximately ten acres. Trees towered over the lush foliage of what would be a jungle floor, with liana vines hanging down.

'Come on, let's go and explore,' said Sandra, eager to see it close up, and she ran through the crop of rape to investigate. She was closely followed by Jake and his father.

On reaching the perimeter, they realised that a machete would be needed, in order to go any further.

Jake ran back to the Land Rover; he kept a selection of tools under the seat, and he had just what they needed.

As they began to walk around the edge, they could hear Fidgit barking deep within. They looked for an opening through which to enter this unusual Somerset jungle.

'I think *Leber* has been playing games,' said Sandra. 'These are not the plants that I researched and gave to Edmund to load into his programme.'

Bill commented that he had watched *Leber* and Moss during the experiment; *Leber* had released something much darker than Moss.

They came upon an opening. It was a pathway which appeared to have been there for an age, a proper jungle trail. It needed no cutting or hacking and led them towards the centre where the sound of Fidgit got closer and closer.

When the three reached the middle, they were surprised to find *Leber* and three reasonably well-dressed native Indians, in a clearing. Each was being entertained by a little one scrambling up their arms and over their shoulders, while Fidgit bounced around expressing his concerns.

'Ah, ehm, good day to you,' said *Leber*, 'allow me to explain.'

It was not in his nature to apologize, but on this occasion, he conceded that he may have slightly altered the original planting arrangement. There was a reason, he said.

'These three young men are all that remain of the Royal blood line. They have survived vicious persecution and are very suspicious of any plans for their lands, and rightly so. It was only by assuring them that I was sincere, and the proposed event would actually happen, that they agreed to accompany me through the fabric, and investigate.'

He had promised to show them what their land would look like afterwards. *Leber* actually sounded quite sincere, and it was difficult for Sandra or Bill to be annoyed.

The three men spoke very good English and introduced themselves to everyone. They were Shaman, of the Awa tribe, descendants of holy men, and they had been living in exile from their homeland.

Leber asked if they could be escorted back to the Manor, where Moss was expecting them. He had to return to *Tabule* and *Chonga* to finish something; he would meet them back at the house in time for the meeting.

Leber turned and disappeared into what looked like a cave, a huge mound of rocks had been forced up by the sudden expansion of roots underground.

Inquisitive Jake had to investigate.

As he entered the cave, he had the distinct feeling of déjà vu, the atmosphere was that of his time with Henry, in the cavern.

His wrist started to pulsate.

Almost immediately came the sound of water, a spring appeared at his feet and meandered out of the cave and into the dense foliage. This was all a bit too much for Jake to handle. He exited the cave and pointed out that they had better take these young men back to the Manor, as the day was getting on.

Returning along the path on which they came, the machete was required. The foliage had begun to grow over it, and the way back was barely visible.

Returning to the vehicles, Bill offered to take the young men back to the Manor in his car, while Fidget and the little ones didn't mind sitting on the old blanket in the back of the Landy.

And so, the convoy headed back to the Manor house, with its new passengers.

Moss was awaiting their arrival; he asked Jake if he was ok, and that he had felt his recent experience and promised that they would talk later.

Then, having introduced himself to the guests, Moss set about showing them around.

Jake and Sandra went off to the old stable block to prepare it for Henry's new horse.

‘I know it sounds daft, but I knew what *Leber* was thinking. Your new jungle is a doorway to the Amazon, and I reckon it is through that cave,’ said Jake.

‘He has to go back to create a door at the other end, and he needs the help of *Tabule* and *Chonga* to do it.’

Sandra was impatient to explore the results of the jungle. She wanted to catalogue the plants, measure the area, and monitor it on a daily basis.

‘I think you are going to have plenty of opportunity to do that very soon, and on a bigger scale,’ said Jake.

He could see that the future would require their presence and that travel, and adventure were imminent.

He was beginning to accept the visions that his connection with the night flower and the *Burrbesh* were allowing him. Jake was changing, he could feel a new strength of conviction for the planned event that lay ahead. His life had so far, been one of learning, the direction of which all seemed to make sense now. He had always enjoyed his connection with plants, and his affinity with water would become stronger, which would prove useful in the times to come.

Jake and Sandra continued to work in silence, preparing the old stables, both seemed to be somewhere else. It was not until Moss poked his head round the large door, that the silence was broken.

‘Hello you two,’ he shouted.

Sandra was startled by the sudden appearance of Moss, and dropped a collection of old tin trays she was throwing out.

‘You made me jump,’ she said, picking up the rubbish.

Apologizing for his sudden un-announcement, he told them both that Henry and Archie had returned, and the time of the meeting was fast approaching. Time had flown whilst they had been working, both of them had been caught up in thoughts of current events.

It was now approaching five thirty; Moss told them that their presence would be appreciated at the meeting, as they were now an indispensable cog in the machine. He told them that the three young men, who were the first guests in the new facility, would also be attending.

Jake said they would both need to shower and change and decided that they would go home; he had not realised the time.

They both set off in the Land Rover, Jake whistled for Fidgit, who came charging out of the bushes and jumped in with one leap, while they were still moving.

Back in the house, Henry was introducing Archie to the council members who had all assembled in the dining room. *Tabule*, *Chonga* and *Leber* entered the room, having just returned from the village. *Leber* had a decorated bag, full of something, which he handed to MacTavish, instructing him that it was to be taken to the three guests.

Henry and Archie mingled and chatted to the council members who all seemed to have concerns of one type or another.

Jake and Sandra returned refreshed, with news that they had seen two men parked on the side of the lane, looking somewhat suspicious.

'There were two reporters' at the Tavern last night, following the trail of the strange plantings, we don't need them snooping around,' said Henry. 'I shall have a word with Moss to keep an eye out for them.

'By the way, how did the jungle work out? I've not had a chance to inspect it yet.'

Sandra explained that *Leber* had re-arranged the planting, and how it was to be used. Unfortunately, it was not as discreet as she had planned. What should have been a small experiment had turned into a larger, more visible jungle with trees. They might well be seen above the skyline, as they would grow above the concealed hollow in the field.

As the meeting convened in the war room, the contents of the bag *Leber* had brought was now evident. The three young Shaman came in, dressed in robes depicting their status.

Moss began the proceedings by explaining what was being displayed on the monitors and used the versatility of the technical equipment to complement his account.

The views of the estate were also available, including the jungle which now looked very impressive. Several teak trees had attained heights in excess of sixty feet, while the understorey had filled out and was very dense.

Moss continued to explain that the jungle area would provide passage from the Amazon to the Manor; it would allow the direct transition of human traffic.

Any plan to assist mankind was something the *Burrbesh* had not done before, and the logistics would require constant attention.

It was intended that once a successful planting could be implemented, the Manor would become the staging post for many indigenous tribes and their displaced populations.

Some areas to be planted might become impassable from outside, and so a direct access, close to their village, may be essential.

By entering the locations of the villages, and leaving them unplanted, the villagers could occupy that space while the event took place.

As the council members took their seats at the table, which had been extended to accommodate the extra five places, Sandra spotted movement.

Moss zoomed in on two figures who could be seen walking along the edge of the field.

'That's the two from the Tavern,' said Archie.

The two figures now had a captive audience; everyone was watching. The smaller one appeared to be taking photographs, while the tall one began making his way through the rape field to the jungle edge; shorty ran after to catch him up. They both disappeared from view as they rounded the dense foliage.

'I think we should have some fun with these two,' said *Leber*.

'*Marley*, do you have a suitable compound that would entertain our guests whilst we continue with more important matters?'

Marley was only too happy to oblige. He said that he had been cultivating a new strain of *Salvia* which he was very keen to try out.

Sporting a rather large reefer, *Marley*, in a much laid-back way, made his way into the fabric. He did not wholly enter but did so in stages. A leg, then an arm, then his torso, in a disjointed fashion, then his other leg, while his other arm placed the reefer in an ashtray and popped into the fabric. His black, gold and green hat was the last to vanish through the doorway.

Sandra giggled at the performance, commenting that it was a well laid-back exit.

Marley made his entrance into the jungle through the cave, which was now becoming a well-used access point.

He could hear the voices of the two reporters getting closer and decided that he would blend into the foliage. His form took that of his latest experiment, a *Salvia,* a plant which had some unique hallucinogenic properties. He positioned himself directly in the path of the two intrepid reporters. Using his hand as though it were a handkerchief, he brushed the noses of them both as they forced their way through the undergrowth.

The effects were almost instantaneous, the two trespassers slumped to the floor in an arm lock, unable to speak coherently. They babbled to each other, pointing at *Marley* as he walked back to the cave entrance, still in the form of a large plant.

At the Manor he emerged from the fabric as half plant, half *Burrbesh*; pulling himself together, he retrieved his recreation from the ash tray, and with the production of one huge smoke ring exclaimed.

'Dey's gonna be happy for a while.'

And so, the meeting began.

It was to prove the most important that the *Burrbesh* had ever attended.

Chapter 22

The council members made their way to their seats; the guests were invited to sit around the head of the table with *Tabule*, who began the proceedings with a profound statement:

… 'We are now tasked with the job of trying to put right the damage done to this world by mankind. His utter disregard of the fine balance this world requires has reached a point where that balance swings towards destruction. We have attended many natural disasters in this world, and it has always given us satisfaction when that balance has been restored. As a result, I believe that we have developed a soft spot for this world, which may have affected our judgement a little.

And so, it has been decided that the *Burrbesh* shall assist man in his quest to right the wrongs of the many and provide him with the means to do so. Had it not been for the intervention of Henry and his associates, who shall play a major role in this world's restoration, the *Burrbesh* would probably have allowed the destruction to take its course. It may have resulted in the extinction of man, but we are confident that over the millennia, plant life will flourish again.

With the recently discovered technology developed within Henry's company, coupled with the night flower, and the assistance of the Council of Libra, there is a good possibility of success. This will result in man's ability to carry out his own repairs to his world.

Master Henry will now speak and explain to us the intricacies of the proposed plan.'

Tabule sat and indicated to Henry to take over.

Henry began:

… 'There is, within the business empire that I have inherited, a small team of scientists. They were originally charged with the task of controlling the weather. Primarily rain clouds, for irrigation and flood prevention, with some success.

During their years of research, they accidentally stumbled on another use for the equipment they had developed. They found that seed has a magnetic signature. The magnetic field they had been using to control cloud formations, could be adapted to distribute specially treated seed. This would be used to plant large inaccessible areas, accurately.'

Henry continued to explain that he and Archie had visited the research facility, on the way back from London. Edmund was the person more qualified to explain the process; he would be returning next day, with Ivy.

Edmund had assured him that the new equipment was showing great potential; it had more coverage than the prototype and was lighter.

Archie assured them that the plane they had would be able to carry everything required.

Henry referred to the Salisbury Plains episode, where a radius of some twenty square miles had been planted by *Moss*, *Leber* and *Tabule*.

'What area would you, as an individual, be able to cover in one go?' Henry directed his question at *Leber*.

He replied that, 'on that occasion we could only obtain a token number of seed. The night flower had been reproducing and it was not convenient to take more. It was the same for the young night flowers in the greenhouses. With mature plants, and a sufficient supply of seed, any one of us can quite easily cover that area, and then some.'

Henry asked Moss to bring up on screen the area of devastation seen from satellite, which he did.

Everyone gazed in horror.

'You see, this area is approximately seventy-five miles long and thirty miles wide at its extreme. We have calculated that it will require the help of the full twelve members of the council,' said Henry.

Moss panned across the area south of the river; the small settlements that had been set up were just visible. Then, as the picture moved north across the river, Moss spotted activity.

'Looks like loggers are moving into the area of trees still standing, they will not be far away from the villagers,' said Moss.

As he zoomed in, a road, which had been cut out by the machines was just visible under the canopy. Moss continued to guide the image across the barren landscape, as far south as it stretched. Again, Moss spotted activity.

'It is getting to be a busy old place, this one-time jungle,' observed Moss.

As he zoomed in on the area, Sandra suggested that they could be cultivating the land, and planting, what could only be a palm oil plantation. After watching the activities on screen, it became obvious that that was exactly what they were doing.

There were machines preparing the ground, tearing out the roots of the once great trees, bulldozing them into huge bonfires, the smoke from which was now very visible.

Henry explained that each member of the council would need to be in a specific location around the perimeter, with a full complement of seed. The plane would then fly over, members would release the seed, and equipment on board the plane would take over and distribute the seed across the area.

Henry apologized for his lack of technical know-how, but assured the council that any questions they had would be answered by Edmund.

Agi, with her love of water, put forward a question.

'This area is larger than we have attempted in the past, and as you know, we have had some failures. If the ground has no moisture, having been left barren for so long, is there a chance of some failing?'

Tabule answered and explained that he had been to this area and had planted the perimeter of many villages, and the water had returned.

'Besides, young Jake seems to have the touch when it comes to water,' he joked.

Jake gave a puzzled look. He was still unsure of how involved he was, or even of any special gift he had.

Leber mentioned that it might be a good idea for them all to explore the area of the Amazon and get a feel for it. Now that the doorway within the new jungle had been established, it would be a good idea to test it out.

Tabule ended the meeting by putting the motion to the committee that their support would be required and asked for a show of hands to confirm.

It was a unanimous decision for support. The council members then wandered off one by one, agreeing to meet at the villagers' compound.

Tabule and *Leber* continued to scrutinize the images that Moss had brought up.

Henry flatly refused to set foot in one of *Leber's* caves.

Archie was also quite happy with his chosen transport, being his aeroplane.

'We could stay here and watch you on screen,' said Henry, 'but I have a driving test to attend, so I shall see you later,' and Henry left, with Archie, for his test.

'Master Jake, can you take the three Shaman to the jungle? We will meet you there. Oh, and don't trip over any reporters,' said *Leber*, amused by his own humour, laughing as he left the room.

Jake who was still puzzled by the reference to him and water, asked Moss what it meant.

'Sorry, Jake, I was going to explain a few things to you, wasn't I? It has just been so busy. You are now *Burrbesh*, you have reached maturity and your wrist marks your rank. Your gift is to command the water from below; even where water is perhaps miles below, you now have the ability to bring it to the surface. It will take practice to control efficiently, but it is a good gift to have.'

Moss promised to give him some practical tuition as soon as he could. He gave him a reassuring double handshake and returned to his station.

Jake, now proper bewildered, called to Moss that he would see him on the other side.

'Do you have room for one more, Jake?' shouted *Chonga,* who had been transfixed to the screen, and had not made a peep until now.

He rose from a very discreet chair, hidden by Moss's equipment, and joined them as they went to Jake's shiny red car.

The three Shaman and *Chonga* made an impressive sight as they marched out to the red car in their fiery red gowns.

It didn't take long to reach the jungle. They all piled out and Jake and Sandra led the way to the path that had been formed.

Entering the undergrowth, they could distinctly hear singing. As they approached the vicinity where the cave was, the singing got louder. It was "The blue ridge mountains of Virginia," in proper Laurel and Hardy fashion.

They crept quietly until they had a better view. The two reporters were sitting with their backs against a large rock, arms entwined, singing their heads off. The sight brought laughter to them all; Sandra commented on the potency of *Marley's* invention.

'Well, he did say they would be happy,' Jake sniggered.

At that moment *Tabule* and *Leber* appeared; they too, found the spectacle amusing. They all decided to wait for the last verse before entering the clearing.

Everyone applauded the two entertainers, then helped them to their feet. They were still very much in cuckoo land, and so were assisted into the cave where the door to the Amazon was to be found.

As they entered the cave, Sandra noticed a coolness as she passed through a shadowy veil. Then the cave continued towards a bright light, which turned out to be the exit from the cave, with sunlight flooding in.

'How are you both? No ill effects? Only we have had arms and legs go missing, as people make the journey,'

Leber gave a very wry smile.

Sandra was beginning to understand *Leber*, and poked him in the arm, telling him.

'No, they haven't!'

The two reporters were made comfortable under the shade of a large bush, just outside the cave's exit.

'I'll ask *Marley* to come and check on them shortly,' said *Leber*.

The atmosphere was high with humidity and the temperature change was distinctive; it must have been in the high thirties, a bit of a shock to the system.

Tabule explained to the Shaman the principles behind the doorway, and that they could use it at any time. It would stay open as long as required, and it was their lifeline to a new world.

As they approached the village, they could see a large gathering in the middle. Many council members were present and there was a very noisy debate going on.

The three Shaman rushed into the middle of the melée to find out what was happening.

It turned out that the loggers from the other side of the river had paid them a visit. They had told the villagers that they had two weeks to leave. If not, they would return with bulldozers and sweep them all into the river.

There was an element of panic amongst the women.

Those who remembered the first time the loggers appeared, were not about to have the horror repeat itself.

Jake assured them that there would be no bulldozers coming to push them into the river. He wandered over to *Chonga* who was trying unsuccessfully to pacify those villagers who were in a state of panic.

'Can I have a word?' said Jake, dragging him away from the crowd.

'If their bulldozer were to suffer some sort of breakdown, it would not be able to push them into the river. So, I have an idea, but I shall have to talk to Sandra first. You tell the villagers there will be no machinery pushing anybody into any river!'

The whole prospect of the threat imposed by money-grabbing loggers had angered Jake. He marched off to talk to Sandra, he also needed the assistance of *Marley*.

Jake found Sandra consoling a young girl, and asked if she could join him. He needed to talk.

They walked through the circle of vegetation around the village, into the barren area. They both sat on a large stump of a once huge tree and Jake told her what Moss had said about his gift, and the need to practise control. He also told her of his idea to get back at the loggers and would need her help to carry it out.

But first, he needed to check out how his gift worked and gain some sort of control over it. He knew only of one previous happening, where water had appeared spontaneously.

'Perhaps you have to think water,' said Sandra.

Jake stood and rubbing his wrist for inspiration; he attempted to recreate the stream that had happened in the cave.

When nothing happened, he reverted to a tribal rain dance he had seen on TV. The song and dance gave Sandra a fit of the giggles, while the look of sheer determination on Jake's face made her even worse.

Giving up on the wailing, Jake concentrated on recreating his feelings in the cave. He remembered it made him shudder; it was the thought of entering the fabric again.

So, he continued with his dance, but with a different attitude, with eyes closed and going round in a circle.

Suddenly, Sandra's giggling stopped.

'Jake, look!' shouted Sandra.

Jake stopped and looking down, he saw the making of a swamp, there were water puddles on the surface. He grabbed a stick and poked around in the middle; it was like quicksand, the stick disappeared.

He picked up a large boulder and dropped it in. There was a deep splosh as the boulder sank.

'Wow, that's exactly what I was thinking. I thought it might be easier to start with a muddy puddle. I wonder how deep that is? ...This is quite insane!'

An even more bewildered Jake suggested a return to the crowd and to find *Tabule* and *Leber* to discuss his plan for retribution.

No sooner had they re-entered the village compound, than they saw *Tabule* and *Leber* sitting patiently with one of the elders, awaiting their return.

This was one of the oldest members of the tribe; everyone had helped to build him a home and he was entertaining as though he had never left.

'Come, sit with us. Moss has told you of your gift, and I get the feeling you have just been testing it,' said *Tabule*.

Sandra and Jake sat on two carved-out logs that formed part of a circle of chairs around a large tree trunk table, at the front of the elder's house.

'This is Charlie,' said *Tabule,* introducing Jake and Sandra to him.

'He has witnessed the good times and the bad and is what you might call very wise.'

Charlie disappeared inside and came out with drinks in a large woven pitcher. He gestured to them both to drink, and grinned when they both exclaimed how strong it was.

Leber, who loved his alchemy, explained that it was a particular root which was fermented and allowed to evaporate in the sun. The condensate was collected, resulting in a rather strong beverage of unique flavour.

Jake complimented Charlie on the drink and then, rather enthusiastically, began to relay to *Tabule* and *Leber* his plan. He told them that he and Sandra proposed to act as university students on a gap year, exploring the river, when their kayak capsized. They would enter the logger's camp for help, and from there, they could assess the operation and work out a plan from within.

Jake did think that *Marley* might be able to assist, as he had done with the reporters, if it was possible.

But the need to know what they were up against was important for the future of the villagers.

'Sounds daft enough to work,' said *Leber*. 'Oh, and I told Charlie you would make him a well, by his house.'

Jake toasted Charlie and said he would do his best.

Leber and *Tabule* decided it was time to check up on the reporters and make some final arrangements, before returning to the Manor.

'We shall discuss this at tomorrow's meeting,' said *Tabule*, and they went off to find *Marley*.

Jake, now with confidence levels boosted by the strong liquor, asked Charlie where he might like his well. Charlie replied by pointing to a spot round the side of his hut.

'You will have to bear with me, this is all very new to me,' said Jake. He decided not to put so much effort in as he had before, he wanted to keep it small.

And so, he began.

Sandra and Charlie watched intently as Jake shuffled around in a small circle, occasionally looking down to see if there was any sign. After a couple of minutes, nothing had happened.

'Perhaps it was just a fluke back there, outside the camp,' said Jake a little disheartened.

'You must have done something different; didn't you say you had the same feeling in the cave, that déjà vu feeling?' said Sandra.

Jake admitted that there was a moment when his body shuddered at the thought of going through that episode with Henry, all over again.

'Well shudder,' said Sandra, now a little tipsy herself.

Jake returned to the process of shuffling and shuddering; still nothing.

He stamped his foot in frustration.

What happened next, was a spectacle worthy of being filmed.

The ground opened up, Jake disappeared into it, and then, almost immediately, a geyser with Jake at its helm, shot out of the ground. Water, and Jake, were sent some fifteen feet into the air; it then subsided and returned back whence it had come. Jake picked himself up and went over to the hole made by the event.

He joined Sandra and Charlie, who had also been caught by the fountain and were dripping wet.

The three stood around the hole, looking at a distinct level of water which had settled some three foot down.

'There you go, one well!' smiled Jake, dusting himself down.

Jake shook Charlie's hand and suggested that they might return the next day.

Sandra agreed that it was time they returned, and they both set off for the cave and its doorway to the Manor.

Retracing their steps they came upon the two reporters, exactly where they had been left. They looked very cosy in their native tribal dress, and they were painted in the most amazing fashion.

The women from the village had spent a couple of hours at *Leber's* request to dress them. They would be treated as royalty and entertained overnight, with no explanation by the villagers on how they arrived there.

Both Jake and Sandra began to hurt from laughing and decided that it was best to leave them and continued on their way to the cave.

'We shall have to get Moss to put this on screen. We can also check out the logger's camp, and see if there is any more detail visible,' said Sandra, approaching the entrance to the cave.

The darkness of the cave was not very inviting. It had a heaviness, as though the air was thick, and it needed extra effort to proceed.

This was the veil that Sandra remembered, and it was the part she did not like. They passed through this and continued on; the darkness prevailed. They expected to see the entrance at the other side, but there was just darkness.

The opening into the jungle appeared very suddenly. It was dark, the stars were out, and the jungle had an eerie feel to it. They managed to find their way back out and eventually reached the vehicle. Jake checked the clock on the dashboard.

'Do you know it's midnight?' he exclaimed.

'Of course, the time zone,' said Sandra. 'We shall have to work out the difference and bear it in mind for the future.'

Jake suggested they call it a night and go home to get some shuteye. Hugging the edge of the field, Jake made it to the lane. He dropped Sandra off, bade her a goodnight, and then continued back to the farm.

Back at the Manor, many of the council members had returned and were discussing Jake's plan.

Henry obviously had his reservations; he was concerned that they might be harmed by this bunch of thugs. He asked Moss if he could see anything on the satellite pictures.

'It's too dark to see the loggers' camp, but our reporters are dancing the night away.' Moss pointed out the fire and the two crimson clad figures travelling anticlockwise around it.

Chonga, who had left the three Shaman pacifying the women, told Henry not to worry, and that Jake and Sandra need not go it alone. There would always be someone close by to assist them both if their plan did not work. There were small pockets of discussions amongst everyone, as they wandered freely around the Manor, right through to sunrise.

The silence of a Manor deep in thought, was broken by the sound of the breakfast gong. Moss, now the official gong beater, made his debut to the morning.

There had been an overnight shower, which had increased the smell of the countryside, and the damp grass brought its aromatic scent, on a gentle breeze, straight through the open doors.

It was one of those mornings where everybody knew just exactly what everyone else was doing. The scent of the day, the relaxed atmosphere, was something that we all have as a treasured childhood memory.

Jake was in the shower, Fidgit was chasing something edible in a field across the way. Mother was in the kitchen creating the most wonderful odours, which permeated through the orchard, and tugged at Jake's nostrils. Bill, his father was changing the blade in his razor having found out the hard way the previous one was blunt. Sandra, having showered, was having a little pamper time, and after shaving her legs she was now doing nails. Her mother was making a continental breakfast; being the busy woman she was, there was no time for cooking.

Sandra's phone beeped as Jake's early message came through. She smiled contentedly at the knowledge that Jake was hers, they knew each other very well and would be soul mates for life, regardless.

Reading his message, she gleaned that he was at the same stage as herself, about to breakfast, and in a no rush, no panic mode.

Jake wandered through the orchard to the kitchen door, with Fidgit in tow.

'Morning,' he shouted.

Father, by now, had completed his ablutions and was attending the kitchen table with bits of toilet tissue stuck to his chin.

'I'm gonna' buy you an electric razor for your birthday,' said Jake, amazed at the amount of paper a face could take.

Mother thrust the contents of her frying pan on a large serving platter in the centre of the table.

'Eat,' she said.

Returning to the table with the contents of the industrial toaster, she sat and joined the breakfast crew.

'So, what's going on up at the Manor?' she asked.

Jake told them about the cave in the jungle, its connection to the Amazon, with its tribes and loggers, the palm oil plantation that would be creeping towards the villagers, and their fear of losing their lands altogether.

He omitted to mention his plan with Sandra.

Jake finished his breakfast for a king, kissed his mother, shook his father's hand, collected his shadow, and went on his way.

Sandra was waiting at the gate; Fidgit took up position on her lap and stayed there for the journey.

They arrived at the Manor, Fidgit did not disappear into the undergrowth, and he would not leave Jake's side.

'That's strange.' said Sandra. 'We usually don't see him for dust.'

There was a distinct quiet about the Manor house, when they entered. The council members were quietly sitting observing the screens, as Moss navigated his way through the area.

Henry came over to bid them good morning.

'Shall we go outside for a chat?' said Henry.

They all filed onto the patio and positioned themselves on some of the comfy seats.

Archie came out with a piece of marmalade toast in his hand.

'Do you mind if I join you?'

There was no negative response, so the five sat, Fidgit being the fifth.

Henry began:

'Having discussed your ideas throughout the night, the conclusion was that it puts a lot of pressure on you, and we were unsure that it was fair. But having weighed up the possible implications, it appears, that as English students, you might stand a good chance of pulling this off. *Marley* is always keen to help and is prepared to remain in the background and prescribe any relevant medicine that may be needed. You could be putting yourself in danger, but I think you know that. If you are both sure that you want to go through with this, you can count on our support,' said Henry.

They all returned to the war room, where they were still waiting for morning to arrive in the Amazon.

Tabule came over to the group. He expressed his admiration for their mettle and for the knowledge that Jake had taken on board. He was a credit to his great grandfather, without whom, none of this would have happened.

'We are ready to go,' said *Leber*.

The council members made their way into the fabric from where they stood; beginners like Jake and Sandra would have to take the economy class and go by cave.

'Are you coming, Henry?' asked Sandra.

Henry's response was instant, and positive; there was no way he would let them both take this risk on their own.

Archie also had an inclination to try another mode of transport, and said he was not going to miss the fun.

They all piled outside and into the vehicles which were available, mainly one Land Rover and Archie's pick-up.

Fidgit's behaviour was still very clingy, even when they arrived at the field with the jungle.

Dismounting, they continued through the rape field to the jungle entrance. They reached the entrance to the cave and began the weird journey through.

When they reached the other side, it was still dark.

Leber and *Marley* had arrived and were approaching the cave entrance.

'Ah, Henry, you made it in and out, without stopping,' said *Leber* sarcastically.

Henry gave *Leber* a dagger-like look, while Archie commented on how the hairs on his neck had not gone down.

The group made their way to the river. *Leber* and *Marley* said they would see them on the other side and disappeared into the darkness.

The five, which included Fidgit then made their way to the river, where a dugout canoe had been left alongside the riverbank. They all climbed in, grappling with the stability, which proved to be a little hairy.

Eventually they all got themselves balanced ready for the launch, they gently paddled to the other side of the river and tied the canoe to an overhanging branch.

When they met up with *Leber* and *Marley*, Jake and Sandra thought it best if they continued along the riverbank with Fidgit, alone.

Henry and Archie promised to keep a watchful eye from a distance.

Jake and Sandra wandered along the riverbank as though lost. Suddenly Fidgit disappeared. Jake was distraught, trying to call him back with a whisper.

Hoping they would catch up with him later, Jake and Sandra continued until they came to the compound.

They both crept around the area where the loggers had camped; the day was just becoming light.

There was a sectional building on stilts, an impressive camping facility, obviously bolted together like a building site hut. The front door opened onto an extended floor area, creating a patio, while the roof extended over the same space.

There were some very big machines in a compound across from the hut and fairly close to the river, three in total. A bulldozer, of some thirty ton, a harvester of twenty ton and a forwarder of twenty ton.

Everywhere was quiet, you could hear a pin drop on the grass.

Sandra took cover behind a large tree, while Jake explored the compound with the machinery. He wondered if his gift could cope with such huge machines.

And then he began.

He shuffled around the machinery compound, humming and searching for that elusive shudder.

The morning continued to appear, and as the sun rose over the treetops, Jake's exertions were starting to show signs of success.

He had been dancing around the vehicles for nearly an hour, when suddenly there was movement – one of the loggers had come out to relieve himself. He then started walking over towards the machines and Jake. Jake crouched under the bulldozer on very soft and moist ground.

Suddenly there was barking further up the track, it was Fidgit, he had that excited bark of, 'I have found something.'

The logger stopped, then went off to investigate the noise. There was no dog in the camp. The barking stopped as the logger went out of sight.

Almost immediately Jake was accosted by a licking and tail wagging Fidgit. Was he glad to see him?

Jake continued to do what he thought was needed and continued with his efforts.

Soon he began to feel a warm glow, and the ground beneath his feet began to feel softer and more pliable. As he continued, the machinery he was dancing around began to sink. He increased his efforts, and the machinery disappeared even faster. It sunk below the ground and was gone from view.

Jake was keen to make a sharp exit before the logger decided to return from his investigations. He navigated around the now liquid floor of the compound to where Sandra was waiting.

'Did you see that? Fidgit distracted that man. We had better get out before he returns,' said Jake.

'You don't have to worry about that man,' came the voice of *Marley,* who could not be seen.

'Him gonna be happy for a while.' He then stepped out of the greenery; he had been through the hut and tried out his latest invention on five other members of the group.

Henry, Archie and *Leber* came walking over to congratulate them. Archie was impressed with the way the machines had been swallowed up.

Marley high-fived Jake and said he had done fine; then he and *Leber*, saying 'see you later,' melted into the greenery and were gone.

'Reckon it's time to get back to the Manor, Edmund and Ivy will be returning soon,' said Henry.

And they all made their way back to the canoe for the return.

Chapter 23

Returning to the riverbank from where they had set off, they secured the canoe and continued along the path towards the cave.

While making their way back through, Archie commented that it was like being at altitude, that pressure you get in the ear was the same.

They arrived back at the Manor to find that Edmund and Ivy had returned.

Henry was keen to find out how the trials had gone with the new machine, and Archie was interested in where he would need to take the plane to have it fitted.

Edmund was optimistic at the prospect of using the equipment, and after extensive trials, it had surpassed all their expectations. Ivy grabbed Sandra.

'Let's leave the boys to their toys; you can tell me all about the Amazon adventure.' Ivy led Sandra through the house and off towards the greenhouses.

Moss came over and congratulated Jake on a successful outcome. He told the group that *Tabule* and *Leber* were conducting some last-minute alterations to the access roads created by the loggers. They would be back in time for the meeting, which should conclude the business in hand.

Edmund, Henry and Archie went through to the patio where they sat and discussed the plan for the equipment.

Henry needed facts to put to the meeting later. And so, with Edmund's report on the operation and installation of the equipment, and Archie's knowledge of aircraft, the three sat and thrashed out a plan to carry the project forward.

Jake meanwhile was watching the activity within the village, on screen, as Moss navigated around the site.

'You can see our intrepid reporters; they have the crimson clothes.

Leber had requested that they do the dance for life. They would be told that the longer they danced, the less chance they had of being eaten.'

Moss found this very amusing.

He told Jake that *Leber* had arranged for the villagers to make them dance until they dropped; *Marley* would then pay them a visit. He would supply the necessary potion to intensify their experience and dream state.

Afterwards, their tribal clothing and paint would be removed by the women and their original clothes put back on. They would then be guided back through the cave, put back into their car, and left down the lane to recover.

'It may prevent them snooping in future,' laughed Moss.

'Anyway, I need some air, and there is something I need to tell you Jake. Let's go and sit in the summerhouse where we can have a little privacy.'

Moss and Jake strolled on down to the seclusion of the summerhouse.

The few council members that remained were partaking of some rest and relaxation in the conservatory, with the night flower.

When they reached the summer house, Moss continued on down to the river's small beachy area.

He sat on a small grassy step of the bank, and picking up a pebble, threw it into the river. Jake sat down next to him, and they both just watched the river flow, while the occasional fish plucked at flies on the surface.

'I don't suppose that anyone has tried to explain to you the whys and wherefores of the gift that you find yourself in possession of?' asked Moss.

Jake had to admit that it had suddenly appeared; he had no idea that he was responsible for the stream in the cave. He admitted that a shiver had run through him when they entered the cave, but he had dismissed it as a feeling of apprehension.

Moss continued to explain that all *Burrbesh* can summon the deep water when they distribute their seed, the two go together. But, he admitted, it was unusual for a new shoot, like Jake, to have this sort of power.

Most newcomers, in the past, had only managed basic telepathy, and after time, perhaps the occasional planting. This would suddenly appear at random, with no control, and after a lot of effort and straining.

'Come, let me show you some of the basics.' Moss stood and walked to the river's edge.

Clasping his hands together, the water began to rise in a spiral, a small waterspout danced around the surface of the river. Clapping his hands, the river returned to normal. He then walked up towards the summerhouse, instructing Jake to stand perfectly still in the middle of the path.

'You have the ability to summon a little or a lot of water from below. You will need to practise this skill if it is to be of use to you,' said Moss.

He explained that the shudder Jake felt, was the connection he made. It was like the sudden shock of falling in cold water, finding the shower was set to cold, or being caught in the rain and getting soaked. The different levels of that experience would invoke the ground water.

'Once you can control that feeling, you will be able to produce a muddy puddle, or a lake.'

Moss suggested he practised these different levels of shudder while he sat and observed. He poured a large glass of iced lemonade, which had just been brought by one of the kitchen staff.

'Now don't forget, start off with a gentle approach.' Moss made himself comfortable and continued to instruct Jake.

As the afternoon passed, Moss had him jogging in circles, standing on one leg, jumping to a rhythm of four beats and even attempting a head stand. Eventually, Jake, feeling as though he was being put on, a little, wandered over to Moss.

'Well, have you learned anything, Master Jake?'

'I do believe I have,' said Jake, as he dragged his foot in a horseshoe shape around the leg of the chair. The ground instantly turned to mud, and the chair sank, tipping Moss from his cosy cushion, onto the grass.

'Very clever, you see you don't really need all those silly positions.' Moss burst out laughing, which made Jake laugh.

Jake offered him a hand up, and they both returned to the house, chuckling over the event.

They entered by the front door; everywhere was very busy. Most of the council members were milling around, from the war room and into the dining room. Some were deep in conversation on the sofas that were dotted around the hall and conservatory. *Tabule* came over to them.

'Good evening, Master Jake, I feel that Moss has been instructing you in a way that you may not have required,' he grinned and gave a slight nod to Moss.

They went into the dining room, where MacTavish had, as usual, provided a spread fit for a king.

'Moss will sound the gong when the meeting begins,' said *Tabule* and left Jake to meet the others. Ivy and Sandra were chatting to Edmund while collecting food.

'Henry and Archie are outside, get some food and meet us out there,' said Sandra, and off she went with Ivy and Edmund.

Jake piled a plate with goodies and turned to join them. In his haste he nearly lost the lot as he bumped into *Marley* who had come to inform Jake that the two reporters had been put safely back in their car.

'How long will it be before the loggers wake up?' Jake asked him.

'They will both be happy till gone nightfall,' said *Marley*.

Jake said he would love to see the look on their faces when they woke up.

Thanking *Marley*, Jake made his way out onto the patio where everyone had congregated around a large table.

'I've been hearing of your exploits young Jake. They may come in very handy,' said Edmund. Ivy also congratulated Jake, who having not eaten all day, was busy stuffing his face, mumbling a thank you for the glass of red wine Henry had poured for him.

Edmund began by telling Archie that there was an old airstrip at Magnatek; it was for customers and dignitaries, rarely used but well maintained. It was a grass runway which had been built by the previous chairman and was a decent length.

Edmund told Henry that the grounds for this facility were a lot larger than they had seen on their last visit. He said that if it was possible to land the plane there, Max would be able to carry out the installation of the equipment much more easily, plus trials would have to be undertaken.

Archie had been doing his own research into the plane, which was affectionately known as 'the shed,' due to its capacity to carry. It had been fitted with extra fuel tanks, giving it a range of nearly two thousand miles. But its main virtue was its ability to take off on rough ground, especially on short runways.

He said that if the plane had been serviced regularly, there was no reason why it should not be fully capable of carrying out the task. It just needed to be collected from an airfield in Jamaica, where it was stored.

Henry asked Edmund what the state of the runway was at present. He replied that Max told him it was always kept in readiness.

Henry continued to ask questions. How soon could the plane be brought to Magnatek, how long would it take to fit the equipment, would they use Archie's airfield in Venezuela as the base?

Henry was beginning to see the bigger picture. His sudden injection into the world of tech and futuristic anomalies was starting to infiltrate his grey matter.

The organizing was really no different from the old days; the only difference was, in those days, you had to ride a horse everywhere to sort it.

Now you could do it on a smart phone or a laptop.

Henry said he would call Max and find out how soon they could be ready to take the plane for its installation.

He wandered along the patio, with his phone, for a little privacy. While he was gone, *Marley* and *Myck* came to their table.

'I see you support the black, gold and green *Marley*. Fancy a trip to your homeland, Jamaica?' said Archie.

Marley declined, claiming heights gave him vertigo, but he would gladly meet him there. He had friends there and would be quite happy to spend some time with them.

Henry came back with good news; he said Max could take the plane anytime. He told them it was easier to land at twilight. He would put the landing lights on, and with what was left of the day, it would make landing, for the first time, easier.

'That's settled then, I shall go and collect your plane. Would anyone like to join me?' Archie asked.

Jake was tempted. He asked Sandra if she would like to go, 'just for a couple of days,' he said.

'Why not?' she replied. 'But what about the meeting?'

Henry said that they could deal with the meeting, and that they should go and enjoy the experience that Archie offered them.

Jake told Archie that they would be back within the hour. They had just to collect an overnight bag, and they would be ready to go.

Jake and Sandra literally ran to the car and raced home and raced back, and within forty-five minutes, they piled into Archie's pick-up.

Before setting off, Archie explained the agenda: his plane was waiting at Henstridge airfield in Somerset, a short drive away. There would be a few stops and refuels to get to Jamaica. He had plotted a course, and was ready to go, if they were sure they wanted to go, he said.

'Please,' said Sandra.

And so, they set off to collect the key element of this crazy plan.

Moss swung the mallet at the gong, indicating the meeting had begun.

Tabule opened the debate, complimenting young Jake and his efforts to secure the safety of the villagers.

He began to explain to the council members the plan that was being put in place for that area of the Amazon. The council had agreed to support it and now the details would be explained by Henry.

Henry stood and thanked everyone for attending. He told the council that the equipment they had discovered at Magnatek was going to be fitted to an aircraft. Archie, accompanied by Jake and Sandra, had just set off to collect it. He introduced Edmund to the council and told them he would explain the technical side.

Edmund started to describe how everything would work, without confusing everyone too much with technical jargon. He began by explaining how he had witnessed the equipment in operation at Magnatek.

It could send a magnetic field, only an inch wide, a distance of one hundred miles in diameter; it would radiate out horizontally, using lasers.

The clever thing was, he said, that the magnetic field could be manipulated, effectively creating a picture of the garden it was about to create. For each individual species, and by using GPS, this picture could be transposed over a map of the target area. This would result in an evenly dispersed ground cover and canopy, which when processed, would be released as the field was turned off. With the right climatic conditions, the seed will drop into its designated area, and then the growing would begin.

'We have calculated the altitude required to pick up the seed from the council members, as five hundred feet. From there the plane will spiral upwards to two thousand feet, during which time the mapping process will take effect, and log into the GPS. When it reaches that altitude, it will be very visible, the magnetic field, with its seed, will cast a shadow over the ground. This process will be monitored and when everything is ready, the field will disconnect and the seed will fall down to the ground,' said Edmund, who now had his technical hat on.

He continued to explain the roles each of the council members would play. Each would have their designated position around the perimeter of the devastation. The plane would make one circuit, and when overhead, each council member would release their special cargo. It had to be low enough for the magnetic field to attract the seed. Once everyone had released their cargo, it would be up to the pilot, and those operating the equipment to finish the task.

'This will not go unnoticed in your media world,' said *Leber*. 'What plans do you have for after the event?'

Edmund said that there would be very little to link any activity with themselves. The aircraft would have no markings and could return to Jamaica. The equipment would return to Magnatek, and everyone would go about their normal business.

Henry claimed that with the night flower established within the villages, and with the use of their own sprouts, the villagers would be able to maintain their borders. They could even prevent the loggers from infiltrating the jungle; it would be their turn to take an upper hand.

'This is but a small scar on your world, it is probably too small to have an impact,' said *Tabule*.

Henry mentioned the Gypsies, who had for years been friends of Mother Earth. They were currently distributing the night flower across Europe. There were many more lost cultures that would become allies, as the introduction of the night flower increased.

'The trouble is,' said Edmund, 'there is so much devastation, it is easy to become overwhelmed by it all, and I imagine that each situation is going to need a different approach.'

With many of the points having been discussed, Henry said all they needed to do now was await the arrival of one plane. *Tabule* closed the meeting, and everyone wandered off to do their own thing.

Marley said he was going to wander over to his favourite island and wait for the plane collectors.

Tabule and *Leber* appeared to be deep in private discussions at the end of the table.

'Moss, can you zoom into that area where the palm oil planting is going on?' said *Leber*.

The screens on the wall flickered as they synchronised the image, the picture became sharper, and one could see the movements of machines and people milling around.

It appeared to be a small village of workers; the road that led to it was very visible, as much of the vegetation had been cut and burned back.

'I know what you are thinking,' said Moss.

'I'll get my hat.'

It was time once again for the three musketeers to perform. As they walked out through the conservatory, their appearance changed. Moss acquired his large green hat, *Tabule's* coat enlarged and seemed to flow like a sail, as he walked, and *Leber* was suddenly sporting a rather impressive staff. They strode out towards the greenhouses and disappeared through the bushes.

'What's going on?' queried Edmund.

Henry knew exactly. He told Edmund that he would be able to see it on the screens very soon. Henry asked what time it got dark over there; Edmund calculated that in three hours and twenty minutes the sun would set.

'Ah, in that case we have time to visit the Tavern. Would you like to join me?

As I now have a licence, I would like to buy you both a drink to celebrate passing my first exam in four hundred years.' Henry's humour brought a smile to their faces.

Henry knew that *Tabule* preferred to carry out his operations under the cover of darkness.

He was sure that when they returned there would be something rather magnificent to see. They all strolled out to the big blue Bentley and drove off to the village.

When they arrived, the Tavern was positively heaving. The garden was full, the bar was busy, Ivy spotted Barney, who seemed surrounded by strangers.

She wandered over to greet him.

'What's going on? It looks like a convention has come to the village.'

Barney explained that the two reporters had returned with stories of being kidnapped by strange creatures and forced to engage in satanic rituals. They put their story out on social media, and all these strange people descended on the Tavern, believing that it was the epicentre of some dark coven.

Henry and Edmund had been to the bar, and passing Ivy a drink Edmund suggested they find a quieter corner.

Barney suggested his usual table, which was normally in a slightly secluded spot on the riverbank.

As they made their way through the crowd, a booming voice with an American accent called out.

'Yo, Lord what's your name, won't you join us, and bring Barney and your friends?'

Henry turned to acknowledge this invasion and could not believe what he saw.

The reporters, the large American and the short Englishman were sitting at a table, surrounded by odd people.

'What happened to your faces?' said Henry.

The two men had been tattooed, dots adorned their eyebrows, a pretty pattern scrolled down their noses and onto their cheeks and three vertical lines ran down their chins.

'We have been to hell and survived, these are marks of the devil,' shouted the American.

He certainly was the type to enjoy being the centre of attention; not so for the shorter one, he did not appear to be enjoying the media as much.

Henry turned to Barney and Edmund and was struggling to keep a straight face.

Barney admitted that he had omitted a description of their appearance and thought it best if they saw the results for themselves.

'Well, my friend, I am glad you managed to escape the wrath of the Devil, we shall have to leave you, there is someone over there I need to see.'

Henry had to escape the presence of the two reporters before he embarrassed himself.

'I see the work of *Leber* on the faces of those two, perhaps we shall get the full story later,' said Henry.

Ivy thought it might be a good idea to put an electric cattle fence around the jungle and put some signs up to say it is a university quarantine experiment. It might deter any further investigations.

‘Barney, can you find out what these two reporters plan to do next? We don’t really want them snooping around the Manor,’ said Henry.

The look on Barney’s face needed no explanation.

‘Very well, but only because it’s you,’ said Barney, and he shuffled off in the direction of the crowd.

Henry’s mobile phone beeped and, tapping the screen, he announced he had received a text from Archie.

‘He’s just circling Montego Bay; he’s going to book in at a hotel and get a local flight to pick up the plane in the morning. He says everyone is fine, but as they may take a little longer to return, he will call us when he lands.’

Henry suggested that it might be a good idea to return to the Manor when they had finished their drinks.

Surveying the throng of odd people in the garden, they found it surprising that so many people could be wrapped up in such a strange enigma.

They could see Barney having his ear bent and in a moment of guilt, Henry decided to rescue him.

Finishing his drink, he asked Edmund and Ivy if they were ready to leave; he told them his intentions and made his way over to Barney.

‘Howdy, your lordship, have you come to join the audience?’ said the noisy American.

‘Terribly sorry old chap, but I have to drag Barney away, he has to make up the four in our Bridge tournament.’

Henry told him he had just had a phone call and the main player had developed shingles.

‘We shall talk again, tomorrow perhaps.’

Henry ushered Barney out of the garden and into the Bentley.

‘Barney, I should really tell you about the events of late. It may help if you are questioned, to be able to explain some of the truths, but not the full truths.

Besides, I felt sorry I asked you to do some probing on the reporters. Watching you, I felt duty bound to rescue you, forgive me.’

They waited for Edmund and Ivy to exit the melée and they all piled in the Bentley.

Barney laughed as they drove out of the carpark and back along the lane.

'I knew you had something to do with it,' Barney roared with laughter as he remembered the faces of the two reporters.

When they reached the Manor, it was about 21:00hrs. Edmund and Ivy went straight into the war room and Edmund set about synchronising the screens.

It had been dark for a couple of hours in the Amazon, and the palm oil village was quiet.

There was no sign of the three musketeers, especially as they would not show up on any thermal imaging; Edmund could only focus the image as best he could, in the hope of catching a change in vegetation.

MacTavish came in with drinks, Henry and Barney took one each and Henry showed him through to the conservatory, where they sat next to the night flower.

Barney commented what a beautiful fragrance the flower gave, something he thought was the closest thing to perfection. They sat drinking in the fragrance, and a very nice Rioja, as Henry told Barney everything that had happened over the past week or two.

Barney listened intently as the proposed plan for the event was laid out.

'I would very much like to experience that door to the Amazon,' said Barney, and went on to divulge what he had gleaned from the reporters.

He told Henry that the last thing they both remembered was getting into the car at the Tavern. They thought they were going off somewhere but couldn't remember where, then the dreams started, and the monsters came. The whole experience had been enhanced by the application of one of *Marley's* hallucinogenic potions.

'The big one said he dreamt that they had been chosen as the sacrifice. The natives were all dressed in demonic masks with bones hanging from their necks. They were forced to dance the whole day around a fire with a huge pot at its centre. They danced until they dropped.' Barney, now privy to the story, knew it must have been *Leber*, and laughed at the thought of the two reporters being dressed up as sacrifices.

'They came to, sitting in their car down the lane. When they realized they had both had the same dream, and with their faces marked as they were, they were convinced that they had been part of some black magic ritual,' said Barney.

'They have quite a following, they investigate ghost sightings and other strange reports. They have had some success and have been on TV a couple of times.

The big one comes from Mississippi, in the Deep South. He said they have a lot of these sorts of goings on down there. It was he who launched their story on public media, asking for anyone with similar experiences, and giving the name of the Tavern. The result was the crowd which had descended. It seemed to bring all manner of people out of the woodwork.'

Just at that moment *Leber* entered from off the patio, followed by *Tabule* and Moss. They had lost their attachments and had resumed their normal appearance.

'Good evening, Barney,' said *Leber*. 'Are you well?'

Henry explained what had been happening with the reporters and the Tavern.

'Did you instruct the women to tattoo those men?' Henry asked.

Leber said, they were not tattoos, it was a plant extract he had concocted many moons ago. It had been used by a farmer to brand his pigs. He thought it very apt.

'It will wear off in a month or two,' and he went off to the war room.

As *Tabule* and Moss walked through, Henry asked if their evening had been a success. Moss affirmed that it had gone very well, better than could be expected.

Moss was keen to see the screens, Henry and Barney followed, only to find that the night had no moon, and it was too dark to see anything.

'The morning will reveal all,' said *Tabule*. He told them that all the cleared roads which led to the working village had been sown.

'Master Jake suggested removing the radiator caps on the machinery and dropping a little something in; once a root system got into the engine it would render it inoperable. I am keen to see if it works!' There was a buzz of excitement from the three, as if naughty boys had escaped being caught. *Tabule* explained that the area would be isolated, nothing would be able to get through, and there was a good chance they might abandon the work.

They watched the screens in the hope that they would see something, squinting their eyes as if to make the image improve.

Henry's phone rang, it was a video call from Archie.

'Can you put this on-screen Edmund? asked Henry.

The picture filled the screens. There was Jake, Sandra and Archie with *Marley*. They were all sitting on the beach under a palm-fronded canopy, sipping cool coloured drinks with parasols, through straws.

'We are struggling here,' said Archie, sarcastically.

He said *Marley* had appeared just a few minutes before, said he was off to see friends and just stopped by to say hello.

Archie panned his phone around three sixty and showed them the beach and bar.

'I have booked us on an early flight in the morning to Negril, I couldn't land there, the runway was too short. Your legal guys made the arrangements to have the plane fuelled and ready to go, with all the paperwork, fingers crossed, eh?'

With little information on the plane, Archie would have to find out exactly how much fuel the plane held, then work out its range, before confirming his flight plan. He had originally estimated five refuelling stops and a journey time of twenty-five hours.

'May have to stop over on the way back, shall keep you informed.'

Archie's image started to pixilate, and then they were gone.

'Doesn't look like they will be back tomorrow,' said Henry.

'How would you like to see the Amazon tomorrow, Barney?'

Barney hesitantly agreed, and asked if it was safe.

'You will be fine, Barney. I have suspended quandaries for the moment,' said *Leber*.

Henry asked Barney if he would like a lift back down to the Tavern, or home. Without hesitation Barney said, 'home would be good.'

Ivy suggested it was probably time they went too, they needed to be up early, Edmund agreed.

Tabule and *Leber* wandered into the conservatory and settled down with the night flower, while Moss, addicted to the technology, remained scrolling and tapping.

Chapter 24

Henry returned to the Manor, he bade Moss a goodnight and claimed his eyes would be square if he continued to watch the screens. His words fell on deaf ears, and so Henry went up the stairs and retired for the night.

Moss continued to watch the village of the palm oil workers for some time; bored with waiting for daylight to return, he switched over to the cameras that had been installed on the estate. Checking the camera over by the jungle, he observed the nocturnal antics of some of the countryside's inhabitants.

Flicking from camera to camera, he eventually came upon the view at the end of the lane, just past the main entrance. There, parked on the side of the lane was a little Fiat 500; he recognized this as the car belonging to the two reporters. He remembered how inappropriate the size was for the giant of an American. There appeared to be no one in the vehicle, so Moss continued to watch, his curiosity aroused.

The two reporters had apparently walked along the boundary wall, to the river, in the hope of gaining access to the Manor. The wall terminated at the river's edge, with a framework of wrought iron attached. The decorative scrollwork extended into the river with a fan of spikes, preventing anyone from climbing around it. The wall varied from around eight to ten feet high and extended around the perimeter of the Manor.

As Moss watched, the two reporters came into view, having obviously given up at the end of the wall. The big one could be seen gesturing to an area of the wall which was a little lower. Moss assumed that they would attempt to scale the wall at that point.

He roused *Leber* who came in to watch. They sat watching for some time, as the small reporter, with his back to the wall, clasped his hands to allow the big one to scramble up. It took several attempts; the little one collapsed under the weight of the American several times, shaking his hands and blowing his fingers as the strain took its toll.

Moss and *Leber* found the spectacle quite amusing. The American eventually managed to raise his body onto the top of the wall, by using the small one's head as a step. He then pulled him up and they both sat on top of the wall surveying the garden, the small one rubbing his head.

'I have an idea,' said *Leber*, and he melted into the fabric.

Leber appeared close by the wall, unseen in his guise; the two reporters were discussing what to do next. He could hear the big one say they should jump on the count of three.

Leber knew exactly what he would do. He clasped his hands together, blew into them, and stretched out his arms. A thin misty veil enveloped the area, creating a circular cubicle, connecting to the wall either side of the intruders.

Leber, satisfied with his choice of action, returned to Moss, and they both watched in anticipation.

There was an audible count to three, and the two launched themselves from the top of the wall. They landed, not in the garden, but in the lane facing the outside of the wall. They then proceeded to scale the wall, an exact action replay, played over and over again.

'You put them in a quandary,' laughed Moss.

Leber commented that it would keep them out of mischief till morning. He said he was going to see how *Chonga* was coping and told him he would be back later.

Leber walked out into the night and was gone.

Moss remained entertained for a short while, then joined *Tabule* and the night flower for a little relaxation.

In Jamaica, Archie, Sandra and Jake were preparing for the day. Archie had arranged a lift on a supply plane for the three of them. They had to be at the airport for 04:30, so while waiting for the taxi, they grabbed a fruit only breakfast from the restaurant.

They made good time to the airport; their lift was already running his engines.

Hurrying to the plane, they were greeted by the pilot, who knew Archie; they shook hands and after a short banter they all piled into the plane. They had to sit on boxes of supplies, no seat belts, but their destination was only fifty miles down the road, and they were there before they knew it.

Disembarking, Archie thanked the pilot; they all gathered up their rucksacks and made their way to the hangars.

They were greeted by the airport's only mechanic, Otis, with his curly white hair and permanent smile. He had been repairing and maintaining aircraft since he was a boy. He took them round the side of the hangar to the plane.

'There she be. But don't be put off by appearances,' he said, 'she is one hell of a plane.'

Otis went on to list the important points of 'Lady Sherpa'. She had all the up-to-date avionics and autopilot; she would take off and land on a short runway, and on rough ground, and the fuel tanks held one thousand gallons, giving her a range of over two thousand miles. Cruising speed was three hundred miles per hour; he had personally inspected her, and all the paperwork was in order. Flight clearance had been authorised, so whenever they were ready, so was she.

Archie told Otis that his first stop would be his airfield in Venezuela, and from there, he would refuel and pick up a delivery he had promised Henry.

He thanked Otis for his work, who wished them all a safe journey and watched as they all boarded the plane, affectionately known as the "Shed."

It did not take Archie long to familiarize himself with the controls and run the relevant checks. Then firing up one, and then the other engine, they taxied to the runway.

Jake and Sandra took up the flight crew seats in the cockpit, and strapped themselves in.

Air traffic control confirmed that they were all clear for take-off. Archie pushed the throttles forward, the plane accelerated, the power pushed them back into their seats, and in no time, they were airborne. Archie levelled off at five thousand feet and set the autopilot for his place in Venezuela.

'Ok you two, you can unbuckle and explore the plane, just don't open any doors or windows,' he joked.

They had made very good time and were airborne for 06:00 local time; now all they had to do was sit back and enjoy the flight.

Checking the time zones, Archie decided it was not the time to call Henry, but did message him, giving a rough eta at Magnatek, and he would give him a call when they landed at his vineyard in Venezuela.

Back at the Manor, Moss was at his station in the war room, keen to catch the first glimpse of the village, as the sun rose.

When the sun did eventually rise and begin to illuminate the area where the palm oil village was, Moss could not see any signs of activity. What used to be a sandy clearing, with buildings and machinery, was now a green canopy of trees and dense undergrowth. A small amount of the cultivated area, which had been prepared, ready for planting, could be seen. Then the ground returned back to the devastation that had taken place.

'There, doesn't that look better? I do like my trees,' said *Tabule*, who had just entered the room.

Moss continued to scan the area for the roads and access tracks; he found none. In fact, the roads that did lead to the palm oil village, which were originally connected to the main highway, had all but disappeared.

'Mornin',' said Henry, gazing at the screens. 'That isn't the place we were looking at yesterday, is it?'

Moss confirmed that it was, then switched to the security cameras.

His sad sense of humour getting the better of him, he displayed the view on screen. The view was from a fixed camera and showed the outside of the perimeter wall. Suddenly, two figures appeared, and after struggling to scale the wall, and jump down to the other side, re-appeared.

'*Leber* has been up to his old tricks again, I see,' said *Tabule*.

Henry was beside himself with laughter.

'So that's what a quandary looks like from the outside.'

Switching back to the image of the palm oil camp, there was still no sign of life. *Tabule* said he was keen to examine the area and his work on the machines, and so decided to pay a visit. He was barely through the doorway in his rush to exit, when he melted into thin air.

'What shall we do with our two reporters?' enquired Henry.

Moss reassured him that they would be fine. He was sure that a decision would be made regarding their future very soon. He mentioned Henry's quandary experience, which had caused him no lasting ill effects.

'I'm not so sure of that,' remarked Henry cynically.

Meanwhile *Tabule* had arrived at the work compound. Taking a very low-key approach, he found that the place was deserted. He entered what was the living quarters of the crew; there, two trees had grown straight through the floor, and taken the roof up with them. The roof was now some thirty foot up in the canopy.

The windows had creepers growing through them, and most of the glass panes were broken.

The workers' belongings were scattered around, and it looked as if they had all left in a real hurry.

He then wandered out to where the machinery was parked. Master Jake's suggestion had worked well, he mused, as he inspected each vehicle. The roots had grown down into the engine, and as they had expanded, the metal had cracked; the roots had come out in different places. The engines and machinery were now just a heap of twisted metal, and there was no way they could be repaired.

Tabule decided to explore along what was once the road access to this compound. He could weave in and out of the fabric, covering great distances, very quickly. He was curious to know which direction the workmen had taken in their haste to escape.

He began with the largest of the three roads, which was now becoming a very dense jungle, and would have been difficult to negotiate at night.

He had gone no more than three miles along the planted road, when he heard voices. Setting himself up in a suitable vantage point, *Tabule* watched, as ten men hacked and chopped their way through the undergrowth, no doubt cursing in their native tongue.

With his limited understanding of Portuguese, he assumed that their conversation revolved around the disbelief they would experience back home. Unable to use mobile phones where they were, they were also critical of the supplies they had been provided with, mainly the lack of communication equipment.

Satisfied that the men were making a beeline for home, *Tabule* decided to join *Leber* and *Chonga* with the villagers.

On arrival, he found everyone busily carrying stones, of all shapes and sizes, to an area at the end of the village. Searching out *Chonga,* he enquired what was happening.

'Come, I will show you.'

Chonga led him to the heart of the commotion, where it looked as though foundations had been dug.

Huge stones were being positioned to form a wall some three feet wide. It was already some three feet high and must have been fifty feet in diameter. *Chonga* said that it would have timber supports and a roof of thatch, thanks to *Tabule's* perimeter planting.

'They will honour the gods and provide a temple for the night flower. Having witnessed the removal of the bulldozer threat, their confidence has grown, and their convictions with it,' said *Chonga.*

The elders had sent their most trusted runners to investigate the two areas. Some of the runners had returned from the camp across the river; they had excitedly relayed the news that it had been abandoned.

The elders were sure the other runners would bring back similar news of the second camp.

Chonga said that the word was travelling fast amongst his people, who had been forced into exile. More people were arriving every day; the villages that had been created would not suffice, they would need more.

Now that there was some stability amongst the people, it was decided that the three Shaman should be instructed in the secrets of the night flower.

Chonga said he would escort them back through the cave, to the Manor, where Ivy should be ready to receive them.

Leber suddenly appeared, having been to investigate the sunken bulldozer camp.

'It has been abandoned,' he said. He had managed to track the workers some five miles into the bush, but their activities across the river had certainly come to a halt.

'Same as the palm oil camp,' said *Tabule*.

They felt reasonably confident that the main event would go ahead, with little or no witnesses, and the threat to the natives had been considerably reduced.

They both headed back to the Manor. *Leber* was at a crucial point with the propagation in the greenhouses and needed to oversee the final stages.

Tabule had agreed to assist Ivy in the tuition of the three Shaman.

Henry was reading the message Archie had sent him on his phone. He told Edmund that the plane would be arriving the day after tomorrow.

Would he like to join him and travel down there? He might be required to assist with the installation. Edmund agreed without hesitation.

'That's settled then, we go tomorrow lunchtime. It will give us a chance to inspect the runway and have a look at the equipment,' said Henry.

Tabule whispered to Ivy that she might like to continue her instructions on the night flower, the Shaman were with *Chonga* in the new building. Ivy excused herself and left them all to it.

'Ivy and I saw a most strange thing as we drove into the Manor,' said Edmund. He described the apparition of the two reporters.

'Aah,' said *Leber* 'I nearly forgot them.'

Moss called Edmund over to the screens to show him what *Leber* had done.

'Oh my,' said Edmund. 'Will they be all right?'

Henry explained that he had been in a similar situation, not so long ago, and reassured Edmund that they would be fine. In fact, curious to see what would happen next, Henry followed *Leber* into the garden.

'Right, Moss, we have a lot of programming to do,' said Edmund.

The map of the desolation needed plotting, it was essential that the edges were mapped accurately, they did not want any overlapping or gaps; and the coordinates for the villages had to be logged in with all their perimeters, to avoid overplanting.

This was information that *Chonga* was sending, using the GPS Edmund had given him. Edmund and Moss got to grips with the intricacies of entering the new data.

Henry caught up with *Leber* just as he reached the quandary. They both sat on the remains of an old fallen tree and watched the two figures come and go for ages, neither spoke.

Henry was the first to break the silence.

'What were they expecting to find? I don't think any of the villagers have told them any secrets about the Manor. It's just a mystery.'

'Perhaps we should interview them?' said *Leber*.

There was another long silence as they both mulled over questions they might ask. All the time, the reporters were jumping in and out of the garden.

'Mmmm, I agree,' said Henry.

Leber got up and approached the wall; he removed the thin veil of the quandary. Returning to his seat, they both waited for the reporters to jump back down, which they did.

'Good morning,' said Henry.

The two reporters grabbed each other in a frightened hug.

'Can we help you?' said *Leber*.

The two frightened men looked around, somewhat confused. They had begun their gate crashing in the middle of the night, and now it was daylight. There were also the two figures sitting in front of them, who appeared to be waiting for them to arrive. It was the small one who plucked up the courage to speak first; he recognised Henry.

'I'm extremely sorry, your Lordship, but I can assure you we are not burglars. We work for a magazine that has asked us to investigate the strange plantings that have appeared in various parts of the country.'

Well, both of them made a sorry spectacle with their face paints, and their story just added a sombre poignancy to the situation.

'Why did you think the Manor had anything to do with these events?' asked Henry.

The American, now finding his voice, explained that the Manor had been empty for years. All of a sudden there was a lot of activity, which seemed to coincide with the strange happenings. After some in-depth detective work, they had concluded that this area was directly in the path of the phenomena, and by a process of deduction, the Manor required investigation. Plus, they had both witnessed one of these events themselves, on the river bank a few weeks ago.

'Well, gentlemen, I commend your dedication to duty, but I think you should exit the way you came. If you would like to see the Manor, return at noon and I would be glad to show you around.'

Henry and *Leber* continued to sit and watch the amusing acrobatics, as the two ascended the wall, in a flurry of apologies, and then disappeared over the top.

'Is that such a good idea?' asked *Leber*.

As they walked back to the house, Henry told *Leber* that the work carried out at the Manor was all open and above board, their visit would only find evidence of training and research. His company were pioneers in the use of plant-based medicines, and the teaching facility for the students had nothing to hide.

Returning to the war room, Henry told Edmund that he had invited the reporters. We shall just lock the door to the war room and warn the sprouts to behave.

'You could call it a home cinema,' said Edmund.

He then went on to explain what a home cinema was, for Henry's benefit, and assured him that it would cause no concern.

'I shall run the world news channel in readiness.'

Henry wandered out onto the patio; MacTavish was putting the day's post in piles on the table.

'There is post for the Lytes Academy. Are we to suppose that this is the name of the new building?' he asked.

Henry replied that it was probably Sandra's decision, as she had been dealing with the registration of the project as a training facility.

He sat and ate breakfast and continued to deal with the post. His mind drifted to thoughts of Shelta and her travels across Europe. The bond that the night flower provided between those it had touched was quite strong. Henry felt this bond and had tried several times to call her by phone, with no success.

With little interest in finishing the post, he went into the conservatory; the night flower had now increased in size considerably. The three sprouts were climbing in and out of the branches.

'Come on you three, I have a couple of hours to play hide and seek.'

Henry walked along the river, past the weir, and into the fields beyond. The sprouts were dashing in and out of the bushes, jumping out in front of him from hiding places in the undergrowth. Eventually he reached the clearing where Shelta had camped.

He sat beside the river, his three playmates now content to sit with him, and his thoughts of Shelta became even stronger. Now the sprouts had snuggled in closer, it was a perfect spot; he began to daydream, and his mind seemed to be pulled across continents.

Even with closed eyes he could see below him, forests, seas and deserts; it was as though he was standing on a huge TV screen. He remained stationary while all around retreated behind him.

There was the feeling of slowing down, as if someone was applying the brakes. Then the feeling of tumbling forward, as he approached a clearing in a forest, where a group of people were camped.

He recognized Shelta as one of them. He came to an abrupt halt and walked towards her.

On seeing Henry, she stood up and ran towards him with outstretched arms and embraced him. Henry wasn't sure if his mind was playing tricks on him, but the feeling of her hugs was very positive.

After they had greeted one another, Shelta said he was becoming stronger; to be able to travel this distance through his mind's eye was proof of that.

She told him that the distribution of the night flower to other Gypsies across Europe was not doing so well.

She now realised that her kin were travellers by nature, whereas the night flower needed to put down roots in a stable environment.

She said that because of this, they were restricted to planting small areas; they needed the night flower to grow strong and thrive, and it needed a permanent home.

They would have to back track over their journey and find safe havens for each night flower. The only trouble was the border guards of this country would not let them pass; they were trapped there.

Henry enquired as to which country she was referring.

She told him that they had passed through Romania towards the Black Sea and entered the southern tip of the Ukraine. It was a journey she had made many times before, but this time there was trouble in the country.

Henry vowed that he would somehow find a way to help her. The bond began to grow weaker, and Shelta began to fade. Henry had returned to the riverbank before he could open his eyes.

'Well, that was an experience,' he said, giving each of the sprouts a hug.

He knew they had been instrumental in his journey. He thanked them for their support and effort in assisting him to find Shelta, and rising to his feet, declared that they should return to the Manor.

The sprouts dodged in and out of the bushes, playing their favourite game, all the way back to the Manor.

Henry arrived just in time; MacTavish was showing the two reporters through to the patio.

'Good afternoon gentlemen, I trust you have no ill effects from your climbing exercise?' he said, a little sarcastically. 'Can we offer you refreshments, tea, lemonade, beer, wine?' asked Henry.

He shook their hands and invited them to sit. The small one said he thought it was best if they had lemonade and continued to introduce themselves.

'My name is Dr David Loxton, and this is my associate, Bud Langford. May I again apologize profusely for our behaviour; we do not normally resort to such drastic measures.'

He continued to explain that they were under pressure from their magazine editor to provide something of interest before the deadline, next week.

'What are you a doctor of?' enquired Henry.

'Cryptozoology,' came the reply.

Henry made understanding noises, and thought he would ask Edmund later, what it meant.

David continued to explain that the area surrounding the Manor was steeped in folklore and myth, with witches still practising to this day. He believed that there was an ancient order that worshipped the woodland deities, in particular the Green Man, who could be responsible for the strange planting phenomenon.

'Fascinating,' said Henry, and he went on to tell them some of the more recent history of the Manor and its function.

He told them of his work in remote areas of the world, and his return to England, on learning he had become sole beneficiary of the family business. A business which had been founded on plant medicines and had continued down through the generations. Henry had known of the Manor since he was a small boy; he had been told stories by his father, and he knew it almost as if he had lived there. When he returned and explored the place, and the surrounding areas, he felt at home, even discovering local long-lost relatives. He was passionate about plants and how they could affect mankind; it was for this purpose that he felt his knowledge and the research of others, should be shared.

And so, a new training facility had been built to provide students with facilities to carry out research. As a pharmaceutical chemist, and searching for new plants and cures, he had witnessed many things, but never a Green Man.

'Let me show you around.'

He gestured to the conservatory and the three went in to see the night flower. Henry told them they were experimenting with the attributes of this species, all highly confidential and top secret, of course.

As they turned to exit the conservatory, Bud plucked a flower. A tendril from the night flower slapped the back of his hand, and he quickened his step to re-join the others.

Looking back, he saw a distinct shiver run through the night flower. He tugged at David's sleeve and whispered to him what had happened.

Henry had noticed this little incident, and the flower that had been taken.

'Of course, we have to be very careful, the plant is hermaphroditic and very poisonous. It could change a man to a woman or vice versa,' said Henry in his most serious voice.

Bud discarded the flower behind a chair on the way out. Henry was struggling to hide his amusement.

They continued around the grounds, taking in the greenhouses, where the local villagers were working, the river, weir and water supplies. Beyond the hedge line, additional fields were being prepared to increase the land available for planting trials.

Henry explained that they had shipped in some exotic plants from areas of the rainforest. An experimental planting of hot climate plants had been carried out in a secure site on the farm. It was a small section of jungle, now being monitored in conjunction with a local University College.

The two reporters looked at each other as though those words had triggered a memory. Henry finished his tour with a look around the new Academy, where Ivy was conducting experiments, in a workshop, with the three Shaman.

Henry told the two reporters that the facility was not yet open, but already had aroused interest from far and wide.

'Well gents, that's it, as you can see, we shall be carrying out experimental research. It does not always gain public favour, what with the bad press on GM crops. But, using up-to-date genetic engineering, we do hope to find cures for some of the world's most horrible diseases.

Now, if you will excuse me, I have business to attend to. Please, come in through the front entrance if you have any further enquiries.'

Henry showed them back to their car on the drive, shook their hands and bade them farewell. He watched them leave down the drive and turned to go back in the house.

Returning to the war room, he found Edmund, Moss and *Leber;* they had been following Henry around the estate, on the security cameras. Edmund was rather pleased with the camera system; they had not lost sight of the three throughout their visit.

'It works well,' he said, having been in charge of the design and installation.

Henry now turned his attention to the plight of Shelta.

'We have got to do something to help,' he said.

He told of his strange experience earlier with the three sprouts, and his conversation with her. *Leber* acknowledged he had witnessed Henry's connection to Shelta, earlier. Although not a total immersion in the fabric, he felt his presence, and thought it a stunning first attempt for a non *Burrbesh.*

Leber said he would think on it and let him know.

'Archie rang just before you came in. I said you would call him back,' said Edmund.

Henry collected the phone from Edmund and went out on the patio to call him. Archie answered almost immediately. He commented on how clear the line was and then explained the flight plan to him. Henry, a little lost in the details, said he might not remember all he was told.

'Never mind, I shall email it to Edmund,' said Archie.

He told Henry he had just loaded a very nice vintage on the plane for him. They were just refuelling, and they should be on their way by 11:30 local time.

Archie passed the phone to Jake who had a message for his mom and dad. He asked if someone could let them know that they were running a little late, and that they were both fine.

'I shall go around straight away,' assured Henry.

Archie said he would call again when they landed in Fortaleza, hopefully around 18:00 local time.

Henry wished them all a safe journey, then passing the phone back to Edmund, decided to pop round and give Bill and Edna the message in person.

Before he went, he turned to Edmund and enquired what a cryptozoologist was. He explained that it was someone who investigated the strange creatures that were mentioned in legends.

'Mmmm, like dragons?' said Henry, and proceeded out the door.

'We have an email from Archie,' shouted Edmund. He was just in time to catch Henry before he had gone, he put it on screen:

Local times

Depart: Arrive:

Negril, Canaima,

Jamaica 06:00 Tues. Venezuela 10:30

Canaima Forteleza,

Venezuela 11:30Brazil 18:00

Fortaleza 06:00 Wed. Praia, 12:00

Brazil Cape Verde

Praia

Cape Verde 13:00Gibraltar 19:30

Gibraltar 08:00 Thurs. Aylesbury 12:00

'Quite a schedule, can you write it down for me? I can give it to Bill and Edna,' said Henry.

He was given a printout by Edmund and then Henry left for the farm.

Edmund then brought up on the screens the entire plotted area of the devastation; overlaying it on a map it fitted perfectly. The villages had been logged, and showed up with their perimeter planting, provided by *Tabule*; all that was needed now was to enter the data for planting position.

Moss had been working with Sandra on this, and they had produced a plan of the wetter areas. This would enable Sandra to choose which of the moisture-loving plants would be best suited there.

Edmund decided to give each of the plant types its own colour, which he then transferred onto the map. The picture it produced had pockets of unplanted areas; Moss was sure that the information he had been given was correct.

They searched through Sandra's work for the missing data, without success, the blank areas were still there. Edmund suggested they should ask her later when Archie called.

'*Chonga* mentioned there may be more villages required, to provide for the influx of people,' said Moss. 'I think I should find out for certain.'

Edmund claimed that the area once had a population of around forty thousand, so it might be a good idea.

As Moss was leaving, *Leber* called to him. He had been examining the situation of Shelta and required her opinion.

'It would be very nice to synchronize the Amazon event with a number of European events. Of course, each would not be of the same magnitude, but altogether, they might equal it,' said *Leber*.

He explained the circumstance surrounding the Gypsies. He thought, if they were to receive assistance in their quest, the effects of all the events, combined, might be just enough to make an impact.

'The trouble is,' said *Leber*, 'the Gypsies would not listen to you or me, but they would listen to Henry.'

He believed that if Henry could instruct them on the most effective ways to use the night flower, they might just be ready in time for the *Burrbesh* to harvest enough seed to make a difference. He admitted that this would be a busy time, but he thought the council members were ready for it.

He would assist in getting Shelta and her people across the border, while Henry, having proved that he was capable, could rally the other Gypsies.

Moss agreed that Shelta should be helped, and to bring the night flowers of Europe to full strength was a good idea.

He said he was off to check with *Chonga* on a few technical points. If *Leber* wanted to check the situation with Shelta and assess the possibilities, they could put it to *Tabule* when he returned.

Moss wished him good hunting and proceeded to melt into thin air.

Leber had a good idea where Shelta was, he could sense a weak presence of the night flower and the little ones she carried with her. He decided that there was no time like the present and followed closely behind Moss.

Moss, on arrival at the village, was a little overwhelmed at the number of people that had arrived. He found *Chonga* with *Tabule*, they were sitting in conference with the elders outside the new temple.

'You were not kidding when you said that more villages may be required,' said Moss.

He explained that the process of mapping the area was being programmed into the computers. If more areas were required for the construction of new villages, then they needed to be dealt with now.

He told *Tabule* of *Leber's* plan, and the help that would be required for the Gypsies.

'*Chonga*, do you have the GPS device that Edmund gave you to log the village sites? It looks like there will be more needed, judging by all the people arriving,' said Moss.

Chonga waved the hand-held GPS and agreed that he was ready to go.

'In fact, little man, *Tabule* and I were just ironing out, with the elders, the preferred sites for these new villages.'

Moss was impressed; he said that Edmund had programmed the map to accept all incoming coordinates, and he would return to the Manor and await their data.

Tabule placed a hand on Moss's shoulder and told him his knowledge of this new technical language had impressed him, "data indeed."

Moss gave one of his deep frowns and disappeared into the crowd. He returned promptly to the war room at the Manor and informed Edmund that *Chonga* and *Tabule* would be transmitting anytime soon.

'It is becoming quite exciting,' said Moss, relaxing in what they now called 'cinema chairs'.

Both of them spent the next two hours punching in coordinates sent back by *Chonga.*

They watched on screen as the greenery magically encircled each compound; *Tabule* was enjoying himself.

Edmund counted forty-three areas in total. He said the villagers would have their work cut out if they wanted to visit a neighbour, the jungle would be so dense.

At that moment, Ivy appeared with her three students. She said that class had finished for the day, and she thought a trip behind the scenes might be in order.

The three students found the images on the screens mesmerizing. Edmund described what they were seeing and tried to put into perspective their situation.

As holy men for their tribe, they would be responsible for all the villages that appeared on the screens. And, with the population rising by the hour, they would certainly have their work cut out.

One of the Shaman, with a name no-one could pronounce, thanked them for the work they were doing. He said, with luck, their society would return to how it was in his grandfather's stories.

MacTavish came in, and, looking at the screens, expressed his delight at the resurgent population. Looking at the three young students he said, 'we shall have to put some good food in their bellies, shan't we, can't have them fadin' away.'

He announced that food would be served in the dining room, with or without his Lordship, in thirty minutes, and then marched off to deal with it.

Henry, at this present moment, was catching up on some family history, compliments of Edna. He had also been given a rare, guided tour of her cider collection, which was extensive. They were currently sitting with a jug of her favourite, on a bench in the orchard, while the family history poured out. Henry listened intently, and graciously accepted a top- up of his glass, as the time rolled by.

'Blimey is that the time?' It had gone six. 'Bill will be home soon, I'd better get the dinner on,' she joked. Otherwise, he would have her guts for garters.

'You come and join us, Henry, there is always plenty.' Henry, now feeling very relaxed, agreed. He would love to, he said. They walked round to the kitchen where Bill had already arrived. On seeing Henry's car, he guessed they might be in the cider house, and thought he would leave them for a while.

Henry sat listening to Bill's tales of the old days, while Edna produced a banquet of food from nowhere. The three chatted for ages; Henry felt a sense of belonging for the first time, and drank in the atmosphere, which had a distinct cider flavour.

As the sun began to set, Henry's phone rang; it was Archie telling him they had landed safely. They were going to be looked after by an old friend who had a house on the beach, not far from the airport. He said Jake and Sandra were fine and would he like to say hello?

Archie passed the phone to Jake, who greeted Henry and enquired if he had been to see his mom and dad.

'Funny you should mention that,' said Henry and passed the phone to Edna.

Caught a little by surprise, Jake and Sandra chatted for a while with his mom and dad, in a four-way conversation.

Finally, Bill and Edna wished them all a safe journey. Henry finished by telling Archie of his and Edmund's plan for the next day, and he would speak to him again soon.

Henry, almost forgetting the flight plan in his pocket, handed it to Bill. Both Bill and Edna scrutinized the schedule.

'Jake has never been further than Minehead,' said Edna. 'Now he's gadding off all over the planet. I do hope they'll be all right.'

Bill gave her a reassuring hug and told her that they were in good hands. Henry thanked them both for their hospitality and said he would have to get back to the Manor.

'Your cider house is a veritable treasure trove,' said Henry and gave Edna a hug. Shaking Bill's hand, he bade them goodnight and left.

When he arrived back at the Manor, he told Edmund he had spoken to Archie, and everything was on schedule. Edmund told him that he needed to speak to Sandra regarding some missing data. Henry tried to phone him back, but with no luck; Edmund concluded they must be in a black spot, and he would try again in the morning.

At that moment, *Leber* came into the room, and approached Henry.

'I believe we are going to have a problem extracting Shelta,' he said.

Chapter 25

'It would appear that Shelta and her companions have been detained,' said *Leber*. He had spoken in detail with her, and she had informed him that their papers had been held by the border guards. They had strict instructions not to allow anyone in or out of the country: the result of a civil uprising.

There were four guards, and they were camped at the side of the roadblock; two were on duty all the time.

Although there was a way through the woods on foot, to take the four horse-drawn caravans through was nigh on impossible.

Leber said Shelta had tried to befriend them. She had taken them foraged food from the woods, and even shared a tot of Poitín. But they were under fear of court martial from their superiors if they disobeyed.

'Had any other soldiers been to the roadblock and witnessed the Gypsies?' asked Henry.

Shelta had told him that the soldiers suddenly appeared seven days ago, and she had seen no-one else. They were to expect a supply truck every fortnight, which would bring them their meagre rations, water and other necessities.

Henry was devising a plan:

'If Shelta were to pay these guards one last visit, a bit of a farewell party, she could explain that she and her companions would be moving on, deeper into the country. If she was not going to cross the border, they might return her papers. She could then provide them with some nice food and drink, with knock-out drops in, and when they were out cold, Shelta could escape.'

Henry went on to explain that the soldiers would not miss her, and with little or no recollection of events, they would not need to report it.

'Damn good idea,' said *Leber*, and went off to deal with the arrangements.

Henry, meanwhile, had just remembered a promise he had made. Excusing himself and wishing everyone a good night, he wandered out to the Bentley.

He drove down to the Tavern, which now had a reduced clientele, and no reporters. Entering the bar, he found Barney chatting with the landlord.

'Evening Barney,' said Henry. 'I've come to fulfil my promise I made you the other day.'

'Oh my,' said Barney.

The rest of their evening was taken up with the trip through the cave to the Amazon villages. Barney marvelled at the spectacle he had been allowed to be part of. Returning Barney back home, Henry bade him goodnight and returned to the Manor.

The following morning Henry came down early. He found Edmund busy at the keyboard, and other than Edmund, the place was deserted.

'Where is everyone?' enquired Henry.

'Moss and Leber have gone off on some sort of mission together. Ivy is coming in later, on the red peril – Edmund's affectionate name for her scooter. The three Shaman had a late night, and *Tabule* and *Chonga* are busy making villages. There was another elder here earlier, I think it was *Myck*. And I could not sleep last night, so I decided to work.'

'Shall I get sir another pot of coffee?' said MacTavish, who was standing in the doorway.

'Make that two,' said Henry, surveying the picture on screen. The village areas were now dotted all across the desolation, in readiness for the villagers to occupy.

Edmund brought up the map of the planting that would take place. He explained to Henry that the highlighted gaps were where there was no planting; data was missing.

'I need to speak to Sandra when Archie calls,' said Edmund. He expressed his desire to finish the map of the planted area before they went to Aylesbury; he would feel more comfortable knowing it was complete.

As though on cue, Henry's phone rang, it was a video call from Archie. Edmund put it on screen. Archie scanned the airport and then the plane, in great detail; he was very impressed.

He passed the phone to Jake, who said the trip was a nonstop holiday, which he was enjoying immensely.

Passing the phone to Sandra, she made comment on how colourful the plants were over there.

Edmund asked her about the gaps in the planting programme, and was there some data that he had missed somewhere? He thought it was the aquatic plants, but they did not appear to be in any of her files.

Sandra told him she had forgotten her laptop and had downloaded the files from college, onto a disc. It was in her CD storage box, and he could not miss it, as it had a photo of her horse printed on it.

Rummaging through the CDs, Edmund gave a shout of delight, as though he had just won the lottery.

Archie said he would let them know if there were any problems but would call again when they reached Gibraltar. Henry wished them a safe journey, and the call ended.

Edmund was busy tapping away at the keyboard and muttering the sequence of data inputs, as he kept checking the screen.

'Yes,' he exclaimed, after a long silence.

He indicated to Henry that all the gaps had now been filled, the map of the new jungle was on screen. They sat there examining the intricacies of the colours which would be the new jungle, as the image moved across the screen.

Edmund broke the silence as he acknowledged the arrival of Ivy. Her red peril made a distinct sound which was instantly recognizable.

She joined the two in the war room, and after her morning peck on the cheek from Edmund, proceeded to sit and watch in amazement the image on screen.

It was not long before the three Shaman joined them.

Edmund provided commentary for them, pointing out the different areas, and explaining the colours allocated to the planting. He described where and where not, the jungle would start and finish, and then finally produced a slow CGI animation of the completed project, with dense foliage and tree canopy.

'I saw something like this by Monet, at an art gallery years ago,' said Henry.

It was truly mesmerizing, the group continued to sit in silence for ages, examining every pixel of the picture.

The room more and more resembled a cinema; even the sprouts came to observe.

MacTavish entered to announce breakfast, but was stopped in his tracks, and even he, sat and took in the spectacle.

Edmund stood, clearing his throat, after becoming a little emotional. He said, 'If it turns out half as good as what we have witnessed this morning, the world will be a better place.'

Henry declared that it was time they should be preparing for their trip to Magnatek. Edmund admitted that he would have to return home to pack, the thought had totally slipped his mind in the chaos of the lost files.

Ivy suggested the Shaman might like to wander the grounds of the Manor and explore, while she assisted Edmund.

Comfortable that things were progressing well, Edmund had no qualms about leaving Moss to take over operations while he was away with Ivy.

Promising to return as quickly as possible, Edmund and Ivy left. Henry led the three Shaman outside; he indicated the direction they should go, along the river, and described areas of interest. As Henry turned to go back into the conservatory, *Leber* and Moss appeared, looking very pleased with themselves.

'So, what have you two been up to?' enquired Henry. Moss said he would let *Leber* explain and continued through to the war cinema.

Leber, eager to tell, began to fill Henry in on the picture surrounding Shelta and her companions. He had taken Henry's advice and put his plan into action, with the help of *Myck* and an amazing mushroom-based concoction. A veritable feast had been laid on for the guards; they had eaten and drunk their fill, and had all slept very soundly, while Shelta and her crew drove through the border. They would be none the wiser, they would assume that they had been just a little greedy with the free grog. The Gypsies would be miles away before the guards woke up.

'Shelta will be making her way back now. She is going to leave her cargo of night flower and little ones with her cousins. They have settled in a remote part of the valley and the night flower will be most at home there.'

He continued to explain about the need to instruct the other groups, who also were travelling with the night flowers. They would need to find sanctuary for their cargos too, and very soon, if there were to be a combined effort with the Amazon event.

‘It is you who must convince these people Henry, they trust you, I shall guide you to their locations. Shelta’s night flower has produced many more offspring, and only a few of those have settled, the remainder are still travelling,’ said *Leber.*

He went on to explain that there was a good side to this situation, and that was, that Shelta had not been idle. While awaiting her rescue, she had chosen sites for her people to settle on, adjacent to areas of devastation, which would allow easy access. With all these events, it was crucial that the night flowers produced well, for there would be a huge amount of harvest required.

Henry was trying to work out how long they had.

‘I shall be back tomorrow with Jake and Sandra; it will take some time to fit the equipment to the plane. I reckon that we are looking at two weeks, possibly, to the event,’ said Henry.

He agreed to start immediately on his return.

‘Would two weeks be enough?’ asked Henry.

‘Yes,’ said *Leber.* He had a little something that Henry could give to the Gypsies to boost the night flower.

‘I shall accurately locate each group and plot our course through the fabric. It should help to speed up the process,’ said *Leber.*

Henry commented that it was not long ago when *Leber* would have left him to rot.

‘Times change and you have proven your worth, I shall see you tomorrow,’ said *Leber.* Leaving Henry to continue with his plans he marched out of the conservatory.

Henry wandered into the cinema. Moss was filling a glass with water and looking up at Henry. He said, ‘that is the first time I have heard him say anything nice to a human,’ and then went back to his station.

Henry collected his overnight bag from the hall and proceeded to the Bentley to await Edmund. He did not have to wait long.

Edmund pulled up next to the Bentley in the open-fronted garage. Giving Ivy a hug, he promised to call later, and, throwing his bag in the back seat they both set off for Aylesbury.

Ivy went off in search of the three Shaman; she caught up with them in the walled garden. She had to admit they did not really look like holy men. Wearing Nike trainers, basketball and ice hockey T-shirts, with distressed jeans, they would blend in anywhere. She rounded them up and took them off to the greenhouses, for some hands-on maintenance.

Henry and Edmund's journey to Magnatek went without a hitch. They chatted, and Henry told Edmund of Barney's visit to the Amazon. Then he had a message from Archie, letting them know that they were on schedule, and were just leaving Praia airport.

Before they knew it, they had entered the gates of Magnatek and were driving up the long road to the house, where Max was waiting for them. He seemed a little agitated.

'Is everything all right?' asked Edmund.

Max was keen to take them both down to the lab and said he would explain there. He said the porter would take care of their luggage, and leading the way, he set off at a brisk pace. They entered the lab and were greeted by Henri.

Max began by explaining that there was an unknown element in their calculations. They had been carrying out tests using the drone, which had been designed to operate on a scaled down version of the real thing.

Unable to carry out field trials of the magnitude that was intended, they had to rely on the computer doing the work. The computer simulations kept coming up with – insufficient data, unable to compute. The problem was the quantity of seed, its weight ratios, and the power required by the magnetic field to hold it all in suspension.

'The calculations for the weight distribution within the magnetic field indicate it has a strength to hold 3.6 tonnes. This would obviously be transferred to the aircraft, which is at the limit of its load capacity,' said Henri.

He continued to explain that the weight of the seed is an unknown because of its variety and quantity. The area had been calculated by satellite imagery and GPS coordinates – it was two thousand four hundred and fourteen square miles.

The magnetic field had a range of some fifty miles radius and was well within the parameters. The power required to produce this field and hold 3.6 tonnes would be 2.15 Kw. This could be generated using the on-board 115V ac power supply, through an inverter, which would provide sixty minutes of power, at a maximum of 2.5Kw.

'Would this be enough time?' asked Henri.

Henry told them that he had no idea of how heavy this would all be, each member of the council would be contributing their speciality. He would have to speak to *Leber* on his return and try to find out the answer.

Max and Henri then took them to see the actual equipment that would be installed on the plane. They all entered a sterile room, with white walls, slightly bowed in, white floor, and in the centre on a table, was what looked like a small satellite. It was wired up to an array of equipment behind a screen, with flashing lights, computers and keyboards.

'Let me show you,' said Max.

Going over to a keyboard, he explained that the module could be installed underneath the aircraft in the old camera housing. Max pressed enter on the keyboard, which began the process; the top of the satellite rose up like a periscope.

'Obviously, when in position it will be the other way up. The transmitter for the magnetic field has to be a certain distance from the aircraft, otherwise it could knock out the navigational instruments. Once fully extended, the field is powered up, and the sixty minutes start from then.'

Max continued to describe the features of the equipment. At the top of the periscope was a cylindrical structure which housed the main component, the transmitter. The whole thing was very substantial and had to be firmly installed, as it had to carry a considerable weight. The fuselage of the plane might have to be reinforced to accommodate it.

'Has it been fired up yet?' asked Edmund.

Henri said they had run it at ten percent capacity. The walls, which were a foil-covered aluminium foam panel, began to bend inwards. They had to terminate the test but were impressed with the data it produced.

Edmund said he had brought with him all the relevant data needed to program the equipment.

'We do need to run a test when it's fitted to the plane,' said Max.

Henry said the plane should be with them tomorrow, he had heard from Archie who confirmed that they were on schedule.

'Shall we go and have a look at the runway?' said Henry.

They all wandered out of the clinical laboratory and into the warm afternoon sun.

'Where could you carry out a test with the plane?' enquired Edmund.

Henri said they had thought of that and there was a place just southwest of the Isles of Scilly, on the edge of the Bay of Biscay. There, they could turn the machine up to maximum, and run the diagnostics.

Unfortunately, it would not be fully loaded, so they could not test the strain placed on the aircraft. That would remain a wild card until they could program some information in.

As they turned the corner of the last building, there, stretching across the grounds was a line of giant redwoods. They screened the view of the runway and provided shelter for the hangar beyond.

'Impressive,' said Henry. He had seen these trees on many of his expeditions; he knew them as Wellingtonias.

As they walked in between the great trees, the runway stretched out in front of them, like a monstrous cricket pitch: well cut grass in as straight a line as the Romans would have done, with a bright red windsock on a tall white pole, having its afternoon snooze.

'Truly remarkable,' said Edmund. 'One just has to walk to the other end.'

Henry agreed; Max and Henri shook their heads and agreed to meet them back at the lab.

The runway stretched over a thousand yards, the grass was immaculately mown and could easily be the envy of many a top golf club. Henry told Edmund of the dilemma facing the European element, and of his impending activity with *Leber* the following day.

As they walked the length of the runway, Henry flattened the occasional mole hill, brushing the grass with his foot.

They returned to the hangar and inspected the inside. In the corner was a Piper Cherokee, and a glider with its wings stored alongside. It was a substantial building and looked well capable of housing the Sherpa when it arrived.

Henry and Edmund walked along the red shale-covered roadway, through the trees and back up to the main buildings. When they reached the laboratory, there was only Max and Henri there, the time had passed very quickly and most of the technicians had left for the evening.

'I imagine you two are in need of a well-deserved drink?' said Max and suggested that they retire to somewhere a little more comfortable.

They made their way to the restaurant with its wonderful views across the gardens. Sitting near the open French windows, they enjoyed the country's fragrance, and chatted for a while.

Henry's phone rang. He put it on speakerphone and Archie confirmed that they had landed safely in Gibraltar.

After five minutes of four-way chat, Archie wished them all good night and said he would see them tomorrow.

Then, over dinner, the four sat discussing the intricacies and the potential of the new device, which had been five years in the making, well into the night.

The following morning Edmund joined Henri in the lab; they put their technical heads together to load all relevant data into the new machine.

'Do we have a name for it?' enquired Edmund.

'Its technical name in the lab is ATT-15,' said Henri. Edmund shook his head, and said no, a nickname, something affectionate.

'What does it stand for, anyway?' he asked.

'Aerial Technical Transport, prototype 1- and 5-years research,' explained Henri.

'You already have the name, Attis: God of vegetation, how strange.' Edmund had doodled the letters around.

They continued to confer over the input of various files, both enjoying each other's command of technical and scientific language.

Meanwhile Henry and Max had chatted over an extended breakfast. Henry was curious to know the history of the facility, and also, what other research was being carried out in the other buildings on site.

Max agreed to show him around the facility and began his commentary with the history of the building.

Henry followed Max, down a staircase and through a maze of corridors, which took them underground across to the other buildings.

Max told him that the house had been built by an industrialist at the end of the nineteenth century. It was bought by the company just after the First World War and was set up as a research facility. It had attracted Government interest, and grants for research. Magnetics was believed to be the holy grail of the scientific world, and so it had been investigated, at Magnatek, for nearly a hundred years.

They ascended another flight of stairs and stepped out into a large open building.

'These are the other buildings you can see from outside,' said Max. 'The three were knocked through to make one large building. We needed the space, especially when we began work on the train.'

Max explained that magnetics were already used in high-speed trains, but their research was going to take it one stage further.

Henry stood there, gazing at the activities of the white-coated technicians, as they went about their business. What appeared to be a train was floating on a single track; there were cars gliding silently along the floor, above a silver road. All manner of objects and vehicles were hovering above the ground with no evident support.

'It probably looks a bit like science fiction, but the possibility of harnessing the force of magnetism for travel, dispenses with all those nasty gases,' said Max.

He told him of a theory they were exploring. It involved using the magnetic field from the molten iron centre of the earth.

'It is massive and provides us with protection from the solar winds and prevents us from being fried in our beds. If it were possible to create an opposing force, control and calibrate it, then you have another form of propulsion.'

Henry nodded in agreement, as the whole theory just flew straight over his head. He congratulated Max on his vision and wished him luck with his project; he had to admit he was proud to be part of such pioneering research.

Henry thought it was about time for Archie's grand entrance and was keen to be there when he landed.

So, retracing their steps, they made their way back to the lab to collect Edmund and Henri, and all four made their way to the airstrip.

It was 11:30. Henry decided to call Archie on his mobile phone. Jake answered the call and they both put it on speakerphone. There was the background hum of the engines, and Jake told them that they had just crossed the M40.

He joked that he was now the delegated navigator, and according to his calculations they should be within sight of the airfield in about ten minutes.

The four watched the horizon for what seemed an age. Suddenly there was a speck which got bigger and noisier. The plane landed on the well-groomed grass, kicking up a little dust as Archie applied the brakes.

Not needing the full extent of runway, Archie applied power to taxi the remaining distance and park just outside the hangar.

Coming to a halt, the engines were switched off and the landing was complete. The rear door of the plane opened downwards to create a loading ramp, on which the three aeronauts disembarked.

Henry gave Sandra a hug and shook the hands of Jake and Archie.

'That's quite a few days you pair have had,' said Henry. 'Have you enjoyed it, have you learned from it?' he said.

They both agreed that they would not have missed it for the world. They also admitted that flying lessons were definitely to be put in their diaries. Archie showed them all around the plane, inside and out. He said he would arrange for a mechanic to inspect and check it over before the return flight, and there were a few cases of wine which needed to be unloaded.

'We can sort that out for you,' said Max.

He also explained that there was a team of mechanics who were on contract to the company. They attended to customers' private planes, a mode of transport which was becoming increasingly popular.

With the tour of the plane over, Henri and Edmund began scrutinizing the possibilities of the installation; they were off on another planet. Henry tried to interrupt their train of thought, to determine Edmund's plans for return. He was greeted with a vague comment.

'I will be fine.'

Henry had business back at the Manor and enquired who would like a lift back. It was Archie, Jake and Sandra who took up the offer. And so, collecting their bags from the plane, they accompanied Max and Henry back to the lab.

While Henry collected his bag from the room, Max gave them a brief tour, and description of what would be fitted to the plane.

Henry returned and enquired if everyone was ready. He shook Max's hand and told him he would call him later. They all piled into the Bentley for the trip back, and leaving down the long road, they exited Magnatek.

'Thought we might have a bit of music,' said Archie, pushing a CD into the music player. It was proper open-top music, the Beach Boys.

After the first few tunes, Henry noticed through the rear-view mirror, that Jake and Sandra had book-ended onto each other and were sound asleep.

Archie gave Henry an account of the flight and the airports they used. He described them very well, in fact in minute detail, including the creation of the vintage which had been loaded into the boot.

'Aha, I thought you might have forgotten that,' smiled Henry.

The journey back was incident free; they arrived at the Manor, just as Jake and Sandra awoke, and were greeted by Ivy.

'I might have guessed Edmund could not resist the temptation to tinker with the new gadget,' she said.

She grabbed Sandra by the hand, and excitedly coerced her away from the rest.

'You have to come and see; things have really moved on while you were away.' Ivy literally dragged her along to the greenhouses.

MacTavish came to the doorway and told Archie that his vehicle had been delivered by the hire company and was around the side by the stables.

'You might want to check out the boot,' said Henry as he went into the house.

He went into the war room, and the pictures on screen showed a throng of people making their way to the new village areas. A jetty had been constructed on the side of the riverbank to assist in the landing of craft coming down the river.

Jake and Archie joined him, staring at the screens in disbelief.

'Have you seen *Leber*?' asked Henry.

Moss replied that he had been there a moment ago. Henry proceeded through the conservatory, and out onto the patio. He found *Leber* talking to *Tabule* and *Chonga;* they were discussing the sheer numbers of natives returning. *Chonga* was elated, the whole event would serve two purposes; he was happy for his people being able to return to their rightful lands.

Tabule admitted that he had to return to recharge, he had nearly exhausted his planting capacity.

'The night flower is proving to be very useful, one of your better creations, *Leber*,' said *Tabule*.

He commented on how it was in the old days, when time was on their side, and they could recharge naturally, at their leisure.

Archie and Jake joined them at their table.

Tabule asked Archie about the plane and how he thought things were progressing, and what he thought the possible outcome of the event might be.

Archie, ever the optimist, replied: 'Very positive, everything should go perfectly, the equipment will be tested as soon as it is fitted, and then we should be good to go.'

Tabule explained the purpose of Henry's mission with *Leber,* to Jake, to allay any concerns he might have, having not long ago rescued him from the very same.

Tabule also told him about the change in attitude of *Leber* regarding the secrecy of the fabric.

Having heard *Tabule's* reassuring speech, *Leber* stepped in and said:

'There is a duty of care which overrides my beliefs; however, Henry has proved himself. Not that I am admitting I was wrong. Anyway, I think we have things to do, shall we?' *Leber* gestured to Henry and they both walked off into the grounds.

Jake turned to Archie, intending to invite him to the greenhouses, but a gentle snore indicated that Archie had dozed off.

Jake excused himself and went off to find Sandra and Ivy. He caught up with them in the end greenhouse, having followed the direction of their laughter. On entering, he found not three, but many little ones everywhere. The three Shaman had not quite mastered the art of seeing them, and so, they were being plagued. Little ones climbing up their legs, sitting on their heads, swinging off their arms. There was pandemonium, and the laughter just encouraged them to be worse.

The night flowers had grown, they had reached the harvest beyond the seed, and had produced many new offspring. They would all be invaluable in the future if the climate was to be reversed.

'*Leber* has put a curfew on them, to prevent them wandering. They are all set to go to the Amazon villages when everything is ready,' said Ivy.

Ivy announced that it was time to return to the classroom, and so, assisting the Shaman to dust off the little ones, they exited the greenhouse.

She suggested to Jake and Sandra that they should meet up later and have supper at the Tavern, her students too.

The resident sprouts were considerably larger and were not under orders. They accompanied Jake and Sandra, who had decided to enjoy a little terra firma, and take a walk along the river.

Considering everything that was happening, there was a relaxed atmosphere to the Manor. Even the locals at work in the grounds, fully understood the implications of all that was planned. Even though they were not privy to the detailed plan, gossip and the grapevine had allowed certain facts to filter down through the ranks.

Henry meanwhile was running a nonstop tour of the Gypsy camps, campaigning like a politician, the day before election. With the aid of *Leber*, who had already set out a route to maximise speed of travel, they visited each one in turn. Some had already made the decision to settle. Those that had, made Henry's task a little easier, while those that had not, needed some convincing. But out of respect for Henry, and with a commitment to the end result, they succumbed.

Their route across Europe took them further East, with some forty or so camps to visit, Henry was determined to do them all in one go. His last camp to visit would be that of Shelta, for she would be travelling back through Romania. Not that she needed convincing, but Henry thought it might be a suitable end to the day's campaign.

Leber, having agreed to Henry's request to do so, fuelled the enthusiasm that Henry required, to carry out his task; it would be a long night.

Edmund, Henri and Max, and a small team of technicians, were working around the clock to fit everything to the plane. It was now in the hangar and an array of portable lighting lit up every nook and cranny of the plane. There had been some luck with the installation. The existing camera pod, fitted by the military to take high-resolution pictures, had been removed.

Fortunately, the new equipment fitted, with no alteration to the exterior shell, and with minimal alterations to the mountings, which were to be located directly onto the chassis. This was the biggest obstacle expected of the installation and could bring the completion date forward by days.

As the afternoon progressed, the wheels of the project turned, and the outcome looked more and more positive.

With Edmund busy, Ivy took her students, with Jake and Sandra for supper at the Tavern, where Barney listened intently to a detailed account of their flight.

Archie had decided earlier that his time would be better spent with the plane and had left for Magnatek in his hire car.

Chapter 26

Henry had visited all but two of the Gypsy camps. He had discussed with each, the importance of the night flower's health and future wellbeing. They had all understood and were currently making progress in reaching the planned areas that Shelta had suggested. With *Leber's* guidance through the fabric, Henry approached the penultimate camp. He repeated his urgent message and the suggestions from Shelta.

Finally, with the traditional sharing of bread and a toast for success, Henry was ready to move on to see Shelta.

When he arrived at Shelta's camp, he was surprised to see only one caravan. *Leber* turned to him and said that he would leave the fabric open for his return, as Henry was now very familiar with its operation, and then he left.

Shelta's caravan was parked up in a small clearing on the side of a hill, surrounded by forest. The view across the valley was quite spectacular, especially as the sun was just beginning to disappear below the tree line on the horizon. Everywhere was bathed in a bright orange light; it was magical.

As Henry walked over to the caravan, Shelta appeared. She had on a colourful dress which fluoresced under the bright light of the sun. She greeted Henry with a hug and a kiss, and she expressed her admiration for the work he was doing.

'I thought we might steal a little time for ourselves, before you have to disappear again,' she said.

She told Henry that the others in her camp were just a short distance along the road. She had camped early, in order to prepare a feast of the forest for Henry.

Leber had been most helpful in keeping her informed of their progress and expected time of arrival.

'Oh, so that's why he made a sharp exit,' smiled Henry.

He did not mind in the least, for Henry had become rather fond of the little Gypsy queen.

They both sat on large cushions around the fire. Shelta served him up a veritable feast, as promised, and they chatted. The smell of the food, wood smoke and the forest, together with the herbal tea made from lichen, made Henry realise the richness of the Gypsy way.

They lay there, watching a large full moon rise gently through the trees, but then the toll of the day's proceedings caught up with them, and they drifted off to sleep.

When Henry awoke, Shelta was making breakfast. A cup of coffee was thrust into his hand as he explored his surroundings. The early sun cast long shadows which disappeared into the blackness of the forest, with its fragrant peppery smell.

He took a carrot from a box of vegetables hanging off the caravan, and gave it to the horse, while stroking its cheek.

They sat on the steps of the caravan and ate breakfast. Henry said they would have to do this again when there was more time. He had really enjoyed it.

Shelta said she would make her way back to the clearing by the river when she was satisfied with events.

Then it was time for Henry to leave, and, with a hug and a kiss, and a wishing of each other luck, Henry made his way to the gap in the fabric that *Leber* had left for him.

In almost an instant, Henry found himself on the patio of the Manor, and with no-one about, he went into the house. Before he could enter the conservatory, MacTavish greeted him.

'Welcome back M'lord, we wondered when you would return.' Henry, slightly confused by the remark, claimed he had only been gone one night.

'Oh no, sir, it has been three days. Mr *Leber* assured us that you were fine and would be returning soon.'

Henry, now a little unsure whether *Leber* had been up to his old tricks, went off in search of him.

He began with the greenhouses. Ivy was there, and she was busy with the ladies from the village. They were tending to the night flowers, encouraging seed production, as per *Leber's* instructions.

Ivy said he had been there earlier, giving the ladies tips on growing the night flower, but had left some time ago.

Henry marched off to the war room. Moss, who remained consistent to the cause, was at his post. Henry quizzed Moss.

'MacTavish tells me I have been gone for three days, and it only seems like a day. There is a nagging thought that *Leber* may have been up to his old tricks.'

Moss began to explain that the time it had taken to visit the Gypsy camps was well in excess of two days, but time within the fabric was difficult to measure. His time with Shelta had taken the best part of a day, and it all added up.

'It is your first experience of travelling so intensely; you will get used to it, in time,' said Moss.

He was sure that *Leber* had not duped Henry in any way.

Henry had great respect for Moss and thanked him for his honesty; he apologized for his own mistrust.

'Where is everyone? It's like a ghost town,' said Henry, now becoming a little frustrated.

Moss began to fill Henry in on the past three days' events. He told him of the progress that had been made with the aircraft and the installation of the equipment. The plane would be undergoing trials the next day, to test the equipment over the Atlantic.

Jake and Sandra had driven down to Magnatek for the event, as they had been invited to accompany the flight on its maiden voyage.

The Shaman had returned through the cave to their homeland, in readiness for the forthcoming event.

Henry had forgotten to enquire of *Leber* the weight of the seed requested by Edmund for the trial.

'Do you know where he is?' asked Henry.

Moss believed that he had taken night flowers and little ones to the villages where the Shaman were. He would probably be backwards and forwards to the greenhouses most of the day.

Henry was rather keen to be involved with the test flight; he would make the journey, too, if there was time.

'What about you, Moss, would you like to go up in the plane?' Henry enquired.

Moss shook his head, he replied that just standing on a stool gave him vertigo, besides, he had to monitor the trial run.

Henry asked Moss to tell *Leber*, if he saw him, that he would be in the greenhouse, and needed to speak with him.

Henry made his way to the greenhouses and fortunately found *Leber,* just about to enter.

'Good morning, Henry,' said *Leber*. 'Did you have a pleasant return?'

Henry admitted that time within the fabric took some getting used to, he thanked him for his time with Shelta, and was surprised how quickly he had returned.

Henry questioned him about the weight concerns the scientists had, regarding the number of seed which was to be collected. Would it be too heavy for the plane?

Leber admitted that in all his time, he had never contemplated the weight of the seed. He explained that the seed went through a change when in the possession of an elder. He reached into one of his pockets, and with his hand tightly closed, he told Henry to watch carefully.

Opening his hand, a small swirling dark mist appeared and danced across his palm. Grabbing Henry's hand, he placed it on his palm; the mist spun and hovered across his hand.

'How heavy do you think that is?' asked *Leber*.

Henry raised his arm up and down a few times, trying to get some idea of its weight, but he could not feel anything significant.

'Now toss it into that area,' said *Leber*, pointing to an area at the side of the path.

Henry did as *Leber* asked; the mist stopped spinning and changed in appearance as it landed, looking more like a seed that you would feed to the birds.

Henry bent down to retrieve a few grains, and as he stood up, the grain began to grow in his hand, with a definite feel of weight. Throwing it back on the ground, Henry watched in amazement at the speed that it grew.

'Does that answer your question?' said *Leber*. 'It's held on the edge of the fabric, until it hits the ground.'

Leaving Henry to observe the growing, *Leber* continued with his work, and went into the green house to collect more items for the villages. He mentioned his little demonstration to Ivy, who came out to observe.

By the time Ivy joined Henry, the plants had reached over four feet in height. They both stood watching as the plants reached a height of over eight feet, then suddenly burst into flower. *Leber* had used sunflowers for his presentation.

'Very impressive,' said Henry. 'I'm going to drive down to Magnatek for the trials. Would you like to join me?' He said there were a few things he had to deal with first but would be setting off just after lunch.

Ivy agreed to join him. She would make sure her ladies were sorted for their work and would meet Henry for lunch.

That settled, Henry returned to the house. He joined Moss in the cinema; he was watching some activity at the highway, where the track to the palm oil plantation began. Two large bulldozers had just arrived on a low loader.

'It looks like they are going to attempt to clear the track which we replanted,' said Moss.

Henry suggested that it might be a good idea to keep an eye on proceedings; it could take them weeks to clear the miles of track, if at all.

Henry retired to his quarters to deal with matters of business, while Moss scanned the areas of activity.

The repatriation of the villagers created by *Chonga* and *Tabule*, was well under way. There was the beginning of a population taking place.

The formation of buildings and boundaries could be seen, as the villagers began to stake their claim. Each of the village areas that had been created were now very active; one could almost taste the anticipation of the impending event, in the air.

Meanwhile, Jake and Sandra had arrived down at Magnatek. They were greeted by Max, who, having arranged their room and luggage transfer, led them round the building to the grounds at the rear.

Max invited them to join him on the transport he used, a golf buggy, adapted for passengers, claiming his knees were not what they used to be.

Negotiating the red shale road to the hangar, Max made small talk. Was their journey ok, and were they well? And all that sort of thing. He was not used to young people, his life revolved around the Scientifics of this world, so he felt a little uncomfortable.

When they reached the plane, Archie welcomed them with hugs and handshakes.

'Let me show you around,' he said.

He led them around the plane and pointed out the equipment that had been installed in the old camera housing. He explained in aeronautical terms, the effects it would have on the plane, especially when it was lowered for activation: the drag factor, could the engines cope with the increased load? These were all areas to be monitored in the trial. His phone indicated a message from Henry, he would be arriving later with Ivy, and had the information regarding the weight factors.

'His message was rather ambiguous, and I shall have to await his arrival, in order to clarify it,' said Archie.

He led them round to the rear of the plane, where they entered via the loading ramp; there they found Edmund and Henri busy with clipboards. They were checking, and re-checking all the new on-board equipment, which had been installed in record time.

'Welcome aboard you two,' said Edmund, and continued to press knobs and turn dials and write things on the clipboard.

Henri, having witnessed the abruptness of Edmund, continued the explanation of equipment, and apologized for Edmund's lack of decorum.

After having a full tour of the newly transformed aircraft, Jake and Sandra turned their attention to the runway.

Jake had to pass comment on its condition, being a landscaper at heart. He suggested they should both inspect it, in all its glory.

So, leaving the technicals to finish their tests and reports, Jake and Sandra went off to explore.

The testing and retesting went on for most of the afternoon, until a delivery arrived, which got Max quite excited.

Edmund joined him to take delivery of the package. They took it over to a small scaffold tower which had been erected at the side of the rear fuselage.

Archie, his curiosity aroused, came over to where they were, now on the tower platform, and unrolling what looked like a sheet of plastic.

Edmund and Max were each holding an end of the offered-up sheet, which just covered the registration numbers on the side.

'Ok I give up, what is it?' asked Archie.

Max told him it was camouflage, pressing it firmly into place. Edmund used a roller over the surface to smooth out any air pockets.

When it was properly adhered to the side of the plane, and covering the registration numbers, which were still very visible, they got down.

Standing back at some distance, Max instructed Archie to observe. Max tapped his smart phone and began to scroll and tap; suddenly the numbers on the side of the plane changed.

Edmund explained that it was a film, similar to that of the screen on a smart phone or tablet. When activated, you could display anything, just as you would on the screen of your phone. When deactivated it reverted back to a transparent film, returning the plane back to its original numbers.

'That's very clever', said Archie.

'It can be activated after take-off to give some anonymity,' said Max. 'Actually, it is one of Edmund's inventions which the company is keen to take on. We are going to apply for patents; Edmund may become rich and famous.'

Edmund and Henri joined them, there were a few little playful alterations to the video panel, as they put it through its paces.

They had done as much as they could; everything was working, and Edmund was expecting the well-timed arrival of Ivy, anytime soon. They decided it was time to relax a little before supper, and so they all piled into Max's golf buggy and made their way back to the mansion house and the dining room.

Shortly after they had all got comfortable, Henry arrived with Ivy. Henry told Max that he had received some information on his phone, from Moss, on the way down.

He told them that *Leber* had arranged with *Agi*, to be at a particular location during the trials. He had the coordinates, and the intention was for *Agi* and her sisters to help in a seed release. It could then be possible to test the magnetic field, and its capacity to capture and release the cargo.

Archie enquired of the coordinates, and Henry passed him his phone. When Archie read the message, he shook his head. Checking on his own phone, he declared that the coordinates given were in the middle of the Bay of Biscay.

'There must be some mistake,' said Archie.

To which Henry replied.

‘No, no mistake! The plane would have to fly low enough to catch the seed, exactly like the planned event. *Leber* assured me that if you fly over these coordinates, you will not miss the target,’ said Henry.

Turning to Max, Henry told him how *Leber* had explained the weight of the seed, and of its strange journey, from an Elder, to the ground.

Max had witnessed many strange things with the *Burrbesh*, but still found it difficult to get his head around the concept of the fabric.

Jake and Sandra joined the group, after walking the perimeter of the grounds; Sandra said they must have walked miles.

‘Nearly four and a half miles, actually,’ said Max.

There was a subdued excitement in the air; everyone there, had a role to play in the project, and they chatted over dinner until late.

The next morning saw everyone going about their business, quietly, they knew what to do and got on with it. Archie was checking the plane, doing his pre-flight inspection.

Max was on the phone to air traffic control to inform them of the flight plan and receive updated weather reports.

Edmund and Henri were double checking the data input and resetting the lasers to accommodate the new, intended cargo.

Henry had made contact with *Agi*, who, admitting it was a last-minute decision by *Leber,* to assist, was attempting to ascertain what plants would be surrendered to the field.

She told him that the quantity would be a sample, sufficient to make an impact on the area, but not as dense as that proposed for the Amazon.

Sandra required this information to try and program the field to distribute the planting, which would be purely marine, in the most beneficial way. They were going to set the perimeter of the field to its maximum, covering a one-hundred-mile diameter, which would be just over seven thousand square miles.

The area where they planned to carry out this experiment was usually fairly devoid of traffic. Fallout that might land on any vessel within that area would be negligible and might be mistaken for sea spray.

Ivy had the most important job – provisions for the trip and tea for the troops.

She arrived on Max’s golf cart with a tea urn tightly strapped to the back, the tea sloshing around and dribbling down its sides.

‘I thought we needed something British to toast the maiden voyage,’ she said.

By now it was mid-morning, they all congregated around the teashop, and sitting on the grass, they confirmed to one another that their tasks were complete, and that the trial could begin.

And so, with refreshments over, Ivy and Sandra took up position in two of the passenger seats, with a cool bag of provisions. Henry, who had never flown before, was invited into the cockpit with Jake the navigator, while Edmund, Henri and Max strapped themselves to the repositioned chairs, now in front of the fixed equipment.

Finally, Archie entered, having removed the chocks from the wheels, and closing the rear door, he took his position in the captain’s chair.

‘Ok people, if we are sitting comfortably, then I shall begin,’ and Archie fired up the engines.

They taxied out of the hangar and onto the grassy runway. After pausing to do a final check, he pushed the throttles forward and the shed powered on down the runway.

Lift-off was gentle and sweet, the plane levelled off at five thousand feet, and after a short conversation with air traffic control, he set the autopilot. Henry was very quiet.

‘Are you ok?’ enquired Archie.

Henry admitted that he had never experienced anything like it, he was lost for words.

‘Archie, you will have to teach me how to drive one of these,’ said Henry.

Archie said it should take about an hour and a half to reach the coordinates given by *Leber*, so he suggested they should relax, and enjoy the flight.

They watched France as it was left behind. This was Archie’s cue to reduce altitude, as they were approaching the Bay of Biscay.

They would need to keep a sharp eye out for the target, but Archie was still convinced they would not see anything.

As they got closer, Archie reduced altitude to the recommended five hundred feet. Edmund’s instruction to energise the magnetic field was confirmed by Henri.

‘Field energised,’ came the reply. Archie felt a bit of a jolt through the controls when the field was switched on, and as a result, he had to increase power.

They were now very close to the exact coordinates when Archie pointed to an object on the sea. There in front of them was *Agi*, or a very good copy, made of sea water, together with her five sisters, standing some hundred feet high, each carrying a basket under their arms.

‘I hope you guys are ready for this,’ said Archie.

The six figures standing on the sea, cast the contents of their baskets into the air. The dark swirling mist of the seed was captured by the magnetic field and spread across miles, further than the eye could see.

Archie confessed to a sudden strain on the controls and struggled to ascend. He pushed the throttles forward to exert maximum power, the plane responded and gained altitude.

Max said they needed to climb to a thousand feet, then they could release.

Sandra and Ivy were transfixed on the images of *Agi* and her sisters; they watched until they melted back into the sea.

‘Nine hundred feet, one thousand feet,’ came the voice of Archie, as the plane continued upwards on its task.

‘Ok, release,’ said Max.

‘Field off, seed released,’ confirmed Henri.

The plane suddenly lurched upwards, as though in a thermal. Archie soon stabilised the plane and increased altitude to five thousand feet. They made a couple of passes over the area, but there was nothing to be seen. The water giants had gone, the seed, which had created partial shade of the sun, for a moment, was gone, but the data recovered was there in abundance.

‘If I was not five thousand feet up in a plane, I would dance a jig,’ said Max.

Henry said he could dance one when they landed, to which everyone agreed, and a roar of laughter resounded through the plane.

Henri and Edmund had their heads buried in computer screens and data, oblivious to any excitement.

Henry was fascinated by the water giants, and was keen to meet up with *Agi*, and find out what magic she had used to create the effect. A well satisfied team began the return journey, confident in the knowledge that the main event was extremely possible.

Sandra commented that it was a shame they could not see the results of the seed that had been taken and scattered across the ocean. She also, would quiz *Agi* on their return.

With the plane set to autopilot, Archie joined Edmund and Henri and asked them what data they had recovered.

'Well, we managed to cover an area of nearly fifty miles radius, a near perfect circle. It was a simple geometric shape, easy to use for the first time. We are still calculating the weight effects; we are not sure if it was the seed, or the effect of the magnetic field, attracting other particles in the atmosphere,' said Henri.

'Pollution,' said Edmund.

The plane made its way back to the airfield, with a very satisfied crew. After a perfect landing, the plane taxied back to the hangar, where several technicians from the workshops were waiting to put the shed to bed.

They attached the rear of the plane to a tractor and pulled it into the hangar. Max and Henri gathered up the relevant hard drives from the computers and said they would be in the lab if anyone needed them.

Edmund told them he would look in on them before he went, to see the progress on unravelling the data. He was driving back to the Manor with Ivy, Jake and Sandra, using the Bentley.

Archie and Henry had duties at Westminster, an attendance that had been overlooked of late; and as they were halfway, at Magnatek, it was sensible to do the trip while they were there. Besides, there was important business which Archie had been committed to and was due to be concluded. It would release funds for the repatriation of displaced villagers in the Amazon; Archie believed it was perfect timing. They would leave early next morning and should be back at the Manor just after lunch.

Edmund, unable to contain his curiosity, made his excuses and wandered down to the lab. Henri and Max were deliberating over information on one of the screens.

'Anything?' enquired Edmund.

'We have run a few scenarios through the computer, and it is probable that a flock of birds may have been caught up in the field,' said Max.

As the anomaly was small, they did not really have great concerns for it, but would continue their investigations. On the whole, the experiment was a success, and they would begin preparations for the main event.

'I shall be back at the Manor shortly, and you can send me the data,' said Edmund.

He left them to their investigations and went to collect his passengers. He found everyone waiting for him in the lobby, and apologizing for his desertion, he resumed his task of chauffeur.

Chapter 27

Edmund quite enjoyed his journey back to the Manor. He explained at great length, the function of each of the switches, knobs and dials that littered the dashboard and surrounding supports.

On arrival back at the Manor they found a number of council members were in attendance. *Tabule* was at the head of the table, with *Chonga* by his side, and they were debating the upcoming events.

There was to be a council meeting the next evening, with all members in full attendance. The plan to deal with vast areas of Europe in conjunction with the Amazon, would require some working out, plus the supply of sufficient seed from the night flower.

Leber had gone to visit the sites where the night flower had been given a permanent home. He had concocted a new tonic for the improvement and wellbeing of the night flower; his attentions resembled those of a doting parent.

'Ah, Edmund, I understand you have had some success with the new equipment?' said *Tabule*.

Edmund and Jake joined the others at the table, while Ivy and Sandra, keen to return to their work in the greenhouses, left the men to it.

Edmund proceeded to give his account of the successful experiment that they had recently carried out. He thanked *Agi* and her sisters for their input and complimented them on their spectacular display.

He explained that Archie, as soon as the tests were complete, and the plane had been serviced, would be taking it to his airfield in Venezuela. He would accompany him, together with Henri and Max, who would be required to monitor the equipment and program the correct sequence into the magnetic field. The main event should then be ready to initiate, and arrangements could be set in place to coordinate it with the European events.

'The operation across Europe may have to be staggered, due to the large number of venues,' said *Tabule*.

'Some would require the presence of several *Burrbesh.*' He went on to say that *Leber* and Moss would determine the size of the areas, and the numbers required to cover them.

'This information should hopefully be with us this evening, and will be the major topic of tomorrow's meeting,' said *Tabule*.

This collaboration with man had never been attempted before; the *Burrbesh* had always kept a very low key, to the point of being invisible. But, as this problem was man made, and man was attempting to put things right, there was a general feeling of paternal sympathy towards their plight.

Moss entered the room with news that more vehicles had been unloaded at the site of the access road and were making progress towards the palm oil plantation. He estimated the completion of the new road would take around seven days and suggested that they might require slowing down.

'Master Jake seems to be the machinery expert,' laughed *Tabule*. 'Perhaps he has an idea on how we should deal with these invaders!'

Moss suggested that they should perhaps create another doorway at the new road and allow Jake to explore the possibilities.

'I shall mention it to *Leber* when he returns,' said *Tabule*.

Moss required Edmund's assistance to calculate the areas which *Leber* was visiting. He had taken *Chonga's* GPS and was transmitting coordinates of the intended Gypsy sites.

Edmund, excusing himself from the table, went through to the cinema with Moss, and explained how to plot the coordinates on the map, and calculate the areas.

Ivy and Sandra appeared and confirmed that the night flowers in the greenhouses were now at maximum production. The ladies from the village had gone home for the evening, and Ivy suggested that they too, might return home for the night.

Moss then indicated an incoming video call from Magnatek; it was Max. He told Edmund that the flight plan had been logged with air traffic control, and Archie would be leaving for Venezuela after lunch. The plane had been serviced, and all the equipment that was required had been installed, and with luck they should make Gibraltar by teatime.

Edmund confirmed that he would be there, he would make an early start and drive Henry's car down.

Max said he and Henri would fly out on a commercial flight and meet them in Brazil. They much preferred a straight-through flight, rather than a hop, skip, and a jump of Archie's route. When the call was over, the four bade Moss goodnight and made their way to the car park.

'You can drop me at the stables, I need to groom my horse,' said Sandra.

Jake said he needed to take Fidgit for a walk, as he had been neglected lately. Jake arranged to pick her up next morning and they all continued home.

When Jake and Sandra arrived next morning, Fidgit, as usual, disappeared into the bushes.

Edmund, keen to capture as much of the day as possible, had already gone.

Ivy was sitting having coffee on the patio with *Leber*; he was discussing the progress of the night flower at the Gypsy camps.

Jake and Sandra joined them, and listened to *Leber,* as he listed the types of desolation that they would be dealing with.

There were chemical and toxic waste dumps, areas of abandoned industry, opencast mine workings and landfill sites, all of which would need a special type of plant. He had inspected these areas, and he had produced a particularly resilient plant that would thrive in these conditions. He had given the seed to Ivy, who would introduce it to the night flower, which, in turn, would adsorb the properties of the new seed and reproduce it.

'If you have a minute Jake, there is something I have to show you,' said *Leber*.

He explained that *Tabule* had spoken with him, and that there may be a little something Jake could help with, as Ivy and Sandra left for the green houses.

'We can drive up to the jungle and I will show you,' said *Leber*.

They both wandered out to Jake's Land Rover and headed on up to the fields and the jungle.

When they arrived, the Miller brothers were just adding the final touches to the fencing which had been erected around the perimeter. They were fixing signage, claiming that trespassers would be prosecuted, and that the area was dangerous, containing tropical poisonous plants. There was also a large notice, explaining that a joint experiment with the College and the Lytes Academy was in progress.

They walked over to a new gate and entered the jungle; the path to the cave was still evident as the growth of everything had slowed down to normal.

When they reached the cave *Leber* explained that there was a doorway to the left which Jake would be able to access. It would take him to the track where the workers were clearing the way, while the right-hand path would remain open and lead to the Amazon villages.

Keen to test it out, Jake moved tentatively forward, with outstretched arms. The doorway, unseen, was part of the cave wall and allowed him to pass through and proceed forward.

In no time at all, he had exited into the dappled shade of the jungle canopy; he could hear the sound of big machinery not far away.

Stealthily, Jake edged forward to get a better view. He reached a position where he could just make out the yellow colour of the machinery. He could hear the cracking and breaking of trees and branches as the bulldozers inched forward into the forest.

Turning to go back, he could not see the doorway through which he had arrived. He tried to retrace his steps, looking for any sign of trodden ground, with no luck.

Suddenly, *Leber* appeared right in front of him.

'Have you lost your way?' he laughed.

Jake, now a little concerned, had not thought to look back and see from whence he had come, believing that it would be a cave entrance and easy to find.

Leber explained that there could be no visible doorway like the entrance to the cave in case anyone decided to investigate; this was a fabric doorway which required sensing.

'The night flower marked your wrist. It will tell you when a doorway is close by, this is just one of many.

'Now, turn and walk back towards the machinery, for twenty paces, then return and find the door.' *Leber* slipped back into the doorway when Jake turned away.

As Jake turned back, he could hear voices, his pace quickened, and holding his wrist, he expected some sort of sign. He thought he felt a slight vibration; turning right, the vibration subsided, but the voices got louder. He turned left, the vibration grew stronger. He continued forward until the feeling resembled the silent vibration of a mobile phone; it grew stronger as he moved forward. Suddenly, with no warning, he had passed through into the passageway where *Leber* was standing, applauding him with a slow hand clap.

'Sshhh, said Jake.' Turning, he could see the misty figures of the workers walking past the entrance.

Leber told him that the workers would not be able to see or hear him, or even enter the door, as they had no connection with the *Burrbesh. Leber* explained that whenever there was a door in the fabric, Jake's wrist would let him know, the more times he used it, the easier and faster it would become to enter and exit. Jake commented that this was a complete turn-around from his opinion of not so long ago.

'Don't get telling everybody, it is really your bloodline to Henry that gives you this privilege,' said *Leber* sternly, attempting to maintain his hard-nosed-ness.

'Besides this is an opportunity for you to practise your talent and do something about these persistent workers.'

Returning to the entrance of the cave, they made their way back to the Manor. On arrival *Leber* said he was going to check on the greenhouses, while Jake went to see Moss, with a mind to keeping an eye on the workers and their machinery.

Moss agreed to let Jake know the moment the workers left; he thought that they might not work at the weekend.

Jake went into the conservatory and stood in front of the now dense night flower; closing his eyes he breathed in the heavy scent from the mass of flowers.

A young shoot reached out and curled around his wrist, a deep feeling of belonging filled his mind. The vision of a green planet reassured him that the task ahead would be successful.

Suddenly there was another embrace, as Sandra slipped her arms around his waist, and whispered.

'A penny for your thoughts.'

As the night flower gently uncoiled, Jake turned to face her. She asked if they could go to the jungle, as she really wanted to catalogue what was there. Jake agreed and told her of his experience earlier with *Leber*.

'We could check out the village and see if Charlie's well is still providing water. Moss says there has been a population explosion, and they may need a few more,' said Jake.

Sandra went to collect her bag and met Jake at the front, in the Land Rover. There was also Fidgit, and the three little ones comfortably ensconced in the back.

When they reached the jungle, Sandra got out and noticed that the rear passengers remained, they did not charge off into the distance as usual. She looked at Jake, and with head to one side, gave an enquiring look.

'They are under strict instructions; we have things to do,' said Jake.

They all made their way to the entrance of the jungle, Fidgit by his side and the little ones in tow, in a very orderly fashion.

Following the path, they reached the cave; Jake asked Sandra if she would like to go to the village first. Then he, together with Fidgit and his three little helpers, would give her a hand to carry out her survey.

There was, however, something that he had to explore before they went, and it required the loyal assistance of the Fidgit crew. He needed to introduce Fidgit to the new doorway; Jake had to be sure that he could pass through without a problem.

If Jake wandered too far from the exit, he had to admit that he was not a tracker. Finding his way back might be dependent on the nose of a dog, or the magic of a sprout.

Sandra chose to visit the village and said she would wait on the Amazon side for Jake to carry out his experiment. They all entered the cave and Jake showed Sandra where the door was; she put her hands on the cave wall and it felt solid. It was evident from that, that Sandra would not be able to pass through.

However, the little ones were stepping in and out of the wall, encouraging Fidgit, who was making the most horrible whine, head on paws and bum in the air, frustrated that the solidity of the wall would not allow him through. Jake passed through with ease, and bending down he beckoned to Fidgit, with just his head and shoulders protruding from the wall.

By now Fidgit's frustration had turned to a decisive bark of defiance. Jake encouraged him with outstretched arms. Fidgit inched forward on his stomach, until he found his head was in, and the rest of him was out. He had succeeded in overcoming his fear, and standing proud, did a circular dance on the spot, half in half out, half out half in.

Jake, now with just his head protruding like a hunter's trophy on a wall, said he would be back in a min. And, with a sound like squeezing the last dregs of the tomato sauce from the bottle, he was gone.

Sandra continued along the tunnel to the exit, where she took up position on a deckchair-shaped rock in the sunshine, and in the heat of the Amazon, she awaited Jake's return.

She did not have to wait long, Jake and his gang arrived within ten minutes. He expressed his admiration for the intelligence of all concerned and was impressed with his experiment. So, with success filling the air they all set off for the village.

Unknown to Jake and Sandra, things had progressed at Magnatek. Archie and Henry had returned from their successful attendance at Westminster.

Edmund had arrived and was carrying out last-minute checks on board the plane, with Henri.

Take-off was planned for 15:00 hours that afternoon. The plane had been loaded with equipment, checked, refuelled and was ready for take-off. After a brief lunch together, Henry drove Edmund and Archie down to the plane in Max's golf buggy.

Like astronauts being driven to their transport, Archie said perhaps they should call it Apollo 7.

Wishing them good luck on their flight, Henry stood back and watched, as the 'shed' taxied onto the runway, and without ceremony hurtled off down the green beige. Henry stood watching the plane, until it disappeared into the sky.

He returned to the lab and wished Max and Henri all the best of luck; they were booked on a flight to Fortaleza the following day.

'I shall see you at Archie's vineyard in Venezuela before the event,' said Henry. Having shaken both their hands, he made his way out to the car, and began his journey back to the Manor.

During his trip back he was keen to learn how Shelta and her people's arrangements were progressing. He fiddled with the buttons which he had seen Edmund use, to make a call on hands-free.

Suddenly Moss came across all twenty-four speakers, within the once silent open-air Bentley. Feeling rather pleased with his technical ability, he proceeded to quiz Moss on the state of affairs at the Eastern end of the planet.

The information that Moss had was extensive, the locations of all the sites were under constant scrutiny. Shelta had made good progress after her incarceration and would soon be fairly central to all that was about to happen.

The Bentley purred along the country lanes as if on autopilot, while Henry listened to all of Moss's news.

It was not long before Henry was back at the Manor.

It was his intention to contact Shelta, and hopefully, assist in the organising of the many events she had planned.

'Don't forget there is a council meeting tonight,' said Moss. 'Oh, and your great grandson and his lady friend have gone to the Amazon village.' Moss had just noticed them as he was zooming around the area.

Jake and Sandra were amazed at the number of villagers that had returned. With two little ones on his shoulders and one on Sandra's, they made their way across the compound to Charlie's abode.

'Stay close, Fidgit,' commanded Jake.

As they approached, they could see Charlie and *Tabule* sitting outside, chatting.

'Good day, Master Jake,' bellowed *Tabule*. 'I hear you are tasked with doing some more machinery magic!'

Jake admitted that it seemed to be his thing at the moment, and asked Charlie how his well was performing. Rising to his feet, he beckoned to Jake to follow him. They went around the side of his hut to examine a beautifully constructed well-head, with perimeter wall, wooden frame with roof, and a large handle with rope and pail attached.

It was all Jake could do to stand there, nodding his head in an impressive gesture, eventually congratulating Charlie on his work.

'Some of the other villagers want one of these, so we can keep you busy if you have nothing else to do,' said Charlie, with a grin.

The little ones were barely visible to Charlie; he said Jake was a very special person to have gained the trust of such special beings. He too had known them as a young boy and was glad to see their return; just knowing they were there, bred confidence.

Jake grasped his hand and promised to return; he would do all he could to fulfil the needs of his people.

But, for now, Jake had urgent business back home, namely the cataloguing of tropical plants.

Sandra bade Charlie goodbye, he put his hand up to her shoulder and touched the little one sitting there; he nodded and smiled.

Jake and Sandra then made their way back to the cave with Fidgit in tow, who, it must be said had been exceptional. Leaving the cave, however, was another matter, Fidgit and the little ones charged off into the jungle.

Sandra, with the assistance of Jake and his machete, set out a three-metre square section of the jungle. Then, on hands and knees at times, she photographed and documented everything within, a project which took the rest of the afternoon.

It was early evening by the time they returned to the Manor. The place was busy; there were council members milling around, along with other strange characters, obviously *Burrbesh.*

Henry came over to them and explained that reinforcements had been brought in to help with the event; they had taken leave of their tasks elsewhere at the request of *Tabule*.

There would be a meeting at ten o'clock when details of the event were to be discussed, and Henry said he would like them both to be there.

They both agreed, and as the time was now six thirty, they both decided to freshen up in their room at the Manor.

Luggage from the last trip was still there, and Sandra was desperate for a shower; she was convinced a stick insect was making a nest in her hair.

Jake said he would catch up with her, as he had to see Moss, and arrange for MacTavish to provide Fidgit with his favourite supper. Jake walked into the cinema where Moss was at the com; there were quite a few characters watching the images on screen.

'Aha, Master Jake, no doubt you have come to enquire on the workers?' said Moss.

He told Jake that the workers had left at lunchtime, earlier than usual. He presumed that they had left for the weekend, but he would keep an eye on the situation.

Just as Jake left to go to the kitchen, a video call came through from Archie and Edmund. They had arrived safely at Gibraltar and confirmed that everything was on schedule.

Henry and Ivy came through to speak with them. Henry told them of the additional help that had arrived and of the meeting that was due to start. He wanted to confirm that the date set for the event would be in four days, on the Tuesday, and it would be this date that the council would work towards.

Leaving Ivy to chat with Edmund, Henry went off to find *Tabule*. There was a buzz of excitement flowing through the Manor. As Henry walked through the rooms, he could hear the main topic of conversation; everyone could be heard discussing the impending events.

He found *Tabule* on the patio talking to *Leber*. He asked if he could visit Shelta to assess the progress made with her people. Henry assumed that having been through the fabric with *Leber* many times recently, he could access this form of travel at any time but thought it only polite to ask.

'You have much to learn about the fabric, even now we ourselves have our moments where destinations get confused,' said *Tabule*. 'But, as you have progressed far in the *Burrbesh* way, it may fall on you to be the one responsible for the maintenance of this world. And so, I think *Leber* should educate you in the art of travel.'

Leber with one eyebrow raised, glanced across at him.

'Touché,' said *Leber*.

Tabule left them to it and went off to join the busy groups. *Leber* said that Henry had already made a successful trip on his own, albeit very brief and sketchy. He explained that the main ingredient for successful travel was the mind.

'Focusing on someone or somewhere, then maintaining that focus, will have positive results.

Then, as you have the image firmly in your thoughts, a step forward will take you there. Try,' said Leber, 'you should find it easy to connect with Shelta, as she is receptive to your thoughts.'

Henry stood, closing his eyes to help him concentrate, he took a step forward. Opening one eye, he could see it had not been successful, he had just moved a step nearer the edge of the patio. *Leber* laughed but continued to give him encouraging tuition.

It was the third step when Henry disappeared; *Leber* gave a clap, even though he could not be heard.

Henry appeared close to Shelta's caravan, on uneven ground, which caught him unawares. He tripped, gambolled down a bank and came to rest at the feet of Shelta, who found it extremely amusing.

'So, you can travel now,' she said.

'Practising,' said Henry.

He told Shelta he had to be back for the meeting, and about the extra re-enforcements that had been drafted in.

He was keen to find out the state of the night flowers and their propagation capacity but had to admit that that was not the only reason he had come.

They spent the short time dealing with business. She was in contact with most of the groups by phone, and the results of *Leber's* special formula had had a pronounced effect on the night flowers.

They had all reached maximum capacity, and would, in two weeks' time enter the third stage of harvest, which was just as well as they would be needed within the week.

They enjoyed each other's company until it was time for Henry to leave, and with a parting hug, Henry began the ritual for return. Getting better, he managed it on the second attempt, emerging close to the Manor house, but standing in the watercress beds, water up to his knees. Wading to the edge, he climbed out and made his way to the meeting.

The meeting went on well into the night, with only minimal reference to his soggy feet. Council members were allocated specific areas to manage the dispersal of seed, each having the willing help of numerous *Burrbesh* colleagues, brought in to assist.

Jake's abilities to disable machinery did not go unnoticed; Moss was sure that there would be an opportunity the next day for Jake to operate.

It was late, and a weary Jake and Sandra made their way home for the night, leaving a throng of individuals still avidly debating the events.

The following morning Jake arrived around ten thirty; he had left Sandra at her stables, as she was going riding, with Henry.

Fidgit was told to stay by his side while he went to see Moss and check on the workers at the Amazon.

Moss confirmed his suspicions, the workers had left for the weekend, and it looked as though Jake would have a clear run. Moss refocused the image on screen to the area in question and noticed smoke.

'Oh dear, looks like they have left someone,' Moss zoomed in to the maximum. He could just make out a figure stooping over the fire.

'Looks like he is cooking something. This puts a whole new light on the situation,' said Moss.

He was concerned that things might get dangerous and suggested that they should abandon the idea. Jake examined the image on screen and concluded that the smoke was some distance from the machinery.

He had an idea.

If the machinery continued in a straight line, bulldozing, side by side, as it had been doing, then somewhere, directly in the path of the machines, Jake could create a large quicksand area. He would not need to put the machinery out of action directly but wait for the workers to do it for him. It would mean exploring the intended path of the vehicles and choosing a suitable spot. He would be able to keep a safe distance from the man with the fire.

He would take Fidgit and the little ones as back-up, and also as guides, to find the door back to the cave.

'It could work,' said Moss.

Jake decided that that was what he was going to do and went with Fidgit to collect the little ones.

He could not help but notice how quiet the house was, especially after the night before. He bade a good morning to Henry, who was just coming down the stairs. He then gave instructions to Fidgit to go and find the little ones and bring them to the Land Rover.

Jake told Henry of his intentions.

Did he need any help? was the reply.

Jake reassured him that he had it covered, and said he was quite looking forward to the adventure. Henry wished him luck, and told him that after his ride with Sandra, he would be joining the council at the village.

There was to be a temple opening, to honour the night flower. Just at that moment Fidgit came racing through the room closely followed by the sprouts.

'Aha, the cavalry has arrived. You be careful Jake, and I shall see you later,' said Henry.

Jake ran after them and herded them into the Land Rover and continued on towards the jungle. On arrival, Jake gave his crew a list of instructions; they listened intently, sitting in an arena style on the dry ground.

Then they set off for the cave in a tight formation, so tight in fact that Fidgit kept bumping into the back of Jake's leg. Jake turned to his crew and re-issued his instructions.

'When I said stay close, I didn't mean that close, just, close.' Jake shook his head and continued through the cave to the hidden door.

As they passed through the door, Jake turned and put his finger to his lips. They emerged in a humid jungle, the early morning sun just beginning to cast its rays through the foliage.

'Remember where the entrance is,' he whispered.

They proceeded a little way until they could just see the front of the machinery. Making their way through the dense foliage, in the direction the road would take, they reached a small clearing. It had no trees but a reasonably dense ground cover, a bushy-type planting of around three to four foot high. Jake thought that this was a good place, the machines would obviously pass between the trees, taking the easiest route.

Jake began to pace out a large square between the trees and extending along the proposed road for a good hundred yards.

He planned not to bring water to the surface but for the surface to float on the water. It would be solid enough to walk on, but as soon as heavy machinery drove across, it would collapse, and the machines would sink.

Jake issued instructions to his crew to stay, while he criss-crossed the area doing his thing. It took a while, but when he returned, Fidgit was sitting there on his own, with a whimper that could only be translated as, not my fault, not my fault.

Jake asked him where they had gone. Fidgit, with the composure of a pointer, turned and faced the direction of the machinery.

‘We had better find them,’ said Jake and headed off in that general direction. When the machines became visible, they kept to the undergrowth at the side of the cleared road.

The faint smoke of the worker’s dying fire was just visible. The pair moved through the foliage until they were opposite the fire. They could see a hammock strung between two small trees, with what appeared to be the worker, asleep. And there were the little ones, dancing around him, and in their wake, rose a ring of monster plants.

Jake recognised them as being the giant arum, a plant that flowers once, and smells of rotting flesh. These giant plants were growing to ten feet and producing an impenetrable cage, incarcerating the poor worker.

Jake beckoned to the problem crew and told Fidgit to go and fetch them. They came over to him as nice as you like, not a care in the world. Jake despaired and told them they must now find the door.

They had not gone but a few steps into the jungle when bloodcurdling screams could be heard from across the way.

There was suddenly a most disgusting smell, one which seemed to tear at the nasal membranes; it too, came from across the way.

‘That’s disgusting, whose idea was that?’ said Jake, and although they never made a sound, Jake heard the name *Leber*.

‘Ok, let’s get out of here. Find the way home you lot.’

They could hear the screams of the worker all the way back to the door, which was found with ease, in a joint effort.

Chapter 28

When Jake and his motley crew returned through the cave, he gave them the option of staying with him, going to the village, or going off to play hide and seek. There was little hesitation; the three little ones ran off into the jungle while Fidgit sat looking up at Jake.

'Go on, I'll see you back at the Manor.' Fidgit did not need to be told twice, he turned and chased after his playmates.

Jake turned to the Amazon exit, and made the ten-minute hike to the village, expecting to meet up with Henry.

At the village, there were a good number of council members and their counterparts; it was a hive of activity. *Leber* came over to Jake and told him that his skills would be greatly appreciated by some of the other villagers, namely, his well divining. He asked Jake, that if he was willing, after the temple opening, he would take him on a tour of those villages in need.

They both wandered over to the temple entrance. Henry was there, surrounded by village elders. They had come from the surrounding new villages to pay their respects, and they would take with them, back to their village, a clone of the sacred plant.

Temples would be built at each of the villages, a place of worship and accommodation for each new night flower.

Henry was trying to impress upon them the need to return to their villages as soon as ceremonies were over. He was explaining the urgency in a time frame they could comprehend. He told them that the jungle would return in three moons. Should they not be back in their villages, they would find it difficult to return, as the jungle would grow around them.

The young Shaman came from within the temple, dressed in their finery. They greeted Henry, Jake and *Leber* and invited them for an inaugural inspection of the temple before the ceremony started.

When inside, Jake was amazed at the amount of light that came in. He marvelled at the design of the thatched dormers built into the roof, letting in just enough sunlight.

The sun streamed down onto the night flower, which had grown to a size on a par with its parent at the Manor. One young Shaman told them that with help from the night flower, they now had something to combat the mass destruction being inflicted upon their homeland. Each village would now have the means to repair the damage.

It was a heartfelt statement, spoken with conviction and emotion. The three young Shaman performed the ritual blessing of the temple. The blessing marked the opening of the temple and would sustain it for the future; then the decision to begin the ceremony was made.

They all went outside to enjoy the music and dancing that followed. Jake was a little overwhelmed to be invited to the table by the village elders. He sat with Henry and *Leber*, enjoying the food and drink laid on for the event.

As festivities continued, *Leber* took Jake to one side and suggested they go now and do the rounds of the villages in need. Time was running out, the day was nearly over, and there were just two full days left to make everything ready.

Leber took Jake to around twenty villages; some already had a water supply, which made life a little easier. But, nonetheless, Jake was beginning to feel the effects of his day's work, and as he finished the last well, exhaustion took over.

'Stirling work, young Jake, we should go and re-join the ceremonies and rest for a while. There is a particular drink that they make, which will make you feel a lot better,' said *Leber*.

Darkness had descended, and in the village, a large fire was blazing. In the middle, dancers were performing, and the food and drink was flowing.

The elders greeted Jake and shook his hand, as he and *Leber* re-joined the table. The particular drink was flowing freely, and Jake had to admit that after a couple of those, he felt as if he could do it all again.

As the evening progressed, the amount of people attending the festivities diminished; the pilgrimage to their roots had begun. It was well past midnight in the village when normality resumed.

Only the locals remained, and one of the young Shaman said they would have to enrol like-minded people to form a new order. He was overseeing the return migration and realised that his services were going to be stretched.

Henry escorted Jake, as they returned via the cave. Jake's Land Rover was just where he left it, and it provided their transport back to the Manor.

Daybreak was beginning to appear as they reached the Manor. Jake parked outside the front door. Henry jumped out and walked up the steps and disappeared inside. Jake was in two minds about going home to rest, which he knew he needed, but something compelled him to follow Henry into the house; there was no feeling of fatigue anymore, he seemed to have received a second wind.

Jake found Henry chatting to Moss, who informed them that Archie and Edmund were awaiting the arrival of the two Magnatek delegates. They were due to land on a commercial flight around noon, and they would then join them on the flight to Archie's vineyard airstrip in Venezuela.

Moss jokingly remarked that they should set a countdown timer on screen, zero hour in forty-eight hours and counting.

He pointed to the image on screen, lit by burning torches, a wide canoe had arrived at the jetty.

'Looks like the last delivery of animals. I have given this river lorry the name "Ark." For the past week it has brought animals to the village, in pairs.'

'Talking of animals, I shall have to find Fidgit. I have chores to do, so if you need me, I shall be at home,' said Jake, and went off in search of his companion.

Fidgit was found in the prone position amongst the foliage, with his three comrades in arms, who were well snuggled into the night flower.

'Pssst,' whispered Jake, Fidgit stirred, it was early even for Fidgit, and so Jake scooped him up, and carried him out to the Land Rover.

Having dealt with the most important things, it was time to catch up with some home time. It was still only four in the morning when Jake rolled in, he parked up and made his way to his place in the hedge line. The sky was brightening as the sun announced its impending arrival.

He put the kettle on for that typically English wake me up beverage and sat on the sofa. Fidgit joined him and curled up in his lap. Needless to say, the tea never got made, and Jake dropped off into a deep sleep. He was awoken by Fidgit washing out his inner ear with his tongue, and Mother standing in the doorway.

'You look like you could do with feeding, my lad – running around at all hours. Fidgit has already had his breakfast.'

She told him food would be served in half an hour, and as father was doing his Sunday morning office work, they could all sit down together.

'Great, thanks mom!' Jake wandered through to take a shower.

By eight thirty they were all sitting around the kitchen table, this was a first for over a week. Jake had either been at the Manor or working in another part of the world, so there was much he had to tell.

They sat and chatted, Jake relayed in detail his exploits with *Leber*, and of the expected event the day after tomorrow. Both his parents were impressed, they were surprised at the change in *Leber* and would be certain to watch the news, on the day.

There was the distinct sound of a scooter pulling up outside; Ivy popped her head round the kitchen door, followed by Sandra.

'Morning everyone, we thought we would surprise you.' She said that Henry had asked if they would like to visit the Amazon that afternoon, with lunch at the Manor for starters. Edna had concerns on how safe it was, she did not want to get stuck over there, but Bill was quite keen.

'That's settled then,' said Ivy.

She stayed for a cuppa. Jake and Sandra went off to the cabin and Bill left the women to chat while he went to do his office work. The day progressed at a gentle pace on the farm, a typical day in the country. It was hard to believe that in two days' time a major event would take place.

The event arrangements were taking place across two continents; the progress in Eastern Europe was beginning to attract attention. Some enthusiastic participants had carried out trial runs, done in the name of curiosity, to assess the efficiency of their sprouts. This was Henry's chosen name and had been adopted across Europe.

Local authorities were investigating intense plant growth in small pockets, across the continent, in what were once unusable areas, poisoned by industry. Even the trials conducted over Biscay had raised questions. Renowned for its turbulent and heavy seas during certain conditions, now, the whole area had remained calm, shipping could pass without issue. A survey vessel, which had been close to the area, detected a massive increase in subaqueous fauna.

There was also an investigative programme on TV, hosted by the two reporters, Dr David Loxton and Bud Langford. It had made media coverage purely from their appearance – of tattooed faces, and claims of abduction by forces unknown.

They had picked up on the strange plantings and were actively investigating them; the results of their findings gave them material for the programme.

In their latest broadcast they claimed to be off to investigate the strange occurrences in Europe. Moss had been monitoring these broadcasts and was keeping Henry informed of any progress they made, and in turn, Henry could keep Shelta in the loop.

At lunchtime Moss got the call that Max and Henri had arrived at Fortaleza Airport. They had met with Archie and Edmund and were transferring to the Sherpa and expected to depart at 13:00 local time.

It was Henry's intention to cross over with *Leber*, and meet up with them at Archie's vineyard, the next day.

Around the desolation, the position for each *Burrbesh* had been plotted on GPS, and a flight plan prepared. Henry would deliver this to Archie when they met, and after a brief visit, would return to the Manor.

He had thought of observing the event from Shelta's location, but on reflection, decided he would watch the satellite images unfold on screen.

At lunchtime Bill and Edna drove over to the Manor, picking Ivy up on the way. MacTavish had laid on a regular banquet on the patio, and Henry was the perfect host. They were joined by Moss and *Leber*, who had nothing but praise for Jake, to Bill and Edna's surprise. They chatted for some time, Moss ironing out some of the wrinkles in *Leber's* personality, which made Jake's parents more at ease with the whole situation.

It was around two o'clock, and after being fed and watered with some of Archie's excellent vintage, they all set off to the jungle, in the Bentley.

When they entered the cave, Henry gave a running commentary on the areas that they were going through, while *Leber* and Moss attempted to explain how they were going through.

Once out of the cave, *Leber* and Moss made their excuses and carried on to the village, while Henry took the others down to the river. Edna expressed her gratitude to Henry; she had heard many things of this great river and was glad to have seen it. Henry then took them to the village, where they were introduced to the elders, as Jake's parents and grandparent; they were all given the royal treatment and made to feel part of the village.

It was a brief visit, but one which Jake's parents would treasure. They made their final farewells to the village elders, as the doorway to the Amazon would be restricted once the event had taken place.

Henry guided them through the scrub, to the cave, and drove them back to the Manor. Bill asked Henry if he would like to join them for a drink at the Tavern, later; they had arranged to meet up with friends to round off the day.

Henry said he had to make contact with Archie and was expected to meet him at his vineyard, which might not be until later. Henry was a little apprehensive about travelling to Archie's, and said if there was any time left, he would love to join them.

Bill thanked him again for the day, and opening the car door for the ladies, he told Henry he might see him later. Only short of a chauffeur's hat, Bill drove off down the drive, with the ladies in the back. Having dropped Ivy off, Bill and Edna met Barney and his lady in the Tavern; it nicely rounded off the day, as they compared their experiences of the Amazon.

Henry did not go to the Tavern but spoke with Archie and Edmund at length. They had been delayed, refuelling at the airport, and were still en route, eta 20:00 local time. Henry decided to meet them the next day, after speaking to *Leber*.

Early the following morning, the Manor was bustling with life, there were odd *Burrbesh* characters coming and going. Henry was with Moss, who, back at his station, was running a programme set up by Edmund. It coordinated the phones of all the Gypsies and their locations.

Shelta had instructed them all to allow access to their locations, something that not all enjoyed the prospect of.

Up on screen came the map of Europe. Moss explained that the red spots were the locations of the night flower, and the shaded grey areas were the intended targets.

They covered nine countries, carefully chosen by Shelta for their destructive impact on the land; most of the sites had been abandoned for decades.

The areas ranged between fifty and a hundred square miles, it would require the additional support of twenty-seven *Burrbesh*, and Moss was in the process of allocating areas to each individual.

It had been decided that the whole event would be synchronised to happen at the same moment. Given the different time zones, it made things a little more complicated. It was decided that zero hour would be 12:00 GMT; this would allow all operations to be conducted in daylight hours.

Moss then switched the view on screen to a video call which was coming in from Shelta. She had arranged for the other camps to network the call and so there were multiple images of people on screen.

They all confirmed that everything was ready and going to plan. The night flowers were ready to provide their harvest to each *Burrbesh,* as they arrived, and the army of sprouts were bursting to go.

Shelta told Henry that she was making her way through Austria and hoped to be back in England two days after the event. Henry told her that he had intended to be over there with her, but now, he would be monitoring everything from the Manor, and so wished her a safe journey.

Jake, Sandra and Fidgit arrived around 08:30, with Ivy close behind on her little red thing. Ivy and Sandra were going to be busy in the greenhouses, as the last of the third harvest were to be taken to the villages in the Amazon.

Leber joined them both, as it was, he who would take the cargo, and he would be unable to accompany Henry to Archie's vineyard.

Henry told him of his apprehension in travelling to Archie's vineyard alone, it would be his first unknown destination, and he asked if *Leber* had any advice he could give him.

'As I told you before, Henry, focus, that is the key. But with so much traffic going through at the moment, even if you do make a wrong turn, there will be someone along soon to put you right. You will be fine,' said *Leber* and disappeared through the doorway, in the direction of the greenhouses.

Henry joined Jake, who had taken a seat close to Moss; he was eagerly awaiting the sunrise, and for the workers to begin their shift.

'The pictures appear much clearer and closer, Moss,' said Jake.

Moss said that Edmund had sent him a link to another satellite connection, and he admitted that the quality was far superior.

‘With a bit of luck, we may see the expression on their faces when they find your little surprise, Jake,’ said Moss with a smile.

Henry enquired if the quality was the same where Shelta was.

‘Unfortunately, no, we are stuck with an old Russian spy satellite link, a bit grainy most of the time,’ said Moss.

Jake asked how long it would be before the workers started.

‘Sunrise in one hour fifty-two minutes,’ said Moss.

Jake decided he would check on the irrigation from the river, make sure it was not silting up; it should take about an hour and a half. Henry too had an hour or so to kill before he made the trip to Archie.

‘Mind if I join you, Jake?’ he asked.

There was an element of anticipation starting to crowd the atmosphere, the need to stay busy was a necessary distraction.

They picked up Fidgit and his crew on the way out, then wandered the grounds, dropping in on Ivy and Sandra, walking the greenhouses, while all the ladies from the village went about their tasks.

They sat on the side of the river, by the weir and watched the sprouts torment Fidgit in the water. They chatted about things that had been and those that were about to happen; it was a bonding, there was an ease with each other’s company.

Time slipped away and they both needed to resume their agenda. Returning to the house, Henry wished Jake luck with his plan, and picking up a package from Moss, he returned to the garden, and was gone.

Henry had taken the advice of *Leber* and focused; he had picked up on the four as a group, and it nearly worked.

He exited between lines of grapes, much to the surprise of four workers, pruning and tending the vines.

He could actually see the house, so it was not a total disaster. Slightly embarrassed, he bade the local workers a good morning and made his way towards the house. Walking in between the vines he could see that they went right up to the surrounding gardens.

On exiting his corralled pathway, he entered the lawned area of the gardens, and there in front of him was the plane.

As he got nearer, Archie shouted to him from the cockpit.

‘Come in, come in. We didn’t see you arrive.’

Henry had to admit that his arrival was somewhat haphazard, but for his first trip to a new place it went ok.

Edmund came from the rear of the plane.

'Morning, milord,' he said with a grin. 'You had fun arriving, I hear.'

Henry handed Edmund the bag with the information Moss had provided. Eager to test it out he went back into the plane, and beckoned Henry to join him.

'Let's see what we have.' Edmund proceeded to connect the contents of the bag to one of the laptops on board.

'Where are our two scientists?' enquired Henry.

Edmund admitted that they were not so early at rising as he and Archie.

He seemed satisfied that all the information on the hard drive Henry had brought with him, was fine.

Archie came in to greet Henry.

'Come, let me show you around,' he said.

They walked along the lawn which passed through two lines of trees, it then opened up into a concrete airstrip which disappeared into the distance in a heat haze. Either side of this were row upon row of vines as far as the eye could see. To the right, a hangar nestled discreetly in the corner, surrounded by trees and bushes.

Archie took him alongside the hangar, down a path through dense bushes and trees. The path was grass, cut very neatly, the sides were pruned and trimmed perfectly; it led eventually to a large lake. A well-groomed path led all the way round, with some elaborate planting.

'This is one of several lakes across the estate, fed by bore holes and used for irrigation. It has a bonus of being well stocked with fish, if you like a spot of fishing. It is my escape, and my favourite vineyard, you must visit when we conclude this business,' said Archie.

Henry was overwhelmed with the attention to detail, he commented that he must have a really dedicated workforce. Archie told him his grandfather had originally planted the vines; he employed most of the local villagers who were now third generation workers and very loyal.

They returned to the house where the two late risers were sitting at breakfast, with Edmund.

'Good morning, Henry, we didn't hear you arrive.'

Henry told them that he landed some distance away and found his way through the vines. He asked how their flight was, and if they were all prepared for the big day.

He told them that there were numerous *Burrbesh* now involved, and they had decided to synchronise all the events to happen at the same time. Everything seemed to be organised, and everyone knew exactly what to do; Edmund now had the final coordinates, and they were in countdown mode.

Max said he was not overly confident with the Sherpa but would subdue his anxieties and concentrate on the main feature. Edmund told Henry that he had fitted cameras, inside and out, to record the event for future research, and they would all be live during the proceedings.

'There is little more for me to do at this time gentlemen, I shall bid you good day, and the best of luck for tomorrow.'

Henry made his way out accompanied by Archie. He told Henry that the plane was all fuelled and ready to go; he had the best of advice on board and could see no problems. Henry shook his hand.

'You're a good man Archie, I shall keep in touch.'

Henry made two attempts to return, without success.

Turning to Archie, he shrugged his shoulders and began to say 'bugger', when he disappeared, and the air made a popping sound as it replaced his presence.

Henry returned back to the Manor and appeared right next to Moss.

'Don't do that, you could give a person a fright,' said Moss.

He told Henry that there had been developments whilst he had been gone, with the workers in the Amazon. Jake had been waiting patiently for the return to work of the drivers of the big machines and his patience had been rewarded. Moss had recorded the event and offered to play back the recordings from the satellite, for Henry.

'Oh yes please,' said Henry, taking up a chair with a good view.

Moss ran the recording. It showed the arrival of four men. They appeared to be searching for the security guard who had been left over the weekend. There was obviously no sign of this person, as their number remained four.

Moss relayed the story as told by Jake, of the three sprouts and their instructions from *Leber*.

Eventually the four men could be seen approaching the machines; they positioned them side by side and set off into the greenery. It was total annihilation, a wide swathe appeared as the machines flattened everything in their path.

Then they stopped, the men could be seen jumping off the back of each machine and just standing there, as the yellow metal disappeared from view.

'Oh, well done, Jake,' said Henry. 'Where is he by the way?'

Moss said he had gone into town to collect some fencing materials for the paddock, and he had taken Sandra with him. Henry could not relax; he told Moss if he needed him, he would be in the greenhouse. Henry went off in search of Ivy, he knew he could rely on her to take his mind off things.

Moss continued to monitor proceedings on screen; the activity between the villages, had started to die down. People were returning to their homes, in readiness for the following day, and the impact it would have.

All those involved were now at a heightened state of apprehension, it was all they could do to get through the day.

The comings and goings at the Manor continued throughout the night. Some returned home, some could not rest and walked the grounds. But still, time ticked by, and morning appeared in all its glory. A perfect day.

Jake pulled up outside his grandmother's front garden, Fidgit, knowing he would be spoilt with biscuits, had already reached the table.

Ivy and Sandra sat finishing breakfast, and Fidgit was not disappointed.

'Morning, ladies,' said Jake, pouring himself a cup from the huge teapot.

The conversation revolved purely around the events due to take place at noon; there was no other subject more important.

They were to expect a video call around 09:30 when the plane was ready for take-off.

It was 700 miles to the area on the Amazon River, and they hoped to be over the target zone by noon GMT.

The European element of the event seemed a little disconnected, they had not been so hands-on involved as the Amazon group. Most had only seen the grey event areas on screen, and had memories of the Gypsy folk, from the party.

Ivy was concerned for the safety of Edmund and the others. She said she would busy herself at home until it was time for take-off. There would be little she could do at the Manor, and she had given the ladies the day off.

She thought the constant in and out of some of the stranger looking *Burrbesh* might scare some of them.

Jake said he had fencing to occupy him for a while, and Sandra said she had bits to do in the Academy.

'It is rather exciting though, isn't it,' said Ivy. 'I mean what will it do to the world, will it make a difference?'

Sandra confessed that it could be of substantial benefit to the greenhouse problems, but there were many other areas which needed addressing. These events were to try and repair man's destruction, but there were other factors, of a natural origin, which also affected the atmosphere, and which man had no control over. It would be interesting to see the outcome.

Jake said he rather fancied observing the whole thing from the cave entrance, as it was on the perimeter of the devastation.

'Who would like to join me?' said Jake.

Sandra admitted that she found the whole concept too good an opportunity to miss. Ivy said she would think on it.

Jake and Sandra said they would meet her in the cinema around 09:00, and left for the Manor, with Fidgit close at their heels.

On arrival at the Manor, Fidgit made his traditional exit into the undergrowth, while Jake and Sandra went through to the cinema and greeted Moss.

He had the estate and vineyard of Archie logged in; it was still dark, but the lights within the grounds illuminated just enough to make out the plane.

The image then changed to an area of scarred earth, then to another area of similar destruction.

'I have all the proposed site coordinates entered for the Eastern sections, and the images are scrolling through at ten second intervals, clever, no?' said Moss, his expertise seeming to have no limits.

He told Jake that the workers had abandoned the site of the palm oil machines; all was quiet. He had scanned the perimeter of the desolation, and other than the villages, there was no other movement, it looked as though they had a clear field.

'What time is Archie making the video link?' enquired Jake.

Moss said it was expected at 09:20.

Both Jake and Sandra agreed to be back for it; they could not just sit around waiting, they would go mad.

They both left and went to do their thing, bumping into Henry on the way out.

'Moss showed me the footage of your machine sabotage. Very good. Remind me not to park my car in your way,' laughed Henry.

Henry had been practising his travel skills; he had made a short trip to Shelta, who had moved on from her last position. She was on her way to the largest of the eastern event sites, intending to observe.

At nine o'clock the familiar sound of Ivy's red peril was heard to pull up outside the Manor. As she entered, she was joined by *Leber*, who had been in the greenhouses all morning. He asked if she might help him after the video call.

The place was very busy, with characters coming and going.

Suddenly there was the sound of the dinner gong, which silenced everyone, and MacTavish made an announcement.

'Tea, coffee, water, biscuits, nibbles and breakfasts shall be available during transmission, I thank you.'

A light humoured acceptance passed around the room. As the staff wheeled in trolleys of food and drink, the ringing of an incoming call turned everyone's attention to the images on screen.

It was Archie; the screen then split into four as the on-board cameras kicked in on the plane. One camera was facing the cockpit window so would give an image outside, one was positioned under the plane in the camera bay with the machine. The other two focused on the operators of the equipment, namely Edmund, who gave a wave, and Henri and Max, who looked a little tired.

Archie enquired if they were getting the images, Moss replied that they were, and all looked fine. Archie could be seen entering the cockpit, and Edmund took up the other seat as co-pilot.

Archie began his pre-flight check, it was 04:30 local time, and he told them his eta would be 07:00 at Caiambé, the nearest point to the desolation.

They were fully fuelled and should have enough for the round trip. The cameras would remain on and there would be half-hourly updates on progress.

With all his checks done, Archie fired up the engines, and after a final instrument check he taxied down the lawn to the runway. It was still dark, and twilight was still a half hour away. However, there was a single line of runway lights down the centre.

Having made sure everyone was buckled in, he pushed the throttles, and the Sherpa lurched forward and began to pick up speed. It did not take long before the plane was in the air, the thrust kept its occupants pushed back into their seats, climbing to five thousand feet.

Once they had reached altitude, Archie gave the instruction that seat belts could be released, and they should sit back and enjoy the ride. Edmund reset the tail numbers to something completely untraceable and, turning to inspect the passengers, he confirmed that both Henri and Max had nodded off.

'Not the best of early risers,' commented Archie.

Back at the Manor, the pictures from the plane were coming through very clear, even the ground was starting to become visible.

It would be at least two hours before the plane reached its destination; most of those involved wandered off to prepare.

Ivy accompanied *Leber* to the greenhouses, to assist in the preparation of the night flowers, and their harvests.

He explained that with nearly forty *Burrbesh* needing to acquire seed, the night flowers would be stretched to the maximum. Those at the villages were still young, as were those over in the East. *Leber* estimated that between them they should provide a good fifty percent of the seed required, the other fifty percent would have to be provided from the Manor.

He asked Ivy to coax each one, they were after all, very sensitive, and as she was involved in their propagation, she would have a maternal attachment to them all. Ivy agreed to do what she could.

'Sandra was also involved and could assist,' she said. *Leber* agreed to find her and ask her to join Ivy.

The morning seemed to pass very slowly, Jake had busied himself with the fencing project, and he now needed equipment to complete it.

It had just gone eleven, Jake decided that he would check out the cinema and see the progress. Moss told him that they were currently on schedule and would be in position within the hour.

Jake told him of his intentions to take Sandra through the cave to observe from the edge. Moss warned him not to venture within the area of desolation, as he might find it tricky to extract himself if he got caught up in the event.

The images on screen showed the sunrise as the plane headed due south; the brightness lit up the cockpit through the portside window.

Edmund and the two scientists were now at their individual computers, and very focused. Archie was trying to tape a piece of paper to the window to reduce the glare.

'You may as well go and find Sandra and get yourselves in position,' said Moss. 'There is nothing more that can be done now. I believe you will find her in the greenhouse.'

Jake went off to fetch Sandra.

As he approached the greenhouses, there were numerous odd characters coming and going. He entered the first greenhouse, and there, standing in front of a night flower was what looked like a female *Burrbesh;* it had the most enormous earrings. The night flower was discharging its seed in a fine black mist, and the earrings were absorbing it.

Jake made a sharp exit and entered the next greenhouse. Each individual had their own method of collecting the seed, hats, scarves, staffs, bags, coat pockets, but he thought the earrings the most bizarre.

Still looking for Sandra, he entered the third greenhouse; she was in there, halfway down. He wandered down to her and found her with a young night flower entwined around her wrist. Jake gently moved his hand down to hers and held it; the tendrils of the flower moved towards him, examining his hand and wrist briefly, before releasing them both.

Sandra said this was the last one to be coaxed, a request by *Leber* to assist with the supply of seed.

As they left the greenhouse, the last two *Burrbesh* entered, giving a slight nod to them both as they continued to collect their cargo.

Jake and Sandra made their way to the Land Rover.

Fidgit was ordered to stay at the Manor while Jake and Sandra made their way to the cave, and a suitable observation point.

Henry had decided to observe the proceedings from the cinema; he was currently chatting with *Tabule* and *Leber* in the conservatory.

They had both come to collect their cargo from the mother plant, *Tabule* with his coat, and *Leber* with his extraordinary staff. They confirmed that all *Burrbesh* were now carrying a full load, and they themselves would shortly be taking up their positions.

The time was approaching midday; Henry wished them luck and returned to the cine/war room.

Moss had the images from the on-board cameras displayed, with Archie on speaker. He said that they had made good time and were five minutes early; he was going to reduce altitude and make the first pass around the perimeter.

Edmund was in control of the laser magnetic field, and Henri and Max were monitoring the mapping and coordinates of all the villages and perimeter.

Moss confirmed that all the twelve council members were in position and ready to release the seed on his command.

Archie brought the plane down to five hundred feet and began the planned run within the perimeter. Moss instructed each of the council members to release as soon as they heard the plane, and the magnetic field would pick it up.

Edmund confirmed that the laser was now active and lowered ready for pick-up; the inverter was on, and the sixty minutes were counting down.

The area was huge; it would take nearly an hour to complete the run. Because of the irregular shape of the desolation, Archie had made a professional guestimate on the time it would take to collect all the seed.

Archie guided the plane on the route set by Edmund; the plane's GPS and autopilot were now connected to the computers on board, and all Archie could do was to make sure the controls didn't falter.

As they flew over the first collection point, the seed was released and captured by the magnetic field.

Edmund confirmed that everything was fine and holding. Archie confirmed that the controls were showing no signs of stress and was good to go.

As the plane continued to track over each collection point, seed was released and captured by the magnetic field. After the tenth collection point,

Archie reported that the weight had increased, he was turning off the autopilot and taking over manual control.

Edmund confirmed the laser field was behaving normally. Archie, having judged the feel of the plane, agreed that it was beginning to behave a little sluggishly, but was responding to his slight alterations.

Back on screen, at the Manor, the pictures from the camera under the plane were of a wide thin film, swirling and cutting out the daylight beneath it.

Archie flew over the eleventh pick-up point and again he felt a weight through the controls. He said it was holding, and Edmund confirmed the magnetic field was also holding.

Henri and Max now had sufficient material to plot the overall map of the seed dispersal; they confirmed that mapping was going to plan. Archie had one more pick-up, it had taken nearly an hour, and used more fuel than he had anticipated.

The final pick-up was collected just above the village where it all began; Jake and Sandra could just see the plane through the dark cargo below it. The black cloud suspended below the plane stretched as far as the eye could see.

'Inverter has six minutes remaining,' said Edmund.

Archie began to struggle with the controls, he now had to gain altitude to two thousand feet before the cloud could be released effectively. Archie pushed the throttles forward, but they were already as far forward as they would go.

'We are losing altitude,' he said, 'the cloud is too heavy.' He pulled back on the controls and the altitude stabilised, but still the plane could not gain height.

'I think you ought to buckle up,' said Archie. 'I have one last thing to try.'

He leaned across the cockpit and lifted the cover off a very red switch and pressed the button beneath.

'Ok gentlemen, hold on, it will either work or the plane will explode,' laughed Archie.

'Inverter has two minutes remaining,' said Edmund.

There was a sudden surge, as though the plane was just taking off. Archie pulled back on the controls and the plane sped skywards at an angle of forty-five degrees. It was not long before they were at two thousand feet.

'This will only last for thirty seconds, so are we ready to release?' he shouted.

Henri and Max confirmed that they were all good, and Edmund too, confirmed that the field was holding, although there was a moment when he thought it might have fallen away.

The plane began to stutter, the unanimous decision was to release, which they did, and the plane resumed a gentle purr as if nothing had happened.

The camera below the plane tracked the cloud down to the ground. Henri concluded that the perimeter coordinates were dead on target. Max had been monitoring the mapping and confirmed that all the villages were untouched, and that mapping was a complete success.

Edmund exclaimed that there were twenty-two seconds remaining on the inverter before the field would have collapsed.

Archie breathed a sigh of relief.

There was a small applause from behind Archie, and the question from all was what the hell happened there.

'Noz', said Archie, 'Nitrous Oxide, it works a little like rocket fuel. I had my mechanic install it, just in case of emergency, at Forteleza, that's why we were running late at the airport.'

Back on the ground, Jake and Sandra had chosen well. Their observation point had been yards away from the descending cloud, which, when it reached the ground, burst into an abundance of foliage.

Back at the Manor, Moss was now scanning the area through the satellite link. The green that had begun almost instantly, covered the whole area, and it was not going to stop in a hurry; in fact, he had to reduce the magnification.

The images then reverted to the European events; all the sites that had been allocated were showing the same. A mass of green, covering vast tracts of land, all carried out by individual *Burrbesh*, who had joined together in threes and fours to carry out the plan.

Archie made an observation. 'Fuel is low, we may have just enough to return, if we go now.'

Gaining height back to five thousand feet, Archie set a course for home. Jake and Sandra investigated the perimeter of the foliage, it moved and grew, and they decided it was not a good time to go any further and made their way back to the Manor.

Shelta had witnessed an amazing event, and if it was the same throughout all the sites she had chosen, she would be happy.

As for the villagers on the ground, it was a time for great rejoicing.

Henry looked on at the images sent back by satellite, in awe. *Burrbesh* began to return to the Manor, and *Leber* and *Tabule* joined Henry as he observed the returning greenery.

'It is nice when a plan comes together. This is what we have done since the beginning of time. Satisfying, isn't it?' said *Tabule*.

The image on screen began to pixilate, the greenery was replaced with a small walnut headed man in orange robes, sitting cross-legged on a stone altar. It spoke: 'Henry James, I have been following your progress since last we met. I must congratulate you on your current successes.'

'Ten-Zin is that you?' said Henry.

'Yes, it is. This world is changing for the worse, our way of life is under threat. I believe we may have need of your services.'

Epilogue

In total, the events covered an area of some 10000 sq. miles, it also effectively neutralised the toxic greenhouse gases created by the pollution at some sites.

The Sherpa and its crew arrived safely at Archie's vineyard in Venezuela, they ran out of fuel at the end of the runway and were unable to taxi back onto the lawn.

The sudden appearance of dense vegetation sparked an immediate investigation by reporters and scientists across the world. The twenty-year advance in growth rates had subsided after twenty-four hours, and all the plants and trees had adopted a standard growth pattern

By the time the investigators examined the fauna, it was perfectly normal, and would be indigenous to its area.

The *Burrbesh* returned to their tasks of finding new worlds to plant, in the hope that they might develop another, like Earth.

The Sherpa was returned to the airfield at Negril, and Archie retrieved his own plane from Sangster Airport, a Citation CJ-4, which returned everyone, including the equipment, back to Magnatek.

The scientists would continue their research into the laser field, and would, hopefully, apply it to the more deserving nations who were struggling.

Everybody involved returned to their daily routine. There was nothing to connect Lychee Manor to the events.

The Amazonian villages, within the now profusely dense vegetation, remained isolated for some time.

The villagers eventually created a network of connecting pathways, but no roads. Their culture would remain protected, any infiltration by loggers or palm oil planters would be thwarted. They would join together and with the assistance of the night flower, would replant where necessary.

Profuse news reports and images of the events were covered by the media networks.

Monitoring of the atmosphere was carried out in great detail, and satellite and radar scans were made, covering the particles in the air. Recordings of pollution levels were considered essential in cities surrounding the events.

After some weeks of testing and analysing the data, scientists concluded that there had been a small increase in the stabilisation of greenhouse gases. Weather patterns could possibly decrease in severity, and a gentle calmness was set to prevail, but only if man did not bugger it up.

The Academy at the Manor would become a recognised training facility and continue to assist those cultures which had been uprooted. It would be these groups, who had an affinity with the Earth that would be its saviour.

Those at the Manor, would be called upon again, to assist in the repatriation of indigenous tribes, while the night flower would continue to be produced at the Manor and distributed to those in need.

The news media speculated for a long time on the possible cause of the planting.

Investigations into satellite images of the area at the time had experienced a strange anomaly.

There appeared to have been a blackout for over an hour, where the only image displayed was of a small man, who sat cross-legged and dressed in orange robes.

There was a particular programme hosted by a small Englishman and an American, who had chased across Europe prior to the event. They had investigated a strange planting in a disused quarry, and claimed to have discovered convincing evidence of the Green Man.

In actual fact the greenery had been the result of an enthusiastic Gypsy.

They subsequently missed the main events, lost their tattooed faces and credibility, and with it their airtime.

The Council of Libra believed that a balance had begun they would monitor the situation and leave Henry in charge.

Archie was to become a good friend to everyone; he too was fast becoming a victim of ruthless governments and corruption.

But that's another story.

OTHER PEOPLE'S MEMORIES

by Paul Templeman

"Remembrance of the past kills all present energy and deadens all hope for the future."

- Maxim Gorky

TABLE OF CONTENTS

6

Prologue

October 1998 - Moscow

SMOKE DRIFTED IN the air like the aftermath of an artillery bombardment, presided over by the ghoulish features of a nightmarish Politburo of the dead and the damned. The busts of Lenin and Felix Dzherzinsky surveyed the nightclub with grim disapproval from their perches high up. Instead of the boom of shellfire there was the boom of the bass and the scream of a guitar. Searchlights danced upon the faces of revellers and not bombers. A lone girl peeled off her clothing on stage in a pool of white light. Men jostled for position at the edge of the stage, swilling beer and vodka shots, their faces cast in shadows under the low lights.

Grigor carved a path through the mass of shuffling dancers and voyeurs towards the bar meeting little resistance, like a Soviet ice-breaker oblivious to spilled drinks and shattered egos. He was a bear of a man, leaving a trail of cigar smoke in his wake. A porcelain limbed girl stood aside with a fragile smile and murmured a greeting that he didn't hear. He nodded at her, and her eyes sparkled, reaching out a hand that didn't touch him. Her male companion glared.

A gaunt barman in a stained white jacket signalled Grigor with a wiggle of a glass and he nodded, bouldering his way to the front of the crowded bar. It was a busy night at Red Nights, and for that he should be grateful. The barman poured a shot then slammed the glass and a bottle of Stolichnaya vodka on the copper counter in front of him. He settled on a bar stool and knocked back the vodka, savouring its icy passage as it slid down his throat. It was just past eleven. Olensky was late.

A small clearing had formed around Grigor's place at the corner of the bar, and he sat there with bloodshot eyes watching Fyodr work the doors, drawing on a thick Cuban Cohiba. Fyodr was on face control duty: they could afford to be selective about their clientele these days. No riff-raff. They should put a sign on the door, thought Grigor.

He glanced at his watch the instant Olensky appeared at the doors. Twenty-past-eleven, and Fyodr raised both hands in a forlorn shrug, looking across the room at Grigor as Olensky pushed past with a phalanx of heavies packed around him like extras from 'On the Waterfront'. A crowd eddied and thrust behind Fyodr and he turned back to admit two men and block another who remonstrated loudly for effect but left in a hurry. Grigor waited for Olensky and his bodyguard to make their way to the bar, without standing up.

Olensky had a twisted, equine face with a long nose and nascent beard and was half a head smaller than Grigor. He wore a long overcoat. His men were larger and wore short leather jackets that must have been stylish in America at the time of Elvis Presley. Olensky gave a curt nod but said nothing. Tina Turner sang 'Private Dancer' and in another dimension a girl performed a naked cartwheel. Grigor stepped down from his stool making a casual gesture as he led the way through to his office at the rear of the club.

Grigor's office was insulated from the noise of the club, but even so when he closed the heavy oak door the thump of the music was all-pervasive. Olensky seemed about to seat himself behind Grigor's desk but he caught Grigor's warning look and changed his mind. There were deep leather couches around the room and a Soviet era steel filing cabinet that looked as though it had been rescued from a war zone whilst an ochre Afghan rug that really had been, covered the bare boards. On the desk a pile of bills was anchored by an army issue pistol. Grigor sat down and glared at Olensky who remained standing. The other men lowered themselves into couches, looking bored.

'So what do you want, Arkady Ivanovich?' said Grigor at last, addressing Olensky.

'I like what you've done to the place,' said Olensky. 'Nice. And you attract a good crowd.' He perched on the side of Grigor's desk. 'Peaceful too,' he added with a pointed note.

'That's what I'm paying you for,' said Grigor. From a drawer he extracted a bottle of vodka and a single glass.

'Thirsty work,' said Olensky, looking at the bottle with undisguised longing.

'The bar's open,' said Grigor pouring himself a shot and nodding at the door.

'You've made something quite special here, Grigor Vassilyich,' pursued Olensky, choosing to ignore the snub. He seemed to be chewing something. An idea, or a wasp, thought Grigor. Olensky stood up and began pacing the room, looking at objects in a proprietary way: He patted a bust of Andropov on the head. 'Looks like nostalgia sells—even Soviet nostalgia.'

'It's worked out so far.'

'I'll be honest with you, Grigor. I'm seriously thinking about taking it off your hands.'

'It's not for sale.'

'Who said I was going to buy it?'

'It's my place.'

'Lenin said 'The land belongs to those who will till it.' I want to till it.'

'Lenin was full of shit.'

'We can reach some kind of understanding. You can still manage it if you want.'

'Get the fuck out of my nightclub,' said Grigor, reaching for the gun on the desk.

Olensky nodded at the gun, 'Does that antique work?'

'You don't want to find out,' said Grigor, pointing the barrel. The men in the couches tensed and leaned but didn't reach for their weapons. Olensky looked unperturbed.

'Our protection fees just went up,' said Olensky heading for the door. 'You'll be hearing from us.'

'It's been nice chatting,' said Grigor.

Chapter One

October 1998, London

SHE TOOK HER seat, felt the carriage lurch and rock, and tried to make up her mind who was following her.

A lesson she had learned from her inner, other life: How to watch without watching. The train ground its teeth and the lights wavered, jumping and jarring so she rocked with the motion. She reassured herself: it didn't happen here. Not in London, and not to her. There was nobody following her. But the paranoia lingered all the same, and the thought of it made her skin prickle.

A shabby, grey jowled man in the seat opposite was staring at her. She crossed her legs and he blinked, coloured, then looked away. When he touched elbows with a woman in a bear-like coat she flashed him a savage glance and he mouthed an apology. Not him. They never apologise; never explain.

The woman opposite pulled her string bag closer to her for security: inside it a copy of Vogue and two tangerines was visible. What they used to call a '*perhaps bag*' in another world. A bag for impromptu bargains. For the queues that were so problematic for her watchers, she had once welcomed them as a way to smoke them out. Her mind drifted.

'What are they selling?' She remembered asking a woman at the end of one such queue that stretched and shimmied for 100 metres along an ashen faced block of offices then dribbled around the corner. Snowflakes like scraps of tissue floated in the air, and her stalker had faltered, some steps behind.

The woman shrugged. She had mottled, crimson cheeks and a baked-in grimace. 'Who cares? Must be something good. A queue this long. You're last in line, you know?'

'Yes.'

Her stalker had been wearing a shiny black coat that fitted around him like the wings of a cockroach. He seemed to be debating something with himself. A moment later he walked up and joined the line. Soles slapped against the crystallised pavement for warmth: shoes, not boots, she noticed, like he had a car parked nearby. She wished him a good day, which he acknowledged with a nod. His jaw was rigid, eyes front, looking past her. 'You're following me,' she said to the side of his head. He fixed her for an instant, then looked into the middle distance, saying nothing. 'I'd like to ask you: Is it for my protection?' she said. 'Or something else? It would be nice to know… that I'm *safe*.'

'You're mistaken, Comrade.' he said, 'Nobody's following you.'

But they were. They had been her constant companions. You were meant not to notice: to pretend at least that you didn't notice. It was their game. They made themselves instantly forgettable with the clothes they wore; their blank expressions. She used to pick them out in the streets and in the supermarkets. Never quite pursuing but accompanying. Not following but rejoining. Reappearing as faces in a shop window or at a table in a cafe. The same faces, over and over. Was she mad to think like this, even now? People at the Club where she worked thought so. They talked about her behind her back. Maybe, in truth, she *was* a bit odd. Different. They called her crazy - and not in a nice way.

So, was she safe? It didn't make much sense, but she imagined herself older in her memories than today: more capable than now and familiar with the routine. Safer perhaps for that reason. She breathed in sips and kept watch on the passengers out of the corner of an eye. A bespectacled type, pinstriped and buttoned-up, sloped from a grab handle: respectable on the surface – but aren't they all? At the Club, for instance? *I know you look at me when you think I can't see you.* Tugging at the hem of her skirt, she willed herself to return his stare and when he looked away she felt a quiver of triumph.

The train emerged into London Bridge, brakes squealing, carriages banging. A gaussian blur smeared the line of travellers at the platform's edge. She sought something in the carriage that seemed always just out of sight: a gesture; a look. Evidence.

In the reflection of her window, bulked up against the cold, they boarded and alighted limp-limbed, briefcases, handbags. A chill swept in. She shuddered, half closed her eyes, absenting herself, abandoning all hope.

But there was no escape, because all at once there he was, distilled in the reflection in the window. A sullen-faced man in a corner seat who sank into the upturned collar of his overcoat. A glance that she was meant not to notice.

She caught sight of her reflection. Did she look crazy? Paranoid?

There was no mistake this time: he was looking at her.

They assessed each other in turn without pretence, he with a secret glint she felt sure was meant just for her. There was a message for her in his look. A message she didn't want to acknowledge.

He was over fifty. Plump, which was unusual—but she guessed he had once been lean because he had sunken eyes like a reptile. Close-cropped dark hair, receding. And when he glanced at an expensive watch that seemed out of place she observed that he moved with economy, wary of attention. A trait they all shared, she was sure. Almost sure, at least. Those memories were at once flawed and conflicted. She looked again and he didn't shift his gaze. An inflated feeling in her chest made her realise she had been holding her breath. She exhaled. Her whole life she had fought what her mother had christened her 'misrememberings'. They were imagined. False. And yet, they seemed no different to her recollections of just a moment ago. An hour ago. They were her shadow memories and they lied.

The doors slid shut with a rubbery bump and her neighbour's shoulder nudged against her as the train pulled away. Pale light allowed a glimpse of the sooty cables in the tunnel. Grim, swaying passengers, hooded eyes in the glass. Surveillance on all sides, but mostly in his eyes. She was scared.

How to leave the train without him following? He had positioned himself in a seat by the door, and she watched him move with the rhythm of the train, staring at the floor. But she was careless. He looked up and held her gaze for an instant too long. Long enough for her to be doubly sure. Pulse racing. Nowhere to hide. Like on stage at the Club. Gawky. Trapped in the spotlight. On stage she had trained herself to look away. At the lights; the ceiling. So she read the advertisements: 'Yellow Pages. Let Your Fingers Do the Walking'. A picture of a girl with a broken smile pointing to an open directory. And: 'Become What You Want to Be. London South Bank University.' But every time her eyes strayed from the ads, there he was lying in wait, and he smiled. A crocodile smile that stirred an uneasy recognition.

But surely *they* didn't smile. They never smiled. Maybe it was her imagination? *Get real*, she scolded. Nothing to be afraid of. Not here. Not anywhere. She clenched her fists until her nails left indents in her palms. She had lived with this for so long: anticipating the moment when her false memories would blend with the real; when the containment of her other past would fracture. She made an effort to return to her magazine, but her mind was blurred with dark and light and traces of words she half read and instantly forgot. *'Become What You Want to Be.'* Urged the advertisement. Out of the train she would be safe. Out of sight. She grasped the handle of her sports bag. '*Let your fingers do the walking.*'

Next station was Borough: Not her stop, but close enough. She stood, pushed her way through winter-coats, stepped with care on her high heels around briefcases and bags. Muttered apologies. Then the train jerked to a halt, doors juddered, and she had to steady herself with a hand on the door as she stepped down. It wasn't too much out of her way: A twenty-minute walk to her apartment.

But as she stepped off the train with a heavy breath, hurried along the platform, she imagined she caught a glimpse of the man over her shoulder, a hulking silhouette of all her fears.

She stopped, searched around for the 'Exit' signs,

then walked with purpose, urging herself not to look back, heels tapping on the concrete. A draught tangled her hair, flapped the tails of her coat. Like a child she held her breath against the sour air as the approaching train pummelled out of the tunnel. Quickening her pace she turned off the platform, listening hard for his footsteps. A sign defaced with graffiti said the lifts were broken. She didn't look back, walked faster, heading for the stairs behind a man with a stainless steel briefcase and the acrid smell of cigars. Only once, she couldn't stop herself from looking – and there he was. Angular. Purposeful. Long strides. Tipping his head back as if about to shout something, but if he did his words were swallowed by the noise of the train.

Mutterings and footfalls echoed in the stairwell. She clanged up the steps almost tripping. Somewhere in the distance she heard an accordion braying half familiar chords. She always knew they would find her one day. Whoever they were. Pungent smell of sweat from the man above made her want to retch. His heels were splintered and worn, the expensive briefcase a facade. He was slow and she couldn't pass him. Almost collided with his back when she reached the top. He paused, fumbled, thrust his card into the barrier. Ticket in hand, she reached out. Then a hand restrained her.

He was taller than she had expected. A hint of garlic on his breath. He said:

‘Katya?’

A name straight out of her misrememberings. ‘No, no.' Trying to shake off his hand. ‘I’m not…’ But his grip didn't falter.

'It's you, isn't it, Ekaterina Ivanovna? I’d know you from anyone.’

There was something strange about the way he spoke. Something ill-formed. Awkward. Drunk?

‘I’m sorry. Bit of a hurry… You've got me mixed up with somebody. Please…’ she panted, trying to find a way around his wide body, avoiding his eyes, but he laughed and side-stepped into her path.

‘Still, you understand me pretty well! You speak Russian? Some coincidence, yes?’

She froze. The twisted, sibilant consonants and long vowels of her dreams. Felt herself turned around somehow, his hand taking her other arm.

'Let me see you properly, Katya.' He stopped short. 'But how can you look so young? It's impossible.' When she steeled herself to look at him there was a mystified look in his eyes. Not a complement but something else. 'It's incredible … But look, Katya, you have to believe me—I was overcome when I heard. Overcome with worry. I didn't sleep at night. When they said you'd been taken. Imagine how surprised … and now here you are! Just exactly like before. *Exactly* like before. *Younger* even, if it's possible!'

She felt her mouth open but no sound came. She stumbled. Recovered, righted her heel and cast around for assistance. A ticket collector regarded them with casual interest. She should call him over. Enquire about something. Envelop herself in his reality. 'I.. I don't know what you mean.' But she had betrayed herself already.

'There's no need to be frightened. Not of me—of all people. It's Dmitry. *Old* Dmitry. You don't recognise me? But of course you don't. I'm fat and bald.' He passed a fleshy hand over his head. 'And old. Whereas you.. How did you?' He trailed off and looked at her.

And she felt like she was emerging from underwater. Dmitry Yevdokimov. A name buoyant with recollections from a past she had never lived. Some kind of doctor… flash of a white coat. She thought she remembered other things too: a grim-faced eighth-floor apartment, plumbing that banged and grunted in the night. She said:

'You can't be him.' It was the first time the other, parallel memories had left the tracks, crossed the line into what she had been taught was reality. Could she be dreaming after all? She was peculiar. Crazy. Everybody said so. Bordering on what? Schizophrenia? Was that what she had?

Dmitry's laugh bounced off the tiles. The ticket barriers buzzed and clicked as commuters ticked past, jostling for position in their winter bulk. 'So what? I'm mistaken?' He leaned into her and she flinched when their eyes met. Long lashes, like those of a child. Like those she now recalled as Dmitry's eyelashes. 'What did they do to you Katya? I always wondered. But of course there was the child too. The birth I mean. All that pain. How you must have felt. Then when you disappeared I was sure you were done for. We all were sure.' A collective she could not bring herself to contemplate. 'I even thought there might be some repercussions. For me, you see? You know what they were like ... How it was?' He glanced around him as if nursing a paranoia of his own, then made an expansive gesture with his free hand. 'Now - here we are in London. Here *you* are in particular, more lovely than even I remember. Old scores forgotten, yes?'

'I really don't know who you are—what you mean. I'm not who you think |I am,' willing herself to maintain the protest, but she realised she had stopped struggling. He saw it too, and released her, fished inside his jacket. Expensive, well-tailored. Not like in those misremembered days…

'Take this.' He produced a business card and gave it to her. 'I'm at the embassy. You know which one. Give me a call. You *should*, you know. There's a lot to talk about.' He hitched up a sleeve, consulted the wristwatch that had seemed so incongruous before. Blue bezel. 'Shit. I'm late. I must run. But you'll call me, won't you? You *must* call me.' He was leaving already, making parting motions as he backed away. 'I have new masters these days. Maybe you didn't read about it, but we *all* have new masters. Everything's changed. Exciting times. You don't need to hide anymore.'

With a final wave he disappeared down the staircase. 'Call me, OK?' she heard him shout.

She thumbed the embossed surface of the card. 'Dmitry Andreyevich Yevdokimov. Vice Consul.' When she flipped it over, there were Cyrillic letters on the reverse. As if observing herself in a mirror, she noticed her hand was quivering.

Chapter Two

Moscow

THE PRIVATELY AIRED consensus in the smarter cafés of the eclectic, imperial-inspired vicinity of Kitai Gorod in Moscow was that General Borilynko was a kingmaker without a prince. Soviet, old Russian, but he could be a New Russian if you wanted, plying his influence with intelligentsia and bureaucrats alike - red or white affiliations made little difference to him. Certainly corrupt some believed, but then who in his position could resist the incentives that must have passed his way? Of course this private consensus was known to Borilyenko, and even the whispered dissent that travelled on careless tongues through the corridors of the Kremlin, for the eyes and ears of the *Bureau,* the security services, were everywhere and they were his organs.

'To the Soviet Union!' The General lifted his glass once more to a dozen sombre-faced veterans of lengthy campaigns of war and of peace and drank a contrived toast to lost empires and a revolution staged by fathers they could scarcely recall.

A meeting of the Feliks Group had passed with nothing new, and little of substance debated. Geriatric revolutionaries, he thought—himself included. His deputy, Major Kvitsinsky the exception in a roomful of old men.

They stood around a magnificent, burnished table thinly effaced with the scratches of generations of resolutions, and scattered with the debris of notebooks, pens and water jugs.

'Comrades, tomorrow is the anniversary of the Great October Socialist Revolution. We've finished our business. Let's take some time to remember the heroes of those days. A toast.' General Borilyenko raised his glass in a challenge to each of them in turn, and watched them drink. 'It didn't turn out the way most of us expected. The way our ancestors planned. But they lived in different times. Now it seems the wolves are already sniffing around the new man.' Yeltsin still the new man to Borilyenko, even after five years as President. 'The President is a sick man, and the wolves are scenting blood.'

Gavrilenko said, 'Aren't we the wolves? The silent opposition? Shouldn't we leverage one of our own? Otherwise, what's the point of us? I'm sick and tired of this talking shop.' A petulant man in a sharply cut black suit, prickles of sweat on his forehead, Gavrilenko was of a certain generation that prefaced any nostalgic reflection with: 'In Soviet times…' A deputy of the Russian parliament, the Duma. He wore a party pin in his lapel like a badge of honour, but it seemed more like a badge of antiquity these days - like a 'sell-by' label. Borilyenko thought he found something glamorous about belonging to some kind of underground movement. A frustrated revolutionary.

Across the room, Vrublevsky leant his fists on the table and said:

'Just what kind of candidate should we put forward, Comrade Gavrilenko? What kind of *silent* candidate for the silent opposition, if there can be such a thing?' General Vrublevsky wore his officer's tunic unbuttoned, famously refused to wear medal ribbons or decorations. A grizzly war hero with a demeanour that seethed with rage in any circumstance. 'A silent opposition is no opposition at all,' he grumbled.

A lieutenant-colonel with yellow nicotine-stained eyebrows said: 'There's a man I heard of in Uglich owns four of only 18 water utility contracts in the country.'

Somebody said: 'So what?'

'So how did he get them? I ask myself. Some kind of minor procurement bureaucrat. That's what he was. What does he know about water?'

' What are you trying to say, Colonel?'

'They say he's worth a billion dollars. Has his own helicopter. I don't know much about that. But it's that kind of thing. That kind of thing the Feliks Group should be opposing.'

Ignoring the Colonel, Borilyenko said: 'Maybe you're right, Comrade Gavrilenko. What's the point of the Feliks Group nowadays? What are we doing here? Why don't we have that debate?'

'Many times we've had that debate.' The weary-eyed Justice Minister passed a hand through his silver hair and and settled in his seat. He flicked at a glass, and it left a wet trail on the veneer as it slid in the direction of a half empty vodka bottle. Kvitinsky moved to top up the glass. 'You invited me to be a part of this group so the justice we dispense can carry a measure of legitimacy. And I still believe. I still believe *somebody* needs to make a stand against the corruption we see everywhere. People think we make summary assassinations. Compare us to terrorists. It's even in Pravda. But we know it's not like that. We consider the facts. The risks to our country. Even the risks to the current administration. We make public a few sordid revelations in the guise of 'research documents' from our fictitious intelligence officer. Ivan Ivanov. A public service. That's what we're providing. So we kill a few gangsters. Justice, as I see it. Setting off some fireworks to show we mean business.'

Gavrilenko said: 'So what are we, then? Revolutionaries or policemen? Was Feliks Dzherzhinsky a revolutionary or a policeman when he founded the secret police?'

'There's no place for revolutionaries in modern Russia.' Grumbled Vrublevsky. 'What are we? A group of the party faithful, clinging to the coat-tails of Lenin and hoping for another chance of power? I don't think so.'

'I suppose this was always my project.' Said Borilyenko. 'The Feliks Group. Not much more than an extension of my official duty as head of the President's security, when you come to think of it. Except our mandate is the security of the State, not the President. Especially not the President. What we're opposed to above all is the erosion of order. The criminality. The high levels corruption. The kind of thing we see every day. The kind of thing this Government condones.'

'Guardians of the State.' Said Gavrilenko, and

Borilyenko couldn't make up his mind whether he was being ironic. He looked at him with suspicion. Gavrilenko dabbed his forehead with a handkerchief, looked at the Minister for Justice for support but received only a stare.

'If that's what you want to call it. But I want us to be clear: There must be no more bombs in apartment buildings. The Minister for Justice is right - in the press the Feliks Group has been compared to terrorists. Mafia. We don't want that.'

'If he's so sick, the President,' said Gavrilenko, 'why not put him out of his misery? You're in the perfect position. We've talked about removing the Prime-minister before. Why not the President? I'm speaking amongst friends, or so I hope.'

'Now is not the right time. We need to consider who would fill that void, now that the Communists are strong again in the Duma. Do you see the current leader of the Communist Party leading Russia?'

'I can think of worse leaders than Gennady Andreyevich.'

Vrublevsky said: 'I can't believe we're even having

this conversation. There would be a civil war. And Gennady Andreyevich is no Lenin.'

The Minister for Justice said: 'I hope this is not a serious proposition, Comrades? It's not something I would put my name to.'

'Shall we put it to the vote?' said Borilyenko.

Vrublevsky looked around the room. 'I wouldn't want to dignify it with a vote.'

'I agree. Then the meeting is over.' He nodded to Kvitsinsky who was now standing in a corner of the room at the side of an ancient Korvet record turntable that had a distinctive tonearm shaped like a globe. Kvitsinsky lowered the needle and the bars of 'Hymn to the Soviet Union' began. Cracked and tuneless voices took up the refrain:

'Sing to the Motherland, home of the free,
Bulwark of peoples in brotherhood strong.
O Party of Lenin, the strength of the people,
To Communism's triumph lead us on!'

The General watched the faces.

'Be true to the people, thus Stalin has reared us
Inspire us to labour and valorous deed..'

The old version, of course, before Stalin's name had been expunged by the liberals. He felt invigorated as he sang, lifting his chin and recalling the stature of the man he had once met. A powerful man. Fearless. And - ‘The Boss’ - not that he, Borilyenko, would have presumed. But in those days it’s what *they* would have called him. The Politburo. The man who decorated him 45 years ago. Was it so long? He sang, and sang well.

After the anthem and the toasts and the grim calls to action. After pledges of allegiance, and more. After all of these things, the men filtered out of the room, with a desultory handshake here and there. All except Kvitsinsky and the General.

Once the heavy oak door was shut the General poured two large vodkas and slid one across the table to Kvitsinsky. Like the great man would have done, he reflected to himself with satisfaction. Like the Boss. Then he moved to stand at the window, framed between the heavy drapes that, for all he knew, dated from the time of the Tsars. He looked out over Prospekt Marksa. Watched the Mercedes and BMWs cutting through the streets far below. Fewer Russian cars than ever. Volgas - mostly yellow taxis; the ubiquitous Zhigulis. He breathed heavily. Almost to himself he said: 'Do you remember something called Project Simbirsk?'

Kvitsinsky sat at the foot of the table, a reflection of the light from the windows shimmered on the tabletop. He inhaled the mellow odour of beeswax, sawdust and leather. Examined his glass. 'I heard about it. I thought it was just a story.'

The General nodded to himself. ‘A story. Is that what they are saying now?’ He glanced over his shoulder. ‘A story?’ The sudden emphasis made Kvitinsky twitch. The General returned to the sparring traffic below. ‘It was more than a story, Comrade. Much more. It’s been on my mind. Sometimes I ask myself what would have happened if we’d been successful.’

‘I didn’t hear… I mean I don’t know much. ’ Kvitsinsky said.

‘Of course you don’t, Comrade. Project Simbirsk was a state secret. There was a silence. ‘But we were successful in some ways. More than anyone would have believed possible. So tell me what you heard. About Simbirsk.'

'Just rumours. That they were trying to… well, to bring Lenin back from the dead.' He looked at the General as if for validation: It sounded ridiculous. Hare brained. But in the Soviet Union everything had been possible, even when it wasn't, and he had learned not to be openly cynical. 'To bring him back to life.'

'Not quite.' The General said without turning round. 'But I'll share a secret with you, Comrade. Simbirsk was real. Not some kind of Frankenstein experiment like it sounds. What we were doing…' He glanced over his shoulder. '…what *they* were doing, I should say. It's no exaggeration to say it would have rivalled the space programme in scientific achievement. Our scientists were the best. The very best.'

'So what happened?'

'Treachery. Sabotage. The usual suspects. Still there might be a way…'

Muffled sirens from the street. The traffic backed up. Some incident out of sight. He sighed.

'We've got to face facts.' said the General. 'We're

not revolutionaries any more. Most of us never were. You think Russia needs men like us? Old men plotting implausible conspiracies? You think Russia *wants* another revolution? After '91 and '93. I was there, remember, standing alongside the President on that tank in '93. In spirit, I mean.' He waved a hand then reached for his glass, emptied it. The vodka numbed his throat. 'Look at our flag, and what d'you see?' The scarlet banner of the former Soviet Union still hung in a corner of the room. 'A relic! How many hammers do you see in industry these days? How many sickles in the fields? The sole purpose of our flag is to intimidate the uninitiated. We need to be looking forwards, not backwards at the fields and factories of the past. What good are we? We're as much relics as our symbols. I think Gavrilenko was right to question what the Feliks Group is about.'

'Comrade General?'

The General swept up the bottle and refilled both their glasses.

'I'm sorry, Yevgeny Vassillov,' The sudden use of Kvitsinsky's patronymic made him start. The General saw his surprise. 'Don't worry, I don't place you in the category of a relic. I'm talking about my generation. But it's time, I think, to dispense with the Feliks Group.'

A knock at the door and a uniformed FSB officer took a tentative step inside, wary of the weight of rank and power.

'The President, Comrade General. He'd like you to call him.'

Vrublevsky was leaning in the corridor talking to another Duma deputy. When he saw Borilyenko he fell into step with him, placing a confiding hand on his shoulder. He bowed his head so close that he couldn't help but notice stray hairs on his chin that had escaped the razor.

'Don't be too troubled by what was said in there. In the heat of the moment. We face difficult decisions in the service of our country.'

Borilyenko knew all about the burden of difficult decisions, and he was still visited by phantoms from Soviet times, when his only thoughts had been the security of the state.

'What we're doing,' said Vrublevsky, 'is necessary and worthwhile. Some day it's sure to be recognised. If not, we hold our heads high.'

In his office Borilyenko made the call to Yeltsin, who was, it seemed, barely lucid. Nervous about the plans for the parade tomorrow. Much the same each year. He strained to hear the rambling voice at the other end. Threat levels. TV broadcasts. Borilyenko issued platitudes and reassurances. The parade would pass without incident as it had every year. He laid down the phone and looked up at the black and white photograph on the opposite wall. He and the geriatric president. He was holding Borilyenko's hand and grinning. Yeltsin was so drunk on that occasion he could barely stand. That's why he was gripping his hand so firmly it hurt.

It was ironic that as head of the Presidential Security Service, Borilyenko presided over the security of a government that he privately regarded as illegal, and a president he despised.

Once he ran the 9th department of the KGB, responsible for government security. One of the few senior officials to make the transition to the senior ranks of the new services after the traitor Bakatin under Gorbachev disbanded the KGB. Borilyenko had made all the necessary political allies. Pulled some strings. He made himself the obvious choice to head the new Presidential Security Service, spawned from the old KGB. Promoting himself as a new liberal, he had carefully severed his public links with the Communist Party, and had been quick to forge new alliances in Yeltsin's circle. For the past three years, alongside the head of the FSB, which replaced most of the functions of the old KGB, they had virtually run the country.

To overthrow the government, he first had to infiltrate it, and that was the secret task that he had once set himself.

That was in the days when he had fostered political ambitions of his own. Andropov had risen to power from the ranks of the KGB. Why not him? But he was old now, in his declining years. Older even than Andropov had been, he speculated. He wanted to leave some legacy.

Anyway, he was no longer sure he had the energy for leadership. And the resurgent communists had become a dangerous and suddenly realistic threat as the State began to disintegrate. Russia needed a strong man to take control, like Stalin, white or red. But there were no more Stalins.

So he bred his quiet brand of insurgency through the medium of the Feliks Group, a collection of disenchanted former and current KGB and GRU officers, like a band of brothers, and waited for a leader to attach himself to. A term had been invented for such people: The *siloviki*. The Hard Men. He thought it set the right tone.

The phone rang.

'Yes?'

'There's a call for you, Comrade General. Dmitry Andreyevich Yevdokimov. He said you would know him.'

A tingle of foreboding. A name from a past that he thought had been sealed shut. 'I know him.' He said.

'I'll put him through, shall I?'

Dmitry Andreyevich: a political officer, in the days they'd thought such things necessary. He had worked for the General in the days of Project Simbirsk over 20 years ago. Probably reported on him.

'Hello, Comrade General. It's been a long time. Not since Soviet times… How are you? I read great things.'

'Dmitry Andreyevich. Sounds like they are Westernising you with their pleasantries. My health is fine if that's what you mean. Next thing you'll be asking about the weather. Where are you? What do you want?'

'London. I work at the Embassy. And if you want to know about the weather here it's *Pizdec*. Fucked up.. Always raining. You never have to ask about how it is. Just assume it's *pizdec* raining. But everyone asks here, all the time. Platitudes. The English have a name for such things: 'political correctness.' Dancing around things. Never saying what they mean.'

'I don't want to know about the weather.'

'Of course not, General. I'm phoning because I have interesting news for you. It was difficult to get through to you…'

'Dmitry, I'm a busy man. What do you want?'

'I'm sorry, Comrade General.' And Borilyenko imagined a smirk. 'You remember in the old days we had a scientist who worked at the facility? Comrade Borodina? Pretty girl.'

'Of course.'

'The one that escaped.'

'Disappeared, Comrade, if that's what you mean.'

'Disappeared, yes. That's what I heard. But she must have escaped to the West because I saw her in London yesterday. Difficult to believe, after all this time.'

'Impossible.'

'Pure chance. I saw her on a train.'

'When was this?'

'Yesterday afternoon. Up close she's unmistakable. But here's the thing - young! Like she hasn't aged since the old days. 25 years - they never touched her. Whereas me, whereas I.. All of us.. Regardless - it's beyond question it's her. You know we… well we had some kind of thing. So I knew her better than most.'

Unable to resist the opportunity to censure, The General said. 'We knew about your indiscretions.' He drummed his fingers on the desk, impatient to get the full story. 'You spoke to her?'

'In Russian.'

'In Russian? And she said she was Ekaterina Borodina?'

'Denied it. Said I was mistaken. But I swear it's her!'

'Young you say? Unchanged? She knew who you were?'

'Of course she knew. She recognised me on the train. Tried to get away but I followed her.'

The General thought for a moment. 'You know where you can find her?'

'No. But she promised to call me. I was caught unawares.'

'Some kind of intelligence officer you are. Wait for her to call. You just allow her to walk away…' He felt a tightness in his chest. He worried sometimes about his heart. Placed his palms flat on the table. 'Never mind. Let me know if she gets in touch. As *soon* as she gets in touch. Find out where she lives. Find out everything you can. Thank you for calling me, Comrade. It's very interesting. And we must meet..

When you're next in Moscow. To chat about old times.'

Afterwards he sat in silence tracing the implications. He'd imagined they'd taken care of her. They got as much out of her as they could, but her work had proven almost impossible to replicate. She'd been thorough. Everything destroyed. All those records. Years of research. Could it really be that with the help of some insider she'd managed to get away? He couldn't be everywhere. Hadn't been present when they executed her. Didn't like to be present on those occasions, if he was truthful. He presented his squeamishness to himself as some kind of humanitarian weakness.

Then he poured himself a generous vodka and drank a silent toast to Lenin. A master he wished he could have served. The architect of his youth - a happy time for him.

Chapter Three

London

OUT OF HABIT she checked off the models and registration numbers of the cars parked along her street. *White Fiat. Broken wing mirror. Ford Sierra. Miniature of Chelsea football kit hanging in the rear window. Red Citroen hugging the kerb, gashed driver's door.* Familiar cars. She didn't know what drove her to do this. Some instinct. *G364 XPP. K960 CNH.* Like a compulsive urge to cover her tracks.

She thought about the man on the train. A Russian: but how would she have known? His language had brushed against her parallel memories. Ignited them. She experimented in her head: A mangy dog that started at her in a shop doorway translated to *sobaka* in Russian. The familiar line of cars along the street became *mashini*. She shuddered. *Po Ruski. Ja gorovju po ruski,* I speak Russian, she told herself. And she was uneasy because something wild and tethered inside her had broken free. And it felt like a violation to have this other voice in her head.

She walked unhurriedly, lost in memories of corridors she was sure she had never walked, cement-floored lobbies where she could never have waited for arthritic elevators. A reluctant tourist in a land of the false memories that her parents had warned her to hide away, she tried now to fit herself inside them to put them into context; she wondered why her parents would never talk about her 'misrememberings'. Tried to figure it all out on her own. How she hated that her mind was so cluttered: she craved clarity. Certitude. But it wasn't normal to have these memories. *Nenormalnaya.* She tried to block out the Russian, but the words kept coming, like some kind of Tourettes affliction, shouting in her head.

Her earliest childhood memory was gazing up at a tall brass object with intricate curves. The pinnacle was a spike, and in the middle it stretched dome-like and shining in the light. The distorted reflection of a young child returned her stare: bloated cheeks and impossibly round eyes. She used to like to move and watch the image alter. High above her, an old lady with a very straight back and a slender neck drained liquid from a tap. She felt a great affection for this person, but she had no idea why. The old woman's shoulders were draped in lace, and she wore flowery skirts that brushed the floor when she moved, as though she was gliding across the room. But it was almost *beyond* childhood, she thought. Further back. Like she could reach beyond birth. Sometimes the memories were involuntary. At other times they came to her only with a supreme effort. Memories or dreams? Real or imagined? *Pravda ili lozh?* shouted her new companion in translation.

This event had no place in Kate's real childhood: It was a jigsaw piece from a different box. She was ordinary. Grew up in an ordinary English village with unremarkable parents. Early memories of birthday tea parties and scuffed school shoes that pinched her feet. And yet all of her life she had harboured vivid memories of other places, places she knew she could never have been. Ragged, sooty cities; ranks of ashen apartment blocks pitted with blank windows and beyond them frosted plains that stretched as far as she could dream. Incongruous palaces, more exotic than in fairy tales with gleaming minarets and swathes of pastel colours. As a child, she had supposed that everyone had memories like these. She even wrote about them in English essays.

Her best friend in Junior School was Laura Parker. They used to hide from the other children in the stairwell of a classroom block during break times and tell each other stories. Laura had a parallel life too: but hers was full of castle keeps and rescues and dashing princes. It was a made up world. She wanted so much to be like Kate. Followed her like a puppy dog, and listened to Kate's stories, slack-mouthed rapture, as they sat on the stairs side by side. Between them they invented an acronym for the episodes in these parallel lives: TIKINDs - Things I Know I Never Did.

'I remembered a new TIKIND today.' And Laura would sit on a stair with her knees together and shining eyes.

'Tell me. What happened?'

'Well, the city was gripped by a big snow storm…' she would begin in her narrative voice. 'Everything was twinkling and there were no footprints in the snow. It was smooth like ice cream.'

'Where were you?'

'In the park near our house. We lived in a very big house but lots of families lived there too. That day, Mummy told me not to touch the climbing frame with my nose because of the frost, because it would stick. I don't really know why she thought I would do that. But afterwards I was *drawn* to it. I wanted to put my nose on the frozen climbing frame just to see what it was like. It made me scared.'

'So did you do it?'

'No. But I always think of it when I see a climbing frame.'

'Is that all?'

She shook her head. The story didn't stand up on its own so she embellished it. The problem was that embellishments sometimes got mixed up with the real thing. If it could ever be called the real thing. 'There was a big brown bear. Dead in the snow. The snow was pink around the body. I touched him…'

'You didn't!'

'Yes. And the fur was all matted and rough.'

'Oh Katie, that's horrible! What could it mean?'

'I wish I'd put my nose on the climbing frame. To see what happened.'

She told her father about the climbing frame TIKIND, including the made up part about the bear, and he had laughed and told her what a vivid imagination she had. That it never got that cold in England. But as she grew older he had become frustrated with her stories, and there had grown a side to his moods that was half anger and half touched with anxiety. What could have troubled him so much?

Mr Travers once made her stand in a corner for two entire periods of geography because her essay had been a pack of lies. Mr Ogden (they called him ('Ogden the Ogre') gave her a beating for a flawless maths paper once. She had copied. Cheated! Where did she get the answers? Who was helping her? An emphatic glare at the class. Who dared? Nobody dared. Not for Kate. Her classmates thought she was strange. Always in a world of her own. Which some of the time she was.

It wasn't exactly an aptitude that she had for mathematics. It was more a kind of learned competence - even to the point that she was aware of using techniques that were different to the way they taught her in school. Techniques that seemed to work just as well if not better.

After that she got into the habit of making deliberate mistakes so that her coursework accurately reflected everyone's perception of her. She was a grade 'D' student. Anything else was too much heartache.

'So this is your real work then, is it?' said her chemistry teacher once with apparent satisfaction, awarding her a 'D' at the foot of her red-lined exercise. 'At least we know what we're dealing with now, Kate. We have a starting point – something to work with.

Well done for effort, Kate, well done.‘

It made her feel good. Made her feel proud to have failed so spectacularly, and to be praised. She felt normal. It was good to be normal.

Looking back, she found that so much of her growing up was pre-empted by fully formed conclusions and recollections. She experienced her first memories of sex when she was only eight, which tainted her transition to adulthood. At eight she recalled the stifling weight of a man who panted with hot uneven breath, and a feeling of damp rimmed constipation. She woke up crying when these visions stole her dreams, but some instinctive shame prevented her from revealing them to her mother. As a teenager she wondered if she had been abused: but by whom? And when?

She had to learn to partition her life, in particular the jumbled, accumulated misrememberings that formed a kind of parallel universe in her mind. But often the fiction became muddled with fact. There were times when she would submerse herself in her other life, so that it became difficult to distinguish between her 'false' memory, as she came to know it, and the stories she had started to invent about it. But her false memory had the same reality as her everyday memory. It was like being able to dip into two separate books and make sense of them.

There was moisture in the air, and the sky was bilious and grey. She felt the icy pinprick of rain on her bare legs as she walked. Her pace lengthened. Passing the familiar blocks of terraced houses now, with soot-stained plaster, dark windows already stippled with rain. She could see at the end of the street the angular, sepia block where she lived. She hated the way it loomed up like a penal block. The very sight of her building awakened in her the smell of boiled cabbage.

Unwanted associations seemed to attach themselves to buildings and everyday things. The smell of chocolate, for example, conveyed to her the image of a view from a bridge across a wide and puddle coloured river. It was a memory she coveted, as though from her earliest childhood – but the actual taste of chocolate always left her unfulfilled.

If she spoke Russian, then what else did she know?

Dance, of course. That was another unexpected skill. Her parents had enrolled her at a drama school with some misguided conception that her imagination could turn out to be an asset. She discovered that she could dance: It wasn't that she was rhythmic. Like the maths it was a technical competence that she had - without teaching. Changements and Échappés that made her dance teacher clap her hands in delight. 'Well done Kate. Wherever did you learn to do that?'

At Livingstone House she mounted the steps two at a time, skipping around the fast-food containers and crushed cigarette packets. The staircase was rank. She passed along an open corridor, feeling the cool of the now teeming rain outside. Past the rows of scratched, identically painted red doors with aluminium letterboxes and safety glass windows.

She saw him at once, slouching in the passage outside her door. A man in Nike trainers with a heavy paunch, chin sparkling with silver stubble. He watched her approach with a dour look. She steeled herself. Felt his eyes assess her. In passing had to turn to face him. He didn't make an effort to move. Stale coffee lingered on his breath.

'Excuse me.'

Without turning back she passed her door - Number 29. She could sense him watching the swing of her haunches as she passed out of the other end of the passage. She couldn't go home now.

Clipping down the rancid steps to the next floor, stumbling, suddenly unsteady on her high heels. *What now?* Another passage, identical to the first. Scratched doors. Heady smell of ozone.

At number 17 she stopped and knocked. The wind carried a flurry of rain into the open passage and she shivered. She wasn't dressed for this weather. A net curtain at the window flipped aside, then came the rattle of a door chain and the door swept open to reveal Manda, diminutive in the dark doorway, looking at her with hard round eyes. She was short and trim and her arms were crossed tightly over her chest. Ginger hair slicked back like a twenties moll. She waited.

'Bailiffs,' Kate said at last. 'There's a bailiff on my doorstep.'

Manda snorted. 'He'll go away. They always do.'

She didn't move. Kate wondered if she had a man inside. A punter, maybe. She looked past her into the bare hallway. A rusty bicycle was propped up against the scuffed wall.

‘It's Thursday.’

Manda's face softened a little. 'Of course,’ she said.

'I can't let my daughter see me like this.'

Manda's stare flicked over her. Tiny skirt. Thick make-up. Black stilettos. 'I'd let you have something of mine,’ she said at last. 'But I don't have anything that would fit.' Resentful. She stepped aside. 'I'll see what I can do. Probably gone by now, anyway.'

But when after a too-milky cup of tea they returned to the next floor, Kate peeked around the wall and he was still there, kicking the heels of his trainers against the wall. 'He's there!' She hissed at Manda.

'It's all right.' She grabbed a coat from a hook overloaded with drab garments, and edged out of the front door.

Kate watched Manda head towards the man, jangling a set of keys. She stopped at number twenty-nine. Kate saw only her narrow back. Heard her say,

'You want something?'

The man reached inside his jacket and produced some folded papers. 'You Kate Buckingham?'

'What if I am?'

'I've got a warrant of execution.'

'What's that?'

'Means I can seize your "goods and chattels"', with audible speech marks around 'goods and chattels.'

'Let me see.'

Kate watched as Manda manoeuvred herself to the man's other side, pretending to read the papers.

'Fuck you.' She said suddenly and snatched the papers, ripping them apart in one deft movement. Stuffing her keys in her bag she strode past him.

The bailiff was scooping up the damp sheets. 'You bitch!' then hurried after her, ''Oy!' When they were out of sight Kate splashed through the puddled walkway to her door and let herself in. *Good old Manda.*

Manda was a whore, but she hadn't always been. They had danced together before at White's. Manda was older though, and her appeal hadn't lasted. Then, when the bookings stopped for good she'd started to accept the odd trick - just to get by. Now she was a full time whore, and still she didn't get by because she was cut-price. Had to be, these days. But Manda was also the only real friend Kate had. Who else would steer the bailiffs away from her door?

Everything in its place in her room. Scatter cushions on the bed in autumnal colours, and a red alarm clock that had stopped months ago: She always woke up when she needed to. On the back of the door a flannel nightgown gown that carried the aroma of fabric softener. At the dressing table, where an array of expensive cosmetics stood in a neat row, she pawed the make-up from her face in the mirror, with cotton wool dipped in cleansing lotion. She thought only of Becki now. Tried not to think about Robert because it always made her feel encumbered. Their marriage had been stillborn, but they had a child. Poor Rebecca. Becki.

She leaned back on the bed and dipped out of her skirt, then hauled on a pair of blue jeans. One day, when she had enough money, she planned to take Becki away. She would pick her up from school and magic her some place where the sun always shined and they could be together all the time. She would feel guilty about Robert for a time, because he was a good father. But the guilt would pass, and she supposed that Robert would forget them both in time.

Major Nikolay Sokolov aligned the transparency and flipped on the light of the overhead projector. It buzzed. Ageing technology. Who in these days of PowerPoint presented using transparencies?

'Here's the latest one.'

Projected onto the grubby wall was a press cutting from Pravda, still the main outlet for the allegations. The other two men tried to hide their discomfort. They hadn't asked to be on this investigation and were assessing the implications. It was hot in the room. The iron radiator ticked and there was a smell of singed clothing in the air.

'The following research report was released by the Feliks Group,' read the slide, *'purportedly attributed to the usual source, one Ivan Ivanov, Intelligence Agent:*

'New information has been uncovered by this officer

regarding the activities of the usurper Andrey Polivanov, Foreign Minster in the illegal Yeltsin government. This officer has already made revelations in the past about Polivanov's role in the Moscow narco group, and his shameful involvement in large-scale drug trafficking. It can now be confidently reported that Polivanov holds foreign currency accounts in Luxembourg, Gibraltar, Cyprus and Antilles, housing the substantial gains of his criminal activities. It can also be reported that his interests in several major Russian banks have been used to channel large quantities of illegitimate funds out of Russia. This agent has uncovered detailed evidence of significant numbers of fraudulent transactions totalling many millions of rubles. The information will be transmitted to the proper authorities for their action.

'Why does there continue to be so little initiative from this government to stamp out corruption and organised crime? Is it because every member of this coterie of thieves has his own interest at heart? As a former General in the KGB Polivanov continues to be permitted to use his influence in the intelligence

services and the government to feather his own nest. This officer demands that he be arrested and tried for his misdemeanours.'

Sergeant Dikul read it with dismay. 'You don't think there could be any truth in all this?'

Dikul was a truculent officer with a defiant manner that bordered on insolence. But resources were limited, and he and Chernov, the diminutive Georgian, were the only two officers that could be spared. So he would make the best of it, like he always did. With a sigh he perched himself on the edge of a scratched and splintered desk.

'And what if there is?'

'It wouldn't be the first time. I read Pravda. This Ivan Ivanov character is some kind of folk hero, like Stenka Razin.'

'As I said: That's not this department's concern. Our orders come from the very highest authority..'

'From the accused.' Interrupted Dikul with instantly stifled laughter. 'From Polianov?'

'From the Foreign Minister, yes. We need to identify the people behind the Feliks Group. And put an end to these press releases. And the killings.'

‘Which means investigating General Borilyenko?' Said Chernov, the other officer.

'If that’s where the investigation takes us.'

'Comrade Major, can I ask you something?' Said Dikul, rising to his feet. He had an enormous belly and the buttons of his shirt stretched like vertical wounds.

'If it's relevant.'

'Did you ask for this assignment?' Sokolov switched on the lights, and the projector image faded to grey. 'Because it seems to me we're between a rock and a hard place. Here we’ve got Polivanov. Didn't he used to be head of the Fifth Chief Directorate?' He knew he did of course. They all knew. The Fifth Chief Directorate of the KGB once had a special mandate for the persecution of dissidents. 'And here,' continued Dikul without waiting for an answer, 'we've got General Borilyneko. Head of the Presidential Security Service!' He threw his hands in the air. 'Yeltsin’s personal bodyguard for fuck’s sake who, last time I heard, had political ambitions of his own. This is political warfare. Can't the FSB investigate themselves? They're supposed to handle internal security for Christ's sake. We're SVR. I thought we were supposed to deal with all the exotic foreign intelligence? Or did I miss something. I mean I joined up to go to Paris and London. Not to get a death warrant.'

'Ask for this assignment? I'd have to be crazy. But you know full well the FSB can't be trusted to investigate one of their own.' He looked at Dikul. He could sympathise. He had had the identical reaction. 'And the police… well. I don't need to go there. Somebody's got to do it.' He said. 'And we're the only department I suppose Polianov thinks he can trust. It's been going on for months, these so called press releases, as I'm sure you both know. And it's not only that. You've heard the stories. The Feliks Group has been associated with other things, including murder.'

'Let me tell you what I think.' Said Dikul. 'As Foreign Minister Polianov treats the SVR like his own personal army. He gets pissed off by some story in Pravda and decides to mobilise. To take the war to the enemy camp. Never mind that he's a corrupt little shit.

Never mind that he's…'

'Careful.' Said Sokolov.

'Never mind careful. I stopped being careful after the wall came down. Whatever happened to glasnost? They wanted openness, now they complain when it opens up things they don't want anybody looking at.'

'Well I've personally got some sympathy with Feliks.' Said Chernov. 'Seems like they're doing a fine job. The police should be doing what they're doing. Whoever they are. Some of this stuff just needs to be told. And some of those people deserve what they get.' Chernov looked around for support but saw none. 'I just thought I had to say that. Sorry sir.'

'Thanks for that perspective.' Said Sokolov. 'But none of this changes anything.'

'I'm just a simple intelligence officer.' Grumbled Dikul. 'I haven't been paid for two months. But still I was hopeful of one day collecting my pension. When I joined the service I thought I'd do some international travel. Spy on some Americans. Instead this.'

Sokolov nodded. 'I know what you mean.'

Chapter Four

ROBERT OPENED THE front door knowing it was Kate and hating that he couldn't look at her after all this time without a a rush of longing.

'Hey,' she said like she always did, looking diffident and cold in the pale light from the hall. Her eyes were a little crazy, and she glanced around, making connections he tried hard to follow.

'Hey,' he echoed, cursing himself for the clot in his voice. He stood aside and breathed her perfume almost guiltily as she stepped past him. The fragrance of another life.

He saw her fleeting look around the hall, and wondered if she noticed the minor changes he had agonised over and for which he harboured an irrational guilt, for he lived here alone now. It was just a hall. A bit grand. Grandfather clock. Chinese ceramics. Probably bigger than the living room of the wretched place she lived in now. He felt he should apologise for something.

She looked at him and hooked her hair behind an ear. Smiled. Politely – not like before. Smiled like she would at a stranger. Frictionless. He smiled back. How do you make a smile warm? Forgiving? How do you make a smile say what you mean?

Becki's stockinged feet rumbled and thudded down the stairs; she almost fell over the last step.

'Mummy! Mummy!'

Then he watched Kate sweep up their daughter and hug her, brushing cheeks. A flash of jealousy made him flinch.

'I've got a new Barbie doll. *And* a new coat.' Becki said with precision.

'I know. You had those last time.'

'Yes. It's a nice coat. Daddy says it will keep me warm as toast, but I like it because it’s red.’

'Did you miss me?'

'Yes. Daddy missed you too.'

Robert swallowed hard and Kate flashed him a look. Accusatory, he thought. 'Did you, daddy?'

'That's not fair. You know I miss you very much.’ And he was on the point of telling her she should come home, that he loved her, that he wanted her more than anything in the world, when he was reminded of the hopelessness of their relationship. Of the restless nights he had waited for her until 5 and 6 in the morning, still with a day’s work ahead of him. Of the credit card bills that slipped through the door with their deadly payloads. What had she bought? Who had she been with? How could he trust her? She chose to leave. It was because of trust. No one could trust her. Still he would beg her to come home, if only she would. And if only she would give up the dancing.

Kate lowered Becki to the floor, who started back up the stairs at once. ‘Shall I show you my new Barbie, mummy?’

'I've seen it sweetie.' Bewildered. Then '...Sorry,' with a forlorn look. She knelt and began the usual nonsense game only mother and daughter shared:

'My telephone began to ring

Who's there?

Elephant.

From where?

Camel's place.

What do you want?'

'CHOCOLATE!' Becky interrupted with a squeal

Robert watched them play. 'What *is* that?'

She shrugged. 'Just something I know. A nonsense story.' She seemed to dip inside herself, seeking something. 'It's called Telephone.' She said. 'For whom?' she continued to Becki.

'For my son!'

'You look wonderful.' He said from a distance. It was something he always said of course. Couldn't help himself. Once she had made him promise that he would tell her she was wonderful every day. These meetings were dogged by ritual. She finger combed her long hair that the wind had tangled, and glanced around for the mirror that had once hung in the hall. Mirrors spooked him these days - reminded him of her. She looked neat and homely in a black leather jacket over a blue cashmere sweater and jeans, as though she had just stepped out to the shops. She looked like she always had when they shared a home together. Not this empty place, but a proper home. A year of bliss, so fulsome it seemed longer to him: It seemed to occupy half his memories.

'Thanks.' She glanced up the stairs with a deep seated unease. 'Where's the mirror?'

'I moved it. I didn't like it there.'

'Oh. How's Becki been?'

'The same. It's just a week since you saw her.'

'I know. But I worry. You know I do.'

'She's safe.'

'Of course she is.'

'I didn't mean..'

'I know.'

Becki appeared again at the top of the stairs gripping a doll with tangled hair. Like her mother's hair. 'I've got my new Barbie.'

Robert led her into the living room where they sometimes made love on the sofa. He bit back the thought of it. 'Can I get you something? Coffee?'

'I thought we'd go straight out. Maybe have Sushi. Maybe some bowling. She likes that.'

'Sure.' They always went out, of course. It was Kate's way, he supposed, of maintaining their separateness. 'Can I come?' but he knew the answer.

'You know what they say?' she said. 'Three's a crowd.' Words felt like they had jagged edges: they didn't fit together easily like they once had. And sometimes they injured. She smiled to let him know she was joking, but he knew she meant it all the same. Even so, he tried to read into it some reticence, some trace of sadness. There was none.

Becki tumbled into the room wearing her mother's grin. She held out the doll with both hands.

'Do you like my new Barbie?'

'It's very nice. But you showed me last time. Do you want to eat sushi?'

'Can I have a drink with it?'

'Of course.'

Robert fished in his pocket. ‘Take the car if you want. It's still insured for you, you know.'

'It's ok. We can take the bus can't we?' she addressed Becki.

'I like the bus, don't I Mummy?'

'Yes you do. How about you take me bowling?’

‘Yay!’

Becki was hustled into her coat and shoes while Robert watched, feeling superfluous. On the doorstep, kissing Becki goodbye he asked as casually as he could, 'Still dancing?' He had a reflexive urge to kiss Kate too, but he knew it was out of the question and the impulse died stillborn.

She shot him a fierce look that said 'back off'.

'You know I am. What else can I do? It’s what I did before I met you.’

He wanted to tell her that he always thought she judged him for being at the night club the night they met. He wanted to tell her that it was just the one time, even if it wasn’t true. But these were some of the thoughts that were never aired, and the conversations they may once have sparked turned around and round in his head, until he almost persuaded himself that they had taken place after all.

Then in a noisy exodus they were gone. The two people he loved most in all the world.

Chukovsky, she thought. That's where the nonsense poem came from. She'd been scouring her memories ever since they left the house. A children's writer from a long time ago. A rhyme she'd known all her life and now Becki would know it too. The clack and rumble from the bowling lanes and the strident eighties music diverted her. The screens above the lanes flashed improbable scores - improbable to Kate, who was poorly equipped for bowling with her manicure and her skinny jeans. She helped Becki to manoeuvre a metal ramp into position and set her ball on the rails. Becki pushed at the bright orange ball with two hands, and it drifted towards the pins, bouncing off the cushions, then tumbled gently into the pins, which collapsed. She clapped her hands and jumped up and down.

'Strike mummy. Strike!' She held up both hands to

do a high five, and Kate touched against her hot palms, laughing.

'Good girl!' she said.

In the next aisle two fat teenagers with round cheeks were pulling on the straws of giant fizzy drinks in paper cups. Their father performed a pointless jig before letting his ball loose with a straight arm, and cursed as it pitched down the gully. Kate watched a waitress in a tight 'T' shirt and a piercing in her nose bring the family a tray of food, piled high with spindly French fries, and the teenagers descended on it at once, before the care-worn mother had time to find her purse.

'Can we have chips, mummy?'

'Let's wait and have Sushi, shall we? You know it's your favourite, and you need to make room.' She lifted her own bowling ball, and let it roll down the lane, collapsing a handful of pins. She didn't look up at the score. 'Are you looking forward to going to school? It's not long now.' she said, waiting for her ball to return.

'Daddy said I'll have lots of friends to play with at school. And I've got to have a special bag for my books.'

'I'm sure daddy's right.' Becky looked so earnest that she couldn't help laughing. 'I'm sure you'll make lots and lots of friends,' she said through her smile, and stooped to plant a kiss on her forehead. It was as she straightened up that she caught the edge of a look from another aisle that made her start.

' What's wrong mummy?'

Two men were playing a serious competitive game. The scores were littered with strikes and spares when she looked at the monitor. They were sturdy and had crew cuts like soldiers, and took no pleasure in their game. Maybe she was mistaken. She was used to attracting the attention of men, after all.

'Nothing. Nothing to worry about, sweetie.'

But she had seen that look before. She had seen how they watched her, not in the usual way, but in the way of professional watchers - indirectly through reflections in glass or mirrors, or straight through her as though looking beyond her at something else. When they spoke to each other she strained to hear them, but the background noise was too loud. Meat Loaf bawled and curdled *Anything for Love.* Everything was normal, she told herself, and she hustled Becki to finish the game, which made her feel guilty.

When they left, the two men were still slamming out strikes, and made no sign of interest or recognition as they passed their aisle. Kate felt a little ashamed, but as they passed a glass faced wall she saw one of the men look at her, and the paranoia took hold of her again. 'Let's go, sweetie. Let's grab a taxi.'

As they headed towards the door, a loud bang made Kate catch her breath. She looked this way and that, half crouched without knowing why.

'Mummy you're hurting.'

She looked down and realised she was squeezing Becki's hand tightly.

'It was a balloon Mummy,' said Becki with a pained, mystified expression, and she began to cry.

Samantha padded across the bedroom naked, to fetch the cigarettes from the dresser. She had a thick waist, observed Dmitry with sudden repugnance, sitting up in bed. She lit a cigarette and offered the pack to Dmitry, but he shook his head. He felt her cold body rummage and settle beneath the quilt beside him.

'What's the matter with you tonight, darling?' she said, breathing smoke into the stale air. She had the burr of an English dialect that irritated him. He didn't know where it was from and he didn't much care.

'Nothing. Just ghosts.'

'Ghosts?' She propped herself up on her elbow and took another drag.

'I met someone I haven't seen in a long time.'

'A Russian?' She prickled. He had noticed she seemed to resent anything Russian, like she felt excluded by it. Sometimes it amused him to use Russian that she couldn't understand. He savoured her hurt.

'Somebody I knew in Soviet times.'

'A she?'

'Yes, a she.'

'Who was she?'

'Her name was Ekaterina Ivanovna Borodina. Katya. A scientist - where I used to work.'

'And now? Why's she here?'

‘That’s what I’d like to know. It wasn’t a long conversation.’

'Were you lovers?'

'What does it matter?'

'I see.'

‘No. You don’t see. It was a very long time ago.' He thought of their chance meeting. Almost to himself he murmured, ‘Hard to believe. Just the way I remember her. Exactly the same. I don’t know how it’s possible…’

'Pretty?'

‘Not aged at all.’ He registered her question: ’Beautiful.' He said, looking at Samantha with a faint smile. ‘Prettier than you’ll ever be, Suka’

She recoiled. ’What does that mean? *Suka*?'

'It means bitch.'

'Bastard.' She swung her fist at him but he was too quick for her, and he snatched her wrist. She yelped.

‘That hurts!’

He squeezed tighter before releasing her with distaste.

She rubbed her wrist on the quilt and said, 'You

don’t play fair.’ He glanced with satisfaction at the rosy imprints of his fingers on her arm. ‘Sometimes I hate you,’ she said.

‘You can always leave.’

‘You’d like that.’

He shrugged.

‘What happened?’ she said, ‘With you and her?'

'She did something stupid. Then she had to leave. We could be unforgiving in those days.'

'Like what? What did she do?'

'It doesn't matter anymore.' And he meant it. It didn't matter to him what she had done. ‘All ancient history.'

'What kind of scientist was she?'

'A good one.'

'You never tell me about the old days.'

'No.' He could feel her waiting for him to continue. Finally, he said 'It's because you’re too stupid to understand.' It was said with humour, but there was an edge to it. There was always an edge.

She ignored the insult. 'Did you talk to her? Will you see her again?'

'What's it to you? You think you own me because

we sleep together?'

She grimaced. Folded her arms over her breasts. Over her *glaza*. He felt a strange and overwhelming urge to speak in his native language. To be with Russians again. Not embassy people. Maybe with Katya. A surge of tedium swept over him. 'It's not even good sex.' He added, meaning it.

Samantha thrust herself out of bed, flinging aside the bedclothes. 'Right! So that's it!' She stabbed out her cigarette on the bedside table. 'Forget it. I never want to see you again.' Now she was plucking items of clothing from the carpet and from the chair. He watched her thick stomach crease as she stooped. 'I've had enough Dmitry. How do you think you make me feel? You think I'm made of stone? Well you've done it this time. It's over.'

'Stop it! Just stop it, OK?' Then, more softly, 'You know I don't mean it. Any of it.' And he cursed himself for being so needy. What did he want with this woman? Where was it leading?

She paused, still naked except for her blouse, which parted in front revealing the shadows of her breasts. 'I never know when you're teasing.' She wavered, caught in the question mark that separated staying from leaving.

'No. You don't.' He felt suddenly aroused. 'Come back to bed, *suka*, so I can fuck with you some more.'

She leapt onto the bed with a laugh and sat astride him, but even then his heart wasn't in it, even as he tugged her hair and fondled her breasts. He was pre-occupied.

He needed to decide what to do for the best. About Katya.

Chapter Five

IN THE WINGS of the stage, Gold squared his shoulders and barely glanced at Peaches as she ducked out of her 'G' string, tipping her chin at the audience. She cast away the last of her clothing, flipped the lacy thong into the audience, then performed a naked pirouette and launched herself onto the pole. She revolved there, hair streaming, then descended upon the stage. The bass beat thrummed and stuttered so you could feel the vibration in the back of your teeth. Kate thought Peaches' breasts were uneven. A bad boob job.

Gold was a West Indian with short, tight dreadlocks

and a huge, rugged body. Gold was short for something, she guessed, but nobody ever asked what. He attended to the music and the lights as Peaches thrust her torso, splayed her legs, caressed herself, eyes half-closed. But no matter how hard she tried it wasn't erotic but formulaic.

Was that even a word 'Formulaic'? Nobody would use words like *formulaic* in her world, so she would have to imagine how it would sound. She needed to imagine how a lot of words sounded, words she never heard spoken. Like the Russian vocabulary that now snagged her thoughts. What about Latin? She knew some - for reasons she couldn't begin to guess - and she didn't know how that ought to sound either. Somebody called out, 'Yay!' and Peaches stepped from the stage. A few men clapped but not many. Some shifted stance, or looked abandoned like people do at the end of a performance, when the lights come on.

Gold ruffled through CD cases, dismissing some with a clatter. A mixed crowd at lunchtime in Whites. Some laddish groups of office workers in suits, necking beer and pretending to be oblivious to the stage, and when they were not oblivious sharing sniggers and grins like schoolboys in class. A few older, jaded types separated themselves from the others during the dances and came closer to the stage. An ever present hard core stared like they always did, perched on stools at the edge of the stage, nursing drinks like stage props.

In her tiny skirt and thigh length boots Kate passed around the jar for tips, watching Gold out of the corner of her eye as he glowered over his CDs. She didn't croon over him like some of the others. Why did they do that? For tricks she expected. Favours. She didn't need favours like that. She danced. That was the deal. No contact. Definitely no sex.

She came up to a man with a sprinkle of dandruff on his dark suit, brushed against his sleeve. He didn't look too bad. Expensive suit. 'Maybe a private dance?' She said in his ear 'What d'you think?' She exercised the smile she used for the punters - the same for them all. But it was wasted: he didn't take his eyes off the stage. He inclined his head.

'For what?' He had to shout to make himself heard

above the pulse of Sade’s *Lovers Rock.*

'A table dance.' She tugged at his sleeve so that she could reach his ear. 'In private. C’mon.' She gave a dispirited twirl.

He glanced at her with indifference. A prospective purchase: comparing, discarding. ’Not now.' Then his attention went back to the dancer on stage. He had that absent look she saw all the time here.

'Okay. But don't forget. For twenty quid you get me all to yourself.' *But you don't get to touch. You keep your hands to yourself.* She patted his cheek with a disheartened smile and went on collecting tips.

She could clear a week’s rent on a good day at Whites. Good money. And no tax, but sometimes 14-hour shifts. She hunted around the men in the bar. Nobody escaped for free. Not on her watch. And she wouldn't let them get away with silver.

'Is that all you think I'm worth?' She said to a small man with a grey moustache who had flipped a fifty-penny coin into the jar. He dipped into his pocket at once and produced a pound.

'Sorry.' He addressed her breasts in a cracked voice.

'You have beautiful eyes.' But he hadn't seen her eyes, and she didn't offer a private dance. Selective. Staying safe. He gave a beery belch as he dropped the coin into the jar.

'Thank you.' She blew him a kiss, turned, and weaved through the bar looking for signs of affluence. This was the hated part of the job. She didn't mind the dancing, because she was on her own up there. Doing it for her. But down here in the bear pit it was different. *There's one. I bet he's a groper.* She could tell them at once. *Keep your distance or I'll set Gold on you.* Because Gold could handle any of them.

At the end of the bar two girls chattered about the merits of bleaching their hair with lemon juice, sipping alcohol free cocktails in the colours of sunset. One of the girls looked at Kate with an appraising, improbably eye-lined eye.

'I like that. Where's it from?' Reaching out a hand to sample the silk of here dress between her fingers.

'From Sally. Eighty quid.' She said, wondering why she felt the need to monetise - but they all did it. Sally's sideline - a tawdry rail of lycra and lace that she peddled around the clubs and bars.

‘Nice.’

‘Mm. Quite sexy.’ Said the other.

Kate shared a look with Jenny, doing her first spot for more than two months. She was edgy, and when she smiled back it didn't touch her eyes. A petite girl who Kate liked. She put her all into the her dances, but the make-up struggled to hide the crow’s feet, and Kate was afraid to mention she’d begun to notice the spread of cellulite on her thighs under glare of the spotlights. Jenny had begun her decline to the bottom of the booking list and Kate had heard she was doing the rounds of some of the seedier places where security was arbitrary, and the rules were few. Soon Jenny might start accepting Gold's tricks. If he ever even offered. which was doubtful. Gold had his favourites. When she had teased and flirted and cajoled enough to make her arches ache in her stilettos, she joined Gold at the corner of the stage just in time for a scrawny girl with an uneven fake tan to finish her act to a desultory round of applause. The jar was so heavy in Kate’s fist that her knuckles were white. Gold bared his teeth in a grin.

'Aw right?' His melodious baritone was the kind of voice you wanted to draw out. You wanted to close your eyes and just listen. She leaned on the console.

'Not bad.'

Gold moved the microphone close to his mouth. He barely needed it at all.

'Let's give Leanne a great big hand. One of our lunchtime favourites at White's!' He winked at Kate. 'Next up in a few minutes we'll be having the very lovely Sapphire do a full striptease for you. So don't go away.' Sapphire was Kate's stage name. All the girls had them - not to add mystique but distance. For her it was like another identity to manage, and she tried to segregate the memories. She watched Leanne haul herself off the stage with her knickers in her hand and wondered about her tan. As she passed Kate she rolled her eyes. A tough crowd.

At the push of a button a projector screen lowered behind the stage. In between acts they had Sky Sports on the big screen. Today it was Rugby League. The punters broke into their groups and some peeled off to the bar and away from the stage. Some of the hard core stayed, nursing their beer glasses.

‘Y’know I can still get you tricks if you want?'

'I know you can.'

'Not pervs. *Businessmen*. Know what I'm saying?'

As if there were a difference.

'I don't want to get into that. Slippery slope.'

He sniffed, nodded at the curtained booths. ‘Not much different from in there, my opinion. More money too.’

‘It’s different.’ Her stomach tightened. ‘They can’t touch me in there. Strictly no contact - you know the rules.’

Gold threw his head back with a laugh. ‘Depends on the girl, innit? Some of ‘em... ‘ and he nodded towards a Polish girl she half knew, working the tables. Somebody had told Kate she did heroin. ‘*You* know what they get up to back there. Anyway. Your choice. Just don’t say I didn’t offer, a’right?’ He shrugged his meaty shoulders and changed the subject. 'See your kid yesterday?’

She nodded.

'Bet she's a doll,' he said.

'She is.'

'I got a kid.'

Peaches was collecting now, coursing through the punters in a cheap frilly negligée that she might have bought from Ann Summers.

'You never told me that.'

Gold shrugged. He was watching Peaches with a proprietary air. 'Yeah, well. Don't see him much, do I? Lives over in Lambeth with his mum and some ... loser. Must be five now. Is that school age?' He flashed her a brash grin that she saw through at once...

'Gold?' Kate thought he looked sad, but he didn't meet her eye. 'Yes. Should be at school.'

Gold waved a hand. 'Whatever,' and was distracted by a commotion in the bar. Peaches was yelling at a tall man in a dark blue suit. Kate was about to say something to him, but the DJ platform was empty. She turned to watch him cut a swathe through the bar. The man in the suit was a head taller than Gold, but Gold had a firm fist around the back of his neck and had rammed the man's right arm behind his back. Other men made frantic space. Peaches was spitting. Snarling. He’d probably touched her. Sneaked a hand inside her knickers maybe. She shuddered. It happened all the time. Gold propelled the man, twisting and cursing to the doors. It was almost casual the way he did that. She’d seen him do it a hundred times, calmly, almost without a trace of aggression. One of the other girls was soothing Peaches, an arm around her narrow shoulders, leading her to the end of the bar where the girls eddied and fussed, sharing righteous curses. Then it was over.

Gold swung himself in front of the record deck, unruffled.

'Fucking pervert,' he said. Then: 'You're up next, Kate.'

In the evening, cornered in a booth with a man in a loose-fitting linen suit that was wrong for the time of year, sipping at a glass of sweet sparkling wine that masqueraded as Champagne, Kate found herself confronted with the usual questions. He put his hand on her knee and she let him leave it there because she liked how he looked. He had a clever mouth and a large mole on his cheek like Al Pacino, and she felt safe. But she wasn't kidding herself: There are no white knights in Whites.

‘You mean what’s a nice girl like me doing in a place like this?’

'Something like that. I suppose you get asked all the time.’

'Yes. It’s an old line.' She hooked a lock of her hair behind her ear and took note of her action because she realised it was in danger of becoming an irritating habit, a social tick.

'So?'

'So. Not much to tell. I was a drama student. Not far from here.'

'Guildhall?'

'Maybe. My grant didn't cover the rent on my shitty bedsit. I ate leftover pizza sometimes for breakfast. A friend of mine did this. Called it dancing not stripping. She said it was cool and I could earn good money. I did it once for fun when I was drunk. It wasn't as bad as I thought it would be. Now it's what I do.'

'Ab inconvenienti.' Kate registered the Latin phrase. Trying to be clever.

'Out of hardship?' She translated. 'Not exactly. I got by. I could have gone on benefits.'

'How did you know that? Latin I mean.'

'I didn't know I did until a minute ago. You think because you're a what—?'

'—a lawyer.'

'You think because you're a lawyer you're the only one who knows some posh Latin words?

'I apologise.' And she felt sorry for using the word 'posh' 'But you're not a student any more?'

'I wish. My ambition was to be an actress. Or a dancer. A proper one. That's what I used to tell people if they asked - everyone these days is intent on having a plan, aren't they? Makes me sick. But I don't think I wanted that. Not really. I didn't know what I wanted to do. Did you? When you left uni?'

'I did actually.'

'OK, but a lawyer? Of course, you were studying law so you must have had an idea.'

'So what then?'

'Graduated. Did a few auditions. A *lot* of them, in fact. And answered hundreds of ads in The Stage, but none of them ever came to anything. So, I got to do more and more of this while I played occasional bit parts in Eastenders.'

'Really?'

She laughed. 'Just walk on parts. I made the best of them but you wouldn't have noticed.'

'But you're so....'

'Young and beautiful and I have a great sense of humour.'

He laughed 'I was about to say you have a great body.'

'If you see any girls in here who don't fit that description you better complain to the management. Next you'll be telling me I should be a model.'

'Is that what everyone says?'

'Yes.' And she laughed again to take the edge away. 'The world's so full of young and beautiful girls they should turn the sidewalks into catwalks. There's a glut of prettiness in case you hadn't noticed. I blame cosmetics. That, and cheap breast enhancements.'

'What do your parents think?'

'About breast enhancements?'

'You know what I mean. About what you do for a living.'

'What do your parents think about you hanging out in places like this? Or your wife, for all I know?'

'Touché.'

'Sorry. They don't like us to talk like that to the punters. No offence. I haven't seen my parents for a long time. I'm not proud of what I do, and if there was another way I knew to make a living, then maybe.' But she missed out the fact it was easy money, a few days a week. You needed to learn to compartmentalise, or it would drive you crazy, and not define yourself by what you did. But she thought she managed pretty well. If anything, sometimes she found the job empowering because she had something that men all wanted. She was in control. That's the part they don't warn you about. That's what makes it addictive for a few of the girls. 'Who's in charge here? Who says what goes?' she said.

'You are. You do.'

She lifted her empty glass. 'And who's paying?'

'I'll order another.'

'Exactly. Seems to me like I've got the better end of the deal.' But neither of them believed it, even though he was quick to concede she had a point.

'What's your real name? It can't be your real name. Nobody's called Sapphire.' He summoned one of the waitresses who glared at her. The waitresses hated to see the dancers making money. Every drink he bought earned her another fiver and postponed the prospect of a private dance. Gold announced the next act and the music started up so she had to cup her hand and lean in to his ear:

'What's the difference?'

He shouted, 'I'd like to know what to call you.'

She cupped her hand again, raised her voice. 'Call me Sapphire.'

Chapter Six

‘GOOD TO SEE YOU again Katya. So good,’ he said, leaning his elbow on the table and bunching up his shoulders. His use of Russian alarmed her. It seemed surreal to be having a conversation in a language she never knew she spoke.

'I'd rather speak English,' said Kate. ‘If that’s alright. And it’s Kate, not Katya.’ Even so, the name was familiar. Like discovering a favourite doll she’d played with as a girl but finding the dress was a slightly different tone of pink and the nose was more pointed than she remembered. Familiar, but different.

Dmitry was smug. He leaned back. She noticed now that when he smiled, he revealed a gold tooth, and she wondered when he got it. '—whatever you're comfortable with,' he said. 'But I'm glad you called.'

They sat on tall stools. Café customers unfolded newspapers, sipped at oversized china cups, made bland conversation. The menus were plastic and slotted between the salt and pepper. Dmitry lay the menus on the table so they could see each other better. They ordered drinks. Vodka for Dmitry - straight up, no ice, and the waitress pursed her lips because it was before midday. Mineral water for her - with a dash of lime. How could she not have called, she wondered? Here was some clue to this woman she had never known but who squatted in her dreams and her memories. Ekaterina. Who was she, and how did she inhabit the shadowlands of her dreams?

'This feels strange.'

'What does?'

'You. Me.' She picked at the corner of the menu. Still wearing her working clothes. At least, wearing the kind of clothes she wanted to be seen in when she arrived at Whites. She dressed the way she thought a stripper *should* dress, off duty. Still making movies. Into character. People were looking. Men were noticing her, in the way that they did. Like she was naked. A gold iguana dangled in the crease between her breasts, and she watched Dmitry's attention flicker.

'What about you and me? You look amazing by the way.'

'I can honestly say I've never seen you before in my life.' She picked her words carefully. The word 'amazing' grated. Shifted earth. 'That's what's strange. I don't understand how I seem to know so much.. so much about you.' *The apartment block. Olga - stern, but delicate. Dmitry at work, in a white coat. A doctor?* The memories were building, one on one. *Simbirsk. Who or what was Simbirsk?* 'A doctor? Were you some kind of doctor?'

'Not really. I was in the lab. Assigned to your project. Amongst others.' He said with business-like haste, and frowned. Thick, black eyebrows that she wondered if he dyed. Then his face broke into lines and he laughed, so loudly that one or two people turned around. 'You're joking with me?' He leaned across the table and she moved back. 'What we shared.. it's never been the same. Not with Olga. Not with anyone. And look at you. Look at you now. Like you're no more than 25 years old.'

'I'm 32.'

'Sure you are,' he said with a surly look. 'So what's the secret? Surgery? Diet?'

'I'm Kate Buckingham. I'm 32 years old. I dance in a club. I'm wondering why I'm here. That's all.'

He was tapping with his fork on the table. 'I couldn't help it you know. What happened. It wasn't my fault. I had orders. Come on. Let's be frank - we all had orders. For a while I thought it was a set up. You and me. I thought they'd arranged it to spy on me. Boilyenko. He never liked me. He shook his head. 'Who knew who was spying on who? I wouldn't have betrayed you, the way you think I did.'

'Who is Borilyenko?' No answer. Just a dark look. The conversation had taken another oblique turn. 'You couldn't help it,' she repeated. 'But I don't know what *it* is. None of this makes any sense. And what project?

Is that what you called it? What project were you assigned to?'

'Where are you living?' The waitress came and hovered with her order pad.. 'You want to eat?'

She shook her head. 'Nothing.'

'Club sandwich,' he ordered, without looking up. 'And another vodka. Large this time.' He watched Kate, waiting for the waitress to leave. 'You work? Dancing, you say?'

'Just tell me - who is this person that you think I am? What did she do?'

He folded his hands on the table. 'Who indeed?' He began to play with his fork again. 'We're not going to get far like this.' He conceded. 'So I tell you how we'll do it, I'll make a deal with you. If you stop denying who you are and answer me some straight questions I'll tell you whatever you want to know?'

Kate thought about this. It was plain he wasn't going to be shifted from his perspective that she was someone she wasn't. She might as well play along.

'Ok,' she nodded. 'I'll be this Ekaterina, if that's what you want.' She gave an ironic wave of greeting.

‘Hi. Pleased to meet you.’

He pounced. 'There! I told you so. So how did you escape? Who brought you to England? You led them a dance, you know, back then.' He laughed. ‘Well done you, I say. So tell me. Tell me everything.’

The subdued light made the colours vibrant and saturated, like a technicolor movie. Dmitry's face was smudged, like there were two Dmitry's. One younger. Thick hair. Sallow cheeked. And this one. Brash. Plump cheeked.

‘This Ekaterina – me if you like - did she do something bad?' she ventured.

Dmitry whistled, shaking his head. 'Oh yes. Yes.' He leaned forward again. 'Yes, yes.' He licked his lips. 'You betrayed your country.' He pushed back against the table. The diners clinked and muttered from their distant planet. *Simbirsk.* That was a name she remembered above everything.

He smiled at last. ’But as the poet said, "That was in another country and besides the wench is dead."' He paused. 'The country you betrayed only exists in the history books. That's why we can be friends again.

More than friends if you want. Like before. Carry on where we felt off.' A glint of the gold tooth. After a moment's consideration he asked: 'What did they do to you? Afterwards? You don't have to tell me if it's painful.'

She said: 'I don't think I much like you. Did Ekaterina like you?'

He shrugged. 'Please yourself. Maybe the spark is gone. Maybe it will come back. Who knows? Why did you ask me here if not to resume our game?'

'Our game?'

'I even thought you loved me once.'

'How could I love you? I don't even know you?'

'Here we go again. I thought we had a deal? Who arranged this new Kate Buckingham identity for you? I like it. Suits you. Was it the British? The Americans? What did you give them in return? Tell me, Ekaterina. Remember, I'm your friend. We *were* friends, weren't we? In spite of everything you must think. Lovers, once. Not just friends. TELL me Katya. Please?'

She noticed he seemed to have forgotten to smile, as casually as you might forget to open the curtains or to put out the waste. At length Kate decided she had had enough. She stood up. Robert used to say she had poise. Dignity. Mustering the remnants of her poise and dignity, she said, 'I think I should go.'

Dmitry glanced up at her. 'It's your prerogative.' He said, without looking at her. 'They tell me it's a free country, although really I don't see much in the way of evidence.'

She scooped up her coat from the back of the chair, thrusting her arm into a sleeve.

'Don't go, Katya. There's so much to talk about. I don't know what they did - maybe wiped your memory. Maybe they can do that - I'd believe anything of them.'

'Before I go. One thing….' She looked down at him without much hope. 'What is *Simbirsk*?'

'You see! *Simbirsk* is a secret that only a few people share. How would you know about *Simbirsk* if you're not Katya? Something we share, and that we can never talk about to anyone else.'

'So what is it?'

'Think about it. Think hard and you'll remember.'

She stepped into the darkness of the street, half expecting him to follow. *Because that was the way his moods used to work,* she caught herself thinking. *Controlling.*

Dmitry nodded to the couple sitting a few tables away, and they stood up to leave.

It was the same Katya, he reflected, despite her denials. But suspended in time: so credible he almost doubted himself. But how could it be otherwise? She looked the same. Spoke Russian with a distinct Moscow drawl, just like he remembered. She knew about Simbirsk - or at least the name. It was like she had woken up after a coma, and re-learning everything from the beginning. What had they done to her?

The faltering engine of the Zhiguli and the rasp of the fan were the only sounds. Agents Dikul and Chernov sat in a blast of stale hot air that didn't reach their freezing toes, watching the road. Chernov was sulking. They'd been sitting this way for almost an hour, and Dikul had a low-down ache in the pit of his back that occupied all his thoughts. The seat was drawn back as far as possible, but his stomach still touched the rim of the steering wheel.

Chernov muttered something to himself, probably in Georgian, and Dikul didn't bother to ask what he had said. He wanted to be home and warm.

A black Mercedes swept past, rugged, and heavy as a battle cruiser. Low to the ground, weighted with armour.

'We're off.' Muttered Dikul, letting off the handbrake and revving the engine. Chernov snorted and watched some faraway space, retreating further into his big black rug of a coat.

They followed the Mercedes the short distance from Red Square to Arbat, maintaining a safe distance, letting themselves be overtaken to put some traffic between them. Dikul watched the sudden roll of the limousine as it rounded a corner, and was threading the steering wheel through his hands in pursuit, when a Volga pulled across the turning right ahead of them, tyres scrabbling for grip.. He hauled the wheel and the Zhiguli veered sideways and lurched to a halt parallel with the Volga. Dikul swore. Slammed the steering wheel hard with the heel of his hand. Then he heard Chernov yell.

'What's going on?'

Four men had leapt out of the car in front and were approaching with outstretched hands clasped in front of them. Dikul realised too late that they held guns. He reached inside his coat in an instant, but the closest man was shaking his head at him through the glass, mouthing the word: 'Nyet.'

'*Krysha*, Mafia.' Announced Chernov in a dull tone that lacked emphasis.

The doors were tugged open. Dikul half stumbled out of the car. A stolid man in a military style fur hat yanked at his coat, and he felt the barrel of a gun pressed into his neck as he emerged, bashing his head on the roof of the car.

Two men propelled him by both his arms over the bonnet of the car. His forehead almost collided with Chernov's, whose face was ripped in a stripy red grimace. He caught the sour reek of vodka on his breath. Cars swished past, the traffic compensating for them, unrelenting.

'What do you think you're doing?' Someone was demanding, as heavy hands rifled his pockets. Dikul's arms were pinned behind his back. There was a searing pain in his joints. He glanced at the Volga and noticed the blue license plates. Official license plates.

'You're in big trouble.' Dikul managed to respond with venom. 'You'll see.'

Somebody laughed. Dikul tried to move his face away from Chernov who was gagging or coughing. 'In trouble, he says. You hear that?' a balanced voice continued. A Northerner, remarked Dikul. St Petersburg. Not Chechen, at least. But not a Muscovite either. Official plates. But a Volga - the Mafia drove expensive German cars. Maybe not mafia. The pressure on his arms increased and everything became suffused. A red haze descended. Then he was let loose and he managed to push himself from the bonnet of the car. When he found his feet he found himself confronting two men in long dark overcoats. The traffic dodged around them, giving a wide birth. No one would stop, nothing was more certain. An everyday occurrence in modern day Moscow.

A thick-set man with a bulbous nose was looking at him, pointing a gun. The other man, was inspecting Dikul's papers with casual interest. He was bare headed, grey and lean, with a commanding air. The tails of his coat eddied around his ankles in the icy wind.

'So now you know.' spluttered Dikul as importantly as he could. There was a tightness in his chest that alarmed him. 'You better return those..' he said, nodding without much hope at the two pistols that had been placed side by side on the roof of their car. The man ignored him.

'So now we know.' He returned instead, without looking up. 'We are in the company of Sergeant Yevgeny Nikolayevich Dikul of our renowned Foreign Service.' He seemed to consider this for a moment with a hint of irony. 'And you were following whom?' He paused, then watched Dikul with intent grey eyes. 'General Borilyenko, for example?'

A wave of nausea swept over him. He shot a glance behind him and saw they hadn't released Chernov, who had ceased to struggle and was watching him with swollen features like a stuck pig, eyes red-rimmed. Two thugs stood meanly at his back, their shoulders bunched. Not Mafia, he told himself again.

'So, who the fuck are you?'

The man sighed. He looked past Dikul and spoke quickly to one of the men. From behind he heard Chernov wheeze as he was released. Then he started to swear in a thick Slavic slur. Someone must have hit him then because he stopped swearing and began wheezing again. Dikul steeled himself, refusing to allow himself to turn around. 'It's not important. What *is* important is your interest in General Borilyenko.' The headlamps of the early evening traffic lanced around them like they were a traffic island. Dikul caught the soviet blindness in the eyes of the drivers. Another unseen Moscow heist. Another Russian widow.

The reality, when it came to him was even more unwelcome than Mafia. Borilyenko's men. Not directly, but almost certainly FSB. And there in the grey man's eyes was the yellow reflection of the Lubiyanka.

'You are fat and most probably slothful.' he observed to Dikul in a tone that suggested this conclusion was the result of lengthy study. 'You should be at home with your Russian wife, who is also fat, and your revolting children. I say this without criticism, you understand.' Dikul wondered whether this demonstration of knowledge about his family was intended as a threat. 'I advise you now. Speak with your superiors. Have yourself re-assigned. Tell them you're not cut out for surveillance, which you're not. Sometimes it's necessary to choose your friends carefully.' Dikul felt strangely apologetic, like he'd been caught out. The man looked into his eyes with a mixture of empathy and contempt. Then he pointed first to Chernov's assailants, then to the Zhiguli. Dikul still didn't look around, even when he heard a car door open and shut. 'Remember this advice. It's good advice.' And he collected up the weapons like abandoned toys from the roof of the Volga and ducked into the car, which pulled away at once. The Zhiguli followed close behind, pink in the glow of the Volga's tail lights. Dikul turned to find Chernov sitting cross-legged in the gutter looking miserable and clutching his side.

Chapter Seven

THE PARANOIA HAD descended again as she left the café so she avoided the subway and hailed a cab, and as she bundled herself inside, she felt sickened - a feeling of ant-climax and unspent adrenaline. The meeting with Dmitry she had awaited with so much anticipation had revealed nothing new, except that there was much more to be uncovered than she ever dreamed. Her parallel memories were crystallising, glacier-like in her head. They were gaining in depth too. Toughening up. It would take a bigger effort to deny these new imposing memories.

'All right luv?' The cab driver was looking at her over his shoulder. He had a mad flock of ginger hair and deep-sunk eyes. When he looked at her he looked directly at her breasts.

'I'm fine.'

'Where to?' The driver burbled.

She felt herself colour and gave the driver her address, then she glanced around, as drivers do when they are passengers, looking for a space in the traffic. A blue Volvo flashed its lights to let them pull away from the kerb. She settled back and immersed herself in her diverse memories, looking for clues. She recalled again the reflection from her childhood, sliding over the glossy brass. Then the old lady, sweeping past in her long skirts. *Keep away from there, Ekaterina. You'll scald yourself.* She froze. She never remembered the old lady speaking to her before. And certainly not in Russian. *Keep away from there, Katya.* She replayed the memory like a video in her head, and it was the same each time. The child's reflection. The trophy like object seated above her on a lace covered table. The old lady, stooping to draw some liquid from the tap. Then the imploring voice. *Keep away Katya. Katy: what Dmitry had called her.*

The blue Volvo had drawn alongside at the lights. In the yellow streetlight she glanced at the car and glimpsed two shadowy figures behind rain-spattered glass. Then the cab jerked forward again, and the Volvo slipped into their wake.

They made good time across London. She watched Livingstone House materialise ahead with a feeling of foreboding. She didn't want to be alone in her bleak apartment, but there was nowhere else to go. It was almost nine when she stepped into the damp night and paid the driver, clutching the front of her coat.

Rushing towards the steps, looking over her shoulder as the cab splashed away. Then she paused just an instant, gripped with an odd sense of anticipation. Two cars passed, before the blue Volvo. It seemed to slow, then sped around the next corner with its taillights ablaze. She couldn't be sure, but she thought there was only a single occupant. Or maybe it was a different car altogether.

She shouldered her way through the swing door and

rattled up the steps to her floor. Then she stopped and listened, holding her breath. There was a pulse in her head. A baby wailed in the distance. Otherwise, silence. After a few minutes she turned to go. It was then that she heard it: from the foot of the steps the shudder of the door opening and closing. She wasn't mistaken after all. With sudden electric energy she ran to her door along the passage, scrabbled at the lock with her key. Burst inside. Messed with the chain and the bolts. Then strained to hear any slight sound of movement outside, leaning with her back against the door as if to fortify herself. She must have stood there for half an hour. Her mind was a blank: She found herself repelling the memories, even the safe ones. She didn't want to know any more.

When at last she was satisfied there was no one outside, she wandered from room to room trying to persuade herself that everything was normal. Her limbs were taut, strung out like her nerves. Finally she discarded her coat on the floor in the bedroom, and threw herself on the bed, in a hurry for sleep to consume her…

The children stood in line with wide eyes outside the grey-green double doors with steel handles, trying hard to suppress their excitement. They were each identically dressed in school uniform of dark-blue dress with a white, Edwardian style collar, and white aprons. There was no giggling or chattering because it was explicitly disrespectful. A uniformed guard in a long coat stood at either side of the doors, stony faced and silent. The children's' toes ached from the cold, and their noses and cheeks glowed.

Watching their breath form wintry clouds in front of their faces, they waited shivering at the head of a long and ragged line of people that stretched behind them across the road. It seemed like an hour or more before they were admitted. Finally, they were permitted to file into the yellow lit chamber in a crocodile, their shuffling feet resonating.

There, with his head propped against a pillow, in a glass sided coffin that resembled the elongated head of a giant lantern, its base swathed in silken drapes, was the wax-like doll that was all that remained of the leader of whom they had read and revered so much. Eerily lit: His face seemed to shine. Like an angel, Ekaterina pondered with awe, staring past the reflections of her classmates at the tranquil figure. She tried to hold her breath at first, scared she would breathe in the smell of death. Then, when her lungs could not hold out any longer she breathed out in a rush, panting for breath. The other children milled about, shoulders pressed together, their reflections mingling with her own. She wondered what it would be like to touch Lenin, and she reached out her hand, feeding her imagination. Her belly felt taut, and she felt a little nauseous. She swallowed some bile.

When she lowered her hand to touch her stomach, she noticed it was bloated, swollen up. She felt with both hands in sudden panic and found her abdomen round like a football. No children around her anymore. Only adults with gruff voices. Some wore military uniforms, some white coats. They were all watching as the glass coffin was opened. She knew now, instinctively, that she was pregnant. Her breath became uneven as she struggled for air. There was something obscuring her face. Cloth of some kind. A surgical mask.

Kate awoke in a sweat, pawing the bedclothes from her face.

Chapter Eight

COLONEL LISAKOV PUSHED a padded brown envelope across the desk. The mouth gaped open to reveal the grey barrels of the two confiscated Makharov pistols, emasculated in the bland package.

'I can't apologise enough, Comrade Major, for this misunderstanding. This *incident*. Most regrettable.' Sokolov thought that Lisakov appeared jubilant.

'I wish to put on record, Comrade Colonel, that my officers were assaulted in the course of their duties. Assaulted by your officers. By the FSB.'

'You wish to put it on the record. Of course you do.'

Lisakov repeated. He sniffed. Nodded. 'I agree they may have been over-zealous. But you must appreciate it was only out of well-meaning concern for the security of General Borilyenko.' He folded his hands on the desk and as he did so Sokolov tried to estimate the value of the Rolex that his sleeve exposed. The Colonel had silver hair and wore steel rimmed spectacles that flashed in the light from the window. He gave an impression of being metallic and invincible, from the sheen on his suit to the flash of his watch. 'Sadly, Comrade Major we live in violent times, despite the best efforts of my department. We have to be vigilant at all times.' He made a helpless gesture and smiled without humour. 'We can't be everywhere. We do what we can, when presented with certain *scenarios*. These new *freedoms* we have in modern Russia have brought unexpected challenges to the security services, as I'm sure you know. In many ways we are victims of our new liberties.'

With both hands Nikolay gathered up the envelope, and stood up.

'I understand, Comrade Colonel. But it was clear

these men were official. There were engaged in a sensitive operation which your officers may have compromised.'

'If there is any assistance the FSB can offer in your operation, then I would be glad to make amends. In confidence, Comrade Major.' Lisakov proceeded in an affable tone, 'What is this operation? Just why was it that your officers were tailing the official car of the Comrade General?'

It was hot in the Colonel's office, which had a collegiate, academic quality. Leather armchairs. A bookcase lined with legal and political volumes. There was even a copy of '*Das Kapital*', Sokolov noticed. The room seemed out of keeping with the Lubyanka. Under his jacket his shirt felt damp.

'You'll appreciate, Comrade Colonel, I'm not permitted to discuss matters of an operational nature. But you must be mistaken. Nobody was following the General.'

'Oh, I don't think my officers are mistaken.' Sokolov had his hand on the door when in an abstract tone Lisakov added, 'Actually, I feel rather sorry for you. You've been handed an impossible assignment. Everybody says so.'

'With respect, Comrade Colonel, what would people know about confidential assignments of the Foreign Intelligence Service?'

'Only what they would be expected to know, Comrade Major. Nothing more.' Sokolov was already leaving, 'And I wish you luck, Comrade Major. Really I do.' Lisakov called after him in a tone laced with irony.

'Thank you, Comrade Colonel, for your offer of assistance.'

Outside Lisakov's office, Sokolov's rubber soles squeaked on the tiles. There was a pervading smell of carbolic in the corridor and the walls were painted a pale green that cast a sickly glow. He walked briskly, took the stairs, waved a dismissive hand at the two uniformed FSB officers as he stepped through the doorway. The air was crisp but tainted with petroleum. He headed in the direction of Lubyanka Square, past the main building with its yellow façade and rows of black windows. The prison was still there - lines of cells on the sixth floor. He wondered who they incarcerated there these days. Below, the basement. It used to be said that the Lubyanka was the tallest building in Moscow, because from the basement you could see Siberia. In the old days it was the basement where they carried out the executions. For all he knew there were still executions there all the time. He passed the empty plinth that once carried the statue of the intelligence service's founder, Feliks Dzherzhinsy. There were calls from some quarters to restore it. Russians hungered for the strength of past leaders, past glories. Across the Square was Children's World, the largest children's store in Russia. He crossed briskly to the south side of the square, and passed beneath the concrete arches of the Lubyanka metro station, part of the original stage of the Moscow metro, once a triumph of the Soviet Union. People, bulked up against the cold, came and went, flicking through the barriers, with empty eyes. In the vestibule, resonant with the shuffle of boots and coughs, a bust of Felix Dzherzhinsky remained. He would will himself to walk by without a glance. It was no use of course. Each time he passed he caught a glimpse. Hard to believe that within his own lifetime this metro station had carried the name Dzherzhinskaya - a celebration of the life of a murderer and a tyrant. But who was he to think this way? He'd served for long enough in the very organs that Dzherinsky had created. Acronyms had come and gone, but not ultimately the organs were intact. He was still KGB when it came down to it.

He travelled south to Yasenevo, some 20 kilometres across town, changing once at Kitai Gorod and then at Oktabyrskaya.

Yasenevo district was where the headquarters of the Foreign Intelligence Service was situated, an imposing skyscraper out of town. It pained him to be so far from the centre. The SVR was the poor relation now the dust had settled on the cold war, and Yasenevo had become an outpost.

When he reached his office Dikul and Chernov were waiting for him. They didn't get up. He offered the lumpy package to Dikul.

'A misunderstanding.' He said, without much sincerity.

'Don't take off your coat.' Said Chernov.

'You'll never believe who wants to see you.' Dikul took a shameful peek inside the envelope. He was tapping his heel, his knee bouncing like a nervous tick. Chernov too looked uncomfortable. 'You'll have to go back into town. Right now.'

'Don't tell me that Boris Nikolayevich Yeltsin has requested the pleasure?'

'Not quite the President…'

Chapter Nine

KATE FELT A perverse impetus, but even so she paused with her hand on the wicker gate of the cottage where she grew up. There were symmetrical stripes on the lawn, the rows of miniature shrubs that lined the pathway were precisely spaced. And there was the dreaded black door with its shiny brass fittings. She hadn't been past that door in years. It was just the same as she remembered. A quiet pool of suburban respectability. A tumble of Austrian blinds at the windows. Gleaming black panes like still water. Once as she stood poised outside the gate, she thought she heard a movement behind her, and her heart leapt. But when she turned around there was nothing. Just an empty street and banks of lawns that eddied around tiny cottages just like this one. And what would she say to them, after all? A part of her hoped they might be out. But they never went out. Not since her father had retired in fact. They closeted themselves together in their tiny fortress in Tring and shunned even the neighbours.

A fresh resolution drove her forwards, but then she found herself pondering again, hand poised at the slick, bony doorknocker, marvelling at its gleam. She remembered how her mother, wrapped in a florid apron she wore almost all the time, would polish it with Brasso. Then it was the turn of the letterbox in an invariable sequence, a ritual of cleanliness. She was always busy around the house. 'Cleanliness is next to Godliness' she used to tell her. It was as though she was trying to atone for something every hour of the day. Father would just sit with his long legs crossed, outstretched in defiance of the vacuum cleaner, engrossed in his Times and drawing on 'that filthy thing' as her mother called it when she appealed in vain for him to put out his pipe.

She wondered how the routine had changed in her long absence. How long had it been? Taking a deep breath, she was about to knock when the door opened, and there was her mother in that same florid apron and tight grey curls. She stood at the door unsmiling and without a hint of greeting or surprise. For a moment Kate thought she might ask if she had forgotten her key again. She might point out that it was late. Too late to be coming home at her age. But instead, her mother said nothing. She just waited in silence and judged her without words.

'Hi Mum.' Kate thought her voice sounded forlorn. She hadn't meant it to sound that way. She could scarcely look her in the eye.

'Your father's in the drawing room.' Her mother said, inching aside for her to pass. Kate though she caught a hint of distaste in her look, even though she'd made an effort. No trace of make-up. A simple sweatshirt and blue jeans that were not too tight. A red skiing jacket she had bought one winter when she'd been meaning to take a holiday, but never got around to it.

Her father was sitting in the chair by the window where he always sat, smoking ‘that filthy thing’. When she came into the room something strange happened. At first there was almost the flicker of a smile, and then his expression seemed to alter at once, as though he had noticed something in her demeanour. He uncrossed his legs and stiffened, leaning forwards in his chair.

‘Kate?’ he said, and she could sense an unvoiced question hanging in the air.

‘Dad. I know.’ She said, watching his eyes. The eyes had aged. There were crevices around them that she didn’t remember. Like they’d been sketched in pencil. *What? What did she know?* ‘I know about Russia.’ She said at last. Hoping it was enough.

He got to his feet in silence and positioned himself in front of the empty fire grate, arms behind his back, with military poise. He seemed to swallow hard before he spoke.

‘Then you’ll know there’s nothing for you here.’

‘I need to know the rest. Everything. I want to hear it from you.’

From behind her then her mother's anguished voice. 'Tell her Bob. It can't hurt now. It was all so long ago.'

His face closed up for an instant, and then his eyes misted over and his face became somehow flaccid: it seemed to her that he avoided looking at her. 'If you're sure. If you're really sure you want to know,' he said, as much to himself as to anyone in particular. Then he sighed. 'Sit down.' He gestured at an armchair. 'Please, sit down.' But she stood all the same, waiting, until reconciled, he began: 'Your mother ... we couldn't have children. She ... we were desperate to have a child. Of our own. It seemed the right thing to do. And when they told me about you… well…' He coughed into his hand. There was a long silence before he began. Kate was about to say something, feeling an urgent need to fill the void of silence, but stopped herself in time.

'They smuggled you across the border just after midnight.' He began again, 'Maybe the border guards had been bribed because there were no questions. They didn't search the bags which was also too good to be true. I was waiting, of course. Alone, because it was impossible for your mother to come along, even though she wanted to.. even though she begged me to let her come. It would have been too dangerous. For everyone.'

Kate had no idea what to expect. She was struggling to interpret what he was saying.

'The border..?' It was all she could think of to say.

'They took you through Turkey first of all.' He explained, as if that were the most natural thing in the world. 'It was safer than Germany, in those days. And I had contacts, you understand.' He sucked on his pipe, but it had gone out, and he stooped to bang the ashes into the grate. 'Through the office.'

She knew her father had worked in the Foreign Office for years. A minor bureaucrat, he used to tell her. Nothing very important. 'So..? What happened?' she prompted with a gnawing feeling inside.

'It turned out to be simpler than I thought. Kris came out too of course. He had to. He knew he could never go back. He brought you out in the bottom of a small suitcase with holes punched for air. A tiny bundle wrapped in white, like a doll. A tiny Russian doll.' Her father looked at the ceiling with unseeing eyes. 'I was shocked when I saw your face. All wrinkled. I'd never seen a new-born baby before. Thought you were ill, to start with. Five days old, when Kris brought you out. Sleeping, peacefully. Maybe they'd given you something—' He was rambling now. 'Getting you out of Turkey was always a concern, but I needn't have worried because Kris had all the right papers. Kris was a professional. Then Heathrow … well that was never going to be a problem. Not with the Job.' He said, looking away. *Something at the Foreign Office. Just paperwork. Nothing important.*

And that was when it dawned upon her what she was hearing. She should have seen it sooner. The strangers that she had known all her life were just that – they were strangers. She was an orphan. She felt giddy but she pressed him. '—and my real mother? My real father?'

'We *are* your real parents.' Came her mother's voice from behind. 'It doesn't matter who conceived you. We clothed you, fed you.' She paused. There was a click in her voice when she added, 'Loved you.' It sounded odd coming from her.

'But who were they? What happened to my parents?'

Her father shook his head. 'They never told us. Russians? Maybe not. Maybe diplomats? But it didn't matter to us who they were. They were gone. We were all there was. We are your parents, Kate. We're all you have.' He opened out his hands, then seemed to notice them and clasped them behind his back. Embarrassed to be caught out.

'When I got you back to the UK we registered the birth as our own. Kris had prepared us for this long in advance.' He nodded at his wife. 'Your mother had to go away during the 'pregnancy' to make it look right.

'Who's this Kris?' she said.

'Kristofer Njevjedovski. He was—well he was a contact of mine. In Russia. Not Russian you understand, but Polish.'

A thought occurred to her for the first time. It seemed ludicrous. She could barely conceal the incredulity in her voice when she said: 'So were you some kind of spy?'

Her father coughed again. Just office work, he seemed about to say. He laughed, but it had a hollow ring. 'Not really a spy. Not really. But I was involved in the *intelligence* business.'

In spite of everything it was hard to believe that her father had been some kind of James Bond. And that she was a Russian girl smuggled at night across some ragged border post. But there was more to it than that. Much more.

'And this..Kris you called him? Is he still alive?'

'He's alive,' said her father. 'So far as I know.'

'Where can I find him?'

'It won't do you any good,' he said.

Chapter Ten

SOKOLOV LEFT THE metro at Tverskaya because he wanted to kill time before his meeting. Crossing under the road, stepping around puddles of muddy water, he passed the usual morose and restless lines outside cut-price kiosks selling anything from cabbages to vodka.

On the way to the Kremlin he ducked into Gazetny Lane where he paid a ridiculous sum for two large vodkas in a tourist café. The bar was empty but the barman ignored him until he slapped the counter with his hand.

'Are you serving, or not?'

‘What’s the hurry?’

‘I just don’t want to die here waiting for a drink.’

The barman said something under his breath and pulled him a grudging shot. He wore a green apron like a waiter in a French Bistro and was bald and surly.

As he delivered each shot, Sokolov threw back the vodka in a single gulp. The vodka failed to enervate him as he’d hoped it would. A summons to the Kremlin was not a common occurrence for him, and he thanked the stars for that. He caught the barman’s stare.

‘Another?’

‘Now it seems you’re in a rush to serve me.’ He pushed the glass across for a refill. ‘This place is empty.’

‘So what if it is? It’s Tuesday.’

’What days does it get busy?’

‘It’s usually like this. Until the tourist season.’

‘When’s the tourist season?’

‘How do I know? I’ve only been here a couple of months.’

He drank his final vodka, unable to put off his meeting any longer.

'Comrade.' He said to the barman with a dark nod, and he turned to leave. The barman returned his nod and watched him go in silence.

The Prime Minister of the Russian Federation, Viktor Chernomyrdin was not alone. A sharp-suited man with slick black hair was sitting at his side, behind a long table. Sokolov noticed that this man's eyes were the same shade of blue as his shirt. He was sure he had seen him somewhere before. A log shifted in a fireplace behind them, spitting out a flurry of sparks.

Chernomyrdin acknowledged him. He was restive. His skin was the colour of parchment, and he didn't look as assured as he did on TV.

'Thank you for joining us, Nikolay Sergeyevich. You probably know already who I am, but to save you any embarrassment, my name is Alexander Ivanovich Lebed.' He had a bass undertone and a lugubrious, studied look. Now he came to think of it Sokolov had never seen Lebed out of uniform, which is why he hadn't recognised him at once. Lebed the hero who had, if his press was to be believed, single handedly brought the Chechen war to an end, only to see it fall into conflict again in recent months. Still Lebed had done what he could, and stepped to one side to watch other politicians scrabble over the mess that could easily be another Afghanistan. Lebed the leader. 'I hear your officers had some difficulties yesterday?'

Sokolov remained standing. 'It was nothing, sir.'

'What happened?'

'They were tailing Borilyenko. Then they were ambushed by the FSB. There were some bruised egos, that's all.'

'Colonel Lisakov?'

'I saw him earlier. He was apologetic.'

'He's a tricky one. Careful of him.' He turned to Chermonyrdin as if to bring him into the conversation. 'The Prime Minister thought the important nature of your assignment should be made clear to you. He thought it appropriate to see to this personally.' Lebed looked at Chernomyrdin, seeking affirmation, but the Prime Minister looked disinterested. He cleared his throat as if he felt that something was expected of him, and said:

'Listen to what the General has to say.'

Sokolov had a sneaking respect for the Prime Minister. An old communist who had worked hard and seemed so much less burdened after the old regime had fallen away that he spoke out, sometimes unfortunately, leading to a reputation for malapropisms, many of which turned out to be succinct. In 1993 after a disastrous intervention by the Russian Central Bank he had explained in a speech: 'We wanted the best, but it turned out like always.' It was the best-known assessment of Russian Economic Policy and the phrase had become legendary.

Lebed leaned across the desk and offered a soldier's clenched handshake, then gestured towards a cracked leather armchair with bowed cushions. 'Please.'

Sokolov sat down. He could feel the hot breath of the fire. Chermonyrdin spoke again:

'There are people that would love to see Russia return to Communism. People with vested interests. They behave like puppet masters. Some of those people are behind the Feliks Group. Destroying the Feliks Group will help to throw our backward direction into reverse.' Said the Prime Minister.

'What the Prime Minister means…'

'Yes, I get it, sir. But why are they such a threat? Who are they?'

Chernomyrdin was looking out of the window, and Lebed answered. 'Some people think it's a mythical organisation. But it's not that. And it's not a harmless bunch of well-meaning patriots as the occasional press releases would suggest. They kill people. Believe me when I tell you that Feliks is a real threat to Perestroika. To any surviving chance of a Democratic government in Russia. A retrograde movement, made up of renegades and terrorists, mostly from the old KGB. We know this for a fact.' He patted the desk with his palm, stood up and walked to the window, where he looked down on Red Square. 'We're certain that Borilyenko is responsible. Which presents us with a dilemma. ' He turned around and looked at Sokolov. 'You see, without proof we can't do anything. Our President and the General have history. Yeltsin won't hear anything against his chief of security. His bodyguard. I know, because once I was favoured in the same way, until I tainted myself by aligning with the political opposition. So we must have proof—your proof, I should say.

There was a silence. Chernomyrdin was peering at him, forming an assessment, he thought. Sokolov wondered if it was favourable.

'I founded the political party 'Our Home - Russia' to be sure to capitalise on the advances we've made since Communism. It's an attempt to promote the principles of freedom, property, legality. Legality above all. It's not an exaggeration to say that these principles are at risk. Our tragedy in Russia is that whatever organisation we try to create, it ends up looking like the Communist party. My party of course is supportive of the President and his reforms. We need to discourage elements that seek to undermine him. Only then can we build the framework for democracy to hang itself on.'

He saw Lebed smile to himself at Chemonyrdin's turn of phrase.

'I'm not political, sir.'

'Good. Russia needs the apolitical.'

Lebed said: 'You must be asking yourself why you've been chosen for such an important assignment. Why you?'

'Something like that. I'm not a policeman, and I'm not FSB either.'

'Hah!' Lebed pointed a finger as though this was what he expected to hear. 'Then of course you must wonder. I know all about you, Nikolay Sergeyevich. I've read your file. Your time in London. Washington. An impeccable record. Successes. What's attractive to the Prime Minister and me is that you don't have the wrong kind of allegiances. With the old comrades I mean. Or with the Silioviki. The hard men. We think that you…' He tapped his temple with a finger. '..you're a free thinker, Nikolay Sergeyevich. Not easily fooled. We need men like you in the new Russia. In influential places, if you see where I'm going.

'It's going to be dangerous for you. You recognise this already. Of course, there are powerful men involved. But it won't be without reward when you are successful. It goes without saying your investigation must be conducted in the utmost secrecy. No more clashes with the FSB – and absolutely nobody must be aware that either of us is in any way connected with this enterprise. The stakes are higher than you can possibly imagine. But you're on the winning side. The right side. Trust me, Nikolay Sergeyevich, and you will be rewarded for your loyalty.'

Chapter Eleven

A SHABBY TERRACED house in SW19 with un-curtained windows, inky black like dark pools and impenetrable. The door was rugged and lined with furrows that may have been made by a dog's claws, and there was no sign of a bell or a door-knocker. When she pushed the flap of the letterbox twice to announce herself a stale smell seemed to seep into the cold air. She waited some moments before she tried again, but there was no sound from within. The front path was bordered by a low and shambling white brick wall. Some of the bricks had crumbled away. She hopped over the wall and peered through the window. A sturdy worn couch and an armchair. An electric fire in an iron grate with two bars glowing. And a half-imagined shadow at the door. She stepped back over the wall and gave the letterbox another prod.

The door opened and she was confronted with a tall and gaunt old man who reeked of iron-filings. His eyes were unnerving, glancing around as though they were independent of each other. She took a step backwards.

'So. You.' He said in a sombre tone. 'I knew you would come.' He had a strong Slavic burr. He screwed up his eyes to look at her, then threw a fleeting, haunted glance at the road. 'Come in. Come in.'

Inside the stale smell was stronger. He seemed to sense her distaste. 'I not leave the house so much anymore. No reason. I buy food sometimes. Newspapers.' He shrugged and showed her into the room she had seen through the window. One eye seemed to keep watch on the street, while the other appraised her. 'You look how I thought.' He said after a moment.

'What do you mean?'

‘*Nothing*. Nothing. I don’t mean nothing.’ He waved a hand, then settled himself in the armchair and folded his hands together as though preparing himself for some kind of tedious entertainment. The threadbare carpet was strewn with old newspapers and a plate with the remnants of some meal or other. There was a saucer of salt in the middle of a coffee table. She thought she had read – or dreamed - that it was a Russian custom to keep salt for guests. The light struggled to penetrate the room, despite the un-curtained windows. Perched on a sideboard was a tarnished, vase like object that she thought for an instant that she recognised. She felt a little afraid of this old man who looked at her with hunger and clasped his bony hands together as though in desperate prayer. ‘Understand first: I have nothing for you. No comfort. Nothing to offer you,’ he said in his cracked voice. ‘I can't speak about these matters. I am pledged to secrecy. You must know such before you begin.’ He seemed to lose his composure for a moment and when she followed his gaze she saw the photograph and jolted. Unmistakably her. She reached across and in a single movement plucked the fussy bronze frame from the mantelpiece.

'Where did you get this?'

It was a monochrome print. The clothes were unfamiliar – they had never featured in her wardrobe, and she was standing on a bridge she didn't recognise – but there was no doubt it was her. Looking at the print she had the strangest sensation - she imagined she could smell chocolate. The old man grunted.

'Your mother gave she to me. For memories.'

She scrutinised the picture again with a frown. It was an old photograph. The face in the picture was her. But it couldn't be.

'She looks so...' she trailed off. 'And you keep it on your mantelpiece? It looks like me.'

He shrugged.

'But it can't be me. So, who? My mother? Is that who this is? Where was it taken?'

'On a bridge. You can see this.'

She could see that it was pointless to pursue this line of questioning. She replaced the photograph. 'Tell me about Ekaterina.' She demanded. He averted his eyes for the first time, darting towards the window.

'I don't know nothing about Ekaterina.'

'Then tell me about my mother and father.'

'They don't alive. That's all I know.'

'They were from Russia?'

'You are from Russia. From Russia with love,' his throaty laugh at this attempts at humour mutated into a coughing fit. She waited for it to subside.

'And you brought me here?'

'I brought you to border. From there it was your father taking you.'

'You mean Bob?'

'Robert,' he said.

'So, what happened? What happened to my real parents?'

The old man shrugged again. He rose then with a hoarse cough and peered out of the window into the empty street. 'I cross border same time as you. I don't go back. I can't go back to this place.'

'I need to know about Ekaterina.'

He was still at the window. He looked uneasy. 'I told you. I not know her.'

She felt light-headed. Empty. She hoped she wasn't

about to cry. 'Please… there are things I just can't explain. Things I need to know. I have these.. *memories*. I don't know who I am. You have to help me.' She entreated.

He shook his head without looking at her.

Then: 'I met a man who mistook me for someone else. This.. Ekaterina.'

He threw her a sharp, attentive look. 'Who?' Both his eyes were pinned on her.

'He works at the Russian embassy.'

'Russian?'

'Yes.'

He abandoned his vigil at the window and stood over her – reached out to her with his bony hands. 'Leave it alone. There are devils in the past. Sometimes maybe better not to know. Don't speak with this man. Don't speak with *nobody* about what is in past. Past is dead. Keep inside like you did before. I speak like your protector. I help you before, long time ago. Now I protect you again.'

She had a vision of the old lady in her sweeping skirts. *Keep away.* 'But I have dreams…' She began again.

'We all have those.' He said as though from a very long way away. For the first time she experienced a stir of recognition. Something welled up inside her, and she almost shouted in desperation: 'Russian! I speak Russian. How is it possible? If what you say is true, I was just a baby when I left Russia. And I know things too. I know ... places.'

For a brief moment he seemed to lose his composure. 'I never thought would work such like this—' But he swallowed his words. 'What things? What things you know?'

'Things like—' but her second set of memories had abandoned her altogether, leaving her beached and incoherent, and she floundered. 'Just memories. Memories of things that haven't happened. Not to me. Not to anyone I know. Or maybe they only happened in dreams. I can't explain the way they feel. As real as yesterday's memories.'

The old man looked about him, then pursed his lips and sank back into his armchair, staring in his odd, disorientated. She realised that the interview was over.

'Leave me alone. I cannot speak about such things. It does not help.I am glad to see you safe and well.'

'You *must* help me.'

But the old man had retreated into a sullen silence in his chair in the half-light, and seemed to be about to fall asleep.

She was at the door when she flung a final glance at the picture above the grate. She had an unsettling impulse. 'Do I have a sister?'

There was no answer. He had closed his eyes, as if to shut her out. His head was nodding.

Chapter Twelve

NIKOLAY WAS ROUSED from a fitful sleep by the sound of the telephone. He sprang out of bed and through the bedroom door in his shorts to rescue the phone on its dying ring from the plastic veneer coffee table by the TV.

'Sokolov,' he answered.

'Did I wake you?'

Nikolay looked at his watch. It was after six in the morning. He was nursing a hangover that had only just begun to assert itself. A vodka bottle lay on the carpet. 'Who is it?'

'It's Lebed. Get dressed.'

Nikolay was already shrugging on a creased white shirt. 'Sir? What's going on?'

'There's been an execution.'

Nikolay paused. 'What do you mean an execution?'

'A Director of the Uvyerenny Bank. Viktor Bukovsky.'

Nikolay was perplexed. His forehead was tight. A litre all alone in his bare apartment last night. He caught sight of himself in the mirror. His eyes looked sore. 'I don't understand…' Was all he could manage, his eyes flitting around the room as though seeking inspiration.

'Do you have a pen?'

Nikolay scrabbled in a drawer for a biro and wrote down the address in Old Arbat that Lebed dictated.

'Respectfully, what does this have to do with me? Like I said before, I'm not a policeman.'

'Just go there.' Said Lebed with a warning note. 'Ask some questions. Make a nuisance of yourself. Make it known that you have an interest.'

'And do I?'

'If we say you do, then you do.' Lebed rang off.

The house in Old Arbat was crumbling but still grand and the grey dawn lent it a monochrome hue. Nikolay parked his car behind a police car with a relentless flashing light at the other side of the empty street. A policeman slouched in the doorway of the house and tapes cordoned off the gate. An ambulance waited at the kerb with its doors spilling open, its exhaust pumping thick white clouds into the air. Nikolay was surprised to see Lisakov presiding at a distance. When he saw him Lisakov beckoned with a cheerful expression.

'What a surprise, Major. That our esteemed Foreign Service should trouble itself with miserable domestic business like this!'

Nikolay joined Lisakov at the side of his parked official Volga. 'Good morning, Colonel.'

Lisakov smiled, but his gaze didn't stray from the house. They were bringing a body out now, swathed in a soiled sheet that flapped in the wind. Two paramedics man-handled the stretcher down the steps with bad grace. Nikolay said: 'Is that Bukovsky?'

'Him or one of his bodyguards.'

'Bodyguards?'

Lisakov threw him an odd glance. 'Bukovsky was mafia. Even if he wasn't he would have needed a 'krysha' himself. A roof. Protection. He was vulnerable.'

The paramedics had deposited the corpse in the ambulance and were returning to the house without urgency, presumably for the next victim. Nikolay cleared his throat and attempted to sound like a policeman. He didn't think he was very convincing. 'What do you think was the motive?' It sounded trite. Like he was playing a TV cop.

Lisakov laughed. 'The usual one.' He put a gentle

hand on Nikolay's shoulder. 'And what is your interest in Bukovsky exactly? You think perhaps he may have been a Western spy?' His eyes opened wide with playful intrigue. Nikolay found it difficult to answer, even to himself. 'Or is it,' Lisakov continued in a casual tone, 'is it his patronage?'

Nikolay froze. 'I don't know what you mean.'

Lisakov shrugged and removed his hand. 'It's no secret that Bukovsky was a friend of our Prime Minister.'

Nikolay attempted to change the subject. He felt miserable, and he had no idea what he was doing here. He huddled inside his overcoat and shivered. 'What happened?'

Lisakov seemed to evaluate him for some moments, as though trying to resolve a puzzle. Then he sighed, and replied in a detached voice: 'They sprayed the front facing rooms with automatic fire while two of them broke down the door. Then they worked their way through the house room by room. Household. Bodyguards. They're all in there..' He nodded at the house as the paramedics emerged with another corpse, as if on cue.

Nikolay waved a hand at Lisakov as though he had seen enough. There was nothing for him to do here anyway. What had Lebed been thinking of?

As he walked back to the car, he passed a construction site, with a semblance of building work – a few upright girders holding up a concrete platform that would have no doubt become a ceiling had the builders not run out of money. It was clear that this site had been abandoned for some time. He noticed that a small fire was burning, and he stopped. A man was hunched over the fire.

'Hey!'

The man hauled himself to his feet and lumbered across the rubble. He looked a big man, but he was wearing so many layers of clothes that it was hard to tell. His face was lined and cracked and he wore a shabby fur hat. He could have been seventy, Nikolay supposed, but equally he could have been thirty. A medal was pinned to his shabby coat. Ordinarily Nikolay wouldn't have given it a second glance. There were plenty of vets on the streets these days. 'Where did you get that?'

The man looked down and seemed to notice the medal for the first time. 'Afghanistan.' He replied in a challenging tone.

'What does a man have to do to win a Medal of Honour?'

'Not much,' he said. 'Lose his dignity. Be a Russian.'

Nikolay noticed that the man's left sleeve flapped empty at his side. There was a moment's silence. The man looked hard at the ground, the way people used to in the Soviet era when they were confronted with authority. 'Did you see what happened over there?'

'I saw nothing. I heard nothing.'

'I'm not the police.'

The man raised his head at last and assessed him. 'You dress like a Westerner. Are you a newspaperman?'

Nikolay shook his head.

'A Chekist then.' The man concluded. In some quarters the old term for the secret police had never died. The numerous official manifestations - Vecheka,

OGPU, NKVD, KGB, FSB, SVR, FSO - all of these were encompassed neatly in the old word, 'Cheka'. ‘I saw you talking to him..’ He nodded his head in the direction of the house.

‘He asked me some questions.’ Nikolay fumbled in his pocket and pulled out the only note he could find, crumpled into a ball. When the man smoothed out the 20 rouble note he cursed himself, and the man seemed about to return it but Nikolay waved it away.

‘What do you want?’

‘I just want to know what happened. And he’s not going to tell me that.’

‘For the record, or for something else?’ said the man. Then he drew a deep breath, and thrust the note into his pocket. ‘I saw the Spetsnaz storm that house.’

Lisakov had a sudden feeling of foreboding. Special forces. ‘What makes you think they were Spetznaz?’

‘I’ve seen them often enough.’ He said. ‘Take it from me, whoever lived in that house must have upset someone special.’

‘But what makes you think they were Spetsnaz?’ He persisted.

The man cackled. ‘I’m an old soldier, see? They had AK47’s for instance. Not the usual kind. Short stocks and barrels. The kind they give to Special Forces. If you were Mafia you would maybe use something more.. *modern*. Like an uzi.’ He snorted. ‘Also they left in an unmarked van. It was a Chekist van. I would swear.’

‘Nothing else?’

‘Only that they made a clean sweep of the place. Nobody survived in there, you can be sure. They did their job.’

‘Thanks.’

The man grinned, exposing gaps in his teeth. ‘Good luck, Comrade,’ he said, with irony.

Chapter Thirteen

OLD NED SAT in silence for a long time after Kate had left. *Old Ned.* He had learnt to become accustomed to that name. It was the way in this hated country that people hadn't the patience to grapple with foreign names. When he had worked in the factory, turning lathes it had been 'Ned the Pole'. Now, in the fag end of his days, it was just '*Old Ned.*' That was when anybody referred to him at all, which was not often.

He nursed her photograph almost without noticing. The girl had turned out just the way he always imagined, of course. How could it be otherwise? If they could see her now in Moscow … if they knew...

The thought of Moscow seemed to crystallise something, and he sat bolt upright, listening. He could hear the scraping of the second hand of the wall clock from the kitchen. The buzz and vibration of the refrigerator. Now and then a car swept past the window. He settled back into his thoughts.

A single act of heroism illuminated a bleak past. It was true he sometimes yearned to return to Russia. Ironic that when he came to England he had exchanged the white coat of a medical researcher for the almost identical white overall of a factory worker. Every day he dissected the newspapers for news of home. He was a Pole by birth, but his spiritual home was Russia. He had read about the new climate of democracy. Perhaps it wasn't out of the question for him to return? But what would he do there? His scientific knowledge was crusted with time. On the one hand he knew too little. And then, on the other hand he knew too much. He knew too much...

The bang of his front gate made him start and he hurried to the window. One of the men caught his eye at once as he advanced down the path. They looked like policemen, he thought. The man that caught his eye was ruggedly built beneath a light raincoat, with the drawn expression of a late-night card player, his hair raked back in greasy furrows from his forehead. His coat tails flapped in the breeze. The other man was smaller and darker, with sharply defined features that gave an impression of an inquisitive bird.

One of the men hammered on the door. Old Ned paused in the hallway, half inclined not to answer, but the hammering continued without respite. He felt a tightening in his chest as he reached to release the catch, and it was only then, too late, that he thought he heard a curse in Russian. '*Pizdec'*

The door was rent aside, and the men burst inside. One grabbed him by the wrist in an iron grip. The other just barged straight past.

'What did she want?' The big one demanded over his shoulder in a bad accent. 'Where did she go? You better tell us, old man.'

'Who are you?' But he was certain he knew, as he was hauled down the passage by his forearm like a rag doll.

'It's enough we know who *you* are.' said the other man in Russian. 'You are the dissident Njevjedovski.' The big one was in the living room, hurling Kristov's few possessions at the walls after a cursory examination of each. 'We are your worst nightmare, old man. Tell us what we want to know and we might let you live.' His eyes lighted on the photograph and he snatched it from him and flashed it at his colleague. 'This her?'

The other man strained over the picture with his eagle eyes, gripping Old Ned's arm. 'Looks like.'

Then the big one squared up to Kristov with a wide gait. 'What did she want?' he demanded again, this time in Russian.

Old Ned had a vision of the KGB Border Guards that night long ago. He remembered the pale light on the snow. He remembered the shabby cardboard suitcase that felt so fragile in his grasp. He remembered all of this, and he thought it was worth it. He clenched his jaw.

The crash of the fist on his jaw wasn't so painful as

he had been expecting. He didn't attempt to resist. Where would be the point? He just folded on the floor and made a silent prayer. A Russian prayer. He felt himself being dragged to his feet, but he made himself a heavy load, and his legs flapped beneath him so that they let him drop back to the ground. His cheek rested against the threadbare carpet, and he inhaled the acrid dust of his long-time squalor with a perverse satisfaction. Far above him the ritual played itself out, but already he was oblivious to their questions, which they asked repeatedly in the mother tongue. Perversely it was almost a joy to hear Russian again to this old Pole. And in-between each question they kicked him, and the strange thing was, that even as the kicks became more frenzied, they seemed to lose their edge. There was just some all-consuming ache that was like a tiredness in his bones. He remained there curled on the floor and awaited the inevitable onset of unconsciousness. He didn't feel nauseous at this stage. In fact, he was surprised to feel almost exhilarated. Once, he tried to peer up at them, through a single swollen eyelid, but it wasn't worth the effort. There was just some haze of movement and the sounds seemed to get louder, so he closed his eye and allowed himself to drift away.

Late last night she had endured Robert's ritual pleading in a vodka trance, lying on her small pink bed with the phone clamped to her cheek, not really listening, contemplating the ceiling that was smudged in the corners with the effects of the vodka. It was like that now, except that the smudged ceiling had more to do with the welling of tears than alcohol. Her bed was pink because it was intended to remind her of her childhood, but it didn't succeed; small because she didn't intend to share it with anyone. Not anymore. Not for a long time. She couldn't imagine a time when she would sacrifice this solitude. For anyone.

Robert wanted her to come home. What he called home. He wanted them to try again. He was willing to try, why wasn't she? It frustrated her that she couldn't make him understand why it was impossible – she barely knew herself - so his argument exhausted itself as it usually did. 'For Becki' he would plead. 'For our daughter.' She wondered if he was drunk. The irony of being drunk together at either end of the phone made her bite her lip. Robert had emitted a strained note then that ought to have wrung some sympathy from her if she had any to spare. Then he had hung up - or maybe she did, she couldn't recall - but she had kept the receiver against her ear, listening to the tone, followed by the recorded voice instructing her to hang up. She had felt tearful then, like today.

It was the anniversary of something today, although she struggled to remember what. There were anniversaries that she celebrated in the quiet of her mind, not with champagne and streamers but with the instinctive acknowledgement that one day or other was significant for some reason. Today had once been a cause for celebration, she knew. It was 12 September. She frowned and swung the vodka bottle to her lips, but it didn't stir her memory, just dimmed this sensation of special-ness.

Vodka was a habit she had acquired almost without noticing. Perhaps it had started at drama school. It seemed like she had always drunk vodka - neat with no ice. She had taken to keeping the bottle in the freezer. Even so, it never seemed cold enough.

She ought to love Robert. She supposed she once had, although it was difficult to imagine when. He had done his best to make her happy, but in a way it was the wrong kind of happiness. It was to settle for something. She couldn't ever explain that to him - she wouldn't have known where to start. To shore up their crumbling relationship he pressured her into having a child. She tried to believe that she loved Becki, but it seemed to her that even there something was lacking. It was as though she had once known a deeper, more profound love that surpassed everything, and reduced anything less to something trivial.

Her thoughts were erratic. She thought of her visit to the old man's house – except that when she tried to remember the face of the old man it had shed its lines and hollows and it was a much younger man that she remembered: Kris. She felt an odd warmth towards him, like he was someone she had known all her life.

How did it change things now that she knew that she was a Russian orphan, and that Kris had risked his life to smuggle her across the border? What strange passion had driven him to do that, she wondered? She screwed up her eyes, like she was trying to focus on something. A number assembled itself in her head in a rhythmic two-digit sequence. Some impulse made her sit bolt upright and she dialled International directory enquiries for the dialling code for Russia. With a tremulous hand she tapped out the number that by now had crystallised and become urgent and unforgettable.

When she found the number was dead it was with a mixture of relief and disappointment. Who had she hoped would answer?

And then it was as though some inner membrane snapped. Faces and voices filled her mind – people she had not had the time to meet – each accompanied by a rush of associations. Murmured confidences over dinner. A shared litre of vodka. Street names. Relationships. Lives that were filled with trivia and pathos. She clutched at her temples as if to stem the tide. And then one overriding memory seemed to break free and shatter everything. The tarnished object that her eyes had lighted upon amidst the clutter of the old man's house came back to her, and she realised that it was almost identical to the one in her dreams. It used to be commonplace in Russian homes. It was a simple tea urn. A samovar.

She didn't have time to absorb this—didn't recognise the significance—before she remembered that it was time for her to leave. But how could she leave, now that her dreams were beginning to melt into her real life? She glanced at the clock with its teddy bear face. Midday. She needed to be at the club.

It was Kate's turn to dance the graveyard shift—the afternoon shift—but nobody was dancing because of the old man. Nobody was dancing EXCEPT the old man. He was a minor sensation. The girls and the punters gathered in knots to watch him. He wore a cheap grey suit that had gone baggy at the knees and elbows, and no tie, and his shoes were worn to paper soles. Just outside the door to the club he writhed and kicked in a striptease parody that the girls giggled over. His face was toothless and mischievous, and he jutted his pointed chin out as he danced, grabbing his crotch and rubbing at his concave chest in all the right places to the music that blared out onto the streets.

Vanessa nudged Kate as they stood and watched. 'Could be you in a few years.' Kate thought the old guy must be fit to keep going this long.

Gold had been observing from the pool table with a listless grin, but it had gone on for too long already. As he shambled to the door the girls and punters parted for him and booing went up. He grinned. 'Yeah all right all right. Maybe I'm just gonna book 'im. As an act.' He waved them away and strode out on the pavement towards the old man, who, when he saw Gold coming, stopped dancing and took a few paces backwards. Gold was too quick for him - with a swift movement he had gathered the old man up under his chunky arm. Kate strained to see what was happening over the shoulders of a balding punter in a brown suit who scarcely seemed to notice her bare flesh. She saw Gold laughing with his head thrown back, and patting the man's narrow shoulders with his big paw. She saw him press a note into his eager hands, although she didn't see the colour. Then the old man scuttled down the street shouting something in his mad language and sawing his arms in the air like a windmill, and Gold returned to a minor ripple of applause. His face was a row of white teeth. He nodded at Kate, raised a quieting hand. 'It's you, innit? You got an impersonator.' and he swung himself up to the music deck, murmuring into the microphone with a voice that was holding down a gurgle.

'How much did you give him?' she whispered as she tripped onto stage with her painted punters' smile.

'Something and nothing,' said Gold, still grinning.

'Maybe I should take up pavement dancing.'

He covered the mike with his hand. 'You'd get raped, you would.' And he giggled. Which was meant to be a compliment.

When Kate finished her shift at six 'o' clock she gossiped in the changing room with the other girls for a while, slipping out of her gossamer threads and pulling on her jeans. She felt sticky and dusty at the same time, and she was sure that the occasional hint of body odour that she caught was her own. She wouldn't shower here though - not since one of the punters had rampaged through the changing rooms. It didn't feel safe. Not that she ever felt safe anymore. Paranoia was a moment away. *The samovar... what was that all about?*

Outside a fine drizzle fell and the passing cars used dipped headlights. She started to set off in the direction of the tube station with her head down and the muffled music of the club just behind her. A car drew up to the kerbside. As paranoid as she was, she looked up in time to see two men emerging with their eyes on her. One of the men seemed to flap like a vulture in his long coat as he came around the car, trailing a hand on the bonnet. He had a hooded expression and a barrel chest. His hair was as glossy and grey as the wet pavements. She took a step backwards. The other man was closer. He was dark and tightly packaged with lean features and a nose like a beak. Without a word he grabbed for her but just brushed her arm as she drew away. Her heart leapt. She cast around her, still retreating but not daring to turn her back on the men. Images flashed in her mind like she was channel hopping on TV.

'We just want to talk,' said the smaller man in a thick

accent, pinning her with his beady eyes and reaching out again for her arm. She backed away. The vulture flapped behind him. 'There's nothing to worry about.' But she could tell there was everything to worry about. The car still murmured at the side of the road, its headlamps painting a pool of yellow on the tarmac, wipers juddering across the glass. The driver's door and the kerbside back door hung open. She wrote tomorrow's headlines in her head. *Stripper abducted.* A hand seized her wrist and her stomach churned.

A voice yelled out behind her 'What's happening? Everything alright, Kate?'

She struggled to turn around and there was Gold. He was standing with his legs apart like a gunfighter. Her wrist hurt. There was a lump of a cash bag hanging from one of Gold's arms. 'Help.' She choked. The vulture lingered a few metres away, watching and waiting.

Gold closed the distance between them in a breath. Her captor tugged her arm. Gold swung high in the air and the cash bag smashed into the side of the man's face with a chink. He let go of her wrist at once and made a sound like air coming out of a balloon, then staggered with his head buried in his hands and Gold took a handful of him and threw him like a mannequin into the gutter where he collapsed in a heap. Weighing the cash bag in his arm Gold was already advancing towards the vulture, who took a faltering step towards the car. Then the vulture seemed to change his mind, and squared up to Gold. He was reaching inside his coat.

The blast, when it came was like the noise of a traffic collision. Gold met the impact with a grin and then a grimace, then heaved himself to the left with his arms flailing as though he was about to perform a cartwheel. Then he dropped in a lumpy pile on the pavement and didn't move. The cash bag landed with a metallic thump beside him.

Even the traffic seemed to fall silent. Kate was transfixed. The vulture looked at her once, as though trying to fix her location in his mind. The gun had disappeared into his coat. Then he tugged his friend to his feet and bundled him into the rear of the waiting car. He leered at her before he folded himself into the driver's seat.

'Dos vidanje.' The door slammed and the blue Volvo sped away with its tyres scrabbling and spray in its wake.

She hadn't noticed before that people had begun to congregate on the pavement. A murmur struck up. A man had crouched at Gold's side with a grey, anxious look. A thick black puddle had accumulated around the wreck of Gold's body. Somebody tried to put a comforting arm around her shoulder but she shrugged it off. Without thinking she hefted the cash bag out of the road, looked fleeting around her, and then ran from the scene as fast as she could, the rain wet and cold against her forehead ... a commotion behind her suggested that she was being chased, but when she looked back all she could see was a huddle of people gathered in the pale light that seeped from the club.

Chapter Fourteen

"IN A LITTLE over a week, two bankers have been killed in Moscow, including one who was the president of one of the largest banks in Russia. A wave of terror is picking up force. Obviously, this is a crime wave. The Feliks Group has evidence that shows that the criminal world is no longer satisfied with its take from legitimate businesses but wants to control them outright. The murder of Uvyerenny Bank president, Viktor Bukovsky, was clearly intended to send a message to all businessmen that the mafia will stop at nothing to take over. Unfortunately, we believe that

law enforcement agencies are implicated as well. Their inaction and involvement with the criminal world have created a situation where criminals can kill with the knowledge that they'll never be caught. In 1991, every example of corruption was a media sensation. Now, there is so much that no one even comments on it. Cases are announced but never brought to trial. Senior officials steal and go unpunished. And in this sense, Yeltsin himself must share some of the guilt for the murder of Viktor Bukovsky. Immediate and effective responses to crimes are needed but nowhere to be found. Instead, Yeltsin has appointed a crony rather than a specialist to head the FSB and names a similar man as minister of the interior. We can't expect any changes until there have been elections for the parliament and the president. We demand action. Ivan Ivanov."

Nikolay read the new 'intelligence report' from the Feliks Group in Izvestia, which was accompanied by a lurid photograph of the aftermath of the killing in Arbat. Who stood to gain from this? He wondered.

It was early in the morning. Layers of fine dust

particles danced in the morning sunlight that peered through grimy sash windows. The office had the impression of an evacuation. Desks piled high with case files were silent and abandoned. Telephones went unanswered. Nikolay perched on the edge of an unoccupied desk with a cup of foul liquid masquerading as coffee. A few solitary insomniacs were bowed over their desks in silence.

Could it be, he wondered, that there was a connection between General Borilyenko and the Feliks Group? And were these murders perpetrated by the Feliks Group as some kind of perverse publicity stunt? And why had Lebed instructed him to be on the scene?

Chapter Fifteen

ROBERT WAS CHOOSING a sandwich for lunch without much appetite when his mobile phone rang. He flipped open the Motorola, tugged out the antenna and pressed it to his ear. A woman standing next to him made a disapproving expression and reached across for a cellophane wrapped green salad.

'Robert? Where are you?' said Sally. In an effort to get a better signal he swapped the phone to his other hand, then stepped outside the shop. He stood with his back to a window display of pastries. Across the road was a temporary traffic light. Cars lined up at a red light with idling motors and the boom of muffled radios. One played 'Don't look Back in Anger'. He raised his voice above the traffic:

'Down the road. Grabbing a sandwich. What's up?'

'Are you coming back?'

'Of course. Why?' He waited. The line hissed. The traffic lights changed. A boy in a hot hatchback gunned his engine.

'The police are here.'

'Police? What do they want?'

'They want to talk to you.'

'Did they say what about?' He turned to the window as though to shield the call from any onlookers.

'They didn't say. Well... They don't, do they?' She sounded doubtful. 'But they say there's nothing to worry about.'

'Nothing to worry about? They would say that wouldn't they? Even if there was.' He was now hurrying back towards his office. 'I hope it's nothing to do with Becki,' his first thought. But she was at school. 'I'll be there in five minutes. Tell them five minutes, OK?' He lengthened his pace and ended the call, almost colliding with a woman loaded with shopping bags. 'Sorry.'

When he reached his small estate agency, he could see past the property boards in the window two men sitting in front of his empty desk. They turned as he pushed through the door, and when he looked at them they stood up, one hitching up his trousers.

'Mr Chambers?' Said the other, taking the lead and holding out a hand in anticipation.

'What is it? Not my daughter?'

They exchanged looks. 'No, no. Nothing like that. I don't think there's any need to worry,' said one, without much enthusiasm. 'Is there somewhere we could go?' glancing at Sally. Nobody else in the office.

'Sally, why don't you go to lunch,' said Robert, taking the hint. Sally unhooked her coat from the stand by the door, eager it seemed to be gone.

'You need to phone Mr Henderson about Portland Avenue.' She said, leaving in her wake the peachy aroma of cosmetics as the glass door shut out the road noises. Robert locked it, asking over his shoulder,

'So, are you going to tell me? What's it all about?'

The taller officer produced a warrant card and presented it to him. The other officer had resumed his seat, propping his arm over the back of his chair in an over-casual gesture that irritated Robert somehow. 'I'm detective constable Trent - and that's detective sergeant Morris,' nodding towards the seated man. 'We're here to talk to you about your wife.'

He looked from one to the other. 'Ex, actually. Ex-wife now, that is. What's wrong? What's happened to her?'

'Well, firstly we need to know her whereabouts. We wondered if you might know where she can be found?'

'Found? What's she done?'

Morris picked up the conversation, as though they had reached the crux of the matter. 'There was an incident yesterday in which she may be a key witness. We need to interview her as soon as possible.'

Robert narrowed his eyes. 'What kind of incident?'

'Do you know where she is, Mr Chambers?' he said with an edge.

'No. I don't. What kind of incident?'

'When was the last time you saw your *ex*-wife, Mr

Chambers?'

'It must be… I don't know. A few days ago. What day is it today?'

'Tuesday.'

'Then Thursday. Last week.' He said, trying to count the days but the arithmetic refusing to work. 'Please… she's still… I mean she's my daughter's mother. What's happened?'

'Close are you? You and your ex?'

'We have a daughter. So we try to keep... on good terms, if you like. We talk. We're friendly.'

'What is it...? An *exotic* dancer, is she? So we're told.'

Robert flushed. 'So what?'

'So… So, maybe some criminal types might be associated with the type of establishment she works in. What do you think?'

'I've really no idea.'

'Possible she got mixed up in something? Over her head?'

'Like what?'

Morris shrugged. 'You tell me. Know any of her

friends do you? Anywhere she could be staying? A *boyfriend*?' He added with a tone that Robert resented.

'What exactly happened?'

'That's a no then, is it?'

'Yes. A no. So, are you going to tell me what this is all about?

'A weapon was discharged, Mr Chambers. Somebody with whom we believe your wife to have been *familiar* was critically injured.' He paused to scrutinise Robert's reaction. 'Critically.' He repeated, making sure that Robert had registered its implication. Somebody dead.. But who? Somebody she knew… 'Need money does she? So far as you know?'

'Not more than usually.' He looked from one to the other but their faces were blank.

The constable started to speak but Morris interrupted. 'It was a serious incident, Mr Chambers. Involving loss of life. But we only want to talk to Mrs Chambers as a potential witness.' He stood up. 'At this stage.' He produced a card. 'If and when she gets in touch, please ask her to call us at once. And, let us know. If she does get in touch. It would be very helpful.'

The two policeman went to the door and waited while Robert unlocked it. Morris pointed to one of the properties listed in the window. 'Nice.' He said. A detached five bedroom in Rickmansworth.

'Interested?' Robert replied with what he hoped was irony, holding the door open wide.

'Not on a policeman's salary.' Morris touched his forehead in a mock salute. Trent nodded at Robert with a trace of sympathy. 'Be in touch then?' Said Morris, unlocking a Ford Mondeo parked right outside on a double yellow line.

Chapter Sixteen

THE BARMAN WATCHED her table with lascivious, sunken eyes. A bald, fat man in a stained business shirt open at the collar, he slouched at the corner of the bar challenging anyone to disturb him. There were few enough customers: a scrawny young couple in a corner whispered over their empty glasses, and touched hands. A man in a shiny suit was feeding money without much hope into a fruit machine. To get to this smoky bar in Kensington she had taken a circuitous route on the London Underground, changing trains and lines several times, without any real sense of purpose or direction. A strategy she'd read about in some spy novel to throw off a tail. She was going to go straight home from the club, but when she caught sight of a blue Volvo parked in her street, she had turned back at once to the tube station at a half run. Overnight at a drab bed and breakfast, where she had paid cash, and whiled away the morning just walking the streets. Now she lingered over a glass of tepid vodka, tracing circles on the tabletop with her finger.

She should call the police. Next to her glass on the table her mobile phone reproached her with its silence. She had a full signal in this place - there was no excuse. And how would she explain herself? Why had she run away? Who was she running from? What did the men want? She shuddered as she recalled the appraising look that the vulture-like one had given her just before he hauled his friend into the car. And the fleeting *'dos vidanye'* that confirmed her fears. This was all connected in some way with her inner life. Poor Gold. Poor, poor Gold. She steeled herself against the onset of tears. Out of the corner of her eye she caught the barman shifting, taking a n interest. She flipped back her hair, lifted her glass to her lips and swallowed the vodka straight down. The man at the fruit machine shot her a secret glance when her chair scraped back. The barman raised his eyebrows.

'Another please. A large vodka. Do you have any that's cold?'

'You want ice?'

'No, not really. It doesn't matter.'

The barman shrugged, hitched up his trousers, and pulled her a large vodka from the optic. She paid and took it back to her table near the door. If not the police, then what? She couldn't stay on the streets. But she couldn't return home either. She had to resolve this whole thing on her own. Whatever it was.

The mobile phone trilled and her stomach turned. She looked at the number in the display. *'Home'.* She pressed the red button to terminate the call. *'Home'* meant Robert. It was one of the things she kept meaning to change. Somehow too painful to do. Like the door key that she hadn't removed from her key ring. It didn't open anything now except old wounds, but she kept it there nonetheless. She waited for the familiar beep that told her that Robert had left a voice message, which he always did.

Gold was dead, she reminded herself. She kept reminding herself at odd intervals, because she felt she owed it to him to keep him alive, at least in her head. To repeat that one horrific fact. *Gold is dead.*

When the phone bleeped she stabbed the voicemail button with her thumb and clamped the phone to her ear.

'You have one new message.' The voice informed her. Then a faint hissing before she heard Robert's voice. 'Kate where the hell are you? The police have been round. What's going on? What kind of trouble are you in? Phone me as soon as you get this message.' There was a pause. Then in a more measured tone: 'Please, Kate. Whatever it is. Phone me. Maybe I can help. They wouldn't tell me anything. Just asked a lot of questions. Phone me.'

She tossed the phone onto the table with a rattle that made the scrawny couple in the corner look at her with a shared frown. She smiled at them and they turned away. Of course the police would want to talk to her.

She was a murder witness. She shivered and threw back the vodka. She could only hole up here for so long. With a sneaking realisation she thought the police may also want to talk to her about the takings from the club. She had the moneybag in her sport bag beside her. As she absorbed this, another thought occurred to her: Beside herself who else had seen Gold's attackers? And if the police didn't know about the two men, then who's to say that she hadn't shot Gold herself, to steal the money?

Some half-formulated idea made her pluck up her phone again and called up Manda's number from the memory. Everything pointed to Russia. Her 'false' memory. The man who thought he recognised her on the tube. Gold's killers. The samovar. Her newly reconstructed past. It seemed to ring for an age. Kate was on the point of giving up when there was a click.

A tired voice said: 'Hello.'

'Manda it's Kate.'

'Oh... hi Kate.'

Kate tried to detect anything unusual in her voice, but she sounded as disinterested as ever. 'Manda I'm in trouble.' She tried to keep her voice low. She felt that the whole bar was listening in.

'Why am I not surprised? You only ever call me when you're in trouble.'

'This time it's different. This time it's really bad.' Manda's silence implied a shrug. 'Manda I need you to do something for me.'

'What is it this time?'

'I need you to go to the flat.'

Across the road from the pub, outside the anonymous entrance to the Russian embassy, the visa queue snaked around the block.

Chapter Seventeen

'Amateurs. Fucking amateurs. This isn't the Wild West. What did you think you were doing?' Dmitry was shouting, spittle flying. He picked up a file from his desk and raised it as though to throw it, then seemed to think better of it and slapped it back on the desk in exasperation. 'What were you thinking of?"

'We were picking the girl up. Like you told us,' said Petrov. He sat with his legs open wide, slumped in the chair.

'And in the process you shot up the town like some Wild West cowboy and killed some guy.' He pointed two fingers across his desk at Petrov and made a gesture of a gun recoiling. 'Fucking John Wayne. In London!'

'Just some black guy. Look.... You weren't there. We had no choice. You should see Sasha's face. What he did. An animal. Bigger than a bear.'

'Our all-powerful KGB. You must be crazy.' He screwed a finger into his temple in demonstration. Then, 'What did you do with the gun?'

'It's safe. In the river.'

'And the car?'

'Well of course, the plates were fake, but I had someone take care of it. Don't worry.'

'Don't worry, he says after starting a fucking war with Great Britain. What am I going to tell Moscow?'

'I guess you'll tell them we fucked up. Sorry Dima. Sometimes it happens.' Petrov shrugged.

'Don't tell me "Sorry Dima we fucked up" or I'll fuck you up for sure.'

He had been putting off reporting this latest development to the General, but there was no choice. He picked up the phone. Looked at Petrov. 'Still here?'

Petrov stood up. 'I did what anyone would have done.'

'Anyone without a brain. Get out. You make me sick.'

The General answered the phone on the first ring. 'Borilyenko.'

'General, there was an incident.'

'I heard,' Said the General. 'You're speaking to me only now?'

'I wanted a full report. From the officer.'

'I already had a full report. From another source. It's not acceptable.'

'I'm sorry.' The receiver whined, and he wondered if it was tapped. More of a probability than a possibility. A question of *who* was listening, rather than if anybody was listening.

'Yes. Tell me something. When you met with our friend?'

'General?'

'Did she describe anything of her memories. Anything you can think of?'

'She mentioned Simbirsk that's all. Wanted to know

what it was.'

'You're sure she didn't mention anything else about… well about our *facilities*?'

'I'm sure.'

'And if she did, you would tell me? At once?'

'Of course, General.'

'Sooner I hope than in the case of this latest incident.'

'I'm sorry General...'

'Yes. It's noted. Tell me something else: when you left town, all those years ago. After you were *reassigned.* Did you have any further contact with, shall we say, former *residents*?'

'It was forbidden.'

'Well yes. It was. But you didn't answer my question.'

'Of course not General. I mean, I didn't have any contact.'

'Good. Keep me closely advised of developments.' The call ended with a click.

Dikul peeled off the list of names with undisguised

relish, with barely a glance at his notebook, and watched Nikolay's eyes widen involuntarily. It served him right. They were messing with the wrong people. Now he would see sense.

'But what were they doing there?'

Dikul indulged himself in a shrug. 'How the fuck should I know? That's who we saw. Right Andrei?' He turned to Chernov for assurance, but Chernov seemed to have discovered an unnatural interest in his fingernails. 'That's who we saw.' He repeated in a reproachful tone. He turned to his notebook and read aloud, 'At nine-forty-five Minister for Justice - Minister for Fucking Justice,' He bracketed unnecessarily, 'Yuri Chaika followed General Borilyenko and,' he paused archly, '*others*, into the building.' He looked up at Sokolov. 'The Minister for Justice,' he repeated again in wonder. The jangle of the phone startled him out of a kind of reverence. Nikolay snatched up the receiver in annoyance.

'Sokolov.'

Dikul counted the moments and traced the hairline cracks in the walls with his eyes trying to display disinterest.

'Good. I'll send someone over. Yes, yes,' Nikolay was saying, drumming his fingers in frustration, and his eyes darted about the room. Dikul secreted a smile. 'Me? No, I don't need to come. Why should I?' A pause. Sokolov frowned and looked directly at Dikul, but with unseeing eyes. 'For what reason? No, of course you don't. But do you know who? Well, I suppose I could find out.' Dikul flung Chernov a sly look, but Chernov was inscrutable. 'If you're sure. OK – then I'll be there.' Sokolov laid down the receiver thoughtfully.

'I have to go into town,' he said. 'To interview a foreigner.'

Chapter Eighteen

MANDA STEPPED INTO the apartment, thrust the keys into her jacket pocket and pushed the door closed behind her. She stood there for a few seconds absorbing the silence, listening for the slightest disturbance. When she was satisfied, she padded down the passage and put her head around the door of the bedroom. Everything orderly and tidy. A bedraggled teddy bear was perched on the white duvet, looking disconsolate. The curtains were half open and the grey sky weighed against the glass like a threat.

She passed into the sitting room and glanced

around. The vacant TV met her gaze from the corner. A stack of fashion magazines lapped over the edge of a coffee table. A pale blue cashmere cardigan lay over the back of the sofa, neatly folded. She knew it would be cashmere because that was Kate.

In the kitchen there was an empty coffee cup in the stainless-steel sink. The window looked out onto the dingy walkway. She knew where to look.

Under the sink, in a plastic bucket filled with a jumble of cleaning products was a folded brown A4 envelope. She felt around inside for the familiar shape of a passport and a thin wad of banknotes. She crammed the folded envelope into her handbag then as an afterthought reached up and opened and closed the cupboards one by one, purely out of curiosity. Nothing there to betray Kate. There was a general absence of personal items, personal touches. Except for the teddy bear. Manda had known Kate for years, but when she tried to call her to mind there was almost nothing she could recall about her at all. She had a daughter. A failed marriage. And now she was in trouble.

Chapter Nineteen

GRIGOR SAT ON his usual stool at the bar with a bottle of vodka and a meaty cigar, drifting in a narcotic trance. A few of the girls arrayed themselves along the bar, lithe and animated with smooth bare limbs, exchanging inanities and smiling at the guys. The guys puffed their chests and sucked on beer bottles, watching the show or trying to catch a girl's eye. The music was loud and the tracks were all the same to Grigor's ears.

A mercurial shape shifted in the spotlight, melting and twisting on the stage. Once he had found it sexually stimulating to watch the girls, but no longer. He had slept with many of them, and his curiosity had waned. He shrank from the sham of the false connection: he had nothing in common with these girls, just a prehistoric desire fulfilled, and then in the morning there came the usual void.

The lights pulsed, throwing shadows on the faces of the grim statues of past Soviet leaders that passed for macabre decoration, lending them expression. The barman picked up Grigor's empty bottle and raised an eyebrow.

'Another one, Boss?'

He nodded, and the barman slid a full bottle of Stolichnaya across the counter.

He didn't see the girl at first. A persistent presence at his side, waiting. When he looked at her she seemed to wipe away a tear, leaving a thin track in her make up. She wore too much make up for Grigor's taste. Lipstick the colour of blood. When she leaned towards him he recognised the perfume, sharp and enervating.

'Can I talk to you, please, Grigor?'

He guessed she was less than 20. She had an

alabaster look about her, fragile and pale. Her eyes were liquid, and she had a tiny scar on her chin that was becoming.

'Pull up a chair.'

'Not here,' she said, looking afraid. 'Privately.'

'What is it?'

'It's personal.'

'I don't do personal. The other girls must have told you that. You're new here?'

'Yes. A couple of weeks. But the girls said I could talk to you.'

'They said that?'

'Can I have a drink?'

'Help yourself.' He signalled to the barman who stopped serving a customer to get him another vodka glass. He filled it and she drank it in one. He watched the contraction of her throat and felt a sudden desire.

'They said you understood.'

'I'm surprised they'd say that.' And he was.

'My boyfriend was in Chechnya. In the army.' She had to raise her voice above the music, putting her mouth up against his ear. Her breath was hot and smelled of spices. A girl on the stage bent double, splaying everything. More biological than sexual, he thought.

‘So?’

‘On Monday he comes home on leave. He’s changed.’

‘Chechnya changes everything.’ He didn't bother to raise his voice so she had to come closer to hear.

‘What?’

‘Chechnya. It changes people. Everything. It changes everything.’

‘Have you ever been?’

‘I was there.’

‘He’s violent. Hits me. Last time he broke my arm. He did this,’ pointing to the tiny scar on her chin, ‘with a knife.’

‘He’s a soldier. Soldiers can be violent.’

‘I'm afraid, Grigor. I’m afraid next time he’ll kill me.’

‘Leave him.’

‘I would, believe me. But where would I go? I don't have any money. As it is I pay all the bills. In the daytime I work in retail. His wages he just drinks away. It wasn't always like this.'

'What's your name?'

'I'm so sorry. My name is Lizok.' She offered him a slim white hand but he didn't take it.

'What do you do here, Lizok? Dance or what?'

'Up to now just dancing. But I'll do whatever it takes.'

'What do you want from me, Lizok?'

'I have to leave him. But I need money. To get another place. A deposit. A loan. I can pay it back, I promise.'

'I can't help you Lizok. It's not my policy.'

'I'd do anything Grigor,' tipping her flawed jaw at him. Another tear traced her cheek.

'Anything?'

'I could make you happy.'

'I can't help you.'

'I understand.' She turned away, and as she crossed the room Grigor tried not to look as a man took her arm.

'Hey. What's wrong beautiful?' he heard. Tears are

attractive to some men. Her reply was lost in the blare of the music, and soon she was lost too, somewhere in the crowded space. But he didn't forget the man. He had untidy red hair and a tattoo on his arm. A military tattoo of some kind with a dagger. His face was bloated and he had a gut that jutted over his waistband.

Later that same evening Alexei steered the red haired man into Grigor's office. The man was trying to shake off Alexei's hand, but Alexei was strong.

'What is this? What the fuck's going on?'

Grigor leaned against his desk.

'Let him go, Alexei. I'll take it from here. Thanks.'

Alexei left the room shutting the door with care. The man's complexion matched the colour of his hair. He looked hot and dishevelled. He put his hands on his hips.

'What's going on? Who the fuck are you? Is this some kind of shake down?'

'I own this place. And a few others.' He poured a shot of vodka. 'Drink?'

'I'm an American citizen.'

'You don't say,'

'What do you want?'

'You're with a girl.'

'She's not under-age is she?' he looked nervous.

'I doubt it.'

'So what then?'

'Her name is Lizok. I don't care what transaction you agree between you.'

'What do you mean transaction. You mean sex?'

'Yes. Or a private dance. However it turns out.' Grigor took an envelope from the desk. It was open and he flipped through it to show it was full of dollars. He flipped out a hundred dollar bill and held it out to the American. 'This is for you. For your trouble. The rest - there's a thousand dollars here – you're going to give as a tip. To Lizok. You won't mention our cosy chat. You're just a generous guy. And she lucked in. Understood?'

The American looked suspicious but took the hundred dollars and the envelope full of cash. 'Why?'

'Because that's what I want. It's my business. Just give her the money. And believe me I'll know if you don't do exactly as I say.’

‘Are you threatening me?’ He looked at the envelope. Flipped through the greenbacks. Changed his stance, one leg advanced. ‘So what's the catch? You can't fool me. I'm an American. This is some kind of scam, right?’

Grigor regarded most Americans with contempt. Maybe because of the Cold War, even though it seemed like a generation ago. But he hated the synthetic toughness. The naïve self-assurance. ‘Go and find your girl,’ he said.

Grigor left the night club to look in on a new project: a glossy fronted casino on Odessa Street. There he patrolled the tables for a few hours, watching pallid men exchange their cash for plastic tokens, spoke to a few of the croupiers, and spent an hour looking at the books with the manager, before leaving with a feeling of renewed propriety, and a conviction to find an additional site. He wondered why he hadn’t thought of this before. Gambling. With gambling there was no product: only cash flow.

When he got back to Tverskaya Street there were three police cars parked outside his club with their blue lights spinning. It was just after three in the morning, and normally at this time there would still be a small queue of men waiting to enter. His first thought was there had been a fight. It wasn't unheard of.

He drew up in his SUV close to the rear of a police car, almost touching, then barrelled towards the entrance. Nobody on the door he noticed with rising anger. What was going on?

Inside the lights burned bright and the music was silent. People with startled faces milled around, trying to assemble themselves into two orderly lines, one for the men and one for the women. Police officers were taking details at the head of each line.

'Name? ID?'

'Who's in charge here?' Grigor said to one policeman. The policeman pointed with a pen to a Lieutenant standing alone, and Grigor approached him with rising fury. 'Would you mind telling me what the fuck you think you are doing here?'

'Who are you?' the lieutenant was young and his

uniform was freshly laundered. He had red cheeks.

'This is my club.'

The lieutenant consulted a notebook. Alexei and Fyodr appeared, looking ashamed.

'Sorry Boss,' said Fyodr. 'They just burst in waving a warrant.'

'Grigor Vassilyich Malenkov?'

'That's right. So what's happening here?'

'We've had a report about illegal prostitution taking place in this night club.'

'This is a respectable place.'

'Well we've had a report, and we have to act on it.'

'Who from?'

'A foreigner.'

Grigor guessed at once. 'An American.'

'Not that it matters - but yes. An American.'

'You can't do this.'

'I need to take some details from you, as the owner,' said the lieutenant.

'I'll give you some fucking details.' Grigor took out his mobile phone and dialled a number from memory.

'What are you doing?'

'I've been raided,' said Grigor into the phone. 'I can't speak to you now because I am too fucking angry. Talk to this person. He wears the uniform of a lieutenant.' And Grigor held out the phone without looking at the policeman. The lieutenant took it and put it to his ear.

'I am Lieutenant Pavel Petrovich Kirov of the Moscow police. Who…' He stopped speaking and listened. Grigor felt a little sorry for this young policeman as he watched his demeanour change. The confidence, what little there had been, drained away. He cupped his hand around the mouthpiece and turned his back on Grigor. 'Yes. But I didn't know. Nobody told me…. Yes of course… but we had a complaint… ' He was silent several moments. 'Yes sir. I understand sir … Yes, he's right here.' The lieutenant turned again to face Grigor and gave him back the phone. When he put it against his ear the receiver was hot and a little slippery with perspiration.

'Colonel?'

'The misunderstanding has been resolved.'

'It's not over Colonel,' said Grigor.

'I understand. See to it however you see fit.'

Grigor terminated the call without saying goodbye. The lieutenant was waiting for him. 'I am very sorry sir. Nobody told me.'

'Just take out your trash,' he said, meaning the other policemen and regretting his words. But he didn't apologise. 'What are you waiting for?'

'Of course sir. I am very sorry to have disrupted the evening.' He clapped his hands for attention, and shouted. 'Everybody can go back to what they were doing. My officers - meet me outside. I apologise for the inconvenience.' The lines of erstwhile revellers evaporated almost at once. Some men, Grigor noticed, headed straight for the exit.

'You need to be more careful.' Said Grigor. 'You're new around here I think …. Even so there must be some kind of list. Places that are - what? Let's say *regulated* by the FSB.'

'You're right, I'm new. I was assigned here from Uglich. A promotion.' He was ashen faced. The lights darkened. A voice over the PA encouraged everyone to carry on having a good time. There was a surge of people towards the bar.

'No harm done.'

'I don't like to ask.. But there'll be no formal complaint, will there? Only it's my first assignment as a lieutenant and…'

'It's nothing. Not your fault. I just want to get my place back to normal before I lose all of the night's trade.'

'Thank you sir,' and the lieutenant walked over to where some policemen stood in a superfluous group'

Alexei put a hand on Grigor's shoulder.

'Boss - in your office. I'm sorry but I let her wait there.'

And when Grigor entered his office there was Lizok quietly sobbing. She stood up when he walked in. Her eyes glistened. 'Grigor. I don't know what to say. I'm so sorry. And so grateful.'

'What do you mean?'

'I know what you did. I know it came from you.'

He poured himself a vodka. 'I don't know what you're talking about.'

'But I couldn't have sex with that man. Even for

money. And he got angry. Still gave me $1,000. He insisted. Told me you'd instructed him to give it to me. But I couldn't … I'm sorry. I know it was him that caused all this. I caused it.' She started crying again. 'You must want your money back…'

'Keep the money. Find an apartment. But don't tell anybody. Nobody, understand? I don't want anyone to think I'm going soft. Go and dance. Make me some money.'

She rushed up to him before he could stop her, and planted a damp kiss on his cheek, then left the room. This was not the right business for her, and he should have told her to go home. But how else does a girl survive on a shop worker's money in Moscow? He had done the sums, and they didn't work.

Chapter Twenty

WRITHING IN HER lumpy seat, she listened to the announcements first in Russian then in accented English, and understanding them both couldn't help but feel a little proud of her new found linguistic skills. The safety information in the seat pocket informed her that she was flying in an Aeroflot Ilyushin 62 jet, which had been substituted after a two hour delay at Heathrow for the modern Boeing 737 was described on her boarding card. It was a full and restless flight.

Throughout the journey it seemed to her that the pilot had been in the habit of turning the engines on and off in mid flight, leading to unpredictable descents and ascents that made her ears hurt. Maybe in an effort to save fuel, she speculated. A wide-bodied man in a sheepskin coat was picking his nose, his elbows planted on a large aluminium briefcase on his lap. Throughout the five hour flight he had drummed on the briefcase with plump fingers, paying her no attention. Now they were drawing to the end of the flight. The crew made languid preparations to land.

She turned her attention to the undulating scenery below, trying to awaken her alternative memory, searching for some vestiges of déjà vu but none came. The plane banked. Below the land was green and wild looking, sprinkled with what looked like ramshackle country houses. They were flying low, and the misty greens and greys sharpened as they hurtled up to greet them. A sudden wave of apprehension swept over her. She wondered, not for the first time, what she expected to find in Moscow. It was as though she was trying to locate questions for a series of answers that she had known all her life. There was an ethereal umbilical cord that attached her to this place, and recent events had given a sharp tug to that cord. Something in her 'false' past had led to this.. *pursuit.* And who was pursing her? It had led to Gold's murder. His *murder* for God's sake. She tried to work up some extra emphasis in an effort to make it real. But it wasn't real. It was like a part of the memories that she had set aside: vivid, and realistic. But not genuine. Lacking *credibility* somehow. She frowned.

The plane landed with a jolt at Shermetyevo 2 airport to a ripple of applause in the cabin and taxied with an undulating roar towards an orange and grey terminal building. The man beside her was oblivious, drumming his fingers. Drumming, drumming, drumming.

She was surprised to find that the airport was a modern building, alight with the gleam of chrome and glass. There were police and guards everywhere. She steeled herself, trying to awaken her false memory, but it seemed to have evaporated altogether. She was Kate Buckingham from England, she reminded herself. She retrieved her single bag and joined a lengthy queue at customs, where she waited in line for almost two hours to be processed. Most of the passengers waited in silence with blank stares. It occurred to her that nobody complained. Everyone seemed remarkably calm, even the customs officials whom she watched as they unpacked each bag with methodical care.

When it was her turn, she began to unfasten her bag. It was then that some intuition made her look up in time to catch a glance, real or imagined, exchanged between the customs official and a man in a brown suit beyond the barrier.

'It's ok. Go. Go.' The Customs man was waving for her to continue.

'You're not going to search me?'

'You may go.'

Bewildered and uneasy, she hauled her bag off the table.

'Welcome to Moscow,' said the officer with a grim stare as she passed him. She looked around for the man in the brown suit, but he was nowhere to be seen. Perhaps she had imagined it after all?

There were people milling everywhere with assorted bags, labouring at the handles of overloaded trolleys. The pavement was punctuated with fossilised gum. She had a strange feeling of abandonment. Just then a man with a bushy grey moustache and shaved head rushed up to her. He was stocky and angular, wearing an olive green military style coat with a red and white kerchief tied around his neck. 'Taxi?' He said in a thick accent. She tried to wave him away, but he produced a handful of creased snapshots and thrust one at her. It was a picture of three toothy children. 'Look.' He said, 'My family.' He was grinning at her, in such an ingratiating way that she paused for long enough for him to snatch up her suitcase and steer her towards the exit by the arm. 'Yes? With family like this I cannot be Mafia, OK? No problem.' He laughed. 'First time in Moscow, yes?' He tapped the side of his nose, talking to her all the time over his shoulder. 'Is good to be careful in these times. OK? OK. No problem.' He was waving his unencumbered arm around in a placatory manner. She protested at first, but then she reasoned that she needed a taxi after all, and he seemed harmless enough.

'American,' he pronounced with authority as he opened the boot of a battered Lada and threw her case inside.

‘English,’ she corrected.

He nodded in stern affirmation. ‘It’s OK. No problem.’ He pointed at the passenger door. ‘Please..’ and she tugged at the door, which opened with an alarming creak. Before getting into the car himself he rummaged in the glove compartment and produced two windscreen wipers, which he attached with intricate care to the front of the car. As if in explanation he looked at the sky. ‘It will rain,’ he predicted. The car smelt of dogs and gasoline, and she noticed with an uneasy glance over her shoulder that the seats were matted with fur. The driver settled himself on the beaded seat behind the wheel with a deep sigh. ‘Thieves everywhere. Where we are going?’

For the first time she realised how ill prepared she was. Maybe she had been hoping that her other set of memories would take over and fill her head with familiar places, but her thoughts were unambiguous. She was simply Kate Buckingham from England after all.

‘I ... I don’t know. A hotel. Somewhere ...

reasonable. Maybe you can recommend somewhere?' she said.

The taxi driver was unperturbed. 'You have dollars.' He said in the irrefutable way he seemed to have.

'Pounds,' she said.

He shrugged as though it was all the same to him. 'Of course. So, you will stay at good tourist hotel. I know such a place. No problem.' The engine fired with an angry rasp and he pulled into the traffic with not even a cursory glance over his shoulder.

And still the memories refused to stir. They drove along wide boulevards choked with traffic, beneath lurid banners advertising cars and casinos, past tall grey apartment blocks with cracked plaster, and incongruous statues and monuments. After they had been travelling for ten minutes the driver shot her a sidelong glance and announced with a grin: 'I am called Leonid.' He gestured with sudden triumph at the windscreen. 'Look.'

'I'm sorry ... what?'

'It rains. No problem,' and as if to emphasise the fact he slapped the windscreen wiper stalk with his hand which fell off at once. This left him delving in the floor-pan to find it with one hand on the wheel, his shaved head bobbing up and down to keep an eye out for the traffic, which did not prevent the car veering erratically. Since every other car on the road seemed to change lane without indication and for no apparent reason, it seemed to make no difference. Sometimes they would weave around a broken-down car in the middle lane.

Along the route Leonid proudly pointed out landmarks, like a tourist guide. 'Tank traps.' He gestured out of the window at a row of angular concrete constructions. 'For stopping of Nazis in Great Patriotic War.' He raised his chin, throwing her a sidelong glance. 'Germans stop here in Great Patriotic War. In tanks. No problem.'

After 40 minutes or so, when she had started to relax, he cut across 3 lanes of snarling traffic and careered to a halt in front of a broad art nouveau facade with a green roof. She gazed up at the rows of windows and counted 8 floors. Leonid gestured down the street as he propelled himself out of the car. 'Red Square there. Not far. OK? No problem.'

While she stepped into the street, Leonid wrested her bag from the boot. 'You have dollars,' he asserted.

'I have roubles ... and … and pounds.'

'Of course. No problem.' He nodded, and she produced a twenty pound note which seemed to be enough, because Leonid accepted it and secreted it instantly inside his jacket without looking at it. 'No problem. Here..' And he fished inside his coat before thrusting a creased card at her which featured a picture of a limousine and a telephone number. The limousine was a world apart from the asthmatic yellow Lada. 'Please.. if you need car. Call Leonid. No problem,' and he deposited her bag outside the glass doors of the hotel and gave her a cheery wave. 'No problem. No problem.' He said again, in response to her thanks, and he levered himself into the taxi and revved the engine as he pulled away.

She tugged her wheeled case through a revolving glass door and into a galleried atrium lobby. She wondered how much this smart hotel was likely to cost, and made an effort to tot up the afternoon takings of

Whites, which she had exchanged for notes in a bank in London, so distracted as the teller had counted them out she had no idea how much money she had.

At the desk a tall darkly dressed man in a pearl grey tie and with what seemed like a perpetual sneer eyed her suspiciously when she told him that she had no credit card. The tariff was listed in dollars on a polished wooden board behind the desk.

'You will pay the full room rate in advance.' He instructed.

'I'm sorry – I don't have US dollars.'

He shrugged. 'We couldn't take them if you had them. It is the law. We accept only Roubles.' He tapped some numbers into a calculator and announced a number in Roubles that sounded like a lot, and she counted out the grubby, unfamiliar notes, disappointed not to feel faintest awakening of her false memory.

After leaving her bag in her room, she took to the streets, seeking a flame that might re-ignite her absent memories. Perhaps she was mistaken after all. Perhaps Moscow was not the city of her past? She had to make a plan anyway. She had to see if Ekaterina Ivanovna was a fiction.

Her 'false' memory drove her to a corner of Gorky Street. Except that when the Cyrillic letters melted into meaning it wasn't Gorky she read, craning up at the sign, but Tverskaya. Her relief tainted with despair, she watched the fleeting traffic on the broad, tree-lined highway and wondered which way to turn. Tverskaya Street wriggled with colour and people. The evening sunshine cast long shadows. Above the growl of the traffic rang the clangour of construction work. This unexpected air of industriousness took her breath away. Everywhere she looked the sky was intersected with gallows like cranes. Scaffolding scarred the facades of once elegant, soon to be again apartment blocks. She sniffed the abrasive, gasoline-tinged air. A thump of rubber made her start. She stumbled out of the path of a wide-bodied BMW mounting the kerb to avoid a pothole out of Gasheka Street. Disorientated, she turned south along Tverskaya Street looking for evidence that this had once been Gorky Street, weaving through a Moscow that seemed all wrong. The bread queues of her memories supplanted with designer boutiques and jewellery shops. Maybe the others had been right all along? Maybe her 'false' memories were nothing more than dreams? She quickened her pace, her heels tapping, as though in flight or pursuit. Which was it? A street trader alongside a barrow dripping with fruit and vegetables devoured her with greedy eyes. Out of habit she smiled and swung her hair behind her. She passed a sushi restaurant, a shoe shop, a café. Every other building she observed was racked out with scaffolding, long chutes disgorging rubble into skips and dust into the air, as though they were busy dismantling the entire city. Further down the street she thought she saw a banner that she recognised: Pizza Hut. She could be in London. This could be yesterday.

Then, just as she was giving up hope, her memories were brought back into focus. Outside the offices of Izvestiya she came to an abrupt halt. A man behind her cursed, almost collided, then shot an angry glance over his shoulder as he passed, muttering something about tourists. Izvestiya. Anonymous, shabby offices with grimy windows. And just across the street, the rugged, red-brick City Hall building fronted by white pillars that looked like a monstrous portcullis. Above them hung the tricolor of the Russian Federation, no longer the hammer and sickle. She felt vindicated - but there was something odd too. Something about her thoughts. It was as though they had taken on an angular, ill-fitting property. Then, when she glanced above the glittering window of another jewellery shop and read the sign "Tsentr Yuvelir" it came to her with a shock. Her thoughts had slipped into Russian, as naturally as if it were her mother tongue.

This realisation made her stop sharply. She looked all around. At the cafes and shops. At the pastel buildings. No longer grey but golden. No longer grim but garish. The pedestrians wore colourful clothes. She looked up, at the clear sky. Was this where she belonged? In the gentle breeze a red flag swayed above an entrance. She picked out the hammer and sickle and it sent a shudder through her because it was as though her other past had interceded. The sign above the door said 'Red Nights'. She shuddered again and pushed against the heavy glass door stencilled with Stalin's portrait, because it seemed the most natural thing to go inside.

As she stepped through the door she was struck by the acrid hint of disinfectant in the air, with an undertone of stale tobacco. She entered a vast room with parquet floors and spindly tables with chairs scattered all around. At the far end of the room, flanked by two giant concrete statues - one of Lenin, one of Stalin - was a stage with a backdrop of red curtains. Two men sat before the stage smoking cigarettes in a halo of smoke, hanging in the air like gossamer There was a bottle of vodka between them on a table. One of them swore, in a deep down, scathing voice. '*Na Hui!* Fuck you!' He stabbed out his cigarette angrily. 'Show me again.'

A girl on stage crossed to a music console and pressed a button. She had spidery limbs and long dark hair. She was a plain-faced girl with pointy features. When the music began with a resounding blast she leapt into the centre of the stage flashing a big fake grin at the two men, pivoting her long legs around. She was naked.

Kate watched enthralled, like she was watching her own performance from a world apart. She watched the girl perform all the usual stunts, pushing up her butt into the audience and peering from between her legs, laying on her back with her legs splayed. The men watched too, inscrutable and in silence, as she played out her routine. Her act was wooden in spite of her efforts. Stilted. Not like her own smooth motions she reflected, her dipping and kicking.

One of the men turned and saw her standing there. He had a broad forehead, like a Labrador, and vast shoulders hunched over the table. Smoke obscured his features. Without a word he lifted a thick arm and beckoned to her. The other man turned then too, narrower, smaller. He looked surprised. She began to back away, knocking over a chair. It fell with an alarming clatter. With her heart in her mouth she turned and fled towards the door. She heard the laughter of the two men above the music as she flung herself through the doors into the street. One of them yelled at her: 'Come back. It's OK.' What had she been thinking of?

She hurried down the street - in the direction of Red

Square she was certain, because now she seemed to recognise the side roads. Many of the names had changed, she realised, but there remained enough familiar ones to reinforce her memories.

She tried to formulate a plan, more composed now. She would go first to the police. She remembered the taxi driver's card. Leonid he said. She would call him from the hotel.

Chapter Twenty-One

WHEN BRAD SPENCER left his hotel, it was a crisp Moscow morning, but there was an aftertaste of petroleum in the air. His regular driver was not waiting for him outside, and he cursed the lazy Russians. He waited 10 minutes outside the hotel, refusing the approaches of cab drivers in one of his sparse words of Russian 'Nyet.' He didn't know what they said to him in return and he didn't care.

A black Mercedes swept to the kerb, tyres crackling on the icy road. The window was down and the driver was smoking. Brad saw him look over.

'Mr Spencer?'

'That's me.'

'They sent me to pick you up.'

'OK great. You're late, you know?' He crossed to the back door and waited an instant but when nobody made any move to open it for him he hauled it open and got in, swinging his laptop bag onto his knees. The car smelled of leather and stale tobacco. 'Better hurry,' he said, 'Where's the regular guy?'

'He was unavoidably detained,' and the car pulled away with a jerk of sudden power.

Brad watched the busy street without much interest. There were long lines at the bus stops. He wondered how the women all dressed like cat walk models in spiky heels and sometimes calf length boots. Yes sir, the women were more beautiful in Moscow than back home. Then he lost his train of thought, just drifted. 'Where are we?'

'We're taking a different route today.'

It irritated him that the driver was still smoking. The driver's window was open a crack, but it didn't stop the fumes from reaching him. 'Would you mind putting that out?'

The driver didn't answer.

'I said would you mind...?'

The buildings they passed were more like he had expected to see in Russia. Crumbling concrete blocks. The roads were more broken up too. The driver veered around a deep pothole, and it caused him to reach out for the grab handle.

He saw the driver glance in the rear-view mirror and smile. 'Mr Malenkov sends his regards,' he said.

'Who?'

'The owner of the night club that you visited last night.'

Everything tightened up at that moment. Everything concertinaed. There was just this moment in the back of a Mercedes with a belligerent Russian at the wheel. He had heard about heists in Moscow. Everybody had warned him. Why did he phone the police last night? Some stupid false bravado. His stomach churned.

'So where are you taking me now?'

'Mr Malenkov thinks that you need some education.'

The car swung into a bumpy side road between a series of tall apartment buildings. They blocked the sun.

'What kind of education?'

'A Russian education.'

They reached a piece of wasteland. There was a burnt out car, hard to tell what make, and a discarded mattress.

The Mercedes stopped, and the driver turned and grinned at him. Brad pulled at the door catch, but the doors were locked.

'This is where you get out.' He said. 'But before you do, there's something you should consider.'

Brad tasted the saliva in his mouth. He felt sick. 'What?'

'Some people would call Mr Malenkov a gangster. Some people say Mafia,' said the driver. 'And there are gangsters I know personally who would cut your tongue out for what you did last night. There are gangsters that would dump you in the Moskva river and not even give it a thought.' He paused. 'Give me your wallet.' Snapping his fingers.

Brad obeyed without thinking, and the driver put it in his jacket pocket without looking at it.

'So you are very lucky to be dealing with a *civilised* gangster who is not as *insecure* as others might be. In a minute, I'm going to leave you here. Without money and without ID. I warn you, it's not a safe area. And you don't speak Russian, which will make it more interesting.' He pushed open the drivers door and came round to the back, opening Brad's door. 'Get out.'

'Is that it?' He knew he was trembling and bunched his fists to stop himself shaking.

'Maybe,' said the driver. Brad saw now that the driver was a head taller than him, and thick chested. 'Now get going. And if I were you I would fuck off back to America as soon as you can. I respect Mr Malenkov, but sometimes I think he can be too restrained. If it were me, I can tell you I would at the very least break some bones. Do you understand?'

'I understand.'

'One more thing.'

Brad had turned away, and when he turned back he was horrified to see that the man was holding a gun.

'What?'

The driver grinned at him like before. Pointed the gun at his head. A dozen feet separated them. 'Take off the shoes. Maybe I want them as a souvenir.'

Brad took off his shoes.

'Toss them over here.'

He did as he was told.

'That's all. Now fuck off and I never want to see you again.'

Brad limped away, the concrete hard beneath his stockinged feet.

Chapter Twenty-Two

'YOU HAVE COME, let us say, to report a disappearance?' the officer spoke in a tone of unfounded suspicion. He was a man with frosty hair in his fifties wearing what passed for a tweed jacket and a greasy brown tie. His fingernails, Kate noticed, were bitten to the quick. There was a reek of tobacco about him. After several attempts to make headway in English Kate had submitted to Russian, and was shocked to find it felt like coming home.

'The disappearance of Ekaterina Ivanovna Borodina.'

He had Kate's passport in his hands and was laboriously reading each page with unmerited concentration. He turned the pages slowly, sometimes turning back as though he had missed something. They were sitting across a desk strewn with documents, mostly hand-written in cramped Cryllic script. An ashtray was brimful with unfiltered cigarette buts. The police station was chaotic. The phones rang constantly but nobody seemed to answer. Everybody seemed to be in a rush about something but it was hard to see what. Some uniformed officers levered a huge drunk through the doors protesting loudly and hoarsely. A few detectives hurried to assist and lent their shouts to the commotion. The officer in front of her seemed oblivious.

He snapped closed her passport suddenly with the air of someone who had finished reading a book with an unsatisfactory ending.

'You are a foreign national.' He concluded with infuriating logic.

'You know that already.'

'Exactly. I must find an appropriate person to deal

with your allegations.'

'I'm not making any allegations. I just want to report a missing person.'

'I must find an appropriate person, all the same,' he said darkly, then stood up and ushered for her to do the same. 'You will kindly follow me.'

He led her through another office, almost identical to the first, then to a corridor that was eerily silent. He opened a door. 'You will wait here.'

It was an austere room with a desk and two plastic bucket chairs. There was a single barred window, high up and almost out of reach.

'Can I have my passport back?' she asked in sudden panic.

The officer grimaced. She suddenly realised that he was no longer holding it, and she wondered what he had done with it.

'Soon,' he said. He gestured to a chair with a stubby, nicotine stained forefinger, then closed the door silently and she was alone. She felt strangely abandoned. Her breathing was laboured. She walked around the perimeter of the room like a caged animal.

She tried the door once, and was relieved to find it unlocked. When she put her head out into the corridor it was empty. She ventured out almost on tip-toe, Listening intently to the silence, then returned at once to the relative sanctuary of the room.

In order to see out of the window she had to put a chair up against the wall. The window looked out upon a small courtyard with two identically battered police Zhigulis parked side by side. A row of high windows like her own spanned one wall. The walls were grey. The tiled floor was grey. The metal table was grey. A symphony of grey. The colour of detention.

She looked at her watch, believing that she must have been in this room an hour already, but only ten minutes had passed.

Time sauntered. Sometimes she sat at the table. Sometimes she walked around the room. She supposed she could leave if she wanted to. She wasn't a prisoner. But then she reminded herself they had her passport. She might as well be a prisoner. She listened for a sound in the corridor, but there was nothing to hear except the buzz of the neon light. It was a mistake to come here, she decided. A mistake to come to Russia at all. What had she been thinking? She looked at the white plastic clock on the wall that measured each minute with an irritating buzz and a click and a wavering minute hand that was maddeningly never pointing precisely to the minute markers. It was set to the wrong time, as though time here was meaningless, and checked off the passing of the minutes in somebody else's time zone.

She remained there alone for almost two hours, thirsty and miserable. She was about to brave the corridor again when the door was flung open by a surprisingly elegant man in his thirties. He wore an affable smile, vaguely apologetic. He offered his hand which was smooth and warm, and looked at her with grey eyes that seemed to see beyond her.

'Traffic, I'm afraid.' He excused himself in flawless English. 'I'm sorry you've been detained for so long. I am Captain Nikolay Sokolov. Can I offer you some coffee?'

'Thank you. Yes please.'

He disappeared for a few moments then returned

bearing two steaming polystyrene cups, pushing open the door with his knee. 'No milk I'm afraid.' He shook his head despairingly. 'You don't want to know what they have in that fridge.' He set both cups on the table making puddles around the bases.

'Now,' He laid her passport carefully between them like a peace offering. 'I'm told that you wish to report a disappearance?' He had switched to Russian and she barely noticed. She was getting used to this, she thought with a rush of dismay.

'As I told the officer. Of Ekaterina Ivanovna Borodina.'

Sokolov had produced a form from somewhere and was examining it as though working out which parts needed to be completed. 'And she is what? A friend? A relative?'

Kate hesitated. 'A relative I suppose?'

'You suppose?'

'Of the family.' She completed hurriedly. 'I myself have never met her.'

'The officer was right about one thing.' Said Sokolov with a strange note. 'Your Russian is impeccable. May I ask where you learnt?'

'In school.' She lied. The coffee was thick and black and scalded the roof of her mouth.

'Remarkable.' He shook his head again, this time in apparent wonderment, and studied the form closely, then produced an expensive looking pen from inside his jacket. 'First, some formalities. Your full name please.' He had reverted to English again.

She watched him closely as he filled out the form with meticulous care.

'And you last heard from Ekaterina Ivanovna when?'

'I didn't ... I mean I haven't. She disappeared some time in 1966,' she finished hopelessly, suddenly feeling rather foolish.

Sokolov lay down his pen and pushed back his chair. He looked tired. 'A lot of Russians disappeared around that time. Maybe you know something of our history?' he said after a long pause. She had a sinking feeling. 'It would be impossible to investigate every disappearance. Even if we had the resources. Which we don't.'

'So you won't do anything ?'

He sighed and held up the form. 'I will fill out a report if you want me to. It won't do any good.'

'I'm sorry to have wasted your time,' she said with bitterness.

He tapped his pen thoughtfully. It was obvious that he wasn't finished with her. 'Why did you come to Moscow, Miss Buckingham?'

'To find Ekaterina.'

'No other reason?'

'No.'

'Have you heard of the FSB?'

'No.'

'The KGB, of course?'

'Of course.' *Komiter Gosudarstvennoi Bezopasnosti* the words strung themselves together in her head involuntarily, and she tried to suppress a shudder, which she thought he couldn't have failed to notice.

'The FSB is the same thing. The new face of the KGB – there have been many faces.. NKVD, MGB, Cheka.. take your pick.' He sighed. 'Have you any idea why the FSB might have an interest in you?' He was watching her attentively. She felt an ominous tingling sensation.

'In me…? But they can't have. Why would they...?'

'Why indeed?' He pursed his lips. 'You think it could have anything to do with this person you are looking for?'

'But why?'

'That's what interests me.' He thought for a moment then seemed to reach a conclusion. 'I'm going to tell you something that I will later deny. I have not been brought halfway across Moscow just to investigate your disappearance report. It's a hangover from Soviet times. When a Westerner of your ... profile comes to the attention of the authorities.' He caught her puzzled frown. 'Your excellent Russian, for example...' He waved a hand. '—it's thought you must either be a spy. Or if not, then perhaps you could be induced to spy for us. So, we are informed of course. And we send someone. More for the sake of form than anything else. A waste of everybody's valuable time.' He coughed into his hand and then laughed, almost to himself. 'As

I said—a hangover from Soviet times.' There was a pause. 'But this time I came personally because I'm informed by the police that you were followed here by agents of the FSB. The police are not stupid. Not always anyway. We often make the mistake of assuming they are. If they say you are being followed by FSB then it is certainly true. It's unusual, to say the least. Foreign nationals are the responsibility of my department, you see.'

She felt a queasiness in her stomach, a quivering in her bones which she was not sure was visible. Was it possible that the men in London had something to do with the FSB? She dismissed the thought out of hand, but not without a lingering doubt. Poor Gold.. Had she imagined the man at passport control who had seemed to be observing her? He was observing her closely. She crossed her legs and gripped herself tightly with her arms around her torso in an effort to ease the shivering. She willed her other set of memories to admit her, but all she could remember was the here and now and an ordinary childhood in Tring, Hertfordshire. She was all deserted and alone in Moscow, she reminded herself, but the city harboured no more connotations than an encyclopaedia entry. Solokov's expression was sympathetic, and somehow sorrowful.

'Is there anything ... anything at all that you wish to tell me? Anything you *can* tell me, I mean? That might shed some light on why you are being followed?' he ventured.

What could she tell him? That she was being *haunted* by another person's memories? In vain she looked inside for something that she could confide, something that would help. But there was nothing. She felt empty. She said: 'I think I may have been born here in Russia. I can't explain it...'

He picked through the pages of her passport and referenced the place of birth without saying anything for what seemed to be a long time. The hands of the clock on the wall fizzed and clicked, paused endlessly, buzzed and clicked, with a fateful resonance. Finally he said: ' They're waiting out there. A blue Volga across the street. You're not in any danger. At least, not as far as I can tell, not as far as you've *told* me.' He held up the open passport. Frowned. 'What do you mean when you say you think you were born in Russia?'

She flashed him a doleful smile. Her back ached. She felt very weary. She felt a need to unburden herself to somebody. 'A man I've known as my father all my life told me two days ago that I'm an orphan, smuggled across the border from Russia as a baby. Into Turkey.' As if that wasn't enough to convince him she added: 'I've always felt—different.' She couldn't quite bring herself to talk about the memories.

He tapped the edge of her passport on the desk thoughtfully. 'And Ekaterina Ivanovna? What's she to you? Who is she?'

'I honestly am not sure. I think she might be.. might be an aunt. Or something. I don't know. She might know the answers. That's what I'm hoping..'

He looked at her as if from a long way away. 'And what are the questions to which you seek answers?' She picked at her fingernails nervously. Captain Sokolov sat back in his chair and sighed. 'I'm going to try to help you, Kate Buckingham. I'll make some enquiries. Nothing guaranteed. I'm curious. But there's something you are not telling me. I hope perhaps you'll learn to trust me.'

Outside the sun was low in the sky, and as she pushed through the doors, she looked around for Leonid without much prospect. But there he was languishing against his cab in his thick parka as though she had been away only minutes. The evening traffic snaked past. Leonid looked anxious.

'It's OK? No problem?'

'No problem.' She said, glancing across the broad street at a blue Volga with its nearside wheels on the pavement. The occupants were looking straight ahead out of the windscreen and not at her. So it was true.

Petrov stood in the doorway with his legs slightly apart and his hands deep in the pockets of a short leather jacket. He nodded. 'Dmitry.'

'What do you want?' He looked out into the corridor, left and right. Petrov shifted a little.

'Are you going to invite me in?'

'You shouldn't be here. What if you were followed.'

'I wasn't followed.'

'I can't believe you would come here.'

'I have my instructions.'

'Instructions? What instructions?'

In a fluid motion Petrov took his hand from his pocket and raised a small gun with a snub double barrel which he pressed hard into Dmitry's forehead. Dmitry took a deep breath. Stepped backwards into the apartment. Petrov followed pulling the door closed behind him. 'Bathroom.'

'Let's talk about this,' Backing down the hallway.

'Nothing to say Dima. I can't talk to you. It's not personal.'

'You work for me, Petrov.'

'We all work for Moscow. This it?' He pointed to a closed door. 'Open it.' The barrel still solid and cold against Dmitry's forehead. He fumbled with the door handle. Tried to un-jumble his head. Evolve some plan. 'Quickly.'

'Please…' Petrov with outstretched arm pushed him into the bathroom. 'You don't need to do this.'

Then the gun discharged with a harsh echo and the

blood left an intricate pattern on the white tiles.

The car bumped over a broken section of road, and stuttered to a halt beneath an apartment block that stretched to 20 stories at least. Leonid tugged at the ineffectual handbrake, and the car rolled backwards a few inches when he removed his foot from the brake. Surrounding this block were smaller blocks of 5 storey buildings with precarious looking balconies in serried rows.

'Krushchoyovki.' He muttered through his moustache, half to himself. 'After Kruschev he make them when there were not sufficient house for everyone in Moscow. Now just rot and nobody repairs. What you do here?'

Kate and Leonid had developed a protocol when it came to language. Kate would speak in flawless Russian, but Leonid would continue to struggle with his flawed and heavily accented English. Each time she implored him to please speak Russian, he would tell her it was 'no problem' and would continue undaunted to speak in English.

Kate emerged from the taxi gingerly, and gazed up at the cream and brown building, shading her eyes against the sun. There was an alarming rift across the entire width of the building, over halfway up. The rows of black windows spanned the building like pock marks. She felt a frisson of excitement. This building had the day-worn familiarity of an old pair of shoes. She turned around, and there before her was the patch of scrubland that served as a park, just as she thought she there would be. Some twisted framed children's swings occupied the centre of the park, and a colourless wooden roundabout with slats of wood missing.

'I used to live here.' She said with assertion, pursing her lips in emphasis.

Leonid laughed in the merry, hearty way he had that reminded her of Santa Claus. 'Not live here. Not you. This Kruchchoyovki. *I* live in apartment like this. It was good times. You are from USA. Not live in Kruchchoyovki.'

'No, really,' she said, wishing he would speak Russian, 'I lived on the twelfth floor. I feel it.' She pointed in the direction of the building, but Leonid laughed, and opened his arms in a shrug.

'No problem.' He said with a laugh.

She walked across the street, and Leonid followed, protesting. She had a blurred vision in her head of the building without the crack in its plaster, and with fresh paint. Instinctively she knew where to go. It was the identical feeling she had had when she returned to her parents' home in Tring after so long.

A chocolate brown painted steel door led onto a stairwell. To the left of the door was an entry-phone and keypad, but it was broken and the door hung open. There was an elevator of course with room enough for two slim people, but a handwritten sign taped to the door said simply 'Broken.' Apologies were unnecessary. 12 floors to climb, then.

Leonid said in surprise: 'You go up?'

She glanced back. ' Thanks, Leonid. Can you you wait down here?' He looked relieved.

'It is not so dangerous.' He pondered. 'No problem.' And he turned to the car, quickly before she could change her mind.

She focussed her mind, looking up at the unevenly cast steps with cracked and pitted plaster. Suddenly she was a child. A child with a vision of a golden samovar in her mind. The destination. The objective. A cramped room with a samovar, up 12 flights of steps. 306 steps! She remembered with an unconscious smile of delight. She remembered that she counted them once. Who counted them? She frowned, interrupting the dialogue building in her head, and the memory dissolved at once. She was standing on a flight of broken concrete steps with the odour of cabbage and urine and rotten plaster ripe in the air. She was still Kate Buckingham after all.

Up the steps. Twice she encountered women struggling down the stairwell. There were no nodded greetings, just hostile, incurious stares. She wondered why they would not be in the least bit curious. Each landing was scattered with cigarette ends, and cracked windows hung awry from their frames overlooking a bleak concrete landscape.

When at last she reached the 11th floor she found it sealed off with scaffold poles across the steel door and a sign that said 'DANGER NO ENTRY'. Her heart leapt as she remembered the fissure across the width of the building.

She ran rather than walked the next flight of stairs, panting for breath, her heart thumping. But when she reached the 12th floor to her dismay it was the same. Rusty scaffolding was wedged across the doorway. She felt sick. The taste of blood mingled with her saliva. On each floor the stairway was exposed to the outside, and she looked out across suburban Moscow with a sliver of recognition. She turned back to the door and pulled at the scaffolding pole, without much hope. It was firmly seated, and anyway the door was padlocked. There was no alternative but to descend.

As she reconciled herself sadly to another wasted journey and began to make her way down the steps, she thought she heard a rustle from the steps behind her. She turned around to see an old lady in long black skirts negotiating the stairway with stoicism. The old woman looked at her in a strange way, then stopped, several steps above Kate.

'What brings you here?' she said, without a flicker

of friendliness.

'Do you ... Do you remember me?' she ventured.

The old woman continued her descent. Screwed up her face. 'She lived here. Your mother. Not you.' Kate took a step down, keeping pace. 'That floor's been shut for years. And the one downstairs. An earthquake, they said.' Kate took another two steps down and wondered how long it took for the old lady to get to the ground. 'Your father lived there too. Drank too much,' she added.

For some reason it had never occurred to her that Ekaterina had a father. 'My father?' she said.

The old woman paused in her descent and looked at her for a moment. Her eyes were bloodshot. 'Grandfather.' She corrected. 'Worked at the University I think. Didn't have much to do with the likes of me.'

Kate slipped further down the steps. 'So where did she go? My mother?'

'Where did any of them go? How should I know? Maybe they moved them to a better apartment. Maybe *something else*,' she said, darkly. 'I'm not told. I don't ask. I'm still here.'

'But you knew her?'

The old woman could have been any age between fifty and eighty. She had an uncompromising look about her. The air of someone who had experienced continual despair, and had determined to plough on in spite of everything. When she came within a few steps of Kate she could smell stale linen tempered with the scent of lavender. It somehow called up an apparition of the samovar again, distinct and real this time. A real memory, not a false one.

'I lived on the 12th floor until they moved us. Too dangerous they said. Now I live on the 14th floor and the elevator works less often than it doesn't work. I'm too old for these steps. Your mother lived a few doors away. She wouldn't remember me.'

'So why do you remember her?'

'She was the *scientist.* We all knew about the *scientist.*'

'What kind of scientist?'

The old woman leaned against the wall with her hand, pausing between steps. She looked at Kate.

'How should I know? If I knew that maybe *I* would have been a scientist too.'

Moving down the steps again, Kate tried to console the old lady. 'What else can you tell me?'

The old woman was getting back into her stride now arching her back and steadying herself against the wall as she negotiated each step. 'Nothing. I can tell you nothing. Your mother lived here. Not for long. And then she went away.' Lean. Step. 'It wasn't a sociable time. Paid to mind your own business.' Lean. Step. 'Why would you come here?' Lean. Step.

'I'm trying to find out what happened to her. That's all.'

'Dangerous to know things in those days.' Lean. Step. 'You didn't want to know too much. Just leave it I say. Don't ask. I never knew anything about anything. I survived.' Lean. Step. 'Keep myself to myself. That's what respectable comrades do.' Lean. Step.

'Would anyone else remember her?' Asked Kate with a flicker of hope.

Lean. Step. Lean. Step. The old woman paused to catch her breath. 'All gone.' She said weakly. 'They've all left. Why would they stay?'

'And do you.. Do you keep in touch maybe?' Attempting for a foolish moment to apply Western standards.

'When they go, they're gone.' Observed the old woman with bleak determination. 'Wherever they go. Me, I keep myself to myself.' Lean. Step. Lean. Step. Her feet echoed in the stairwell.

Chapter Twenty-Three

GRIGOR WEDGED HIS bulky frame into the passenger seat of the Volga and scratched his beard. 'You're late.' He observed, hauling the car door shut with a tinny bang. He had a fearsome headache, and he worried that he might try to take it out on someone soon.

'Affairs of state,' answered the driver with an ironic smile, looking straight ahead.

The car felt claustrophobic.

'I heard about Yugorsky bank.'

'News travels fast.'

'In Moscow it does.' Grigor reached inside his

leather jacket and produced a thick envelope. 'Anything to do with your people? Yugorsky Bank I mean?'

'I would conclude it was intended as a message to those that don't pay their dues. A man of Ivan Bokovsky's stature should have invested more in his health, I think.' Lisakov accepted the package. 'It's a sad business.'

Grigor grunted. 'It's the second banker in less than a week.'

'You should be careful to trust your money to the right banks.'

'How is anyone to know which are the right banks?' Grigor complained bitterly.

Lisakov glanced at him. 'Be guided,' he said. 'There are criminals everywhere in Russia today. Criminals everywhere.' He patted the pocket into which he had secreted the envelope.

Grigor craned to look over his shoulder. The rugged grille of a Range Rover filled the rear window, and he felt comforted to see Oleg with his forearms hanging over the steering wheel. The perpetual lines of traffic swept past in the yellow dawn. He turned back to the windscreen and shook his head slowly. 'You're all just a bunch of gangsters.'

'Speaking of which..' Lisakov fumbled inside his coat and took out the envelope Grigor had given him, appraising it for the first time and weighing it in his hand. 'How is business?'

'We get by.' Grigor felt a swell of anger and clenched a fist, unseen.

'Sometimes it's hard to tell who the gangsters are and who the businessmen.'

'And the policemen,' added Grigor.

Lisakov settled himself back in his seat, with a supremely dignified air. 'That too,' he agreed.

'And what if I were a legitimate businessman? What then?'

Lisakov sighed. 'We do our best. But we don't have the resources. Sooner or later the mafia would launder money through you, or sign an agreement with you that you wouldn't be able to refuse. You know how it is. That's capitalism I'm afraid.. What's to be done?'

Grigor pressed himself into the seat to make more

room for his knees. He said 'I think I'm paying for too much protection.' Keeping a wary eye on Lisakov's reaction.

'You can never have too much protection. You of all people should know that.'

'Now there's Olensky feeding at the trough.'

'I'm sure you can deal with him.'

'Isn't that what I am paying you for?' Said Grigor, bitterly.

'I like to think of our relationship more as patronage than protection.'

Grigor laughed out loud. 'What the fuck does that mean?'

Lisakov flashed him a dangerous look. 'Whatever I want it to mean.'

Grigor returned his look, calculating just how easy it would be to snap Lisakov's neck. It would take no more than a movement. A strategically directed elbow. What he was trained to do. Over in a second. Then he would be closeted in the Range Rover in the whiff of leather and wood, and whisked away . It would be a popular murder. Instead he reached for the door handle.

'I'll deal with it then. But I don't want any trouble.'

'*That* is what you pay me for.' Lisakov smirked.

Chapter Twenty-Four

KATE HAD SPREAD her money over the bedspread, a rainbow of banknotes, Pounds mixed with Roubles, Queen Elizabeth rubbing shoulders with Peter the Great, fretting over how she could stretch her resources.

For the past few days she had pored over maps and telephone directories. Borodina was a common name. She had made countless abortive phone calls. Leonid had dragged her on pointless excursions through the altered streets of the outer reaches of her memories, to dingy, broken stairwells of half familiar apartment blocks, spoken with harried, frightened people that proved to have no connection with Ekaterina Ivanovna at all. She had phoned Nikolay Sokolov half a dozen times, but he had no news for her, and when she left messages he never returned her calls. She wondered if he even made the slightest enquiry. Why should he, after all? What was she to him?

And everywhere she went, there followed in her wake a Volga or a Lada with blue official license plates, not even trying to conceal their presence. Sometimes they parked immediately behind Leonid's taxi. Always there were two of them, reading newspapers, chain-smoking while they waited, resting their elbows on the open windows and shedding cigarette butts into the street.

The city was only half remembered. The same shape, but the parts had different functions, different names. Sometimes she would follow a promising trail, delighted with a flood of recollections, breathless with anticipation, only to find the building she remembered so vividly had been demolished, or had been refurbished, changed purpose beyond recognition.

As she sat in her hotel room counting banknotes, she wondered if she should go home. She had an open ticket to London. Then she remembered Gold's murder. She remembered the vulture like man and the struggle. Nothing could put that right. It was a mess that was waiting for her return. She wasn't safe in London. She wasn't safe in Moscow – but in Moscow was the answer. In Moscow she could find out why this was happening to her. In some ways the men that were following her were a comfort. They were proof that something existed to be discovered. Nikolay had told her she was not at risk. So she felt she could turn their presence almost into a positive. Maybe they were seeking the same answers? Maybe they were watching and waiting for her to show the way, to shine a light?

She had to play the hand out, and Moscow was where all the cards were to be found. The trouble was, she was running out of money. She couldn't sustain herself for more than another 2 nights at the Tverskaya Marriott.

And now she thought the memories were just beginning to assert themselves, to sharpen. They were seeping into her dreams just as her dreams used to seep into her memories. Everything all mixed up. She remembered a white pole with what looked like twisted orange and white ribbons wound loosely around it, as high as a tree. Like a huge maypole. Next to it was a long, wide sign in Cyrillic. She was trying to decipher it in her head, but it was jumbled up with other signs. It began with an 'O' she was sure. Or an 'S'. She knew it was a gateway to something… to somewhere. It had been important to her once. Or at least, important to this other someone that inhabited her memories when they lost their focus.

She went to the window and yanked back the net curtain. All along Tverskaya Street the boutiques and cafes were shaking off the shadows, letting in the light. The stream of traffic crawled at its usual pace. An official car, or an Oligarch's car, raced down the middle lane with a blue light flashing. People marched single-mindedly towards their private destinations, with as much or as little hope as any city dweller in the world. As she strained to see further down the street, in the direction of Red Square, she caught sight of a limp red flag above a doorway. Then she had an idea.

Chapter Twenty-Five

'IT'S CLEAR THAT this group needs to take positive action to prevent the traitor Viktor Chernomyrdin from attempting to succeed the President.'

The room was silent for some moments. A bluebottle was clearly audible, buzzing at the window, tapping against the glass.

'When you say positive action..' ventured the Duma deputy. Borilyenko silenced him with a savage glance.

'It's unthinkable that this illegal regime should be perpetuated through the second millennium. Gentlemen, it is left to us to prevent this proud nation from being *destroyed* though the cynical and corrupt offices of its leadership. The Feliks Group is a voice in the wilderness that needs to swiftly demonstrate that it is in fact the voice of the people.' Borilyenko was tapping the table with the heel of his clenched fist in a restrained but powerful gesture. 'It's time we made plans. Time we made the way clear for a new leader.'

Vassillov observed Borilyenko , and thought that he looked somehow re-invigorated. A spark that had been missing had returned.

'You mean we should plan for the assassination of the President?' said Vassillov slowly, vocalising the dreadful course of action that was festering in the minds of all of them. The room was hushed. Even the bluebottle had gone silent.

'I mean we should prepare the way. Remove the .. *obstacles*. In a short time the president will step down. I am sure of this. But there are many *pretenders*. Many that the President has been grooming to assume his mantle. It is this that we must prevent. We need to escalate the activities of the Feliks Group. We need to prepare. We need to take action now.' He looked around the stern faces. 'Are we agreed, gentlemen? Are we *united*?'

There were mumbled approvals, and each man knew that they were sanctioning murder. The murder of the prime minister. And others. Maybe Lebed. It was a renewal of a kind. A communal feeling of renewal. The chairs scraped back. The usual toasts.

After the meeting Borilyenko phoned a number at the Lubyanka and Lisakov answered. 'What news of the girl?' he said with suppressed anticipation.

'She's an assiduous tourist,' replied Lisakov. 'She's been driven around to.. to various locations. I have a report. It's difficult to see how these places are connected. It would perhaps help if you could tell me what we're looking for. What's her importance? It would help.'

'It is not for me to tell a KGB officer what to look for.'

'FSB.' Reminded Lisakov with a hint of irony.

'Of course.' Borilyenko paused. 'Let me have your report tonight. If we can't determine the purpose of her visit here, then we need to pick her up. Give it another day.'

'Yes General.'

After Borilyenko had laid down the phone, he thought about Project Simbirsk, and the more he thought about it, the more he thought that it must have been a success after all. Not a complete success.. but one that could be replicated. One that could be harnessed. He would be a custodian. Keeping the faith.

Chapter Twenty-Six

GRIGOR MALENKOV SAT in his office with his boots on the desk in a tobacco trance. There was a poster of Stalin on the wall which someone had defaced with devils horns. Smoke spiralled from a large Havana that festered in an ashtray, and the desk was strewn with documents and scraps of handwritten notes. A handgun doubled as a paperweight. The smoke from the cigar shifted and swirled as the door opened and Oleg leaned in the door frame, grinning in that manic way he had.

'There's a girl out front. The one you frightened off the other day.'

Grigor frowned, then remembered the pretty blonde that had scuttled out of the club when he called out. 'The cute one? What does she want?'

Oleg shrugged. 'Says she wants to audition.'

Grigor plucked his cigar from the ashtray and reflected upon it. 'We're always interested in fresh talent. Has she done it before?'

'In England, she says.'

'England. What the fuck? OK then. Let's take a look' Grigor stood up and pushed the gun into the back of his waistband. He slotted his cigar into a corner of his mouth and followed Oleg down a short corridor and into the club. A stocky woman was washing down the bar, overlooked by a rocky bust of Lenin. Leaning against the stage was the same girl that had ventured into the club a few days before. She had sharp inquisitive features, and an animated look about her. Her blond hair tumbled over her shoulders. He stopped at the other end of the stage from the girl and smiled. 'Welcome,' he said, his voice sharp and resonant in the empty club. 'I'm Grigor.' He looked around him with a proprietary air. 'What do you think of my collection of memorabilia?'

He watched her perch herself with a balletic leap on the edge of the stage. 'Interesting,' she said, sniffing the air as though catching a hint of something unpleasant. Grigor sauntered over to a statue of an impish man with a pointed beard and a cap tipped back on his head adjacent to the club entrance. He gestured to it with his cigar.

'My favourite,' he said, assessing it as though he were inspecting a soldier on parade. He glanced at her with a raised eyebrow. 'You know who he is?' When she didn't reply he said: 'Allow me to introduce the infamous Felix Edmundovich Dzerzhinsky. *Iron* Felix. The architect of the Cheka. The KGB. Still keeping an eye on us after all these years, aren't you Feliks Edmundovich.' He patted him on his shoulder. 'He was the first. The first of the statues. It was him that gave me the idea ... you know, of a *themed* club. Red Nights. These days there's a lot of.... nostalgia about Soviet days. Misguided of course, but still ... It has its appeal. And then there are the tourists of course.' He turned to the girl and rubbed his hands together. 'So! Oleg tells me you dance? What's your name?'

'Kate. Kate Buckingham.' She smiled a smile that didn't seem to touch her eyes.

'And where are you from, Kate Buckingham?' He felt like a compére on a TV talent show.

'I'm over from England.'

'Oleg – can we arrange some music? Any preference, Kate Buckingham?

'Do you have "Sexual" by Amber?' She said, getting to her feet. Grigor thought she looked a little fragile. But she was slim and pretty, and seemed to have a way about her. Grigor settled into a chair at the very front of the stage, where the hard-core clients sat.

'Good choice. We have that.' Yelled Oleg from the deck, and as the music begun to play Kate begun her routine, skipping on her toes across the stage, loosening her clothes.

Grigor tapped his foot to the music, and watched Kate writhe to the rhythm, discarding her clothes on the stage. Her skin had a pale sheen, and she swung her long legs high in the air – like a real dancer, Grigor thought. Grigor had a sensation as he watched her of being a voyeur. It was a feeling he hadn't remarked in himself before, and he wondered if he had blocked it out. She performed all the ritual moves, caressed herself, splayed her legs. It was like always, but somehow lacking. Then all at once he knew what was missing. She was lacking *pornography*.

When the music stopped, and she gathered up her clothes, Grigor's slow and stark clap echoed. She was beautiful, there was no doubt. She stood there naked on the stage, trailing her clothes in one hand, head on one side, almost a little gawky without the rigour of her dance routine. He felt a tautness in his stomach.

'So?' She said. 'What do you think?'

'Thank you Kate Buckingham. Please get dressed.' Grigor left his hard-core position at the front of the stage to pour himself a vodka behind the bar, jamming his glass under the optic, and watched Kate as she stepped into her jeans. He raised his glass to her but she didn't notice him at all. Oleg fussed with a pile of CD's at the deck, shuffling the cases. He caught Grigor's eye and gave him a thumbs up.

When Kate was dressed she looked around her and

Grigor beckoned. 'Over here,' he pronounced loudly. 'Drink?'

'A vodka please.' Kate propelled herself from the stage and crossed the room, wriggling onto a bar stool. 'Did I pass?' she enquired with her lifeless smile.

Grigor considered for a minute, pouring himself another shot. He passed a hand over his beard. He'd decided for no particular reason that he did not want her on his stage. He was a man of impulse, and he refused in his head to justify his attitude. He pushed a glass of vodka across the bar, and the glass scraped on the tiles.

'You're talented.'

'Thank you.' She tipped the glass in his direction with irony. '*Davai*!'

'*Davai*!' He returned, and drained the glass. He slammed the glass on the bar. 'But it's not quite the dance for "Red Nights". I am sorry.'

'Not the right dance,' she repeated.

'Not for our audience, no.' He ran a hand though his shaggy mane. 'But I have something else that you could do for us...'

She looked nervous. ‘I don’t do sex. Not for money.’

Grigor laughed. ‘That would be unusual here. Another reason why it wouldn’t work out for you at “Red Nights”. But it’s not what I had in mind.’ He ruminated on the ways he could keep her to himself. ‘I think that you could do some other work for us. Some *courier* work. As a Westerner you’re almost beyond suspicion these days. And you’re unmistakably a Westerner. A Russian girl as pretty as you would be far more.. chic.' He saw her injured expression and let out a sudden guffaw, touching her knee in a conciliatory gesture. ‘Nothing personal. But your clothes are chain-store not designer.'

‘What do you want me to do, exactly?’

‘Oleg!’ He summoned with a bark that made the girl start.

Chapter Twenty-Seven

'IT'S ABOUT A girl.' Nikolay ventured, sitting opposite General Artur Blodnieks. The General had bloodshot eyes and a heavy jowl. Nikolay had been summoned to review the progress of the investigation into General Borilyenko. He felt empty as a shell crater.

'Isn't it always?'

'From the archives...' Nikolay produced a black and white photograph of an attractive girl standing on a bridge. He slid it across the desk. Then he produced another photograph in colour of the same girl, this time walking down a busy shopping street. 'Recent surveillance.'

The General looked at both photographs without much curiosity and sniffed. 'Pretty.' He commented.

'These photographs were taken at least 20 years apart.'

The General looked at him without a flicker of interest. 'Nikolay, are you going to get to the point sometime soon?' He gestured to a pile of buff folders. 'As you can see, I am busy.'

'The point is that Borilyenko is having this girl tailed. This one,' he continued, tapping on the black and white print, 'disappeared around 20 years ago.'

The General leaned to inspect the two photographs, squinting his eyes. 'Are they not the same girl?'

'The similarity is remarkable, I agree. The first is Ekaterina Ivanovna Borodina. She was a microbiologist. Her file is—incomplete. She was engaged in some classified project before her disappearance. The other girl is from London. Kate Buckingham. She came here asking questions about Ekaterina Ivanovna. Our investigations have revealed that the surveillance of this Kate Buckingham was ordered by Borilyenko himself. Why the special interest?'

'You think she might be working in any intelligence capacity?'

Nikolay shrugged. 'She seems to be only interested in finding out about Ekaterina Ivanovna.'

The General grunted and pushed aside the prints. 'All very fascinating, I'm sure – but I think there are more important matters when it comes to Borilyenko. What of his involvement with the Feliks Group? Is there evidence?'

'It's difficult.'

The General rubbed the back of his neck with his hand as if in an effort to relieve some tension. 'You don't say. It shouldn't be for us to pursue this type of enquiry. We've become embroiled in some political manoeuvrings, and I don't like it at all.'

'You don't have to tell me.'

'That Borilyenko should position himself as a presidential candidate...'

'Unthinkable.'

'Some believe so.' There was a lengthy pause. The

General looked at Nikolay.

'General, I also believe that the FSB is in some way responsible for the recent murders of bankers. In particular, the Uvyerenny Bank. Colonel Lisakov was at the scene, and I had the distinct impression that his men were there to tidy up.'

Hotel Rossiya, she knew, was the largest hotel in the world. Splayed along the banks of the Moskva River and overshadowing the Kremlin to the rear, it covered over 30 acres of the once important, historical district of Zaryadye. The hotel reminded her of the base layer of a huge mouldering wedding cake. Inside, she clicked through the murmuring marble lobby with its gambling machines that blinked and tumbled, avoiding the stares, and caught a lift to the eleventh floor. The attaché case hung at her side. It was heavy, and she wondered what was in it. Whatever it was, Grigor was paying her $150 to deliver.

At the end of the corridor the *babushka* sitting on a wooden chair glared at her. The whites of her eyes were marbled and her lips had the in-grained pucker of a chain smoker. Kate ignored her and walked along the corridor where she paused at the door of room 1127, listening to the rumbling of voices and laughter from within. She glanced back and tried to gulp away the dryness of her throat. When she tapped on the door the room fell silent, and she wondered if it was in her imagination that she heard the kind of metallic click that signalled the loading of automatic weapons in the movies. But that was in the movies.

When the door opened the acrid smell of stale tobacco stung the air. Traces of smoke drifted from the room. A man in an Adidas track suit held open the door, looked her up and down. Shorter than her, but barrel-chested, he stood with his legs apart as though preparing for a gun-fight. He had crimson, hangover-rimmed eyes.

'Grigor sent me.' She told him as instructed, trying not to catch his eye.

'Of course.' He made as if to execute a stiff bow and stepped aside.

It was a large room with a bay window with crimson

drapes that were swept aside to reveal a view of St Basil's Cathedral. Everyone was smoking. There were five men in the room lounging on beds and couches. A bald man was sprawled on one of the twin beds nursing an empty bottle on his chest and dribbling into his stained shirt. Empty vodka bottles and stub-filled ashtrays littered the tables and the floor. A TV babbled unregarded. American football. The door to the bathroom was open and there were towels on the floor. She felt all eyes upon her as she stood in the centre of the room. The man behind her snatched the attaché case.

'I'm Olensky,' he said. 'This—' he announced to the room with a gesture towards her '—is mine. Apparently.' and she felt the heat rise in her face. A man with rusty hair and bad teeth got up and came up to her with a grin. He stopped, and examined her with clinical curiosity, like the men at the club would do when they thought she wasn't watching. But this man didn't care that she was watching. He seemed to be making his mind up about her. She took a step backwards. Without warning he made a grab for her and his hand slipped inside her skirt and clenched her buttocks with sharp fingernails. An involuntary yelp escaped her in a single breath. From behind her she head the click of the attaché case. Then she rammed her knee as hard as she could between her assailant's legs. The hand on her buttocks froze, but the man didn't move. He didn't double up. Just inches from her face the reek of vodka on his breath was nauseating. She remembered the Russians had a word for this smell: '*peregar.*' All colour had drained from the man's rocky features. A sickly grin formed. She felt more terrified than she had ever been in her life. She pulled at his arm. It was unshakeable. Opened her mouth to say something. Then there was a shout that caused the man to retrieve his hand and straighten up.

'What the fuck is this?' Olensky was ranting. He thrust a handful of banknotes at her. 'Who does he think we are?' Kate noticed only then that he was brandishing a heavy looking pistol. He pointed it at her and she flinched as he pulled the trigger. There was a hollow click. She tasted bile. Somebody laughed. Olensky turned to him, a long faced man with a thin beard. 'Don't you laugh!' He shouted, pointing the gun with a straight arm. 'Don't you *ever* fucking laugh at me!' The man shifted backwards in his seat, and she saw he was afraid.

'Sorry, Boss.'

Olensky swung the barrel round at each man in turn. 'Anyone else see anything funny?' Then he cursed and tugged out the magazine. Kate was horrified to see that it was full of bullets. A misfire. She could be dead. She backed away as he slapped the magazine back into the gun with his palm. He pointed the gun, but she saw his anger had subsided. 'It's disrespectful, that's what it is. Nobody disrespects me. Tell Grigor that. Tell him our business is in dollars not roubles,' he began, 'and tell him that I'll keep his fucking roubles as a forfeit.' He thrust the gun at her forehead. 'Not in payment. As a forfeit. I should send his messenger back in a box to insult me with this monopoly money. But I won't. Not this time. You're lucky.,.' He tucked the gun into his trousers in a swift gesture that made her flinch. His eyes were misty. 'Tell him that I want the money by noon tomorrow at the latest. Or there'll be a fucking war. Now piss off before I change my mind.'

As she was leaving the room he stopped her. 'And bring it yourself. Tell Grigor we want *you* to bring it.' He winked at the rusty haired man. 'Let's call it a condition. I think Rubletsy here has taken a liking to you.'

As she hurried down the corridor, under the suspicious stare of the old woman, the tears were welling in her eyes, and she was sniffling and shivering all at the same time. All she could think about was the click as some mechanical fluke had saved her life. The hotel was a blur. In the lift a wave of claustrophobia came over her and she almost stopped at the next floor. When the doors parted she pushed through two waiting guests and crossed the lobby.

When she emerged from the hotel she found herself gasping for air. It was cold and the cars droned along the broad Varvaka Street with its scaffolding clad monuments. Her eyes were watering either from the cold or from fear, she wasn't sure. She looked around her, and set out with her head down in the direction of the Kremlin.

The Hotel Rossiya seemed to occupy the whole of the street. When she reached a corner she glanced towards the banks of the Moskva River to her left and then up at the hotel, seeking out the eleventh floor, wondering if they were watching. She hated Grigor. She would never go back to Red Nights.

And then the eleventh floor of the Rossiya Hotel threw up over the shabby street in a stream of glass and rubble, with a bang that resounded like two cars colliding. She almost slipped on the pavement in front of a dark windowed Mercedes, craning her neck. At least three rooms were eviscerated. A tangle of metal and blackened, ragged brickwork. The sky revolved above her. People in the street were looking up. She could hear an urgent rasping sound. Then she realised that someone was calling her.

'Kate! Get in! Hurry!' The passenger door of the Mercedes was open and a man was leaning over from the driving seat, beckoning. 'Get in the car, fuck your mother!'

She dipped into the car. Sat down. The man reached past her pulling the door closed. The traffic noise deadened.

'Vanya.' He introduced himself. 'Don't worry. Grigor sent me. Let's go.'

A muted roar and they pulled away with a sharp jolt. Jumbled pieces in her mind assembled themselves, as though the bomb in the hotel had ripped her thoughts apart and they were settling back into place. She looked at Vanya. He smirked.

'Did I—? Did I have anything to do with that?'

The driver's smirk spread wider, but he didn't answer.

'Of course I did. Oh my God..' Rain stippled the windscreen. A fire engine with its horns wailing passed them at speed in the opposite direction, splashing the windows with rain that the wipers swept away. 'I killed them. I killed those men didn't I?'

'Grigor will be happy.'

She shrank into the leather seat, feeling child-like. She had murdered those men. And who else? Who was in the other rooms? Two police cars and another fire engine flailed past, bathing them in blue light for an instant. Inside the warm car it was like watching a movie. 'One of those men almost killed me.' Her voice was quivering, and she realised that her whole body was trembling.

'Scum like that.'

'What about the other rooms?'

He shrugged. 'Similar.' He said. 'They have rooms in that hotel permanently blocked out. For… meetings.'

The leather creaked as she twisted to look out of the rear window. They had passed out of sight of the hotel. 'Who were they?' There was a tremor in her voice that she found impossible to control.

'Mafia.'

'And Grigor.. is he Mafia too?'

'You could say that,' he admitted. 'But not like Olensky.'

'Why not? Why not like Olensky.'

He turned to her with a big grin that exposed a gold tooth, and his eyes crinkled up so she couldn't see into them at all. 'Because we're the *good* guys.'

They sped through the afternoon traffic in silence while she absorbed this, keeping her mind away from the bomb. The good guys. She recognised the broad sweep of Tverskaya Street. They swung right into Kozitsky Lane with a lurch, and stopped. The driver leaned on the horn. They waited. In a moment an iron shutter ground open on their left. The engine growled and as the tyres thudded over the threshold, they were engulfed in darkness. She glanced over her shoulder at the descending shutter. Yellow lights flickered on, and Vanya thrust open his door ushering in a smell of rubber and petrol and spent exhaust. They were in an underground garage with room enough for four cars. Parked next to them was a mean looking Range Rover with gleaming chrome and dark windows. Inches from the three-pointed star on the bonnet was a set of iron steps where a wiry man in a leather bomber jacket languished, hand poised over a bank of light switches. He was grinning. She could hear strains of Russian folk music from somewhere. Through the windscreen she saw him put up his hand. 'Welcome back.'

A gentle touch at her elbow prompted her to get out of the car. She was finding it hard to perform simple functions. She tugged a few times at the door catch before she could make it work. When she stumbled out of the car she allowed herself to be directed up the steps, feet clanging on metal. They ascended a staircase with greasy walls.

'Where are we going?'

'I'm Fyodr.' Said the man at the stairs, as if in answer to her question. He had a voice without edge. 'Like Dostoevsky.' He added with mock pride. At the top of the stairs Vanya flung open a wide door and the music crashed and echoed off the walls. She followed him in a daze into the brightly lit Red Nights bar, and a ripple of applause broke out. Grigor was there. He shouldered his way towards her, a vodka bottle hanging from his arm, and stopped after a few steps, looked at her, his broad forehead angled down in earnest appraisal. Intent. Then without a word he crushed her in his arms, lifting her from her feet, so that all her breath escaped in a grunt. She wriggled, trying to touch the floor with her toes, and he released her.

'We'll be celebrating thanks to you.'

'I don't understand. What was it for? What did I do? Why me? The money ... the bomb. How could you…?'

'Protection money. Only as it turns out it wasn't us that needed protection,' he laughed, guided her to the bar. She blinked at the faces all around her and it was an all male cast. It hardly occurred to her that it was unusual that many of the men were carrying guns. Grigor himself, she noticed had a large pistol tucked into his waistband.

'Drink?' Without waiting Grigor edged behind the bar and took a stubby glass from a shelf, splashed vodka into it and offered it to her. She took it with both hands because she was still trembling. Threw back her head, letting the spirit course down her throat. It seemed to make her feel less shaky. Holding out the glass Grigor filled it again.

Nodding at Grigor's gun before she took another gulp she said: ‘Everybody has guns.’

‘That’s right.’ He pulled the pistol from his belt and waved it with pride. ‘This is a Browning .380. You can't imagine the damage this can do.’ He inspected it with reverence. ‘You can’t imagine,’ he repeated, half to himself.

'But why?'

Grigor eased the gun back into his belt and looked solemn. 'Possible repercussions. Just a precaution, but who knows? They'll regroup. Have to. A new leader I expect. And then they'll come after us.'

The atmosphere in the bar was taut. The music was merry and the vodka was flowing, but there the faces were steely, and men sprawled at tables without talking. At either side of the empty stage the statues of Lenin and Stalin presided. Lenin had a yellow streamer hanging from his ear. The red flags hung above them like becalmed sails. She felt sick.

'Why would you send me to do something like this? Horrible. It was horrible.' She was shaking again.

Then she heard a thumping at the door. A rattle of weapons being readied. Somebody turned off the music. She backed towards the stage and crouched at Stalin's granite feet. Her throat felt knotted.

Somebody banged again. There was a muffled shout. Grigor nodded to Fyodr and another man who lifted the bar from the doors, and when they tugged open the doors they stood well back.

A silver-haired man in a long fur-trimmed coat

strolled into the club with his hands deep in his pockets, his heels squeaking on the parquet. He paused and looked around him until he caught Grigor's eye. He nodded. Fyodr and the other man peered into the street behind him, then pulled the doors shut and barred them again. Most of the men in the club had lowered their weapons, but Kate could tell he was not a welcome visitor.

'Well, Grigor. A successful day for you?' His sharp tone resonated in the big room. Grigor leaned on the bar. He shrugged.

'Not especially.'

'That's not what I heard. I came straight here, of course.'

'Vodka?' but the silver haired man ignored him and paced in Kate's direction. He stopped. looked up at Stalin’s bust and gave an ironic salute. Then for a fleeting second he caught her eye, and she thought she imagined a glimmer of recognition. He seemed to lose his composure, but then he turned and paced back to Grigor. Drank the vodka.

'What are you talking about?' said Grigor.

‘I need a few minutes of your time, Grigor Vassilyich.’ The man headed towards Grigor’s office. Grigor said:

'I’ll be right back.’

Kate watched the office door close behind them.

'Who's that?' She asked a haggard looking man with an AK47 propped over his shoulder.

'KGB.'

‘So who’s the girl?’ Said Lisakov when they were alone.

‘The girl?’ Said Grigor with surprise. ‘Just a girl.’

‘Trust me,’ said Lisakov narrowing his eyes. ‘that girl is not *just* a girl. There’s more to her. If I were you, I would be careful when it comes to that girl.’

Grigor was taken aback. What would Lisakov know about some scrawny tourist from London? Did he suspect that he had used her to deliver the bomb?

‘She’s just a girl,’ repeated Grigor, watchfully.

‘Anyhow. The bomb.’

‘The bomb?’

‘It was a bit public.’

Grigor shrugged. 'He was well protected. Anyway the Rossiya could do with a little *renovation.*'

'It may be expensive.'

'It's always expensive.'

'I will ensure there are no loose ends.'

'All I can ask.'

Lisakov stood up, brushing off imaginary dust from his trousers. 'I'll head over to the Rossiya to supervise. It's important that we find out who is responsible for this outrage. Round up the usual suspects, as they say in the movies.'

'Do you have a preference?' said Grigor, without getting up.

Lisakov smiled. 'We'll see.'

Boris Yeltsin mopped his neck with a towel as he limped from the tennis court, racket hanging from his left hand. Borilyenko's eyes were drawn to the two missing fingers no matter how much he tried not to notice. An accident with a grenade they said. Not heroism but a boyhood stunt.

Yeltsin landed next to him on the bench with a

grunt.

'Not bad for an old man.' He punched Borilyenko in the arm and it hurt. 'We old men can still give the youngsters a run.' His shirt was sticking to him, a gluey mess, and his chest heaved. The sweatband around his head made Borilyenko think of a coronet.

The youngster he had given a run today was a rugged man in his 40's who saluted with his racket as he left the court. Yeltsin leaned and buried his head in the towel whilst he steadied his breathing. Droplets of the president's sweat made dark patches on the concrete floor.

'All that running around,' he muttered between his knees. 'Even five years ago, it would have been nothing. I'm an athlete.' He looked up at Borilyenko with rheumy eyes. His face was strained. '*Was* an athlete. Did you know that? Takes a younger man, Yuri Ivanovich. This game. Tennis. More importantly this—this high office. The thing about getting old ... I used to make things happen, now things just happen to me.' He made a wide gesture, voice thin, raspy, but still resonating amongst the courts. He leaned in. 'You're an old man too, Yuri Ivanovich. But not sick, like me.' Then like a disclaimer, 'Sick? That's what the doctors say. Sick and tired more like. Pah!'

'What are you saying, Boris Nikolaevich?'

'All this terrorism. Bombs. It has to stop. I lost money, you know. Uvyerenny Bank. I was an investor,' he continued with a sigh, 'International terrorism. Domestic terrorism. Then Chechnya. Feliks Group. It's all around. Needs a strong man with a belly for violence. I say we need to come down hard.' He slammed the handle of his tennis racket on the wooden floor. 'Put a stop to it. But what I always say is: you can build a throne from bayonets, but you can't sit on it for long.' A stale expression that Borilyenko had heard before. Yeltsin swivelled his eyes. 'I'm not the man for this task. Used to be. Not anymore. Not now. When I was an athlete..' He grimaced. 'Maybe you could build that throne, Yuri Ivanovich? Think you could?'

'I'm at your service.'

Yeltsin coloured. 'It's not about *my* service you idiot. No about one man. Just like it wasn't about the

Party before. The Communist Party ... that was just an idea. Pie in the sky. I told them that. Saw through it at once. You people ... those people.. It's about the State. About Mother Russia. Take hold!' Exasperated he made a fist of the hand with the missing fingers. 'Somebody needs to… somebody.' Then seemed to falter. 'You know, Yuri Ivanovich, if you want it, it's yours. I can make it happen. But you have to really want it.' He looked dismal.

'Are you offering me the presidency?'

'It's the heart you see. People - I don't care what they say - people think it's the vodka. But it's the heart. And these drugs they give me. You know this to be true, Yuri Nioklaevich. I swear.' He seemed to drift. 'Somebody needs to take hold.' a mantra, repeated to himself. 'If not me then who?'

'I thought Chermonyerdin?'

'Yes, yes. Everybody thinks that.' Dismissive. He thought for a moment, eyes narrowing, watching tennis balls thrashed around. He nodded at the courts. 'How long do you think Viktor Stepanovich would last out there, on the tennis court? Chermonyerdin - he's got seven years on me. Man's senile. Dribbles in his kasha. No, no no. Not him. For God's sake, not him.'

'If not Chermonyrdin, then..?'

Borilyenko thought he heard Yeltsin mutter 'Speak of the devil' as he rose suddenly to his feet. Borilyenko stood up as a taut, compact man with a bald head approached wearing immaculate tennis whites. His expression reminded Borilyenko of a picture of a fox in a children's story book. Yeltsin shouldered past Borilyenko so that he had to step aside, and embraced the man. 'Vladimir Vladimirovich. Welcome.'

'Thank you, Boris Nikolaevich. I flew in from Petersburg this morning and came straight from the hotel.'

'Good. Good of you too come. Let's play a couple of sets, then go to my office. Maybe I have a proposition for you.' He gave a wave in the direction of Borilyenko. 'Take care of it. The Feliks Group. I want it stopped, and I'm relying on you, Yuri Nioklaevich,' and he realised that he was dismissed as the two men headed for the courts, Yeltsin with a paternal hand on the other's shoulder, or maybe for support. Borilyenko felt abandoned. Who was the stranger from St Petersburg, he wondered? And what to do about Feliks?

Chapter Twenty-Eight

THE EARNEST MAN with neat brown hair leaned across the coffee table with his hands clasped together. Robert eyed him warily. It was odd, but if he turned away even for a moment, he could not recall a single feature about the man in front of him, except the colour and length of his hair. He had already established that he was not a policeman. He had met various types of policemen over the past few days, asking about Kate.

'Your wife..'

'Ex-wife,' reminded Robert.

The man began again, with just the hint of a foreign

accent that was almost indiscernible. 'Your *ex*-wife. Do you have any idea where she is?'

'As I've already told the police, I've no idea. Who are you anyway? You didn't say...'

'I can tell you where she is. Your wife. Your ex-wife.'

Robert was taken aback. 'What is this? What's going on?'

'Kate is in Moscow.'

Moscow? Why in the world would Kate go to Moscow? His Kate? 'I don't understand.' His brow furrowed and he leaned towards the man, mirroring his posture. Two men hunched over a coffee table.

'She's quite safe. For now,' he added.

'But what is she doing there?'

'That's what we're trying to find out.' The man reached inside his plain, dark jacket, brushing aside a plain dark tie, and produced an identity card with a bland photograph, surmounted with a gold crest surrounding a blue globe. He laid it open on the table. The letters looked like Greek. Or Russian. Definitely Russian, he thought. 'This won't mean much to you,

I'm afraid,' he said. 'I work for the Russian security services, and I'm hoping that you can help us to help your wife.'

'So you're what—KGB?' He hazarded in a whirl.

The man smiled, showing a perfect row of white teeth. 'That particular acronym is behind us now, thankfully.'

Robert swallowed. He felt as though he had been swept away on some wild excursion. This was not his life – this was like something from a movie. He was an observer. 'What about the police? They want to interview Kate. Will you tell them where she is? Can you put me in touch with her?'

'Let's treat this as our secret for now. I don't suggest that you or I communicate with the British police until we have done some detective work of our own. We want to help. Do we have a criminal at large in Moscow... or something else?'

'A criminal? Kate? What can I do?'

'All you can do is to give me some background. Tell me about Kate. Anything you like. Anything you know. We're looking for something in her background. A connection. We don't know what ... but we think Kate may be in danger. We know of course about the *incident*. We know about the unfortunate death…' He paused. 'It's most probably connected with her visit to Moscow.' He smiled as he said: 'We are—how do you say it? Trying to join up the dots.' He smiled over Robert's shoulder. 'And who is this lady?'

Robert turned to see Becki standing in the doorway with a curious expression.

'Please go and play,' he said, gently.

'You can call me Pavel.' Remarked the visitor, producing an A4 notebook and a pen from his bag as Becki scurried down the hall. 'Now, let's … let's begin at the very beginning. Where was Kate born? Who were her parents? Was there anything unusual about her? He glanced up as Robert sat there in silence. 'It's background. If we're to help Kate, there's nothing that's too trivial.'

Something trivial. Without thinking, Robert said with a sinking feeling, 'She used to have these dreams.'

Chapter Twenty-Nine

'YOU'RE LYING TO us, old woman.'

Emila Alliluyeva sat very still with her hands in her lap and her eyes averted.

'What do you want me to say, sir?' She said with a cracked voice.

The officer stood up, towering over her, and grimaced. 'We want you to tell us the truth, of course.'

She looked up at him with pleading eyes. 'Just tell me what truth you want to hear. Tell me and I will say it for you.'

A man in a long dark overcoat had just entered the

interview room and he paused in the doorway. The interrogator glanced at him and nodded.

'You did not leave your post?' he said to Emila, 'Not even for a moment?'

'Never.' She hesitated and looked for inspiration. 'At least I don't think so. Please just tell me what you want.' Her interrogator's face was blank.

'I think you saw nothing,' he said. 'You made up the girl to hide the fact that you neglected your post.'

'I saw nobody. There was no girl,' she said.

'Wait.' Interjected the newcomer. 'Wait just a moment.'

Emila looked from her interrogator to this man, wondering where she should place her faith. This new man looked to be senior. Important. He swept over to her in his outdoor clothes, as though from another realm and spoke kindly. He had intelligent eyes.

'Please describe to me the girl you saw,' the man said.

She glanced at her interrogator who had stepped back to accommodate the superior officer. The officer was tall and well groomed, with silver hair like a doctor. Or a fox. 'There was no girl,' she mumbled at last, looking at the floor. 'I left my post. I will be punished.'

The man knelt down beside her. 'You will not be punished. Trust me.'

Emila looked at him. Could she trust him? She saw no threat in his expression, only empathy. She bit her lip. 'I think I may have seen a girl in the corridor. She may have entered room 1127.' There, it was out. She shrank back a little as if expecting a rebuke.

'Good. Good. Now please describe her,' said the man.

'A foreigner. A Westerner.' A Westerner—to her it was almost a curse. She didn't approve of the new ways. She didn't approve of Westerners here in Moscow, treating the place as their own. Everything was better before. Life was easier then. 'She was tall, with long blonde hair. Pretty, I expect, to a certain type of man. Carrying a big briefcase. She looked wrong. Like a prostitute, but not. I see these girls come and go in my line of work.' She shook her head. 'Not a prostitute, this one. Something else.'

The man seemed to consider for a moment. 'Please think hard. When the girl came out of the room, did she still have the briefcase.'

Emila responded in an instant, anxious to please now. 'No. I thought it was strange. In a hurry, she was. And upset.'

Lisakov rose stiffly to his feet, and Emila looked up at him, but he headed towards the door. 'Thank you for your cooperation,' he said amicably. He nodded to her interrogator as he opened the door, and it was then that she noticed a fraction of a shake of the head. A brief communication passed between her interrogator and the other man, and she had an eerie feeling that her fate had been sealed in that tiny gesture. She felt breathless. She started as if to get up, but didn't seem to have the energy, the will.

'Wait!' She called, but the door had clicked shut. The room was silent. Her interrogator was looking at her with an irritated expression, his hands planted on his hips. She looked at the dusty floor and steeled herself for what was to come.

'This girl you have an interest in. She seems to have got herself mixed up in something.' A stark voice at the end of the line. Borilyenko raised an eyebrow.

'What kind of something?'

'She is ... well she appears to be involved with a criminal gang.'

'Mafia you mean?'

'Yes.' There was a pause. Borilyenko waited. This was a completely unexpected development. 'She's—well, it looks like she carried out an execution.' There was a cough at the end of the line.

'A what!?'

'There's no doubt I am afraid. She delivered an explosive device to a rival gang. It was successfully detonated, probably remotely. Six fatalities.' The voice was impartial. Factual. Why would she do that? How would she get involved in something like this? Borilyenko hunted for possibilities where none existed. There was nothing in the girl's background that would lead her to this…

'I don't understand. It doesn't make sense. Let me think about this—how has it been presented?'

'My people were on the scene. We don't want panic. It was made to appear like an unfortunate incident. A gas explosion.'

'Were there witnesses? To the girl's involvement I mean?'

'There was one. The *dezhurnaya-* the corridor matron.'

'They still have those?' said Borilyenko perversely, his mind still turning circles. In Soviet times every hotel had a woman on each floor that monitored the comings and goings, collecting and dispensing keys. These were the *dezhurnaya,* but it was a practise long since discontinued in most hotels.

'In the Rossiya, yes. They've been useful to us in the past. Sadly, on this occasion the witness suffered a heart attack on the way to the police station. She was not able to throw any light on the identity of the perpetrator before she died. It's a pity.'

'A pity. Yes.' Borilyenko reached a conclusion. 'I think we may need to abandon our surveillance plan and bring her under our control. Her safety is paramount. She is of vital importance to National

Security.'

'National Security,' repeated Lisakov. 'Of course, General.'

Chapter Thirty

IT WAS A fine day. Ekaterina paused outside the glass door of the facility, framed in the rugged concrete lintels of the porch, enjoying the silence and the warmth of the sun on her face. She gazed at the orange and gold and green shrubs that spilled over the brick wall of a square, decorative bed in front of the entrance. It wasn't much of an effort, she thought, but at least someone had tried to brighten the place up. She crossed to the bed and stooped to tug some scrawny weeds from the crumbling dry earth. Not much of an effort, but something. The moss and weeds between the slabs that formed the quadrangle were entrenched. A losing battle. She kicked at some of it and the moss lifted and smeared the grey concrete with a deep green.

Her appointment with the doctor was at 11:00am and so she took her time, walking along the cracked pavement towards the apartment blocks: nine identical buildings, etched with rows of windows, in the centre of a patch of scrubland surrounded by a few wilting trees. Some rickety picnic tables had been placed there for optimistic lunches. She looked up, calculating where her apartment was, halfway up the second building from the left, at the front. Everywhere was still and silent. Everybody working. Or sick, she reminded herself. Half of Sorsk was sick like her with influenza. If it was influenza.

The other side of the apartment block there stretched for several hundred metres a single storey block with shuttered steel windows on one side of the road. The State Research Centre for Applied Microbiology. Even with her clearance she was not admitted to that block, but she knew the nature of the research carried out there. She knew what happened behind those shutters that the sunlight could not penetrate. Everybody did, but you didn't talk about it out loud. Those that worked there were regarded with a little distaste by those engaged in more acceptable projects. And was her own project acceptable? Did it satisfy her own peculiar moral criteria?

Across the road was Building Six, a drab concrete and glass structure five stories high surrounded by an electrified fence. Some of the windows were cracked or broken. The entrance was guarded by two bored looking uniformed KGB officers. They watched her pass without much interest. She could hear the electric fence humming.

When she reached Keldysh Street she turned right and entered an anonymous building with a scrappily painted grey door. She passed through a corridor with scuffed walls and encountered a grim faced woman glaring over a reception desk.

'I have an appointment with Dr Korolyov.'

'Name?' The receptionist spun a rolodex with authority. Ekaterina cursed her. She knew very well who she was. There were not so many residents in

Sorsk that each of the patients could not be recognised.

'But you know who I am. And I know who you are, Comrade Lebeda.'

'Name.'

'OK, OK. Ekaterina Ivanovna Borodina.'

Comrade Lebeda plucked a card from the rolodex and squinted at it. Then she picked up the phone. 'You're early.'

When she was directed to the Doctor's office, she made her way along another corridor, her footsteps resounding in the passage. She knocked at the door and waited, but there was no answer. She knocked again, louder this time. For some reason, she felt a rising panic. Something was gripping her tightly inside. She was hot and flustered. She knocked again. Her forehead was damp and sticky to the touch. She began to bang on the door with the palm of her hand.

Bang. Bang. Bang.

Still no answer. Her breathing was shallow. She gulped. Raised her hand to the door..

When she awoke she was in a hotel room and somebody was banging on the door. She looked around, bewildered and confused. Her clothes were draped over a chair. She was naked and cold. The air-conditioning was fierce.

Bang. Bang. Bang.

Sorsk slipped into its allotted place in her memories. She looked at her watch. Two am.

Somebody banged again on the door and called her name, but she couldn't tell who it was. She grabbed a bathrobe from the foot of the bed and wrapped herself in it before rushing to the door, where she paused. 'Who is it? There was no answer. More banging. She made a decision and pulled open the door.

Grigor filled the frame of the doorway. His broad head was more pronounced than ever. His beard, she noticed, was flecked with grey. He leaned on the frame, clearly drunk. In the corridor a door opened a crack, then clicked shut again.

'It's late,' he said. 'Sorry to wake you.'

Still trying to extract herself from her dream, Kate at first stood firm at the threshold, and folded her arms. 'What do you want?'

His eyes were bleary. 'Do you have a drink?'

She ought to feel afraid but she didn't. She made an effort to rationalise her lack of fear. There was a gangster at her door at two am. She stepped aside and he brushed past, sucking in his stomach, headed straight for the mini-bar in a heavy footed stride that seemed to make the room tremor. He pulled out several bottles from the mini-bar, examining then discarding each one. Finally he held up a miniature bottle of champagne 'Want one of these?'

'What do you want?'

Grigor flipped out the cork with plop, and poured a glass for her with an unsteady hand. It splashed her hand when the took it. Then he twisted the cap from one of the bottles and emptied it into a glass. 'Sorry it's so late.' He repeated, and thrust himself into the single armchair in the corner.

'It's two in the morning.'

'Is it?'

'What do you want?' Trying to feel angry. 'I'm so angry with you.'

Grigor shook his head. 'I don't know. To apologise. To help. But first of all, to apologise. I was wrong to get you to deliver the bomb. It was a kind of joke.'

'A joke?' She knew she had tears in her eyes now. 'I killed those men.' It was the first time she had vocalised it, and it made it real.

'Not exactly a joke. A test. *Like* a joke I suppose ... a bit of a prank amongst men. Not that you're a man, of course. More like a test.' He let out a deep sigh. 'I don't know. Like lots of things it seemed like a good idea at the time.' He looked at her. 'I can't explain. I can only say I'm sorry.'

'People died. How many people died?'

'People always die. Story of my life. In my business ... well anyway, let's look at the people who died, shall we? Worthless people. You need to know this. Gangsters, all of them. I don't know how many were there, but each one of them deserved to die that way. Vermin. In fact it was a good thing that you did, whether you believe it or not. Anyway, I apologise all the same. It's different here. From what you're used to, I mean. You come from a place where policeman don't carry guns.'

'But you - you're a gangster as well. Just like

them.'

'Not like them.' He shook his head, looking at the floor. 'I don't think of myself that way. A businessman, yes. I want to make you understand...' He ventured. 'In Russia today, it's not like anywhere in the world. Not even like the Russia where I grew up. The Wild East, they call it. Anything can happen. You just have to get through each day. Who's guilty? Who's innocent? Who the fuck cares? I like to think we're the good guys,' he said, echoing what the driver had said in the car outside the Hotel Rossiya. He pressed the small, empty bottle against his brow and rolled it from side to side to cool his forehead. Kate thought he looked like a man undergoing something that wrenched him. He sat up again, aimed the bottle, and it rattled against the sides of the waste bin. 'Maybe you don't care—I wouldn't blame you—but I came here to try to make you understand.

Not too long ago, I was a soldier. Like my father. I come from a military family. Then I wasn't a gangster like you call me - I was a Major. A Major…' he repeated. 'Not just a Major in any old army, but

Spetsnaz. Alfa. That's Special Forces, like your English SAS. The sent me to all the worst places. They sent Alpha first. Afghanistan. Chechnya.. wherever. Dropped us behind the lines. Look.' He fumbled with the buttons of his shirt to reveal an angry furrow that spanned his chest. 'I was wounded many times. I believed in what we were doing. They told us we were liberators. Told us we were peace-keeping. Told us so much shit. Of course, I saw a lot of people die. Good men mostly. On both sides good and bad men dying all the time. You didn't try to get close to anyone because they could be gone the next day. Killing was as commonplace as emptying the latrines. Unpleasant. But part of our routine. I don't take it seriously any more. Death. Some lives are not even worth thinking about. There are men from the Mujahedeen that I'd rate way above the filth I see on the streets in Moscow.'

'But you kill people.' Kate steeled herself to remember every so often that she was here, sitting opposite this big, sad angry man in a hotel room in Moscow. She missed her home, she realised. She wanted to be back in London. She remembered the

Champagne and gulped at it in wistful, unshared celebration of occasions not yet met, or those that had foundered untoasted in one memory or another.

'It's true. And they called me a hero for it. But listen, when I left the army I expected a hero's welcome. I was entitled, wasn't I? After everything. All the terror. All the people I killed. They gave me medals to prove it.' He nodded at the window. 'And all this? The way Russia is today? The funny thing—I blame myself. No, really. Not solely of course, but I bear responsibility. Back in '91 I was with Alfa under Karpukhin, and they ordered us to storm the White House. To murder Yeltsin and the others. Well. I don't have much time for that drunken bastard. Sorry.' A brief smile. 'But we decided, all of us that day, to disobey. We rebelled. Karpukhin too. It was the first time for me that I ever disobeyed an order. Things could have turned out differently. Karpuhkin was a hero too then. All heroes together making history. Yeltsin on that fucking tank.' He laughed. 'Tank 110 it was. Afterwards they rounded up all those criminals who tried to make it happen and put another bunch of criminals in charge. All for nothing. Here's to fucking heroes.' He took another bottle of spirits and tilted it at her and said again. 'Here's to heroes.' He threw his head back.

'When I came out, joined the civilians and of course there wasn't any hero's welcome. None of us realised just how unpopular our wars were, back home. We were too busy defending the motherland to appreciate that nobody thought it needed defending. Not by people like us. We were pariahs. So, these days the bars are full of vets telling their tales, showing off their collections of medals. Their wounds.' He patted his chest, where the scar was. 'But nobody gives a shit. They're tired of hearing about it. We're left with the medals and the scars and there's no work for war veterans. Not anywhere. We find other work to do. You know - I employ girls in my clubs to take their clothes off for tourists … one of them is a physician! One an engineer! There should be more respect.

'And so everybody does what they can.' He shook his head. There was a distant look in his eyes. 'Me? I take what I feel should have been given. I'm not a bad man.. Not in the regular sense. Do you think I'm a bad man, Kate Buckingham?'

'Why are you telling me all this? I don't understand.'

Grigor looked at her. 'I don't know. I like you. I wanted you to understand. I was thinking and thinking. Thinking.' He kneaded his forehead with the heel of his hand. 'Then I decided to come here. I don't know why it matters. Or even *if* it matters. It seemed to matter at the time.' He planted two meaty hands on his thighs and rubbed them. 'So, am I forgiven?'

'Of course not. How could I forget what you made me do.' The debris pattering on the pavement beneath the hotel. The moment of realisation.

'No not forgotten. Nothing's forgotten. We all have our *memories*.' He grinned at her. 'I've paid off your bill at the hotel. Stay as long as you like. It's taken care of.'

'Why would you do that?'

'Why wouldn't I? It's a big thing you did.'

She was a murderer, she thought. 'And the police? What about the police? Surely there'll be an investigation.'

'You don't need to worry.' He stroked his beard. 'Now,' he said, 'is there something else I can do for you?'

'What do you mean?'

'Everything's not what it seems with you, Kate Buckingham.' He shot her a sly look. 'You did know that you're being followed? By the FSB?'

Nikolay spent a loveless, sexless night with 2 hookers in a downtown nightclub. It wasn't sex he wanted, and it wasn't sex they wanted. He just craved the company of two pretty girls that were fun and intelligent and undemanding. He paid a premium price for the vodka, and they helped him to consume it without making him feel guilty.

Two 'o' clock in the morning. Too late to go to sleep. Too late to be awake. The music pounded and smoke hung in gossamer layers. The club had a Soviet theme, pandering to the Western businessman's image of Russia. Reclaimed statues lined the walls, of once notorious Soviet officials. He recognised Krushchev and Brezhnev with their heavy jowls scowling at him, and he raised a glass to them.

Nadya, who told him she was a law student by day, was toasting the health of the president, her irony not lost on anyone. A freckled girl with an angular jaw that made her every expression emphatic in some way. Everyone followed her toast because old habits die hard in Russia. '*Davai!*'

Nikolay's head was swimming, but he wanted to preserve this state of half sensibility indefinitely. To his left sat Irina. She was dark and sincere, and made all the usual small talk. The shadow of her breasts reached low into her silk top, and he had to check himself more than once when his eyes strayed too deeply, trying to stretch the shadow to its source. Irina wanted to make small talk about his family, and raised her voice above the pulsating music, leaning into his ear. Her nicotine breath lingered in the air. Since Nikolay had no family other than an elderly aunt in Volgograd, he was happy to invent one for her, just as his training had taught him. And as the inane conversation washed around him, and as he half-heartedly fended off the attentions of Irina and Nadya, his mind turned once more to the

English girl, and the connection with Borilyenko.

On stage, a long-limbed girl in a KGB peaked cap was making swift, angular movements in time to the music. Her milky, naked limbs gleamed where they were caught by the spotlight. Nadya tugged his sleeve and asked him if he thought the girl was sexy. He flashed her a grin.

The report from London had done nothing to reveal any possible connection. Except for the odd dreams of course, which were fascinating but hardly relevant. Then there was the Russian scientist with the classified file. Why would a stripper from London flee to Moscow in search of a dead scientist, pursued by the FSB? Why would the head of the FSB be interested? It made no sense.

Nadya asked him in her emphatic way for a private dance, and he shook his head.

'What is it you do, when you're not dancing?' He asked her.

She smiled. Everybody asks. They also ask what she is doing working in a place like this. He knew the answers already. She was a medical student or a law student. Maybe even a doctor. Or she was an engineer.. mostly it was the truth. Here in today's Russia the professions barely generated enough Roubles to pay for a miserable apartment in a shabby Moscow suburb. The girls came here and places like it for as long as their beauty and youth endured, to supplement their incomes. To get by.

'I'm a micro-biologist,' she said.

A microbiologist. Like Ekaterina Ivanovna, he thought. He looked at her faintly freckled face, and saw that she was older than he had first noticed. Thin lines were discernible through the make-up. It was quite feasible that she might really be a microbiologist.

'Interesting,' he said, and Nadya pouted. 'No, really.. That's really interesting.' Although he didn't understand why. 'Where are you working?'

'I'm doing a research project just now. At Moscow State University.'

Nikolay considered for a moment, twirling his empty glass in his fingers. A question too ludicrous to vocalise was on the tip of his tongue. She was looking at him through half-closed lids. 'You are a microbiologist,' he intoned with infinite care, the way that drunks pronounce unfamiliar words. 'And what is your specialist area?'

'Genetics.' She said without any hesitation, throwing back another vodka.

It was too late now. The question had crystallised in his head. There was nothing else he could say. 'Have you heard of a woman called Ekaterina Ivanovna Borodina?'

Music played. People danced and drank. A short-lived flurry as someone was ejected from the club. Nothing out of the ordinary happened at all. It was a simple question, after all. Irina thought for a minute, wrinkling her nose. 'I think so...' she said at length, pushing her hair back. 'The name's familiar. I think I've seen a paper... Who is she?'

Nikolay felt as though he had been roused from a deep sleep. He straightened up. Nadya looked startled.

'What was the subject, do you remember? This paper, what was it about?'

Nadya had shuffled sideways on the bench. 'Does it matter?'

'I'm sorry. I think I'm very drunk. Do you remember anything? About this paper?'

She flashed him a broad smile, and took up his hand between her soft warm palms, leaning inwards so that his eyes were drawn to the shadow of her breasts. Her scent was heady and intoxicating and his nostrils flared. 'Let's forget about genetics.' she said, and wriggled back towards him, cosying herself against his arm. Irina looked away, bored. She was chewing gum.

'There's an English girl in Moscow. Called Kate. She's looking for Ekaterina Borodina.'

She released his hand, and the mood had changed again. Her smile had vanished. 'Kate,' she repeated. 'What's your interest in her?'

Nikolay's eyes were leaden. The music resonated inside his head. He felt like he was underwater. 'I don't know.' He shrugged. 'Maybe nothing.' He pulled at his glass, knowing that he shouldn't drink any more.

Suspicious, she said: 'Are you Cheka?' Then she thought for an instant, and seemed to make up her mind about something. 'Wait.' She stood up, grasping her purse. ' I will be only a moment.'

'It's OK.' Avoiding eye contact Nikolay watched the dancers, as they weaved around the bar, whispering heated confidences and touching the arms of the men, tugging a sleeve. Nadya sashayed to the other side of the bar where she was lost in the shadows and the throng. The music wailed. 'Iron' Felix Dzherzhinsy glared down from his perch with disapproval. Nikolay glanced at Irina, but she had lost interest and she nursed her sickly cocktail, seeking out a new man to signal her with his eyes.

After a while he felt a light touch on his shoulder, and Nadya stood like a shimmering phantom at his side. She beckoned with her chin. 'Get up. You need to meet somebody.' And without waiting for him to struggle to his feet she swept away. He found he was unsteady on his feet and put it down to cramp. She led him to a heavy door. 'He's expecting you.' She said, and turned to walk away. Over her shoulder she said 'Good night, Nikolay.'

He took a deep breath, and was on the point of knocking, but instead pushed open the door. Through a haze of cigar smoke a gruff voice said: 'I hear you're looking for a friend of mine?'

A giant of a man raised himself from behind a desk, and pointed to a chair. Nikolay noted the Makharov PM pistol on the desk. He glanced around at the heavy wooden furniture, the leather sofas stationed around a glass topped coffee table that seemed to be fashioned out of a huge shell casing. The smoke irritated Nikolay's eyes.

'Drink.' The man wiggled a bottle of Stolichnaya at him as he sank back into his seat. It sounded like an order rather than an invitation.

'Why not?'

The man grunted and splashed vodka into two glasses, leaning to push one across the desk. 'I am Grigor Vassiyivich Malenkov, proprietor of this fucking dump.'

'Pleased to meet you, I guess.'

'And whom do I have the pleasure of addressing?'

'I'm Nikolay.' He stretched a hand towards Grigor, who grasped it briefly and firmly. 'Nikolay Sergeyevich Sokolov.'

‘And who exactly is Niokolay Sergeyevich?’

Nikolay shrugged, feeling the weight of the man even from where he was sitting. ’I’m nobody.’

‘You here on official business? Or would you say you’re just another punter?’ Grigor swung around in the chair and rose to his full height, pouring himself another drink as he did so. He did not offer Nikolay another.

‘Official?’

Grigor sniffed. ‘You smell like a Chekist to me.’

‘No. I’m not a Chekist.’

’You were asking about the English girl. In there.’

‘I mentioned her.’

‘Funny. Everybody’s mentioning her lately.’

‘What’s she to you?’

Grigor shot him a look. ‘She works for me. I’m a caring employer. If she’s in trouble I’d like to know about it.’

Nikolay made an effort to focus. He could hear the thump of the music outside, but it was as if from another world. He felt shipwrecked here in this office.

‘Maybe we’re both looking out for her.’ He said at

length.

'And in what capacity would you be dong that?' And when Nikolay remained silent Grigor laid a heavy hand on his shoulder. 'I could have you searched. I could even beat it out of you.' he said, but it was with a casual humour. 'If you're not a Chekist - then maybe you don't know—those guys have an interest in her.' He said, leaning on the desk.

'I know.'

'So what's to be done? If we're both looking out for her, then maybe we should lay some cards on the table. What do you think?'

Nikolay said: 'Sounds like a plan.'

'So maybe you can start by telling me who you are?'

'I'm with the security services. Not FSB but something else. All I can tell you.'

'I knew you were a fucking Chekist. What's your interest in this girl?'

'She was brought to my attention when she entered the country. She came here to look for somebody. A scientist from Soviet times. Some kind of expert in genetics. All I know is the scientist was engaged in something so secret that there's no access to the files. She says that this person is a relative. I'm not so sure it's the truth. I said I'd help to find her... But of course, you know. It's an almost impossible task to find out what happened.'

'I was with Kate just a few hours ago. At her hotel. We talked.' He made a vague gesture with his arm, and Nikolay realised that he too was drunk. 'I like her,' he said, and grunted. 'Anyway, for some reason the FSB is very interested in her. They're tailing her everywhere. She's no idea why. She seems ordinary enough. Maybe to do with this scientist. Her work?' He paused. 'You're some kind of policeman?' Looking up from his chest.

Nikolay shrugged. 'Not really. But it seems that's what they want me to be right now.'

Chapter Thirty-One

BEFORE THE EXPLOSION that ripped through the house on Privett Avenue, Ralph had spent a lot of time standing at the front window and not sitting in his usual armchair. He chewed the stem of his pipe, but rarely lit it. When Hayley entered the room he had remarked on seeing strangers in the street.

'He seems in a hurry,' or 'They don't look quite right as a couple, d'you think?' She had given it little thought, appeasing him now and then with a word of consensus.

There was something awkward and ill-fitting about the days, and he had a feeling of foreboding that he put down to a kind of resurgence of his training from the old days, like dementia in reverse. He found himself looking for small signs in the street that something was out of place. In particular, there was a blue Volvo he had noticed more than once, one morning idling at the kerb for almost two hours across the street and some way down, almost out of sight. Two male occupants.

He'd been thinking a lot about the Job, and about Kate. Disappointing how it had all worked out. He had such high hopes in the early days, such optimism. Kate would have gone to University of course: she would come to visit at the weekends, sometimes with a new boyfriend. Eventually with grandchildren. A good job: something in medicine, he always imagined, even when it looked like she was never going to be an academic. And she would never know about her past. About the secrets that would expire with him in accordance with the terms of the Official Secrets Act. A minor diplomat. Hayley knew the truth about the Job but nobody else. It was the Job that had brought them Kate, ultimately.

Apart from Kate, he couldn't claim to have done anything of significance in his career. A secret intermediary was all it amounted to. Passing secrets from one party to another, never truly being in the know. Never possessing the knowledge that he so freely shared. But they taught him to observe. The importance of covering one's tracks. He had thought all that was behind him, a long time forgotten, but as it happened they'd programmed into him some residual instinct that something had awakened now.

Hayley hovered behind him on one occasion as though searching for some common thread. It was easy to slip out of the habit of conversation, and not so easy to resurrect. Kate was the unspoken subject of all of their communication, carefully set aside as a topic that they had plenty of time to consider over dinner or at breakfast. But somehow they brooded in silence and picked at their food instead, suffering Kate's absence.

'What do you see out there?' she had asked.

'I'm not sure.'

'All this time, looking out of the window. You ought to know what you're looking at by now.'

'Not looking at. Looking for.'

'So, what're you looking for?'

He didn't answer. There was a number for Kris that he'd never used up to now, and when he tried it the number was unobtainable. Well, and why not, after all this time? What would he say anyway? He wondered if Kate had been to visit. Considered making the journey himself, but reluctant to shake the shadows. He didn't like to use the phone - another precaution they'd instilled in him, a mistrust of telephones - but even so he phoned Kate every day with no reply.

They said it was a gas explosion, those who knew about these things. The elderly couple that once lived in the prim cottage keeping themselves to themselves were both killed in the blast. Recorded in the local newspaper with a picture of the carcass of a bedroom, but never made the nationals. There was a daughter, the papers said. Police still trying to trace her.

The banging and creaking of the pipes kept her awake for most of the night. The pipes seemed to make an unnecessary amount of noise about performing their function, and yet delivered precious little as a result in the way of heat. She tugged the bedclothes around her tightly and stared up at the cracks in the plaster. Dmitry was sleeping on his back with his mouth open, and his throat cracked softly when he breathed. Sometimes she thought she despised him, like now. But there were so few people she could talk to, and even fewer men that were remotely attractive. Dmitry was remotely attractive, she thought. It was the best that could be said of him – the best she could do here in Sorsk. So when Olga was away in Moscow, which she was frequently these days, she and the political officer engaged in acts of sordid gratification that made her feel empty in the morning, like a husk.

She pulled herself onto her elbows, but the blankets slipped away and it was bitterly cold in the sparse bedroom, so she shuffled back beneath them and lay there on her back What kind of life was this? It was all about her work, she supposed. But what did her work represent? Was it morally justifiable? Who was she to play at being God? It was a dilemma she had turned over and over in her mind, ever since she had confirmed that she was pregnant.

They knew so little about the science. It was more about physical mechanics than science. They were working in the dark. For instance, they had no idea what elements, what *characteristics* of the cell donor would be replicated from the cloned cell. *Her* cell, in this case, she reminded herself with a grimace. What is the container of the soul, if there is such a thing? The container of the soul.' She turned the words over in her head, pleased with this new turn of phrase. Should they be meddling in such things at all?

Dmitry stirred, and she hoped he wouldn't wake. His breath stuttered, and she held her own breath for an instant until she heard that familiar rhythmic patter of his breathing resume. She wondered, not for the first time, if she was Dmitry's *assignment.* Was Dmitry assigned to keep a watch over her. Who would trust a political officer? Even if she accepted they were lovers in the conventional sense, she would still have to be wary about confiding certain of her innermost thoughts. Olga's convenient absences were almost too convenient, allowing them to pursue their clandestine relationship with impunity. She frowned. Something was wrong. Something was *missing*. She reached out to touch Dmitry's warm body but the bed was empty.

She sat up with a start, her eyes darting around the empty room, restoring things to their proper places in her head.

Hard to judge precisely when her dream had morphed into a memory. Hard to judge precisely how long she'd been awake. Boundaries between her false memories and her here and now were slipping away. Was she dreaming still? She clutched her temples, wanting to banish the other memories that flooded her head. Was she going mad? With a wrung out feeling she remembered Grigor late last night. Was that a dream too? A memory? If so, whose memory was it? It was all mixed up in her head - the real, the imaginary, the quasi-real. Why would the Russian security services be interested in her? The Major she had met before - he had said the same thing. Maybe this was what triggered her dream. Her brow was damp with perspiration. An irrational fear had taken hold of her. A feeling she was under observation. It was KGB no matter what label they put on it. She shuddered. Dmitry was KGB. A blast from her other set of memories.

She had tried not to notice that if she concentrated really hard she could slip into her other set of memories at will. Sometimes she couldn't help herself, and achieved this level of concentration in spite of her fears, like prodding at a bad tooth with her tongue. The memories were still fragmented, and she couldn't control at exactly what point she would arrive because she had no bearings, few reference points: but as each memory hardened into reality, the reference points accumulated, and she was beginning to find new and unexpected depths to her memories. Once inside her other self, she found that she could direct her thoughts forwards or backwards, which alarmed her at first.

The phone beside the bed startled her. She glanced at her watch as she fumbled to pick up the receiver. Nine a.m. 'Yes?'

'I've been thinking some more,' said the gravelly voice in flawed English without preamble. For some reason she felt flustered. Did Grigor come to her room last night or was that a dream too? Perhaps this whole KGB story was a dream too?

'And drinking?' she ventured.

He laughed. 'You think I was drunk?' He sounded offended. 'You never saw me drunk.' He muttered. There was an awkward pause, before he went on in a conciliatory tone. 'I'm sorry. Last night.. I hope you didn't mind..?'

That settled one thing. 'I didn't mind. But now..?'

'I need to talk to you. I want to help. Believe it or not.'

She remembered that Grigor had settled her hotel bill. The bomb... 'You've helped me enough.'

'Not with money. I'm worried for your safety. These men… I know them. They wouldn't waste time with somebody like you unless there was a good reason. There must be something…. '

'I'll meet you at the club.' She said at once, surprising herself.

'In an hour.'

'OK.' She rang off, and almost immediately the phone rang again. She lifted the receiver warily.

'Kate?' said a familiar voice 'Kate, is that you?'

'Robert?' She swung around and sat rigidly on the side of the bed. Part of her was horrified, and part of her happy. 'How did you find me?' The line wavered and clicked.

'Kate, what's going on?' he said anxiously. 'The police..' He stopped, and began again. 'The police have been around. Asking questions about the doorman at the club. The murder. It was in the papers. Then you were gone and…'

'How did you find me?'

'Somebody else came. A Russian.'

'What? A Russian? Who?'

'Said he was from the Security Services. Showed me his badge. Could have been anything I suppose... he said he wanted to help. The police.. they don't know. I haven't told anybody anything. Are you all right?'

'I'm OK. This Russian—what did he want?'

'He knew where you were. The hotel and

everything. He said you were being watched. That you were in danger... but he wasn't sure why.'

'How's Becky?' She interrupted. It would be mid-day in England. She would be at playgroup.

'Becky's fine. She's fine, really. I'm worried about what you've got yourself into... I'm really worried Kate. Russia. Why are you in Russia? What's going on?'

She glanced at her watch. 'It's difficult. I don't really know myself what's happening at the moment. But you don't need to worry.. if anything, this trip is helping me to come to terms with some things.. you know, with my *past*.'

Robert knew that when she mentioned her past in this emphatic way, it wasn't her past that she meant, but the other past that he had found so difficult to believe in. 'I see.'

'But you don't see,' she said flatly. 'You've never seen. Nobody has. Nobody *can*. You don't understand how *real* all that is to me—' she trailed off. There was a pressure behind her eyes. She wiped away a tear. 'It's *real* Robert. This person inside my head she's real. She died, I think. But she was real. I know that now. That's why I'm here. That's what I'm trying to find out.. what happened to her.. what it all means.'

'What about the Club? What happened there? The doorman.'

'I have to go.'

'Please come home,' pleaded Robert. Kate laid down the received, pulling her hand away like it was electrified, and when the phone rang again she let it ring for a long time before Robert must have finally given up. She pictured him alone in the house, sitting amidst the stage set of another stream of memories, worrying about her. Wondering about her. He wasn't to blame. He probably thought she was crazy. He'd even tried to get her to see a doctor. A *head* doctor. But she wasn't insane. Her memories were real. She was convinced more than ever. Somehow this Ekaterina Ivanovna was living inside her head. She was as real as Kate Buckingham ever had been.

The phone rang again several times while Kate showered and dressed, and she steeled herself to ignore the shrill bleating. It was still ringing as she glanced around the hotel room one more time, checking for her key before clicking the door to.

She was quietly fretting about Becky and Robert when she took the lift to the ground floor, and as she weaved her way through the tourists milling in the lobby, a familiar face appeared at her side. Nikolay Sokolov shunted her with his shoulder and apologised, touching her gently on her shoulder – the good-looking officer who had interviewed her at the police station and promised to help. In English he said hurriedly:

'Why don't you answer your phone?' Then he brushed past, saying fleetingly out of the corner of his mouth, 'Follow me. And don't make it obvious.' Instead of heading directly across the marble lobby, he weaved through the armchairs and coffee tables.

A glance around the lobby, and she was just in time to spot a badly dressed man with a florid complexion catch her eye then avert his gaze. She thought he wasn't trying too hard. Nikolay pushed his way through the revolving doors, and after waiting a few moments she followed, keeping a furtive watch on her tail in a shabby grey track suit, lounging in a corner seat with one striped Adidas trainer propped on his knee. He uncrossed his leg and leaned stiffly forward in his seat in preparation to rise and follow her from the hotel.

Out in Tverskaya Street where the traffic boomed relentlessly, Nikolay had already hailed a taxi, a bright yellow Volga with a missing wing mirror and a cavernous dent in the rear door. He was stooping over the driver's door and straightened up as she emerged from the hotel.

'I'm sorry.' He said with an open handed gesture. 'If you're looking for a cab, you're welcome to take mine.'

She thanked him, playing along, and ducked into the back seat, propping her handbag on her knee. The damaged door creaked. No sooner was she in her seat than the driver rammed the column mounted gear leaver into gear and edged the car into the stream of traffic without a word. Then suddenly he careered across the road, turned sharply into a small side street, tyres squealing, and made two more swift turns that sent Kate scuttling across the plastic seat, reaching out for the seat in front. Afterwards he drove for two blocks in silence as though nothing had happened, then pulled into a narrow street where he wedged the stocky Volga between two abandoned SUV's.

'What now?' She said hesitantly.

The man shrugged. 'We wait.'

'Are you a real taxi driver?'

He glared at her. 'Of course.' He said without seeming to care if she believed him or not.

Out of the rear window she watched the traffic crawl past on the main road. After fifteen minutes or so a red Volkswagen turned into the street, and she saw Nikolay mount the kerb and leave the car without locking it. He slipped into the back seat of the taxi behind her.

'Amateurs.' He said, in an almost injured tone. 'I could never have gotten away with that in the old days.' He gestured out of the window. 'He's not following now.' He glanced at the driver meaningfully, who sighed and levered himself out of the car into the street, where he lingered, leaning against the bonnet and lit a cigarette. 'We spoke with your husband in London.'

When Lebed arrived at the offices of the Russian Democratic Union Party offices on Arbat Street flanked by two beefy bodyguards, a tall, silver haired man in a long coat was presiding over the breaking open of a row of steel filing cabinets. Colourful campaign posters of Lebed in army uniform adorned the walls. The bodyguards looked at Lebed for the lead.

'Stop. It now,' he commanded, with a calm inflection that suggested he was used to being obeyed. The intruders faltered, appearing uncertain. They hadn't expected he would show up in person. Their leader was unfazed, abandoned the filing cabinet, and approached with an affable smile, snapping open his ID with its twin headed eagle.

'Good morning, sir,' he said breezily. 'I am Colonel Lisakov of the Federal Security Services. We have orders, I'm afraid.' One of Lisakov's men was engaged in levering open a cabinet, and it made a retching sound like someone clearing his throat loudly as the metal buckled. Lebed barely glanced at the ID. He assessed the situation unhurriedly, like the General that he once was, running scenarios and outcomes through his head. Three FSB men and this Colonel. The FSB men looked unprofessional, thuggish. Not much of a match for his own men, if it came to it. Then he said:

'Please instruct your officers to stop what they are doing.'

Lisakov shrugged. 'I'm sorry sir. Orders…'

'I'm not without influence you know, Colonel.' Lisakov looked a little uncomfortable. Lebed put back his head and laughed. Lisakov started. 'I know your kind Colonel—what is it—Lisakov? You think you have some useful patronage, some mandate. But you don't. You don't have anything. Borilyenko would drop you like a hot potato if you caused him the least embarrassment... ' He paused, and glowered at Lisakov from beneath dark forbidding eyebrows. 'Whereas I could have you transferred in a moment to some god-forsaken outpost of Russia to work with some hick militia outfit in the snow...' Lebed snapped his fingers. 'In an instant.' He said, regarding Lisakov with his intent poker stare.

Lisakov gestured to his men. 'Wait,' he said.

The windows in the taxi were already steamed up. Kate made a porthole with her glove. The traffic rolled past, giant trucks with throaty growls, tantalisingly close to the parked cars.

'Robert,' she said.

Sokololov smiled. 'He was of no help to us. I thought you should know. But he's very worried about you.' He paused. 'He told us about the…. Incident in which you were involved. Before you left. To come to Moscow.'

'So it was your people that told him where to find me?'

Sokolov coughed into his hand in a small gesture of discomfort. 'I didn't see the harm... But if it was me I would have played things differently.'

She threw him a sidelong glance. He looked somehow forlorn, with a far away look in his grey eyes, and a strange empathy stirred within her. The collar of his blue suit was turned up, like a small act of rebellion.

'I have a meeting,' she said. 'What do you want?'

'So.. I've been doing some research, Miss Buckingham. Like I promised I would.'

'You found her?' she started.

'I really don't think that will be possible,' he sighed. 'The person you are looking for disappeared in, well… what I guess were predictable circumstances for the times.' He glanced at her. 'But I have found out something about her.'

'So, she's alive?'

Sokolov shook his head. 'No, no. Doubtful I think.'

A silence ensued. She listened to the traffic. Sometimes the car would rock in the wake of a heavy vehicle passing, its exhaust spluttering.

'Ekaterina Ivanovna Borodina.' He paused, and for a moment Kate thought he was addressing her by this name. It felt reminiscent of something. 'She was a scientist. And so far as I can tell she was well regarded in all of the right places. By which I mean the Party. She distinguished herself at University. And went on to specialise in genetics. Then... she is lost to us.'

'Lost?'

'Miss Buckingham, (can I call you Kate?) in my

position I have a long reach. I can access many things that to others would be inaccessible. But in the case of Ekaterina Ivanovna.. I've drawn a blank. Which means that whatever work she was engaged in was not for for the usual consumption. Highly secret.' As if for emphasis he repeated, as if with some relish, 'Classified.'

She frowned. 'So what are you telling me?'

He grinned unexpectedly - a wry, boyish grin. 'I was rather hoping you could do the telling. Is there anything you can tell me about Ekaterina Ivanovna? For instance, why do you come here looking for a scientist who most probably died a long time ago, and whose background is a mystery?'

'Ok … So I told you before she's a relative. An aunt most probably.' She lied 'I wanted to find out what happened to her.'

'An aunt. Most probably.' He sighed, and wound down the window to summon the driver. 'Can we drop you somewhere?'

A rainy day in November. Warm for the time of year.

They walked to the Registry office, not hand in hand but with a joint determination. Kate was 8 months pregnant. He wore his long overcoat, a suit but no tie. She looked beautiful with her long hair in ringlets and her sweeping red silk dress with the plunging neckline.

He remembered the swift professional execution of the service. The exchange of rings. The desultory walk back to the cold apartment. It was a day that he had longed for. It was a day that he had dreaded. It was a day that passed like every other in a series of gestures and images of happiness and despair, culminating in a night that was curtailed too soon by a bleak insipid dawn. Their wedding day.

He watched the clouds skim past the cabin window. The plane was on its descent into Shermetyevo 2 and the passengers were restless, packing away their books and magazines. The chime of the seatbelt warning sounded and a sultry voice made a lengthy announcement in Russian.

He felt a chill pass through him. Flipped through his passport to where the newly appended visa filled up a whole page. Wondered again why he was here.

Chapter Thirty-Two

LAYERS OF TOBACCO smoke hung wispy in the air like angel hair, half-remembered from the Christmas tree when she was a girl. It lent a dreamy feel to the cavernous nightclub with its empty chairs and tables and the open jaw of the stage, where a row of empty Baltika beer bottles stood at the edge like green teeth.

The door banged behind her. From their perches in the wings the sentinels of Soviet history acknowledged her with stony grace. The statue of Iron Feliks glowered. She ventured forward, feeling like Alice lost in some strange and vaguely threatening world. She heard her voice resonate. ‘Anyone here? Grigor?’ It seemed harsh and uneven and didn’t sound like it came from her. When her thigh bumped against a table the sound made her start. The air was tinged with disinfectant and stale sweat. When Grigor appeared at the office door she was relieved at first, but at the same time felt a frisson of apprehension.

Grigor had a way of occupying space, even large spaces. His sound and size and energy eclipsed his surroundings. And yet somehow he made her feel at ease, with his bluster and bulk.

‘Welcome,’ he said in English, and beckoned to the open door of his office. ‘You’re late of course - but I knew you’d be here.’

She allowed herself to be steered into Grigor’s office, his large paw in the crook of her back like he was leading her to the dance floor. Then he pulled out a chair for her, and seated himself behind a broad, heavily carved, mahogany desk. A large gun rested on a sheaf of envelopes and paper on the desk. Two empty bottle of Stolichnaya were upended In the wastepaper bin. He looked at the bottles and snorted.

'Yesterdays' empties.' Then he sat behind the desk and scrutinised her. She held his stare until he said. 'Tell me everything. Tell me what is so fucked up in your life that you end up here in a strip joint in Moscow, with a KGB tail.'

She felt a sudden impulse that made her want to unburden herself. Here with Grigor she experienced a perverse feeling of security.. She longed to air her other past in front of somebody that might believe her.

'Everything?' she said, instead.

'OK. Let's start with why you're here. In Moscow, I mean.'

She shook her head. 'That's a hard one. Difficult to explain. I'm not sure you'd believe me anyway.'

Grigor made an inviting gesture with his hands and sat back in his chair with a creak of old leather, like he was preparing for a vigil. He moved his legs as if to rest them on the desk, and then seemed to think better of it. 'Let's try. Because there are guys out there,' he nodded towards the door, 'who seem to have an unnatural interest in you. For whatever reason. And now you've brought them to *my* door - which considering my business activities isn't particularly welcome either. I'd like to find out why they think you're so important. From what I see you're pretty ordinary. If that's not insulting.'

'It's not insulting,' she said, feeling slighted all the same. Where to begin? 'I think I'd give anything to be just ordinary. It's going to sound weird, but bear with me: you see, for as long as I can remember I've had these… dreams.' She began. 'No, not dreams exactly - because they come to me when I'm awake as well. The first one I remember was a dream I kept having about a samovar. I didn't even know what a samovar was. I dreamed I was looking up at my reflection in this big urn thing, and an old lady wearing a long dress was walking around. Busy.' She frowned. 'There were lots of other dreams. What you might call ordinary dreams, most of them. But the samovar dream was different. It was *real*. It was in my dreams, but it felt like a part of my past. Then there were daydreams that were more like memories than dreams. Mum used to call it... misremembering. I misremember places I've never been to. People I've never met.' She glanced up, flustered. 'See? I told you it was weird.' She said.

'Keep going. Let's hear it.'

'So it turned out it was more than that. More than misremembering. You know...' She paused, took a breath. '..nobody *taught* me to speak Russian. I just... well I speak it like I speak English. Seems like I always have.' She wondered what he must be thinking, but he said nothing. 'And then there's maths. Science. I know things about biology and disease that had my GP reaching for his text book. I've known the periodic tables all my life. Nobody taught me them. Nobody *could* have taught me these things - except, I remember learning them. I misremember learning them I mean. I misremember schools I've never been to. Teachers I've never known. Books I've never read - stuff from Dostoevsky, Turgenev, Pushkin, Lermentov. I can even quote you lines of verse.' She was on the borderline - almost in tears. She recounted more from instinct than memory:

"I have outlasted all desire,

My dreams and I have grown apart;

My grief alone is left entire,

The gleamings of an empty heart."

'You think I'm crazy don't you? Everybody does. It's very beautiful - but I don't even know what it is. If I thought about it maybe I could remember…'

'It's Pushkin,' said Grigor. 'Yes, I like this poem. But I remember only:

"I live in lonely desolation,

And wonder when my end will come."

From the same verse. Beautiful. So you must have learnt it somewhere. Where did you go to school? Not in England but in this other world of yours. This alternative past, if that's what you think it is.'

She answered without thinking. 'School 66.' And a vision of the iron gates came to her at once. Waiting in a snowstorm for them to open, pounding the packed snow with her heels.

'Could be,' he said. 'But only if you were a lot older.'

'But I didn't. I didn't go to that school at all. I went to St Andrew's junior school. In England - and then to The Highfield School. Not a school with a number. But I *definitely* remember it, School 66. Every detail. There used to be a crack in the wall a few inches wide above the entrance, maybe five feet long. It scared us and we used to be afraid it would collapse. That's why we were always in a hurry to get through the doors. The teachers thought we were keen, in a hurry to get into class....' She stopped. 'You see? Even small details. And I wasn't even aware of that detail until this very moment. It came to me just now.'

'So where do you think they come from? How do you come to have these dreams? Something you read? Somebody you know?'

'I don't know. It's like being haunted. Possessed. I've never read anything about Russia. Never known any Russians. It's like there's another person in my head. I think I even know her name.'

'What name?'

'I met someone recently. Somebody real - but someone I seemed to know already from my misrememberings. He works at the Russian Embassy in London. Some kind of diplomat. And he mistook me for this person - this person that lives in my head. He called her - he called *me* - Ekaterina Ivanovna. *Katya*, he said first. And I knew her. I *felt* her if that makes sense. Like she was part of me. That's when I realised these memories must be real. I *understood* him. That's what I still can't get over. He spoke Russian and I knew what he was saying. And after that, things started to happen. People following me. Sorry. I don't know why I'm telling you all this.'

'Never mind. It's getting interesting.'

'It made me look at myself. Look at my past. I discovered my English past is every bit as much of a fiction as my misremberings. I'm not who I thought I was - at least, it turns out I was adopted. As a baby. I don't know how they could have kept it from me for so long. Those hypocrites.'

'So who are your real parents?'

She shook her head. 'I don't know. But I know one thing - I'm from here. From Russia. I was smuggled out of the country as a baby.'

'Why would they do that?'

'That's what I was trying to find out. Before they killed Gold.'

'Gold?'

'Somebody who tried to help me when they…' she sniffed away the panic that had gripped her at the though of Gold. 'When they came for me. When they tried to take me away.'

'Slow down. Who tried to take you away?'

'No idea. Russians. And they shot Gold.'

'Some Russians killed him? And they shot him for helping you?'

'He tried to stop them taking me.' Gold, thrown backwards and left bleeding on the wet pavement. 'He tried. Poor Gold. I felt so… he was…' She faltered. Thought about the son she never knew he had. What was to become of him? 'Anyway, I ran away and somehow managed to escape - but I just knew they'd be back - That's why I decided the only thing to do was to find out why they were after me. Find out what it was all about. It led me here, to Russia. But it's different here. Not like the Russia I remember. The Moscow in my dreams. Even the street names. I'm no further forward. Not really. And people are still after me. You said so yourself . Those men outside.' She checked Grigor's face for signs of disbelief.

'Maybe you need to tell me more about this Ekaterina Ivanovna. Her work, for instance.'

'I was a scientist,' she said at once, before correcting herself. 'She, I mean. She was a scientist. In Sorsk Gorod. That's where she worked. And lived.' And as she said this she realised that this was a brand new recollection, something that she had uncovered like wiping away a layer of snow on a tombstone.

'Sorsk?' He said. 'I never heard of it.'

She lifted her chin, as though straining her neck to see over a barrier as she said 'It was a ZATO. A secret city. We were involved in secret work. Nobody even with a foreign passport was allowed to go there. It wasn't…' She checked his face to see that he wasn't laughing at her. 'It wasn't on maps.' She paused. Felt awkward. 'I'm not making this up. I don't think so anyway.'

'I know about ZATO's. *Zakritye administrativno-territorialnye obrazovaniia.* There were lots of them in Soviet times. You needed a permit to enter. And to leave. And you're right - they're not on maps. Usually they're known just by a postcode.'

'That's right! The postcode. It was: Veliky Novgorod-120.' With sudden certainty, her misrememberings, having acquired a fresh vigour.

'It means,' he said, 'that it was probably 120 km from Veliky Novgorod. I say probably, because sometimes they changed it. For EXTRA camouflage.' He laughed. 'So tell me about this secret work?'

'It was…' she began, 'I was…' But the source had died up. She concentrated hard. Closed her eyes. She was wearing a white coat, like a doctor. She was working. Working…' Her mind drifted. 'It's too difficult.' She shrugged. 'Sometimes it's like they just dry up. The memories. They stop coming.'

Grigor hefted himself out of his chair and stood for a while, just thinking. She watched him, angry at herself for revealing so much in the vague hope of some miracle. Finally he said:

'I can't explain any of this. The only thing I know for sure is that there are some serious government people who are interested in you, and it can only have to do with what you've told me.' He paused. 'If you were smuggled out of the Soviet Union as a baby, there's got to be a reason. Maybe…' he said, 'maybe they were experimenting on *you*. Seems like science fiction I guess, but maybe, I don't know, *thought implants* or something. They did crazy things in those days from what I know. Especially in those ZATO's. Nobody was accountable for the damage they did.'

'So what do you think I should do?'

He thought for a few moments. 'I think we should go and find Sorsk.'

It was cold in the apartment. The fire in the grate barely reached out to touch the chill of the room. She looked at her reflection in the bulbous metal and inclined her head, watching her left cheek inflate, and pulled a wide grin.'

'Keep away from the samovar Katya. I've told you before. It's very hot,' said a kind voice.

'It's funny'

The long skirts whisked past her, and she felt a firm hand on her shoulder. 'You won't think it's so funny if you are scalded Katya darling. Come with me and I will make you some supper.'

'I'm cold. It's warm here.'

'I will put another log on the fire.'

'Why is my face backwards?'

From above came a rippling laugh that made Katya feel warm inside and diminished the cold of the room.

'You're looking into the mirror world Katya. The samovar is like a window on the mirror world. Everything there is topsy turvy.'

'Can I go there?'

'To the mirror world?'

'Yes. Where it's topsy turvy. I think I'd like that mama. Can I go there?'

Then a big laughing moon-like face swept down from above, and Katya's mother was there at her level, pushing away a wisp of hair from her face. Katya thought her mother was very beautiful. 'You can go wherever you want darling. So long as you are safe and happy.'

Katya reflected for a moment and glanced back at the samovar. 'Will you come too mama?'

'I will always be with you darling...' And Katya felt her mother's warm lips pressed against her face, and then she was swept from the ground and carried away…

The sheets were damp and crumpled when she awoke, and she worried that she might be sickening for something. She felt as though she'd been tugged from safety and deposited here in this bleak hotel room. She ached to go back - to lose herself in her dream again in that topsy turvy world of her other life. She looked at the clock on the bedside table. Only 11:45 pm. She sighed and tried to immerse herself in sleep, but conflicting images stumbled and collided in her head. Moscow then. Moscow today. London seemed like a lifetime away.

Chapter Thirty-Three

'WHY WOULD YOU be interested in this girl?'

'She works for me,' said Grigor, tapping the gun on his desk with a pen. The gun was a relic. A souvenir from Afghanistan. He had his feet up as usual on the corner of the desk and a large Coriba smouldered in the ashtray. After Kate had gone he had sat for a long time before phoning Lisakov.

Lisakov laughed down the phone. 'Many girls work for you, Grigor Vassilyich. What's special about this one?'

Chink. Chink. Chink. He tapped the gun. 'I don't

know, Comrade Colonel. That's what I'm trying to find out. What *is* special about her? Maybe you can tell me. There must be something—you said so yourself, after Olennsky. At the club.'

'You're asking the wrong man.'

'Then who do you think I should ask?'

'I don't think you should ask anyone. And I've already forgotten that this phone call ever took place.'

'Give me something Colonel. I pay you.' With a playful, cutting edge.

'Not for this you don't.'

'It's not enough?'

'It's never enough Grigor Vassilyich. It will never be enough.'

'You people have been following her since she came to Moscow. Do you deny it?'

'I don't confirm it.'

'She's just some Western bimbo. Not a spy. Not anything at all.' He laughed. 'What can you possibly want with her?'

'Is she pretty?'

'In a Barbie doll kind of way.'

'So I can guess *your* interest at least.'

Grigor grunted. 'Maybe. But what's yours? That's what I'd like to know. That's why I'm phoning.'

A pause. 'Grigor Vassilyich, I'm thinking about this very carefully, and I don't believe this girl is for you. Find another Barbie doll. You have a wide choice at your establishment.'

'You're not going to help me?'

'I don't think I can. But I'll tell you all I know.'

'What does that mean?'

'I mean.. What I know is nothing. I have orders, and I follow them. You remember what that's like? Probably not. I represent other peoples' interests - not my own.'

'Whose orders?'

'Leave it, Grigor Vassilyich.' And the line went dead.

Grigor pulled on his cigar and watched the smoke fold upon itself in the air. Where did the smoke go to, after it disappeared, he asked himself? What happened to a secret city when the secret was out? He checked an ancient rolodex, pulled out a card and picked up the phone again, dialled a number.

'Sergey Ivanovich. It's been a long time.' and after the usual exchanges of old comrades, after enquiries about the expired and the soon to expire, he said, 'Tell me what you know about a ZATO called Sorsk Gorod?'

Robert put his head in his hands. 'I don't know what you want from me.' It seemed like they had been in the airless room for days, playing and replaying the same questions and answers.

'We just need to be sure, that's all. About what she told you,' said the man with a face like a gnarled oak.

He fought against a wall of frustration and anger. 'But she didn't tell me anything. She sometimes had these dreams. I told you everything I know about them. They were just dreams. Like I told the other guy. In London.'

'Other guy? What other guy is this?'

'From Moscow. Asking me all these questions. About Kate. About her dreams. Not KGB he said, but something else.' He tried to remember. 'Just not KGB. Said his name was Pavel.'

'Describe him, please.'

Robert could see that the man was paying close attention. 'I don't know. Not tall. Brown hair. Personable. Excellent English.'

The man waited. Robert floundered, searching for more to give.

'What did you tell him exactly? About the dreams. This is very important.'

'Just what I've told you. What is there to tell?'

The man with the oak face stooped to look into his eyes. He saw his eyes had flecks of yellow. Saw empathy there, but maybe it was only something he projected for his own comfort. Robert's vision faded briefly - there was a blackness around the edges. Tiredness. He wanted to be somewhere warm and he envied the man his thick coat. The man raised himself again to his full height.

'Tell me about *Simbirsk*.'

Robert shook his head. 'I don't know what that is. I told you a hundred times.'

'You're sure she never mentioned it?'

'Never.'

'*Simbirsk* was the birthplace of Lenin. Now Ulkyanovsk. Kerensky was born there too—and what about *Pustinja*? Did you ever hear her mention this?'

'I don't know what that is either.'

'She didn't talk about it?

'No.'

'*Pustinja*,' he repeated. 'You're quite sure? And this other man in London, he never mentioned it?' He said looking hard at him. Robert shook his head.

'No. I never heard her mention that name. What is it?'

'Everybody's worst nightmare. It means "Wilderness"' He turned to one of the guards and said something in Russian. The guard nodded and left the room, banging the steel door behind him. 'At length he said, 'So… when she talked about these dreams - they were always about the same thing?'

'No. Different. Always about different people. Places. Except for some childhood memory. Some ornament. She seemed to have that dream quite often.'

‘A samovar, maybe?’

‘I don’t know. I’ve never heard that word. What is it?’

’A Russian tea urn.’

Robert shrugged. ‘If that’s what it was.’

‘And you thought these dreams were what? Her imagination?’

’Like I said: She’s always had these dreams. Like another memory. Since she was a child.’ He remembered the wistful expression that would descend upon her sometimes when she entered that world that he couldn’t penetrate.

‘What are you thinking?’ he would say.

‘Nothing. Just misremembering,’ she would reply. By then he knew about misremembering.

’So what, exactly?’

‘Now? I’m remembering the circus.’

‘Circus?’

‘Yes. A man fighting with a small bear. The bear was wearing a red neckerchief like a pioneer.’

‘A pioneer?

She looked at him like he had caught her out. ‘Yes.

It just came to me. A pioneer. I don't know - it's natural for a pioneer to wear a red neckerchief, I suppose. Isn't it?'

And these were the conversations they used to have about her dreams. If they were dreams.

'I just played along,' he said, and the self reproach made him look away from the yellow flecked eyes.

The man grunted, thrust his pink hands into his coat. Then the door opened and the guard appeared again, this time accompanied by a vaguely discomfiting man in a crumpled suit, who followed at a respectful distance. When he saw the man in the long coat he acknowledged him with a flutter of his eyelids. The man looked at Robert in what he sensed was a meaningful way. 'You'll have to excuse me,' he said. Robert felt deeply emotional for some reason.

'You're leaving me?'

The man articulated a smile, and left, and then the man in the crumpled suit regarded him with a dutiful expression, assuming responsibility for him. His hair was grey but streaked with silver. His face was grey like concrete, and scoured with thin lines like somebody had skated there before the concrete had set. He had with him a scuffed plastic case - what used to be known as an attaché case, and which he swung onto the table, clicked it open. Robert half expected him to whistle. He strained to see the contents. He wasn't tied down, but he felt as if magnetised to the chair and each time he moved he glanced once at the guards, feeling the pull of invisible restraints.

'Roll up the left sleeve,' said the grey man, and Robert rolled up his sleeve almost without thinking, his whole being shivering. 'It won't take long.' And the man took his arm and pressed a needle into a vein.

Robert had the urge to do something heroic, but he did nothing heroic. He willed himself to struggle and prayed that nobody would judge him later. There was nothing he could have done, he told himself. There was no escape. And Robert sailed blissfully into oblivion with the guilt of somebody leaving their baggage on a train.

Borilyenko walked alone down the corridor. Wilderness. Project Pustinia. Everybody's worst nightmare: that's what he'd told him. His own worst nightmare: he hadn't told him that, although it was implied.

He remembered the weighted muzzle of the mask that chafed and pulled and filled with moisture when he spoke. Yellow flames lapping out of windows. A wall of heat. His skin slippery with perspiration inside the NBC suit that crackled when he moved. The troops looked like mutants with doleful round eyes and long snouts, clad in wax ponchos. It was lunchtime and the canteen building was full. A strident voice through a megaphone was giving orders: 'Stay inside the building. Do not panic! This is a drill.'

A soldier fumbled with his weapon, made intricate by thick gloves, then directed it at the building. Some people hovered at the doors, torn between flight and the concrete security of the building. A child shouted for his mother. A woman sobbed with loud gulps of distress. Above everything he could hear his own hoarse breathing.

Then the rocket ignited blanking out the screams.

Colonel Borilyenko clamped his hands over his

ears, ducked his masked head, then looked up through steamy goggles in time to see the roof erupt. Empty windows filled with bright light, white then yellow. The heat was like a slap. He took a step back. The building crumpled and baked and a haze of heat surrounded the concrete like a halo.

The looped red sign above the doorway had turned to black, buckled but still legible: 'Stolovaya'.

And it felt—lke Stalingrad. For the greater good. A city burned and smouldered all around him, like Hades.

A Zil fire tuck drew up behind him and waited with its big diesel idling.

Every last living organism, he told himself. Everything must be exterminated. The alternative too horrific to contemplate. A necessary evil. A necessary contingency. Cleaning up after himself.

And now the general found himself cleaning up again, covering his back.

An officer unlocked a door at the end of the corridor.

Chapter Thirty-Four

THEY DROVE PAST serried blocks of Krushchoyovki apartments, steep barracks with empty eyes and sooty faces. The traffic had thinned out. She settled herself in the deep upholstery and looked down at the other vehicles as their SUV powered past. Grigor steered the car with calm authority, the engine little more than a murmur, rasping now and then when he accelerated past other cars or swung the wheel to weave around a pothole or a broken-down car. Soviet relics with smoking engines. He threw her a glance.

'Soon we'll be out of the city.' He waved a hand at

the window. 'See those houses? Meant to be temporary. Five storeys of misery. Freezing in the winter, hot in the summer. I grew up in a place like that. Bathroom down the hall.'

Hard to imagine this rugged bearded man as a child, she thought. 'How long is the drive?'

'Who knows? Maybe two or three hours. Depends on the roads. The trucks. They won't all be like this..' And as if to emphasise the fact, the tyres rumbled where the road had been broken up for resurfacing. A solitary red and white bollard stood in the centre of the road and Grigor flipped the car around it. The wheels thudded when they re-joined the surfaced road. They slowed in the wake of an 18-wheel truck in a brown fog of exhaust, and the undertow of sludge spat at them smearing the windscreen. The truck's engine laboured, changed note. Acrid fumes tainted Kate's tongue. As they passed Kate caught a glimpse of the driver, stolid and oblivious, staring straight ahead, both hands planted on the wheel.

Sorsk. She thought about the name, hoping to awaken some memory, but it just whispered to her, composed itself in her head in Russian characters, *Сорск,* empty of meaning. 'I'm not sure what I'm hoping to find there. Not even sure if it'll be there at all.'

'Maybe you'll find nothing.' He shrugged. 'Maybe everything.'

'I just hope it's not a disappointment. Hope *I'm* not a disappointment.' She said with a sidelong glance. Grigor said nothing. 'You say the location of these places is some big secret?'

He shrugged. 'You had part of the secret already. You knew the name. There are no secrets without the people that keep them.'

'Do you know a lot of secrets?'

'A lot. In this case, I know somebody that knows about these places. Closed cities. He's from my network. Reliable until now. I told you I wasn't a gangster all my life.' he finished the sentence with a clearing of the throat.

A road lined with birch trees. Up ahead a line of girls, teetering on pointed heels and bare-legged in the freezing weather. Snowflakes spiraled. A ragged blonde in thigh length boots gestured as they passed, seemed to shout at them.

‘Prostitutes. They’re always here. The police try to stop them, but it’s no use. Ordinary girls. Shop girls.’ He shrugged. ‘Sex is better paid than selling beetroots in the supermarket.’

‘Where do they come from? There’s nothing around here. Not for miles.’

‘From the town. *Chornaya Graz.* It means Black Dirt. Describes it perfectly.’

Now there was a line of mournful shopfronts, facias of grimy blues, oranges, yellows, that flapped with paper bills. An ironmonger’s wooden porch cluttered with rattletrap lawnmowers and a tired cement mixer. A baker’s empty window.

‘It’s debatable whether there’s life beyond the Moscow ring road.’

A hotel with a statue of a golfer and an empty car park, then a timber yard.

‘What do you think about those girls back there? And the ones that work for you?’

‘For me a lot like places. Some colourful. Fun to

stay one night, but that's all. Some places sophisticated. Spend a week there and learn something new every day. Then there're the ones where you live. Familiar. Habitual. I had a wife like that.'

'From your club?'

'Not mine. From another club.'

'What happened?'

'I was always away. When I was a military man. It's rough on the women.'

'Did it have an effect - the work she did before? From the club, I mean?' Drawn to the question.

'Never thought about it. A lesson from the army. Nobody wants to find where the bodies are buried, so we don't dig in those places.'

The interior smelled richly of leather. 'Grigor. You've been so helpful, and I'm grateful. But why? Why are you helping me?' picking up an abandoned conversation.

Eyes glinted in the lights of a passing car. 'Curiosity. About the dreams. About you. Also about the attention you're getting from those guys at the Lubyanka. You need a friend here, whether you know it or not.' He reached and brushed her hand but didn't take it and she felt a tremor so fleeting it could have been imaginary.

'My hero,' she laughed. 'So you want to be my friend?'

'If you want it.'

'Anything else?' It sounded arch. He didn't answer, and she was glad.

She thought hard to dredge up some vestiges of her misremembered past that would prove helpful when they reached Sorsk but her head was empty. 'How does it work for you?' she said. 'Remembering? I mean the mechanics?' Hard to articulate what she meant by the mechanics. Hard to know what she meant. Did people remember things in a different way to her?

He threw her an odd look. 'I just remember. Or sometimes I don't. Maybe choose not to. Vodka helps to carve out some of the worse bits. Each day we add to our memories by taking a cut from the future, like another deck of cards. Also sometime we invent our past to fit our present. Make it fit who we think we've become.' He shrugged. 'My experience, that's all.'

'I like that. Making it fit. For me it's not so easy. The mechanics. I have to really concentrate. It's an effort to recall things. Then sometimes I think so hard about the process of remembering that I forget how to do it. Or not forget, exactly. Just not remember. I'm not making much sense. When it happens it's like breaching a membrane - I get this flood of stuff. New memories - but they're not new. Memories can't be new. That's stupid. They've been with me all my life. Just… misplaced.'

'You're making my head hurt.'

She laughed. Wanted to laugh so much. 'Ordinary people.. I mean other people - they accumulate.. what would you call it? Terms of reference. With waypoints. Then they use the waypoints to locate their memories - that time on holiday in Rome; that time at school. Except for me there aren't any waypoints with my other memories. That's what makes it so difficult to remember.'

They drove on for almost two hours, Kate drifting in and out of a stupor that passed for sleep. Grigor left the highway once, and drove along a straight, single track road. She awoke when the car turned onto a deeply pitted road with alarming ruts that made the SUV dip and buck.

‘Is it far?’

‘Who knows? I wasn’t even sure this road existed. No signs. Sometimes there are roads on maps that were planned but never built. Other times there are roads like this that aren’t on any maps. At least the road’s here. But Sorsk Gorod? That’s not on any map. If it ever existed then we’ll find it. Trust me.’ And she did.

The road swept around to the left, and afterwards there was an abandoned checkpoint, with rusted red and white poles standing upright and two guard houses with empty windows. Grigor sped through the gates and the road widened into two carriageways again. The surface was surprisingly smooth, although the central reservation was overgrown. Brown tentacles crusted with fresh snow, tumbled over the outside lane.

‘Like a highway,’ he said in disbelief, accelerating. ‘Without any traffic. But some tracks in the snow. Look.’ He nodded, and there ahead of them was a single set of tyre-tracks. ‘Seems like at least one other car came this way today.'

The snow had begun to assert itself, and seemed to close in around them so it was like travelling in a gauze bubble, landscape a streak of brittle-backed frozen fields and leaden skies, a blur of snowflakes. She shivered, even though it was warm in the car, huddled into the folds of her coat.

'Soon,' he said, turning his head briefly. 'Maybe,' he qualified.

They drove for another hour on the straight road, and Kate dozed again. She awoke with a start when she sensed the motion of the car had stopped. 'Are we there yet?' Like a child's refrain, she thought.

Ahead was a checkpoint, this time occupied. The road had narrowed to a single lane each way and there was a guard house on each lane. Barriers barred the route in both directions. At the side of the road there was a parking area, and a battered Lada with a blue light was parked at an angle taking up two spaces. Above the checkpoint hung a sign pronouncing 'SORSK GOROD'.

'Looks promising,' said Grigor.

They edged forward, snow crunching under the wheels, and a uniformed guard emerged, adjusting his fur cap with one hand and swinging an automatic weapon over his shoulder with the other. In front of the barrier he raised his hand. A crooked yellow sign at the side of the road read ‘Contaminated Territory. Access Prohibited’.

‘Contaminated?’ she said.

With a creak of leather and a burst of cold air, Grigor manoeuvred himself out of the car.

‘Wait.’

When Grigor approached him the guard unslung his weapon and pointed the barrel at him, then yelled something Kate couldn’t hear. Grigor walked with his palms aside, as though showing he was unarmed; slipped once on the frozen road, and the guard tensed at the unexpected movement. Kate looked around, but there was nothing to be seen except the checkpoint and a line of black and barren trees on either side of the road. The engine ticked as it cooled. She watched Grigor stop a few paces from the guard and thrust his hands into the pockets of his leather jacket. He looked relaxed. Kate tried to put down the window to hear what they were saying, but without the engine running the electrics were off. They mouthed silent words at each other, and appeared to share a joke. The guard hoisted his gun over his shoulder again and gestured a few times in the direction of the town. Grigor turned towards the car. The guard looked. Then Grigor produced a packet of cigarettes and offered one to the guard which he accepted. Grigor pushed the packet on him and the guard first pushed the pack away without much conviction, then accepted. They smoked, standing together in the falling snow, the guard stamping his feet now and then. He seemed friendly enough. Then they shook hands, and Grigor turned back towards the car. The guard threw his cigarette butt into the wind, where it faltered and blew back at him, then swung the barrier up as just as Grigor tugged open the car door again.

'Let's go,' and the instruments beeped and blinked as the engine burst into life.

'What happened? What did he say?'

'Not much. He's been assigned here a year. They

don't get visitors, so he's pretty bored sitting in his cabin. Plays chess with himself; drinks plenty of vodka by the smell of him. Lives in a village a couple of hours away. A bitch of a commute, but there are no traffic jams and he gets to stay warm in his cabin. Nobody's lived here for years. He doesn't know how long. The area's contaminated he said, but he's not sure with what. Thinks maybe radioactivity, but he doesn't really know. He says he's not ventured much further than the guardhouse because he's nervous about the contamination. He's got orders to stop anyone from going in. The whole perimeter's fenced off beyond the checkpoint, so this is the only way in or out.'

'Why did he let us through?'

'My natural charm,' he said, baring his teeth in a grin. 'He's just a boy. A conscript. We talked about army shit. I asked him for a favour, one comrade to another. He didn't take much persuading. I told him my girlfriend used to live here when she was a kid, and wanted to see how it looked now. He told me it's your funeral.'

'Girlfriend?'

'That's what I told him.'

'Is it dangerous?'

Grigor gave a wave as they crunched past, and the guard made an ironic military salute, then hauled down the barrier. 'Whatever happened here, it was a long time ago. Even Chernobyl's safe enough now, so they tell us - although you wouldn't want to live there.' They passed three ancient soviet military trucks hunkered down at the roadside with flat tyres and rust flaked paintwork. 'Your funeral, he said to me. Our funerals. We can go back if you want?'

'No.. no. If it's OK with you. Let's go on. We can't go back after coming all this way. Anyway, I 've *got* to see it.'

He shrugged. Then as they drove over the brow of a hill Kate seemed to recognise an imposing white edifice with a faded mural of a rainbow on its cracked white plasterwork, pitted and fragmented with exposed brickwork. The rows of windows were desolate and soot stained. 'I remember that.' She breathed. 'I think I do.' To their right was a series of fossilised shacks, and blackened skeletons of once meaningful structures. Abandoned military vehicles lined the road. Grigor stopped the car.

'A war zone.'

Something was welling up inside her. A queue of memories jostling their way to the forefront. A long grey building. 'Over there. Turn right.'

They passed what had once been a children's play park. A swan's head on a ride-on had been deformed into a monstrosity, and the seat had burned away to reveal only a charred metal chassis. The swings were reduced to blackened chains hanging from a buckled frame. The snow had settled like a thin layer of icing sugar, turning the scene into a black and white print of Armageddon. In a half-hearted attempt at looting or rescue or both somebody had dragged some furniture from an official building with un-timbered doorways and windows, and the charred remains spilled over the stone steps. Some twisted pieces of furniture lay in the road: The bones of an office chair; a twisted metal cabinet with stove in drawers. The mangled letters along the facade of the building showed that this had once been Administrative Headquarters. In front of the building a bronze statue of Lenin gestured to the sky like a fruitless plea, from a fractured concrete plinth. She pointed.

'Borilyenko worked there.'

'Borilyenko? Here? You mean *General* Borilyenko?'

'I don't know. He was in charge. He wasn't a General. At least I don't think so.' A monstrous Zil fire truck with its ladder half extended was mounted on the kerb, scorched grille like an angry grimace. ' I used to come here a lot. He had a big office overlooking a small park at the back. I mean.. *she* used to come here. I think. Have you heard of him?'

'Borilyenko?'

'Yes. Him.'

'General Borilyenko. Of course. He's in charge of the Presidential Security Service. KGB. A big man. Maybe even a presidential candidate on day. He was here, you think? In Sorsk?'

Kate wasn't listening. 'Look! Drive over there.' She pointed to a charred building with a long empty frontage that had once been glass. The road was littered with debris.

'What happened here?' he said steering the car around humps in the snow. A spindly dog was sniffing at the wreckage. It bared its teeth, and was joined by another, which stood and watched them pass. 'This is not like any closed city I've ever seen. More like Chernobyl.' He stopped the car.

'It used to be a biological research centre. Part of Biopreparat.' Half-familiar words assembled themselves in her head. 'There were lots of projects. I was working on…' she thought for a moment and the name came to her in an instant. '*Simbirsk*. I don't know what it means. Does it mean anything to you?'

'Only the city. It's the old name for Ulyanovsk - before they renamed it after Lenin. His real name, Ulyanov. Simbirsk is where he was born. Kerensky was born there too, but of course they named it after Lenin and never changed it back to Simbirsk. Not like Stalingrad or Leningrad.' He shrugged. 'That's all I know.'

'*Project Simbirsk*. That's what I was working on. I mean that's what she was working on. Embryo research. It was called *Simbirsk* because they were planning to make a human clone. From cells taken from Lenin's embalmed remains … They planned to build a clone of Lenin.'

Grigor barked once. A humourless laugh. 'What kind of science fiction is that? What kind of bullshit?'

'It wasn't science fiction. I think it was real. I remember… I feel it was. We were doing stuff with human cloning. Experiments. We'd come a long way, and the next stage - it was the first real implanted embryo. Not Lenin. That was going to be later. Sounds crazy but.. ' She remembered the operating table. Remembered staying awake through the process in wonder at the culmination of her work. Remembered pale green curtains at the windows of the ward. How she must have felt afterwards with her swollen belly. How she would wrap her arms around the unborn foetus. How she would whisper to her unborn child at nights. She took a deep breath. The memories swam and merged. She felt she was one with them. 'She was my mother." She started, with sudden resolution. "I believe my mother was called Ekaterina Ivanovna.

Maybe she cloned herself and produced me. And then somehow - something they never thought about - somehow I've inherited her memories, like they were embedded in her DNA.' She stopped, looked at the shell of the former research centre and remembered the long glass window gleaming in the sunshine, shrubs lining the entrance. 'It explains everything. She shook her head slowly. 'We go through life thinking we're unique and purposeful. But in the end we're just composites. What makes us who we are? Where's our personality, our memory bank, our strengths and weaknesses? Where's all that stuff that we've been cosseting - where's it all kept?' Shattered buildings; foraging dogs; broken paving and silhouettes of trees. Tears began to come, and she buried her face in her hands. Who was she? Kate. What kind of abomination of nature? And she wept for an imagined past that would haunt her forever, a new past that was not hers to own. Who was she? Her dreams, her memories belonged to somebody else.

A weight around her shoulders. Grigor had his thick arm around her. She felt the bristle of his beard touch her forehead.

'It's OK,' he said.

But it wasn't OK and it never had been. This was all that was left. *Sorsk Gorod.* The ravaged shell of a life never lived, but which had lived inside her all her life. She felt cold when he pulled away. Then the door thudded; she heard the squeak and splinter of boots on fresh snow. The engine was still running and when the door closed the warmth was restored at once. The aircon laboured. She looked up, wiping her eyes; saw Grigor through the streaked windscreen stepping through the rubble towards the Embryonic Research Block; saw him pick his way up the stone steps. A dog with sparse fur and pink blotches pricked up its ears; took a few faltering steps towards him, but decided to keep its distance. Grigor disappeared inside the building. She stepped down from the car. It was fiercely cold but the temperature invigorated her and she breathed hard. A dog barked. Should she be afraid of these creatures? The place was familiar to her now, derelict as it was. She followed Grigor's footprints up the steps, seeking the struts of metal that would have supported the wooden handrail she remembered, and finding the buckled metal beneath a thin layer of snow with a perverse feeling of satisfaction. She reached out a hand, as though to place it on the wooden rail, and imagined her mother as she would have stood there over a quarter of a century ago; trailing her hand along the rail, ascending the steps. Now they were slippery and she climbed them with care. At the top, she turned to face the once imposing columns of the Administrative Headquarters, misremembering Dmitry with his bulging attaché case and stern poise standing in the doorway consulting his watch. Not a flashy Western watch like he had now, but a *Chaika* watch, made in *Uglich*.

A guttural snarl made her start. A large brown dog down on its haunches, fur bristling, fixing her with a malevolent stare from a few metres away. She stepped backwards, but the dog edged forward. She felt breathless. Took another step, heart pounding. Scrabbling of claws. A howl. The dog launched itself. Stumbling. Raising her hands. Colours making fast patterns.

An explosion.

The dog landed in the snow in a halo of pink, its body limp and useless. It made no sound, not even a whimper. She bit the back of her hand. For an instant she couldn't understand what had happened.

'I thought you were in the car,' said Grigor from the doorway, a pistol hanging from his right hand. He looked at the lifeless dog. 'These dogs are dangerous. They're wild and starving.' She looked too, wondering what would have happened if it had connected with her.

'Good shot.' Her throat was parched. 'I didn't know you had a gun.'

'I always have a gun.' After the detonation of the gun, everything seemed silent. 'Come and take a look.' Grigor turned back into the building. She trailed after him, keeping a watch behind her, looking for more wild dogs. She felt unsteady, hands trembling. Inside, there was nothing that was recognisable, just a vast expanse like a factory, with no interior walls. The exterior walls were scarred and blackened by fire. Grigor's boots crunched on broken glass, harsh and resonant in the empty building. Where before there had been a reception desk there was only rubble. No carpet, just a vast bare concrete space littered with broken masonry and mangled, rusted metal. When she looked up, the ceiling was gone, and the floor above was exposed. Charred timbers hung from above like a thickly drawn spider's web.

'What do you remember about the layout of this place?' he said.

She closed her eyes, trying to visualise how it had been. Left of the reception the security doors with criss-crossed safety glass. She would have swiped a card for entry, then headed down a corridor. She moved in that direction, picking her way through the wreckage. The labs would have been along here. She heard his heavy boots grinding glass and debris. 'Here. I think.' She stopped. The cold was a deep down numbness in her bones. Grigor was at her side. He stooped to pick up a fossilised relic in a gloved hand, turning it over. It was unidentifiable. He tossed it far into the shell of the building where it bumped and skittered, echoing off the walls.

'If there was one thing you could rescue from a burning building, what would it be?' she said.

'I don't think I have anything that means that much to me.'

'I feel like I'm all washed up. I don't have anything to cling on to. Nothing to rescue.'

'It doesn't look like a regular fire.'

'What do you mean?'

'There's not a single thing. Nothing intact at all.' He gestured back to the entrance. 'And it's not like they didn't try to put out the fire. That fire truck.. I've seen damage like this before. In Afghanistan. And in Chechnya.' He pointed to the open sky. 'Bumblebees. The first thing that happens is they blow the roof off.'

'Bumblebees?'

'Rocket propelled flamethrowers. We used them to clear occupied buildings. Or to destroy evidence.' He nudged a twisted haft of metal with his boot. 'Creates a hell on earth. 2000 degrees Celsius. We used to call them Devil's Pipes.'

'What evidence would you want to destroy?'

'I'm not proud of it. We followed orders, that's all.'

'I see. But what makes you think they would use something like that here?'

'Maybe I'm wrong. It's the only way I know to incinerate an entire city. That's what they've done here.'

They made their way back to the car, where a mangy dog eyed them with curiosity. Kate avoided it in a wide arc. They drove slowly around the empty city at her direction. Turning into precincts and boulevards, lined black eyed apartment blocks and windowless shopfronts. She pointed out landmarks to him. Here a school. There a supermarket - well stocked, not like Moscow in those days. More labs. An athletics stadium. All hollow and soot stained. A devastated, post-apocalypse landscape. Wilderness. Some half sketched association made her shudder. They passed a few more Zil fire trucks and many other soviet era vehicles, some burnt out, some atrophied and scoured by the elements.. 'They left a lot of kit here,' Said Grigor. 'Like they were in a hurry.'

May day in *Sorsk*. Gleeful radiant faces along birch lined Marx Prospekt, crowds flapping red flags.

Military bandsmen who smiled into their instruments with pride, and belted out Tchernetsy's Jubilee March. Brightly coloured balloons floating past the pharmacy and the bookstore. Feeling special and privileged. The warmth of the sun, but with an edge that was winter's legacy. Rows of marching soldiers and sailors, tight lipped and severe - but sometimes with a playful wink for a child or a pretty girl who was cold but determined to air her summer dress for the first time since September. Kate's other set of memories flowed.

There were no trees on Marks Prospekt any more, only a few ragged black stumps like crows. The pharmacy and bookstore were not distinguishable from the other empty windowed stores and offices, with soot lined doorways open to the street.

'*Sorsk* was a nice place to live. Believe it or not.'

'These memories? You're remembering now?'

'Yes. I remember this street well. They had parades here. It's like having *real* memory. These are memories like you have memories.'

'Unbelievable.' He frowned. 'So do you think you can remember what happened here?'

‘Whatever it was - it must have been after I was born. After I was born I have only one memory. My own memory. If that makes sense.’

‘None of it makes sense to me. I’m just a gangster, remember? So you remember everything your mother knew?’

‘Well. Not quite. Memory plays tricks. Sometimes we make things up and they get mixed up with the past. And I don’t remember everything - just like you don’t remember everything. It’s improving now. Now I believe in it.’

’So about Borilyenko - it’s possible he wants you for something you may remember. Or because you validate his experiments?’

‘It’s strange. I remember my mother’s childhood better than I remember her adulthood.’

‘What about Borilyenko?’ he pressed, ‘What do you remember about him?’

‘I didn’t have so much to do with him directly. He wasn’t a scientist. But he was interested in our work. Other projects took up much more of his time. Project Simbirsk seemed like a bit of a plaything. Not entirely serious.'

'What kind of projects took up his time?

'It was better not to ask.'

'Why?'

'Those days…' she trailed off 'People didn't ask.. and this was a military facility - look. Stop.'

'Stolovaya'. The blackened metal sign with buckled loops and curls was still there, edged in snow - almost festive. She stepped down from the car. The building was little more than four scorched walls.

'Like the rest,' she heard him say. 'Like every building here. Worse than Grozny.'

'Beyond belief,' She murmured. Where she had eaten almost every day. A cavernous place alive with the rattle of cutlery and crockery. Long tables and benches she remembered. And Yevgeny.

Yevgeny was a Jew but almost nobody in *Sorsk* cared. It was said his father was in the camps. Yevgeny it was that inserted himself on the bench beside her that time, slamming his loaded tray on the table.

'Everything good?' He said, pushing back strands of hair and looking at her through thick lensed glasses.

'Couldn't be better. How's life on the Hill?' They called it The Hill because it was the highest point in *Sorsk* but it was an ironic label as the hill was no more than an incline.

'The Hill is bracing,' was his invariable reply. 'Actually,' he said, lowering his voice and looking around 'we have some issues up there on the Hill, if I'm honest.'

'Issues?' She didn't know the nature of Yevgeny's work. Never asked. Everything in *Sorsk* was a closely held secret,

'Yes,' he said, spearing a cube of meat with his fork. 'Quite serious.' He raised an eye as though seeking her complicity. 'I've been meaning to talk to you. To *somebody* anyway.'

She watched a vast breasted woman ladling anaemic dumplings onto plates from behind a row of steaming steel dishes. Somebody shouted something unintelligible, and another person laughed.

'Will you take a walk with me, Katya?'

She felt wrong footed. An unexpected invitation. Looked at her watch. 'Now?'

'In a minute.'

'I'm expected. I have some technicians...'

'Just for a short time. OK let's leave now. I'm ready. Come on - you don't want to eat that shit.'

The food was coagulating on her plate. She lay down her cutlery. It couldn't do any harm. After all, she liked Yevgeny, and she was intrigued. 'Five minutes.'

He dabbed at his mouth with a paper napkin and stood up, tossing the napkin on the table. 'Let's go.'

As they emerged into the bright sunshine, Yevgeny leaned into her. 'You know what they say, don't you? About my father?'

'What about him?'

'That he was in the camps.'

She nodded. 'I heard that.' They were going down the steps to the street.

'It's not true.'

'No?'

'Sometimes I wish it was. I know it's a terrible thing to wish for, but it's true. This way.' He guided her to the right at the foot of the steps.

'Where are we going?'

'I wish he'd been in the camps in preference to where he really was. He was a scientist. Like me.' Now he was walking briskly. Not a casual stroll. 'He worked for them. For the Nazis. Of course, they forced him to do it. I can't blame him for that. He was working at a secret underground base. They had a nuclear weapons program - did you know that?'

'I read about it.'

'He was working on developing a nuclear warhead. They already had rockets, you know. It's a blessing that the war ended before they could use them.' They walked in silence for a few moments. Yevgeny had a habit of thrusting his upper body forwards when he walked, as though to give himself extra impetus. They were heading in the direction of The Hill.

'And today,' he continued, 'I find myself working in much the same line of business.' He stopped. He had an earnest expression. 'Do you know? Have you any idea what we do, up there on The Hill?'

He was very close to her. She took a small step backwards. 'No. I … you shouldn't talk about this, I suppose.'

'I have to tell somebody,' he said, walking fast again. 'Even if it's the *wrong* person. I can't live with it anymore. And now we have these *problems*.'

'You said that there were some issues.'

'It's my project you know. *Project Pustinia*. Wilderness. It's a horrible name but it describes the objective perfectly. If we ever get to use this weapon, God forbid, then it will lead to a wilderness. The consequences are too terrible to think about.'

'So are you going to tell me? About these issues?'

'You sure you want to know?'

She wasn't sure. It was forbidden to discuss their work with anybody outside their immediate group. She found that they were standing before a compound with a barbed wire fence. There was a long low building inside with blacked out windows. A dusty military truck was parked outside with a covered loadspace. He held her arm. Glanced around. The street was empty. 'Let's keep walking. Know what that is?' he said.

'An eyesore?'

He didn't laugh. 'It's a hospital.'

'But there's a hospital on Potemkin Street.'

‘Not an ordinary hospital. More of an isolation ward.’

‘Isolation?’

When he glanced at her she thought she caught a tear in his eye. ‘It’s out of control, Katya. We thought we could control it but we can’t. And there’s no cure. People go there to the isolation ward to die. We’re manufacturing the mother of all diseases. And now it’s killing people. Our people. They take the dead away to be buried in bleach at night. I don’t know where they take them. Katya, I don’t know what to do.’

She heard Grigor say: ‘You OK?’

‘I think I might have an idea why *Sorsk* had to burn.’ She said, looking at the burnt-out refectory with regret.

Chapter Thirty-Five

"HUMAN CLONING TECHNIQUES

Professor Ekaterina Ivnaovna Borodina

Moscow State University 28 August 1962

Procedures employed in cloning human embryos have much in common with the cloning of animal embryos, with the exception of the zona pellucida. The methodology would require that several sperm cells and mature egg cells are gathered from donors, and combined in a petri dish using in vitro fertilization procedures to form an embryo."

Nikolay had acquired the paper through the

Moscow State University Archive. It was a print from a microfiche, and the images of the pages were lop-sided, speckled with background, but legible nonetheless.

"An alternate methodology, provides for pre-produced embryos from volunteer donors that have embryos left over from prior in vitro clients. The embryo would be placed in a petri dish and allowed to develop into a mass of two to eight cells. Next, a chemical solution is added that dissolves the zona pellucida enveloping the embryo. The zona pellucida is a protective protein and polysaccharide membrane that covers the internal contents of the embryo, and provides the necessary nutrients for the first several cell divisions that occur within the embryo."

He sensed a presence at his desk and looked up to find Dikul hovering there, dour faced and petulant.

'What's up?'

'A press release from our famous "intelligence agent" Ivan Ivanov.' He laid a single printed sheet of A4 on top of the microfiche copies. 'Printed in Izvestia. I had it typed up.' A single paragraph:

"From out of the ruins of our once glorious Soviet Empire, a criminal state is evolving the likes of which the world has never experienced. Witness Yevgeny Nikolaievich Kirilov, Chief Executive Officer of the Narodny Mining Corporation. This officer has evidence linking Mr Kirilov with narcotics, racketeering, embezzlement and money laundering. His criminality is blatant and far-reaching, but even so Kirilov appears to seek election to public office in the Duma? Please be in no doubt, that if the authorities refuse to acknowledge the criminality of this individual and to take action against him, then the Feliks Group will take it upon itself to restore order."

'What does it mean do you think?' Said Nikolay 'Restore order?'

'I guess it means they'll take him out.'

Nikolay sighed. 'I'm not a policeman. This is a case for the police, not an intelligence officer.'

Dikul sniffed and hitched up his trousers. 'Borilyenko. You really think he has his hands in all this?'

'I think that's what we're supposed to find out.' He

pushed aside the press release and looked at the microfiche copies again. 'I wonder what interest the General could have in a girl from England who's looking for a scientist from the Soviet days?' He put his hands behind his head and sat back in his chair. 'What do you think about human cloning? Do you think it's possible to make a replica of a human being?'

'Cloning? Replicas? I find it difficult enough to master the photocopier.' He said with a snort. 'What's it about?'

'The general is keeping close tabs on a girl who has travelled from England to find a distant relative. The relative was a soviet scientist who wrote a paper on human cloning whilst at MSU. She has these dreams..' He began

'Dreams? We all have those. I dreamed I would have a posting in some fucking embassy abroad. A warm climate with beaches maybe. Not this ...' He waved his hand to indicate the office and the building generally. 'About making replicas of humans. I don't think it can be done.'

'Why not? We sent men into space before the

Americans could make a decent car.'

'They still can't make a decent car. Anyway, if you want my opinion, it's Science fiction. Take it from me. The General has an interest in a girl, why doesn't he just pick her up. Ask her some questions?'

'Why indeed?'

'*Sorsk*! What would they be doing in *Sorsk*?'

'My officers followed them only as far as the gates. They were afraid to risk going inside the perimeter.'

'Risk? What kind of risk?'

'The sign said it's contaminated, they said.'

'That was decades ago. The instructions were to keep her under surveillance. Why did your people not follow?'

'Like I said… but also it would be difficult to keep a watch on her without being noticed. The town is empty after all.'

'I suppose so.' Borilyenko ran through the implications. Another breach. It was becoming as difficult to contain as the disease itself. He pressed the telephone to his ear, as though in an effort to prevent anyone overhearing, although Borilyenko's office was empty. 'And this gangster? What's his connection?'

'Romantic I would guess. I know him well.'

'How well?'

'We do some business from time to time. You know how these things are. He owns a few clubs and bars. A casino on Odessa Street.'

'Who else knows about *Sorsk*?'

'I don't know, General. I doubt Malenkov would have discussed it with anyone, but you never can tell for sure. He's impetuous.'

'Does he have a big network? Of people he might talk to?

'Nobody close. Business associates. He's a vet. Alpha in fact.'

'Alpha. So he should know how to keep his mouth shut.'

'I should say, yes.'

'All the same… this gangster—what's his name again?'

'Grigor Vassilyich Malenkov.'

'Malenkov. He needs to be eliminated. Does it cause

you a problem?'

'Not me. It doesn't cause me any problem.'

'As for the girl. It's time I met her. As soon as possible.'

'Yes General.'

'Your people - are they still there?'

'I imagine so. I haven't given them further instructions.'

'Tell them to look for them in *Sorsk*. Deal with the gangster. Bring me the girl alive.'

'Bring her to the Lubyanka?'

'Yes. And another thing. About *Sorsk* - it never existed. There was never a town by that name.'

'That goes without saying, General.'

The General sat a long time after the call. Loose ends. Every time he cut he created another loose end. What to do about Lisakov, now that he knew about *Sorsk*? Something he would hold over him. And the others, Lisakov's people. Where would it end? Cut, cut cut.

In the distance they heard it: the buzz of a car going slowly, the engine whining through the lower gears. It seemed like the only sound in the universe.

'I thought this place was off limits?' said Kate.

'For some people there are no limits.'

They listened, in front of the scorched '*Stolivaya'*, for the car to get closer. Sometimes it seemed to get further away. At other times it sounded like it could be in the next street. Then they watched a black Volga with blue license plates turn in at the top of Chukovsky Street, and weave its way down the cratered road. Its headlamps were pale and dim and they lifted and fell as the car negotiated unseen debris, humps in the snow, bouncing hard on its suspension. 50 meters from Grigor's Range Rover it halted and the occupants sat huddled in the car for a few moments. The windows were steamy and there was a jagged smear in the centre of the windscreen where they had tried to clear their view. Two men got out. Both wore long dark coats and fur hats. They stood either side of the car, watching. One man had his arm on the roof.

'So, comrades.' Grigor called. 'Seems like you must

be looking for us, since there's nobody else here.'

The men looked at each other, then seemed to make up their minds, and walked towards them. They were both carrying pistols in gloved hands. Kate noticed Grigor tuck his gun into his waistband beneath his coat and leave one hand on its handle. A few paces away they stopped. They looked cold and ragged, and they pointed their weapons without much conviction.

'You both need to come with us.'

'In that fucking thing?' said Dmitry, nodding at the Volga.

'We'll take yours.'

'I wouldn't trust the Cheka with an expensive car like that. So, what if we decide we don't want to come?'

'It's not an option.'

With great care, watching for a reaction all the while, Grigor removed the gun from his waistband and slowly levelled it at the man who had spoken, who glanced with unease at his companion.

'Now we have an impasse.'

The man had a prominent forehead that made it hard

to discern the direction of his eyes. It gave him a look of intensity. When he spoke he pronounced his words deliberately, swallowing his 'G's like a Ukrainian. 'What is this place? What happened here?'

'It was a *stolovaya.*' Said Grigor.

'Is it dangerous, do you think?'

'I doubt it. Not anymore.'

'Not much left of it. Not much left of anything.' The man looked around him. He seemed to have forgotten about the stand off entirely, although his gun still pointed in their direction. 'It's the same all over. We drove around for a while, looking for you.'

'Looks like somebody didn't want to leave any clues.'

'Devil's Pipe.'

'That's what I thought. You were in Afghanistan?'

'A few places like that, that I would rather forget about.'

'So what happens next?'

'I have instructions to bring in the girl. As for you…'

'Whose instructions?'

‘Does it make a difference?’

‘I expect not.’

The man lowered his gun. His face seemed to relax. ‘You know…’

The first gunshot made her ears buzz and the second seemed muffled, far away. She clamped her hands to her head. Felt like she was under water. The two men had dropped where they stood. Both were still. Kate took a step back. The snow lent the scene a graininess, like an old photograph. Monochrome. Except for the blood. Silence, except for the ringing in her ears.

‘Why did you…?’ she began. There was a tremor in her voice.

Dmitry was looking at the two corpses with a clenched jaw. ‘It was a signal. When he lowered his gun I saw the other one flip off the safety. It was them or us. Them or me at any rate. I don’t think they would have killed you. Not yet. A pity I had to shoot them. This guy did the right thing. Just orders.’

‘That’s how it is with you people? Just orders?’ Kate was angry.

‘What else is there? We need to live our lives by one

rule or another. There have to be rules. Look at what happens when there are no rules. This place.' He was bending over the body of the first man, rummaging in his pockets. He withdrew a white envelope and opened it.

'Theatre tickets,' he said. 'Moscow Art Theatre. For tomorrow. What a fucking waste.' She didn't know whether he meant the tickets or the life. He bunched them up and tossed them in the snow where they fluttered and fell. He flipped through a cheap leather wallet.

'What are you looking for?'

'Some ID. Would be nice to know who I shot. This guy was careful. A professional. Doesn't carry ID. You don't find many like him anymore. A nice set up. They sat there in the car agreeing the plan. Lowering the gun like that for a distraction. Then: bang. The other one was stupid to have the safety engaged. Could have been a different story.'

'It's a game,' she said, her stomach tight. She was trembling, and not from the cold.

Grigor looked fierce. 'A game of life. I'm just trying

to survive it.' He had started on the other corpse. 'This one's not so careful.' He flipped open a booklet, flashed at her the sword and twin headed eagle emblem, then threw it in the direction of the *Stolovaya*. 'No surprises. *Parporshchik* Medvedev. Yegor Ivanovich. A Checkist.'

'But these killings. Don't they mean anything to you? You… you root through their clothes like they're just tailor's dummies.'

'To some people the act of killing is incidental. Others carry their corpses to the grave.'

'Which are you?'

'I have a broad back but I promise you I struggle with my burdens.'

He slipped his hands under the Chekist's armpits, and began to drag him in the direction of the abandoned Volga. The heels of the man's boots carved twin trails in the snow. She felt rigid and frozen inside her coat. Her coat felt as if it had grown in size. Grigor sprung the boot of the car, and hauled the lifeless Chekist over the lip, then he stooped to arrange him inside like baggage. He came back for the first man.

'What are we going to do?' She said.

'I'll move the car. Then we'll head back to Moscow.'

'You mean just leave them?'

'You want to bury them?'

'What if somebody finds them?'

'Go and wait in my car. Switch on the engine. You look frozen.' He reached out and put a hand on her arm. 'Go. It's a long drive and it's late already.'

Grigor parked the Volga in the burnt out shell of a building, and when they drove to the barrier the gatehouse was deserted. He climbed down and swung up the barrier so they could pass though, then padded around the gatehouse leaving crusty bootprints, peering through the windows, before getting back behind the wheel. The Lada was still parked where they saw it earlier, now swathed in a crisp white shroud.

'Nobody at home,' he said. 'Maybe some more tidying up, poor bastard.' Kate felt her eyes widen, but she said nothing. The heater rasped, blasting warm air in her face.

Chapter Thirty-Six

IT WAS THE EARLY hours of the morning by the time they joined the Garden Ring Road and headed towards Tverskaya Street. The traffic was sparse and the Garden Ring was 10 lanes.

'I can't leave you alone tonight,' said Grigor.

'I'll be OK,' said Kate.

'They'll come for you again. It's not over.'

'I know. But I don't know what to do.'

'Go back to London. If they'll let you.'

'You think it's possible?'

'I know somebody in the FSB. A Colonel. Maybe

he can help.'

'I'm scared Grigor.'

'Stay at my apartment tonight. They won't expect that. You'll be safe there. At least for now.'

'No. I prefer to stay at my hotel.'

'Then I'll stay with you there.'

'No, really.'

'You're afraid of me?'

'Of course not.'

'Then let me take care of you.'

'I can't'

'I'll take a room next door.'

'You're very sweet.'

'Nobody called me sweet before.' He laughed. 'I'm not the kind of man that makes that kind of description trip off the tongue.' Grigor braked suddenly and they were outside the Marriott. In the lobby were the usual prostitutes, looking bored. They went to the desk.

'I want to take a room next to this lady. She is room 4661.'

The clerk assessed him critically. 'I'll see what I can find.' He tapped something into the computer. Paused.

Kate thought his face tightened. 'I can give you three doors down. 4664.'

Grigor handed over his ID and a credit card. The clerk entered it into the computer, then handed him a key and announced with a blank face:

'Room 8001. Presidential suite. You have a free upgrade.'

Grigor slid back the key. 'I don't want it. Just give me the regular room. 4664, you said.'

The clerk shrugged. 'You're the boss.' He tapped at the keyboard. Issued a new key. 'Have a nice stay.'

They travelled up together in the lift to the fourth floor. Outside her room they stopped.

'I don't know how to thank you, Grigor. For everything.'

He took both of her hands. Squeezed gently. She saw his eyes were bloodshot. He leaned in and she let him kiss her. His lips were softer than she expected—had expected firm and parched. She stepped backwards, pulled her hands away.

'No Grigor. Not like this.'

'It's OK. Get some sleep. I'm down the hall.

Tomorrow we'll decide what to do.'

An elegant girl with translucent limbs and burnished golden hair played harpsichord and the music rippled through the restaurant. Nikolay thought Mozart, but he was no expert. The walls were lined with leather volumes like a library and the light had a copper hue. He hardly thought that places like this existed in Moscow. He weaved through the tables to a corner where Lebed was standing to greet him, head slightly inclined, holding his napkin in place with one hand while the other was extended in greeting. Nikolay thought he had a politician's smile and it was hard to recall the warrior from before. He felt ashamed of the coarse wool of his suit and his thick soles. This was not a place for thick soled shoes.

'Nikolay Sergeevich. Thank you for giving up your evening.'

They sat, and a waiter in a crisp white apron appeared at their table at once with an improbably large menu.

Nikolay glanced at the businessmen at the next

table, and recognised at once they were not businessmen at all but the security detail, a shared bottle of mineral water and a basket of bread on the table between them. They didn't speak to each other.

'Thanks for inviting me, General.'

'Please. It's Pavel Ivanovich here. But what will you have to drink? Some vodka?'

'Just water.'

'I thought it would be more amenable than the office. You know this place?'

'There are too many noughts on the menu for my rank.'

'I like it because they're discreet.'

Nikolay read the menu, looking more at the prices than the food. 'I'll have the Olivier salad, please. And the chicken.'

'Good choice,' said Lebed, and Nikolay had the impression that he would have said the same if he had ordered stale bread. 'As for me I've already ordered.'

When the waiter had gone, Lebed lowered his tone, speaking more to the table linen than to Nikolay.

'The Prime Minister would like to know about

progress. What have you found out?'

'I briefed General Blodnieks on some of my findings.'

'Yes of course. Blodnieks. But better to hear it from the horse's mouth I always think.'

'General Blodnieks is my superior.'

'I don't have superiors. I'm as high as it gets, except for Boris Nikolaevich. You understand what I'm saying?'

Nikolay sensed disappointment in Lebed's tone. 'I'm sorry, sir. Look.. this is speculation - but my view is that General Borilyenko is at the heart of some kind of conspiracy. And the people are involved are mostly old communists - at the highest levels. Cronies from the old days. It seems probable that this association is responsible for the Feliks Group communications, and for some of the recent atrocities.'

'Yes, yes,' said Lebed with impatience. 'You have proof?'

'Not yet.'

'We need incontrovertible proof Nikolay. And we need it quickly.'

'We've done our best to keep General Borilyenko under surveillance. But it's not easy. He uses the FSB like his own personal bodyguard. It's my belief that the murder of the banker Bukovsky was carried out by Russian Special Forces on his orders.'

'Spetsnaz you think?'

'There were indications. Like the weapons. The procedure.'

'I see.'

'There's an FSB officer. A Colonel. He's everywhere. He had two of my men intercepted whilst they were in pursuit of Borilyenko's car. He was also at the Bukovsky murder scene.'

'Name?'

'Lisakov.'

'I'll see about him.'

'And this conspiracy—if that's what it is—may involve people like Yuri Chaika. I have to say I feel completely unqualified…'

'You're doing a great job, Nikolay Sergeyevich. An important job.'

'There's something else. Something odd. I don't

know if it's important yet.'

'Go on.'

'As I already reported to General Blodnieks, General Borilyenko seems to have taken an interest in a Westerner. A girl. She came here from London some days ago.'

Two waiters brought the first courses and set them on the table. One of them poured some water into Nikolay's glass.

'So, this girl you were telling me about. What kind of interest are we talking about?'

'Not the usual kind. He's having her followed. But she's just ordinary. A nobody. I've been trying to work it out. She came to Moscow to trace somebody. A relative, she said. But I don't believe her.'

'So, what's the connection?'

'I wouldn't even mention it. But the person she's looking for disappeared in Soviet times. Some scientist. A geneticist. Good degree from MSU. She wrote a paper on the viability of human cloning back in the '70's. I found it in the University archive. It's the last mention of her I can find anywhere. Like she dropped off a cliff. I appreciate many people disappeared suddenly in those days.'

'Human cloning?'

'I don't know what the connection could be. But look…' Nikolay produced the same photographs he had shown to General Blodnieks in his office. 'You would think it's the same girl - and yet these pictures were taken 30 years apart.'

Lebed studied the faces. 'Remarkable.' He sat back in his chair. 'What I know is that General Borilyenko headed up a secret biological research facility in the 70's. Not much else is known about it. Almost nothing about the work they did there. All highly classified. I'll try to see if I can find out anything else, but any light you could shed…'

'You think it might be important?'

'We need to know everything about Borilyenko. Anything we can find out could be something we could use against him.' He glanced again at the photographs before returning them to Nikolay. 'Pretty girl.'

'I didn't know who else to call.'

‘Then maybe you called the right person,’ said Nikolay.

‘A lot has happened since we last met.’

‘It doesn’t surprise me.’

‘Can we meet?’ said Kate.

‘If you want.’

‘Maybe there’s a library in town? I want to check some things.’

‘There are many libraries in Moscow. The biggest is the Russian State Library.’

‘I’ll meet you there. At 11:00. Where is it?’

‘It’s not hard to find. It’s a landmark. Can’t you tell me anything now?’

‘Nothing. Except—can you do something for me? See what you can find out about a man named Yevgeny Peshevsky.’

‘Peshevsky. Patronymic?’

She strained for the memory but it didn’t come. ‘I don’t know it. Just Yevgeny Peshevsky.’

‘Who is he?’

‘A scientist. I think he was a colleague of the person I’m looking for. And another name too: Andrei Illyich

Sverdlov.'

'I'll see what I can find out. See you at 11:00.'

'One more thing…'

'Yes?'

'They tried to pick me up yesterday. The KGB. FSB. Whatever you call them.'

'What happened?'

'There were two of them.'

'And?'

'They're dead.'

'I'll come for you now.'

'No. I don't want that. I'm safe for now. Let's meet at the library.'

'Kate, you're going to need a lot of help.'

'I know.'

She put down the telephone. Tried to phone Robert's mobile twice but there was no reply. Then she phoned for Leonid who said everything was OK, as he always did, and that he would be there in 20 minutes.

It would take Nikolay half an hour to reach his rendezvous with Kate. That left him with two hours.

He called Dikul.

'Find out everything you can about two people. Yevgeny Peshevsky and Andrei Illyich Sverdlov. Drop everything. Both were scientists in Soviet times. Most probably in the seventies.'

Then he called Lebed on the private number he had given him.

'The dissident Sverdlov? I remember something about him. I'll see what my people can dig up.'

'Is there any way we can protect the girl? In the meantime?'

'From the FSB?'

'From Borilyenko.'

'Not a chance.'

'They tried to take her in yesterday.'

'That's good.'

'Good?'

'Something's about to break. What happened?'

'I'm meeting the girl in a couple of hours. I'll know more then. But the FSB agents are dead.'

'Dead?'

'That's what she said.' After he put the phone down

it rang almost immediately. It was Dikul.

'We think that Yevgeny Peshevsky is Yevgeny Pavlovich Peshevsky, and he has no file.'

'What do you mean, no file?'

'I mean there's no record of him beyond his birth. He was a German Jew. At least, his father was. His father, Pavel Ivanovich Peshevsky was involved in secret work. We don't have much of a file on him either.'

'Is he dead? Alive?'

'There's no record of his death. But there's no active record for him either.'

'And the other one?'

'There we had more success. Andrei Illyich Sverdlov. Born 18/01/19 in Uglich. Also a biologist. Executed 15/06/78 for counter revolutionary activities. Some nonsense about Darwin had him exiled to Siberia. Then he made a name for himself spreading malicious rumours about a doomsday bug developed at some closed city. Details are sketchy. Probably went a bit crazy. He was tried and executed but the file's been removed.'

'On whose authority was the file removed?'

'Nobody's authority. It's just not there.' A pause. 'Don't read anything too much into it. If you spend any time looking at the archives for that period you'll see there are many missing records. More missing than not, in fact. Some of them just misfiled by some drunken clerk. Nothing sinister. And counter revolutionary activities could mean almost anything. Like reading George Orwell.'

'It's no problem,' said Leonid, when she told him to take her to the Russian State Library on Vozdvizhenka Street. 'The Leninka.' He corrected over his shoulder, because people still called it that.

The windows of the taxi were mottled with grime, so that shapes of cars and buildings were ghostly, blocky shadows, but when she put the window down the cold took her breath away. A few flakes of snow wet her face like spittle. She worked the window winder again but it stuck with a centimetre to spare and the air roared through the gap. 'How far is it?'

'Yes. It's no problem,' and she wished he would speak

to her in Russian instead of pretending to understand her English. The ride lasted at least 40 minutes, stopping and starting and grinding gears.

Leonid pulled up at last, tugging at the useless handbrake, at the foot of the steps to a long and angular stucco building with square columns and tall windows. The statue of a grim-faced bearded figure sat on a plinth before the entrance. Kate leaned over to pay, while the engine rattled and the exhaust stuttered. 'Dostoevsky, ' said Leonid with a kind of pride, reaching back to take the money. 'The statue. Very great Russian writer of…'

The rear door was tugged open. She shrank. A man reached inside. She felt his grip hard on her arm. Caught sight of a burnished wedding ring as she tried to free herself. He was strong and he hauled her from her seat. Leonid let go of the roubles in a flutter. Stretched out his arm to grab her.

'What the fuck?' he yelled in Russian.

She fought so hard her arms ached, floundering with her fists, but when another man came and held her from behind it was useless. She was powerless when he manoeuvred her towards a black Volga that stood behind the taxi with its engine ticking. Leonid leapt into the road with improbable speed, cutting in front of the Volga. A whirlwind of grimaces and shoulders and prods and pushes. Leonid took one of the men by the shoulders and tried to pull him away while Kate kicked out blindly. Now she was being wedged into the Volga. Her assailant turned his back, made a swift movement with his right arm. A shot. Leonid buckled. Kneeled on the tarmac. Free now, the other man came around the car, kicking Leonid aside and threw himself onto the back seat next to her. The seat creaked. She screamed, but the man forced his hand over her mouth. 'Shhh.' Tried to bite but his grip was firm.

Straining to see what had happened to Leonid she felt the car jolt and pull out onto the road. A horn sounded and the driver made a gesture. The engine rasped as they accelerated into the traffic, leaving a puff of black smoke in their wake, and Leonid lying half on the pavement.

'No need for struggle,' said one of the men in fractured English, breathing heavily, so close to her that she could smell pickles and alcohol on his breath. He looked over his shoulder and said in Russian, 'Somebody's following.'

'Call Igor,' said the other man.

'She'll scream if I let her go.' He looked at her. Shrugged. Took his hand away and raised a warning finger. She turned in her seat and didn't scream. The kidney shaped grille of a silver BMW. She thought it was Fyodr, driving close. The man fumbled in his leather jacket and took out a Nokia.

'The girl's with us. Some asshole following. Maybe the gangster's men. What do you want us to do?' He looked at Kate while he listened to the phone. The whites of his eyes were yellow. 'OK… Not long.'

She looked back again at the BMW, willing it to catch up, but a red Lada slotted in front and they fell back. Then she saw a Volga pull into the middle lane with a blue light flashing, and she knew they would cut off Fyodr before he could reach them. She wondered if Leonid was alive.

The cigarette smoke inside the car was stifling and it stung her eyes. She wanted to explain her tears to the men. That it was the tobacco. She felt the need to persuade them she was strong. Not some tearful girl. But her cheeks were wet with tears all the same.

'OK, OK. Seems like he's gone.'

As though picking up an earlier conversation the driver said, 'The BMW is faster than the Mercedes in a straight line. It was an M750i.'

'You're right. But the Mercedes - it's better engineered. Turn left here to avoid the jam on Petrovka. I prefer the Mercedes.'

'Doesn't matter how fast your car is in Moscow. You still have these fucking queues.'

'Better to be comfortable then. I think the Mercedes is more comfortable. Maybe it's a better choice for Moscow roads.' Talking like she wasn't there at all.

'Who are you?' She said, trying to control the shake in her voice.

'No need to worry,' said the driver over his shoulder. 'We're official.' He laughed. 'Hear that, Stefan? Us, official? That's what we are.' Then he shouted at the windscreen 'Fuck you!' and rammed his hand on the horn. 'Out of the way fuck your mother!' A small hatchback pulled out of their path. ‘Sorry,’ he said under his breath as an afterthought. ‘Sorry for my language.’

Chapter Thirty-Seven

'EXCUSE ME BOSS.'

'I'm busy.' Fyodr still languished in the door frame with a wry grin. It wasn't a humorous grin. 'We got some trouble.'

'What kind of trouble?' said Grigor.

'You need to come to the cellar. We had a delivery this morning.'

'What the fuck? Now you want me to supervise deliveries? What's going on in your head, Fyodr?'

'Andrei thinks he can defuse it. I hope he can.'

'Defuse it?'

'Instead of beer they delivered around 500 kilos of

RDX. If Andrei can't defuse it then we won't be opening for business today. Or maybe at all.'

'Jesus, Fyodr. Why didn't you tell me? Let's get everybody out!'

'I've got a lot of confidence in Andrei. It's on a timer he says. Quite primitive. Set to go off an hour from now. So, we have an hour. At least.'

Grigor leapt to his feet and reached instinctively for the ancient Makharov pistol. *If there was one thing you could rescue from a burning building, what would it be?* He remembered her saying.

'No need to panic Boss. I think Andrei is a good guy.' Grigor pushed past Fyodr, who followed him. 'It's nobody we know. Nobody we know would use RDX in these quantities.'

'It's sure as Hell *somebody* we know.' Grigor led the way down a narrow passage past the toilets, to a private door which he pushed open. 'Who took the delivery? Was it the regular people?'

'Arkady let them in. He didn't say if it was the usual people.'

'We should be more careful.' They hurried down a

flight of stone steps. Grigor ducked his head beneath a steel beam. The yellow lights gave them a jaundiced cast and illuminated a long low room with a line of steel barrels and plastic pipes. There were crates of beer and mixers still shrouded in plastic packaging, and piles of boxes. At the end of the cellar, Andrei was crouched over a wooden pallet loaded with oblong white bricks like wax.

'Igor saw it first,' Andrei said without looking up. 'Ripped open the packaging to check. Lucky that he did. It was just the bottom case. The rest was beer. I fucking hate Baltica.' He had a small electrical screwdriver in his hand and a bright flashlight in the other. 'It's not very clever. Not booby trapped as far as I can tell. We weren't meant to notice. Laziness I call it,' he said with the scorn of a professional. Andrei shared the scars of the Soviet campaign in Afghanistan.

Feeling superfluous standing over Andrei with the heavy gun hanging from his arm, Grigor said 'Who d'you think might have done this?'

Andrei sat back from the pallet, admiring his own handiwork. The bare wires of an LCD timer connected to a detonator in an aluminium sleeve lay twisted and exposed. 'It's safe,' he said with a weary sigh. 'A lot of explosive. Enough to take out the club and a few places each side. Somebody wanted to be sure. Hate to say this, but smells to me like Cheka.' He, turned his head to look up at Grigor. 'Unprofessional too. I would have booby trapped it. Schoolboy stuff.'

'Good job. What are we going to do with it?'

'Here's as good a place as any. It's very stable. We can dispose of it when we want. Maybe we can use it for something…?'

But Grigor wasn't listening. He headed straight back to his office and phoned Lisakov.

'Everyone is still alive.'

'Should I be surprised?'

'Your outfit filled my cellar with RDX today and I want to know why.'

'Why would we do that?'

'That's what I'd like to know.' There was a long pause. Grigor wondered if Lisakov was consulting with somebody.

'I can send some people. To check,' said Lisakov at

length.

'To check what?'

'Forensics people. Maybe I can help find out where it came from.'

'I have my own people to do that.'

'I suppose you do.'

'It was KGB. There's no question. Which points to you.' Another long pause. 'Are you still there?'

'Yes, yes. I'll come to your club. Let's see what can be done.'

'When?'

'An hour or two.'

'Come alone.'

'Of course.'

Grigor laid down the phone. 'Fucking snake.' He crossed the room and opened the door. 'Fyodr! Get in here.' He needed to make some plans.

An old and craggy man with a very straight back walked in, followed by two men in blue-grey uniforms. A door banged somewhere far away, followed by an angry interchange. She couldn't make out the words.

The old man smiled at her, and she hoped he didn't notice when she brushed away an involuntary tear. He was wearing a bulky black overcoat over a squarely cut grey suit, and a red tie. He clasped his hands together in front of him and they were red and gnarled, then he greeted her softly in Russian.

'Hello Miss Buckingham. I'm sorry that you were brought here this way. We'll try to make you as comfortable as we can. I'm sure you'll soon be going back to England. If that's what you want.'

She felt reassured by the mention of England. 'Who are you?'

He seemed to consider for a moment, gimlet eyes taking in the room. 'You can call me Vladimir,' he said at last, pulling up the chair opposite her in a leisurely way.

'Is that your name?' she said with suspicion.

The man simply smiled. The two men in uniform had placed themselves behind her, one either side, their faces inscrutable when she craned her neck to see. The room was empty except for a cheap laminated table and two hard chairs streaked with the grime of past occupants. 'Can I order some refreshment for you? Some Tea? Coffee?'

'What am I doing here?' Her voice echoed off the blank walls.

'Vladimir' shifted uncomfortably on the chair. He pulled his overcoat around him and thrust his hands into his pockets. It was cold in the room and her breath formed a fleeting mist in the air. 'You don't have to worry,' he said. Another uniformed officer came swiftly into the room without acknowledging anyone, deposited a pile of notebooks and some pencils on the table, turned on his heel and left. His boots squeaked on the tiled floor. 'You're in safe hands here.'

'They shot that man,' she blurted. 'My driver. Leonid.' The emotions swelled up in her. She was trembling.

'That was unfortunate.' He said, nodding, without emphasis. 'I wish I could change that, but I can't. I understand he was trying to be—gallant. One of my officers was overzealous. These things happen from time to time. Nothing to be done about it.'

'Is he dead?'

The old man shrugged without interest, and from his coat pocket he produced a miniature tape recorder. He held it up for Kate to see, raising an eyebrow. 'Do you mind?'

'Why should I mind? I've got nothing to hide. But Leonid… is he alive?'

He placed the recorder delicately on the table and pushed a button, waiting for the red light to flash. 'There.' He said with a smile. 'Now…' he continued, settling himself into his coat, 'Forget about the taxi driver. I'm sure he'll be taken care of. I want to ask you what you know about Project *Simbirsk*.'

Since her visit to *Sorsk*, the name had haunted her. *Simbirsk* - a city on the Volga now known as Ulyanovsk, notorious for being the birthplace of Lenin. Project *Simbirsk* – perhaps the rebirth of Lenin. She looked at the old man again, and recognition stirred: another misplaced jigsaw piece from that other set of memories slotted into place.

She couldn't help herself from saying out loud 'Comrade Borilyenko!'

His eyes widened a fraction. Then he shook his head

in wonder. 'Do you know me, my dear?'

The sombre, spacious office with its twin portraits of Lenin and Stalin. The smell of new carpet. Borilyenko with hands folded on the table. Smooth skinned. Eyes so sharp they could make incisions. A leisurely dignity. Unmistakably the same person ... cracked at the edges now, and forlorn, like a sepia portrait, but the same man.

'I seem to remember...'

Borilyenko leaned forward in his seat, his eyes flashing. 'This is remarkable! You—*remember me* you say?' he said. 'So unexpected.' Kate watched him, thinking that he didn't look surprised at all. Then he seemed to sharpen up. 'What else do you *remember* Kate? - You don't mind if I call you that? - What else can you recall from those days?'

She bit her lip. What else? How much should she tell him? How much did she know? She frowned and concentrated. 'Why are you keeping me here?' Was all she could manage. 'Why have you brought me here?'

Borilyenko looked around him as though noticing the bare room for the first time. 'Here? It was just convenient. My office is upstairs.' He pointed upwards as though to the heavens. 'It's safe. But I'm sure if required we can transfer you to somewhere more comfortable for a full debriefing. Would that help?' He smiled with that benign look that he always used to have.

'What do you mean by a full debriefing?'

'Well of course you hold the key to a lot of state secrets, if these memories of yours are to be trusted. In many ways you're state property.' He smiled as though to soften the implication. To take away the bad taste.

'Is that what you think I am?'

'Of course not. A joke. In bad taste.'

A thought occurred to her. 'What happened to her? My mother?'

He looked at the tiles and rubbed his hands. 'Your mother. Yes. So she was, I believe. So she was, my dear. Well, those were difficult times Kate. For us. For our country.' He looked sincere. Sad.

'She was definitely my mother? Ekaterina Ivanovna?'

He looked up. 'I should think so, yes. The

resemblance is… quite remarkable. It might be her sitting here.'

'In some ways it is, isn't it?' Something shifting in her stomach.

He nodded slowly, appraising her with a kind of fascination. 'Yes. Yes that's right. I suppose it is.' He sat up. 'So… you remember me. Does that mean you remember other things about your mother's life?'

'What happened to her?'

'I'm afraid to say she did some foolish things. Towards the end. It was taken out of my hands. Those were dangerous times ... but your memories—are they what you might call detailed? I mean, eating kasha for breakfast—those kind of memories?'

She shifted in her chair. The cold was inside her, gripping her with icy fingers. 'They're not always clear. Maybe sometimes they get confused with dreams. Or present day things.'

'At what point do the memories stop?'

'Older memories are clearer than more recent ones. But my last memory of those times—the most recent memory—that would be in the lab. It would be when I biopsied my skin cells for use in some experiments. I remember because it was a big dilemma for me at the time. Cloning my own DNA. HER own DNA, I should say—' she trailed off.

'And after that?'

'Nothing. Just my own memories. At that point it's like a kind of separation.'

A silence. She heard one of the guards stir behind her. A sniff. A shuffle of boots.

'What about your earliest memory? Think carefully Kate.'

'That's much clearer. A samovar. Looking at my reflection. I've always been kind of distracted by my reflection. I think it's because of that memory. I used to like to watch my reflection in the samovar. An old lady is always there telling me to keep away. It was dangerous because of the hot water, she said. An old lady.. My mother.' Then, 'Grandmother. *Her* mother.' She corrected. She remembered the face vividly, close up. A powdered face with grey, kindly eyes. High cheekbones. Smiling. Always smiling.

'No, that's not your memory Kate.' Like a slap. 'Try

to focus on your own memories. Your mother. What do you remember about your mother?'

'Not much to be honest. Not much at all. She must have sent me away very young.'

'Any tiny thing that you can think of would be helpful. Her appearance, for example.'

'Her appearance?'

'Yes, yes. Was she fat? Thin? Dark haired? Light haired?'

'We're identical in every way.'

'How can you be certain? Maybe she was ill. Or pregnant.'

'Pregnant?'

'A bad example. Like I say, any tiny thing you can remember about her may be enormously helpful. Any condition. Conditions are things you wouldn't share would you?'

She felt empty and forlorn. She tried to imagine her mother - tried to imagine herself fatter or with different hair. Or pregnant.

'There's nothing.'

Borilyenko seemed pleased. He lay his hands on his

stomach and leaned back in his chair. 'I'm interested in what you can remember about Project *Simbirsk*. The experiments. The processes. Can you remember any of that?'

'I remember,' she said. 'I remember the objective. To manufacture a clone of Lenin from the DNA of his embalmed remains.'

The old man leaned over, his eyes glinting. 'And what do you remember about the success of those experiments?'

'We validated all of our findings with practical experiments. On rats. Everything in line with expectations. The final step was to clone a human being. It had never been done, even in the US. Let alone working with DNA samples that were over 50 years old. That was the ultimate plan, of course. We were ready to take the first step, I remember.' She looked at the old man and saw a fierce intensity. It took her back to Borilyenko's office in *Sorsk*.

'Why wait?' she remembered asking. We're ready. We just need a donor.'

'Some ethical concerns have been voiced. At a high

level. We just need to satisfy all of those concerns before we can proceed.'

'What kind of concerns?' She had been protective of her project. Prickled at any hint of criticism or doubt.

'There's no need to concern yourself, comrade. In a matter of days, we'll get the mandate we need, and we will find you a donor.'

But it hadn't been a matter of days. Weeks passed without word. Lab technicians played chess and card games. Morale melted away.

'And so, your mother took matters into her own hands, and you are the result. Quite incredible. She was an exceptional scientist. One of life's pioneers.'

'That's how it seems to me.'

'But we could never have imagined that memories were somehow embedded in the DNA. What else? The soul? If there is such a thing.'

'We couldn't exactly interrogate the rats.' Her head was tight. She was making an effort now to block out her own memories, pushing away the here and now. To live inside the head of her mother. It gave her a head ache.

'So far as anyone knows you are the only clone of a human being in existence.' There was something of a challenge in his voice that caused her to wonder what he meant.

'So, is that what I am? A clone? A copy. Not a person in my own right? Property of the State.'

'You're much more than that, Kate. You are TWO people. Now Katya, think carefully. This is very important. Do you remember hearing about Project *Pustinja*? Project Wilderness?'

'I heard about it. I don't know what it was.'

'Yevgeny Peshevsky? Does that name mean anything?'

She felt like she had been connected with electricity - like she read the KGB might do for interrogation purposes. She tried not to register her shock. *A walk to the infirmary. Have you any idea what we do, up there on the hill?* She frowned. 'I'm not exactly sure,' she said.

'Think about it. Write it down—write everything down that you can remember. It wasn't part of your work, of course—I mean, your mother's work. But it helps to build a picture. Of those times.'

She looked at the scratched surface of the table. Borilyenko was thinking. At length he said: 'I apologise for the way you have been treated. The way you were brought here. Your driver. That's unfortunate. We'll make contact with his family. Some compensation, perhaps. And this—' He made a wide gesture, '—cell. You're not a prisoner. Not exactly. But we'd like you to stay a while. To debrief. To rebuild what we know about your mother's research. And other things you might remember. Wilderness in particular.' He raised himself to his feet, placing a frail hand on the table. 'We'll move you to somewhere more comfortable soon. I'll see to it. We'll prepare somewhere you can work. In the meantime,' he nodded at the notebooks, 'it would help us a lot if you could begin to write down what you remember. About the project. About the science. About Wilderness.'

'Compensation? For Leonid?'

'If it's appropriate. The least we can do. A tragic accident.' He stood over her, waiting.

Leonid. *It's no problem*, she remembered with a stab of guilt. But it turned out to be a problem, after all. 'Surely you have your own records? Of my mother's work?'

'Sadly not.' He shook his head. 'Everything was burned. A long time ago. Nothing remains at all from those days. All destroyed. You saw yourself the state of that place. A terrible thing.' He waved a hand at her as he moved to the door. 'I'll see you tomorrow. Tell the guards if you need anything. Anything at all. Then we'll get you installed somewhere more pleasant.'

'You said pregnant.'

'I'm sorry?' He paused at the door.

'You said to tell you if I remember my mother being pregnant. Why did you say that?'

'I also said fat.'

'There's another one, isn't there? Another clone.'

He stood up.

'You are quite unique, Kate, I assure you of that. Please write down whatever you can remember. We'll talk again in the morning.'

And he left the room like a phantom.

Chapter Thirty-Eight

'I WARNED YOU about the girl, my friend,' said Lisakov, easing into a chair in Grigor's office. He looked relaxed.

'So it's about her? About Kate?' Grigor was leaning over his desk. The radiators clicked and muttered. 'Why the fuck would the KGB be interested in some girl from a village?'

'It's not my business to know that. Knowledge is a dangerous thing. This… situation is evidence of that,' said Lisakov. 'Anyway, she's out of reach. Yours and mine.'

'What does that mean?'

'Take it from me, you don't want to be mixed up in this.' He paused. 'She's in the Lubyanka.'

'She's where?' Grigor hadn't made up his mind how he felt about the English girl, but suddenly he was enraged and alert and he felt something churn deep inside.

'In the hands of the FSB. But more than that: she's been taken by General Borilyenko. Anyway, never mind about her now. We have our own situation. You and I.'

'Borilyenko? Jesus. And the bomb - I take it that was yours?'

'I'm sorry about that. Really. I could lie to you, of course. I could tell you we'll hunt down the perpetrators. We will anyway, if you report it. But you were a soldier. A practical man. You understand we can't question orders. Otherwise there'd be chaos. And I had instructions.'

'To kill me.'

'Not just you.'

'Who then?'

'Everybody. Your associates. No survivors.'

'And now what?'

'Yes, what now…? That's rather the question, isn't it? What happened in that place? *Sorsk*? I sent some people, who never came back.'

'We met them.'

'Lozik in particular was a good man.' Lisakov looked wistful.

'That was his name? The Ukrainian?'

Grigor plucked the Makharov from the desk, weighed it in his hand and pointed it at Lisakov, looking down the barrel and flipping off the safety with his thumb. Lisakov was still and unfazed. Grigor held the gun there for a few seconds, then lay it down again.

'I didn't know. That he was Ukrainian,' said Lisakov.

'So what do you suggest? Now?'

'Well.. We could have a war.'

'You brought some help?'

'Outside, of course.' He changed the subject. 'So what did you see on your excursion?'

'Not much. Burned buildings. Nothing I haven't

seen before.'

'*Sorsk* was a closed town.'

'I know.'

'I've been trying to find out what happened there.'

'I thought that too much knowledge was dangerous?'

'The problem is, as your girlfriend is finding out, you can't *unknow* something. And I'm beginning to worry I already know too much. It was made very clear to me that I should forget everything I know about *Sorsk*. But like I said, we can't very well unknow things. So I've had a hunt through the archives. Top secret archives. I have clearance at the very highest levels. And I've drawn a blank. There's no file. No such place.'

'Looked to me like there was a thorough clean up.'

'Yes. But who did the cleaning up? There's no record of any operation like that.' He took up the previous conversation. 'So, we could have a war. I'm sure you're prepared too. That you've taken sensible precautions.'

'Just as you'd expect.'

‘I think that’s the outcome the General is expecting from this meeting.’

‘Or?’

‘Or we could cooperate.’

Not a prisoner... Borilyenko had assured her. But confined to a cell all the same. Finding it impossible to sleep on the iron bedstead with the thin mattress, she lay on her back, avoiding the prospect of the inevitable use of the bucket in the corner for her toilet. The light built into the wall just above the bed could not be extinguished. They had left her with a ceramic jug of water and cup on the shelf beside her, and the pad of paper and pencils.

She thought about Yevgeny, earnest and riven. She now knew how much courage he had needed to tell her about Project Pustinja. She remembered how many times he had come to her seeming to be on the brink of something.

'Katya. It's a pleasure. Not with Dima this evening?'

‘Called to Moscow.’

Yevgeny seemed relieved. 'It's a good party.'

Sipping his vodka like a fine wine and seeking something of interest to point out in the small crowded apartment. Shostakovich played in muted tones. ‘Everybody's here.' But in reality there were notable absences, fearful of association with Sverdlov, who was marking his departure from *Sorsk* with a small celebration. ‘Comrade Sverdlov is a good man,' he said.

'Do you think so?' she said, wary of entrapment.

'Of course. I've followed his work for a long time. I'm an admirer.'

'Comrade Sverdlov should be less outspoken, don't you think?'

'You mean about that Darwin nonsense? I thought after Stalin we were supposed to be more enlightened. Surely the modern view is more progressive? He expressed his view of religion in the context of Darwinism. So what? In fact there are people that say that Darwin purposefully left the door open for a religious interpretation.'

Katya drew away from Yevgeny. Did people openly express these views? Even whilst Comrade Sverdlov was discredited?

'But you think I'm reckless.'

'No, just… It can be unpopular to express support—
'

'—for poor Comrade Sverdlov, you mean?' Yevgeny laughed. 'I'm sure in time the Party will recognise him for the genius he is. And if we can't engage in some harmless scientific dialectics, then what was the revolution about?'

Katya willed him to lower his voice. Instead he helped himself to another glass of vodka from a bottle on a coffee table, excusing himself as he reached past other guests. 'It's time we acknowledged that Stalin is dead.' He said in a voice that seemed to silence the room. In reality, faces didn't turn and conversations didn't falter. The world continued on its regular course around the sun.

'Please don't ever talk like this when Dima's here.'

'Sometimes I think you're a dangerous lady.' Yevgeny's voice was tainted with disappointment. 'Your association with Dmitry for example… our resident Party thug. As for me I always say what I think,' he said. 'There's nothing they could do to me. I wanted to talk to you about something... But maybe now's the wrong time. I'm tired, Katya.'

'Dima's no thug,' was all she could bring herself to say. Then Sverdlov joined them. A tall, rugged man with a high, broad forehead. He was beaming and his cheeks were pink. 'Well my friends. Thank you for your support.' He put an arm around Yevgeny's shoulders and pulled him tight. Yevgeny was a head shorter than Sverdlov and it made him look like a child. 'Good of you to come, Yevgeny.'

She tried to sleep on her side, but she could still feel the ridges of the steel skeleton of the bed beneath the mattress. Poor Yevgeny - he thought his work made him invulnerable. He could say anything. But in the final reckoning it was his work that destroyed him. And her work? Did she even have a view?

'You're a geneticist. You must have a view,' said Yevgeny that night.

'I take the Party view,' she had said.

'Even the Party can't really decide. Hitler decided of

course. He at least had a definitive view. About Darwinism.'

Sverdlov recognised the direction of the conversation and became fidgety. He had a very deep voice, full of self assurance normally, but she caught a waver in his tone as he said 'Let's keep the evening light.' Then he walked away, a little unsteady on his feet.

Yevgeny, the tragic Jew, driven like his father to develop more and more destructive weapons to support a system that they both doubted.

What more could Borilyenko want from her? She could see where his questioning might lead, and everything led to Yevgeny and the Wilderness Project. Pustinja. But she knew so little. Nobody knew anything. At least, nobody alive. So what would happen, after she told him everything she knew?

She picked up a pencil and knew that she had only to concentrate and the memories would come thick and fast. Withdrawing memories like files from the archives. She began to write. Ponderously at first, and then with a fury in cyrillic loops and curls that she had never learned to make, but that struck her as ornate and satisfying.

'I was transferred from Moscow to the closed town of Sorsk to administer a scientific project, codenamed Simbirsk. Simbirsk was the town where Lenin was born, before it was renamed Ulyanovsk in his honour. The objective of the project was to create a successful clone of a human from the cells of Lenin's embalmed remains.'

'Do you think it's even possible?' she remembered Colonel Borilyenko asking. It was her first day in *Sorsk*. She had been allocated a comfortable two room apartment in *Karl Marksa* Street, and had left her bags unopened inside the door while Dmitry waited outside with the engine running to take her to the headquarters building.

'I wrote a paper on the subject, Comrade Colonel.'

'And I read it, Ekaterina Ivanovna. It was most interesting - but only theoretical. Do you think it's really possible to recreate a human being from the cells of another?'

'I certainly believe so.'

‘And then there are other challenges that we theorists tend to disregard, if you don’t mind me saying. Nobody has even begun to think, for example about the consequences. There may be moral questions. What do you think about moral questions?’

‘I don’t think about moral questions, Comrade Colonel. I leave such things to the Party.’

‘And so you should. But even so, there are interesting dilemmas. Where is the repository of the so-called soul? Is it contained in a single cell? Can we, *should* we recreate dead souls? Can we influence the personality, the biological make up of a cloned human?’

There was a series of framed certificates and photographs on the wall of the office, and she saw that Borilyenko had a degree in physics from Moscow State University. She saw also that he had been made a Hero of the Soviet Union, and wondered what he had done to distinguish himself.

‘You’ll have every resource at your disposal. Anything you need, you only have to ask.’ He leaned across the desk at her. She thought he looked evangelic

'You're about to make history, Ekaterina Ivanovna. How does that feel? More than that… you are going to *recreate* history. Just think of it: to bring back Lenin from the dead. A new Lenin. What do you think of that?'

'I think it's exciting work Comrade Colonel and I thank you for this opportunity.' She meant it, but it sounded trite. He didn't seem to notice.

'You'll find there are many scientific projects here at *Sorsk*. Most of them are much more mundane than your own work - but equally secret. You've met Comrade Dmitry Andreyevich of course. He 's probably explained already that he's the Commissar here - he does so at the first opportunity with any new visitor,' said with a forbearing smile. 'He'll be giving you the usual security briefing. This facility is top secret. I hope you'll find the community of *Sorsk* to be interesting and stimulating, but you mustn't on any account discuss the nature of your work outside of your immediate colleagues. Is that understood?'

'I understand, Comrade Colonel.'

'Good. Then your first task is to start to build your

department. Anybody you need to work with you from outside - any specialists or technicians - just give me a list. We have a laboratory for you but it's a shell. You're the expert - you decide how it evolves. Make a list of everything that you'll require. I'll see to it personally.'

'Thank you, comrade Colonel.'

Afterwards, alone in the spartan apartment that smelled of wood shavings and mothballs, she stared out of the window at the empty street lined with spiky saplings and indulged herself in daydreams. She was so proud to be here. So proud to be chosen. And for such a project…

'*The principles of the research were at first firmly established in rats. After 2 years research we had successfully cloned sustainable living rats from skin cells.*' They named the first ones Gagarin and Titov, she recalled. Pioneers, like the cosmonauts. Unlike their namesakes however they were sadly short lived and had died within the week.

'But the project had stalled because sanction was withheld for experiments with human DNA. We went nowhere with the project for weeks. There was

resistance to the project from somewhere, but I wasn't told where.' She wrote, and writing she learned, because it seemed that the memories flowed directly to her pen bypassing conscious deliberation. *'We had progressed to the point in our work where the only logical next step was to experiment with humans, I was frustrated because I knew that we were ready. That's when I decided I would be the donor, and that I would continue with my work in secret.'*

The nocturnal visit to the laboratory. Alone in the cavernous room with laminate faced work benches and rows of petri dishes, and a tiled floor that magnified every footfall. It was cold there at night and the harsh neon lights threw distinct shadows she had never noticed in the day. She must have paced the laboratory for hours, busying herself with minor tasks, fighting off the moment of decision. And then, preparations complete, she laid out the instruments on a sterile tray. The iris scissors, suture, needle, punch biopsy instrument… all set out in a neat row. Then the anaesthetic. The jolt of pain as she inserted the needle.

After that moment she remembered nothing at all.

She had reached the buffer zone.

A key scraped in the lock and she guessed it must be morning. Her eyes were sticky but she felt an electric alertness. She put down the pencil and sat on the bed with her feet on the floor. A guard opened the door and stepped aside for Borilyenko to enter. He seemed more familiar to her than ever now, a memory ignited and burning bright.

'Good morning, Ekaterina Ivanovna.'

'I'd rather you didn't call me that. It's not my name.'

He was sympathetic. 'No. It's not. I apologise.' He seemed at a loss for a moment. 'Please follow me, Miss Buckingham.' And he turned and walked out. She followed him into the corridor, and they walked past a row of cells. The guard followed. 'I'm sorry you had to stay here overnight. Later we'll…' but he didn't complete the sentence. Instead, he opened a door and ushered her inside. 'Please,' and she recognised the room where he had questioned her the previous day.

She sat down at the scored table where she had sat

before. ‘I’m hungry,’ she said.

‘I’m so sorry. It’s very thoughtless of me. I just wanted to get on. I was forgetting…’ he turned to the guard and ordered him to arrange some food. He left at once, without saying anything.

Borilyernko was reading her notes, and she wondered how it was that she hadn’t noticed him pick them up. There were several pages of closely covered cyrillic, and she was surprised at how much she had managed to write. He shuffled the papers and then lay them on the table.

‘This is quite incredible,’ he said. ‘Your recollections are much more detailed than I would have ever imagined. And your Russian is… did you ever have lessons? I mean in England?’

’Just French. At school. And I don’t remember much of that.’

‘Quite incredible. I would never have expected…’ He leaned forwards, his elbows on the table. He seemed to drift for a few moments. His skin was sallow in the artificial light, and there were folds in the skin of his face, like valleys. ‘Even the grammar is perfect…’

he mused. 'And after this you remember nothing.'

'After the laboratory that night. After the biopsy. There's just me. Kate. The other memories seem to just cut off, no matter how much I try.'

'I see.'

'When can I leave?'

'It's because those memories—your Russian memories—must have been contained in the DNA sample that your mother took. Your memories - your mother's memories in fact - were replicated, just like everything else. You're a complete clone of your mother, including her memories. Quite extraordinary.'

'You didn't really say, what happened to her. I'd like to know.'

'What I'd like to know - what I'd like to talk some more about - is whatever you can remember about Project Wilderness. It's very important, Kate.'

'I need to know what happened to her.'

Borilyenko got to his feet. He placed himself with his back against the wall, opposite Kate.

'I was sorry about your mother. But she brought everything upon herself. Her unauthorised experiment. But then to bundle off the result of her experiment to the West. Well you must understand that we couldn't allow that. When I say the result of her experiment - well that means you, Kate. Ultimately.'

She felt sick. The result of an experiment. What she was. 'So, what did you do?'

'Not me, Kate. First Dmitry. He was Commissar. We needed to find out how she had got the baby out of *Sorsk*. The route. The identities of the collaborators. But Dmitry of course was conflicted. In fact we reassigned him shortly afterwards. So, we had to send her here, to the Lubyanka. The KGB were given the task - to question her.'

'And then?'

'Sad to say, many records are incomplete of those sent here for questioning in those days.'

'But you must know what happened to her?'

'Many people do not survive the rigours of questioning.'

'They killed her? *You* killed her.'

She stood up. Gulped down a silent scream. Ekaterina Ivanovna.

'You must appreciate the position she put us in.'

Once in Trubanya Square there was a Palace, where now there is a vast, gloomy derelict house with sunken window frames and snowdrifts that hunker up to the walls. A moment's grizzled speculation and a glance over his shoulder and then Grigor kicked aside the timber doors and he led his men into a vast hallway. A spartan chandelier, empty of jewels, hung high above them. As their boots resounded through the empty rooms Grigor wrinkled his nose at the stench of urine and looked at the rubble and burst and abandoned mattresses all around. Vague shadows in military fatigues, weighed down with bulky sports bags followed.

'That room,' growled Grigor at last and he pointed the way through a broken doorway into what may have once been a library. Splintered panelling and a network of empty slatted shelves lined the walls. The stone floor was littered with rubbish. They dispersed and drifted around the room watching their feet, no talking, looking for signs. Then in a corner of the room Grigor found what he was looking for.

'Here.'

One of the men set to work on a slab of flooring with a tyre lever, and soon it scraped aside releasing a foul breath.

'I'll go first.' Each man produced a mining helmet from his pack, and began to fasten battery packs for the lamps to their waists. All of this was carried out in silence. Grigor illuminated his lamp and descended into the hole, shifting his bag to his back. Vassily Gronsky had told Grigor that he had discovered this tunnel years ago through studying some archaeological books and making some deductions. There was a story that the master of the palace had built a subterranean passage to the Kremlin where he had carried on an affair with Tzarevna Sofia.

It seemed that as soon as his head disappeared below the surface his lungs contracted. The steps were steep and narrow and slippery beneath his boots so that he had to descend them as he would a ladder, face down, clinging to the wet stone as he felt below for the next foothold. His breathing became laboured. Above him he heard the echo of his comrades' boots and the rush of their breath. As he climbed he tried to direct his thoughts to Kate. What was she feeling now? Had she lost all hope?

For five minutes he climbed downwards. It felt as though he was entering an ice compartment. His clothes felt clammy. He shifted his bag with a shrug and a clang of metal.

Suddenly a voice rang out. 'Welcome Grigor Vassilyich!'

Grigor looked down and strained to fix the beam of yellow light in the direction of the voice. He caught a glimpse of a shadowy figure, then solid rock some metre or so below. He jumped the remaining distance, stumbling with a clatter on the greasy surface, but quickly regained his balance. The beam followed the movement of his head, skirting around what appeared to be a bell shaped cave with a high ceiling. Then it lighted on his friend, Vassily Gronsky. He was tall and wiry and wore a shabby Red Army greatcoat two sizes too big from The Great Patriotic War. On his head he wore a fur hat with earmuffs sticking out absurdly like rabbit's ears. A wreath of rope was slung over one shoulder. Over the other hung an AK47 secured by a length of string.

'You look like a *zek*,' said Grigor. A *zek* was what they called the prisoners of the Gulags. He embraced him tightly. At his back he heard the others leap to the ground one after another. The cave reverberated with the sounds of their boots and their breath, spiralling endlessly, turning upon themselves in the darkness beyond. There was steam on their breath that was thick and grey in the lamplight.

'We don't have much need for your western fashions down here,' said Vassily, not without bitterness Grigor thought. There was a hint of madness in Vassily's expression that may have been a trick of the light, but it made Grigor wonder for the first time whether Vassily might lose them in the labyrinth that he knew they were about to enter.

Grigor looked all about him, lighting up the entrances to passageways that seemed to head in all directions. Obviously the system had expanded since that single lover's pathway. 'Which way?'

'We'll head out first for the Neglinka River.' Said Vassily with confidence. He produced a wooden shaft with a lantern on top like peasants once carried. As he lit it, only then did it occur to Grigor that Vassily had been waiting down here for them alone in complete darkness. He fixed the shaft into an empty holster in his belt. 'Let's go.'

They followed him towards the mouth of a tunnel that redefined itself as the light played upon the shadows. Then for some 250 meters they proceeded sideways, crab-like, because the tunnel was so narrow, although it was at least four meters high so they were able to hoist their equipment onto their heads. Grigor felt the coarseness of the rock rubbing against his clothes, and when he looked down the lamp revealed that his tunic had acquired a slimy sheen. He tried not to think about the popular legend of rat-mutants in the caves below Moscow. Instead he tried to focus upon the plan. He tried to focus on Kate.

The slime on the walls down here was a peculiar yellow. Sometimes scraps of it fell upon them from above, disturbed by who knows what. Grigor picked a length of it from his shoulder and it felt like a length of soapy hair. He heard the others cursing behind him in low murmurs that had a harsh resonance, as they scraped through the tunnel until finally they emerged at another cavernous junction. This time there were other sounds, and other lanterns, and grotesque shadows flickered on the walls. Grigor looked around in bewilderment. It was a strange underground community. Vassily appeared not to notice them at all.

'We need to head over that way.' He said pointing. 'We'll pass under the Maly Theatre. Over there is where the tunnel joins with Metro-2.'

'Metro-2?'

Vassily glanced over his shoulder. 'Built in Soviet times. A secret metro system that connects to Vnukovo-2 airport, amongst other places.'

'I heard about it. Thought it was a myth.'

'The trains still run from time to time. You can hear them.'

'Who uses it?'

'Whoever needs to.'

'What about these people down here? Who are

they?' A cackle rang out from somewhere, and a shout.

Vassily shrugged. 'Illegals. Dispossessed. Who cares?' Then he grinned, and Grigor caught a glint of madness again. 'Sometimes the militia do a sweep. But they've never come this far. My private quarters are not far from here.'

They passed odd people carrying out mysterious acts that they carried on in oblivion. Grigor noticed a woman stretched out naked upon a table, surrounded by black robed figures like jackdaws, muttering vague obscenities. The woman wore a black mask, and there were black candles burning around her.

'Satanists.' Vassily said in casual explanation over his shoulder. 'Sometimes I've known them bring children down here for sacrifice.'

At the entrance to another wider tunnel, a bearded man with long greasy hair sat idly nursing a pistol. They passed him without comment. The caves seemed to whisper urgently all around them. Grigor glanced uneasily behind him. 'Wait.' He called, unhooking his bag and heaving it to the ground. The shuffling behind him stopped abruptly. Vassily looked back, waiting.

Grigor stooped to unzip his bag and removed the weapon which he strung around his shoulder.

'Afraid, Comrade Major?' asked Vassily.

'Not afraid. Careful.' His men followed his lead and began to arm themselves. He heard the rattle of cartridges being inserted, checked. 'How far now?'

Vassily shrugged. 'Not too far.' He turned, holding his lantern aloft like a tourist guide. *This way for the Lubyanka tour*.

They proceeded in silence for about twenty minutes, tramping along the glistening tunnel. Grigor fixed his eyes on the ground, watching his step. Finally, brandishing his lantern before a huge door with a rusted lock Vassily stopped the column at last. He glanced at Grigor, as if in affirmation of something, then kicked at the door which submitted at once.

Further ahead the way had once been bricked up, but now there was a crumbling arch and lumps of masonry. Vassily picked his way through the rubble with exaggerated care, then trailed his hand along white stone as they walked, looking for a breach.

'Here!' He stopped abruptly and hauled off a broken

section of the wall. Then another, a cloud of dust swirling in the light of the lanterns. Behind it was a rugged steel door, stippled with rust. 'This door will not have been opened for a hundred years at least.' He traced his fingers down the door as though admiring some artefact. 'We can have a go at the lock. Or we can just blow it away.' He looked at Grigor with his mad eyes.

There was restless scuffling behind him, the creak of leather harnesses of automatic weapons. 'Let's try the lock first. Yegor!' He called over his shoulder.

'Here boss.' The whisper was close to his ear and made him start.

'See what you can do with this,' ordered Grigor, pointing to the lock.

It took just a few moments for Yegor to release the lock, scrabbling with steel and complex instruments like a dentist. Then he twisted the handle, but the door wouldn't budge. He stood, put his shoulder to it, and finally it burst open sending guttural reverberations through the tunnels behind. 'We're in, boss.' Grigor sensed a collective intake of breath.

They emerged into a dimly lit pale green corridor with chipped masonry. At intervals there were wooden doors with square grilles. Their boots echoed starkly in the tiled passage.

'We're on the lowest level. There are 8 floors below ground. She's on six,' said Grigor, leading. 'This floor is unused.' They came to a sturdy pock marked door with two locks. Above it was an ancient Soviet made security camera. Grigor took the handle and paused. 'Now we'll find out if Lisakov can be trusted.' He opened the door. The hall was deserted. There were two steel elevator doors and doors that he knew led to the stairwell. Another camera watched them from the ceiling.

'What about these cameras?' Said Fyodr.

'I was told not to worry about them.'

'You have some pretty good sources, Boss.'

Chapter Thirty-Nine

HE WAS IN A dismal bar in Serafimovicha Street when Dikul called him on his mobile.

'What have you got for me?' said Nikolay.

'Sverdlov. There was an administrative error,' said Dikul.

'What kind of error.'

'He wasn't executed.'

'So he's alive?'

'Transferred.'

'Where is he now?'

'He was sent to Perm. Then in 1986 there was the

General Pardon.'

'He was pardoned?'

'That's what it looks like.'

'So what happened to him?'

'He lives in Moscow,' replied Dikul.

After the call Nikolay slapped his glass on the bar and shrugged into his coat as he pushed through the doors into the street. He followed his own tracks in the snow back to his car, which had acquired a phantom like property beneath a thin, translucent layer of snow. He wrenched open the door with an alarming crack, had already half frozen shut. In the car, his breath steaming, he called Lebed and told him the news.

'Get to him. Make sure he's safe.'

'I'm on my way there now, sir.'

From the glove compartment he pulled out a map, and it took him almost ten minutes to find Borisova Street. It was hard to focus after half a litre. He closed one eye as he drove across town in a hurry, randomly changing lanes.

If Sverdlov had spent time in Perm he was likely to be a shell of a man. And how old now? Would he in fact be any use at all?

Borisova Street was a collection of grey blocks on the edge of town with precarious balconies some of which had been enclosed with windows. A deserted play park was situated in an open space in front of Sverdlov's block. Icicles hung from the swings. Only a handful of vehicles were parked along the street, and there was single set of tyre tracks passing by the building. He stopped right outside the entrance.

When he pressed the intercom there was no reply, so he stabbed at the buttons for other apartments until somebody simply buzzed him in without bothering to answer. In the damp concrete lobby he saw there was a row of tin postboxes and one was marked 'A I Sverdlov'. Somebody had sprayed a line through each mailbox, and a meaningless circle on the wall in blue paint. The paint was old and nobody had made an attempt to remove it. He tried to reach inside the flap of the mailbox but it was too deep. He pressed the button for the lift, and it made agonising progress. The doors rattled when they opened and he stepped inside, pressed the button for the fifth floor.

The door of apartment 512 had a brown fake leather fascia studded with buttons. He pressed the bell, then after a few moments banged on the door with the heel of his hand. He heard bolts pulled aside on the other side of the door, and then it opened to reveal a tall, emaciated old man.

'Andrei Illyich Sverdlov?'

The man squinted at him. 'Who are you?'

Nikolai held out his ID, and Sverdlov looked at it without much interest. 'A Chekist.'

'Something like that.'

'You're drunk,' admonished Sverdlov as he held open the door and Nikolay slipped inside. The interior was gloomy and had a raw metallic smell. There was no carpet and the sound of his shoes on the boards sounded vaguely intrusive. Balls of fluff moved in the draught. 'You want to see my papers?'

'No. Nothing like that.'

'What then? What do you want?'

Nikolay was ushered without enthusiasm into a small bare room containing two armchairs and a TV on the floor. One of the armchairs was worn and shabby.

The other looked almost unused. He chose the unused armchair and sat down.

'It's about *Sorsk*.' It was very cold in the apartment – as cold as the lobby. Nikolay thrust his hands deep into his coat.

'*Sorsk*.' Sverdlov said without emphasis or recognition.

'You were a scientist.'

'I've been many things. Lately I was in geology. I broke rocks. Where was it you said?'

'*Sorsk*. A ZATO. A closed town.'

'A closed town. I wouldn't know anything about a closed town, would I?'

'It doesn't matter anymore.'

'If I knew about this place – what did you call it?' He leaned forward as though to hear him better.

'*Sorsk*.'

'If I knew about a place like that I might find myself back in Perm.'

'Perm is closed permanently.'

'Some other place then. They're all the same.'

'You have my personal guarantee...'

‘The guarantee of a drink sodden Chekist? That’s comforting. What use is that when I’m digging trenches with my bare hands?’

‘I mean there are people at the highest levels…’

‘They change like the wind. What did you say your name was?’ Sverdlov stood up and went to the samovar on a primitive veneer cabinet. He put his hand to the side of the samovar and grimaced. Then he stooped and produced a half full bottle of Stolichnaya from the cupboard underneath. Nikolay was sure the gesture with the samovar was an act. It was tarnished and looked like it was rarely used. Sverdlov found a glass and slopped vodka into it without offering Nikolay a drink.

‘You know this room is bugged?’ he said, after drinking.

Nikolay looked around, feeling it was an unlikely prospect. ‘Bugged?’

‘Of course. You people. Now you're trying to trap me.’

‘Nobody's trying to trap you.’

‘I wasn’t born yesterday. You're here to take me

back, aren't you?'

'To where?'

'To Perm. Once a zek always a zek, eh?'

'Perm is closed.'

'My suitcase is packed. I always have it ready.' He had sunken eyes but they glinted with intelligence.

'Alexei Illyich, I'm not here to arrest you. Perm is gone. So are all those places. Since Gorbachev's time,' although he wasn't sure that was true. The labels changed but the confectionary tasted just the same.

'I'm not afraid.'

'There's nothing to be afraid of. I need your help. With *Sorsk*.'

'Never heard of it.' He poured himself another vodka. Lifted the glass in Nikolay's direction. 'Catching up.'

'Andrei Illyich, we know you worked there.'

'Show me your id again.'

Nikolai produced his ID and this time the old man squinted at it, holding it close to his eyes. Seconds later he handed it back.

'Impressive, Major. And not KGB. Different

letters.' A bark to indicate irony, but without humour.

'The KGB was disbanded.'

'Not gone. Just hiding. Different badges. Different acronyms.'

'If you believe that, then you really must help me. Because you're right.'

Sverdlov put a finger to his lips and indicated the small room with a frantic gesture. Pointed at the door and rose from his seat.

'I think you should go now,' he said.

Nikolay went to the door and Sverdlov accompanied him outside. He locked the door with particular care, and they went down in the lift.

Out in the open Sverdlov walked fast with a wide, urgent gait, and Nikolay struggled at first to keep up.

'Where are we going?'

'For a walk. Away from prying ears.' They passed a row of run down shops. In the window of one was posted a picture of a line of leggy girls displaying the winning numbers for the latest Goslotto draw. There was a wooden kiosk up ahead and Sverdlov stopped and bought a half litre of Stolchnaya and some cigarettes. Nikolay stamped his feet to keep warm while he waited and hoped Sverdlov was the sharing kind. He needn't have worried as Sverlow took a deep tug at the bottle and passed it to him. The spirit slipped easily down, and it felt like kindling, lighting up his stomach. He reminded himself that he hadn't eaten. Sverdlov resumed his pace with a sidelong glance at Nikolay.

'Not discreet, are you Mr chekist? The question is, are you here to bury or to praise Caesar?'

'Not to bury,' said Nikolay, thinking that Sverdlov was an unlikely Caesar.

'I don't want to go back to the camps. If you're here to trick me, then you should question your humanity.'

'I'm not here for that either.'

There was a bench at the side of the deserted street, and Svedlov sat down. On the other side of the road a few spindly black trees stood out against the white landscape.

'Tell me exactly why you've come, Nikolay Sergeevich. No bullshit.'

'I need to find out about *Sorsk*. What happened

there. Why they would burn it to the ground.'

'Is that what happened?' Sverlov passed him the bottle. It was half empty already. Sverdlov had eyes like oysters. 'I'm not surprised. It would have been the only way.'

'The only way?'

'I worked with Peshevsky on a biological warfare project known as Wilderness. Our task was to take the naturally occurring Ebola and Marburg viruses, and to genetically modify them. They're haemorrhagic fevers with no known cure, leading to internal and external bleeding and vomiting. With ebola death occurs in six to 16 days. It's a painful death. The disease is transmitted through bodily fluids, and this was not ideal for our purposes.'

'Didn't we sign up to the Biological Weapons Convention?'

'Of course we did. We signed up to anything to get hard currency. But we paid lip service. There were Military compounds all over the Soviet Union working on biological weapons programmes. Look at Biopreparat - this was a completely open, public agency for biological warfare! Military compounds produced hundreds of tons of Anthrax. Who the fuck cared about the Weapons Convention? Our task at Sorsk was to weaponise Ebola and Marburg. We were trying to genetically alter the virus so it was capable of airborne delivery. And the particular function of my department was to develop a vaccine.' He shook his head sadly, looking at the ground. 'I'm sorry to say I failed. But we had some minor breakthroughs. Ebola is a particularly virulent virus. Then I was transferred to Moscow. Which proved to be a euphemism.'

'So what happened? With the virus?'

'I don't know. Yevgeny's work was gathering momentum. But without a vaccine I thought it was a hazardous strategy. Made the mistake of saying so. So did Yevgeny, but you didn't question orders. And Colonel Borilyenko was an ambitious man.' He threw Nikolay a twisted grin. 'So they burned it? The City? Is that it?'

'I understand so.'

'Then I would suggest that maybe the project got out of hand. It would be the only way to eradicate the disease. To burn it. Once it was airborne… wilderness.'

'I think you should go and get that bag you packed,' and when he saw the sudden panic in Sverdlov's face he rushed to reassure him. 'There's nothing to worry about. Nobody's arresting you. But I think it may not be safe for you to stay alone in your apartment for a few days. You were right about Borilyenko. He was ambitious. Still is. Have you any idea what he's doing now?'

'I read the newspapers, Comrade.'

There was a scrabbling at the door. Not like keys but something else. Kate swung her feet onto the floor and waited, feeling sick. Her back ached and it was cold in the cell. Somebody pushed open the door and it slammed against the wall. She started. A bulky man in military fatigues filled the doorframe. He wore a gas mask, and a heavy automatic weapon hung by a leather strap from his shoulder. He threw something brown and ragged into the room, and Grigor's voice, suppressed but recognisable said:

'Put it on.'

'How did you...?' she picked up the ragged object and unravelled a gas mask.

'That will be the first thing they try. Gas. We would use Kolokol-1. I don't know what they'll use in here. Time to go Kate. Hurry.'

She pulled the mask onto her head, fumbled with the straps, and an eery isolation imposed itself. Grigor reached out to her, and she looked back once at the iron bed before being led out into the corridor. There was a huddle of men in the corridor wearing camouflage and masks like hers. Every movement resonated. Nobody paid her any attention. Guns spiked in all directions.

'That way.' She wondered how they knew. How did they get here? How would they get out? She allowed herself to be pulled along. 'Did they give you anything? Drugs?' She shook her head.

Far ahead she heard the sound of a pneumatic drill. Except she knew it wasn't that. A downward pressure on her shoulder propelled her to the floor. Her wrists stemmed her fall. They hurt.

'It's started.'

When she looked up she saw through the twin

portholes of her mask a body in a pale blue uniform curled like a foetus at her level. The sawing sound she heard was the panting of her breath. Some people were shouting. A single gunshot was followed by another burst from an automatic weapon. There was a sour smell in the air that reminded her of bonfire night as a child. Boots thudded past her head, and she saw two men running up ahead, crouching. They reached the turn in the passage, stood with their backs against the wall. One of them threw something blindly around the corner. An explosion. More shouting. The men launched themselves around the corner and there were more bursts of gunfire. She tried to press herself into the cold tiles but found herself plucked to her feet like a package.

'Come on.'

A voice she didn't recognise said: 'We need to reach the stairs. You need to run fast, OK?'

There seemed like many people surrounding her, but she thought that after all there were less than 10. Kit jangled and rattled. The edges of her goggles were steamed up, and threw her periphery vision out of focus.

'Everything will be OK.' Grigor's disembodied voice. Echoes of Leonid's reassurances. She tried to believe it. Her lips were trembling. He gripped her arm and they pressed forward.

They reached a door. Somebody kicked it open and sprayed shells into a hall. It was empty. There were elevators there. Grigor bundled her through the door, directing his weapon, suspended from its sling, with the other hand. He fired at the surveillance camera which shattered into fragments which clattered on the floor. Her hair was sticking to her brow.

'Can we go back to the tunnel? Or do we need to find another way?' somebody said.

'That's the best route. But we'll need to fight our way down the stairwell. Now's the time, before they bring in reinforcements. It's unlikely that they will use gas on the stairs. Let's do it.'

Two men were already pushing open the doors, tentatively. One of them threw something onto the stairs, where it skittered and bounced. Then silence. She watched them advance through the doors, one with his weapon pointed upwards, the other downwards. Nothing happened.

'I think it's safe for now Grigor.'

She felt herself thrust towards the doors. 'Come on,' said Grigor. 'Looks like Lisakov came good for once in his life. By now this area should be swarming with Chekists. Quick. Down here.'

She almost lost her footing once or twice as they hustled her down two flights of stairs, scuffing against the walls, heavy tramp of boots, clap of hands on gun shafts as they changed the direction of their aim. She was tall, but felt dwarfed by the men.

They crashed through the doors on the lowest level, and emerged into a passageway with black and white chequered tiles and rows of wooden doors with heavy iron locks. The fluorescent lights flickered. Then a single shot rang out. The returning fire was a deafening cacophony. A door was pushed open and she was pushed into a cell. The others backed in after her. Another series of shots rang out. Then silence. The cell felt stifling.

'What now boss?' She thought she recognised

Fyodr's voice.

A hoarse voice said: 'Next they'll use gas.'

'We wait.' Said Grigor. 'We'll be hard to dislodge from here. We're not in Grozny now. This is the centre of Moscow.'

'How will we get out?' she said.

'I'm hoping that there'll be an intervention,' said Grigor, 'but first we're going to have to defend our position for a while. I don't know for how long.'

'An intervention from who?'

'Your friend Nikolay.'

'We understand,' said Lebed at the other end of the line, 'that you have a situation at your offices.'

'I see.' Borilyenko was at his desk. 'And where would you have acquired this information?'

'Our sources are impeccable.'

'There's no situation here.'

'My sources tell me the Lubyanka is under siege.'

Borilyenko laughed. 'A siege, you say? I'd hardly call it that,' he said. 'A few militants managed to break though our security. Everything's under control.'

'A rescue party we're told.'

'I don't know where you get your information from. Who would they be rescuing?' the fresh implications were running thorough Borilyenko's head. The leader of the opposition party in Russia had somehow found out about a misguided assault on the Lubyanka. That was bad enough. But what did he know about the girl? What could he infer about Sorsk? 'There are no princesses to rescue in the Lubyanka.'

'An English girl, I'm told.'

'An English girl?' how much did Lebed know? How much had leaked beyond the corridors of the Lubyanka?

'I think we should meet, General. Before this causes a diplomatic incident.' Said Lebed.

After an hour that seemed like a day, the lights went out.

'No torches. Use infra-red.' said Grigor. 'We'll see them coming if they use lights.

Kate felt claustrophobic inside her mask and with no light at all.

Fyodr heard it first. A soft hissing sound in the corridor.

'Here it comes,' he said. 'Gas. Like I said.'

Grigor whispered in her ear. 'Don't panic. I know it's easy to say. Trust that your mask will protect you. The darkness is to scare us. We have lights if we need them, and we have infra-red.'

'They'll give it 10 minutes for the gas to do its work, then they'll come.'

In the blackness her mind drifted. She worried about Becki. Where was she? Would she see her again? Why did Robert not answer his phone? What about Gold's son? Death was life's punctuation. Gave it its rhythm. Pauses. Questions. But never a full stop. She could die here today, she and her mother, and life would go on. But she wasn't her mother, even though she was grown from her cells. She knew it. For her mother she was no more than a memory store. Ekaterina Ivanovna didn't share her pain or her aspirations. Her life was over, but she had left a record in her daughter's genes. She knew she wasn't her because all she felt right now was her own raw fear, and not anybody else's. She dreaded her own loss but it was her loss, unique and strident. She was alone in the darkness.

Grigor? She wondered. What did he dread?

'You OK?' He said, as if awakened by her thoughts.

'When will it end?'

A scuffling in the corridor then. Occasional tiny sounds. A muffled footfall. A brush of clothing.

She didn't see the movement but she felt a disturbance in the air.

Then an explosion. The bomb in the hotel Rossiya. Like that. And white flashes. A sustained burst of detonations. Ringing in her ears. Tinnitus. Curses. A scream, rising and falling, like a banshee. Movement all around. Darkness, pressing in on her, amplifying the sounds. She pressed her back against the wall and it felt cold and hard through her clothes. More gunfire, the sound bouncing off the walls. A crash. An urgent shout. It seemed to last no time at all. Then silence and blackness, like a shroud descending. Becki. Her gappy smile. Her assertive manner. Where was she? Gold. The gunshot that brought down such a big man in a fraction of a second. She was tense against the wall.

Then a hand touched her arm. The rumble of Grigor's voice.

'Now we wait again. Be brave Kate.'

Little was said in the pitch black cell. She felt afraid to be alone with her thoughts and tried not to think at all. But she kept seeing Yevgeny, the last time she saw him. He was waiting for her outside her apartment.

'Hi Katya. Do you have a few minutes?'

She was surprised to see him there. Surprised he even knew where to find her.

'I'm on my way to the lab.'

'Mind if I walk with you?'

'Of course not.' But she felt somehow cautious.

It was a bright day and she felt the pleasant warmth of the sun on her bare arms. Yevgeny was wearing a short sleeved shirt and Western blue jeans. She wondered where he bought them.

'My work is going well.'

'That's good to hear.'

'Too well.'

'That's bad,' she wanted to tell him to go away. She

wanted to surround herself with ignorance. She wanted to unknow what he had told her that last time they took a walk on The Hill.

'The virus is airborne. We're trying to contain it. Experiments take place in an airtight environment. We're very, very careful.'

'Yevgeny… you shouldn't be telling me,' she felt an irrational anger at him.

'But still,' he went on, 'Sasha was put into the isolation ward yesterday. He has influenza symptoms. That's how it starts. Sasha's a technician. A friend of mine. Do you know him?'

'I don't think so.' She walked quickly, and he kept pace.

'Katya..'

'Yevgeny, what do you want me to do? This isn't my area. It's not my responsibility. I shouldn't even *know* about it.'

'A few years ago I ran an experiment. On the Moscow Metro. We released an influenza virus.'

She stopped walking.

'On the Metro?'

‘We wanted to see how quickly an airborne virus would spread. Just a harmless virus.’

‘Somebody told me. A friend. Everybody seemed to have a cold one year. It was you?’

‘We calculated that 87% of the population contracted the virus within 7 days.’

‘Yevgeny…’

‘Imagine if it was ebola and not influenza. Imagine if it was *my* virus. In London. New York. Here in fucking *Sorsk*, Katya!’

‘You have to control it.’

‘We’re trying. And a vaccine - that’s my number one priority. Sverdlov was doing good work on that. It was a catastrophe to lose him when we did. He was a genius.’

The memories were clear, but lacked definition around the edges. Some of the detail was absent. The colours. The sounds. Dreams had more depth.

Then the lights came on.

There were measured footsteps in the corridor. Figures around her came to life, cradling weapons, standing, kneeling. A voice from outside.

'Don't shoot. I'm here to talk.'

From Grigor 'Lisakov?'

'Who else?' the voice was calm. Self-assured. But muffled all the same, and Kate guessed he must be wearing a gas mask.

Grigor pulled one of his men away from the door and stepped out into the corridor. He had a large pistol in his hand, but she noticed he wasn't carrying his automatic weapon. She heard them talking.

'Is this your idea of cooperation?'

'I can't supervise every activity of the FSB.'

'They used gas.'

'You have masks.'

'So what are you doing here?'

'A negotiating team has arrived. Upstairs.'

'Who?'

'Lebed is here.'

'The politician? What the fuck has he got to do with this? What do you suggest we do?'

'I think you should leave the way you came. Fight your way back.'

'Fight?'

‘I’ll do what I can to ease your passage. But so long as Borilyenko is still in charge, I can’t guarantee what will happen. You need to be prepared for anything. I’m here to formally request your surrender. I’ll take the message back that you’re considering our proposal. My men will be stationed beyond the doors. It means you can reach the tunnel without opposition, in all probability.’

‘In all probability. Thanks for that assurance.’

‘The best I can give you.’

When Grigor shouldered through the door he stood for a moment. Kate thought the mask gave him a look of melancholy.

‘Let’s get out of here.’

Hunched men straightened up in readiness. Equipment passed from hand to hand. Nobody said anything as they pressed through the doorway. Somebody placed a hand on Kate’s back and urged her forward. She knocked her shoulder against the doorframe and felt a dull pain. Faster now, they moved down the corridor until they came to the door to the tunnel. Grigor hauled open the heavy door which scraped on the floor, then stood aside and motioned for each of his men to enter. Kate was last, and she felt him grasp her arm. He peered at her through the grotesque eyeholes.

'You know—' he began. She felt his grip tighten.

Then a sharp reverberation; Grigor's head whipped back. She reached to keep him upright, but he was too heavy, and he sagged to the ground. She tugged at his clothes. Another shot. Two more. She was trembling, eyes stinging. She heard her breath, shallow and sibilant. The smell of cordite seared her throat. Another shot, and she backed into the tunnel - saw Grigor's hand twitch on the tiles. Somebody was yelling from behind but she couldn't make out the words. Her face was wet inside the mask. She felt hands grappling with her, then pulled backwards. A bulky shape pushed past her and levelled a gun around the door. A deafening volley. She caught the swift movement of an arm, and there was a loud explosion in the corridor, followed by the patter of falling plaster. She backed deeper into the tunnel, and found herself propelled in the path of dancing flashlights into the darkness, her head full of

Grigor, slipping out of her reach. From the corridor she heard a drawn out moaning, like a Muslim call to prayer. She recognised Fyodr's disembodied voice.

'Katya, we have to go. The Boss is dead.'

Chapter Forty

A PROCESSION OF glossy black vehicles stopped at right angles outside the main entrance of the Lubyanka. Nikolay hung back as Lebed, flanked by assistants and security men, converged upon the teak double doors, his coat tails flapping. Nikolay thought it looked like the arrival of a delegation from Washington.

The guards were expecting them but still made a show of examining papers.

'Don't you recognise me? Do we need to go through this charade? You must have seen me on TV,' said Lebed. The guard just handed him back his papers in silence and nodded towards the interior. When Nikolay passed through he exchanged a secretive smile with the guard that had held up the Great Man, and he barely glanced at Nikolay's ID.

Their shoes stomped in the marble reception hall and their voices boomed. A single uniformed FSB officer greeted them at once, and directed them up an ornate staircase to the third floor offices.

They were shown into a wood panelled ante-room with chairs around the wall. A secretary sat at a desk to one side of a double door. She had sharp birdlike features and her fingers pecked at a keyboard, ignoring them.

The FSB officer accompanying them stood in front of her desk and waited. She sighed. Looked up.

'General Borilyenko is expecting…'

'Two men,' she said. 'Not this pack.'

'They're together.'

'Not in the General's office they're not. They'll have to wait there.' Still not acknowledging Lebed and his entourage, she stood up. She was tall and slim and Nikolay noticed that her nails were perfectly manicured. ‘I’ll tell the General they’re here,’ she said to the FSB officer, and opened both doors to enter the General’s office, offering Nikolay a brief glimpse of a rugged mahogany desk and a hammer and sickle flag. The doors closed behind her. Lebed was fidgety. He looked at him.

‘She better be quick.’ But without much assurance.

Three uniformed officers entered the ante-room. Two of them took their places at either side of General Borilyenko’s office and the other remained just inside the entrance door. Their faces were impassive and they avoided looking at anyone. Nikolay thought they were not regular guards: They were wide shouldered and poker straight and had a combative air about them. One had a purple discolouration over half his face. He recognised a red and silver ribbon representing the medal For Distinction in Military Service. A war hero.

The doors to Borilyenko’s office opened again and the secretary emerged, followed by an FSB Colonel. The secretary resumed her duties.

‘I am Colonel Kvitinsky.’ He did not extend his hand, but stiffened just enough to acknowledge

Lebed's rank. 'Please follow me - just General Lebed and Major Sokolov. Everybody else can make themselves comfortable here.'

'These men are with me,' said Lebed

'They'll wait for you then,' said Kvitinsky, turning back to the office.

'A town of 150,000 inhabitants,' said Lebed with incredulity. Outside the window the sound of the traffic undulated. 'Just wiped out.'

'Necessary casualties. The disease had to be contained at all costs. *At all costs*. I did what I had to do for the sake of the Soviet Union.'

'You did it to protect yourself General. Why was nobody else informed? Nobody in government. This was your dirty secret.'

'The KGB was a state within a state in those days. We looked after our own.'

'Even Comrade Andropov - the head of the KGB at the time. Did he know what was going on?'

'Not precisely. Comrade Andropov would not involve himself with day to day matters.'

‘Day to day matter? A doomsday scenario?’

‘It was contained. There were many incidents, in those days.’

‘About the clean up operation,’ said Sokolov. ‘there’s no record of such an operation at all.’

‘It was of course classified. As many things were.’

‘So far as we can tell it was not even known about by the Politburo. Not by Comrade Andropov himself. Nobody.’

‘It would have been unthinkable to implicate the Party in such a thing. And I had everything under control.’

‘So, what happened to the men that implemented your clean up solution?’

‘After the operation they were redeployed.’

‘Redeployed to where?’

‘Oh look. It was a time of mass migration throughout the USSR. It was common for specialist troops to be deployed throughout the Union. Wherever they were needed.’

‘But these particular troops? Where were they deployed?

‘It was no more than a Company. Perhaps 200 men at most.’

‘So what happened to them?’

‘They were sent to assist our colleagues in the DDR. At Wismut.’

‘The uranium mines?’

‘Their expertise was invaluable there I’m informed.’

‘How many survived.’

‘It’s not recorded.’

‘So you were responsible for the deaths of 150,000 residents of Sorsk and perhaps the deaths of a company of specialist government troops?’

‘Less than that. Much less.’

‘How many people died in Sorsk?’

‘It’s not recorded.’

‘Not recorded,’ repeated Nikolay.

‘It is also not recorded how many people would have died an agonising death if I had not implemented the necessary containment strategy. Throughout the USSR. Throughout the world perhaps. Not to mention the negative impact of the exposure of a mishap in our biological weapons programme.'

'A mishap?'

'An unfortunate set of circumstances.' He looked up at his interlocutors. 'Let's not forget this could have been a global environmental disaster with implications for all humankind. The outcome of not taking appropriate action cannot be exaggerated.'

'And *Project Simbirsk*?'

Borilyenko laughed. 'A naïve aberration. A pet project of mine, I have to admit. Soviet advances in DNA and genetic manipulation led the world. In secret of course. But the application of human cloning was unorthodox at that time. My idea to clone Lenin. Something of a personal crusade. Well. It could have been done. I've been proven right.'

'Because now you have your human clone.' Said Sokolov.

'That crazy bitch.' Said Borilyenko.

'Were there others? Other human clones?'

'It's not recorded.'

'It seems that for a scientific research centre not much of anything was recorded.'

'It's the nature of the kind of secret work that we carried out.'

'Tell us about *Project Pustinja*. What was the nature of the work exactly?'

'I can't tell you about that. It was classified.'

'We've talked about *Sorsk*. There'll be an investigation. It's my belief that you were criminally negligent.'

'Think what you want. You're too young to understand the imperatives of those days. The sense of duty. And what is there to investigate? A few charred buildings. The evidence of the daughter of a dissident? Will anyone believe this cloned memory fabrication?'

'I believe her.'

'But who are you? A war hero, I concede. But outside the army you're just some mouthpiece in an expensive suit. Maybe you made the most of your popularity. It's not the same as power. You're just a flawed legend.'

'Whereas you?'

'Whereas I'm still in charge here. Whatever it may look like.'

'And what about your connection to the *Feliks Group*?'

Borilyenko laughed. A cracked and mirthless laugh that left barely a trace on his features.

'A myth. Invented by dissenters and enemies of the state. My department has fully investigated this non-existent cabal.'

'Colonel Lisakov?'

'Amongst others.'

'He'll testify to the contrary.'

'I doubt that.'

Nikolay suddenly realised that Borilyenko was a sad and lonely old man, increasingly isolated.

'The real criminals,' he pointed to the floor, 'are down there.' I need to resolve our security issues in this building. So, if you'll forgive me…'

'Tidying up some more loose ends you mean?'

'I've heard enough.' Borilyenko pressed a buzzer and looked at the door, but nobody came. They waited and Borilyenko buzzed again.

'As I said. Lisakov will testify. I think he wants your job,' said Lebed.

'Lisakov. Who does he think he is?'

'In addition to the testimony of...' Nikolay hesitated, unsure how to refer to her, and felt awkward when he settled on: 'the former Ekaternina Ivanovna Borodina, we've located a reliable witness to the work that was being carried out on *Project Pustinja*, and to the former status of the closed city of *Sorsk*. We've enough evidence for the Prosecutor General to launch an enquiry.' He felt like a policeman, and found himself couching his words in a contrived, legalistic way that was not his own.

'What witness?' said Borilyenko, adding 'The Prosecutor is a good friend.' His tongue flicked out to moisten his lips in a manner that reminded Nikolay of a lizard.

'Andrei Illyich Sverdlov was a scientist engaged in the development of a vaccine for the virus that was being developed at Sorsk. The work on this virus was in breach of the Biological Weapons Convention.'

Lebed watched Borilyenko.

'Sverdlov was executed.'

'I'm afraid not, General.'

‘He was a traitor.’

‘Some would argue, a patriot,’ interceded Lebed.

‘It’s impossible to condemn all of the judgements of all of the courts back then, just because of a fashionable hostility towards the Soviet Union. Sverdlov was judged to a be traitor to his country. Do we need to cast doubt on the judgements of murderers also? The rapists? The thieves? You think all of the judges during those years were corrupt or incompetent? The man was a traitor and deserves to have been executed in accordance with the court’s sentence. As for me - you think you can hold me accountable for a breach of the Biological Warfare Convention? No more than a Colonel at the time. You think I wasn’t just obeying orders?’

‘Why don't we let the President decide,’ said Lebed. And at that moment the phone on Borilyenko’s desk shrilled, making Nikolay start. For several rings the General seemed to ignore it. Then without taking his eyes away from Lebed he lifted the receiver.

‘Borilyenko.’ He shifted his gaze away at once towards the window. ‘Of course Boris Nikolaevich.

May I ask the nature.... No, no. I understand. I'll be there at once.' He lay down the receiver with exaggerated care. 'I have been summoned to the Kremlin.'

Lebed laughed without humour. 'And you're going? In the middle of a siege? In the middle of our meeting?'

The General raised himself up. 'The FSB will tidy things up. The President wishes to see me.'

'And what about our meeting?'

'You mean interrogation.'

'If you want to call it that.'

'I've had enough of it for today.' He flapped his hand at them and walked to the door.

Nobody tried to stop the General leaving his office. Nikolay heard a flurry of activity in the ante-room. Some barked instructions.

'That went well,' said Lebed, after the door had closed.

Somebody must have led them back through the tunnels, but she had no idea who. The anaemic light from a flash lamp danced ahead, casting cameos in the darkness. She was surprised to see there were other people down here, huddled in crevices, bulked up in heavy clothing. Muttering unintelligible greetings or imprecations.

Hobbling on the uneven surface, she reached out a hand to steady herself now and again, then pulled back her hand, repelled by slime or debris. She wondered if they resented her for the death of Grigor. It was her fault. When she felt a hand on her back, prompting her, she wondered if it wasn't a shade too unrestrained, betraying more than just impatience. The guilt attached itself to every small thought and gesture. Grigor had come to rescue her, and now he was dead.

Nobody spoke, unless you counted the occasional curse when toes were stubbed or hands were scraped. Sometimes metal jarred or scraped against the walls, and she thought that it was their weapons that did this, whenever the passage narrowed. They pressed forwards.

She was glad to be rid of the gas mask. Even the foetid air down here was fresh compared to the mustiness of the mask. It was very cold - her fingers throbbed but when she thrust her hands into the pockets of her jacket she felt unsteady. And when they emerged from the tunnel, what then? It wasn't over. No final resolution. And her misrememberings, no longer misremembered, were with her forever. A life pre-lived that wasn't in her power to dismiss. Her mother's life. The gleam of the bowl of the samovar.

Two of the men fell back at intervals, nervous about an assault from behind, then rejoined them in a rustle and jangle of equipment and heavy footfalls, flash lamps playing erratic patterns on the stone walls. She imagined once that she heard the rumble of a train.

What time would it be now, out there in the real world? What time in England? She wished she wore a watch. She couldn't return to the hotel, like nothing had happened. Would they be waiting for her? Her feet ached.

The man in front stopped, and held up a hand. Somebody shined a light on him and she saw he had a ragged grey moustache and a washed out monochrome face. Unlike the others he wore a mangy fur hat with a red star, and a long coat. She had never seen him before. Everybody listened to the silence, broken only by the sounds of breathing and the faint scrabbling of a small animal. She shuddered at the thought of rats down here. There must be rats out there in the darkness, beyond the range of their torches. Somebody trained a light in the direction they had come, and it revealed an empty void. Then they moved on.

When they finally hauled her from a hole in the ground, like Alice she thought, the world was so stark and white and loud she had to blink. The sun was hot on her face, and light bounced off the snow banks along the walls. A toothless, bearded old man wrapped in a plastic sheet sat propped in a corner on a pile of snow watched them without displaying much interest. He was nursing an empty vodka bottle. The faces of her companions had acquired a new vibrance, brought into sharp relief in the sunshine.

'No reception party,' said one.

'What did you expect? Nobody knows about this place. If they come for us it'll be through the tunnel. And it's a labyrinth down there.'

The men seemed to mill around, lacking purpose.

She started to say: 'Grigor…' and it was Fyodr who looked at her with a blank stare that she didn't know how to return. She thought that the impetus seemed to have drained out of him and all of them, and they stood around the ruined house thoughtful and morose.

'What do we do now?' she said.

A short stocky man with closed cropped hair hoisted a rucksack onto his back. 'We load up the cars and get out of here.'

'And go where?' said another.

'Wherever we go, they'll be waiting for us now.'

'Grigor would know what to do.'

'Fuck Grigor.'

'Yes,' agreed Fyodr. 'Fuck him.' And they observed a respectful stillness for a few moments. Kate thought about Grigor's body in the cellars of the Lubyanka and wondered if they had removed it. Fyodr shouldered his weapon and ran a thumb through the shoulder strap. 'Let's go.' He said, and she followed them to where a short line of SUV's were parked in the road. Somebody began to throw kit into the rear of one of the cars, where it landed with a thud and a clink. The oblivious

Moscow traffic buzzed and growled and breathed malevolent fumes into the air. A horn sounded, but not for them. She felt all washed up. A heavy hand on her shoulder, and when she looked it was Fyodr.

'It's not your fault,' he said, speaking to her thoughts.

When she spoke it surprised her that she choked on her words. 'Whose fault is it, then?' Her eyes were moist. Maybe from cold or from the shock. She thought about Grigor.

'We'll wait for them at the Club,' he said, and he helped her to climb into the back of a huge Toyota. 'Everything will be OK,' he said, pushing the door closed. Leonid again. Another life lost.

Chapter Forty-One

A BLACK MERCEDES awaited Borilyenko in the courtyard, issuing two perfect plumes of exhaust from its tailpipes that sailed away in the cold air. A uniformed driver opened a door for him. He wondered how much the President already knew. He wondered how to take care of Lebed. What was the strength of his position? He sat back in the supple leather.

'Let's go,' he said, and wondered what the driver was waiting for. 'The President hates to be kept waiting.' He didn't recognise the driver. He looked at the square shoulders and the shaven neck, and leaned forward to make himself heard. Then the other door opened and somebody slid in beside him, pulling the door to.

"'Good afternoon General,' said Lisakov, removing his gloves.

'What are you doing here?'

'Drive,' said Lisakov, and the driver responded at once, pulling forward with a powerful jolt. Lisakov spoke with brisk authority. Borilyenko slumped, feeling the spirit drain out of him. He had waited a long time for this moment, and it was accompanied by what was almost a feeling of relief. 'I regret to inform you General, that you are under arrest.'

'On whose orders?' but he knew already. There was only one man in Russia that could issue orders for his arrest.

'Surprised? Surely not.'

'I'm an old man. There's nothing left to surprise me. Are we going to the Kremlin?'

Lisakov shook his head. 'Lefortovo Prison.'

The very name of Lefortovo struck terror into the hearts of all who were taken there. But not into the heart of Borilyenko. Not today. 'Do I get to meet with the President at least?'

Lisakov's profile, he thought, was not a worker's profile. He had an aristocratic look about him, an association of privilege. He did not have the look of an executioner, but he knew he was a dangerous man.

'Not for me to say,' said Lisakov.

'What *is* for you to say?'

'Only that you will be required to answer questions about certain allegations.'

'About *Sorsk*?'

'I'm sure Sorsk will feature in discussions.'

The Moscow traffic was at a standstill on the inner ring, and stationary vehicles flashed past as they sailed down the middle lane reserved for official cars. In the other direction cars swarmed around a broken down truck, belching black smoke. Their driver had attached a flashing blue lamp to the roof.

'Am I permitted to learn the origins of these allegations?'

'In time. They won't come as a shock to you.'

'Lebed of course.'

‘I’ve been tidying up, General. Just like you. The gangster that was protecting the girl is dead.’

‘Good work.’

‘As for the girl - I think we’ll repatriate her.’

‘You think it’s wise?’

‘It doesn’t matter what I think.’

Borilyenko craned his neck to look out of the back window. He felt stiff and lethargic. ’This isn’t the way to Lefortovo.’

Lisakov sighed. ‘The prisoner, escaped our custody on the way to be interrogated.’

Everything felt strangely detached, as though he were watching events unfold from the sideline. ‘You intend to kill me?’

‘No, General. That’s not my current intention.’ He glanced at him. ‘The girl will be our insurance policy, of course. And Peshevsky.’

‘Insurance against what?’

‘Against your return, General. I’m taking you to the airport.’

‘What about Lefertovo?’

‘My little joke. I hope you’ll forgive me. You’re

fortunate, Comrade General, to have friends in high places. The Government is in a weak position today. It can't afford another scandal. Not of this magnitude. You would be notorious.'

'Notorious?'

'The extermination of an entire population. I would call that notorious.' He thought he detected a hint of humour. 'And then of course there are your other activities.'

'Other activities?'

'The *Feliks Group*.'

The engine of the Mercedes undulated as the automatic gearbox churned up and down. Borilyenko tried to think of something to say. It was useless to deny anything. Everybody talked eventually. Lisakov said: 'We've known about *Feliks* for a long time. Practically since the beginning. And we've been observing with interest.'

'I don't understand.'

'Comrade General, you know the system better than anyone. Everyone spying on everyone else. Lebed thought he'd stumbled on some epic secret that would remove you from whatever succession plans the President may have had. So he commissioned the other team to uncover your links to *Feliks*. But he didn't discover anything new. The President already knew what was going on. The organs are aptly named. They're part of the tissue of the state. It's like a biological system: Every function interdependent. We know almost everything. I can tell you for example about the contents of your Cyprus bank accounts, your property in Barcelona, your links to organised crime. There are no secrets. You think we're amateurs? Not like the KGB of your era, maybe. Different. Maybe better in some ways. Worse in others. Your precious Soviets failed to make the collective farms work, but they discovered collective policing, and it's acquired a life. A life of its own. When they founded the police state they made spies of all of us. But the *Sorsk* business. That was a surprise. You kept that a secret for a long time. I commend you, General.'

'So if you knew about Feliks why didn't somebody stop us?'

'It suited everyone to have a bogeyman. It was

useful. The oligarchs are out of control. They need to be reined in - and not by the Government, which can't be seen to trample on the free market. You did a good job, and we tried to support you whenever we could. Cleaning up after you, as it were.'

'Why does *Sorsk* make any difference. Such a long time ago. All such a long time ago.' He ruminated.

'I'm no politician, General. I have no ambitions in that direction. But I understand how *Sorsk* might have an *international* flavour to it. How would it look to the Americans, for example - the nature of your work back then? What if it became known that you'd murdered an entire community in a cover up? Sadly the American view has become increasingly important to us. So, you'll understand that the President could not allow you to occupy public office - especially with political pretensions.'

'What now?' the car was already drawing up at the airport terminal. Muffled up families tugged wheeled luggage to and from the taxi rank, bent against the cold wind.

'We understand you have a delightful villa in

Barcelona.' He withdrew an envelope from his pocket. 'We've taken the liberty of booking you onto the next Aeroflot flight. One way. Your ticket's here. Your passport is also in the envelope. Just a word of warning: you'll have company out there. Nice assignment for somebody in our business, don't you think? Just to watch over you. Think of them as a security detachment, looking after your welfare.' The driver opened Borilyeno's door. Lisakov leaned across the seat as he got out. 'Boris Nikolaevich sends his regards, and wishes you to enjoy your retirement in the sunshine.'

He wondered for a moment about *Project Simbirsk*. That should have been the true legacy of *Sorsk*. He was about to lean back into the car to ask, but the Mercedes was pulling away. He could see the back of Lisakov's head. He didn't even merit a glance backwards. His coat thrashed in the wind and his cheeks were numb. A freezing snowflake slipped down his collar and Moscow wished him a chill-breathed farewell as he turned towards the glass doors, contemplating the nature of memories.

She left a pink imprint on a paper cup as she sipped at a scalding latte, taking care to keep her bag close, and with one eye on the departures boards. Her flight was delayed of course. They were playing Gangsta's Paradise in the background, above the rattle of the baristas' jugs and spoons. Sheremetovo was a cosmopolitan compound and Moscow stopped at the perimeter with its exhaust tainted breath.

The copy of Pravda she'd been reading reported the departure of Borilyenko from his role as head of the Presidential Security Service to enjoy a 'well deserved' retirement. The President acknowledged the 'breadth and competence' of the General, and thanked him for his years of service. The appointment of an unknown and recently promoted General Lisakov barely merited a line at the tail end of the article.

The chair opposite was hauled back and she looked up.

'Hello, Kate,' said Nikolay, and the pull of Moscow gave her a jolt.

'They said I was free to leave,' she said, putting the

newspaper aside.

'Free? Of course you're free,' he said, before understanding. 'Oh, I see. You think I'm here for you?'

'Aren't you?'

He sat down, folding his coat and laying it on a vacant chair. 'No. Nothing like that. I've been posted to Barcelona. At my request. A position has become unexpectedly available. My good fortune.' He placed a polystyrene cup on the table. 'If that's what it was,' he added. 'I'm really pleased to see you. You don't mind if I join you?'

'It's your country.'

'Yes, it is, isn't it? And I can't help feeling ashamed of it sometimes. At other times… well, I'm a Russian after all.'

She turned her face away. She didn't know what to say to him. Without Nikolay things could have ended differently, she supposed.

'They gave you a hard time?'

'Not especially. In the end it wasn't about me. It was about Wilderness. I'm sorry, but I'm not allowed to say—they made me sign.'

‘Of course they did.’ He dipped his head and drank some coffee. ‘So what now?’

‘I’ll see my daughter at last. She’s been with her grandparents, all this time. Since … anyway she’s in bits. She loved her father. I’ll miss him too.’

‘I’m sorry, of course. About your husband.’ And she didn’t bother to correct him. ‘So difficult to know what to say. Without knowing him. What will you do? When you get back?’

‘They’ve been generous. The Russian government. On condition that I don’t talk about… well about anything.’

‘That’s good.’

‘I don’t understand how they could let him get away it. Robert was a good man. So many people… There was Grigor too. Even him— he was a good man too. In his way—’ but she welled up and found she couldn’t talk any more without betraying herself. A wide hipped waitress in a stained white apron clattered crockery as she loaded a tray of empty cups and debris at the next table. She added: ‘I suppose I should thank you.’

‘If you think so.’

She fixed her attention on the monitor displaying columns of constantly refreshing flights. 'I don't feel like I'm anyone any more. I feel like I'm in somebody else's body.'

'That must be… strange.'

'What's strange is feeling like I'm not a real person. Like somebody invented me. Like Frankenstein's monster. Property of the State. That's what Borilyenko called me.' And as her eyes became blurred with the onset of tears she caught a man and a woman watching her too closely in the reflection of a mirror. It hardly surprised her. She would never be alone again, in her head or on the street. 'Property of the State,' she repeated.

'I guess it's something you'll have to learn to live with. I don't know how that must feel. I guess that nobody does.'

'He said something else too. Something I've been thinking about it a lot. He wanted to know if I remembered my mother being pregnant.'

'Pregnant?'

'Yes. A strange thing to say.' She felt swollen with

frustration and emotion all at once.

'What do you think it could mean?'

'I think there's another one. I think they used the work my mother did, and they went through with it. They made a clone of Lenin.'

He laughed. Then, 'Your flight…' he said, with a gesture towards the departure board.

She saw in the reflection of the mirror the man and woman gathering their coats and bags and checking their boarding passes and knew she would never be truly alone again.

Epilogue

HE MISSED NADEZHDA. To other people he knew it would seem odd to miss a person he'd never met, but for him it was normal. Nadezhda, the spouse of his benefactor. Beautiful a long time before the sickness ravaged her, but even the bulging neck and swollen eyes which were the hallmarks of Graves disease were dear to him now if not attractive. He thought he needed her practical, forthright nature to make him whole. He longed to ask for her advice. The wife of Lenin.

He liked to walk beside the lake, in summer and in winter. They'd rented a rambling place for him outside

Zurich with a small mooring and a broken-down boathouse. A half-immersed dinghy floundered at the end of a rusty chain, like a mournful mongrel. In summer he would swim off the jetty for hours, and his security detail would watch him through binoculars when they could be bothered. He was embarrassed by them when he went into town. They were boorish Slavs who wore army boots and had shaven scalps that marked them out as soldiers or policemen amongst the quiet suited bankers and the designer set. He was grateful they didn't sit at his table in the cafes, but took a table to themselves where they grumbled in Russian and ordered their vodka and zakuski and no longer needed to explain to the waiters what that meant. They watched him eat with disinterest. He ate alone. There was no space in his life for companions. Instead he read about love and friendship, and that would have to do.

Sometimes, tantalised, he lingered in Spiegelgasse and took a turn past number 14, close to the now rotting Cabaret Voltaire that the record said he had never visited - although he alone knew that Lenin was a Dadaist. Could anyone seriously doubt that his hand was behind the Dada Manifesto, that most nihilist of anti-artistic pronouncements?

A simple plaque recorded that Lenin had lived in the apartment at number 14 from February 1916 to April 1917. Above a butcher's shop, now gone, so that if he had lived here today he would not have had to keep the windows closed during the day because of the smell of carcasses.

The General promised him one day he would go home. There would be street parties and banners, and statues would be erected in his image. But Zurich was his home, not Moscow, and he could live without the statues. There had been enough poor effigies of him created to last an eternity.

It was his destiny to lead Russia again, the General had told him, but he didn't think much of destiny. He'd read all the speeches that he dimly recalled writing, and they left him feeling anxious and morose. He didn't want to destroy state or society – or indeed anything. He preferred Pushkin to Marx.

The General behaved like a father to him, like Pinnochio's Gepetto. He sensed he was ashamed, but like Pinnochio he couldn't help his true nature. Perhaps he was the man that Vladimir Illyich never had the courage to be. Now that the General was in exile in Europe he feared he would be a more frequent visitor, embroiling him in his conspiracies, preparing him for an office to which he had never aspired.

It began to rain, and he turned up his collar. The lake rippled with rainfall, disrupting reflections of black boned trees, trees that shed heavy tears into the water, but not for him. He was not Lenin, even though he shared his head with Lenin’s memories, and he was happy with who he was. Vladimir Tupovsky. No need for patronymics. After all, he had never had a father.

Printed in Great Britain
by Amazon

28527881R00324